EXALTED VIBRATIONS TRILOGY
BOOK 2

# Traversing the Wild Unknown

# LEE KEMTER

# EXALTED VIBRATIONS TRILOGY
# BOOK 2

## *Traversing The Wild Unknown*



Contact: www.leekemter.com

Author Photo by Brent Looyenga

# DEDICATION

*To Valerie Guthrie, my best friend forever.*

*Thank you for always being there for me, especially in our wild, mystifying encounters with the infinitely blazing quantum field.*

*From the other side of the veil, I know you are hovering in that sweet space of ever-evolving consciousness. I'll meet you there.*

# TABLE OF CONTENTS

# PART 1

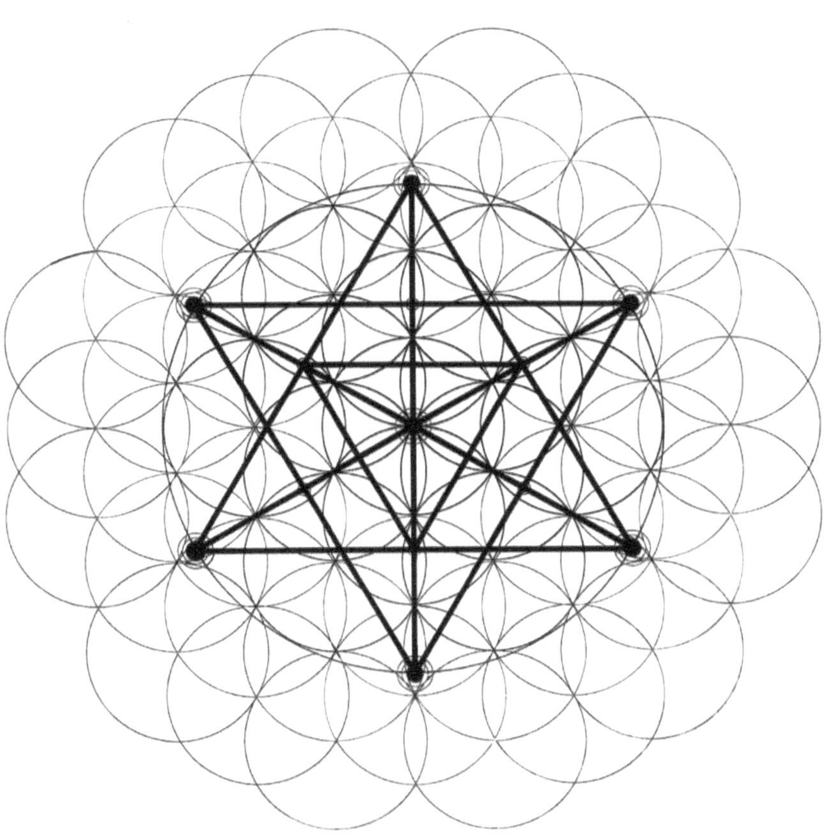

# CHAPTER 1

# PIVOTAL MOMENT IN LINEAR TIME

An eerie current of foreboding rippled through the members present in the Galactic Council meeting. Furrowed brows and an unusually somber tone pervaded the atmosphere of the exquisitely-designed craft in which they were meeting. A daunting topic had become the focus for the galactic community at-large, and the Council had convened to discuss the issue.

The meeting had begun with a propitious update regarding their emissary, Sophia, whose mission to bring codes of ancient wisdom and indispensable *unicity* to the inhabitants of Earth was proceeding well. Sophia, through many incarnations and millions of years, had embodied these codes within her DNA and had been given the task of radiating them to others in order to shift the direction of human evolution. Now, her tight circle of friends had begun to embrace and activate these codes more fully themselves. However, far too many humans remained entrenched in low frequencies manifesting as fear, anger, apathy, or arrogance—rendering the codes impotent.

Normally quiet and pensive in the meetings, Elbon, dark-skinned and blue-eyed, slowly stood up, his hulking figure rising to an imposing thirty feet. His countenance was majestic and his voice so thunderous and deep that the room became entranced as he spoke eloquently and to the point.

"From my perspective, Sophia is doing what is needed most—reaching *many more* good hearts—supporting legions of humans across the planet who wish to raise their frequency, thus advancing their evolution. Militaries and leaders of governments and business around the planet have proved to be more focused on war and colonization than on receiving our ceaseless messages of collaboration and peace. My point is that our intrinsic *connection* to the citizens of the planet should perhaps be our strongest focus.

"Through contact in dreams, we've encouraged Sophia to write more prolifically about the theme of *becoming still inside*. This species has fallen increasingly prey to left brain, unsteady thoughts about anticipated misfortune at every turn. This is juxtaposed with the highly creative right brain, which generates quantum-level solutions based on a mind drenched in silent connection with Essence, the still point of all-that-is. Although many scoff at her, she remains tenaciously thoughtful and kind, and indelibly immersed in *unicity*. The focal point of her writings center on the absolute truth of the inherent unification between all beings on all levels, the understanding of our unified origins as pure Essence and the *unified field* within which we constantly interact and communicate. We all agree, the historic insistence of Earth's military and global leadership on fostering separation and intensified concern for building technologies to harm or overpower each other must end. It is short sighted and will ultimately destroy this noble species."

Human beings had already evolved to receive the rarified DNA codes available to advance their quantum nature, live more fully in elevated frequencies, and use their creative right brain capacities for incalculable problem-solving; and yet they continued to adopt the status quo of left-brain manipulation strategies and intense analytical thinking. The council wondered what could be done to allow this illustrious species, with their unlimited potential for advancing consciousness, to move forward without fear while acknowledging the gravity of their situation. The meeting evolved from bantering back and forth for an answer—which they realized was extremely complex—to a solemn, grave tone arising from an inconclusive inquiry.

Next, Layor came to standing—a twenty-foot tall, Nordic Pleiadian with sagacious blue eyes which conveyed an ocean of wisdom and savvy diplomacy. As the Presiding Emissary of the Council, his character was beyond reproach. He gazed compassionately around the room at his comrades, a varied assembly of highly advanced, noble-minded, galactic adepts. Regardless of his towering countenance, his authentic kindness and obvious care for each member present easily softened the mood. Trusted and loved by all, and as an esteemed elder, they gave him their undivided attention while he assured them of a significant, encouraging update from Sophia's father, Belstar—a venerable, galactic human giant, who vigorously supported his daughter's mission to bring vital codes of wisdom and unicity to Earth at this pivotal moment in humanity's evolution.

He reminded them of an essential truth they had shared in their meetings many times: more than rumination and discussion, this council's *highest vibratory support* mattered to the entire cosmos. Instinctively, the contingent of long-standing, noble comrades paused, instantly entering the still point within themselves. The entire craft and its occupants melted unreservedly into an unfathomable silence.

Having satiated themselves in the resplendent vibrations of their interior world, their consciousness simultaneously emerged, like a flock of elegant birds, back into the meeting space. After collectively offering their highest vibrations to Planet Earth and all its inhabitants, they unanimously agreed that it was useless to dwell further on the actions of a relatively small number of humans obsessed with a destructive paradigm of division and war at all costs. Humanity as a whole was poised to take charge of themselves by focusing on their inner consciousness as an invaluable resource rather than relentlessly expending their valuable life force trying to control the outer world.

Belstar's bushy eyebrows twitched as he nodded to Layor and began to speak in an assuring tone. "As you know, Sophia and her beloved Trahar, known as *Nate* in their recent assignment, have been coming to Gaia for millions of years. When needed, they have helped survivors of brutal ice ages and devastating cataclysms to regroup and regain access to their innate quantum potential. Those two galactic adepts remain dedicated to humanity, especially in the area of elevating consciousness in this important evolutionary process.

"As reported, Trahar was called home, leaving his earth suit and his beloved Sophia. She was understandably distraught. Remember, she does not fully recall her true identity. Bravely and with conviction, she continued without his benevolent support. She found her way to a mystical lake in California where she was hosted by a kind, wise woman, Angelica. Sophia's mission was instinctively proceeding, but she needed opportunities to recall her cosmic past. With the help of her friends, she has been discovering the technologies once decimated by the dark ones in an unfortunate epoch in Gaia's history long ago, as well as the innate, exalted *inner* technologies of the human species to rise above any *outer, mechanical* technologies or oppressive tactics by anyone on earth or from the cosmos.

"As you know, humanity's *inner* technology is imperative to Gaia's survival, and it has been hidden and cloaked by authority figures on and off the planet throughout human history, causing it to be forgotten by this uniquely gifted species. I can see by your faces that you agree. But I invite you to join me in becoming increasingly optimistic about the profound instances of recollection that have begun for Sophia, relating to her personal history, her inherent capacities of perception, and her powers of manifestation. I was allowed to visit her in lucid dreams. I do not want to expend valuable time going over prior report material—I thank you for your unremitting support. Let me assure you that although Gaia's future is unknown, from my perspective all is well. Sophia's mission remains feasible within our projected timeline; humanity still has the opportunity to collectively shift in frequency before the point of no return for the continuation of the species.

"I am happy to share an important update. Sophia has maintained contact with Angelica, an exceptional human being who is an illumined soul indelibly committed to the welfare of Gaia. For your review, I have included her valuable contributions throughout linear time for the advancement of Gaia.

"Sophia is regaining higher levels of memory about the *critical nature* of our solar sister, the sun, as a prioritized ally to Gaia in coming decades. The sun is intimately connected with all life and the subtle and not-so-subtle cycles of Gaia. Like the DNA of all human beings, Sophia's genetics hold memory of millions of years of life on Earth, including bonds with the sun as an invaluable companion.

"Recently, I realized Sophia's memory was coming back online regarding Gaia's extensive history. In her writing, she has featured the much greater lifespan of Earth and humanity—boldly sharing that her broad-minded circle of science-oriented friends and associates recently revealed that Gaia's countless inhabitants, across large swaths of time, perhaps looked and thought differently than humans today. She is posing questions that are causing many readers to shudder, such as: *What if humans are endowed with greater knowledge and have access to more advanced DNA capacities than advanced cultures millions of years ago?*

"She posits that perhaps cataclysms destroyed most evidence of ancient humans yet memory of them can be accessed from the energetic field in and around the human body. She asks: *What if humanity is an advanced species who fell into lower vibrations, yet their DNA and cellular structure holds memory of their inconceivably powerful foundational make-up and genius-level capacities? How long will it take for human beings to realize their biology can quickly adapt to support an inner focus, relying on their limitless powers of consciousness to reach the still point where endless information is stored from the infinite quantum field? While struggling in their current phase of evolutionary metamorphosis, how can global civilizations fathom the inconceivably higher vibrational version of themselves that is swiftly emerging?*

"This is relevant to our discussion today because after the initial backlash from skeptics, the collective memory of Essence is emerging on Earth! They've *reconsidered* information they thought they knew about Gaia's past, the value of their advanced DNA, and are allowing themselves to look *inside* instead of worrying about or incessantly trying to control the *outside* world.

"Moreover, they are openly talking about Oppenheimer and Einstein and a document these esteemed scientists tried to deliver to then President Truman, with suggestions for how to interact with off-planet communities. These scientists knew their cosmic kin clearly stepped in after WWII to prevent nuclear and hydrogen bombs from proliferating. Of course, we know who prevented their letter from reaching the President. When the letter and its profound sentiments began to circulate recently, I experienced long-awaited solace and hope. Encouragingly, millions of humans began discussions about Sophia's publications on a variety of topics, including little-known historical facts like this letter, and documents describing how human consciousness drives AI, not the other way around. Of great consequence to human survival and higher evolution, Sophia's friends remain focused on bringing the truth of humanity's exalted frequencies into the awareness of Earth's inhabitants.

"Sophia's comrades are beginning to recognize and understand her words: *jaw-dropping historical, archeological and cultural patterns across enormous expanses of linear time.* It is clear from responses to Sophia's writings that larger numbers of Gaia's inhabitants are exploring history from a new perspective, letting go of *repetitive patterns* while embracing their DNA's potential, which can consistently support them in experiencing higher frequencies. Her small circle of advanced souls is part of an expanding global network, who are beginning to sense and realize how indelibly their species is connected to each other and the cosmos. They are not willing to be subjugated to the limited thoughts, beliefs and social programing of their leaders or cultures. Through advanced quantum physics, they have come to the realization that a small number of humans who raise their frequencies have immediate, exponential impacts on *the field* in and around them—which then extends to their sister, Gaia, and all her inhabitants.

"Recently, Sophia posed some profoundly provocative questions:

> *"How can humanity expect to develop a realistic approach to the future without considering and exploring thought and behavior patterns and consequences of historical behaviors and beliefs—even if looking back reveals unsettling truths and crushes cherished cultural or religious beliefs and long-held conclusions?*

> *"What is the unfathomable truth about humanity's origins? What patterns culturally, spiritually and personally contributed to the fall of past civilizations and can those patterns be redeemed going forward to avoid suffering and devolution?*

> *"What is the immediate antidote to the rising, debilitating fear of the future?*

"I submit Sophia's writings to you with delight. Having shared my optimism, however, I am realistic that time is running out.

"Humans must focus on moving beyond their *common ground* with *the Opposites*, which cause them to engage incessant divisiveness. *The Opposites* have never lived in a body and they prey on those who live in lower vibrations. Unquestionably, *the Opposites*, existing on and off Gaia, influence the thinking and emotional elevations of humans according to their own distorted world view. Sadly, this leads to focusing on separation and division, developing *us and them* ideologies, and the proliferation of low vibrations such as apathy, anger, heart-wrenching sadness, and debilitating despair.

"Humanity must realize the value of their quantum-level existence and enter this still point at the base of their subtle architecture—without delay. Most of them cannot yet conceive of themselves as a unique energy-being of incalculable light, sound and electromagnetism that arises from the infinite field of all-that-is. In stillness they will discover their perfect equilibrium point between the darkness of the opposites and pure bliss. From that nexus point, universes arise and creation unfurls its cosmic dance of endless potentiality.

"Adhering to our agreement, we will not intervene in the exchange between humans and the invisible *Opposites*. Humanity must learn how to move beyond the negative influence of the *Opposites* in the dreams and thought forms that drift like a plague through the species. But humanity has been gradually, systematically programmed not to believe in anything that is unseen—except, of course, imaginary ghosts and religious adversaries. But these are distractions. By believing that a higher spiritual power must swoop down to save them from these apocryphal negative forces, they inadvertently blind themselves to their own innate power of discernment. This discernment is exactly what is needed in order to develop a state of harmony and balance, which would easily wipe out the influence of *the Opposites*.

"With optimism, I can report that although Sophia and her comrades are not aware of these invisible beings, they are continuing to solidify discernment and equilibrium, allowing them to remain unaffected by either visible or invisible beings with whom they intersect in daily life.

"In addition, essential advancements in science and culture on Gaia are becoming highly creative, as extraordinary as anything we've observed in the past million years. For these advancements to succeed, however, our human brothers and sisters must bravely view each other and their world from a fundamentally new perspective: they must understand elevated frequencies of unicity, collaboration, and mutual care as the *indispensable* foundations of life. They have an unequivocal window in which to come together and allow for an exponential upsurge in their frequency, rising into vibratory levels never before experienced on Gaia.

"Esteemed Council members, I appreciate this opportunity to express my optimism and love for Gaia and all her inhabitants, as well as to share the latest news related to Sophia's profoundly crucial mission on Gaia."

"Thank you, Belstar," Layor said respectfully. He gazed at Belstar with affection. "Dear brother, know that we do not harbor criticism for Sophia or her friends. They are doing the best they can. Any disquietude we emit is simply our way of expressing our deep concern for Planet Earth. As a sentient being, Gaia is our sister, and all humans are part of our galactic family. It is with love and profound respect that we focus considerable attention on them. Speaking as the Presiding Emissary of the Council, I assure you we will support this amazing species forever, regardless of whether they falter and risk extinction, or rise in frequency into the awe-inspiring global civilization they are capable of creating.

"Sophia is progressing exceptionally well. Having to move forward without support from her beloved Trahar, she followed her intuition impeccably and continued with a sense of courage and regality. We find it exemplary that she has persevered bravely without having the benefit of recalling her roots. In spacetime, however, there is a short window in which the codes MUST be disseminated, received, and integrated by humanity. It sounds simple but this is an arduous process. We grasp fully that we are dealing with billions of multifaceted souls."

At the end of that unusually somber council meeting, Layor asked: "Are humans actively seeking unicity with each other, and are they diligently and regularly cultivating their connection to the unified field of energy that underlies all creation?"

Belstar ruminated over this provocative question to which no immediate answer was required, and the meeting adjourned.

✦ ✦ ✦

Shortly after the meeting, Belstar arrived unannounced at Kandor's spaceship, stationed deep within a massive, remote mountain in North America. Belstar sought counsel with his closest friend about how to best appease the council to give Sophia time to fully express her mystical contributions. Although Sophia's current mission on Earth appeared daunting, Belstar was confident in her skills. He also knew that if humanity did not receive her gifts with timely enthusiasm, her presence and extraordinary capacities would also be needed and appreciated somewhere else in the Universe.

With Layor's question dancing in his mind, Belstar greeted his trusted comrade with a sigh of relief. "I always find solace and encouragement in your company, brother. Although I updated you through a brief message about the council meeting and the burning question they left me with, I would like to share a few details about what is happening in Sophia's life."

Belstar recounted that after Nate passed away, Sophia had found her way to an extraordinary lake in California where she met Angelica. With similar interests in ancient Earth history and spiritual growth, their friendship deepened over the years. Kandor and Belstar smiled at each other as they reminisced about Sophia's mystical experiences and burgeoning galactic memory at that ancient lake.

Wrinkling his snowy, bushy eyebrows, Belstar said pensively, "Let's take a look at the holographic screen to see how my dear Sophia is progressing in her mission. The council was respectful of her but I sense they are not totally convinced she can reach her goal in time. Her mission is a tall order even for the most highly skilled among us. In addition, she has DNA from her current biological parents that is similar to most of humanity, without the expression of the unicity gene, and it is possible she, too, could falter. It does seem the unicity gene is expressing itself in her, but she will have to override other genetic expressions from her earthly lineage. I am confident she will do so. Kandor, am I *overly* confident?"

Kandor shook his head. He, too, was certain about Sophia's capacities, as long as she remained focused and alert to her inner state. He knew full well that genetic expressions can be skillfully developed with the right attention.

"About the DNA Sophia carries," Kandor said. "Neither she nor her comrades realize how far back their lineages extend in linear spacetime. We won't delve into DNA from all parallel realities—an aspect of human consciousness that will become available as they quickly rise in evolution. Experiencing parallel realities will require more right brain capacities than most humans have yet cultivated. But the mystery of those facts and the science behind them is emerging on earth. At this point, Sophia and her friends are focusing on their DNA along the vector in linear spacetime they are experiencing.

"Although we meet them in dreams and communicate in subtle ways, they believe it is *their idea* to focus on DNA. Most importantly, they heard us and are embracing the subject with relentless vigor, even if they do not fully recognize the implications of looking deeply into the patterns of their DNA and those of global citizens across epochs of spacetime. DNA holds important codes for survival and evolution, but exchanges of information with the field in the present moment, within stillness, is equally relevant. Unfortunately this task seems so simple that many humans ignore its invaluable magnitude and implications for their higher evolution. However, soon they won't be able to ignore their quantum-level biology and the associated capacities. It has become a matter of survival. For that reason the council is placing more emphasis on Sophia's mission and offering assistance to her and her friends from their extended cosmic lineages—even if, in impending encounters, they do not recognize their soon-to-be galactic comrades as kin."

Watching the enormous hologram display a current scene in Sophia's life, Belstar said, "Although Angelica visited Mystic Cove a couple of times briefly, she did not meet Sophia's friends nor did she go to the cove. Knowing that she had in-depth knowledge of botany, Sophia's trusted friends, Jake and John, are undoubtedly looking forward to meeting Angelica to talk about rare lichen and unusual algae that grow in the caverns. I am interested to see how her skillset can become integrated with Sophia's new friends and whether or not she will fit into this closely knit group."

Belstar smiled affectionately as he observed Sophia's cheerfulness when she caught sight of John—her staunch friend, who had given her a meticulous first-hand experience of the magnificence and power emitted by the giant skeletons they'd found in Mystic Cove. Regardless of the situation, John's humor created a space for childlike playfulness. He and his best friend, Jake—a comrade in archeology, cosmology, astronomy, and mysticism—had become inseparable as their work in the cove steadily unfolded. Together, they perpetually cultivated the art of curiosity—as though the deeper the subject, the more profound the mystery, the more they allowed for an exponential expansion of their worldview.

Another devoted friend of Sophia's, Adele, was part of the unfolding scene on the hologram as well. Belstar smiled, reflecting how, like all of her new friends, Adele came into Sophia's life through astonishing synchronicity. Adele's grandmother, Gilda, was an ex-Nazi spy who later proved to be of extraordinary character. Gilda had helped Sophia to grasp the ramifications of dark secrets of black military projects in the U.S. Equally astonishing, she elucidated what she had learned from close alliances with ETs she had worked with while serving in various military programs over many years. Getting to know Gilda intimately over the course of their friendship, Sophia noticed that Adele exhibited her grandmother's courage and sage-like instincts, her awareness of unseen realms, her open-hearted approach to life, and her persistent drive to find ways to enhance high vibrational living.

The two giants watched as the sun began to rise further in the sky, drenching Sophia and her friends with shafts of warmth and glistening morning luminescence. Belstar noted that the spring equinox had arrived, delivering its wondrous, magical vibrations to the cove. In silent reverie, the circle of friends glanced at soft sunlight filtering through the enchanting trees nearby. With a joyous sparkle in her eyes, Sophia shared that she was looking forward to a longer visit with Angelica who was bringing her daughter, Caitlyn. She recounted sitting with Angelica under magnificent, towering oaks while they pondered the wonders of the cosmos and expressed optimism for the future of humanity.

Sophia, John, and Jake were going to introduce Adele to the megalithic circle at the precise time that the stones would align with specific constellations in the solar system. As they planned the auspicious event at the circle, a text chimed on Sophia's phone saying that Angelica was sick. She couldn't come and requested that Sophia call as soon as possible.

The giants listened to Sophia excuse herself to take the call. When she came to standing, she paused momentarily. Still and serene, she watched the tips of crimson tulips slightly swaying in a soft breeze. Small moments of connection to Earth's beauty and rhythms allowed her state of serenity to remain intact. Sufficiently satiated from her moment of reverie and connection, she stepped inside to make the call.

"Angelica, are you okay?" Sophia asked warmheartedly.

"My goodness, Sophia, I caught an awful cold," Angelica answered with a weak voice followed by a sudden pause as a coughing spell erupted. Collecting herself, Angelica continued, "I'm so sorry to back out last minute. I never get sick. And it breaks my heart because Caitlyn is looking so forward to meeting you and your friends. She's excited, her bags are jammed packed with tons of archeological gear, and she's ready to hit the road."

"Too bad! Given her educational background, I know she must be disappointed to miss this opportunity to explore the cove with Jake and John. I was looking forward to finally meeting her. But I am also relieved that you only have a mild cold! As I connected with you through the ether, I felt something was off." Sophia sighed deeply, releasing the inner tension that sprouted when she sensed Angelica was not well.

"Awww, sweetie, thank you for always caring about me and tuning into me with your highly sensitive cosmic antennae." Angelica said as her voice cracked, "With rest and my herbal remedies, I'll be fine. If it isn't too much of an imposition, I wonder if Caitlyn could come with a friend. I'm not crazy about her traveling a long distance by herself. I know she's a grown woman, but you know how protective mama bears can be."

"I understand," Sophia said. "I look forward to meeting her. Would you rather wait, get well and come together?"

"I would do that but I'm about to begin teaching a botany class locally and that puts the trip off for a while. I'm telling you, Caitlyn is full of anticipation and thrilled to get to work with you and your friends at the cove. This is right up her alley. She's completed her studies and is a full-fledged archeologist. Oh my Lord! She's obsessed with pyramids, ETs, ancient technologies, and all things that indicate how the planet and humanity have evolved over huge epochs of time."

"Have you told her anything about the cove?" Sophia asked.

"I explained that you have archeologist friends and there's a site that's actively being worked. Of course, I never saw it because your friends were not there to show me around. I respect that this is their work, not a tourist site. It didn't sound like a place you run in, look around, and that's that. Tour over."

"That is an understatement!" Sophia said with a wry chuckle. "It's a good idea for Caitlyn to have a traveling companion. Who is the friend she'd like to bring?"

"Her best friend, Avani." Angelica added with a boost of enthusiasm, "You will love her! She's also an archeologist who added astronomy to her repertoire. Since they were small, she and Caitlyn loved to huddle in their blankets on a moonless night. It was hard to get them to come inside because they seem mesmerized—naming constellations or watching meteor showers and shooting stars.

"Oh my goodness, those two darlings complement each other perfectly. Caitlyn is the fearless, brainy go-getter. And Avani is the sweet, kind empath who loves adventure but only if intuition leads the way. She's sensitive and Caitlyn is, too. Get ready, though, they are equally passionate about their fields of study! They were always inseparable, so it wasn't a surprise that they chose similar fields. Each added astrobiology to their repertoire. Getting advanced degrees, one headed east and the other to the west coast to be trained. And yet both ended up working in the Middle East, Egypt, Peru, and the Americas. They continue colliding into each other's world. It seems they plan to keep it that way.

"Their PhD's compliment each other, too. People often think they are related even though they couldn't be more dissimilar physically. Avani is barely five foot five, has a round face and huge brown eyes framed by long, thick black hair—she's Indian by heritage. And then there's Caitlyn, descended from Europeans: tall as a tree, fine blond hair floating around a slender face, and crystal blue eyes with the fairest skin ever. I always felt people picked up on their bond, which is indelible—of that, I am sure. They are inseparable friends; two adorable *soul* sisters."

This was something Sophia could relate to because she and Grace, her lifelong bestie, were always that way; close in heart even when continents separated them.

"That sounds perfect," Sophia said. "I hope you are feeling great again soon and I look forward to seeing you when your schedule opens up. I miss you bunches! Tell those adorable besties to head our way. If they can get on the road soon, they'll arrive before dark. I know you'll be happy about that."

Their conversation sparked the same tone of love and care they'd shared after Nate's death and Sophia's transition from being a wife to a bold explorer of unknown realms. For this new phase of life, she was traveling on her own. Sophia knew it was a blessing to have Angelica's kindness and companion-ship in making the transition from being a partner to being a single woman again. Friendships like theirs, emerging during a time of soulful transformation, can become the foundation for developing a strong tap root that endures for a lifetime.

Sophia began immediately to make notes in preparation for the two young archeologists who would arrive later that evening. She thrived on meeting new people and providing a space for everyone to come together and discover more than any of them could have expected. Her spirits were elevated as she walked with exuberance to share the news with John, Jake, and Adele.

John motioned for Sophia to join them for a quick cup of tea. As she settled in with her aromatic brew, she looked at John and smiled. His anticipation was palpable as he fidgeted, as though he could hardly wait to begin the day's activities.

"When you finish the Equinox event at the stone circle," Sophia said, "I'm thrilled that Adele will be going with you to roam through the cave at Mystic Cove. Today is auspicious! An equinox is gracing us with its potent energies once again, Adele is about to have a potentially jaw-dropping experience in the cave system, and there is more good news. Although Angelica cannot come, her daughter is arriving tonight with her best friend, Avani. This evening we'll have two new archeologists among us."

With raised eyebrows, John said, "Wow! It's turning out to be an awesome day!" Directing a sparkling wink towards Adele, he said, "I guarantee plenty of awe and wonderment! And considering our visitors... No botany but double archeology. I like that tradeoff. Caitlyn's resume looked impressive. I am sure her friend's will be equally outstanding. I promise to come back early so Jake and I can prepare to meet our guests."

"While you and Adele explore the cove," Jake said, "I'll gather the gear we'll need tomorrow so our guests can begin exploring the cove early. Something tells me that they will hit the ground running. I sure hope they are ready for exceptionally unique archeology and open-minded enough to not faint when they see what's down there."

After relishing a final sip of coffee, John came to standing, thanked Jake, and turned to Adele, downloading the details of

Mystic Cove equinox celebrations and everything she should pay attention to. As they talked, the group slowly made their way to the circle of mystical megaliths.

Through the hologram display, the giants watched this small group of altruistic humans tune into simultaneous equinox celebrations being carried out across the solar system. Rays of blinding effulgence streamed between two stones in the megalithic circle, aligning precisely with the constellation of Orion.

Sophia smiled softly, later admitting to Grace that she could not help but think of her dear friend Gilda and the young sage, Kabir, who she'd met in India. Both of them had special connections with the heart of Orion which was now ablaze with light.

The group sat in pristine stillness within the circle as the peak of the equinox faded. Not a bird tweeted nor breezes moved until the cosmic event began to wane.

John rose quietly, and with Adele by his side, headed for their adventure into the mystical cave system.

As Belstar gazed contentedly at the huge, holographic screen, he said, "Extraordinary comrades are entering Sophia's life on schedule. I am happy to see she is magnetizing these marvelous humans to herself. Tuning into Caitlyn and Avani, my heart space expands exponentially. And I predict that Adele is about to enter higher dimensions. I feel more confident that Sophia's mission is unfolding exceedingly well. Do you agree, my friend?"

"Yes, undoubtedly," Kandor said with customary joviality. "I am delighted that Sophia's new comrades are already so attuned to higher vibrations. Sophia's gift of skillful collaboration will serve her mission well. Given the fact that so much of the world on Gaia is in utter chaos and turmoil, we will continue to send blessings to humanity from our megalithic circles. Shall we meet here on the summer solstice?"

As a sense of robustness and fervor grew in Belstar, he released his giant heart's passion in acceptance of Kandor's invitation. He said resolutely, "I would be honored to join you and our star brothers and sisters as we strike the rods creating powerful vibrations to invigorate and bring courage to this incredible planet and all who inhabit her!"

Receiving Belstar's enthusiastic support, Kandor exclaimed heartily, "Thank you! This will be a beautiful solstice!"

Shifting the mood abruptly, Kandor paused, connecting intimately with his friend through a piercing gaze of pure love. With warmth and affection, he said, "I'd like to suggest that you relax your concern relative to council meetings. After all, you've shared Sophia's progress candidly with them. What's more, in my communication with Layor, he's expressed his support for your daughter implicitly. Yet he realizes that ultimately, the future of Planet Earth lies not in Sophia's mission nor with the council's guidance... the human race must raise its frequency and do so quickly. Time is running out. Our only option is to support Sophia and carry on.

"And now, my friend, do you have time to help me solidify plans for the galactic solstice ceremony? From ancient megaliths nearby, as in ancient times, I propose we provide stellar vibrations and quantum codes to thoroughly drench our brothers and sisters in rarefied light. It is the council's desire that humanity have every possible opportunity to resonate more fully with the unified field from which they arise, and raise their frequencies by leaps and bounds! Having bequeathed these high-vibrational photons, if their heart space is receptive, their subtle bodies will recognize the potency of this downpour of pure love vibrations and receive our blessings with effortless ease. I love our work, don't you?"

With renewed buoyancy and a delightful chuckle, Belstar answered resolutely, "Yes! Let's delay no longer! They are about to realize the value of authentic friendship and inner fortitude in developing the mystical gifts that every human is imbued with. My prediction is that their journey is about to amplify in unforeseen ways. Regardless of the challenges and daunting path this species is facing, may we continue forever to bless this extraordinary planet and her inhabitants with exalted vibrations, powered by our deeply-rooted bonds of kinship!"

# CHAPTER 2

# UNFATHOMABLE REVELATIONS

As the sun shifted from its subtle post dawn luster to full mid-morning brilliance, donning sunglasses and tightening their boot laces one more time, John and Adele began methodically descending the slightly rickety staircase. With each wooden step's creak and groan, they noted its number so it could be repaired. Such unequivocal care was given to every aspect of Mystic Cove.

When they finally arrived at ground level near the massive dock and small marina, Adele stood awe-struck as she surveyed the breathtaking, sapphire blue lake. Interrupting her reverie, John led her to a bench near the rocky shoreline. He asked her to join him for a few moments so he could share important details about the mystical cave, the enigmatic skeleton named Max, and prepare Adele with the same information that Sophia received in her first visit. He warned Adele about the powerful impact of meeting Max, an ancient, giant skeleton with an elongated skull.

Soon, they were sliding closely along the giant boulders while dodging the water's edge. As they reached the entrance, Adele was radiant with excitement. She took a deep breath and entered the sacred site. Walking slowly, she let her eyes adjust to the darkness lit only by John's lantern. Gradually she began to take in the vast cavern, the multitude of scents and magnitude of its structure. Then she saw Max. Like Sophia on her first visit to the cave, Adele justifiably fainted.

John was prepared. He caught her, laying her gently onto a sleeping bag he'd brought in the day before. Earlier, he'd shared with Jake that he planned to be ready in case Adele freaked out the way most people did when they met Max. After a few minutes, Adele returned to waking consciousness. John had shifted her so when she sat up she was not facing Max.

Adele was clearly embarrassed. "I'm so sorry, John! I didn't think that would happen, knowing in advance about Max and what to expect in the cave. But the energy is WAY stronger than I expected and my brain just couldn't integrate what I was seeing—the skeleton of a giant, perhaps from another planet. Wow!"

"Don't give it another thought, my friend. Our brains need to make adjustments for the unknown. You had no context in your daily life for this experience. It's normal. When you are ready to stand, I'll help you. If you want to make eye contact with the skeleton, you can sit on a rock nearby and titrate your vision between looking at Max and looking at the earth. Your brain is familiar and comfortable with Gaia. So the ground below your feet can support you and calm your mind."

As they smiled at each other, Adele rose to her feet and headed for the rock. As John recommended, she patiently moved her vision back and forth. After ten minutes, she could hold her gaze on Max for longer periods and after fifteen minutes, she spontaneously stood and approached him.

"John, he is vibrating, isn't he? Oh my gosh, no one could have prepared me for this experience!"

Slowly and carefully, she walked around Max, still glancing between his skeleton and the ground. Then she began to peruse the cave with a look of awe. As John guided her, showing her the cave art, she remained silent.

When they left the cave, she embraced John in a tight hug. With a fiery depth of appreciation, she said, "Thank you so much! This meant the world to me. I don't know about archeology, but I am very familiar with frequencies. This surpasses any place I've visited. I've been to caves and mystical sites but never with a skeleton! This giant is totally off-the-charts! My parents were academics which influenced me to develop a highly analytical perspective. But my mom was a mystic, like Sophia, allowing me to also develop a curious, open-minded worldview. Her influence lets me take in everything I just witnessed with confidence that it will have a radical impact on my life. I am thrilled to have the opportunity to experience such amazing phenomena and I appreciate how incredibly sweet and thoughtful you are!"

Blushing, John thanked her for courageously following her "inherited and cultivated curiosity" into unknown places and experiences.

They scaled the multitude of steps and headed to Sophia's house. Adele plunged into quiet reflection. By the time they arrived, Adele's daughters were home from school, sitting on Sophia's porch, enjoying apple crisps made from fruit harvested and canned during the preceding autumn. The hundred-year-old apple tree grove was just a small part of the abundance of her property. Sophia welcomed the girls to her nurturing abode as her way of supporting Adele, who was navigating life as a single mom.

Kellie, Adele's oldest child, streaked across the yard to greet her mom, while Leisa remained engrossed in the story Sophia was reading to her.

Everyone sampled the ambrosial dessert, and after giving Sophia and John a warm hug, Adele headed home with her girls to begin homework and dinner. With an abundance of smiles and laughter, John and Sophia walked with them to their car.

Adele's eyes danced with enchantment as she turned to Sophia. Her voice brimming with wonder, she said, "I have shivers! I can't believe what happened to my entire energetic being at the cove today. I am still vibrating... buzzing... Did that happen to you? I fainted when I saw Max but I was able to get myself together and look around the cave. Max's presence is palpable. I felt like I was transported beyond this reality. It's wild. Just between us, I felt my mother and amazing grandmother walking every inch with me! They are not embodied on this Earth, yet they were definitely with me."

Pausing to collect herself as gentle tears gathered, she added softly, "We were a family in bliss today. I couldn't say that to John, but I knew you'd understand what their presence meant to me because of your friendship with them all those years ago. You are the only one here who knew the chasm of my grandmother's agony, and her triumph as she recovered her soul from brutal Nazi programming. And you've experienced my mother's amazing intuition, sharp mind, and her profound graciousness and goodness."

Sophia smiled lovingly. She felt comfort and happiness billow up inside as she so often did, sharing such precious moments with close friends, family, and kindred spirits who are also established in the subtle worlds. Sophia and Adele hugged warmly as they expressed their common understanding that, regardless of how the material world appears, everyone remains connected.

Addressing Adele's experiences of a "buzzing and vibrating" effect in the cave system, Sophia affirmed that it happened every time for her as well. "My intuition and study of the unified field theory of quantum physics tell me that we can sense the subtle vibrations of the underlying forces of the universe. This is an enigmatic and profound process. I feel the deeper, inexplicable frequency levels of the field when my mind becomes still. The cave system has such high vibrations that if I align with them, letting go of my analytical mind, a more refined level of the field emerges into my consciousness. This is when the right brain gets to be in charge, overriding analytical thinking. I wonder if Max and his kin were more right brain-oriented than left brain. Regardless of how the experience of the cove unfolded for you, I am thrilled that you experienced it!

"You are definitely a mystic," she said in a softer tone. She paused and her eyes closed momentarily as she entered her internal world. Opening her eyes softly, she said, "Recalling my openness to the esoteric aspects of an ever-unfolding, cosmic reality, I recognize my inner journey in yours."

Sophia invited Adele to return when she was ready for further exploration. Adele responded with a long, warm hug and ecstatic smile.

Walking back to the porch with Sophia, having overheard their exchange, John said, "Adele is a sweet person. I observed she's tougher than she first appears to be. Holy cow! When she got her bearings, she took to the cove like a champ! I have to admit I'm not the best cove guide when it comes to introducing Max. However, the good news is at least I'm getting better prepared! And now we have your friend's daughter and her best friend arriving tonight. I'm wondering if I'm ready."

Laughing and moving into enjoying afternoon snacks, tea and coffee, the sound of Jake's truck paused the conversation.

As he arrived on the porch, he asked, "Okay you two, how did it go? Sorry I could not be there this afternoon."

"Just another day in the cove," John responded.

"She fainted, didn't she? John, I know you too well. Your poker face is pathetic."

Winking at Sophia, he settled into a comfortable porch chair as their customary playfulness and camaraderie continued. Jake and John teased each other unrestrainedly, while the boisterous sound of their laughter lingered until they were gasping for air.

As the radiant luminosity of the sun made its gradual descent behind the nearby mountain, Sophia offered to make dinner for her fun-loving friends while they waited for Caitlyn and Avani to arrive.

"Sure... I'm in," Jake responded in enthusiastic agreement. "John, you can stay, right?" John nodded and flashed a friendly smile towards Sophia.

As they settled into the silence and stillness of evening, Sophia asked, "Do you want to greet our young explorers and get to know each other tonight? It will save time tomorrow and Angelica expressly said that they are *super excited* to meet you guys."

"I like the idea," John answered. "It's better to get the typical small talk out of the way. Hmmm... I better watch that kind of thinking. I envision them being like some of our colleagues yet they may be very different than that."

"True," Sophia said. "Angelica and I are close friends though, and if her daughter is like her mother, you'll love Caitlyn. Besides that, these girls seem gutsy and adventurous. They have traveled all over the world and would presumably be open-minded."

"I have a good feeling about them, too," Jake added. "Sophia, something sure smells good. Thanks for feeding us bachelors. My peanut butter sandwiches and mac and cheese definitely lack pizzazz...You always convince me to eat more veggies, and that garden of yours has won me over. Everything you grow is over-the-top in flavor."

Sophia smiled warmly at his humor and with appreciation for his kind acknowledgement of her prolific garden and delectable vegetables. Without reservation she beamed a smile, sparking a giant love-bomb for Jake and John—as three devoted friends went inside to eat, enjoy their bond of friendship, and wait for their guests to arrive.

# CHAPTER 3

## FRIENDS TIMES TWO

Within the hour, the two budding archeologists arrived. As they stepped into the chilly Idaho evening, a light wind whipped through the trees to welcome them in its embrace. For a minute, they stood silent, absorbed in the atmosphere.

With a radiant smile, Sophia approached and greeted them warmly. "Welcome to Mystic Cove. You must be tired after your long trip. Please come inside. We have snacks and evening tea ready for you."

John approached saying, "I'll grab your luggage."

And Jake came forward with his gregarious way of helping everyone to be at ease instantly.

The girls had eaten on the road, but they were captivated by the wafting scent of Sophia's spiced tea. Soon they were heartily sipping from mugs and talking about their global travels, educational backgrounds, and shared vision for the future. The conversation was filled with optimism for a world Avani described as, "full of high vibe humans and a planet with ever-increasing frequencies of light, sound, and electromagnetism." Their worldview included the unified field theory, in which many fields of study come together in harmony—theories of cosmology, anthropology, psychology, physics, chemistry, biology, and archeology. They passionately shared that everything and everyone is connected at a subtle, quantum level.

But beyond theory, these besties were committed to the *experience* of their expanded, interconnected worldview, and to sharing their discoveries and research with others.

Sophia, John, and Jake glanced at one another with knowing smiles as the girls described their ideas and enthusiasm for encouraging each other to "think outside of the box." Bringing the conversation to a philosophical pinnacle, Jake and John spoke about the necessity for various fields of study to become more open-minded, less dogmatic, and more cohesive as a *team of good humans* (as John called them) ready to dive into inconsistencies and anomalies (like skeletons and flash fossilized giants) which have otherwise been relegated to a tightly controlled scientific narrative.

In a voice illumined with passion, John said, "We think there is a vast repository of ancient knowledge that is being disregarded across the planet because science has become *too narrowly defined.* Why can't we wonder about giants and potential cosmic kin without paleontologists, biologists, geologists, and archeologists coming unglued at the seams? For example, if there were mile-long dragons that walked the earth and who are flash fossilized by massive volcanic activity or other means, why can't we be open to putting research into those sites instead of trying desperately to solidify *only* what we already teach in academic circles? You will soon realize that Jake and I have way too many questions to stay in the mainstream lane. I'm feeling you are on the same wavelength, with a curiosity that causes your peer's eyebrows to explode when offered unforeseen information! We've observed that when that happens, people sometimes tactfully, sometimes in a pissy way, hit the road—never joining us for another dig.

"We don't see ourselves as total outliers like we used to. For example, the theory of a catastrophic flood twelve thousand years or so ago isn't under intense debate. BUT in our neck of the woods, in Montana, some enigmatic discoveries have been made, which relate to that flood. Miles of inexplicable megaliths, huge granite structures, covered in a pink polymer that is clearly not a natural part of the rock, seem to have been part of structures likely devastated by the flood and perhaps many other cataclysms. I say *many other* because the foundational infrastructure of the sites was destroyed, the evidence suggesting they were toppled and moved by tsunamis, three to almost five-thousand feet high, at least once in their history.

"We can't measure the age of this megalithic complex. It's too layered. The oldest megaliths could be millions of years old. After cataclysms came and went, they were possibly rebuilt by survivors. They are definitely vibrating at a high frequency. Imagine that! I'm talking about rocks definitely not shaped like natural stone. Granite doesn't form ninety-degree angles nor stack itself in perfect symmetry, creating walls fit more for giants than for humans of our size. With modern devices, we can read the electromagnetic fields of the stones and the earth grid. This is spine-chilling stuff, folks!

"For example, we saw twin elongated megalithic structures standing perfectly side by side, almost touching. They withstood the flood I mentioned but a lot of the rock around them shifted. What were these megaliths used for? What does the polymer coating do? Why is there so much inexplicable quartz in this polymer's composition? Maybe it ingeniously generated electric current, or perhaps it was an energy amplifier? Then we studied five-thousand ton megaliths supporting a capstone, with the weight resting primarily on one of the stones. We speculate that the pressure of that point generated a massive energetic effect. Was this area a power plant? An inconceivable civilization with endless free energy? Working globally with like-minded archeologists and geologists, we are theorizing a giant-based, energy producing technological wonder. Again, with the overall structure scattered by massive flood waters, it isn't like digging into a site in Egypt or Peru.

"In the cave system in Mystic Cove, we have found megaliths and evidence of giants as well. But what's more astonishing is that here and at the sites I mentioned, ground penetrating radar and other advanced geo scans indicate that there remain intact structures far below ground—circular edifices, living quarters, and possible temples that could reveal an ancient world buried under layers of sediment that covered this area during floods. Similar to MRI technology, these scans produce images of each layer which can be spliced to bring unprecedented clarity and detail. Stone circles, including etchings and small artifacts, are visible. At even deeper levels, skillfully designed structures are being discovered via well-built ancient tunnel systems. With these new technologies, ancient underground structures be-come real rather than speculative.

"We fight tooth and nail to maintain these sites. You see, a lot of them are located in forests owned by the government. But the law has changed so that forests have been relabeled as "multiple use" and can be sold. These days, national forests are not one hundred percent protected and owned by the public. I wonder what Teddy Roosevelt would say about that?! He and others worked tirelessly to maintain specific sites as places of inestimable value for future generations. I committed to memory some of his most powerful words on the subject:

> *It is also vandalism wantonly to destroy or to permit the destruction of what is beautiful in nature, whether it be a cliff, a forest, or a species of mammal or bird. Here in the United States we turn our rivers and streams into sewers and dumping-grounds, we pollute the air, we destroy forests, and exterminate fishes, birds and mammals -- not to speak of vulgarizing charming landscapes with hideous advertisements. But at last it looks as if our people were awakening.*

"If we allow the government to sell, and thus mine these sites, archeological treasures will be obliterated, pristine forests destroyed. Like President Roosevelt, I believe people are *awakening*. And to be clear, we would not invite you two to join us at the cove if we didn't believe you are *awake*, will appreciate the site, and hold it with reverence as we do."

Knowing smiles and nodding heads bathed John in affirmation and camaraderie. Then Jake spoke.

"John and I realized we'd developed a crazy knack for pissing off numerous colleagues. When we were young, we thought we could convince our teammates of the need to explore wider and deeper—but that was useless and arrogant. Instead, we learned to go on digs with true compadres with open minds and curiosity, willing to explore theories about mountains and rocks that seem to be more than natural rock formations. I'm speaking about flash-fossilized giants and animals, and structures that can extend a mile or longer. We never stomped our feet or tried to debunk the traditional theories that implied such things were impossible. Instead, we paid attention to how the remains, *when scaled down*, have an eerie similarity to the anatomy, biology, and structure of similar, smaller humans and creatures. The giant stone hearts of these mega-giants have been found all over the world. We took plenty of shit from colleagues who said we were just experiencing *pareidolia*—which is when you see a cloud that looks like a dog and conclude the cloud is a canine.

"This kind of controversial topic is relevant to our insatiable appetite to dig deeper than other people can fathom or handle. We don't want to waste time chasing every theory out there, but when something is found consistently across the planet and has a foundational basis that bucks traditional theories, we are wide open to taking a closer look. We are convinced there were giants on this planet, whether human or species of off-planet beings who were massive in size. How long did these beings remain here and what caused them to leave or become extinct? We have an insatiable hunger for discovering the deep, mysterious roots of human and Earth's history.

"To be clear, we gather factual data and take science-based approaches, and we have put in hard work to develop a hypothesis that's beyond bias. But this hypothesis may upend our present scientific understanding. The archeological site you'll visit here isn't conventional; we can't necessarily explain the myriads of jaw-dropping discoveries we've made. You need to know we are in for the long haul, and we are sure we're headed in the right direction. As a foundation for our work here, John and I agreed early on that humans are not alone in this cosmos. I can tell you aren't shocked to hear me say such things."

With a luminous smile, Caitlyn said confidently, "We don't shy from anything provocative. But we request the freedom to ask tons of questions. We aren't bound to traditional beliefs about Earth's history, and we don't feel obliged to look through a conventional lens into *giant* mysteries—no pun intended!" She grinned. "For sure... we are on the same page."

Avani's eloquent, coal-black eyes glittered with enthusiasm. Glancing around the group, she shared an unbridled smile of lion-hearted boldness for exploring *the unknown.*

As excited as the whole group was to venture into unknown territory, yawns began to emerge on their faces, especially of the two young travelers. Noticing this, Sophia thanked them for their authenticity and courage.

"Before we conclude for the evening," she said, "I'd like to add another dimension to the discussion. There is something called a *unicity gene* in all of us that is waiting to be expressed. This gene updates the human organism both emotionally and intellectually. From my studies and experience, I've gathered that we are more than flesh and bones; we are made of energy that connects us with the entire quantum energy field in and around us. Fundamentally, we are not separate from this field, which means we have unlimited access to everything everywhere. We are definitely kindred spirits, we are wholeheartedly in alignment, and the cove that you will see tomorrow will reveal why the expression of the unicity gene is critical right now."

Caitlyn and Avani smiled radiantly, folded their hands over their hearts, and for a moment, sat silently in gratitude.

Caitlyn said softly, "I feel that we can be honest with you. It is obvious that you *get us.* I want you to know that we're definitely on the same page. Mom was right. You are totally amazing!"

Avani smiled as her gaze moved purposefully from Sophia to John, and then Jake, silently yet thoroughly conveying her heartfelt, congenial appreciation for them.

The evening came to a natural closure and the girls headed to the guest room looking sleepy yet still in high spirits.

Jake and John both stood as well, glancing warmly at Sophia with gentle smiles mingled with yawns.

Looking relieved, John said, "These are two bright, young explorers—quite impressive. I'm relieved and look forward to working with them. They have integrity and are refreshingly open-minded, making them undeniably well-suited to work in the cove."

"I love their spirit," Jake added, "and they are clearly into a broad spectrum of sciences. I feel better about taking them to the cove. Sophia, I trusted your judgement, but I'm more confident after meeting them."

With hugs, they parted to prepare for the next day ahead.

# CHAPTER 4

# MEETING MYSTIC COVE

Caitlyn and Avani awakened before dawn to meditate and prepare for an adventure into the enigmatic cove they'd heard about. Luckily, they were staying with an intuitive host who had tea and homemade huckleberry muffins ready when they emerged from their room.

After an hour, Sophia sent a text to John and Jake: "I've got two racehorses in my kitchen who've eaten and are pawing at the starting gate. Are you guys up and ready? You better be. I don't know how long I can contain these two!" She added a smiling emoji and two hearts.

Sophia's description was not far from reality. Their gear was waiting on the porch as the besties sat fidgeting and drinking an extra pot of tea—looking expectantly towards the long, tree-lined driveway for John and Jake.

Jake was the first to arrive. Flashing a smile, he shouted, "Okay you two, I can't wait all day. Are you coming or not?"

As they scurried over, Sophia followed them, carrying snacks and water for their visit.

Within seconds, John's old red Chevrolet barreled noisily down the drive, brakes squealing into a dust-filled halt. With a hearty wave and a full backpack, his broad smile stirred their anticipation for the adventure ahead. Leading the way, he headed unflinchingly to the mystical cove.

Everyone followed, moving along the mossy boulder in his wake. At the opening to the cave, they centered themselves for a moment, closed their eyes, took a couple of deep breaths, and calmly entered. The stillness was palpable in the enormous expanse of the cave.

Not missing a beat, Avani exclaimed: "I feel the Essence of this space. My God!" She approached the skeletons. "These remains are speaking a silent language—its vague but familiar to me. It's like I have forgotten how to hear it naturally, but my subtle energy fields hold the memory of it. This is amazing!"

She talked slowly to Max, standing relaxed and still. Her breath was even, sometimes reaching a deep, long cadence.

In a trance-like state, Caitlyn walked rhythmically in a clockwise circle around the skeletons. As her steps became slower, she noticed the perfect boulder for a meditation seat and settled into it, softly closing her eyes. Silence prevailed for several minutes until she began to speak.

"It's gigantic... way bigger than I expected," she said, her voice exuding astonishment.

Suddenly, with a bolt of effervescent enthusiasm, she said, "This cave is epic! Every aspect is designed for giant-sized living. The whole species must have been at least as tall as Max. Avani! Look at the rock formations that form a table and stools. They are at least ten-feet-tall. To be here... to have such incredible access to these giants and their underground world... I'm in awe and deep gratitude for the opportunity to see and experience this site first-hand... Whoa! ... Max has the elongated skull! I've seen one of them but never the whole skeleton. We've both seen giants, but this is amazing to get a close look and know at least a little about his possible history and where he lived."

Avani's eyes had moved passed the immediate area to catch a glimpse of the first pyramid. Stunned into amazement, all she could muster was a whispered gasp, exclaiming with ever-widening eyes, "Oh my God, Caitlyn! I have chills!"

She continued, "We were thrown off-course for a while because we'd heard of red-haired giants in North America and a race called the *Nephilim* described by Biblical scholars. And predominantly Judeo-Christian traditionalist scientists tended to assume the giant bones we saw all over the world in different sites were from those few races. But that appears to be a limited viewpoint. Can anyone step back in time and say that ancient accounts from one *small part* of the planet is an indication of the *entire global story*, spanning vast epochs of time?

"To be clear, we did not look at this giant topic from a religious context. Our research is DNA-based and we looked for patterns where certain giant skeletons were found as well as the archeological technologies of the time period in which they lived. But we haven't seen anything like this site. It is obvious we're nowhere near being able to draw conclusions about giants on or below the surface. My eyes are wide open and in awe of this living complex.

"Part of our research that may be relevant to this amazing cave is that we posit human civilizations could have lived on Earth many millions of years ago. Hang in there with me—I know this is *out there* in relation to mainstream archeology. What if our VERY ancient ancestors viewed themselves and the world as a unified part of the whole? Being more balanced between the right and left hemispheres of their brains, they could have analyzed and gone into creative-thinking when needed, which set them apart from animals. But like animals, they could communicate telepathically, were highly tuned in to sound, light, electromagnetism, and the infinite field in and around them. With this kind of perception, perhaps they created a world that seems sci-fi to us.

"I'm mentioning this because we decided the only way to extract information of value from our digs was to ignore mainstream signs and warnings and head off-road. For example, if we assume these beings are not vastly ancient, that's where our minds will settle. But with an open mind, we can ask, *What if cataclysms destroyed a big part of any evidence of human life. And what if decay and time took their toll on artifacts and other solid forms of proof.* Oh my God! This is giant thinking! And we're getting so tired of everyone assuming historians, paleontologists, and archeologists know our immense history. Maybe we're at the tip of an iceberg of revelations about our roots."

"Holy shit!" Jake exclaimed looking wonderstruck. "I sure as hell didn't expect to hear that maverick side of you. I'm impressed with your openness. I see John smiling like a Cheshire Cat! Tell them why, John."

"Jake and I have a bet going with a very rigid archeologist, who is a professor at a prestigious university. We wagered that everything you just said will be verified in twenty-five years, and he can just go shit himself for shaming us and not being willing to even slightly wonder about the possibility of a past that exceeds our current knowledge. He prefers to tie archeology in a pretty little bow with a conclusive article in a well-known journal.

"Welcome to our world of insane revelations and incalculable mysteries. We ignore the shaming and lack of respect and go forward with our right brains. We're determined to be like the ancestors you mentioned who don't rely only on logic and what they can see with their eyes. We're looking at the world through our relationship with the endless data from *the field* which makes us infinitely powerful and capable of doing things that *seem* impossible in this moment of our evolution."

The group became silent to take in the magnitude of intimate secrets and visions they'd shared—revelations that had often led to ridicule or loss of standing with peers. Without further conversation, they entered further into a series of caverns.

Suddenly Avani's eyes met the next pyramid. "It's like in Egypt and other places! There's no door! Later civilizations added them. It's seemingly solid. The architecture... the technology... it's breathtaking!"

She walked around it slowly to allow her eyes to absorb and assimilate every inch of its architecture. Stopping to stare at it from base to tip, she asked, "How do you enter? Is there water under it? That's what we find most often. The water, along with specific minerals, creates a perfect transmitter of electric charge and subtle information."

Turning to Jake and then John, Avani asked, "How did you manage to keep this site discreet?"

"It's been a combination of events that helped with that," John answered. "For a while we were worried. Then there was a legal dispute and the original inhabitants of this area were given rights to the skeletons, as relating to their ancestors. In addition, the local indigenous people have to be consulted to grant permission for proposed archeological projects in this area. No one can take the skeletons or artifacts and study them off-site. It was clear to others in our field that we had already done extensive documentation, that we knew the site intimately, and that we had a relationship with the local people. So our peers would have to come and work under our supervision.

"There are other factors that deter fellow archeologists as well. Sites like this don't promise placing an archeologist in the spotlight of fame and glory and large grants which usually go to large sites. On request, we share our findings openly and we wrote a seminal paper about the cove, so currently there's not an incentive for our colleagues to come for research. I can't say for sure about the future, but right now, we don't find colleagues wanting to flock here. You must have observed that when you get past the dating of bones, artifacts and other generalities, the research teams tend to move to the next adventure.

"From my perspective, the real value to us in this cave system is that our research adds the perspectives of cosmic archeology, quantum physics, and astrobiology. Often when we try to discuss these relevant topics with colleagues, they start bailing from the conversation, complaining we're not staying within the established boundaries of the field. Jake and I are fortunate to have more broadminded colleagues in fields like astrobiology, cosmology, physics, astronomy, and cosmic anthropology.

"For us, discovering who the skeletons were as a species was important. We wanted to study the artifacts, technologies like megalithic circles, and other hidden clues to uncover how civilizations operated when they were alive. It's not about finding an ancient skeleton. It's about how the being who embodied that skeleton can be placed within human evolution and history. How could getting to know Max and other skeletons in this cave system, including a smaller female of Max's species, influence our understanding of past and present biology, humanity's current advanced technology skills, and our world view of who we are and have been as a species?

"We do not discount Sophia's lucid dreams about these skeletons. She dreamed about Max and the smaller female, seeing them as *beloveds* who walked this planet long ago. Although we have not published her accounts, we are unshakable that lucid dreaming is one method to receive information from the infinite quantum field.

"We also respect the ancient narratives of the local indigenous people. One of their elders, Will, shocked us when he divulged that the bony structure of the female giant was *The Mystic* from their long-held traditions. Hang onto your hats, friends! He also divulged that Sophia and this female giant are one and the same. We've been hit relentlessly with mind-numbing truth-bombs like this and we realize that we have to allow plenty of time for reflection before we can fully assimilate these revelations. Instead of brushing off Will's divulgences as imaginings or simple story narratives, we took his words to heart and allowed questions to arise and further conversations with him and each other to ensue.

"What did our ancestors learn from the giants? How were our forefathers possibly influenced by the skills and wisdom of these ancient beings—who don't appear to be human or at least not one-hundred percent human? Often we observe polymaths and other academics trying to figure out how structures like pyramids were created with mind-blowing accuracy and advanced architectural techniques. Going back to what you said a few minutes ago, are we using too much left brain thinking to understand something they created from highly advanced right-brain perception? When we were young archeologists these questions were off the table, but now we explore potential answers with a few colleagues who we trust implicitly to be open and kick-ass courageous in their willingness to remain outside the box.

"Jake and I want to work with collaborative teams so that anthropology, biology, chemistry, cosmology, and archeology can help paint a broader landscape of these ancient sites, rather than focusing on minutiae or only parts of a whole picture. From the field of astrobiology, as you two know, we gain the insight of molecular biology, biophysics, biochemistry, chemistry, astronomy, and more. We're not considered conventional archeologists. New fields are evolving and the galactic aspect is finally growing roots. You two must be observing this."

"We feel like the historical explorers who first went to the Arctic or charted the glaciers in Alaska in the 1800's," said Caitlyn. "In our smaller circles, we're not being ridiculed. In fact, we're fueling each other with a whole lot of dialogue and enthusiasm."

"For example, we want to know who Max was. Where did he come from, and why did he come? You say he doesn't have human DNA. We've seen these kinds of giant skeletons globally, including the elongated skulls, and all of them, according to current understanding of the structure of human DNA, are not human. What was daily life like for them? What may have happened to the planet at that time? I'm thinking that atmospherically there were changes such as floods, moving ice, massive predators, and other day-to-day survival challenges to contend with. What was civilization like for these beings and everyone else? There are similar artifacts and artwork and ancient texts in the archeological sites in Egypt, Central America, and other places we've explored.

"Apart from that, there are broader questions that can perhaps be answered with clues through artifacts and art, like, How did these civilizations depict the common person's relationship to those of authority? Were artifacts and carvings an indication of how people viewed humans who were their leaders, or even off-planet visitors who came from the sky? Did they see them as mystical gods prophesied by their ancient stories? Maybe they saw them as overlords. What were the foundational structures for the ones who held control? Are they different than the governments and religious institutions that we saw in the Middle Ages, for example?

"I'll share a seminal moment in history to explain why I'm asking these questions about *control*. In a monastery in the fifteenth century, books made from papyrus and other delicate materials were a treasure. The masses were not allowed to read, nor did they have access to books. In my view, this censorship was a means of *control*. How did society find ways to depict this oppression in art and other ways? The truth about the daily lives of ordinary people and the oppressive nature of their culture had to be hidden and carefully recorded through symbolism. Attempts to record it were often fruitless. Art was demolished and books burned.

"One poignant example is that as medieval monks made copies of a document, they could not ask a question about what they transcribed. And worse than that, they could never speak about nor question what they read. If they did, they were flogged or otherwise punished. This created slavish compliance and they all became like zombies. We've seen mass graves from the eleventh century and many other periods in history, the bodies showing signs of gruesome wounds. And for what? Finally, the whole civilization crashed and burned—as did Rome and Mesopotamia before.

"Brutality and oppression always seem to have preceded the fall of these empires. As their world crashed down around them their leaders grasped for more control. These patterns clearly repeat. We researched the constant rise and fall of emperors, popes, and kings. We dug deeper to discover the *role the working class played* in civilizations."

Avani nodded and changed her unusual upbeat tone to one of melancholy as she said, "This gives me chills, Caitlyn. We know this, but most of our friends are so distracted by life they can't see how these failed civilizations overlay perfectly, and forebodingly, on top of ours today. Keep going. Sorry for interrupting. This is so important."

Caitlyn smiled lovingly at her friend in response and said, "My interest in the galactic or cosmic aspect that you've been talking about goes deeper than archeology or any of the sciences. I want to know how we can learn from Max, the ancients, the Middle Ages, and all other times in human history, to avert a disaster looming over our culture and our planet's future. Max is part of human evolution. We're kidding ourselves to think otherwise. How did he view us and how did we view him? Have humans always tended towards being subservient or is that an evolution that happened after cataclysms or for other reasons? How and why did the wealthiest and most surreptitious elites in a civilization control the masses?

"Have you noticed how divided we are today? How distracted we are by our daily life and concerns? There was always a theme in fallen civilizations—people saw themselves as less *than* or *not powerful enough* to overcome obstacles or rise above those who sought to control them. Because they saw their oppressors as *parental figures* or scary overlords, they sought their guidance and got their survival needs met by those who *seemed to be* more powerful than them. How did they develop that dangerously fallacious perception?

"As a species, if we have the unicity gene that Sophia mentioned last night, that means that we have unlimited powers for multiverse travel and communication. We forget that we are more powerful if we expand our focus to include more than the 3-D world, if we stop abdicating our inherent power to others. There aren't enough self-help gurus or spiritual teachers to constantly spoon feed us into seeing the truth of who we are. My point is that we suspect that Max and his beloved came to help humanity find their way back to the source of their greatness. Do the cave art and pyramids give us a way to go back and maybe retrieve our *latent memory from long ago when Max roamed the Earth* so we can step into the evolved beings that we are?

"I know this can sound like science fiction or "woo-woo spirituality," but we are quantum at our core. And it's time to own that truth. Being quantum computers of light is no longer a crazy theory. This quantum-ness is who we are and why we are alive on this planet. This is central to our human evolution.

"Otherwise, we can just go on being distracted by media, limited by our insecurities and our fear of what others think of us. We can get some super-cool computer chip and let someone else think for us. We'll be resigning ourselves to suffer like silent monks in the Middle Ages in a monastery where freedom wasn't in the equation, and life was nothing but unbearable suffering and low frequency thoughts and experiences.

"It's important to Avani and me to look at the past so we can look to the future with a sense of excitement about the possibilities for radical change. Our focus remains on what we're doing *now* because change happens in the present moment—inside each of us. We've had conversations with our colleagues about this a thousand times. It's about focusing on our own contribution. It's not about hating dictators or cruel rulers of the past or anticipating future rulers who will save us. It's about our *individual frequency*. Period.

"Avani and I want to discover and share what the pyramids were about, why Max and others came here, and how we can learn from the fall of civilizations in the past. We worry that our generation may end up being the last civilization on Gaia—that ours is the epoch on Earth when humans become extinct. No way! For us, it's about *both* learning about the past *and* taking personal responsibility for the present.

"If we let our civilization decay, Gaia would still continue her gradual evolution with extraordinary resilience. She and the stars will still align, and she'll remain a vital part of the Universe even without us. When will we quit trying to fix her and instead, fall deeply in love with her? When will we relate to her as a sentient being? Will we align with the Earth and the cosmos before a tragic historical epoch reaches a point of no return for us?

"How far back do our biological roots and evolution reach? We need to explore this through a broader lens. We're feeling that Max and other skeletons could be much older than any of us realize. As Avani mentioned, we also posit that due to countless, massive global cataclysms, we might not find the archeological evidence that proves our true origins, as it remains buried for miles beneath the surface. We can't get to it yet. It's like that in areas all over the globe. When we grasp how much we don't know, how often governments obstruct our exploration, and how each field of science pushes hard to teach only mainstream thinking and to trust only their piece of the puzzle, we get frustrated. It's so freaking crazy untangling and dealing with all of this. Yet we *definitely* do not have the total picture of the planet's past nor our true potential for higher evolution."

Sophia was seated on a rock that seemed to have been hewn into a chair for a human of her size. "I am sitting here on this solid foundation from which to listen and take in wisdom from two wonderful young women. I feel you are on solid footing in your curiosity and areas of focus. My part in all of this is a little different; it's about the *sacredness* of it all. When I think of something sacred, its transcendent nature allows me to dive easily, deeply into my Essence. Sacredness is not about experiencing something on a grand scale like the parting of the dead sea. It's about precious *moments of connection* with each other, with Max, and others from various coordinates in spacetime, and connecting with the quantum-charged protons within my being. I have no problem thinking on scales from inconceivably small to unfathomably huge.

"When I go to the pyramids, participate in an equinox ceremony at the stone circle, or enjoy mind-blowing conversations—without exception—sacred, sublime potentiality is at play. The more I open to higher consciousness, the more I embrace the unknown, which expands my consciousness further. Long-held fear, anger, pride, and apathy melt away and space opens for love and appreciation for a human life to emerge naturally and powerfully from inside me. A simple joy for existence emerges.

"I don't strive for dramatic moments. More than ever, I appreciate the simple, sacred moments while in meditation—connecting to *the field* in and around me to observe the endless potentiality of my ever-expansive nature. There's no end to what you can learn at Mystic Cove about history, the Earth, and yourself.

"Caitlyn and Avani, what priorities do you each have for going into the pyramid? Would you rather spend time with Jake or John working in the caverns with cave art or checking out the stone circles?

"And of course, there are more skeletons, some of which are giants older than Max who have red hair and wore robes. The skeletons are a vast subject for exploration. After a flood over ten thousand years ago, some guarded our survival while others became mentors and advisors. There are many global shamanic traditions that kept that period in world history alive through story.

"Since you have limited time here, where do you want to begin? John, Jake ... do you have ideas of what they could explore today? I can stay or come back later, according to what you decide."

"It's up to our guests," Jake said smiling. "We can show them the first part of the cave system and then go with the flow."

"I'd like to work with Jake and John," Caitlyn said, responding with the speed and directness of a lightning-bolt. "Avani, are you salivating to get into that pyramid? I was worried that it was going to take heavy machinery to get her out of the pyramids in Egypt and Peru." She and Avani laughed at the memory.

Avani stood up confidently and said, "I'm super excited to enter the sacred pyramid. You have my word: I'll be more willing to emerge from this one. It's true. I have an obsession with pyramids and once in, I hate to leave them. But be fair, Caitlyn—at those other sites, they only gave us a few minutes in the pyramids. And the connection with unicity, pure stillness, and infinite space was totally amazing! I was in bliss!"

"Yep, I can't agree more," Caitlyn said laughing. "Enjoy your trip to the cosmos, Avani. I'll be with you in spirit."

"You always are," Avani replied congenially, as she watched Caitlyn adjust her backpack, tighten her boot laces, and prepare for her adventure into the cave system.

Sophia's eyes danced. "Jake, John, and I agreed to let you two take all the time you want for exploration today. No rushing. No questions are off the table. Having fun is also important. Discovery without fun can make this exploration serious and lifeless. This work is *mind-glowing*. I hope your mind becomes illumined and ponders unexpected revelations and your heart gets to enjoy mystical moments and archeological surprises. When you finish working down here, take time to rest, make notes or whatever you want to do. We'll meet at the fire pit at Megan's for dinner at six o'clock. Sound good?"

They all agreed as went in their different directions.

Avani moved towards Sophia, who said with a sparkle in her eye, "The local elder of the indigenous people, Will, taught me the utterances to open the first pyramid. Would you like to go inside?"

Looking intently at the majestic forty-foot-tall pyramid, Avani moved towards it unhurriedly with a gaze and body language that exhibited intense reverence. She folded her hands in prayer over her heart. As Sophia uttered the ancient, mysterious sounds, a spontaneous, radiant smile emerged on Avani's face. Her eyes widened and her eyebrows raised as though a breathtaking sunrise was expanding in electrifying resplendence in front of her. The pyramid opened, inviting her into subtle fields of unlimited potentiality and moments of jaw-dropping astonishment.

# CHAPTER 5

# FIRESIDE CIVILIZATION CHAT

At sunset, gold and pink horizontal streaks spread across the western horizon. A light breeze wafted around the group who were in deep conversation—becoming increasingly introspective by virtue of the roaring fire that John had meticulously created for the evening gathering.

Crystal clear skies set the stage for mystical star gazing followed by the chance for a special meteor shower for those who could stay awake for it. Uninhibited laughter, playfulness, informality, and camaraderie were woven through the conversation.

"Thank you so much," Avani said with her customary charm. "Today was amazing—spending unrestricted time in the pyramid and staring at the drawings until my mind was saturated with questions and ideas for research. Usually I've been supervised or under a time constraint so I can only hit the highlights, and we only work our tiny little area and usually don't get to explore the whole site. I appreciate the way you gave us the freedom to explore the caverns without boundaries today."

Looking towards Avani with a sly smile, Caitlyn prompted her friend. "Tell everyone why the cave drawings and the pyramid so impacted you and why your discoveries today are relevant to both of us."

"Do we have one evening or a few years?" Avani laughed with unfeigned delight as she flashed a smile and a wink towards Caitlyn. "What my bestie is talking about is an unexpected area of study for me in school. Although I was already getting to do exciting fieldwork as part of my career path, like most of my colleagues I decided to acquire further degrees. Luckily, I was accepted into a master's program in Archeology and later, a specialized area of Anthropology for a PhD, both from an Ivy league school."

Looking towards Caitlyn, Avani shook her head and said as if in disbelief of what she was about to describe, "My crazy friend, Caitlyn, kept pushing me to get into the university's world class library, a vast treasure house of ancient documents. Her idea seemed insane at first but ended up lighting a fire in me.

"The idea was simple. I would use resources at the university, including cutting edge DNA research, to trace civilizations related to my Portuguese roots from Goa in India and other influences in my DNA lineage in Maharashtra, India that may trace back to Europe. I would also study Caitlyn's European roots in Portugal, England, and France. We wondered if her DNA was linked with mine—even though we appear to be from different countries and lineages. We've got blue-eyed, blonde Caitlyn with European roots, and Brown-skinned, brown-eyed, Indian me. However, we wondered about *common* DNA; we knew there could be links, maybe *ancient*. How far back would we have to go to find a common link? One reason this idea came up is there were fossils in our digs that indicate humans lived a couple of hundred thousand years ago in Africa. And another site posited a human skeleton was dated to 3.7 million years ago. What if somewhere *way back*, we have common DNA? We were curious for anthropological and archeological reasons.

"Only crazy explorers like us would plunge into the deep, dark waters of ancient history in this way—while working on advanced degrees! There was no way my advisor would let me head in that direction for my dissertation so this was for personal research. We also wanted to explore the ways our ancestors expressed common *emotional patterns* like fear, arrogance, and shame—which can be passed down for countless generations. By the way, my advisor later recanted his objections and encouraged me to publish a paper with my findings. He was so gobsmacked by our research that he began to support me one hundred percent. I was edified... and totally thrilled!

"You likely know that, for a while, scientists believed that some of our DNA was important and the rest was junk, but that *junk theory* is being continually debunked. There is something equally important. The effect of DNA on humans isn't only physical. It affects our emotional state. One study has found that grandchildren of people who suffered trauma during the Holocaust had the same genes for depression and anxiety as their grandparents—which could mean that some mental/ emotional patterns we find running constantly in our heads were initiated by someone else. That truth-bomb torqued on my brain for a long time!

"Recent research has also revealed that thirteen generations carry similar genes. Looking back deeply into our ancestry, Caitlyn and I got excited about research focused on giants and ancient skeletons that do not match human DNA identified today. When we had our DNA tested, we discovered it was similar to theirs. I see by your faces you didn't expect that rad truth! Neither did we! It gets crazier... we were not alone. Other people have been tested for this giant DNA and other unidentified DNA. Using advanced tests which are quite intricate, it may someday be possible to discover a perfect match with giants and very ancient ancestors going back millions of years. Let that crazy idea land! Oh my God! How can that even be possible?! We were particularly fascinated by a giant we saw with unique DNA. It's important to realize that the DNA lab work I'm referring to was NOT examined by one of those online ancestry sites. We worked with innovative geneticists at the cutting-edge and who were interested in our research and hypothesis.

"Since it's likely that DNA is passed down through countless generations, thus bringing through emotional commonalities with our ancestors, we wondered how could humanity be affected emotionally today by DNA from past civilizations? And what subtle, yet vital information is stored in our DNA? One of our colleagues studies biology down to the molecular and quantum levels and she says humans have a vast *library* of information in this intricate net of proteins we call DNA.

"We wondered what cultural norms might have triggered the rise and fall of different civilizations and what *emotional triggers* had a direct influence on the collapse. If we cracked that code, we could figure out how to deal with seemingly insurmountable challenges we currently face as a species. On a more personal level, was there anything in ancient DNA that was emotionally hindering or helping either or both of us? Caitlyn and I have Portuguese and British blood in common, but what about the rest of our DNA?

"One example of unusual DNA that got our attention belonged to a giant in Central America with an elongated head. His DNA was not found on Earth. Crazy, right? Adding to the mystery of this unique DNA is globally documented shamanic history about giants helping and advising many civilizations.

We began to wonder if advanced DNA helped these populations to express *unicity*, which I understand to be Sophia's term for the *connectedness* with everyone, everywhere all at once. It's a big concept and we realized that to research this concept, we'd likely have to enter unconventional arenas of science.

"Wanting to expand our perception, we didn't want to only read established journals and papers. We knew they would be constrained by natural biases and the professional urge to play it safe and robotically support the status quo. We explored letters, journals, historical records, and anything else we could find from a wide variety of time periods. I speak Portuguese, French, and English. Having that advantage, I was interested in reading personal accounts of people who lived among my ancestors. I ran everything by Caitlyn because we wanted to collaborate on this project.

"I'll condense what I found. Oh my God! It was amazing!

"Visiting Goa, I found cave drawings of animals and symbols similar to what we've seen globally, ranging in age from twelve thousand to fifty thousand years old. The same kind of cave art indicating a race of giants was found in Central America. Many people do not know that India has plenty of pyramids as well. Of course, Indian culture and religion is full of stories, assumed to be myths, of celestial wars in the heavens. We can't ignore that the mythological time periods described in such stories correspond to those described by other civilizations similarly documenting flying gods through images etched on stone pillars and the walls of caves. In some very ancient caves, you can look up at a domed roof and see drawings that correspond to known constellations, rendered to scale. Who educated these people? Did they have highly developed biology and advanced mental acuity tens of thousands of years ago, maybe even farther back in time? It appears they knew geometry and mathematics long before the ancient Greeks.

"We carefully examined the cave drawings that depict giants, how their proportions compare to the animals and other people in the artwork. It appears that at least some of them stood twenty to thirty-feet-tall. It may not sound like a big deal that Caitlyn is fair skinned and tall, but there's tons of research and conjecture about the reason for the size of some of the people depicted in these ruins. Are they her distant ancestors? Not everyone in Portugal expresses her physical qualities. Where did this tall, fair-skinned species come from? We tried to find a link with Scandinavia but found none. We also wondered about a link between our DNA and the elongated heads. According to new technologies, Caitlyn may share genes with beings who look like Max. That was mind-bending, for sure. Sounds crazy, right? But stay with me. Who were these beings? Our commitment to keeping open minds led us to dig deeper—pun intended for us archeologists!

"First we went to an underwater site in Portugal. We'd seen images from deep dives there. Like Egypt, Bosnia, China, and all over the Americas, the pyramids under water are enormous—towering sometimes a hundred feet or more. Why so tall? A commonality is that they are surrounded by elaborate carvings etched on pillars and structures within entire cities submerged long ago.

"Over the years, as we went from site to site, we noticed they share common symbols which we believe are not literal. Rather they are metaphoric representations of what life was like when the civilizations were thriving. There's more evidence now that off the coast of Portugal was a part of an ancient *Atlante-an* culture. That is the name given to a culture from eleven to twelve thousand years ago that applied advanced mathematics and physics in building structures—an inconceivably high-tech race of humans.

"We were lucky to hook up with a group who wanted to study how that culture, whose ruins are now under water, interfaced with Egypt, Mesopotamia, the Pacific Rim, and all of the Americas. The similarities are stunning. On all of these various continents, they found the same symbols on pillars and rocks, the same technologies, like stone circles and pyramids, and the use of water to effect electromagnetic fields. These ancient cultures seemed to know where natural cosmic portals occurred in the Earth, where quantum spacetime travel is possible. The swirling vortex of zero point energy of a being could move through worm holes into the multiverse. Sounds like sci-fi, but I want to be clear that there is burgeoning science to support this inconceivable truth.

"Keep in mind, these sites are tens of thousands of years old. At that time, weren't humans supposed to be happily hunting, gathering, and gradually evolving? How did the humans in the places with the cave art evolve rapidly in architecture, intelligence, and civilization?

"If mainstream thinking says people like Caitlyn are not linked in DNA with the long-skulled giants, then who are these non-human beings? Did they help humanity by breeding with us to generate faster evolution? Is that how all of these civilizations manifested across the Earth simultaneously?

"Our curious-minded anthropologist colleagues asked a lot of provocative questions that kept us searching for unpredictable answers. We did tons of research, and although we can't conclusively prove that the DNA of off-planet beings was responsible for this accelerated evolution, we could not disprove it.

"If such visitors were evil, then why didn't they just kill everyone and take over the planet?

"We also wondered why such sophisticated civilizations fell. Was it a natural disaster or were these advanced beings subject to the pitfalls of greed or power when they aligned with certain humans and began to co-lead civilizations? Oh my God! We had so many questions!

"In our quest for answers, we interfaced with colleagues in astronomy, anthropology, and quantum physics. It seemed that two things may have happened to cause the demise of these civilizations. One is natural—a massive, global flood. Another possibility is that survivors were perhaps greedy and manipulative as well as very smart. And most importantly, were they focused on unicity? How does unicity, our inherent connection with all-that-is, fit into evolution and extinction? What was happening to humanity's DNA?

"Some off-planet survivors of the flood may have left the planet. Whoever stayed, along with the humans who ruled, maybe stayed together and perpetuated their lineage through DNA and handing down secrets in underground places via sacred mystery cults. We examined when and how certain symbols appeared and reappeared throughout the centuries. We also looked for civilizations that suddenly materialized, flourished, but mysteriously fell apart and crashed into extinction.

"However, researching civilizations going back more than twelve thousand years was not easy—not to mention beyond twenty-five thousand. So we decided to focus first on the last six thousand years for our research into the DNA of our ancestors—and then we'd look further back, if possible. We realized that because of its massive influence on western culture, we needed to investigate the Roman Empire. So I looked in that direction next.

"Some of my ancestors were Christian... Well, sort of. They were Templar Knights and friends of Templars who settled in Portugal. The Templars were a group of unique, medieval knights. Although they were called *knights* and many historians have written that they were fierce warriors, my research indicated otherwise. It was trippy when I found documents that revealed another side of the Templars. In the twelfth century, a small group of nine knights went to Jerusalem and stayed there for seven years. They were focused on the Temple Mount and later were referred to as the Knights Templar.

"A group of British engineers miraculously got permission to dig under the Temple Mount. This area is sacred to Jews and Muslims. That's why I'm saying it was a miracle to get permission. Oh my God! Within eighty feet into the granite, what they found was stunning—intricately designed caverns dug by hand, stretched for extensive distances. It was clear the Templars had been there, with their famous swords and crosses left behind from a millennium earlier. But the tunnels were so advanced that it was doubtful even mighty Templars could have done the work with the primitive tools at their disposal. Is it possible that the Templars discovered the tunnels and perhaps slightly extended them in specific areas? Rooms were found that seemed to be used for ceremonies, designed to specific geometry.

"Later, Israeli archeologists got permission to explore a particular cavern under the temple that led to a wall blocked with stone and debris. Unfortunately, the authorities would not let them dig through it. They could take photos, but no excavations were allowed. Artifacts showed, once again, that the Templars had dug their way into this sacred area of Jerusalem where Solomon's Temple once stood. What were they looking for? Many said it was the Holy Grail, whatever that was. And some believe they found it.

"It is known the Templars were focused on finding scrolls and ancient wisdom which would offer instruction for how to ascend in frequency without limits. If the grail was a piece of technology that required a savvy, adept mystic to work with its untold power, they would have been qualified for that job. Was it possibly an invaluable, esoteric scroll? At this point, our minds were definitely spinning.

"It's undeniable that Templars were in Jerusalem during the Crusades and that they settled in and under the mystical Temple Mount. We've seen growing evidence that they began creating more tunnels and saving those precious scrolls and other artifacts that likely related to higher consciousness and the mysteries of self actualization. They continually cultivated and experienced the elevation of their individual consciousness to the extent they could elevate their frequency at-will and become alchemists. Mystifying powers were part of their inner circle's experience. However, not all Templars made it into the inner circle. This elite core had to agree to protect the secret treasure of these subtle, esoteric practices with their life. They were more of a secret society than a group of monks. Were they my Goa-Portuguese ancestors and Caitlyn's Portuguese ancestors, too? If so, what qualities did their DNA express?

"When the original nine Templars came to Portugal, they were gifted cities and large tracts of land. As the monastic order grew, all individual knights on every level of the order were required to surrender their possessions which went into an *escrow* held by the Templars. They became known as savvy bankers and financiers as they received money and assets from rich donors, and the order grew quite wealthy. This wealth was allocated to create abundant land, housing, and work for the populations in Templar areas of influence. Their land holdings grew rapidly, and for the sake of time, I'll say generally, by the fourteenth century, they owned a third of Portugal.

"All of this begs the question: Why would affluent land-owners and prosperous kings gift vast amounts of riches and property to the original small band of nine knights? That would be crazy unless those knights possessed something absolutely invaluable—like maybe the capacity to elevate human frequency enough to bi-locate, experience higher states of consciousness, and become superhuman? Likely cosmic bliss and mystical experiences were part of the lure, too. Maybe this mattered more to the well-to-do elites than accumulating resources and prosperity. Whether these capacities were conferred by a scroll, a highly charged electromagnetic box inside an enclosure called an ark, or some other technology, who cares? I couldn't disprove that *something invaluable* was either being sought or protected by the Templars.

"To understand Templar culture and codes of conduct, you should know that married knights were allowed to enter the order, while others became chaste after initiation. Historians found that although quite a few Templars left their wives, others remained married. And some were naughty, if you know what I mean. Plus I cannot find proof they'd be kicked out for sexual mischief. My point is that there were definitely ways that Templar DNA could have been passed down.

"Another interesting aspect of my knightly ancestors is they never agreed to be subject to the Catholic Church."

Pausing, she looked piercingly at Jake. "I can sense you have something to contribute. I've been watching your eyebrows raising and your head nodding. What do you think about what I shared up to this point?"

"Well, to start, I bet the Templar's lack of subservience got the Pope massively pissed off. Back then the church was brutal. You were *in or out*. And *out* meant burned, boiled, or beheaded. I did some work on the Medieval era and there were plenty of papal beasts. Can I add a little more context to see if it sparks something for you?"

"Sure, I'd love that," Avani said with a cheerful smile. "Thanks for entering the conversation, Jake. I invite anyone else to chime in if you want. I'm not here to find a captive audience for my research. I'm all ears! I know you must have looked at these kinds of sites during your career."

Avani adjusted her posture, prepared to pay rapt attention. In response, Jake flashed a congenial smile towards her—which passed like a wave through the group whose faces shone with enjoyment for the subject at hand. Jake launched into sharing his research while John chuckled as though he knew what was coming.

"From my research... holy shit! ... one pope was so bad that his name was taken off the pope-roles! To prevent looking overly scandalous, the worst sixteen of his crimes were never read out loud at his inquisition. Instead, they listed the top seventy such as sodomy, adultery, rape, incest, and murder. Even with all of that, he still had followers. That is typical of human nature. Sometimes we don't like to admit our idols are like us. We put them on pedestals and hate like hell when they let us down. We'll follow them devotedly even when a court of law shows us their crimes or when they confess their atrocities.

"At this point in our fascinating conversation, it's relevant to mention something related to the Medieval Templars. My birth name is Jacob and my father's distant ancestors hail from Jerusalem. I have a fascination with the Middle East which led John and me to engage in provocative digs there. While working in that part of the world, we noticed your Templar buddies showed up. Is this a good time to share our findings or maybe I should wait until you finish?"

"Please go ahead!" Avani said, glancing at Caitlyn with an irrepressible smile that glistened with feverish elation. "Oh my God! Caitlyn and I are stoked to have this kind of exchange of information. Keep going! Tell us everything!"

"Okay, great! We realized that Templars, your potential ancestors, were bad-ass warriors," he explained, "especially when it came to protecting their beloved Jerusalem from Muslim invaders. But we wondered why historians keep talking about them as mighty knights who protected the Catholic Church. We couldn't verify that viewpoint because it seems like they were more interested in Jerusalem as a special place to investigate, building tunnels for long distances underneath it. John the Baptist, Mary Magdalene, and the well-known, Pagan Green Man were embedded into their architecture. Templar rituals and lore provide massive wormholes to navigate. After a lot of digging, we discovered that the churches they established appear to honor John the Baptist, who was revered as a prophet and renowned teacher with a significant following of spiritual seekers during Yeshua's lifetime and beyond. Through his successors, his teachings, values, and spiritual practices were perpetuated for many centuries. To our surprise, we realized that Mary Magdalene was likely the female icon displayed in Templar churches. Adding to those revelations, we surmised they also incorporated rituals related to death, birth, and renewal as part of their mystical spiritual practices. Thus the Green Man is noticeable in their architecture and lore.

"Wanting to take an objective approach to our hypothesis, we needed to eliminate possible ecclesiastical bias from our research. When we arrived in Portugal—Caitlyn's ancestral land—we met astute secular scholars and researchers who shared archeological and historical accounts indicating that Mary Magdalene may have represented to the Templars the mythological figure of Isis from ancient mystery schools. Isis, a Greek name for an important Egyptian goddess, was often depicted holding a child as she represented the mother goddess. Her influence was widespread across the entire region from Egypt into Rome, Greece, and Mesopotamia. At the same time, Mary Magdalene was known as a mystic and highly evolved soul by those who knew her. The reason for the Templar's high regard for her was likely multifaceted.

"The team confirmed the Templars likely spent a lot of time in Jerusalem. They speculated that Templars found documents or artifacts that cemented their bond with John the Baptist and Mary Magdalene. Conspicuously missing was any Templar church conclusively honoring Jesus or his mother, nor were Templars unequivocally in service to the Catholic Church. Rather, Templars consistently displayed an independent stance which kept them at odds with the papacy. I have to say that from what John and I discovered in various archeological digs and in historical research, the Templars were more like *mystics* than *monks*.

"Every city they built or area they cultivated made room for the preservation of the ancient mystery school wisdom, including the teachings related to metaphorically dying to the physical form to allow an initiate to awaken and roam forever in the unlimited space of elevated consciousness. From that standpoint, we came to the consensus that unless further research came forward, it was difficult to view them undisputedly as loyal champions for or followers of the traditional Roman church.

"Another historical revelation about the Templars involved the outer circles of their order who were bankers, navigators, artists, craft-makers, bookkeepers, and architects. Does that sound like monks? They seemed to give a middle finger to the pope, who they tricked into saying they were good guys while they never signed on as loyal members of his team. They had this cheeky style of interacting with the popes, like playing cat and mouse games. Without question, skillfully and miraculously, they stayed one step ahead of the Roman church for a couple of hundred years, until the inquisitions took over like a house on fire, literally.

"More relevant for us is, how did outrageous characters like popes, kings, and authoritarian rulers throughout history dupe a whole population? And how did their successors do the same thing while the working class, our ancestors, suffered and starved in a pit of hopelessness and despair? I love your question about which gene expressions were predominant at the time and which ones came forward in full expression and how that could affect you? What ancestral DNA expression carried forward as raw *boldness* and courage? Does that describe you two?

"If mysticism had been allowed to continue, I wonder if it could have helped our ancestors to turn the tide? Could we have expressed new genes? What if they'd continued their ancient traditions looking to the inner world, where their benevolent hearts could express virtues like compassion, kindness, and love as opposed to savage aggression? How did the masses benefit by following endless church rules, designed and contrived by emperors and councils? If they'd been allowed the freedom to worship as they were inclined to do, maybe they could have experienced their true Self, their infinite glory. We'll never know.

"Were the Templars tapped into this line of thinking? I do not want to digress into an endless wormhole of speculation. We cannot change the past. Based on your research and questions, I'm wondering if their exalted states and capacities for moving through dimensions within themselves, and perhaps bi-locating, are a product of information in their DNA? Has it been passed down? Could it be something you and Caitlyn have in common? Maybe that's what we all have in common? Maybe those rascals gave us something unexpected and difficult to identify and quantify? These are my musings I offer to this absolutely spellbinding discussion."

Lowering his head as though in deep thought, Jake sat still for a moment. Everyone instantly joined him in silent reflection. Even the crickets paused their incessant chirping.

As he raised his head, Jake took a deep breath and addressed Avani saying, "Sorry. Please forgive me for talking so long and throwing out copious ideas and revelations for you and Caitlyn to consider. Can you tell this subject gets my hackles up? Yet more than that, is it apparent that it leaves me completely befuddled? You have my respect and full attention."

"Are you kidding? No worries. I'm psyched you are interested enough in what I've said to add your thoughts. Plus you concisely articulated what we wondered about. Is their DNA providing something more than brown eyes versus blue eyes? Emotionally, it was difficult to do this research because we accessed a clear view of eons of inconceivable, horrendous human suffering. Templar history has been mingled with fiction, religion, and lore—a tangled mess that makes unwinding the truth difficult. However, we had a purpose. We wanted to learn about genetic expression and emotional patterns rather than drown in judgment of what happened to them or how they chose to live and express spiritually. I love hearing what you learned about the Templar-Jerusalem connection. We did not go on site to that region but, like you, we definitely saw a potential connection with Muslims (which I will talk about in a moment), mysticism, and weak ties, if any, to Roman church authorities.

"Because my research is different than a lot of the information about the Templars, I've received criticism. Without getting distracted, I stood by my findings. Every year, we learn more and we can no longer hold current historical accounts and beliefs about our lineages as being unquestionable reality.

"At this point in the conversation, it is relevant to further address my observation that perhaps they were not a devout order of Catholic monks who protected Christian travelers and that sort of thing. I concluded that above all else, the Templars were highly skilled mystics. That relates to what you said about them possibly having advanced DNA that expresses as a capacity for mysticism. Maybe that was the secret to their insane capacity to fight in protection of Jerusalem. As they fought to maintain the city, they may have also discovered secrets in those underground areas of the Temple Mount.

"What hardly anyone talks about in the Templar's history is a link with *esoteric cults originating in ancient Mesopotamia and accepted by early Islam.* Were specific Islamic sects in the Middle East part of a secretive, insider-only wisdom tradition which included esoteric rituals? We found evidence of some Muslims known as epic magicians and ruthless protectors of their occult mysteries. We saw crossover between Templar rituals and enigmatic Islamic influences. But I'm not sure why that occurred.

"One group we studied in depth were the Mandaeans, who lived in ancient Sumer prior to Islam and flourished in the early Islamic period. Historical records show that both Templars and Mandaeans believed John the Baptist was an important prophet—to the Mandaeans, he was the most important. They used baptism as a fundamental ritual, and were known for highly secretive, esoteric practices. As the "Sons of Light," they proclaimed themselves to be the custodians of secret rituals and knowledge—blending Jewish Gnosticism with ancient Babylonian belief systems. Both Templars and this Islamic cult were not considered loyal members of mainstream religions in their respective countries but they were both infamous for practicing magic and focusing on the Divine as being all-pervasive. Immortality is included in both philosophies. And the study of specific, secret, divine knowledge is a lynchpin upon which both Templars and this ancient, esoteric Islamic cult built their traditions and philosophical systems.

"The Templars were teaching self-actualization to larger numbers of initiates, who were willing to take the oath and agree to their secret practices. I'm not glorifying them as benevolent heroes. It's just that they were definitely more than monks, warriors or normal land barons.

"Caitlyn added to our research by going onsite to confirm that, in Portugal, Templars built cathedrals over old stone circles or pagan temples. The Egyptian goddess, Isis, was a powerful and easy-to-find symbol in Portugal and the same applies to Mary Magdalene from the Christian faith.

"Today, quantum science doesn't shy away from looking at time-travel and teleporting from specific locations on earth to other coordinates in space. This is accomplished most easily where a ley line grows strong enough electromagnetically that portals open to other spacetime coordinates. And wham! Those Templars were headed to another point in spacetime. When that sinks in... Oh my God! It also looks like these guys were playing with the fabric of time and carefully trying not to tear it. Instead they aligned with places where subtle quantum travel happens naturally. Where the heck did they get this idea? Were they endowed genetically to have the predisposition for this kind of knowledge? Maybe they were focused enough to express genes that were dormant, like what we've been calling *junk* DNA. Somehow, they were doing some very cool stuff. What was that infamous grail, ark, or whatever they found? We didn't uncover definitive answers to many questions like that.

"For the Templars, the idea of creation and going into a womb-like stillness to be able to generate the cosmic experience of higher consciousness was definitely part of their practices. Who taught them to do that?

"Globally, we often see snakes carved in stone or cave paintings. Iconographers tell us the serpent appears to represent the rising of a subtle energy in the body. This idea has been commonly found in India, but the Templars also used snake-like symbols in the art they created for cathedrals and other buildings. Another surprising image found in most Templar architecture is the Green Man, a Celtic deity symbolizing rebirth and fertility—in effect, he brings a dead, winter-like earth back to spring-like wonder. His head is made of or surrounded by leaves and foliage. Why were Catholic monks obsessed with symbols like this—using them throughout their highly acclaimed architectural projects? You can even find these symbols and other Templar-related art in twentieth century cathedrals in your local area—built under Freemason influence or European artists who perhaps began to accept the prolific symbols as *Catholic culture* here and abroad. That's another can of worms. For this conversation, I'll focus on what we discovered about European Templar culture.

"Caitlyn and I posit that the Templars included the Green Man's symbolism of death and rebirth as a theme in their rituals for initiates of the inner circle. That was a key aspect of ancient matrilineal cultures (where knowledge, sagacity, and name were passed down through the *female line*). In the ancient scrolls or whatever else the Templars found, perhaps these ideas had been preserved. They were walking on blasphemous territory by preserving ancient customs that the masses could gravitate towards and participate in with a sense of reverence and sanctity—this made the Templars even more radical and dangerous to churches and kings. The church adopted specific doctrines and anything else was heresy. No other form of worship was allowed. Period.

"In Templar architecture, they often included shallow carvings hewn from rock about six feet long, with a slab of rock to cover the top. We believe the initiates went into these spaces which were womb-like or even tomb-like in design. After using plant medicines—which they could easily have learned from the culture of the Green Man's pagan legacy—initiates could enter a trance state and have a mind-altering cosmic experience. From there, they could have slowly learned how to reproduce those subtle, quantum-style experiences purposefully through meditation and other practices. What motivated them to do this?

"My research showed that the Templars perhaps believed if they elevated their personal frequency, and could maintain a high enough inner state, they could shift human consciousness on the planet, gradually yet permanently. However, they allowed their communities to choose how they wanted to worship and elevate in consciousness. This was markedly different from the Roman Church's approach of forcing people to obey strict, dogmatic doctrines, while sitting back and watching them starve and suffer. The Templars acknowledged that those higher up in the Church's hierarchy had full bellies, big egos, and were lawless. Templars taught that war, cruelty, and riches at the expense of others was never part of Jesus' teachings nor was it going to create a safe and benevolent world for everybody. If that is what historians and archeologists discovered, why do they continue to depict them as warriors?

"In my research, I observed that over time, they started doing less fighting and way more land gathering, navigating, and banking. Perhaps they'd seen firsthand the horrific violence of the crusades, witnessed the hideous hypocrisy of the inquisitions, and the brutality of a church that allowed its priests, monks, scribes, and the pope to amass great wealth at the expense of the general population. There are documents that indicate that Templars took the church to task for these kinds of crimes against humanity.

"In Europe and at the university library, I read documents, approved by the Catholic Church for publication, that back up the Templars' concerns. The descriptions of accepted practices for ardent followers of the Roman Church and the Pope's Roman Curia were shocking. Accounts of kinky sex, lewd jokes, fondling, and dogs who licked perverted royalty and clergy, giving them erotic pleasure. It sounds insane. I'm too embarrassed to tell you the things they recorded—with the church's permission. I couldn't find church censorship of these subjects. It seems to have been accepted by the church and citizens, too. It's the *acceptance* part that was hard for us to understand. Not only did the scribes and historians write about what was going on, they wrote that only a *mindless idiot* would think that priests and monks should be poor. After all, a vow of poverty meant *poor in spirit*. Seriously?!

"Most shocking was the extent to which the general population was enslaved, too afraid, and brainwashed to do anything about it. For survival and as a form of religious tribalism, the citizens snitched on neighbors and relatives and turned them over to the church's inquisitions for doing things like meditating or using herbs. The mass population, both educated and not, seemed to be convinced that if they aligned with the church, they would be safe and headed for heaven. Ugh! The irony is they were giving the church and the kings all of their power!

"The protestant reformation added to this violent frenzy. Martin Luther and John Calvin became the next level of crazed, torture-hungry humans. They incited hatred in speeches and writings about Catholics. The *divisiveness* seemed endless and brutal. Unicity had vanished.

"Given eons of such tendencies, how can an entire species shift into new expressions of DNA in which emotional patterns elevate? How can a wide range of cultures share ideas, collaborate, yet perceive life from different viewpoints?

"Getting back to the Templars, a defendant in an Inquisition case inevitably ended up brutally tortured and killed. As their benefactors got cold feet from the Inquisitions, the Templars had to flee Portugal, France, and England. In Portugal, many of them were tortured by the Catholic Church's Inquisition and gruesomely put to death by fire. When the remaining Templars realized their security had dissolved, they fled temporarily to a few places where they had friends to count on. Since Templars were architects, alchemists, brilliant scholars, and skilled navigators, they were valued by intelligent merchants and other wealthy elites. We found it curious that Christopher Columbus apparently obtained Templar plans for crossing open waters. That means they were savvy enough to take to the open seas. Purportedly, many fled by ship to Goa in India, one of my ancestors' places of origin, and to South and North America.

"What happened after the Templars were out of favor? After they left, what was life like for the working class in Portugal, France, and England?

"We found that citizens were busy paying taxes and working as serfs for the Lord of the area where they lived. This was the feudal period. Women gave their bodies to the priests, believing it would give them a better chance to get to heaven. And their husbands looked the other way. Can you imagine that kind of behavior being the norm, something that people accepted? The working class gave up their basic human rights and *assumed* that they *should* do so. As though metaphorically blind, they went along with the politics and religion of the time.

"Every uprising was squashed. They had no way to talk to each other over long distances, having no access to writing or reading. As a consequence, the church could easily align with kings or other rulers to destroy a village or annihilate large areas of dissenters. It was a simple and effective way to maintain tight control. Since people could not travel and gather to protest or revolt, the king and church held them like defeated hostages. Kings and Popes seemed to be power hungry and ruthless. And who served them? Legions of fearful people.

"Contrast those living conditions and psychological patterns with jaw-dropping revelations from our research. During a couple of hundred years, the Templars took desolate areas, donated by kings and elite landowners, and transformed them into landscapes of *massive beauty*, filled with art and gorgeous cathedrals with intricate design and skilled architecture. These lands had sustainable farming practices, clean water, and zero poverty. Who taught them how to build the gothic cathedrals that stand as iconic architecture even in modern times? Did they find their way to other coordinates in the multiverse and gather assistance? That's one of our many musings.

"For the citizens of Templar-owned lands, there was no threat of kings and churches demanding taxes and imposing heavy handed doctrines or laws on them. The knights held great wealth, but they didn't seem to waste it on lavish self-indulgences or personal gratifications. There was something about them that seemed to be driven by a sense of purpose. With further research, more questions arose: Why couldn't their ideas and models for society take hold? Why wouldn't people hear about these amazing places of beauty and freedom, revolt and say, *I want this, too!*? The complete truth of the Templars seems to be too deeply buried to be known in current history.

"Our conclusion, based on historical writings, is that the working class felt hopeless, worthless, and alone. Thousands of pages of documentation indicate an ingrained belief that turning against the church meant the possibility of eternal hell and turning on the king meant losing your life.

"Was this tendency for hopelessness passed down genetically? If so, what gave the kings and church incomprehensible leverage to reinforce that degraded state? Why didn't the common people take the initiative towards the personal and spiritual growth that the Templars developed in their community? Did the working class think a better king or new church would save them? If so, it made no sense. Throughout history, we didn't find evidence of a king or pope relenting and allowing the working class to thrive. We cannot find one example of that. Instead, citizens remained slaves in a hideous cycle of poverty and despair.

"Listen to this, though! Suddenly, a monumental, totally unexpected change occurred—bringing with it the potential for a paradigm shift. Word spread about unexplored territory in the west that appealed to bold, adventuresome spirits—what we now, of course, call *the Americas*.

"I've never shared with anyone but Caitlyn the unexpected, totally crazy link I discovered between me, the U.S., and the Templars. We got an opportunity to go to Newport, Rhode Island to join archeologists who were exploring a famous land-mark called the *Newport Tower*. The architects believed it to be linked to Templars. It fit the Templar style of architecture and genius-level building skills. It was pointed out that there are several impressively accurate astronomical alignments that occur throughout the year through the eight archways of the structure.

"The first one caught my attention. On the day of the winter solstice (which happens to be my father's birthday), at 9am, a shaft of light from an archway on the southern side illumines an egg-shaped keystone on the north side. Stay with me, there's more to this story... the same key stone also gets illumined on my birthday, May 1st! Is that a coincidence or was it a clue that could help me find the threads of my ancestry?

"The first of May is celebrated in Celtic cultures as *Beltane*. Templars were known to have celebrated the natural world and seasonal events like this. In my research, I felt gutted when I discovered that by the medieval era, those who celebrated Beltane were tortured and killed. Even if they got baptized and attended Catholic church services, any celebration they participated in that wasn't on the church's official holiday calendar became justification to kill participants. How could that kind of meanness be widely accepted? I wondered if the collective population didn't agree with this aggressive, violent behavior yet were too scared to stand up for my ancestors' right to worship and engage with natural cycles when and how they wanted to. Did anyone realize that the gruesome horrors inflicted on people were likely more about power and control than saving souls through brute force?

"I couldn't help but wonder if being born on an ancient festival day was random or a sign post for me to follow. There will always be inexplicable mysteries in life—yet this one compelled me to dig deeper into my Templar roots. As if what I told you wasn't enough, I was in for another jaw-dropping surprise. I just shared that I was born on May first, but guess *where* I was born? Oh my God! This is amazing! I was born in Newport, Rhode Island where the tower stands and I was born at 7:45 AM, just as the light would be beaming onto the key stone!

"It wasn't until I started sharing my research with my father that he divulged *why* he had brought me to the Newport Tower at 7:45 AM on my birthday every year to see the breathtaking light streaming from the east side onto the key stone. We had always gone there on his birthday as well. Guess his birth time!"

The circle simultaneously shouted in astonishment: "9:00 AM?!

She beamed a dazzling smile and offered a thumbs up before continuing. "Yes! The same time the light from the sun illumines that same keystone. How could I disregard coincidences like these, faultlessly entwining my family with Templars? I thought it was a coincidence that these anomalous cosmic events blessed our birthdays each year with light. But the birth times, too?! As a kid, of course, I had thought it fun to have this special place to visit on my birthday, but my father hadn't elucidated these concrete ties between my family and Templars, except to say that he believed our family shared historical roots with them somehow. I had also never asked about my birth time until he put the pieces of our history together for me. I assume it's clear why I felt unshakably compelled to research the Templars in the U.S. more thoroughly—not to exalt them, but to clarify their place in my family history and uncover information in my DNA that might resonate with Templar influences.

"Before I take you into modern times, I wonder if we can pause for a few minutes. I'm about to share some pretty wild history related to my DNA. I'd like a hot cup of tea first. Is that okay?"

Everyone smiled and nodded in agreement.

"I would love some tea," Sophia said. "Before we pause the conversation, Avani, I want to express my gratitude for your brave, honest, heartfelt exploration of your DNA and your ancestor's past—which most of us here share in one way or another. This topic can become a profound inquiry. From my experience it takes us back in our evolution further than we anticipated and into areas of Gaia's history that are extremely useful for self reflection and reevaluating our perception of reality. Let's have tea, coffee and snacks and reconvene in a few minutes to hear more about your captivating research."

As they all stood, and as though on cue, a meteor shower launched streaks of sparkling photons across the inexhaustible, celestial dome above them. They looked skyward with awe, stunned into silence. The electrifying display and Sophia's cryptic words wafted through the energetic field in and around them, worthy of their attention—an impetus for self reflection before the conversation re-convened.

CHAPTER 6

# CONTROVERSIAL AND PERHAPS MISUNDERSTOOD

The meteor shower faded and everyone sat peacefully around the fire that John stoked into a roaring blaze, supportive of a spellbinding conversation.

Avani settled into her chair with a delicious cup of tea as she began to share more about her ancestors—who she described as "the controversial, definitely esoteric, and perhaps misunderstood Templars."

"We discovered evidence that the Templars left Scotland and Portugal and headed west. This is relevant to our DNA research. BUT I had Goa roots, and that took me into family history that shocked me! I mean, left my jaw dropped to the floor!"

Caitlyn giggled, nodding her head in wholehearted agreement.

"When the Templars went to Goa, some were married and some were not—only the Knights themselves were bound to a vow of celibacy. They settled as best they could into a land quite foreign to them, with a culture formed from the synthesis of Hindu worship and Christianity that had been brought to the continent by the Apostle Thomas. According to my father, one of my ancestors was an Indian woman believed to be a sage from a lineage tracing all the way back to the cave I mentioned earlier with the astrological paintings; she married one of these Templars. The marriage was risky, as she could have been killed for breaking Hindu law, and the Templar was a

Knight who was supposed to be chaste. Times were obviously revolutionary for them. Their story could be part legend, but my father has a Templar artifact that was passed down to him, which I verified as authentic according to its age and motif. I can see you're curious... I sure was!

"This couple was known to be unique, able to both levitate and bi-locate—practices in elevated Hindu as well as Templar inner circles—and they became revered. They transformed the village structure, brought Hindus and Christians together, and consistently performed superhuman acts like manifesting food during famines and thwarting the devastation of monsoon floods by keeping the water levels from rising too far. They had at least six children who inherited their gifts and high-frequency DNA. This Templar was extremely tall with blue eyes. Sounds like Caitlyn's DNA, not mine. Maybe I got a greater degree of his wife's genes.

"They suddenly left the village without their children and grandchildren and no one knew for sure where they went. My father said the Templar was like a king, so no one questioned him. Yet the villagers missed the couple and soon a catastrophic plague hit the area and almost everyone there died. The Templar had told the villagers he would one day take to the ocean. Back then, no one could believe that! According to my father, there were indications he'd gone to North America.

"It turns out Templars were skilled navigators who had been going to the Americas before Christopher Columbus or other European explorers dared to undertake such a dangerous voyage. To substantiate this revelation, we found recent forensic geology that can place the Templars in the U.S. in the fourteenth century—after they'd been murdered en masse in

Europe. We sought out and interviewed several current high level Templars. Among many things, they shared with us that their tradition reveres the wisdom of a scroll called the Zohar, which includes depictions of seven continents and a spherical earth. They said it was from an ancient civilization called Atlantis. All of a sudden, my family's lineage story became feasible and totally riveting for Caitlyn and me.

"My father always felt he was in two worlds, not fully Hindu nor fully Christian. He had been endowed as the keeper of the artifact, and taking little else, he set out from Goa and traveled across the ocean as his ancestor had done. He never shared this with me until he heard I was publishing the paper. After he told me, I heaved with sobs for days. Confirmation had dropped in my lap in an inexplicable way!

"So we had to look at the U.S. in case I could trace my ancient roots here. We were surprised to find Templar symbols appearing in the area of George Washington's birth place. Caitlyn and I both have distant Templar relatives who might have settled in North America. Could this be a link in our DNA?

"In the U.S., public documents indicate that George Washington was the *Worshipful Master* of his Freemason lodge in Fredericksburg, Virginia. This meant he was a leader who initiated new members. Another interesting finding was our research into similar rituals between Templars and Freemasons. From laborious investigation, we know the Templars could have influenced the Freemasons, although it is difficult to verify our discoveries because if you aren't an initiate, it's hard to access their closely held secrets. However, the current Templars we spoke with confirmed the Free Mason-Templar link, without revealing any details.

"It seems there are an endless number of secret societies around the globe. In many such societies today, the wider membership enjoys social bonding and community relationships strengthened by innocuous rituals; yet there are intricate levels of *secrecy* accessible to only a small number of initiates. One of the Templars we spoke to had entered the higher levels of a local membership group. After showing him my father's artifact, he left for a few minutes to retrieve some old books. Smiling in a relaxed, friendly way, he told me that based on the artifact, my father's Templar lineage was from India and likely dated back to the fourteenth century. He unreservedly told me the same story my father had told me about the Templar and his Indian wife who sailed to North America. At that point... Oh my God! He had my total attention!

"I shared with him honestly that researching Templars often felt like crawling down rabbit holes, especially when I'd encounter speculation about their use of black magic. The Templar just chuckled and brushed those ideas off with a sweep of his hand, saying they were categorically untrue. But then he became somber and admitted that political views can infiltrate and influence any brotherhood. His main point, though, was that the core group of Templar Knights, *the highest and most esoteric members*, likely never expanded to beyond three thousand at the apex of their heights of glory in Europe. Ultimately, few Templars had access to the *highest* wisdom, including rituals, scrolls and other artifacts.

"From his perspective, those elite knights perfected within themselves the highly esoteric, elevated levels of consciousness. The man I interviewed was not a Grand Master, but he was also not from the lowest ranks. He assured me that Templars at his level and below knew traditional rituals, but nothing related to dark magic. He said upper level Templars would have access to more information and secrets than he did, and they were sworn to 'protect secrets that the world is not ready for.' He also confirmed that long ago, Templars had been aligned with Free Masons and shared secrets with them. But he was clear that I would not learn any of this kind of information by asking someone at a low level of membership, because they don't know what's above them in the hierarchy, including the information he'd just shared with me. After sharing what he felt I was qualified to hear, it was clear the conversation was over.

"But then, as we were parting, he unexpectedly paused and looked me eye-to-eye, hauntingly, like someone wanting to unload a disturbing secret. My attention was riveted. He almost whispered to me that from his understanding, *the Templar's children* who stayed behind in India with my ancestors were adepts in *high level Templar practices* and Templar tradition says they passed these practices down to succeeding generations of Templars, *like my father's relatives in India!* They definitely were not rank and file members. When I asked if there was anything written about this, he just shook his head, repeating that my ancient ancestors were rare, mystical adepts among his brotherhood. He had become increasingly fidgety. Maybe speaking so blatantly had made him nervous. I got the feeling these guys take vows of secrecy seriously.

"All of a sudden his eyes narrowed to slits of pure angst, he was trembling and his breath came out shakily, like he was preparing for something awful. He awkwardly blurted out that my Templar ancestors from the fourteenth century moved underground in North America—emerging only occasionally to advise his brotherhood. This part of Templar history was passed down orally. His hands were shaking and I was praying he would not lose his nerve, ending this epic revelatory moment. Get ready for his craziest divulgence... he said with even more trepidation that a few Templars settled in cave systems and built tunnels in the Northeast U.S. but the rest headed to an elusive, sacred place in the Northwest. He mumbled something about Templars bending space and time and having access to *wisdom from Atlantis*. And then, looking thoroughly drained of life-force, he proclaimed that we were done! He wasn't saying anything else!

"I thanked him with tears running down my face—making it clear to him that this was HUGE for me! I spontaneously hugged him. Looking depleted and rather sheepish, he turned and bolted through a nearby doorway. Oh my God! Give me a second to collect myself. That was one of those life-moments that takes your breath away."

After closing her eyes for a moment and collecting herself, she continued. "Our research showed that Templars admitted to passing down information and rituals to Free Masons at the level of the stone workers, interacting with them before the Templars fled Europe in the fourteenth century, and advising them further throughout the past few centuries. Yet my father wasn't familiar with anyone in his family with Free Mason ties here, only a few with Templar ones.

"Curious about Templar-Mason ties, we decided to explore anthropology and history that could tie our Templar ancestors to the United States. Could they have brought their *values* here? And did the Templars or their Mason friends establish an *unprecedented, unconventional* kind of world across the Atlantic

Ocean? How can we learn to express the level of high-vibe DNA of those Templar knights that unites us as a species and uplifts the whole planet?

"We continued to explore whether Templars merged with Freemasons to help carry forward their *esoteric* wisdom. But if Templars were here and passed down rituals and beliefs to the Freemasons, why didn't the *values* that led to such vital and flourishing lands of amazing beauty and equality in Portugal take root here? I kept recalling how the Templar I'd interviewed had alluded to the possible infiltration of political views that could have tainted their organization and perhaps the masons, too. Did those influences possibly eclipse the creation of an epic new world in North America? If they gave up one-pointed focus on experiencing higher consciousness, lost interest in achieving the Templar Knight's level of self-mastery, perhaps the original goals for a high-vibe world became increasingly elusive.

"Remember Templar Knights took desolate areas and turned them into awesome places of wealth for everyone, without structures like socialism or other political idealism. It was based on values and heart connection. From our research, doesn't it seem like the unicity gene was turned on and fully functioning in those areas where residents didn't need police and didn't fight each other? This wasn't a competitive environment or a hierarchy.

"We wondered, if the Templars believed in creating *equitable and free commerce* in small areas—like local communities—did they pass down those beliefs to the Freemasons or anyone else? If so, we didn't find proof of it through U.S. history or sociology spanning the past two hundred years. Likewise, we didn't see evidence of the profound Templar spiritual connection with

Essence, unicity, or other cultural values they displayed in Europe. We found their symbols and tales of Templar rituals, but they seemed like empty shells compared to what they had created in Europe. We were beginning to think we'd hit a dead end. Had the unicity gene, after its expression in European Templar communities, gone back to sleep? If so, why?

"Had that sad occurrence created a sense of defeat in our psyche, shifting the way our DNA is expressing today? Our quantum physics colleagues pointed out that all of the trillions of protons within our trillions of cells hold the *entire information data base* of the universe (this has been mathematically calculated), and our DNA is likely the link for our minds and bodies to interface with that field of information. We took time off to reflect and let that revelation settle. The more we discovered about bio-physics, the more exciting the incalculable wonder and quantum potential of being human became. They challenged us to keep going, suggesting we can dip into the field and reclaim dormant tendencies for unicity. This sent us back into research with a boat load of enthusiasm! Even though we had no idea how to do that, we wanted to figure out if there was a gene expression in our U.S. ancestors that was dormant in us.

"We saw the dilemma of the early days of the U.S. The founders of this new nation wanted a free country, but they were backed by (or were themselves) rich bankers and landowners who needed the institution of slavery to make money. Locked into a burgeoning system based on power and control, they had to go along with certain agendas, at all costs, to support their ideologies and way of life.

"Meanwhile the working class held the governmental infrastructure in place, simultaneously losing their voice to the interests of shadowy institutions and a government with murky, convoluted, and fiercely divisive agendas. The ordinary people knew it was possible to disagree and remain connected and caring towards each other; they worked through their differences daily in community—not always pretty and sometimes fractious, but they knew how to get along or perish. They loved their new country and didn't want to fight each other, or foreign adversaries. Yet they began to lose ground in being able to participate fully in decisions about their country's policies and future. Their voice steadily dwindled. How did that downhill momentum occur? How did they get distracted and lose their influence over government?

"To start with, the potential for having agency over their lives slowly diminished when the oppressive *taxation* they had thought to escape crept back into the new country's economy. When land and farming became more expensive, the farmer's revolted in HUGE numbers. The banks and government cleverly found a solution. They "forgave" the taxes, but created a new system called *mortgage*, that allowed the landowners to keep their land. The people at the top, who were creating the allotments of land, wanted to control it for their own profit—of course, this was not optimal for the working class. Immigrants had arrived thinking they'd finally own land, free and clear. No way that would happen! Political systems that curbed such freedom went into place immediately, becoming more embedded as time went on.

"By the early 1800's and into the twentieth century, the average person lived in abject poverty, on the brink of survival. Local groups tried many times to protest and revolt. This sort of information doesn't exactly go in the history books. From the beginning, this was why the working class could not get land unless they took it from the indigenous people. For Caitlyn and me, that seemed like a strange system for obtaining property rights.

"But our research wasn't about critiquing and evaluating systems. We were looking at how citizens turned to fear, anxiety, and hopelessness as a response to all of this. We wanted to know why they didn't see that they were the majority, *united* to each other, and were sacred beings of *infinite gifts*. And how did they not see that they could thrive without annihilating the indigenous people on behalf of the government?

"We'd seen the magnificent society the Templars created when the unicity gene was turned on and people were raising their frequency, evolving out of fear into care and cooperation. Why didn't that take hold in the early U.S.? If upper level Freemasons had access to Templar wisdom, were they cherry picking the fun, esoteric, and brotherly stuff, while forgetting the deeper values? Finding answers felt daunting.

"Helped by a handful of historians, we discovered how the Founding Fathers learned law and developed their own legal system based on a book called *Blackstone's Commentaries on the Laws of England*. This book made understanding law approachable for non-lawyers. It taught that those who owned land, like the bankers and wealthy businessmen should protect their rights to private land ownership even if it violated *the common good* of the whole community. Sounds pretty elitist, right? It was a foundational worldview of those who were at the top of the food chain on this new continent.

"If our working class relatives wanted to survive in their new homeland, education wasn't a possibility for most. Imagine the Irish who thought they were going to the United States to build a railroad and instead were taken to sulfur mines in the south and guarded all day like slaves. When they tried to run away, they were captured and forced back to work. One of them wrote about escaping and walking for over forty-two days, traveling to New York with one dollar in his pocket. Was this the abundance and freedom that he had been sold when he accepted the offer to work for the railroad? Was this distant land the playing field for manifesting his heartfelt wishes and biggest dreams?

"In contrast, the Templars consistently introduced many kinds of opportunities and possibilities for the working class to thrive on the land that kings and wealthy people gave them. We posit that everyone at that time in Europe likely knew the Templars held the keys to *true wealth* in human life. If someone is vibrating with the frequency of courage, higher wisdom, or love, they will not think of themselves as helpless and hopeless. Especially when they join with others in the community who are also raising their frequency. So Templar communities were not filled with downtrodden, demoralized slaves.

"What we do not know and cannot confirm is whether or not the Templars became corrupted. Nor can we be sure that they passed the wisdom of their cultural views on to any other groups, like the Freemasons.

"Caitlyn and I searched for the answer to this question: did the Freemasons and a degenerating Templar clan perhaps gravitate towards and include occult rituals rather than the unicity and higher consciousness aspects of Templar culture?

"As we looked at research spanning the whole country, we found that the immense popularity of the Freemasons caused them to spread swiftly, with lodges popping up everywhere from large cities to small towns. Similar living conditions and attitudes towards the working class were easy to spot. In the western U.S., we discovered that seventy-five thousand Chinese citizens came to build railroads in California and were treated like slaves, living in poverty and inhumane conditions. When would the Chinese be allowed to immigrate, own land, and prosper? The same pattern of slave-style-labor played out on the East Coast.

"Most history books leave out the aspect of the upper middle class, who began to see themselves as a rung or two above poor citizens on the societal ladder. How does it become acceptable socially to promote something like this? Well ... we have to look at who ultimately benefits from the development of a hierarchy in society.

"We noticed that the burgeoning upper class were the pawns of another system that crept in. Take the famous Yale lawyer, Russell Conwell, a wildly popular author and speaker after the Civil War, who said that the poor were in poverty because of their *sins and shortcomings*. That's an interesting belief, right? That opinion led us to explore-further questions: Is this divisiveness representative of antiquated religious beliefs, political ideologies, or propaganda? How could this kind of thinking separate or unite humanity?

"Alongside this ideology, a clever system was taking root and flourishing as a new upper middle class, including teachers, doctors, lawyers, engineers, technicians, and others who were paid by large institutions such as *philanthropies*—which were created by the wealthiest in the country. By helping those upper-middle-class of the ladder to acquire more status and wealth, a new hierarchy could be assured.

"We observed the possibility that unconsciously, the upper middle class began to write about and absorb Conwell's worldview of a lower class who were weak, lazy, and somehow deficient. And the lower class group themselves began to believe those things about themselves as well. It's not surprising that hopelessness emerged and began to flourish in the general population. We engaged psychologists and sociologists in our research who agreed that our hypothesis has merit.

"Does this scenario for the working class sound a lot like the Middle Ages? Those who now owned land and had become wealthy didn't want to lose their status any more than the aristocracy in the Middle Ages had, so they found ways to maintain their social and financial standing through exploitation of slaves, indigenous people, and the laboring classes.

"Another key factor in keeping the lower classes in line was the development of new forms of education focused on producing students who could work in factories and obey rules. The consensus among elites was that most people were deficient intellectually. This is insane, isn't it? The next part is important for understanding the foundation of our current educational system. By the mid-nineteenth century, there was an intentional movement to get teachers on board with the new system and keep students in line. Teachers were made to swear loyalty oaths, show their patriotism, and pass through special certification programs. Rote learning was favored over developing creativity or innovation. History was taught through a patriotic lens; it was not open to question or analysis, which meant no one could question the systems, the authority figures, or the political status quo. History textbooks were not designed to tell the whole story. How can a slanted view of history be useful to a society? From my perspective, such oppression is reminiscent of the Middle Ages.

"The average citizen lost even more human rights through this kind of education, threatened as they were with censure, loss of standing, and no possibility of livelihood if they didn't comply. This was a serious assault on the poor and working classes.

"Books were banned. Hitler and Stalin did not have a monopoly on that. Believe it or not, the more educated people within U.S. society agreed that it was good to burn certain books, but only if their own favorite books were protected.

"Divisiveness was encouraged, and propaganda ran rampant. It was impossible to decipher truth from falsehood. Constant confusion was a diabolical tactic to keep people in line. How much trauma has that perpetuated and how can it be attenuated? A nation divided falls. It falls into the hands of those who master propaganda and know how to maintain tight control over economies and governments.

"Again, doesn't that sound like a repeat of feudalism in the Middle Ages?

"I want to share how our DNA, affected during medieval times, could be continuing to affect our current emotional and behavioral lives. I'd love to tap into your wisdom on the subject of DNA and how it can be altered based on how we feel and respond to particular emotional and psychological triggers from our environment.

"As I said, in our research, it's clear that DNA *is not* mostly junk. It's just that no one has yet perceived the intricacies of how our genetics function. Recently, research has come out showing how genetic expression triggers a biochemical reaction in the body, which produces an emotional response. I realize you may already know more than we do about this burgeoning field of science. For us, it was part of our discovery.

"We wondered what motivated the Templars to seek out quantum portals in the earth where it is easier to connect with innumerable coordinates of spacetime. Did they meet advanced star brothers and sisters? Like I said, they also used ritual to raise their consciousness to higher frequencies. Raising their frequency and living in a flow state could activate the unicity gene along with other genes that promote self-actualization. Suppression of these high frequency genes can be triggered by fear and primal safety issues. There are no records to tell us about Templar motives nor their ultimate success in this area.

"As our country moved forward, the new leaders had elevated their status in the world; or so they thought. Like the Templars, they were driven to discover new levels of personal mastery, but their aim was not to build high frequency communities or access self-actualization. Many of them were Freemasons, but their connection with the noble Templars of old seemed to be negligent at best. Especially considering the next part of our research.

"In the 20th Century, scientists discovered how to split the atom. The message to our citizens was that we had more power and were infinitely safer because of the atomic bomb. Many scientists and humanitarians met the first devastating use of that power with a sense of foreboding, if not outright terror. Of course! At the same time, although most of the world was happy the war was over, they didn't want to see, in that *moment of victory*, the reality of those who'd suffered as a result, nor the inevitable implications for the future. Citizens of the area of the nuclear blast in Japan found themselves devastated, with many dying a grueling, slow death.

"In the U.S., school children now had to practice what to do in case of a nuclear attack. Although the bomb wasn't dropped in the United States, the fear of nuclear bombs penetrated deeply into the psyche of U.S. citizens and everyone across the planet. The possibility of foreign aggression using nuclear weapons became a catalyst for further underlying fear and a sense of foreboding going forward—none of the psychologists we spoke with disputed that fact. Fortunately, humans are resilient, and life went on. The problem is that humans are *gullible*. Often Caitlyn and I found that word to be applicable in our research.

"Throughout history, citizens have fallen for cheap tricks, hook, line, and sinker. After the war ended, President Eisenhower ushered the country into a new era, but at the end of his term, in his farewell speech, he solemnly warned Americans to beware of the growing military-industrial complex. During the next administration, President John F. Kennedy shared similar concerns about this growing threat. Their apprehension was well-founded and bone-chilling.

"After World War II, leaders of the military-industrial complex became enthralled with cutting-edge tech and decided the military branch would divide in two: one division to be the front face of the institution, and the other to be secret from the public. They quite literally moved the secret military activities underground—into tunnels. The U.S. and other global governments were aware of ancient underground tunnels connecting the north and south poles, as well as vast numbers of other tunnels located across entire continents. A number of tunnels, the height of a ten-story building, have been found along the U.S.-Mexico border using newer technologies like *ground penetrating radar* which can reach three miles or more. The military developed bases in just such underground havens for *covert research centers*—perfect for stealth programs with incalculable financial and power-broker-style rewards.

"In 2013, the U.S. government admitted they had lied to the public about their secret military base in Nevada, referred to as Area 51, citing *national security* as the reason they needed to do so. Those two words are used consistently to hide anything they don't want to share. For years, even as unusual sightings were regularly reported in the area, and whistle-blowers came forward reporting both off-world technology as well as reverse-engineered craft in the base, government officials had vehemently denied there was any underground military base. Yet it's gigantic. In fact, it's many miles deep. Although our elders paid for it with their tax dollars while the military swore it didn't exist, the government unceremoniously decided to admit it's been there all along.

"Who was benefiting from *all of this* underground secrecy? On the surface, the working class was struggling to survive, pay taxes, find a job, and keep small businesses alive. In some countries, many people were starving. Sounds to me like the Middle Ages. Why can't we find evidence of amazing genetic expressions like *unicity*?

"From the seventeenth to the twenty-first century, we can link our national leaders and many presidents with Freemasonry and other secret societies. Since they are *secret*, we don't know the multitude of rituals they employ. Nor can we see evidence of important wisdom, if any, they received from the Templars. During the trajectory of World Wars and the rise of atomic bomb research in the twentieth century, two presidents, Franklin D. Roosevelt and Harry S. Truman, achieved elevated degrees of Freemasonry. They were each conveyed the Honorary Grand Master of the Order of DeMolay (Jacques DeMolay was the last Grand Master of the Knights Templar). Perhaps the Free Masons did learn to cultivate *power*, but their understanding of its purpose was incomplete; maybe the Templar rituals and teachings didn't get passed down properly, became distorted, or were purposefully ignored, leading to a continuation of a medieval slave-style society.

"Regardless, we have plenty of thirty-third degree masons among our political leaders, and a number of secret societies that include such leaders and elite individuals among their membership. President Truman rose to the 33rd degree of Freemasonry and, like George Washington, had been elevated to Worshipful Master. Yet none of these high degree Masons delivered anything close to the Templar's awe-inspiring societal creations found in Portugal. With so much evidence of links between high levels of Freemasonry and the Templars, what went wrong? We considered that it could be personal frequencies. Were the Templars who survived developed enough to pass on the elevated frequency necessary to ascend levels of consciousness? We wondered if maybe the unicity gene expresses when we get into a flow state *consistently* and allow ourselves to *raise our frequency* through practices like meditation, which the Templars were known for. That gave us a thread to follow.

"The unicity gene may not have had a chance to express because society was in a steep decline emotionally and spiritually. When a civilization is about to be crushed, their inherent genes hit a crescendo and can either express further, or go dormant.

The latter option means it's game over for sustaining any form of meaningful life for the general population. Included in this scenario is *possible extinction.*

"Satisfied that we'd seen enough, we were bummed-out to realize that the unicity gene and other higher genetic expressions had not manifested in our lineages. Yet we became stoked during a meeting with our quantum biophysics friends. I mean totally stoked! They claimed that new DNA expressions had started to be found globally. As I said, it used to be called *junk,* but it's not. Although still in small numbers, these expressions show that the gene has been in us all along, available if we know how to activate it. We realized we could express unicity rather than choosing to express our ancestor's patterns of self-sabotage, self-destruction, and vicious divisiveness. We didn't need Templar rituals to express those genes. We were motivated and excited as we started to work with the possibility that we could affect our DNA expression by turning particular genes on. *Epigenetics* is the study of the influence of behavior, emotion, and the environment on our gene expression. Our inner and outer environment matters to our genes.

"We created teams involving thousands of people meditating, practicing focused attention to still our minds, and staying in the flow state for extended periods—relentlessly raising our frequency. It worked! That's why I could be here now and enjoy the mystical pyramid in Max's cave. A couple of years ago, there was no way I could handle that frequency. Maybe we're finally cracking the highest-ranking Templar code by creating environments of uplifted people who change the world and thrive in the process. Propagating elevated expressions of genetics can create fertile soil from which more amazing *junk*

DNA can express. We're committed to supporting each other in this process.

"As if that wasn't enough to get us motivated and excited about DNA expression, we started to look at other subtle aspects of genetic expressions from the quantum physics perspective. We want to gather and share information about the potential of up-leveling our DNA. Our DNA is connected in a feedback loop with the quantum field. We forget that we can always access infinite information from *the field*. There's so much more to us than our subordinated genetic expression indicates. Let's express the high-vibe DNA! I have a feeling this circle is *all in*. Would that be amazing, or what?!"

"Avani, I felt your heart in the research you just described," Jake said. He was leaning into the circle with interest, his face saturated with the radiance of endless possibilities for higher evolution. "I admire you for not getting lost in the horrific tyranny that humanity endured; instead, you stuck to the focus of genetic expression and how you finally saw a way through it to help shift humanity's trajectory. You blow me away! You and Caitlyn are concise and thorough. I am honored to be the beneficiary of your results and continued hypotheses. Positive, thoughtful people like you have my deep respect and my heart is all yours. Can I add something? I don't want to keep interrupting you."

Avani nodded with enthusiasm. Her brilliant smile and sparkling eyes were confirmation for Jake to continue.

"John and I share your hypothesis that genes matter for a civilization to evolve higher and thrive over time. The gene expression for unicity was available but we weren't expressing it. We're finally aligning with *the best* of the Templars, rather than their weaknesses. And we have to look at personal and collective ancestral traumas in the face, and dissolve them through pure love. Our traumas don't define us. We have agency over them. No government, pope, king, or anyone else can turn on our genetic gifts, allowing us to express the raw power and splendor of our human potential—we have to do it ourselves

"From my perspective, revelations about our cosmic origins, the possibility that many epochs of advanced cultures like Max's lived on this planet long before us, and the absolute necessity for each of us to take responsibility for our inner state and our actions, are combining to wake a whole bunch of folks up, including myself! I definitely have frustrating days every now and again, but I want you all to know that having honest and sincere conversations like this and knowing you have my back for certain, emboldens me to live my best life. I've never valued friendship as much as I do now. Regardless of the struggles and obstacles I face, I feel this deep connection to all-that-is, to the cosmos, and all of you. I don't want to deny frustrations that arise, but I refuse to wallow in low vibes." He suddenly stopped and said, "Sorry for the rant..." then looked penetratingly at the earth as if it could absorb the enormity of feelings rushing through him.

In a compassionate tone, Caitlyn said, "We all have those moments of overwhelm about how life is playing out. From what I've observed, a lot of people globally are frustrated. However, when we interviewed people, we found that a massive reality check was going on, and most of them were fine with handling the fallout from impending truth-telling that has to emerge into the light of day. I have to admit it's been shocking to see governments finally so completely busted that no one believes their propaganda anymore. Global powers and their bureaucratic departments are gradually imploding and disintegrating into a pile of smoldering ashes. After the firestorm of hearts who felt seriously betrayed by them, healing can finally begin and continue with dignity and unicity. It took a lot of courage on a planetary scale to get to this point in history.

"No one would have believed that the big shift came when the masses united and started talking to each other with respect and open hearts. It started with a few seemingly normal individuals who remind me of the most elevated and luminous Templars. Remember that not all Templars were warriors. Yet they all cultivated courageousness and remained fierce in their oath to love others, to care about their fellow citizens, and to propagate higher consciousness. The Templars witnessed those traits in people like John the Baptist, whose relics they acquired. They honored, respected, and admired him, evidenced by the art and structures they left for us to explore. What interested Avani and me is that they didn't adore him blindly. They deeply respected him and learned from him while focusing on their personal practices of higher consciousness.

"We can learn from many who came before us, yet we still have to do the inner work and personal growth to unlock our unicity gene and allow it to express in harmony with the Earth and everyone and everything living on her.

"As Vatican secrets have been disclosed, it's become clear that the upper echelons of The Catholic Church in Rome, and their highest levels of leadership across the globe as well, have been unmasked. Small groups across the world devised a unified plan to disclose information from the church's carefully guarded archival vaults. These vaults maintained for posterity the inside story documented in jaw-dropping written records. Like a game of chess, checkmate manifested when insiders—awesome whistleblowers—thoroughly thwarted the church hierarchy's carefully formulated plan to maintain control. Finally, their leader and all associates had to come clean with what they knew. For many people, it's been a painful process of assimilating the magnitude of those disclosures.

"Avani and I are relieved that long-held religious and cultural *origin stories* are being reviewed and studied because ancient texts were found in those vaults, while at the same time, recently discovered ancient sites have been uncovered. Undogmatic religious scholars and historians are researching these texts and our methodical, unbiased colleagues are exploring the findings in archeological sites which reveal temples and other ancient buildings that paint a broader and unimaginably extended historical timeline of humanity—and our relationship to the cosmos.

"As the Roman Catholic Church sought to centralize and grow its power over the last millennium, *dogmatic* information about human origins and our relationship to the cosmos was disseminated. However, the church did not know that unbiased religious followers, with an open-minded approach to spirituality, had fearlessly preserved documents a millennia ago. Miraculously, these texts withstood the ravages of time, manipulation, and censorship.

"The Dead Sea Scrolls, for example, were likely collected by a Jewish sect called the Essenes, in the first century CE. The earthen jar used to preserve the scrolls was covered in *bat poop* which provided a protective seal to guard them from decay. Discovered in 1947, these scrolls were held in a museum in France for forty years. As we studied them, we realized they share the *esoteric* nature, philosophy, and practices of our ancestors related to our highest human nature.

"Over time, as whistleblowers have exposed information from once carefully guarded, archival vaults—like the giant one under Vatican City—we've been able to see the origins of humanity expand through a full spectrum of previously undisclosed texts. For many people, it's been a painful process of assimilating the magnitude of those disclosers. Our origin stories and beliefs about ourselves and our world are getting a reboot. For many people, it's been a painful process.

"Concurrent with all of that, whistleblowers in various governments across the globe have disclosed that ongoing extra-terrestrial contact with human society has been occurring *over the past century*. This information can be juxtaposed with legends of galactic visitors *throughout ancient history*—divulged partly through new studies of global archeological sites and religious texts discovered by various sources over the past one hundred years. We got to work at many of these locations, often leaving us in shock and wonder. It became apparent that galactic neighbors have visited our planet during many epochs in Earth's history.

"Adding to these revelations and archeological findings, small pockets of people, primarily children, began to report seeing and receiving messages from *orbs of light*. In recent government hearings, the U.S. military admitted they'd seen these orbs for many decades and had identified them as a form of galactic contact. According to reports, the children were not afraid. More often than not, they said it felt natural to sit in silence with the orb—which allowed for astonishing telepathic messages to ensue. We remain in a global conversation about this phenomenon, especially as it increased towards the end of 2026. This time frame became even more monumental because with all of that happening, our research about genetics was also validated due to new biotech. Max is no longer seen as a *possible* relative, rather he's a *probable* one. As 2030 rapidly approaches, I'm looking forward to it, and beyond, rather than worrying we may not make it to the next decade.

"Avani and I demand personal growth of ourselves through each discovery we make. Maintaining higher personal frequencies is our responsibility. It's not always easy to do when we encounter something that triggers us emotionally, but it's the only way forward for us. We want to feed-forward and receive back high vibrational data from the field continuously. Focus and determination are required to develop this vibrational capacity as our *new normal*. We settle into the stillness of our core, our true power center, as often as possible throughout the day. If our research evokes strong emotions, we made a promise to remind each other of our *vibrational goal* with compassion and solidarity."

"I agree, it's just that..." Avani paused with a wrinkled brow and noticeable concern that caused her capacious eyes to flatten and tighten with tension. She said reflectively, "I feel uplifted but cautious, because the highest levels of the occult sects we uncovered perceive themselves as wildly superior to us; they believe they should subdue us because they are ultimately invincible, god-like beings. This is way beyond lower-level Freemasons enjoying their social club and community service. The people we discovered play a high-level role in national and global leadership; they control science and academia—more vigorously than anyone realizes. They follow a tactic we've seen in most cults: divide and conquer through creating factions that live in righteous anger and conflict; create endless chaos; manipulate the population to believe that leaders—who are just oligarchs and fascists—cannot be rendered powerless. These leaders often strive to develop supernatural powers via the occult. These may seem like *modern* problems, but they actually have *ancient* roots. They are ripe for a massive reboot by a population of innately designed, good humans. We have discernment, and a deep knowing of our unicity, which can overcome anything they throw our way. The occult is real, yet so is higher consciousness. I'm leaning into it as my lifeline going forward.

"Having said that, we were forced into facing frustrating revelations and irrefutable truths. When we researched the influence of the occult, we were astonished at how far-reaching its scope of influence was. I'm talking about over a *majority* of the planet, we found power hungry occultists at high levels in the hierarchy of global power. The power and dark magic these occultists can conjure up is perhaps their last-ditch effort to use esoteric realms to gain control. And they definitely embrace a covert approach to their work. Their use of mystical, superhuman powers for ego-driven control is very different from Templars using esoteric practices for higher personal evolution to support and elevate themselves and humanity.

"Through reliable contacts, we gained access to information about a few prominent cults within global hierarchies in several countries—looking at high levels in the hierarchy who had studied alchemy as a supernatural way to alter levels of reality such as the legendary pursuit of transmuting lead into gold—which is amazing. Unquestionably, gold meant a lot in

Roman times and modern times as a basis for currency exchange. BUT, the *alchemy* that the elite among the Templars studied and applied was a way to *advance their experience* of the material *and* spiritual worlds. This was what they later used to create those amazing societies in Portugal. They practiced *transmuting* the personality into its highest nature.

"To understand this kind of higher use of the alchemical process of turning lead into gold, or *spiritual alchemy*, within Templar membership, we located sources who had access to ancient Templar texts. When I use the term *spiritual alchemy*, I am referring to turning an ordinary life into higher levels of experiential love, unicity and sagacious wisdom. According to those writings I just mentioned, the Templars studied and practiced esoteric teachings ranging from alchemy to entering high-vibe portals; their purpose was to transmute *human consciousness* from fear to invisibility, from division into wholeness, from insignificance into grandeur, pure love, and unicity—the condition of being unified with the unlimited power of *the field*. The Templars described the field as *all-that-is*.

"Instead of producing gold to accumulate wealth, they used it to pay for their endeavors and care for the poor. Their more central focus, however, was on a form of white powder, described as being like manna from heaven, which provided transformative properties they could use to raise their frequencies and accelerate their evolution. Believe it or not, Sir Issac Newton and others throughout history sought to perfect this higher octave of alchemy as a way to expand their consciousness and be in service to the world.

"We followed a provocative link between the Templars and a Jewish sect called the Essenes. The Templars seemed to have adopted the *Essenes'* culture, which espoused the principles of "Do No Harm" and "Love One Another" as primary spiritual and cultural themes. We wanted to understand if there might be a link between both groups' DNA expressions of unicity and their impassioned interest in esotericism.

"A number of modern scholars, anthropologists, and archeologists posit a link between John the Baptist and the Templars. John was considered the leader of a sect *within* the Essenes—who had settled in cities like Jerusalem and the barren Qumran desert. Members of his sect were desert dwellers who allowed marriage (so the group could endure), were vegetarian, and, like all Essenes, were adamantly opposed to war and violence. They were known as adepts, mystics, and healers, and were sought for their wise counsel. Like the Templars, the Essenes created sophisticated and modern architecture and living conditions at a time when this was inconceivable, like systems for accessing water and simple yet comfortable structures within a brutal desert environment.

"Our sources have said that elite levels of current occult groups focus on learning classical alchemy as a way to control and influence the material world, and the higher levels in these membership groups posit that quantum physics will provide clues about how they can master the universe in modern times. Even if some of them don't embrace dark magic as overtly as Hitler, Stalin, and Mussolini did, our sources verified most of them practice the occult and pass it on to their fellow members. We wondered whether they are motivated by a desire to increase their authority or by the impulse to *feel or do something* they consider beyond their everyday experience? Since these organizations are shrouded in secrecy, we couldn't get concrete answers to these questions.

"We have found that throughout history, when leadership engaged in occult practices, science and academia participated, too. In any area of science, when the dark occult shows up, we wanted to ask, *Why?* The opening ceremony of a massive tunnel in Switzerland was brushed off as *artistic expression, acrobatics, a parade, and a blessing.* Why dark occult symbolism and eyebrow raising costumes? Why was that the chosen celebratory *expression?* Was it just to get attention? The media response ranged from not mentioning it to calling it *unusual* or *modern artistic spirit and style.* Yet our colleagues shook their heads, looked confused, and used terms like *bizarre* to describe their response to it. The moaning, screaming horned beast (who represented the Swiss ibex, a native mountain goat), fake dead people, and a legion of people wearing only their underwear who got sexy with each other on stage... none of that escaped our attention as the chosen medium to celebrate a supposedly state-of-the-art, high tech tunnel... We couldn't make sense of it. As if that wasn't enough, there was a ghost-looking, bare chested woman who flew over the corpses of people who represented those who died while building the tunnel. Groups marched eerily like zombies while others carried sticks or antlers. In a separate event, someone faked a ritual murder in front of a statue donated by India to CERN in Switzerland—officials said it was a prank. Why would that be the prank of choice for CERN staff? The only offerings I've seen to a similar statue in India were sacred leaves and white flowers.

"We wondered why the occult is becoming noticeable through influencers and associated with certain leadership globally. As I just mentioned, avant-guard science allowed it to surface as having a place in their domain, too. Dark magic and the occult have been around as far back as we can research. However, we noted that it pops up as a sign of burgeoning cultural change. Remembering leaders such as Hitler and Stalin, when frustration arises at the top of the food chain about how to obtain desired powers and agency over life's ups and downs, a tendency develops to lean into the mystical, dark realms. Their contemporary, Mussolini, cultivated *Mystical Fascism*. There's usually a trickle-down effect of these kinds of heinous occult power structures into many layers of society—with unfulfilled desires begging for satisfaction.

"My overarching takeaway from our occult research is that it creates a sense of coveted specialness for those at the apex—they want to have the highest powers and feel exalted. For others at lower levels of the hierarchy, the practices and mythology bring a sense of agency over life's unpredictable and seemingly insurmountable challenges. In contrast to this, unicity isn't about creating a ritualistic, *magical spell* to override nature or create a bond with ethereal forces. Unicity is based on innate, pure, transformational love. Magical moments and mystifying synchronicities happen as a *by-product* of living with awareness of our innate, unlimited super-nature. In our research, secrecy and trying to bend nature to human will were methods to overcome inconvenient, annoying *limitations*. However, we weren't drawn to that because the *unlimited* quantum reality thrilled us. It wasn't elusive or evasive. High frequencies instantly create a portal to our infinite essence. This became our *modus vivendi*, our habitual way to approach human potential."

Sophia had been listening attentively. She raised her brows and added in a confident tone, "This has been *incredibly* fascinating. You've done thorough research and kept your focus on the unicity gene and elevating the frequency of the global working class. After hearing you speak, I am even more excited for you to meet Adele tomorrow. She holds missing pieces of your research-puzzle. She has conducted phenomenal, in-depth historical research into high level secrecy. Like you, she encountered *the occult* in current governments as well as in ancient history. And her research into current DNA expression will blend nicely with your analyses and evaluations. She'll join us for our fireside conversation tomorrow. It's helpful to be clear about history because it can show us where, collectively, we tend to make recurring mistakes. With her unique historical perspective, we get a bird's eye view of epochs of time and have the benefit of looking out for patterns we never want to repeat. I love the broad range of backgrounds and insights within this group.

"Reflecting on tonight's discussion, I appreciate that you are not lost in the damage that was done, wallowing in blame, and complaining about the past. You are exploring history to learn about your ancestral DNA, considering potential cosmic DNA overflowing with quantum data, and the possibilities for an elevated world when unicity comes fully online. Without doubt, I'll be dreaming of astonishing, thriving ancient Templar communities and a wondrous future. I am grateful for every minute of this conversation. Caitlyn and Avani, I love you! Thank you for creating a thought-provoking and absolutely enthralling evening."

Gazing toward John and Jake, Sophia's eyes were on fire as she launched a resplendent love-bomb their way, saying emphatically and vivaciously, "I love you two very much!"

The circle became animated in coherence with Sophia's uninhibited love. Smiles exploded and the crickets chirped an octave louder. The group frequencies were expanding and the possibilities for a new world felt more tangible than ever.

As the vibrations of the moment emerged back into the still state, the circle of friends dispersed, ready for another day of exploration at the cove, and an evening with new friends, further insights, and inconceivable wonderment.

# CHAPTER 7

# DNA SECRETS

When Megan and Beth crossed the threshold into Megan's home, auriferous hues of afternoon light streamed through enormous picture windows, creating a welcoming, warm ambiance. For the past five years, Megan chose to spend most of her time with her daughters, granddaughters, and great granddaughters. The dogs she'd loved and doted on for many years had crossed the rainbow bridge that connected her to them. She came to the realization that pets were not part of her current phase of life.

"Goodness gracious, Beth!" Megan said with a radiant smile, "Every time I come back, I wonder how I am going to be able to leave. Can you feel the loving embrace of this place? I feel the trees greeting us and the soft breeze is welcoming us home. Maybe we can stay a little longer this time. I love my daughter and my grand-babies yet something here calls me. I need my *introvert* time. How about you?"

"You know me." Beth said, "I'd never leave. It's always been a magical place. Not to mention that John, Jake, and Sophia are the icing on the cake."

Smiling at the kind woman who had been willing to travel as her constant companion after her children were grown, Megan said, "I'd like to unpack, eat something, and get ready for this evening. It seems the group makes a fire, gets cozy, and talks together. I'd love to be there for that."

"Well, I'll be asleep. You can tell me all about it tomorrow," Beth said with a friendly smile and sportive wink.

Footsteps behind them caught their attention as Sophia arrived with her arms open wide to embrace both her friends with one giant hug.

"I've missed you so much!" she said. "Can I do anything to help you get settled? I've brought food. I don't want Beth to have to cook. You two can just relax and settle in."

"Sophia, you are an angel," Beth said as she gave Sophia an extra hug and a smile that expressed their bond of friendship.

"I am going home to do a few things before tonight," Sophia said. "We'll meet at six-thirty this evening. Jake and John are going to clean up at the guest house and prepare the fire pit. I've loved gathering around the bonfire in the evenings—with a clear view of the stars and the enchantment of the grove of nearby trees, the deer and small animals visible by moonlight. The big animals don't seem to be interested in us. I'm thankful for that. I hope you will have enough time to rest."

Megan squeezed her hand as she said with sparkling eyes, "More than enough, sweetie pie! I'm looking quite forward to it. I'll be refreshed and ready for this evening."

With warmth and vigor, Sophia said, "Oh! I almost forgot to tell you that I invited a *special friend* to join us tonight. I don't know if you recall that when I moved here, I spoke about my dear friend, Gilda. In a wonderful turn of events, her granddaughter, Adele, moved to Idaho. She lives nearby with her two young daughters. She calls her grandmother *Anna*, which was Gilda's birth name. It's been amazing to connect with Gilda's legacy through Adele. We've become very close. Her girls are with some new friends tonight so she can have a mama's night out. You will love her. I look forward to introducing you.

"Beth, will you join us?"

"Nope, I can feel my comfy bed calling me. I'm jet-lagged and ready for an early night. Tell my favorite Idahoans, Jake and John, they can expect a gigantic hug and huckleberry pancakes for breakfast."

"I will definitely give them that welcomed news," Sophia said with a warm smile.

Megan turned to Sophia thoughtfully saying, "Please invite your friend to stay in the guest house. I have a good feeling about that young woman. I look forward to meeting her. And you know the way to your room. I shudder to call it a *guest room*. It has your name on it. You can stay up late and talk as much as you want."

They hugged tenderly and smiled with even more radiance and unicity than the day they first met. With hearts satiated by the embrace and warmth of intimate friendship, they parted company to rest and prepare for the night ahead.

John was a master at creating a dazzling bonfire. Luckily, he was blessed with the perfect fire pit in the center of a border of large local stones, some two-feet high. Within the stone circle, Megan arranged a dozen chairs, made from local wood which blended impeccably with the environment. The bonus was Beth's thick, handmade cushions. The fire-lit area became an irresistible space that enticed friends and family with the strength of a resplendent magnet.

Adele arrived as Sophia and everyone gathered around the blazing fire. Megan had already had a tearful reunion with John and Jake—their love for each other and invaluable friendship had been cultivated over years and solidified into an invincible bond.

Caitlyn and Avani joined them, warming up to Megan instantly, and engaging in a lively conversation about their global travels and areas of study. The atmosphere was light-hearted as everyone met Adele and greeted her as they would family.

Bringing more warmth to the circle, Sophia served tea and coffee, and everyone listened entranced by the symphony of insects that masterfully serenaded the gathering. After a few minutes, Sophia asked the group if they were ready to hear from Adele who could add her perspective to the prior evening's conversation. Although Adele knew John and Jake, she'd not met Megan, Caitlyn, and Avani. Sophia was thrilled for Adele to meet the circle of friends. Earlier in the day, she shared with Adele her respect for and immediate camaraderie with her new guests, referring to them as *two brilliant archeologists*. Adele also received a summary of the research Caitlyn and Avani had shared the night before.

Adele sat up straight and directed an infectious smile to everyone in the circle. The group came to life in response to her charming presence. She spoke with warmth and sincerity.

"I am so happy to meet you. Megan, thank you for inviting me to stay tonight. What a treat!"

Megan smiled affectionately in response.

"Avani … Caitlyn … I was fascinated to hear from Sophia about last night's conversation," Adele said, as her eyes sparkled in the firelight; her expression glowed with inner radiance and natural enthusiasm. "I was captivated when Sophia told me how you explored your ancestors with an emphasis on genetic expression.

"I majored in history and minored in anthropology in college, focusing on Europe. Admittedly my bliss zone emerges when I discover clues into influences of religion and politics on a civilization's evolution. It sounded like you demonstrated how current beliefs and emotional responses, initiated by our ancestors, get passed down unconsciously through DNA and cultural norms. Our environment and beliefs matter more than our ancestors realized. Until now, we didn't consider the role of our genes and how we could express latent ones.

"I was glued to Sophia as she told me about your ancestors because I also have ancestors with an interesting past. Adding to the conversation that you began last night, I'd like to share my family's' story. It may fill in gaps of information and be of interest to you."

"I'm totally stoked!" Caitlyn said smiling and leaning forward, poised to listen.

"Oh yeah! I'm all in," Avani said with a look of childlike curiosity. "Tell us everything!"

"Well, it could take us weeks to cover everything," Adele said with a chuckle. "If everyone is ready, I'll dive in and then answer any questions. Sophia gave me one requirement for meeting with you—to be open and forthright. She said you are *truth tellers*, vulnerably and honestly sharing your personal and ancestral history. I love that! Immediately, I knew I'd feel at home with you.

"At first, the subjects I will speak about were quite emotionally triggering for me. In fact, it was hard for my brain to register my research as truth—it seemed more like something from a movie script. I have to admit that my mind struggled to grasp the magnitude of my discoveries: multiple generations of ancestors, spanning four hundred years or more, could be passing on a tendency to express certain genetic emotional patterns and unconscious mental beliefs. Amazing, isn't it? If I don't become *conscious* of them, I may run *unconscious* auto-pilot programs like my family did for centuries. But the best part is that by becoming aware of those patterns, I don't need to be *bound* to them. I feel so fortunate to have the opportunity to change those long-term patterns. When I become *aware* of ingrained patterns that I express, they cannot repeat unconsciously or sabotage my process of higher evolution.

"I assure you that I won't share anything unless I have double-checked the information long ago with my grandmother, my mother, or most recently, through comprehensive research.

"I'm not sure how much Sophia told you about my family, but Grandmother Anna was a Nazi—a full-fledged, diabolical, propagandized member of the Third Reich. Without giving you a lot of history, the bottom line is that she recanted her Nazi ideals and became a spy for the U.S. government. I'm sharing this with you because she had first-hand knowledge of history that was invaluable to hear from her perspective. My mother also worked for the U.S. for many years in an administrative role. Later, near her death, she revealed that she was also covertly involved with the secret space program. I don't want to talk too much about my relatives because I want to stick to my research about DNA and history.

"Since I come from a brainy, scholarly family, I definitely slant towards facts. Because of my grandmother's life and stories, I'm aware of another aspect of historical research: observing patterns and comparing them to personal accounts of people and events to get closer to the foundation that supported and solidified the patterns. My undergraduate and graduate work focused on various aspects of world history. My lineage is German—going back hundreds of years. What most people don't realize is that Germany was comprised of many smaller states. It was only integrated into its present form in the past couple of hundred years, then redesigned again after World War I, and reconfigured again after World War II. We had different languages and customs and when the post WW II integration happened, there was a push to create a unified nation.

"Adding to the discussion you began last night, I'll share a *pattern* that formed in those German states and all over Europe. It was about *secret societies*; a social construct in which *withholding transparency* was rewarded. Lower-level members do not know what the small, upper levels of the society are doing in the dark recesses of their tight, inner circle. I traced back dozens of secret societies that my ancestors were involved in. Many you've heard about, while others are not well-known.

"When I talk about secret societies, I mean a group that makes vows of secrecy they take seriously; they gather as a group to get special information, spiritual knowledge, or other benefits from the group; and they never share what goes on behind closed doors: think Templars and Freemasons.

"And by the way, the lower levels of a secret society are oblivious to upper level operations, yet every level takes a blood oath to never share anything and to pledge enduring loyalty to the group—they wouldn't dare break their vow by becoming a whistle-blower. Potential shame and ostracism are controls for a secret society's continuous evolution.

"I spoke with a historian who said the bond and oaths run so deep that a judge, for example, is obligated not to convict a masonic brother of a crime. He was surprised to uncover the extent of the allegiances that members developed when a couple of masons defected and shared secrets with him privately. His insider information revealed that as they climbed the masonic ladder, the vows change from seemingly insignificant and harmless to more and more dramatic and eerie, solidifying psychological impressions each step of the way as they make continuous pledges backed by their blood and that of their family. The defectors said they felt increasingly uncomfortable with next-level pledges and oaths. They'd joined because many influencers in local business and politics were members of the society—so membership started out as networking and bond-building.

"However, vows are an important part of all secret societies, even if they seem like they won't be acted upon or are harmless when initiates first agree to them. I was interested to discover reluctance to leave the society and the intense allegiance to what post-members described as a *social club or charitable organization*, rather than a *secret society*. Admitting to a being in a secret society may have been unpalatable or would perhaps seem outrageous. My colleague was researching the unexpected *patterns of beliefs* acquired from membership in these societies. This applied to current membership and seemed to be passed down to future generations. Interesting, right?

"I was in sync with him because you may have noticed I mentioned potential *shame* and abandonment for leaving the brotherhood, feeling *honor* and *camaraderie* as a member, and the underlying, unconscious or conscious *fear* of retribution for a broken vow. I wanted to explore these emotional triggers in my ancestors because I know that emotional patterns like these can express in later generations. Had my ancestors passed down an unconscious belief that this kind of blind loyalty and secret initiation were important, or perhaps acceptable or tolerable, to get the benefit of becoming influential in their local area? Through in-depth research into many secret societies, I learned that lower levels were being influenced unconsciously by the upper echelon's ideologies and worldview. In fact, this kind of stealthy influence was part of the society's plan. I'll be talking more about that in a minute.

"The historian shared that the Masons became so powerful in the U.S. that in the nineteenth century, the first *third party* emerged called the *Anti-Masonic Party*. John Quincy Adams later ran for president declaring he'd never been and would never be a Mason. So it must have been a point of contention at the time. Obviously the public expressed doubts about a secret brotherhood overseeing the government—even if most members were likely innocuous. There's also documentation indicating that Masons picked up where the Templars left off and perhaps decided to personalize the ideologies, and change the rituals and codes of belief to make them their own.

"Since Sophia told me that you talked about the Templars, I'll skip that part. Except, remember that the Freemasons, as a secret society, were extremely influential in England and Germany. Otherwise, why would royalty, like King George VI, hold the supreme position of *Grand Master* in his Scottish lodge. His grandfather held the same position in the *United Grand Lodge of England*. They would have to be initiated into the thirty-third degree to attain that status.

"Why did Hitler purportedly attend meetings of the thirty-third degree Freemason meetings as a guest in the early days of his rise to power? He could not take masonic vows because of his vows to the Nazis, his primary allegiance. It's hard for me to ignore that royalty and dictators, who likely kept tight schedules, would make the effort to visit local social clubs without a reason. I wondered if perhaps there was something substantive, or perhaps monumental, that happened in those meetings to entice numerous elites in many countries to join and gather in secret. Keep in mind the thirty-third degree masons were at *the apex* of society—these higher degrees of secret societies matter in the context of what I'll be sharing.

"In our conversation, you'll notice that my ancestors adopted a common pattern in the eighteenth through the twenty-first century. They were part of *multiple* groups. Bankers gravitated to one group and technocrats to another—later they joined each other's secret societies.

"Even in multiple groups, they were clearly one hundred percent secret. Like I said, I kept wondering why they joined and how they benefited. Why would elites of society need this specific format in which to meet? Parties and social gatherings were regularly held. My researcher-brain went crazy with complexities and questions while finding no simple answers or resolutions.

"It was easy to trace my family's involvement in government, religion, banking, and other areas of life from the eighteenth century forward. What got my attention was their use of family artifacts that I found: strange talismans, runes, codes, and paraphernalia from centuries before.

"One Germanic state, previously part of Germany, was Bavaria. In 1776, a small Bavarian group met with a twenty-eight-year-old man, Adam Weishaupt to create a secret society whose mascot was an owl, representing the ancient goddess of wisdom.

"I understand from Sophia that you've talked about the goddess Isis and the Templars. Gods and goddesses seem to play a pivotal role in the rituals and other aspects of these societies. And the worship of these deities is often associated with intersections of different *ley lines*, which are electromagnetic streams of energy on the planet's surface. Specifically, locations where the points cross often correspond to places of deity worship. Isis in Egypt comes to mind, but there are many other deities worshipped all across the planet.

"The intersections of ley lines are power centers whose energy levels can be read by modern devices, but indigenous people everywhere have been able to locate these spots quite accurately, and civilizations around the globe have always taken advantage of them for healing and to raise their consciousness. There seems to be a perennial desire, over the millennia, to connect with the power attributed to ley lines. I'll tell you more about that as we follow secret societies to current times.

"Weishaupt named his society, *The Illuminati*, and he chose the all-seeing eye as one of the symbols for their group. Most of us think this image symbolizes God or a form of the divine. But my grandmother learned through my grandfather that for Weishaupt's brethren, this is the eye of the secret members *at the top* of the society. Those highest level members remain nameless in historical documents. Yet within the group, they are given allegiance and loyalty that defies my comprehension to understand it.

"Weishaupt's group claimed they planned to make men free and happy. Sounds like a great group, right? Well, there's one important detail you should know: they wanted to make these men in their organization into what they called *good men*. And sorry ladies, you were not part of this boy's club. They wanted a world revolution, and something near and dear to Weishaupt's heart was a *New World Order*. In his Utopian world, religion would be wiped out, globally. His clan thought big. Like Hitler, they convinced themselves that they knew the best plan for mankind. No governments would be left. People would no longer be restrained by any social, moral, or ethical ideologies.

"They planned on substituting a form of atheism for Christianity, Judaism, and all world religions, which they saw as superstitious. They saw their form of atheism as *enlightened*. This would allow all men to be equal—although they viewed life from a patriarchal angle. I'm not quite sure where women fit in, except they'd be atheists, too. And the elites in their society would embrace a pantheistic view that God is everything sentient and insentient, a wishy-washy description without a clear view of what that meant to them.

"Their form of daily life, by today's definition, would be considered communistic, which they saw as an enlightened Utopia. With their *enlightened elites* overseeing the world, Weishaupt thought his *good men* would have enlightened capacities and unquestionable infallibility.

"Sounds like the beliefs that the Catholic Church held about the pope, whom Weishaupt wanted to overthrow. World power and being *the best* are themes you'll see many times in secret societies.

"Who knows why or where he came up with all of this? From the research I gathered, it was clear that he and his confidants believed governments and churches had always been corrupt and were useless in helping men to find happiness and freedom. Therefore, the elite of the Illuminati needed complete power over society, including religion.

"Weishaupt advocated absolute concealment. His essays are clear that his society would never appear to do anything in its own name. There would be a cover for everything it did, never traceable back to his beloved *Illuminati brothers*.

"He wrote that he learned from his Jesuit education that mysteries and secrecies in a society help to control people's minds. Weishaupt's voluminous writings consistently affirmed that he believed brainwashing was good, especially since he and his inner circle would be the ones holding the secrets and doling out the mysteries to the butchers, educators, bakers, and all *lower levels* of society.

"Generally, these *lower levels* are commonly known as the *working class*, who would never know what was going on. Which was fine for Weishaupt and this inner circle because his small elite group knew what was best for them.

"I know you've already looked at why and how the papacy had a long history of oppression and corruption. In addition, during Weishaupt's lifetime, the Jesuits were strong clerical authority figures for him and other devout Catholics. They ran schools for students from prestigious families with exceptional standing in society. Weishaupt attended one of them and learned the *art of propaganda* and other tools and techniques for ruling as an elite in society. He often expressed in his essays his deep gratitude to the Jesuits for that wisdom.

"I easily located church and historical documents showing that the Jesuits took blood oaths to protect the pope, which extended to all the wealth of the papacy. Without question, they followed orders of their Superior General (the original title was *Father General*). Taking a vow that requires abdicating their will to all supervisors, they agreed to kill their own mother if asked to do so. They zealously countered the Protestant reformation, vowing to assist the church in reverting to the highest degree of inflexible, rigorous adherence to papal authority and the top of the ecclesiastical food chain.

"You could think of this order of monks as a modern day invincible intelligence agency, replete with weapons and zero compassion for anyone their superior told them to kill. Originally called the *Holy Alliance* (later renamed "the Entity"), the *intelligence arm* of the papacy became thoroughly entrenched as the papal espionage and security arm of the church. They became wealthy and powerful, feared by many because their claims-to-fame were conspiracy and assassination. That was a surprising revelation for me, because clearly there were lower rank-and-file members who were docile, humble missionaries. Since they are a secret society, I can only share historical accounts about them. Documents reveal that they pledged to spy and ingratiate themselves to 'heretics,' including but not limited to Lutherans, Calvinists, and Jews; they would pretend to be one of them to gather information, doing whatever was necessary as a faithful *soldier* in service to the Army of *Loyola* (their founder) in the service of the Pope.

"They also swore to take possession of all lands across the earth for the Pope. From their inception, they seemed to take the society's vows to heart—history indicates they were unquestionably loyal subjects of the papacy. French Theologians in the 17th century wrote extensively about them. Antoine Arnauld asked in an essay, 'Do you wish to excite troubles, to provoke revolution, to produce the total ruin of your country? Call in the Jesuits…' You won't be surprised to know that he had plenty more to say about their character and modes of operation during his lifetime.

"I also discovered they had been in Paraguay a century later, where they were arrested with a coded manual for teaching the local indigenous people how to kill settlers from Europe, while also creating a hybrid religion with the locals. Although there are plenty of controversial and conflicting tales in history about a lot of groups, I cannot ignore the many eyebrow-raising accounts of this secret organization.

"While eighteenth century citizens in the U.S. fought a revolutionary war, Europe was embroiled in the brutal Napoleonic wars. Jesuits interacted with European intelligence agencies in an effort to maintain control of the Papal States. Church and state had become bitter adversaries. During this period, as part of the Entity, Jesuits were intimately involved in covertly securing church authority.

"My grandmother, Anna, knew an ex-Jesuit in the 1960's who affirmed he'd taken their vow. She had shared with him her massive life review and resulting change of direction to overcome Nazi mind-control and intense indoctrination. The reformed priest said, like her, he had realized the allegiances and vows he'd taken had become embedded as absolute truth in his psyche. But through persistent, clearheaded, and often agonizing self-reflection, he realized that secrets were neither necessary nor healthy in order to be in service to humanity. His story was captivating.

"For him, WWII had brought *blind obedience* and *obfuscation* front and center. Although he'd hoped such concepts could be reformed in his religious order, he knew that Ignatius' viewpoints, which he'd studied methodically, left too much room for duplicitous practices. For example, in modern times, a brother who had perpetrated crimes against women and children was secretly moved to a new place without reporting the crime to the secular authorities. Allegedly, his brother in Latin America had systematically tortured prisoners yet denied and hid the facts.

"During WWII, the Jesuit head of the *Entity* was Pope Pius XII's advisor. There were numerous stories of covert Vatican-Nazi chicanery during and after that war. The ex-priest had believed unquestionably that the Pope and his advisors knew best. Yet more often than not, he began to wonder if he was ignoring and falling prey to destructive biases and influences. Consequential secrets and entangled deceptions allow leaders to maintain control while avoiding accountability. Gradually he learned how to discern the truth—building higher personal frequencies and experiencing buoyant vibes and much-needed clarity.

"Unexpectedly, and much later on, he stumbled on a pivotal event that further shattered his hope for maintaining priestly allegiance, when he read a news article exposing Jesuit clandestine affairs, thrusting him into grappling with the costs of modern day secrecy. He and my grandmother had stayed in touch, and he shared with her the shocking article, which was in *La Nación* (an Argentine newspaper). Apparently, during the investigation of an Iranian terrorist attack in 1994, *Argentinian* intelligence agents heard a leaked wire tap of a conversation between two *Iranian* intelligence officers. One of the Iranians had met the head of*Vatican* Intelligence in Argentina and was told that both this Vatican official and a Jesuit named Father Bergoglio were Freemasons.

"Father Bergoglio became the pope in 2013. If he had been a freemason, was he part of both Jesuit *and* covert masonic networks? Vows to Freemasonry are church heresy, so his participation would have disqualified him from priestly duties, definitely from serving as pope. So this revelation made no sense except that perhaps he was given special permission to be a freemason, as Jesuit undercover work.

"The ex-priest further discovered allegations that certain levels of Freemasonry in *specific covert masonic lodges*, along with certain Jesuit priests, were part of a complex, international intelligence network. Why would a religious organization be implicated in political espionage and engage in conversations with government *intelligence* agencies? Disconcertingly, he could not find evidence that the church confirmed or denied the allegations. Agonizingly, he began hearing other Jesuit, shadowy divulgences. His head was spinning in confusion.

"He asked, 'What is the value in upholding and participating in a surreptitious organization in modern times? Given these revelations, getting confirmation from trusted brethren in the society, what should I do?' Such questions and startling knowledge became a haunting reality for this man. Looking to his moral compass as a guide, he left the brotherhood, embarked on a new path forward, living a life of contemplation, focusing on spiritual growth and elevation of his consciousness. As a society, over hundreds of years, Jesuits have purportedly performed both ruthless and beneficial work in keeping with their society's particular beliefs.

"The ex-priest's first-hand account of his revelations helped my grandmother to better understand the path of our Jesuit ancestors' adherence to secrecy and blind obedience as well as our family's acceptance of their behavior and choices—which could be influencing current generations. For me, it transferred the topics of subterfuge and surreptitiousness to a *personal, genetic* level rather than a *cultural* one. The influences of secrecy run like a turbulent current, uninhibitedly headed downstream into my lineage.

"Yet elites in history like Weishaupt wholeheartedly admired and adopted secrecy and concealment tactics. In fact, he wrote about being grateful for the Jesuits' brilliant hierarchy, ingenious methods of maintaining control over initiates, and retaining masterful inscrutability. That makes sense—he basically took on the role of a Jesuit Superior General within his own organization. After all, it was his creation. Being the head honcho suited him to a tee. And, once again in history, the term *enlightenment* became distorted. He wrote about his version of enlightened men. It felt creepy to me, but I'm not *illumined* like he was. As I read his prolific writings, I found it hard not to get a little snarky and judgmental. Sorry. I'll be more careful to drop my opinions about him and stick to facts."

"Dear one," Megan said softly, "we are all likely having similar feelings about Weishaupt's vision and worldview. I appreciate that you want to be factual rather than emotional. Sophia assured me that you have high integrity and a kind heart. My guess is that your good heart is responding to some pretty low vibes. I do not feel judgment or anger coming from you. Please continue."

"Thank you, Megan. I appreciate your patience with my presentation of a difficult topic for me. I assure you that I have processed a lot of triggering emotions that arose during my research. In modern times, sitting comfortably around this gorgeous bonfire, it's hard to comprehend long-forgotten history and fathom the explosion of Weishaupt's seductively powerful delusions—their far-reaching effects thoroughly saturating the upper echelons of European society.

"As though what I've shared wasn't enough, there's more. The Illuminati were part of a strong eighteenth-century emergence of occultism mixed with spiritualism: like Voltaire, Alesandro Cagliostro, and the Count of St. Germaine. Some tended towards personal evolution while others like Weishaupt had other objectives.

"To reach their big goals, the Illuminati needed more members. Weishaupt wrote that he liked the way that the Freemasons were united in their secrecy. Adding to unarguably high aspirations for his secret society, their upper levels were, in his mind, enviable as leadership models for world domination. With that in mind, he directed all of his society members to infiltrate Freemason lodges. So they ventured into France, Switzerland, and Austria, and went anywhere a Freemason lodge was found. Again, these guys had big plans for the society going forward.

"The aim for joining the lodges was to assume positions in the higher levels of Freemasons. They were told to become the leaders so they could slowly bring in their propaganda. And then he went a step further. Think how this relates to current times. He had his members infiltrate library guilds and any place where academia was thriving. In his essays, he said that if someone writes something that is popular but goes against their ideas, they must either bring the author into the fold or if that doesn't work, then they should destroy the author's credibility and standing in society.

"He also wrote about how they slowly indoctrinated and heavily influenced the Lutheran and Calvinist theologians. He wrote that he was delighted in what he accomplished. He saw them as gullible and himself as a pure genius of manipulation. Interesting that he was proud of that.

"I know this seems like enough, but he wasn't finished. He said he would go after the *common people* by means of schools. He'd root out any opposing ideas about society and make his own ideas become commonplace. If that didn't work, he'd use coercion. From his writings, it seems he meant he would win them over one way or another—whether they came along like sheep or as one of his slaves, through fear or coercion.

"As for how he saw the role of women: he wrote that women help to win men over, which he could exploit by making it seem like the Illuminati embraced emancipation of women. Although if truth be told, supporting women was a form of manipulation. And he didn't hide it, even in writing.

"After months of pouring over his words that described his philosophy and worldview, and following his society forward in time, I found it hard to believe that the highest levels in society joined him, giving complete allegiance to the person who'd recruited them. Then they were told what to read and think, and to keep journals about their ideas—only if they matched the Illuminati worldview.

"It wasn't easy to ascend to the higher orders within the Illuminati. Anyone they believed to be even slightly religious or patriotic could not ascend in their hierarchy. And the lower ranks didn't know about the six higher ranks above them.

"I want to be clear that I'm not just assuming these things. There are documents showing that barons, dukes, princes, famous authors, and many esteemed theologians joined this society, as well as lawyers, academics, and physicians. Commoners from *the working class* were excluded.

"Like the Jesuits, if a recruiter or superior gave an order to do something that is normally considered amoral, allegedly the member had to unquestioningly obey. This included murder, theft, or anything else that the secret society deemed relevant to their cause.

"The movement grew from his original five hundred to as many as two thousand members in ten years. The Catholic Church convinced the Duke of Bavaria, Karl Theodor, to ban it five times.

"As I dove deeper into my study of the Illuminati, I had to keep in mind that this was a secret society, and as such, it was impenetrable and tough to eradicate. I kept observing it going underground and then popping back up. I have to admit that it was fascinating to find research showing the church playing *whack-a-mole* with Weishaupt's secret brotherhood.

"Weishaupt's writings were creepy and felt eerily similar to tyrants like Stalin, who killed millions of people, and other modern dictators and totalitarian regimes. Historians indicate that although this group seemed to have dissolved, it likely morphed and carried on. A disgruntled member became a whistleblower and exposed Weishaupt's personal ideologies and massive influence so they had to go deeply underground.

"Weishaupt's *New World Order* felt like chaos and horrific pain to me. What kept me going was my unquenchable desire to understand him because these kinds of societies never seem to die out. They just change their name, the perfect strategy for a masterfully surreptitious organization. I'm sorry to tell you that I have relatives who were Illuminati. Why? And where is this society today?

"I wanted to understand the large-scale tendencies to join a secret society because the unicity gene would not express in these low frequency environments. From childhood, my mother and grandmother taught me about the value of this genetic expression. Did I have genetic tendencies I was not aware of and which may contribute to unconscious patterns that thwarted the expression of extraordinary unity?

"Across the board, regardless of which society I studied, these secret societies morph and then carry on with business as usual. I discovered through my mother and grandmother how some of our relatives kept their Illuminati thread going. It was disturbing and honestly, totally freaky.

"Since I'm sharing their story and confessing my heritage, I have to tell you that among our family were Jesuits scattered here and there over the last few hundred years. One of them was associated with an Illuminati look-alike from Spain, the Alumbrados. They sought ecstatic union: a mystical union with the Holy Spirit. And once they experienced it, they could then have sex, steal, or have whatever they wanted because, from documents I uncovered, they believed themselves to be enlightened and fully connected with the divine. Although this seems twisted, I dove deeply into historical records, and I'm sharing what I discovered. This group was embraced by many levels of society.

"They shared numerous ideas with Weishaupt in that the illumined elite of the Alumbrados would rise to the top, while the others in the society trudged through life continuing to meditate in silence and hoping to experience the ecstasy that was their ultimate goal. That ecstasy was like the carrot of intoxicating bliss continually dangling in front of initiates. This kept the lower levels motivated. These lower levels were, like members of many secret societies, looking for ways to escape the incessant harsh rule of popes and kings. Historians describe these souls as men whose hearts longed for a glimpse of bliss and any form of reprieve from the harsh conditions they found themselves in.

"To understand why Weishaupt and others were getting increasingly confident about heading for the top of the elite-leader food chain, we have to look at church history.

"By the fifth century, the burgeoning Roman Church added original sin to their doctrine, which said that humans were born as sinners. Christians now had that obstacle to deal with. Slowly, more doctrines evolved. The pope's words were interpreted as *infallible* in matters of faith or morals, the idea of *purgatory* was added—the concept that when a Christian died, they might get stuck in a mystical layer of reality, where they could not see God. But of course they could comfort themselves because at least they wouldn't be burnt to a crisp.

"Worse was that the sovereign right to be in communion with God in perpetuity was no longer innate. It was tied to strict rules that must be followed impeccably. If you broke the new rules, you could get cut off from the divine in myriad ways, and through innumerable transgressions. Luckily, the priest would be the intercessor to get you back in good graces.

"An era of incomprehensible oppression was rising into full splendor which was great if you were the pope or the king. Church councils, held every hundred years or so, systematically expanded on the structure and hierarchy.

"By the time of the crusades in 1050, the Papacy was definitely rising in personal glory. Conquest, murder, and assassinations were the norm—which don't seem religious to me. For many years, I never shared this part of history because it is triggering for people. I grew up afraid to venture into this controversial area of our human timeline. Tonight, among friends, I feel safe to speak honestly about my extensive research and the revelations that manifested from it.

"This kind of vice grip on people through religion may be one reason that secret societies became an important part of life for both the elite and working class.

"The papacy wasn't just infallible—it could take the liberty of imperial conquests. The lay population had no input into the Roman church's decisions. In fact, they were kept in the dark about all the church's internal workings. The original New Testament had been passed down for centuries only through the clergy during church services. Even though the lay population in Europe finally got access to a printed translation of the Bible in the fifteenth century, they still relied on religious clergy for biblical study and interpretations of texts since less than twenty percent of the population was literate. Over the centuries, various popes and their inner circles of scholars had written, interpreted, and modified the scriptures, made decrees, and decided every detail related to religious life. Any attempts to defy a church order or question its authority meant certain torture and possibly death. Yet worse was the threat of an endless afterlife of harrowing damnation.

"Perhaps secret societies were a way to deal with mounting oppression. At one point in the Middle Ages, there were as many as three or more popes at the same time, fighting for power in the Roman Church. And whether there was one pope or three, nothing changed for the lay population—my ancestors, and perhaps yours. An uneducated, oppressed population was starving for food, respect, and basic human needs. Consider the effect this must have had on their DNA and the emotional patterns they would pass to future generations.

"The elite of society also found themselves serving the papacy and the kings. These elites were becoming educated with a worldview that shimmered with possibilities for power, prestige, and the finer things in life. However, these are things the papacy and kings wouldn't share. The Popes and royal court were, however, happy to amass land, gold, and the right to enjoy sex and other liberties. Any elite or working-class person would be shamed or killed for similar acts. Looking at the double standards and iron fist of the religious and monarchical rulers of the day, perhaps the secret societies filled a need of the time. Imagine our ancestors trying to manage this emotionally charged conundrum.

"Over the years, such secret societies may have evolved to provide members of the inner circle with the status of popes and kings: their own hierarchy collecting secrets that made them powerful and sometimes feel superhuman. I'll tell you more about that superhuman part in a minute.

"By Weishaupt's time, he was overtly resentful of religion and monarchies. For him, the world needed modern, progressive rulers. And Weishaupt felt he was perfect for that position.

"Rulers like Weishaupt usually rise to the surface following a time when the basic needs of a society are not met. Starved and resentful people create chaos, and revolution easily follows. That seems to be my family's history. Through my research, I observed that my elite and working-class ancestors lived through relentless wars and revolutions, watching new popes, kings, and secret societies roll out incessantly. Did anything change that made a noticeable difference for the working class? Not that I could find.

"Then came the industrial revolution and more recently the tech and information revolution. Across these eras of history, did anything change for the working class in terms of basic human dignity and taking care of their needs? Well, it did for some, but surely not all.

"In many countries, we could buy more things, take out loans, and have more stuff. But were we happier because of that? Were we truly free?

"And the heart-gripping truth is, with each brutal war of the twentieth century, we saw how fragile our lifestyle and safety remained."

Jake squirmed and said, "My mind hasn't wandered for a second since you started talking. But I have to take a quick bio-break, if you know what I mean. This is brilliant! And I've been watching for patterns from the anthropological perspective. Everything you talked about is important to me. Can we regroup in a few minutes?"

The group gave Jake affirmative nods and dispersed for a brief pause.

# CHAPTER 8

## SECRETS SPREAD GLOBALLY

As stars glistened in the vast dome above them, everyone returned to the circle and sat introspectively around the waning fire as John re-stoked it. As usual, Sophia served hot spiced tea with a nourishing touch.

After a few moments of silence, Avani looked at Caitlyn. "Adele found the same low frequency beliefs and mental patterns playing out that we discovered in our ancestors. Transparency, unicity, and trust are central for our survival as a species. This is why we have to continue to make a global cultural shift. For some reason, secrecy isn't just tolerated—it's deeply embedded in our culture."

"Well, there was a good reason for secretiveness on behalf of leaders," Caitlyn said. "Look at what she's talking about. For thousands of years, working class people were propagandized, coerced, and believed they couldn't be free. I'm seeing a pattern of slavery that spans epochs of time. It's like secret societies were always there so the elites could plot how to rule more effectively. And the working class continued to resign themselves to their low status, following their own specific patterns of low-frequency behavior. Why?

"There were always more working class people than leaders. Across the millennia, they only occasionally, when totally desperate, started a revolution; only to accept a shiny new ruler soon thereafter. I'm seeing in myself that when I'm shamed, I'm impotent. The working class joined secret societies, too. They used them for rebellions, like Lenin did to take over Russia. But somehow the elites were master manipulators. They always found a way to stay on top of the game.

"Thank God humanity has seen these patterns of behavior in global leaders of politics, business, and religion—before it was too late. The twenty-first century will be known as the beginning of a new era in human history."

They watched sparks blow in an endless stream of sparkling light from the fire as a soft wind swirled around them. John worked his magic and the fire began to blaze fiercely with a current circling endlessly upwards, sending tiny sparks billowing into the night sky. Nestling more securely into their blankets, the circle of friends settled and Adele continued.

"Let me go back to the Alumbrados for a minute.

"The beliefs of Alumbrados were a sign of the times, which has been true for all secret societies. Humanity is creative and looks for ways to satisfy a desire for connection with the divine as well as with the sacred splendor in each other.

"Throughout my research, I have observed that humanity has always wanted a connection to the ultimate Creator—some refer to this as *higher consciousness*—which could not be usurped by anyone. Instinctually we know it is a sovereign right.

"The bigger question for me was not *how to stop* these groups that take personal or spiritual longings to psychopathic heights of delusion. I wanted to know *why* civilizations had fallen from trust in leadership and in themselves to such an extent they found themselves free-falling into despair, shame, and hopelessness. Human nature can always produce an opportunistic person to emerge with personal delusion and take control. I keep wondering *what makes the masses follow them* in lockstep?

"I asked that question again and again as I watched secret societies come and go and morph once again in slight variations in new places. The Alumbrados were no exception.

"The Alumbrados were banned in 1525 as a sex cult and I noted the future founder of the Jesuits, St Ignatius of Loyola, was implicated. I'll say more about him in a minute.

"Not to be deterred, the society slipped over to France and resumed business as usual. It's important to note that a secret society elevates members, promises them a special power or knowledge, and focuses their attention on a goal that feels appealing to their sense of sovereignty and empowerment.

"In a tangled web of secrecy during the sixteenth century, the Alumbrados' elite had garnered momentum as a self-proclaimed godhead with unfathomable psychological influence over the lower level members. Naturally, if you were an elite member you'd want that status to endure.

"Sophia told me that you've talked about the Middle Ages. I'm glad that I don't have to mention too much about that era. It was a time in history of lords, serfs, inquisitions, crusades, and abject poverty. Humanity's suffering rips at my heart and my mind's capacity to comprehend the willful callousness of church and state.

"I could say more about that, but I want to share my research regarding the Jesuits. My grandmother told me that some of our Catholic relatives in the banking industry immigrated to the U.S. in the early 1800's. Part of their contribution was to help Jesuits overcome obstacles preventing them from participating in this potentially lucrative new world.

"In 1773, after the Jesuits had taken a few too many liberties with their power in Europe, a papal proclamation had banned their order around the globe, officially abolishing their order, including in North America. This meant the Jesuits couldn't come to the Americas and establish a larger foothold in the new territory.

"Not many Catholics had immigrated to the colonies yet, and the Catholics who were in the colonies were in bitter conflict with the Protestants. It was Protestants who had fled Europe at this time in large numbers, to get far away from kings and popes, fleeing persecution. These Protestant immigrants were seeking food for their families, a safe home to call their own, forums in which they could speak freely, and to be able to pray together in peace without risk or danger. For these desperate people, it was a last chance to actualize their basic needs and sovereign rights. Can you imagine how that must have felt? Wow! It gives me chills.

"You likely know that Europe had its own issues at that time. For this conversation, I'll stay focused on my ancestors' story in the United States, gleaned from their personal accounts.

"By the mid 1800's there were plenty of bankers in the colonies—Jewish, Catholic, and Protestant. But my relatives and other Catholic leaders believed that banking needed a boost from the papacy and its global wealth and power structure. And the Jesuits had exactly the training and ethics to build an empire for their Pope while supporting a bigger economic footprint for certain wealthy families like mine in the Americas, so my Catholic banker relatives wanted their expertise. However, the pope had disbanded the Jesuits.

"It took time, but a few years later, the Catholic Church reinstated the Jesuit order and sent Jesuits across the Atlantic, overriding their previous expulsion. Some people in California protested and demanded that the Jesuit priests leave, but ever-resilient, they established themselves across the huge new continent in key cities.

"By the way, I'm not picking on this particular church or group. It's no secret that many churches turned a blind eye to atrocities or helped to get the west settled by Europeans while slowly wiping out or leaving indigenous people in inconceivable poverty and despair. However, I'm sharing my family history to show how the Jesuits used their influence to make a difference in the Roman Church's power structure in the new colonies.

"My relatives lived in New York and Chicago. The Chicago kin, in particular, got my attention. They kept copies of letters from one particular priest, Father Chiniquy. He lived in Canada and, apparently, the kindness and care that he showed to his Canadian community drew many additional followers to the Catholic Church. So he was invited by the Jesuits to join them in Chicago and help them do the same, but he soon became controversial when he started writing books about his experiences. He wrote that a Chicago bishop invited him to come for the purpose of getting Catholics to stop marrying Protestants and to build the church's influence and power in the growing city. The priest kept a diary and saved his correspondence with several ecclesiastical supervisors. He also wrote passionate pleas to Pius the IX, imploring the pope to end the licentious lifestyle of priests in Chicago. His diaries are available online today.

"It's notable that Chiniquy hired Abraham Lincoln to represent him in a case in which a lay catholic accused him of slander. Lincoln persuaded Chiniquy to recant his remarks and the case was settled by agreement. Still, Father Chiniquy continued getting in trouble for being outspoken against the Catholics of his time—accusing them of reckless abandonment of vows, theft of parishioner's money, and lavish retreats with plenty of whiskey and women.

"He didn't back down from his criticisms of the Catholic Church and clergy, but to this day, the Catholic Church doesn't support his side of the story. Interestingly, some historians cite Lincoln as holding the Jesuits responsible for instigating the Civil War.

"Why did this priest, Abraham Lincoln, and the inventor, Samuel Morse, make bold proclamations about the Jesuit order, a secret society within the Catholic Church? Samuel Morse's book, *Foreign Conspiracies Against the Liberties of the United States*, can be found online, in which he wrote extensively about the nineteenth century Jesuits and their surreptitious nature and tainted past. History is full of both accolades and accusations of the Jesuits. When it comes to secret societies with hidden agendas, my grandmother said you cannot ignore the Jesuits. That is why I'm sharing this.

"I'm not telling you about them to get religious or political. I was looking at the secrecy, the vows, and their direct impact on society. In this case, I took a closer look at the secret vows and rituals, especially those designed to subordinate one's own will to that of a higher authority, as well as the promise that such vows and rituals suggest in the consciousness of members that in return they will get special powers, special knowledge, or something else of value to them—something they value so much that they become willing to die before breaking the vow. I don't want to spend time talking about details of their rituals and perceived occult rewards. Let's not linger there.

"I admit that it's not possible to dive deeply into these societies. How can you know the truth when there's immeasurable secrecy and motivation to hide their plans and motives? My focus remains on *the effect* their top-level members imposed on the unsuspecting working class or in the case of the Jesuits, on its own lower hierarchy of monks.

"My appreciation for the lessons I can learn from history is mixed with the effect of these societies—including the Jesuits—on myself, my daughters, and our world. I want to be clear that I appreciate having the opportunity to have studied my family history in depth and for the profound reflection and life lessons that emerged from that exploration. I noticed patterns in myself that I want to up-level. I also don't want to pass down to my daughters beliefs and worldviews that feel antiquated. A pivotal revelation for me happened when I realized the incomprehensibly powerful effect of secrecy—the mind-blowing number of secret societies in my lineage and across the planet for thousands of years. I realized that the psychology and influence of secret societies, whether secular or religious, have influenced my family, thus myself, in subtle ways. I am not trying to say anyone was wrong. Each generation does the best they can under the circumstances in which they live. My mission is to objectively examine the influence of my ancestors' worldviews and the effects of widespread secrecy so I can grow personally and spiritually. Is my purpose clear?"

Adele glanced almost sheepishly around the circle. Looking for encouragement, she found it immediately in Sophia's sparkling gaze.

"It's crystal clear for me," Sophia said resolutely, "and interesting from the perspective of looking at my own ancestors."

"You are in sync with the research that Caitlyn and I conducted as well," added Avani. "I get why you're looking worried. Often our colleagues were slow to grasp why our research included enquiries into secret societies—we were trying to understand the rules of the hierarchal game established thousands of years ago, rules that still affect how each of us responds to life and how we might be able to change course as a species. *Not-so-innocent* vows, absolute secrecy, manipulative power deals are worth exploring."

Looking around the circle of warm, friendly smiles, Adele took a spontaneous, deep breath. Calm and encouraged, she expressed renewed confidence as she continued.

"Thank you so much. I should have expected you to take a bold approach rather than digging your heels in with reluctance to hear me out. Sophia thoroughly warned me about your big hearts and open minds."

Winking at Sophia and glancing around the circle with effervescence, she said, "Sorry for my moment of *intense trepidation!*"

With her customary smile spreading affection and warmth through the group, she created a contagion of resonance with her, while their smiles spurred her onward.

"Rather than continuing with the nuts and bolts of these organizations, it's more helpful to take you forward on the timeline of secret societies and introduce you to some of my ancestor's pretty wild *membership choices*. I'm deliberately making light of a dark subject by speaking this way. It's my method of coping and trying to understand how psychotic manipulation and arrogance could be acceptable to my family line in a modern world.

"I kept wondering if secret society lovers in my European DNA caused the insidious tendency to gravitate towards elitism, a world view in which a few people are entitled to crush everyone else for their personal pleasure and aggrandizement. Inexplicably, these same relatives also expected spiritual enlightenment and to have access to magical powers. Finding other ancestors who were ordinary, working class folks brought a little comfort and balance to our bloodline.

"I mentioned that the occult was gaining traction in Germany. There were several main groups. Quickly rising to a global presence was the Theosophical Society, founded in 1875 by Helena Blavatsky and Henry Steel Olcott. Blavatsky's claim-to-fame was that she professed to have direct communication with ascended masters in other realms who supplied her with information. Of course, she passed on their wisdom and secrets to those in her society. It was like she had intel that no one else could access.

"Now we can jump to the turn of the twentieth century to see *why* many groups like hers were thriving. To give context, the masses were starving, the agony of war loomed unabated, and devastating natural disasters like potato famines painted a gloomy future. Within a few decades, Germany's unemployment soared to forty-five percent. There was immense suffering in the general populace, and even bankers, lawyers, and academics were desperate for solace. They found it in the occult, joining in droves; the working class enjoyed the feeling of having something that made them feel special and provided a sense of cohesiveness, while the elite seized what they saw as a chance to take greater control over the entire Earth.

"Each secret society had unique, esoteric rituals and symbols—which are foundational aspects of secret societies. They're the fuel for elevating the member to a higher status and a better version of themselves. However, for most societies, some form of *magic* was a big part of membership *advantages*. The society promised elite members that they would learn how to become superhuman and how to rule over the masses with ease and grace.

"Astrology, spells, secret rituals of all kinds, seances, crystal balls, pendulums, and a variety of ways to predict the future were comforting. Society was restless and seemingly endless wars had been costly on many levels. Famously, Hitler began to delve aggressively into the occult. He was into astrology, began to dabble in many areas of paganism, and then engaged in the darkest recesses of the occult—beyond normal sorcery or Wiccan magic. For example, to make decisions about military strategies, he decided that he needed a pendulum society. Sound innocuous? The problem came when a pendulum did not give him the right answer and the poor guy who wielded it could end up wasting away in a work camp, or worse, ruthlessly executed.

"Another example of how much Europeans were growing interested in the occult occurred when one of Hitler's top aids, Rudolph Hess, was captured while traveling to Scotland. He was there to locate a ritual that was being orchestrated by powerful witches who he believed were planning to cast a spell on the Nazis. In fact it was a ruse to bait Hess. Cecil Hugh Williamson, an English researcher, occultist, and master of the magical arts had been helping the MI6 intelligence section of the Foreign Office to collect information about Nazi occult shenanigans. He formed *The Witchcraft Research Centre* to help him identify top Nazis interested in astrology, the predictions of Nostradamus, occult magic, and more. Hess fell for the bait, but instead of getting to savor highly coveted English magic, he landed in prison."

Jake chuckled facetiously. "That's what you call a really BAD day for Mr. Hess! I'm not making light of all of this but, frankly, it's torquing on my brain to take in the insanity of it—not to mention the sober reality that this same occult obsession was a growing phenomenon in cultures across the planet. Of course, not everyone dove head first into the dark arts, but as a species, at that pivotal moment in history, we seemed to be longing for something to eclipse or minimize our emotional suffering. In retrospect, it is easier to see this phenomenon playing out, but when a population is in the middle of not one but many insurmountable crises, detachment from Reality can easily emerge. We've seen that happen many times."

"I understand," Adele said. Her tender gaze swept around the circle. "Believe it or not, there's more I can share. How is everyone doing? Should I keep going?"

Everyone nodded with encouragement so she continued. "Hitler required that his core team engage in various occult practices. To elucidate this from first hand knowledge, I brought a quote with me tonight from my grandmother. It is from Joseph Goebbels, Hitler's Minister of Propaganda, expounding his ideas about the occult's powerful influence in the U.S., and referring to a Nazi journalist:

*Berndt handed in a plan for the occultist propaganda to be carried on by us. We are getting somewhere. The Americans and English fall easily to this kind of propaganda. We are therefore pressing into service all star witnesses of*

*occult prophecy. Nostradamus must once again submit
to being quoted.*

"As the occult became prolific in practice and in media, it
found footing psychologically in many countries across the
globe. Grandmother Anna was clear that the Nazi style of occult
practice, as a seminal worldview, jumped Germany's borders,
especially as Nazis spread out across the globe after the war.

"One of Hitler's premier occult confidents who deserves
mention is Heinrich Himmler. He dove into the occult mysteries as though it was a dream come true. He'd always been
attracted to the occult. As if it was an unforeseen twist of fate,
he received the budget and authority to explore esoteric and
mystical areas. The choices of where to put his focus and budget
were so vast that he was like a kid in a candy store.

"He became head of the Schutzstaffel, known as the SS, a
paramilitary group that became the most powerful organization in the Nazi regime. Under his leadership, all SS members
were required to meditate, perform esoteric rituals, and make
vows of obedience to their supervisor. As they elevated in rank,
greater mysteries and enhanced superpowers awaited them.
This was one of many ways that the occult became embedded
in Nazi ideology. Many SS symbols were pseudo-runes indicating various aspects of Nazi ideology and their special brand
of occult mysticism. Among these was the double S symbol for
the SS itself, which was a rune stylized to look like lightening
bolts indicating "victory."

"Hitler and his staff were aware that Germany's cities, towns,
and landscape were planned and designed with geomancy in
mind—aligning with certain power spots which hold frequencies

that allow subtle energy currents to flow—often using rocks, megaliths, and other artifacts to indicate those subtle, high frequency areas. All SS meeting areas, Hitler's headquarters, the young Nazi training headquarters, and Nazi military locations were carefully located using geomancy. Places like Stonehenge in England were their guide.

"My grandmother said when you put occult tools in the hands of a psychopathic dictator, things get weird. She believed it was his addiction to superstitions that led to the fall of his Nazi empire. Her reason for believing that the demise of his empire was inadvertently self-inflicted was that Hitler surprised the head of his research team with a strange decision about the V-2 rocket program—the first surface-to-surface, guided missile program which represented enviable, high-tech genius at that time, and considerable military advantage. Hitler supposedly left his inner circle and scientists befuddled when he cut back the program because of a dream he had that the rockets would cause a disruption of *cosmic ice* and a galactic apocalypse would follow. The *cosmic ice* theory was part of another esoteric view that Hitler embraced.

"As the war turned sour for Hitler, he acquiesced to his inner circle and allowed the missile program to go forward at breakneck speed. My grandmother said history will show that his decision was made too late. She concluded that he inadvertently sabotaged the pace of his own research, foregoing a possible technological advantage. Timing is everything, right? Grandmother Anna said that even the most occult-loving members of his inner circle grumbled about that delay.

"The Nazi worldview was based on what she labelled Hitler's *obsessions with fantasy.* Her perspective was that his low vibe was no match for alchemy and other high vibe subtle arts and practices. It is one thing for Isaac Newton to practice alchemy but according to my grandmother, Hitler wasn't adept at resonating with the kind of intuition required for true alchemy and the sublime high frequency of the subtle arts. One incomprehensible example she shared was Hitler's and Himmler's obsession with Inner Earth. She left a few diary accounts like this one where she said:

> *The Führer was so goddamned egotistical that he thought he could just take over Czechoslovakia, Bulgaria, and anywhere else where caves of metaphysical significance, inner earth giants, and tales of mystical powers were reported... and voila! He'd be the proud ruler of the inner worlds!*

"She believed that Hitler convinced his confidant in *all-things-occult*, Himmler, to study the Hollow Earth Theory. She heard them speak about DeSoto and his escapades with Tuscaloosa and other giants in the America's in the 1500's. The Nazi occult team speculated that giants originated in the inner earth somewhere. Apparently there were tons of Nazi meetings about and budgets allocated for ways to satisfy what my Grandmother described as "psychopathic, delusional indulgences under the surface." Emphatically, my grandmother said in the same diary passage:

> *In the Führer's obsession with the occult, he never realized the accessible, mystical treasure that lies way beneath our feet. For him it was something he could discover, thus use, for personal gain. However, those rarified frequencies of*

*Inner Earth eluded him. According to the ETs I met, they will remain accessible only to those with a frequency match. There were a few caverns within the mantle, earth's crust, where he met like-minded, low-vibe beings. Yet he was nowhere near the Inner Earth described by my ET contacts—the profound, deep realms within Gaia from which legends arose elucidating the incomprehensibly high-vibe Shambala and Agartha.*

"You may be aware that Hitler and Himmler were determined to find proof that Germans descended from an unequalled race they called the *Aryans*, who they presumed to be descended from a high tech race of humans and ETs who purportedly were wiped out when a global flood inundated Atlantis, their home-base. The Nazis spent a fortune to create and develop a pseudo-scientific organization of scholars and scientists called the *Ahnenerbe*, and later, the *Research and Teaching Community for Ancestral Heritage*, in order to prove their racial theories and justify their policies. This organization, which was a branch of the SS, sent select Nazis to India, South America, and Tibet to trace the roots of the what they believed to be the tall, blond, fair-skinned, blue-eyed, superior Aryans. That was Hitler's description of perfection. His views are incomprehensible to me. Sharing this historical information and my grandmother's perspectives leaves me shaking my head in wonderment.

"Part of the Ahnenerbe exploration was to connect with esteemed archeologists. However, they also sought out monks with secret knowledge of magical powers and other forms of occultism, various fields of academia, and expert scholars in areas that ranged from Germanic history to the paranormal.

There is evidence that Hitler sought The Ghent Altarpiece, a painting that was believed by occultists to contain an encoded map of Roman Catholic treasures. He also made a run at obtaining the coveted sword that pierced Jesus' side at his crucifixion. To the surprise of western military personnel, the Ahnenerbe left behind hundreds of artifacts, carefully documented. These fascinating treasures were discovered after the war as a testimony to the Nazis' diligence and persistence in gathering things they believed to be "Aryan"—particularly anything with coveted, mystical vibrations.

"They wanted to create a Neo-Pagan Nazi religion that could influence and entrap the minds of their countrymen for centuries to come. The importance of the Ahnenerbe was its ability to influence future Nazi masses through rituals, some as simple as magical bonfires or lavish seasonal events that exemplified Nazi ideology. My grandmother said she observed Hitler was enthralled with the pomp and circumstance of Catholicism; to which he was accustomed. For his Nazi religion to stick, he didn't want to leave a shred of the past religions for people to turn to. However, he borrowed *aspects* of them which he twisted to fit his own Nazi ecclesiastical organization.

"In December 1940, Gauleiter Weiss proclaimed that the church would be obliterated in Poland because of its anti-German stance. This was an indication of the serious downward spiral faced by religions in the growing number of Nazi-occupied countries. The Polish language was prohibited in church services. Catholic weddings and funerals were no longer allowed. Most of the Polish priesthood ended up in concentration camps. Prayers invoking or honoring Mary, Jesus' beloved mother, were forbidden.

"During the same time period in Norway, Prime Minister Vidkun Quisling and others were promoting a break with Christianity and a return to a neo-pagan version of Norse pantheism; this included using the emblem of the Sun-Cross as the new national symbol, an image similar to the Nazi's swastika. This new religion made bold moves like creating a catechism which required full allegiance to Quisling. As you can see, Nazi-style fanaticism was spreading in Europe with the same tenacity as in Germany.

"Hitler brought back pagan rituals to aid in reconditioning his followers and the populace to take on a new racial ideology; the study and reimagining of rune lore, sacred geometry, ceremonies enacted in sacred mazes, ritualistic summer bonfires, and other rituals collected by emissaries he sent to Tibet to meet with lamas who could evoke a green, mystical being with ancient magic. He hired Wilhelm Teudt to identify sacred ley lines where The Third Reich could build various halls, such as a youth center on the holy island of Rügen (a Pagan sanctuary in ancient times). Such practices and ideas mixed with racial doctrine were integrated seamlessly into all Nazi activities and propaganda.

"Hitler thought big and played a long game. Immediate satisfaction was not his true aim, nor was it for those Nazis who came to the U.S. after the war.

"Hitler's focus on the Aryan race was of course his claim-to-fame. Research into this idea was sustained throughout the war. You see, Hitler believed that Aryans were the descendants of *Atlanteans*. My Grandmother said he saw himself as an elite of that civilization, like a god, and he believed he was born for that role in the twentieth century.

"Of course, there is plenty of evidence for the historical existence of advanced, ancient cultures all over the planet. Sophia said you've been to the sites of many of them, including an offshore Atlantean site in Portugal. These advanced Atlantean humans were the ones who learned how to connect to star beings and who learned the arts and sciences of pyramids, multiverse travel, and so much more. Hitler believed and wanted to prove that Atlanteans were his beloved ancestors, a true Aryan race of 'god-like men.' Hitler would not abandon his beloved Ahnenerbe so it was diligently continued until the end of the war."

John leaned forward. As he met Adele's eyes with a sincere look of astonishment, with his eyebrows raised sharply, he asked, "Hitler believed he was from an advanced civilization? Did he realize what those cultures were like? Over the years we've discovered jaw-dropping archeological sites filled with advanced mathematical and geometric knowledge, clearly beyond the capacities of hunter gatherers at the time. More importantly, the advanced cultures I'm speaking about clearly preceded the Aryan races I've come across."

"Could you say more?" Adele asked quizzically.

"After compiling tons of research, we posit that it's more likely that highly advanced beings, maybe from other star systems, connected with humanity and pointed out powerful spots on the planet—usually where two ley lines cross. These areas became known as locations where intergalactic travel and high frequency energies were available. Contrary to Hitler's hypothesis, from what we've studied and viewed onsite, the technologies were meant to advance everyone in the world, not just a bunch of blue-eyed, blonde Aryans. Ancient Egyptians, for example, could be either light or dark skinned. Thriving advanced societies likely focused on unicity and higher consciousness rather than breeding humans for certain physical traits.

"Ten thousand or more years ago, some form of war was likely waged. Suddenly a great flood spun the world into a new era. It was like being back to ground zero as a civilization except some humans held the DNA and memory for recalling how to continue advancing in evolution.

"In cave art and drawings in various locations, you can see a tall person with smaller people bowing to them or you see people being battered by an animal-human-looking being. Then you find someone in what appears to be space suits hovering above people. This art has nothing to do with Aryans.

"This is amazing to hear about Hitler. He certainly thought highly of his race's supposed advanced state. Absurdly, rather than focusing on what might actually make them great as a people, he felt compelled to pursue power and dominance through magic and ruthless leadership. Given what you said, what I want to know is *how did he pull it off*? How did he convince so many people to follow him? Why did everyone jump lockstep, literally, into aiding and abetting his criminal behavior?"

"I had the same questions," Adele answered. "My grandmother explained that part. I want to be clear that I'm not sharing this just to revisit past atrocities. I wanted to understand the effects of their relentless secrecy and mind control on the DNA of future generations. By maintaining control through *secrecy*, the working class can be kept *off-balance*, enduring constant chaos, demoralization and submission. My grandmother was living proof that the Nazis *held specific core values*, as secret societies do, and their influence expanded surreptitiously across the globe—in clusters that remain in place today.

"Before I share more about current societies, I will answer your question about why my ancestors joined. My grandmother told me that Naziism was a long-term, carefully orchestrated plan to manipulate and brainwash people. Citizens fell for their convincing facades and deceptive tactics.

"Hitler was infatuated with Tesla and the quantum sciences. He already understood that everything is *frequency*, including the *emotional fields* of humans. He knew that shame and guilt generate low frequencies and render people vulnerable to indoctrination and less likely to assert themselves. Further, he knew people are *led by their emotions*. He concluded that the more he kept the masses in lower frequencies, the higher he could rise.

"A crucial step to his success was taking over the media. My grandmother said the public only heard one message. The media was controlled by the Nazis, who told them emphatically what they could and could NOT speak about. A distorted, *unilateral* view was firmly established, inconspicuously ingraining itself into the German psyche. All opposing viewpoints became labeled as dangerous threats to Germany's safety and longevity. Over time, not even the slightest differing view was allowed. As Hitler gained power, fear was rampant. People had mindlessly gone along. Then there was an *eerie tipping point*, as my grandmother described it, when German citizens began to believe the propaganda they were hearing. It became so ingrained in their psyches that they even turned on their neighbors and believed only the government, only Hitler, who they believed was wise and taking care of them.

"For a population traumatized by war, economic depression, and mass unemployment, this confident, invincible leader felt like a safety net. The majority of citizens also ignored indications of Nazi ruthlessness and sadistic violence, remaining in denial until the war ended and the allies *insisted* that the survivors help to bury the starved, tortured, brutalized remains of the holocaust victims—their prior neighbors, friends, and fellow citizens.

"In my research and through interviews I conducted with German WWII survivors, a similar pattern emerged for the whole population. During the war, if you were not Jewish, you initially felt somewhat protected. All propaganda in the press was designed to make Aryan-looking Germans feel safe, special, and part of something noble and praiseworthy. At the same time, the propaganda perpetuated fear about Jews, depicting them as *disease-spreading scumbags*. It feels horrible to repeat that phrase. Yet, this is the gut-wrenching truth of what happens when *propaganda* thrives and *divisiveness* reigns unimpeded. The media, influenced by the government, could make any group seem dangerous and *despicable*. They focused first on Jewish people and how *different* and bad they were.

"As a mom, I've had many opportunities to receive unexpected wisdom through my girls. Recalling the way my ancestors were pitted against each other, I thought of Leisa, my youngest, playing a board game with her older sister, Kellie. Leisa always lost, cried, threw a temper tantrum, and swore she hated the game. Yet if Kellie asked her to play, she jumped right in enthusiastically. Kellie was a triumphantly demonstrative winner to boot! It's been my parenting style, although it's sometimes hard, to let them work things out. One day, I was gathering some of their toys to donate and Kellie brought the board game. Of course, I smiled knowing that Leisa would be glad to be rid of it.

"When I asked Kellie why she wanted to donate it, she didn't get to answer because Leisa came around the corner giggling. She looked at Kellie and they cracked up laughing as Leisa explained, 'I finally read the rules. I could never win without knowing them. When I read the rules and thought about the game, I realized it was lame! Why was I playing?'

"With a good-natured, exuberant smile, Kellie interjected, saying, 'And Mom, I liked winning. But after a while I hated tricking her. She wasn't old enough to know the wicked awesome moves in the game! What I really wanted was to play with her, except I ended up acting like the worst sister ever. We decided to find a new game and now she's old enough to read the rules!'

"Both girls howled with laughter and walked outside imbued with the sweet connection of sister-love they always share. With their childhood innocence and sagacity dancing in my mind, I cried unrestrainedly. Recalling the precious authenticity of their realizations as I worked with the information I was learning, I realized that my grandmother didn't know the rules of the Nazi-game. Worse, though, the rules were hidden and the board they played on had been co-opted by manipulators. My girls learned a valuable lesson that I hope they remember for the rest of their lives.

"My grandmother always wept when she shared the next part. As they were accustomed to doing, she said her fellow Germans looked to authorities for reliable information, and the media was considered to be a source of truth and integrity. At one time, there were four thousand newspapers and magazines in Germany. Hitler reduced the number of outlets to keep them under Nazi control and, over time, the constant narrative shifted German citizens' perception. She was adamant that complicity of the media was a crime against humanity.

"If someone caught a cold, citizens blamed their innocent friends and neighbors, spewing the hateful rhetoric they had been absorbing. There was no science to prove that Jews carried disease. The Nazis made it up, repeated it across all media, and soon it was an *accepted fact*. Yet it remained *pure fiction*.

"This level of propaganda eclipsed the dwindling remnants of compassion, friendship, and even family ties. If either parent was Jewish, for example, the family had a problem. And after a while, a Jewish mother would be sent away and, as the war progressed, she'd be turned in and sent to a concentration camp along with her children.

"My grandmother discovered later that Hitler's psychological manipulation included making those he considered to be pure Aryans feel special, noble, and worthy of honor, deflecting their attention away from any sense of responsibility or empathy for the suffering imposed on others. This is undeniably brilliant manipulation. The ones thus privileged began to willingly turn, sometimes viciously, on their brethren—cursing or spitting on neighbors who only a few years before were friends. If a family member said anything against the Nazi regime or insulted the Third Reich, the family turned them in as dissenters—not realizing the family member would be killed.

"Hitler carefully made sure the religious population felt safe until the time was ripe to kill them, too. For example, he would not let his officers or Nazis leave the Catholic Church. Hitler insisted that both of my grandparents go to church regularly, even though they'd not been attending for many years. It was all about appearances. My grandmother later realized this strategy was meant to maintain the appearance of being in alignment with the Vatican. But once the Nazi's power had grown beyond their need for this deception, priests, nuns, pastors, and religious people of all faiths met their death in concentration or work camps as well.

"The Nazis were clear that people who questioned authority, thought for themselves, or felt independent would not fit into their schemes for worldwide domination. They needed people to feel like a vital part of their overall global agenda with their worldview slowly curated from micromanaged propaganda. Free thinkers needed to be controllable or dead. His plan included creating systems of surveillance and compliance. He would faint with bliss if he could see Artificial Intelligence today, the massive opportunities it provides for power and control. My grandmother said that the psychopaths she knew thought big, envisioning life on a grand scale. The kind of high tech, pro-grammable global systems we now have would be invaluable for their plans for planetary domination—all done, in their minds, for the greater good. At the time, Hitler was proud to have the leading edge IBM punch cards to track deaths in concentra-tion camps. This was one of many innovations employed to streamline his diabolical goals. It's hard to relate, but he felt no remorse for keeping secrets, harming citizens, and other forms of wickedness, normally *shame-inducing* behaviors. Psychopaths think self-centeredly.

"Unfortunately for him but fortunately for the world, he didn't have enough tech to control everyone. The Nazis felt there were still too many citizens who were not Aryan, so they went full tilt developing schemes to murder those that he and his inner circle called the *despicable* people. As his murderous programs continued, Hitler felt more confident and began plans for even more exterminations. I want to emphasize that although some say he was a random, crazy dictator, my grandmother said he had powerful connections and the backing of wealthy, elite people who supported him to enact his plans. These backers might even have dumped him once the population was under control. This subject is complex! It was more than just Hitler. Yet he felt entitled and born to lead this *'noble'* endeavor, and he was the driving force behind what was truly a global movement with global financial backing.

My mother said that after the war, German citizens, including many who had been Nazis, were devastated to realize the extent to which they'd been manipulated and controlled by the propaganda and mind control, and became determined to put safeguards in place to prevent such a disaster from happening again. Even in the 1970's, a unique post-war curriculum taught students to sniff out deceit, lies, and manipulation in news articles and broadcasts, whether in print, radio, or TV presentations about current affairs.

"Mom had a friend in Germany whose teacher was an ex-Nazi who admitted to her students that she had once had a ruthlessness and contempt for humans she labeled as *despicable or undeserving of life.* She committed the rest of her life to sharing with younger generations the dangers of propaganda and the immense value of personal empowerment and self-mastery. She taught critical-thinking skills and techniques to identify tendrils of propaganda that could easily creep into their minds. She ended her course asking a few poignant questions. *Will you rely on news or authority figures for answers to life's challenges or will you demand transparency so you, your friends, and family can make informed decisions? Who are you... at the core of your being? What will you do each day to still your mind and become gentle and kind? If you don't know, you'd better find out. It matters.*

"With profound regret, this teacher said her generation had not believed in their self worth and inherent wisdom deeply enough to demand respect for all citizens. To evolve as a species and create lasting peace on earth, she realized that spying on people and hiding or twisting facts could no longer be acceptable to global citizens. One way to immunize young people against such manipulation was for them to realize their unlimited potential as sovereign human beings.

"Keep in mind that Hitler's beliefs, and those of everyone he affected, had become more than just mental constructs—they had become solidified experiences, altering people's neurological responses. He knew that in order to manifest his personal *dream world* he had to shift the population's *experience* of life into fear, so they would be emotionally dependent and compliant; a belief that the world is unsafe causes people to look for a leader to bring normalcy and safety into their lives. Hitler recognized this neurological tendency. If the population could not love themselves and others with a feeling of safety *on a neurological level,* he could control them, his comrades and followers could take advantage of them, and they would begin to do things that were formerly inconceivable."

Adele looked down. Her voice cracked as she tried unsuccessfully to choke back tears. After a moment, gathering a semblance of composure, she said in a subdued tone that brought the circle to breathless silence, "Sophia, I can't speak about the next part. It's about how Hitler, his backers, and inner circle planned to reduce the population. Sorry... I can't..."

She took a deep, centering breath, wiped her face, and mustered a modicum of equanimity as she implored Sophia to share this particularly dark side of history. She said in a murmur, "Would you tell them the part about the program? And how doctors, academics, businessmen, and the military willingly, *eagerly* followed their political party rather than their heart or prior oaths."

Smiling compassionately at Adele, Sophia nodded in agreement. Pausing for a moment, she allowed the group a chance to prepare to absorb the magnitude of an obviously emotionally triggering subject.

✳ ✳ ✳

Sophia sat with her spine fully lengthened to allow for a deep, centering breath before speaking.

"Adele and I have talked at length about a part of Hitler's plan to create his version of a perfect world, and how to reach his lofty goals. She has two daughters so it's hard for her to speak about this part of the Nazi's plan.

"Hitler decided to interweave professionals like doctors, industry leaders, academics, science, and the military into his Nazi party. These were all *authority figures* and with years of intense propaganda, he got the masses entrained to follow all authorities, without question, even if those authorities had become thoroughly *psychopathic*. The general population of

German people were carefully trained to never think critically for themselves. The Nazi propaganda monster was working Hitler's magic on everyone, keeping them complacent and distracted.

"My friend, Gilda, who was herself a de-programmed, former Nazi, spoke with anguishing remembrances of Hitler's and his Nazi brethren's viewpoint that the Nazi culture needed children to obey, learn rules, and pass rigid, standardized tests. The Third Reich's oppressive tactics were one example of the carefully orchestrated assault on human rights, creativity, and dignity that Hitler propagated ruthlessly. Any educational institution that did not comply with Hitler's eerie vision of a perfect Nazi world was forced to close. To remain open would result in im-prisonment or death for teachers and school administrators. Beyond formal education, Hitler continued to degrade the minds of his Nazi followers by involving the health system in a con-cept that was growing on both sides of the Atlantic—eugenics. Hitler planned to improve the human species by implementing specific beliefs and practices to study and alter human genetics on a massive scale.

"This topic remains unimaginable. No one realized top doctors in Germany would engage wholeheartedly in such madness. These included psychiatrists, and not just two or three outliers. Astonishingly, dozens of doctors and nurses became killing machines. I cannot envision them as humans. It was like they turned into humanoids infected with apathy and disregard for human life. The T-4 project was a program of "euthanasia" in which disabled children and adults were determined to be genetically 'unfit for life' and systematically killed. It was decades in the making, and Hitler wrote proudly about how well the program was progressing. The callousness for human life is reflected in the mass graves it created, which are heart-wrenching to see. No remorse was expressed, which is incomprehensible.

"Hitler defined sovereign beings—those born with the divine right to life and happiness—to be only those whose blood was considered to be purely Aryan. Not only that, but those Aryans had to align with the idea of taking over the world, creating a new world order, with a global classification system in which Hitler and a small group were on top deciding who would be considered perfect, divine, and worthy of love, dignity, and respect. Human rights flew out the window of the Nazi's elite cage.

"One aspect of this program ties into something we should consider as we move forward in time—Hitler was upset that Great Britain and the U.S. were ahead of him in their eugenics programs. He saw it as a competition. Weird but true. In the U.S. between World War I and the 1970s, thirty-two states enacted laws that restricted certain citizens from having children. Not surprisingly, these laws were inflicted on those who were poor, of certain races, or had debilitating physical or mental conditions.

"Starting in the late nineteenth and growing steadily in the early twentieth century, scientists and sociologists became enamored of the idea of *improving* the human species through *culling those with undesirable traits and promoting the procreation of those with desirable traits.* The science of breeding hereditary characteristics into or out of animals seemed, in this view, relevant to human breeding. What started as curiosity, slowly evolved into something more. Courts and doctors decided who could procreate and who could not, even ordering the sterilization of those deemed unworthy. It's worth considering and not glossing over this kind of authoritative structure that denies sovereignty as an irrefutable condition and right of all people.

"In the 1960s the Club of Rome formed, described as a group of thought leaders, researchers, and philanthropic benefactors who wanted to tackle the challenges facing humanity and the planet. Seem innocuous? My father loved it. If you want to dig in, read their literature and you'll recognize recurring themes carried forward from the 1930s to present. Their main focus is what they consider to be the problem of too many humans crowding the planet. My father was adamant about the need to align with this view and his friends joined him in speaking about it often. He said, 'The *crowding problem is absolute truth on which to base decisions and strategies!'*

"Although often worded more subtly today, this perspective is easily discernible in many academic circles and think-tanks. It's *an entrenched belief system.* I wonder how we can shift this view and develop ways to outgrow *limited* perspectives that we've been living with for a long time. After all, the views emerged at a very different time period. I'd love to see us move forward with radically expanded views. Can we ask, *If we had free energy for everyone without governments controlling it, unicity was wildly expressed, and we inexorably embraced our inconceivable, inherent capacities as human beings, what else might be possible for us as an evolving species?*

"I realize that I am pushing the capaciousness of our current societal envelope, asking us to think big and way out of the box. *Is it possible that we have ancestors who predate our wildest imagination? Can we think predominantly with our right-brains as they did and exhibit incomprehensibly high vibrations?*

"I want to entrust this profoundly important inquiry to you, my closest and dearest friends, because we want to look closely at propaganda that began many years ago, ceaselessly bombarding our culture with a *limited* worldview—without questioning its ramifications and validity.

"With heightened global tensions and relentless war across the globe, I am grateful that people are asking these kinds of questions. If it wasn't for brave souls who dared to buck the system and challenge the status quo by digging deeply into well-guarded secrets and intensely crafted propaganda, we may have found ourselves in a really dark place.

"After discussing all of this, believe it or not, my most far-reaching, mind-boggling revelation is that Hitler and all leaders, past and present, believe themselves to be *heroes*, not *villains*. Is it possible they show up for us to see the dark and light in each of us and choose a way forward that's in alignment with unicity, compassion, freedom, and respect for everyone?

"Well, dear friends, this feels like a great point to conclude our conversation. I feel genuinely optimistic going forward as part of an astonishing global species, with you by my side. I love you so much!

"Can we talk more tomorrow night? I want to reveal secrets I've never shared. You are my safe ground on which to stand when I feel vulnerable and raw. If it's okay, I'd like to take a moment by John's mesmerizing fire to be still and regroup after that finale to our conversation."

With respect for her request, the group graciously disbanded. The fire remained full of life with sparks soaring upward into the moonless firmament that engulfed her within its mysterious darkness. Soon Sophia sat alone, motionless, allowing herself to become entranced by the magnificent, alchemical power of the raging flames. With each breath, she allowed her consciousness to expand in all directions, effortlessly soaring as wondrous quantum waves in an infinite ocean of exalted vibrations.

Regardless of what had happened on Planet Earth, the astonishing potentiality for her destiny danced like a wildfire of optimism in every atom of her being. The inconceivable momentum of human evolution she was observing globally thrust her heart into endless waves of bliss and soothing comfort.

She was revisiting a recurring inner vision which revealed a world in an epic upward spiral of transformation and radical unicity.

# CHAPTER 9

# SYNARCHY

With friendliness and hugs, the group coalesced into a fireside gathering with their usual camaraderie. Everyone settled in, organizing their chairs and huddling closer to the fire which John skillfully brought to a roaring blaze. The cool air invited everyone to snuggle into a comfy blanket and prepare to listen from within their warm cocoon.

Sophia arrived last, slipped into her chair unhurried, smiling tenderly at her friends.

The fire was dancing and crackling as a light breeze encircled the group with a nurturing sense of calm. Sophia's eyes closed gently; she sat motionless and her face took on the attributes of a serene moonlit lake. Synchronizing with her, the group became still and introspective.

After a few minutes, John noticed Sophia's eyes gradually opening with the softness and radiance of the mystical, golden dawns they'd come to expect at the cove. He broke the silent reverie saying, "Sophia, I don't want you to feel that you have to talk about something that is too much for you to handle."

"Thank you, sweet friend," she replied in a soothing tone that spread over the circle like a comforting blanket. "I'm okay. Until last night, I wasn't aware of the magnitude of buried emotions hiding in me about this subject. I'm not willing to gloss over humanity's darkest periods because they are *multi-layered teaching moments*. That's what Gilda used to say. However, when Adele's grandmother told me about inconceivably grievous events, Nate was very sick. I was overloaded emotionally so *feelings* associated with those subjects didn't get thoroughly processed. After unrestrainedly venting an unforeseen, hidden cache of pent up emotions, I dreamed of disturbing atrocities in our world that are playing out unrelentingly. Yet I realized our circle is asking *why* and *how* we can elevate our frequencies as individuals and as a species. That propelled me into a higher state of awareness. Definitely, excavating my grief and sorrow helped to dislodge emotions ingrained in my psyche and emotional field.

"This evening I am super-curious to dive further into our conversation. *How can we raise our personal and collective frequencies in novel ways? How can we learn from patterns in history, elevate in frequency, and express new genes in the process?* This is huge! It's immeasurably exciting!"

Settling the group instantly through her engaging, reassuring smile, she began. "We've certainly covered a broad time frame. We went from the lost continent of Atlantis to medieval European history, and into World War II. Now we'll move forward. There's a thread in all of this—*secrecy.* Adele shared her concern about potential genetic expressions inherited from secret society members in her lineage. The motivation for sharing my story is a curiosity that arose about why secrecy has become so important to our DNA expression and our future as a species.

"In every era our circle reviewed, the working class struggled to survive, thrive, and lived in unrelenting mental and emotional suffering... and unfortunately many still do. *Why?*

"Recognizing *our programmed belief patterns* about ourselves and historical events can be a clue to the answer. The end of World War II led to a stronger middle class in North America—a burgeoning *consumer class*. There were parties to celebrate the end of a devastating war, and fresh production consumer goods, including chemicals to help rid the new consumer class of everything from pests in their gardens to cleaner teeth and spotless bathtubs. All areas of media boosted advertising like never before. And the amount and variety of things to be purchased was unprecedented—which looked good on new television screens. Everyone started striving for more stuff. In fact, if you watch TV shows from the 1960's, having a mortgage and credit was glorified as the ultimate *American Dream*—the most seemingly innocuous, popular sitcoms wove this into their scripts.

"All this programming shifted the consumer from simply striving for food and fulfillment of basic human needs, to striving for a success only achieved through acquiring more things, more money, more comfort and pleasure.

"A new epoch was upon the citizens of Planet Earth. This gets us to the part about my family secrets. What I wanted to share first is about specific secret societies and how they play into everyday life, now more than ever before. Although they are in the backdrop of life, they influence us in unseen ways. Over the past few years, since the upheavals in stock markets, currencies, and all of the challenges we've faced, secrets matter more than ever. What I can share about my family's ties to secret societies may help to put pieces of the puzzle together.

"I need to take you to Europe for a minute. My mother's family was French, a highly pedigreed lineage of bankers and industrialists going way back. If I told you her maiden name, I would be name dropping—it's recognized internationally, with a multitude of connections to high society. I don't want to get sidetracked so I won't take us there. I want you to know her as a person, without her title and lineage. Mom was beautiful in all ways.

"Even as a child, I could tell that she had a hard time dealing with my father's aloofness and hardened heart. He met my social and financial needs, so some would say he was generous—yet assuredly not in an emotional way. Being married to my father meant mom had to rely on a few close friends who brought out her joyful, light-hearted side.

"I recall one morning overhearing my mother's conversation with her Dutch friend, Gertrude. Gertrude told my mother to 'watch *The Bilderbergs.*' She said it was important because they had been active for at least a decade and they were only going to get more influential.

"Many years later, through Nate, I discovered that the Bilderberg group was comprised of political, business, and academic leaders who had been meeting annually since the 1950's in secret, ostensibly to prevent another world war. He called it a secret society because they met his criteria: they are totally secret, make vows, never disclose anything, publish no notes or information about their meetings, membership includes privileges and information nonmembers have no access to, and members don't apply but have to be invited. There's almost no published information about them except from media organizations that are not mainstream. An itinerary is the only information available and is distributed after the meeting starts—which is always held at a posh hotel that has security like Fort Knox.

"The members of Bilderberg group work in intelligence agencies, global media companies, the entertainment industry, the food industry, petroleum, technology, and more, yet they claim not to represent those companies or agencies. Oh, I almost forgot to include the key policymakers in global governments who attend as individuals, supposedly just hanging out and sharing ideas. These are the *movers and shakers* of a global *who's who* of influencers in every sector of international business and world political leadership. Because the society's membership is broad and undisputedly influential, journalists naturally scrutinize this group, to no avail. Review of a PhD dissertation—linking their meetings to unforeseen, *coincidental* subsequent events in the world—reveals staggering benefits to members. It's a deep dive into the belly of high-level secrecy where members agree that they can use information acquired but cannot report who shared it.

"Nate was dumbstruck by *the coincidence* between their gatherings and global changes. And he realized that, like most secret societies, they share cross membership with other clandestine societies, expanding their network of influence. Gertrude wanted Mom to stay alert to their agendas yet how is that possible? Nate also was emphatic their vested interests matter. Of course, Gertrude would be elated he was paying attention. Nate was not saying they called the shots, maybe they met to decide how to carry out strategies made above their level within the hierarchal structure of global leadership. However, they were often rising stars in the upper echelons of politics, finance, and industry.

"Nate and Gilda were clear—history had revealed the involvement of secret societies in orchestrating wars and ongoing instability in culture, reaping the associated rewards. According to Gilda, Lenin used the Oriental Lodge of Freemasonry as his underground network for communication and planning. Trotsky didn't like the idea and advocated for keeping their movement transparent and accessible to all citizens. Take note of who made it into leadership and who didn't. Some historians say the Masonic Lodges and members were Lenin's secret to success.

"Learning about the role played by such societies in wars helped to make sense of the times when I heard my parents argue over my father's 'involvement in the war.' I was confused because he never served in the military. I didn't realize that, as a member of several societies, he was involved in a *covert* way. It's an understatement to say that his involvement made her angry. I still cringe remembering his terrifying, guttural voice, full of roaring rage as he threatened to *shut her up*. I can hardly count the number of times that I sat in my bedroom shaking—horrified by their fierce arguments about financing wars. I'd hear glass shattering as an expensive vase or delicate work of art hit the wall. At times, I'd hear her blood-curdling screams—followed by bone-chilling silence.

"Mom had no contact with her family in Europe. It wasn't until after Dad died, and she was quite old, that she told me our family secrets. Sharing it prior to his death would place both of us in a cauldron of danger. My instincts to be terrified of my father were justified. He had indeed hurt her viciously several times. But her feisty nature overrode her survival needs. Without speaking up, she felt hopelessly complicit in his work which was agonizing for her. Yet she knew she couldn't thaw his frozen heart enough to shift his worldview.

"In France, her family had been involved in a secret society that my father's family eagerly joined as it grew in power and influence.

"She called the society *Synarchy*. My mother said that her exalted relatives in the banking world did not believe that human beings were innately endowed with sovereignty. For them, no one had a divine right to freedom or to live and express themselves as unique contributors to society. In the Synarchist's world view, the working class was just a resource, like cattle or corn. There was no empathy or any form of corporeal relationship with them. The common people served the society through their labor as soldiers in time of war, producers of goods and services, and procreators of working class labor.

"Again, I'll take you to France where she explained her understanding of how Synarchy started. Apparently no one knew anything about its secrets until the murder investigation of a banker who had been known to belong to several secret societies. As I mentioned a few minutes ago, it was common for members of one group to be members of several others. The murder victim fit that pattern.

"In the banking, finance, and corporate sectors, the top tier met in secret, could conspire with friends and allies, while remaining bound by secret oaths and other occult-bonding mechanisms like rituals. After the banker was murdered, a small leather bound book was found in his bedside table. The words, *The Synarchist Revolutionary Pact*, were written in gold embossed letters. It included one hundred pages of what appeared to be a manifesto.

"Getting a peek into this group was chilling. They had a plan, and it was clear that they likely had the power to see it through to its egregious goal. The society's horrific outcome for humanity, which my mother and father fought furiously about, was clearly outlined in that manifesto."

Sophia's gaze moved around the group as she connected with piercing profundity. She paused and gently closed her eyes for a moment, then continued her story.

"The Synarchy's hierarchy is eerie. I will share how Synarchy is playing out, from my mother's perspective. This society is not merely something from the past. It is alive here and now. Their basic goals are to unify Europe and then dominate the world within a specific global structure.

"Bankers, considered to be the smartest and most noble, are at the top, then industrialists and technocrats, followed by the collective global population. The working class would live in a supposed utopia where they would enjoy being led by immense propaganda and a pseudo-pagan, occult religion led by oracles and priests.

"By the late 1800s, Synarchy found firm footing. Secrecy was its hallmark. No one openly admitted to being in the group. As part of their strategy to gain global control, they didn't want to start a group from scratch. They decided to hand pick the top people already invested in secret societies like Freemasons and the up-and-coming Martinists, and convert members whom they felt were a good match. They also invited technocrats from any political party as long as they'd been vetted and were trustworthy. Occult rituals were part of the magical allure and a promise that members would be prestigiously bestowed with superhuman powers.

"My mother's grandfather was a member of a French Synarchy Society. He groomed my mother's father to join them. My father's family later joined the society, too.

"In the beginning of the twentieth century, a rift emerged between the Synarchists of Russia and those in Europe. Russia had ousted the Czar and the People's Socialist Party was going into power. Stalin's and Lenin's horrific reigns of terror resulted from Russian revolutions which set the stage for new governments.

"Hopes for a global alliance of Synarchists was dwindling. With determination, the French began to regroup. There were plenty of Freemasons, Catholics, fascists, occultists, gullible technocrats, and banking elite to enlist. From the members, they would carefully develop, cultivate, and rank them with bankers at the top.

"Keep in mind that only a small fraction of members rose to the upper ranks of the society. Just as the Freemasons are divided into thirty-three degrees, the Synarchist Empire Movement had hierarchal ranks as well, with a select, tight-knit few at the top. The ranks below them knew nothing about what was going on at the elite level—except through carefully curated communication fed down through the membership. Part of the allure of secret societies, remember, is that members feel special, and enjoy a sense of camaraderie as exclusive members of an influential group. Don't forget the amazing secret powers, prestige, and privileges always dangling before them, like constant, delectable bait for hungry fish.

"The French government decided to have their intelligence agency track the Synarchists to assess the range of their membership and influence. The French Ministry of Justice received the report which showed that Synarchists had woven themselves into every aspect of the government, including the inner circle of the Vichy Head of State. More than that, they were astonished by the large number and specified names of alleged members from the biggest French banks, like the one my grandfather and his father worked for.

"The report didn't dive into a bunch of information about a group of eccentric occultists. Instead, it completely stunned the Ministry of Justice by divulging the names of powerful elites in banking, finance, and big business. It was clearly run by high-ranking banks at the top.

"Synarchy was a movement that planned to do away with governments across the planet and impose their own brand of global authoritarianism. Mom called them, *The I Know Best Society*. My mother said that their goal was not to use violence, which was too tumultuous for their liking. Instead, they would surreptitiously take over global banking, all currencies would be dissolved, and they would gradually take ownership of the global monetary system. Their weapons were secrecy, a stealth-style of communication, massive propaganda, and making all countries dependent on this central group. They were fine for their plan to simmer and bake slowly until it fully materialized. As with Hitler, they accepted a long-term game plan.

"Bankers like my great grandfather and grandfather were sitting at the top of the society's pyramid structure. The industrialists, the giant corporations they invested in, were below them; and a group of elite technocrats, groomed by them, were on the next level down—with the rest of us at their disposal.

"As I look at the shock and blank stares on your faces, I remember being in your shoes. I get it. Imagine seeing the face of the French Ministry of Justice who first read the report. It probably didn't seem even possible. Wow... out of the blue... I am feeling my mother sitting here with us."

Sophia paused to collect herself as delicate tears, like glistening drops of morning dew, landed softly on her cheeks. In a hushed tone, she said affectionately, "It's time for her voice to be heard, even if it's through me, and many years past due."

As they watched her captivating eyes shut with elegant tenderness and her breath assume a soothing smooth cadence, the group became mesmerized, patiently waiting for her to continue. The fire ceased its crackle, crickets ended their chatter, and the breeze froze... silence engulfed the gathering that was motionless, nearly breathless, submerged in an ephemeral moment of timeless spaciousness.

Without warning, caught by a sudden soft wind, the fire started to roar and emit its rhythmic, mellow crackling. As if on cue, Sophia gently opened her enchantingly guileless eyes. Her voice was soft as its gentle lilt sent a wave of warmth and comfort that soothed and entranced the circle of friends as she continued to speak.

With unshakable clarity, she said, "Without a choice... through Synarchy... the global population was destined to deal with occult priests who mom said would strategically guide the religion. Imagine that the world collectively would forever grapple with a multitude of rituals and rules to follow. And whether they were happy or not was inconsequential. Recall that human beings were not considered to be sovereign. They were resources described as categories like chicken and wheat. Along with the air, water, and land, human rights would belong to the highest echelons of banking and business.

"What the French investigation uncovered was that this society of elites would create disasters and wars to bring constant instability. They funded particular factions, often on both sides of a conflict, to keep wars going consistently. In fact, a theory evolved that Synarchists had deliberately sabotaged the economy in France before the war. This led to France's unexpected and swift collapse in 1940.

"Revolution would become a device that they could employ to weaken governments, which required diverse factions; plenty of infighting was a great boon for them. This instability, revolution, and division within countries, including many civil wars, was part of the long game that I mentioned. They would rinse and repeat this pattern many times.

"It is believed that within a year, the intelligence report was complete and it was dispatched to the Vichy Head of State. Unfortunately, the Synarchists had infiltrated his inner circle and he never saw it. The group's goal to solidify an international brotherhood of financiers and industrialists was gaining traction.

"There were other societies that my mother's synarchist family joined. She thoroughly informed me about Synarchy because as it crossed the Atlantic it had far-reaching tentacles and deep roots that took hold in the United States. When my mother shared the story that I am about to tell you, I thought it was from a movie. Why didn't I hear about this remarkable event in history class?

"It was called the *Business Plot of 1934*. It starts with a retired U.S. Marine, Major General Smedley Darlington Butler. He was from a Quaker family of civil servants, lawyers, and congressmen. He'd won two congressional medals and was held in high esteem as a man of personal integrity and courage. This is the kind of guy you don't want to confront because he's not only tough-minded, but he also had a heart and soul of pure gold.

"After his retirement, he had second thoughts about military service. He did a deep dive into the subject of war and into some the countries he'd fought in. He arrived at the surface of this research with a change of heart which he explained in his short, powerful book called *War is a Racket*—with chapter titles that are engrained in my memory, like the last one, *To Hell With War!* Butler researched all the way to the underbelly of wars that he'd fought in, and he was changed forever. He saw beneath the surface of the actual conflicts and, with meticulous care, unearthed the guts of the beast of war.

"As a general and thirty-year veteran, he revealed the truthful mechanism of war to a country whose population was left dumbfounded and shaken by his words. Regardless, they believed him—he was deeply respected, especially among the military. At the end of each conflict, he explained that he consistently found himself looking into the eyes of the same societies of people—Wall Street and global banking elites and financiers—who 'raked in' enormous power and profit.

"The civil war had been no exception. He kept researching and shared his eyebrow raising research to veterans who conveyed their astonishment and dismay. His natural capacity to express bold, unbridled passion drew people to him in droves. He stood strong, regardless of the reality that loomed over him. He was not naive to the fact that the top levels of Wall Street and those he called their puppets in government would seek to crush him. Like a cornered mountain lion, he would not back down. I guess that's how he got two congressional medals of honor.

"I'm not getting off track by speaking about General Butler because my mother talked about him in the context of Synarchy.

"Records show that instead of striking back, the top Wall Street players contacted Butler through a Wall Street stockbroker. The proposal was mind-blowing to General Butler because they invited him to join their A-Team. Yes… they wanted him to join the team and be at the top of a military command. Amazing offer, right? Butler's mission—should he choose to accept it—was to use his enormous popularity to raise an army of nearly one million veterans to march on the capital in Washington to install a corporatist government that aligned with the Fascism happening in Italy and Germany at the time.

"A dictator would be needed. Wall Street was satisfied that they'd found the perfect candidate to suit their wants and needs. He was General Hugh S. Johnson, a retired U.S. General who understood how to work with the military and was intimately tied to elite Wall Street bankers and financiers. Importantly, too, he spoke openly about the merits of Fascism. As though that isn't inconceivable enough, there's more. Johnson, the proposed dictator, was President Roosevelt's first head of the National Recovery Act.

"At first, Butler listened, stunned and in shock.

"Behind Gerald C. McQuire, who had extended the invitation to Butler, was Wall Street powerhouse, Grayson M.P. Murphy. Murphy was purportedly backed and supported by a legendary figure on Wall Street, Mr. J.P. Morgan. Butler later shared that the French DuPont family were financial backers of the plot, too.

"Remember that I mentioned a report about the Synarchists given to the French Government—the report that went nowhere. It did not escape Mom's attention that an elite French name was mentioned in this U.S. report along with upper class U.S. family members and others who were part of the financial backing of a new U.S. government, with a bona fide dictator at the helm.

"Those Synarchist families are part of the Wall Street elite. Mom was alarmed because they brazenly moved forward with the plot. She believed they were savvy business people and must have believed their chance of success was pretty high. Her trepidation came from realizing that it would take a highly organized, secret network to pull off this kind of audacious scheme.

"Butler said the affluent Wall Street brethren were willing to contribute up to thirty million dollars to this noble cause. These financiers proclaimed they were philanthropists. They were just trying to help. Their plan was for *the good of all*, right? Like Hitler, Stalin, Mao and many others, these families saw themselves as heroes rather than villains, entitled to make the world a better place based on their world view. And this was the messaging about them in media—these well-to-do families were depicted as praise-worthy and saintly for their philanthropic efforts.

"Well... Mom emphatically said she didn't think so.

"This may surprise you, but one of her most poignant comments about the upper echelons of elite society was about their *misery*, at a very deep level. In her view, my father's inner circle employed constant manipulation, which after a while, undoubtedly depleted their inner tranquility. In her encounters with them, and while living in their uniquely prosperous world, they never seemed relaxed and happy. From what she observed, nothing was ever enough—not enough entertainment, sex, pleasure, food, or power. From her perspective, they were driven to a form of self-inflicted madness, believing themselves to be remarkable, noble, matchless. With this distorted worldview for some and societal indoctrination and peer pressure for others, she said they easily rationalized and justified their actions. You may want to keep her observations in mind as we continue. Her insights were helpful for me to understand my father's peers on a deeper level.

"Now, I'll continue to tell you how this amazing general responded to the lucrative offer to get the chance to be part of elite U.S. and global society, becoming a powerhouse in the upper echelons of government. For a year, Butler strung the Wall Street elites along to see how much intel he could collect about the plot. Finally, he went to Congress to expose the whole thing.

"Do you know what happened?"

Sophia observed everyone's furrowed brows of confusion; except Jake who was smiling.

"Okay Sophia," Jake said, "Son of a bitch! I heard about this plot years ago and thought it was ridiculous. With all that we learned about our government's fabrications and cover ups over the past one hundred years, I'm all ears! What did Mom say? If it's okay, I'll add some pieces that she may not have known.

"Please welcome her to the circle tonight. I appreciate hearing her invaluable perspective. She saw this happening and no one in the press or in leadership had the balls to fully disclose this stunning reality to the public... and then kick some ass! So, thanks, Mom. On behalf of our tight little circle under the stars, I can say, we love you! We appreciate you!"

"From Mom and me, *thank you, Jake*," Sophia continued while beaming a loving smile at him, her voice still wrapping the group in a cocoon of care and an embrace of comfort that sustained their capacity to absorb inconceivable history. "One reason the public blew it off is because that's what Congress did—one hundred percent. Mom was clear this was part of a highly strategic coverup and an attempt to hide an elephant in the room. We have to wonder why their concealment worked? Where was everyone's attention? What had captivated the minds of the U.S. population?

"It gets more intriguing… Congress never called any Wall Street bankers or anyone implicated to testify. Justifying their complacency, the Congressional committee declared that since the plot didn't happen, how could they prove a crime was committed?"

Sophia was becoming more animated inciting the circle to enliven and listen with rapt attention. "Okay, hang on, my friends. It gets crazier. Their *official findings* stated there was an attempt to create a fascist organization in this country. Plus they admitted there had been discussions about this fascist regime takeover, specific plans had definitely been made to remove the U. S. President, *and they knew who was involved*. Keep in mind we are talking about a takeover of the U.S. government and kidnapping the President. That is no big deal, right?

"Listen to this part carefully: they also note that this fascist coup d'etat had *financial backers* to support the planned takeover. But congress decided not to mention the names of conspirators in the public records. Seriously? No one in the executive branch, *including the Department of Justice* and President Roosevelt, took the results forward. The New York Times dismissed it as a hoax, like it was disinformation or misinformation rather than indisputable, scary, inconceivable facts backed by tons of documents and irrefutable testimony.

"Butler helped U.S. citizens to peak behind a curtain to discover who was pulling the strings in government. Despite this astonishing revelation, everyone yawned and went back to sleep. The president could appear as the victim of a conspiracy and his connections with Wall Street remained behind a veil of secrecy.

"Mom's further stunning revelation was that during this time, a well-known U.S. stockbroker headed to France to meet with bankers and financiers. This was the time to create a rock-solid plan to fund World War II. She said emphatically that authoritarianism, power, deceit, and control were in safe hands within the Synarchists' brotherhood. Her concern with all secret societies was their link to rituals and occult power. How could relying on those rituals and a tightly knit group create a global foundation for unicity and massively creative, diverse thinking?"

Sophia paused and looked quizzically at Jake asking, "Why are you looking so dazed? I can tell by your gnarled eyebrows that something isn't sitting right with you. What's going on?"

"What the hell, Sophia!" Jake exclaimed and then continued in a softer tone, saying, "Thank you for vulnerably sharing this part of your family background, without guilt or judgment. I appreciate getting the perspective of what happened and realizing how easily we can look the other way when we don't want to deal with something shocking, confusing, or overwhelming. But disregarding this egregious hubris gave it power to come back fiercer than ever, biting us in the butt today.

"During these conversations, I have been getting super pissed off! But I just had a giant epiphany and conscious shift in perception of a wormhole I'd tumbled into. It was all about *right versus wrong* and *low vibe judgment* that felt like crap! I kept recalling our conversations about quantum physics, higher frequencies, and without warning, my consciousness morphed into a spiraling perspective of higher frequency. As you were speaking, I settled into a still state for a few minutes.

"Our history lessons around this fire are about perceiving patterns in society and more importantly... *repetitive patterns in myself*. Patterns either eclipse or foster unicity with all-that-is.

If I contribute higher frequencies to the collective population of this planet, an immediate shift in *the field* occurs. I know that energetic shifts matter. It's quantum science 101. So why the hell would I do anything except focus on getting still and raising my frequency?

"Getting a closer look at our historical family and global DNA, it's clear that we have genetic expressions that are rough around the edges as well as highly elevated ones. It's those high-vibe expressions that are going to f**king change our world for the better! I hope you can feel the assurance of that like I do!

"And Sophia, I was reflecting on how you don't seem to have to strive for higher frequencies. I'm sitting here shaking my head. Somehow, it's easy for you. My guess is that you are mastering the art of high vibe living because you enter inner stillness with the tenacity of a dog on a juicy bone! I know few people who unapologetically get quiet whenever they feel the need to do so.

"As I entered into stillness a few minutes ago, I had an epiphany related to my judgments about people and events. More than that, it was painfully obvious that I need to focus more on *stillness*, dropping into zero point—the ultimate still space of my consciousness—to be able to gain vital insights. This is such a big f*cking deal!

"Without fail, we're willing to dive into the most uncomfortable topics and see the mental patterns in us that play out in the situations we're discussing. Holy shit! I appreciate you all so much! My perception of Reality and my relationship to it shifted, irreversibly higher. The part of me that feels *less than* or *a victim* of authority got a solid reboot. If it's okay with you, I'd like to take a few minutes to pause and let this settle into every fiber of my being. My whole body is vibrating, letting me know that a recalibration is occurring. What a gift, my friends! Thank you for being here to support me and bear witness to this watershed moment. This kind of awesome quantum shift always comes at the most unexpected moments. I guess it is because I inadvertently get out of my head and the true Reality gets to surface. Damn! This is some deep shit, my friends!"

John looked around at his friends who'd been stunned into silence. He said, "Folks, on that note, I need a beer. This wild, unbridled conversation calls for more than Sophia's tea."

His honest, humorous response brought a blazing round of laughter to the group.

"I'm okay with tea," Avani said with a sprightly wink, "Considering tonight's conversation, please make mine extra strong."

Caitlyn walked amiably with Sophia to make a stronger brew, remarking on the "crazy, sort of sad, enlightening conversation—including an unexpected, honored, ethereal guest ... which was the best surprise ever!"

Softening her tone, with sincerity and gentleness in her voice, Caitlyn said, "It meant a lot to me to feel your mom with us. I hope she can hear my voice from the ether because I want to thank her for giving us you—a very cool, totally epic, inner archeologist."

Putting her arm around Sophia's shoulder, they proceeded to the kitchen to create a potent beverage that would uplift everyone's spirits and energize them for the dialogue they were about to enter.

# CHAPTER 10

# SOVEREIGNTY

Rekindled firelight was swirling upwards and expanding into the night sky—heat and energy were the centerpiece for a conversation that was on the verge of blazing even higher. After the beverages of choice were served, everyone settled in cozily.

The circle waited for Jake to come alive, as usual. Yet his eyes remained unflinchingly shut as though his awareness had dipped into another dimension of his consciousness. Suddenly, becoming aware of the present moment, he evoked a sense of poignancy as he spoke. His expression was unusually subdued and the tone of his voice created an atmosphere of foreboding.

"As I recall mountains of intense research, at the turn of the nineteenth century, *the occult* was spreading wildly in popularity. It offered hope to its followers. Mysticism, rituals and secret societies emerged all over the world. Like Adele mentioned, through the occult and associated societies, the working class could find a modicum of relief from the daily grind. And the elites could turn to the occult to propagate awe-inspiring superpowers. As Adele also pointed out, Hitler thought this was possible. Maybe we ought to talk about something else."

Sophia smiled amiably and urged him to continue, with the assurance that he could safely share conflicts and concerns he'd grappled with for a long time.

Clearing his throat and sipping water to refresh his voice and composure, he said, "In this divisive madness, our ancestors attacked each other, sometimes viciously. Those wounds within our *collective* DNA need healing. I can't help but wonder if through the work we're doing, we can model the value of raising our frequency and invite others to join us in extraordinary possibilities for a radical, inconceivable future. Damn it! We're all incomparable beings imbued with quantum-level power, unified at our core. We cannot deny this any longer. We have to somehow embrace it… or live in an endless cycle of misery and suffering. With so much information about the nature of Reality, why do we still play so small? What will it take for us to shift enough in frequency to end this insane cycle we've been wallowing in for too long?"

After pausing for another rejuvenating sip of water, with uncharacteristic somberness, he sat mute and motionless.

Observing that Jake clearly needed more time to regroup and reflect, John bumped him lightly shoulder-to shoulder and asked, "Can I tell them how we met?"

Jake nodded, remaining embraced in introspective silence. His clenched fists rested on his knees and his eyes were cast downward with a penetrating gaze, as though allowing the earth to absorb his inconsolable agony. His customarily spirited eyes seemed crestfallen and sullen, contained by the same dam that had been holding back all the tears repressed persistently for decades.

Without the slightest inhibition, John glanced at his closest comrade with palpable feelings that arose as a natural element of their enduring friendship. In an instantaneous flash, the circle launched into soft, reflective silence. John let the tranquil hush culminate naturally, and after strengthening his resolve with an emotionally fortifying breath, he spoke.

"I was a young archeologist on a dig in Ireland, which is my ancestral place. Jake and I met at a pub. We got to talking about the dig, anthropological history, and my love for unearthing hidden, outlandish artifacts. It was obvious that our ideas and aspirations were perfectly aligned.

"As the dig continued, something shocking happened. We—my team and I—uncovered a mass grave. Of course, we had to stop. We were looking for an ancient pagan site where they performed rituals to attract ETs. That peaked my interest because during my whole life I've been drawn to anything that cannot be explained. My mother said I was too curious for my own good. Hey, it's just me. I can't turn off my curiosity. It's my juice for life."

He smiled at the group, knowing that they knew he was more inquisitive and full of wonder than a four-year-old seeing the endlessness expanse of the ocean for the first time.

"I realized how big the site was, so I immediately reported the findings to the local authorities. I ran into Jake again and shared our findings with him. He was blown away by the magnitude of what we'd found, and joined me at the local library to find out more about the region's history, particularly archeologic sites. Later that afternoon, while talking to locals in the town pub, we learned of other historical details preserved in local lore spanning several millennia.

"Jake's mother's relatives lived near the site. He wanted to take me to meet his mom's family line and inquire about this area. Neither of us was prepared for the devastating truth they shared, which was not part of the official record. Although this was a sacred spot of worship millennia ago, it was also a place where Catholics had been slaughtered; more than once. Before that, though, Romans had brutally conquered the local residents. Even later, bloody wars were fought for independence from the Crown of England.

"Covert technologies were widely applied in military weaponry. Jake's mother told us that an ex-British government intelligence officer admitted that, in the 1960s, they used low-dose microwave weapons on Catholics; not killing them... well... not right away. A year later, the victims developed cancer or neurological diseases, without being able to track the source of their suffering. We wished his story was not true. But why would he make that up?

"My team and I were staying near the site and one evening at dusk, just as the sun was throwing its crimson blanket over us, I saw a silhouette that I'll never forget. I went closer and saw it was Jake, a budding archeologist with a giant heart. He was sitting near the pile of bones, his legs pulled tight to his chest and his head was tucked down. He'd heart-wrenchingly curled into a fetal position. I could hear excruciating sobs from a hundred yards away. My eyes automatically filled with tears as I heard and felt his harrowing state of being. I'm empathic to a marked degree, did training in remote viewing, and all kinds of techniques to move my mind into stillness to connect with a person or a place. I connected fully with Jake and..."

Having to pause to allow his emotions to settle into a more serene state, John glanced tenderly at Jake who was still motionless. John's bond of kinship with Jake was powerful enough in its child-like innocence and indefatigable kindness to engulf the atmosphere of the circle—while also bringing glistening tears to the entire group as he continued, speaking softly enough to drench the atmosphere in compassion. His voice was saturated with a sense of honor and solicitude which he spread like an invisible blanket over his closest friend.

John said devotedly, "I didn't want to intrude on Jake's obviously life-altering experience. As I turned to leave, he thrust his head back and let out a howl, a scream of agony, echoing across the landscape like an earthquake. Making a heart-to-soul connection with the horrific suffering of those people, violent and uncontrollable body tremors arose in him from profound emotional pain. My friend, sitting next to me, is one hell of a compassionate, kind, empathetic soul. I stood in awe of what he was doing and who he was on the deepest levels of his humanity.

"As I walked away from Jake that night, I realized that he was crying out and physically expressing incomprehensible grief... his... and theirs... and all those who'd lost loved ones. He wasn't angry; his heart had cracked open, without its shell to protect the innate, unlimited power of pure love and unicity. We'd uncovered a shocking, massive, secret grave. How many of them were all over Europe, and how many were all over this country and other continents?

"How had humanity escaped seeing these people as sovereign beings who deserved to worship or live as free people? Who thought it was anyone's right or perverted duty to kill people like this? When does ideology, religion, or philosophy become a valid justification to punish, harm, or kill fellow human beings?

"As an archeologist, I saw evidence of mass killing and war throughout the world. Could that change? If I kept digging, could I find clues to a higher path, beyond endless misery and insanity? It was a game changing moment for me. I wanted to literally unearth secrets that no one wanted me to find. I have always had that kind of spunk in me.

"After that dig in Ireland, I didn't care if my peers thought I was crazy, I was going to continue digging deeper. I've definitely pissed off a few people along the way. I decided not to censor myself or play safe to be palatable to my colleagues. That's horseshit. By applying cutting edge technology and a lot of hard work, I can say that ETs are real, mass graves matter, synarchy-style secrecy must be exposed, even if certain heads of industries, elite military brass, and others want global citizens to remain impotent, confused, and fearful. From that moment, I latched onto my own sovereignty and committed to relentlessly honoring humanity in all work that I engaged in."

Suddenly the fire danced fiercely and trees started to swirl haphazardly in the night breeze, while the circle became utterly motionless. No one could muster the motivation to speak. As quickly as nature animated herself, she became tranquil, surrounding and embracing the group of intimate friends with pristine stillness for several minutes. A respite from recalling humanity's pain and a fresh chance for rejuvenation were nature's gifts to the group as they reflected for a few moments on what they'd heard, without the slightest sound to interrupt their reverie.

While creating a space for the group to enjoy a moment of quiet repose, nature's spontaneous serenity provided Jake with the inner resources to fully regain his composure. After taking a long, rejuvenating breath, he spoke in a soft, reflective tone. He said solemnly, "I knew on that dig that I could not go back and study law or banking. My father's side of the family was a tightly knit banking and finance lineage. My dad joined a small cluster of alpha males in our family—hardcore Wall Street power brokers.

"After attending a meeting in Washington, my dad died by drowning in the Potomac River. Knowing what I know now, drowning in that river isn't like drowning in the sacred Ganges during the raging monsoon floods in India. Dad was an athlete and a skilled swimmer. Maybe he said the wrong thing or knew something that was above his pay grade within the company he worked for. Who knows?

"When I got back to the U.S., I told my mother what happened and she openly shared details about our family's past; *the good, the bad, and the ugly.* She was brutally honest, revealing that my father was definitely murdered—and, luckily, she was not a threat to his business associates. As I prepared for a career in finance and banking, they were watching me to make sure I didn't know anything about Dad. Sounds crazy, doesn't it?

"My mother's Irish relatives later shared stories from our family lineage who emigrated to the U.S., along with their accomplishments and heartbreaks—providing the basics of what I just shared with you. Their worldview and human nature crossed the Atlantic as it did for everyone else. There's no good guys versus bad guys in my story tonight. I want to explore with you the beliefs, habits, and patterns they embraced—which may not be worth clinging to in modern times.

"Consider that their expressed, heartfelt hope for my grandmother was to marry an upper class banker in New York, allowing her to live carefree with endless luxuries. They admitted this was an enviable situation. But the beautiful, blue-eyed redhead never corresponded with her family, never visited, and lost contact with everyone overseas. Near her death, she confided in her favorite niece—describing the profound sorrow and regret she experienced as the result of her perilous, bleak marriage.

Her married life was fraught with danger, always. Skullduggery is the hallmark of my family history on Dad's side.

"From that point forward, I wanted to excavate hidden facts and realities in our world. Eons of global secrets and my family history left me fired up to become a *bearer of truth* in this world. It's okay to have faith in humanity. Yet I can also practice discernment in relationships and all areas of my life. After a while of floundering and soul searching, I left Yale and took time off for personal growth. Finally, I landed at Berkeley in California to study archeology, which I viewed as constructive digging. Of course, that was a damned good choice because it became my passion.

"After I changed my focus of study and graduated, I arranged to join John to dig in Egypt and Peru. As we got to know each other, we decided not to marry or have kids. We didn't want to pass down our lineages' patterns through our DNA. I know that sounds strange but we were rogues in our profession. We added master's degrees in anthropology and cosmology to our studies and I branched out into cosmic archeology. It was easy to convince John to get enthused about that.

"That's why Max became so important. He was not just a skeleton. He was a pioneer of some sort. Who was he? Why did he come? What had he shared with our ancestors? I'm so f**king sure that our ancestors, a very long time ago, were badass technological geniuses and I wanted to figure out how they accomplished quantum-style, amazing feats. So I jumped into the *unified field theory* of physics and dragged John into that, too.

"Max became our hero. When we realized that we also had the pleasure of meeting his wife, we felt like it was family time. The cove was our dream job."

Jake paused and looked at the group, touching the entire circle with his gaze, "Over the past few years, I noticed that people became extremely divided. Fear escalated to epic proportions; confusion was rampant. Who can you believe? World events make no sense. Folks, it's a power-game that's been played for eons and we, as the working class, didn't know the rules. And if we did, we let the upper echelons win, like it was expected of us to play small.

"My question to myself was: *What can I do?* Excavating particular sites to put puzzle pieces of history together felt right for me. Over the years, I did a lot of work on myself. People call it personal growth. I call it personal excavation. I looked at who I was as a soul and began to meditate to still my mind, to hear Truth from within rather than from the media.

"Equally important, I learned from indigenous people globally about how to be in touch with the natural world and less invested in modern war mentalities from my banking legacy. Digging into the earth was easy but digging into my beliefs and response to life, to people, to injustice... Well... that was damned tough. And I also know that if I don't continually do my personal excavation and reveal the truth of myself, both wounded and eternally perfect, I'm part of the problem.

"What surprised John and me was that as we worked on sites where we believed there were ancient ET influences, we began to think more from a subtle, quantum level and less from a solid, physical perspective.

"I think that I can speak for John when I tell you that we began to realize the majestic nature of a human soul. We worked on ourselves to get past cultural taboos of guilt and shame, and the deeply ingrained assumption that we're somehow born sinners and inherently flawed. Instead, our conclusion was that we are sovereign, masterful beings of pure starlight. We're photon-miracles of intense emanation and manifestation. To each of you, I want to say that I feel your goodness intermingling with mine. Our conversations stir my soul in immeasurable ways. We own our shit and we fully own our infinite glory. Many times in the cove, you've shared tough times that made you stronger. You are the excavators that the world needs right now.

"I didn't want to leave you with the low frequencies of humanity. And I appreciate that none of us are here to bash anyone. For me, our conversation is about a sober look at past patterns, and making sure we go forward informed and clear about what worked and what didn't. The present has seeds in the past, and its *patterns* float within the infinite unified field as a possibility for the future.

"My questions are:

*What am I creating in the present moment?*

*Do I interact with the field from the flow state where new possibilities manifest endlessly, or from lower frequency states of shame, anger, or egotism?*

*As I tap into the field consistently, how high is my frequency and how deep am I allowing my consciousness to drop towards my silent core, where infinite information is accessible, waiting to reveal itself to me?*

"Going forward, It seems obvious that the time for secrets is over. Our world is at the precipice of excavating whatever needs to come into the light. We can do that while holding dignity, elevating ourselves with such intensity that we are like a dog on a bone, and expanding in frequency like there's no end to it. We are creating something radically new.

"War is a racket, as General Smedley so eloquently pointed out. When I absorbed the truth of his words, I realized that as a collective, we fell into fear rather than staying buoyant in the flow state, plus everyone took the easy path of looking the other way. But responding this way didn't resolve anything and kept us locked into a global war paradigm.

"Whew! We've explored some deep shit tonight and I appreciate the chance to dig into it with you. Having copiously shared my history, and the world's... in full transparency, it sure feels like bedtime to me. How about you?"

He looked around at his friends who were chuckling warmheartedly. His endearing solidarity with them allowed the unity they shared to reach increasingly visceral levels.

Unanimous head nods and warmhearted smiles answered his question.

For a moment, in silent friendship and appreciation, all eyes were lovingly set on Jake and John, who exemplified the immense freedom found in intimate friendship and the miraculous nature of unicity.

Without further conversation, the group disbanded to rest and rejuvenate before dawn rose majestically over Mystic Cove.

# CHAPTER 11

## BOHEMIANS

By lunchtime, a fierce storm was roaring with intensified speed towards the lake. Ominous clouds were forming, churning, and darkening by the minute. Megan texted the group telling them to come to the house ahead of the rainfall and high winds that were predicted to arrive imminently.

As everyone gathered, having dropped their gear in a storage shed nearby, the wind roared, lightening pierced the earth in rapid bolts, and thunder rumbled deafeningly and frequently. As rain hit the windows head on, trees bent to the breaking point.

Lunch was already on the table. Although immensely grateful, no one seemed surprised. Megan always showered her friends generously with care and kindness.

Because the storm was becoming increasingly deafening, attempts to have a meaningful discourse were rendered impossible. While Megan's formidable abode kept everyone safely contained within its sanctuary, everyone found a place to enjoy the meal—to the backdrop of the tempestuous sounds of Mother Nature.

After half an hour, the rain became lighter yet remained steady, and the winds calmed to an audible threshold that allowed for conversation. It was the perfect time for Beth to serve peach cobbler and chocolate chip cookies. Her hot tea and coffee brought the chilly winds outside into a neutral zone of comfort. Everyone gathered spontaneously in a circle where the stormy afternoon's conversation could unfold.

"Sophia, tell us about Truman," John said, leaning forward with interest. "I have a feeling you have some compelling revelations. It seems from what you've shared with Jake and me, between Nate, your mother, and Gilda, you learned a lot about the inner workings of government and corporate life in the last century—before, during, and after WWII. I'd like to know what aspects of that historical era remain relevant today. With all that's going on these days, I'm more interested in this time period than I would have been ten years ago. How do you feel about sharing?"

"Let me sip some tea," Sophia answered, "and finish my last bite of cobbler. I'd like to fully savor the taste of sweetness before I share this part of history. There are definitely surprising, hidden secrets and captivating, bewildering revelations that my husband, my mother and Gilda helped me to grasp. They are worth knowing as we explore how we arrived in the current state of world affairs—including the emotional effects of our ancestor's struggles on modern DNA."

John grinned amicably and affirmed her with a spirited thumbs up. The rest of the group joined his supportive affirmation. Aligning with them, she adjusted her posture, emanating a pleasant smile yet a solemn timbre as she began to elucidate hidden truths.

"Wall Street is where my family's DNA was dramatically transformed for the past hundred years. To be clear, there are secrets that must be revealed and understood by *all of us*. Our ancestors were indisputably affected by the events and situations in the story I will share. The challenges were common to everyone—there is no escape from collective anguish and turmoil."

Pausing, she looked at Jake quizzically. She realized that something had inadvertently triggered him. He fidgeted uncomfortably, his brow was wrinkled, and his eyes were narrowed—perhaps it was frustration.

"Jake, do you want to share something? If not, it's okay. But the way you started squirming in your seat and your face became noticeably flushed, I sense you could be feeling an urge to share something. When you get an inner nudge to speak, followed by a sheepish grin, you usually have something potentially consequential to add to the conversation. Is that true?"

Gathering composure, he looked at her, astounded by her forthrightness. Shaking his head as though his feelings had been unwittingly exposed, he said. "I better grab some lemonade and cool down. Here I go again, getting my hackles up. You sure as hell know me inside and out, Sophia. I'm sensing this conversation will be yet another opportunity for personal growth."

He chuckled heartily and said, "Bear with me friends, I can explain. When I think about Wall Street, everything they did was plotted in secret to benefit a small group… which reminds me of something. It's personal and definitely embarrassing. Now that I'm laid bare before you, maybe I should go ahead and share it. Is that okay?"

Everyone nodded graciously.

"I'll take that as a Yes. For our newer friends, a little background might be helpful. As you've heard in our conversations, many companies in the twentieth century used *cloak and dagger tactics* and I tend to take it personally. But I'm determined to fully process my habit of getting pissed off when confronted by secrecy. Here's why…

"When I finished college and was entering grad school, I met my girlfriend, Serena. I was enchanted with her. I gave her gifts and leant her money, which she never paid back. I was so smitten with her that it was easy to ignore her tendency to be aloof—meaning she was not emotionally available in a way that allowed us to have a deep and meaningful relationship. But friends—she was hot!"

Jake blushed and wiped his forehead with his tattered red bandana as he composed himself after that clearly embarrassing revelation. He continued, shaking his head and smiling wryly.

"Although she was aloof, she was also up for fun, like dancing for hours on end, and she was always eager to join me at archeological sites, which meant the world to me. As a fresh grad student, I put her on a pedestal because she was literally a genius at math and sciences, my unfortunate weaknesses at the time. She tutored me in those areas and she had a knack for making it seem less daunting. The field theory of quantum physics was her professed obsession, which we shared. Seriously, we couldn't stop talking about it.

"The dark side of our relationship was that Serena took full advantage of my innocence and devotion to her. True confession: deep down, I knew something was off. But it wasn't until I caught her cheating on me, red-handed and red-faced, that she owned her deceit. Worse than that, I had to own that I looked the other way for WAY too long. As an insecure young guy, my need for her love felt like survival, and life without her was devastating. I was like a whipped pup! It was scary as f**k to lose her because I was so emotionally attached to my world with her in it. As you can see, that breakup was pretty damned devastating on an emotional level. I was head over heels in love with that woman!

"After my romantic debacle, I would remember her whenever I heard a story about secrecy or certain people having secret knowledge. Basically, I don't like the feeling of vulnerability that comes with trusting someone blindly.

"My takeaway was that people can take advantage of me if I look the other way when my intuition is screaming for me to look more closely. Over time and with inner growth, I realized a brutal truth—my girlfriend took advantage of my gullibility and innocence. I trusted her. As life moved forward, I realized that beating myself up for being blind and gullible was useless. I developed confidence and authority over myself by becoming more discerning about *who* I chose to trust, and *why* I did so. I began to let my gut instincts and intuitive heart lead those choices.

"Because of this, I choose to pause when I get triggered by lies and deceit. Within our conversations recently, I realize that it's time to look more closely at my triggers again. I have a heap of emotional pain, fortified over time in layers, which is related to other painful events as well. I tend to be hot headed so my emotions need my attention when they come roaring to the surface. When John and I were younger we thought this kind of inner exploration was for pussies. But life kicked us in the butt often enough that we began to think otherwise. I'm observing that you youngsters take this shit seriously and handle yourselves differently than we did. I want you to know that I respect that in you. When Caitlyn, Avani, and Adele spoke about horrendous subjects, I didn't detect judgment or triggers. Good job! Seriously, it's a big deal!

"Sophia, please keep going. I was getting riled up when the subjects of trust and secrecy resurfaced. I want to diffuse the emotions as they arise and not let them have free reign to lower my frequency. Thanks, sister. I'm settled down and all ears."

Smiling at her fiery yet profoundly kind-hearted friend, she continued, "Jake, your story is apropos based on the subjects I'll cover tonight. Thank you for being willing to confide in us. I sense it's still a tender wound, which is understandable. As always, I respect and appreciate your willingness to notice knee-jerk patterns of responding to past emotional pain. That's no small feat, my friend. From my perspective, part of this intimate circle is to have a safe place to notice and raise lower vibes—from old patterns that eclipse pure love and unicity.

"Keeping your analogy in mind will be illuminating for us as I tell you about my family's Wall Street rich-and-famous clan. They definitely used strategies that could turn the economy in their favor. Like your girlfriend, they focused on their own needs and desires while mastering the art of manipulation. My mother was clear they operated with cleverness, cunning, and in absolute secrecy.

"Unfortunately, they took advantage of people's innocence and trust, like Serena did with you. The unsuspecting citizens looked the other way as the tycoons took advantage of them. Does that sound like you and your girlfriend?"

Jake chuckled and smiled as she continued.

"Before I describe politics, it's important to mention a name in the historical Wall Street business culture, Brown Brothers Harriman. Mom called them *BBH*. This was a private investment group comprised of twenty-five to maybe thirty *elite families*. Keep BBH in mind. You'll hear more about them as I share my family's history."

"The main players are important. The CEO was George Herbert Walker. The lawyer was Allen Dulles, with the law firm of Sullivan and Cromwell. Keep those names in mind as the story unfolds.

"My mother was the first person who explained to me the shocking level of influence an oligarchical elite played in the early twentieth century in the United States. An oligarchy is a system of power in which a few individuals or groups hold disproportionate power over economic development, government, and societal structures. Leaders of big business and banking, religious groups, and other large organizations end up calling the shots in government and in how economic structures will be developed. It often coincides with fascism—in which a strong leader colludes with such groups for mutual advantage—or puppet rulers, presidents or prime ministers who do the bidding of the oligarchs in order to retain their own status or authority. I keep wondering how a system like this will advance the human species? How can it evoke our super nature, extraordinary creativity, and foster a global wave of far-reaching innovation?

"The question Mom had was where and how does the working class fit into such power structures? You will definitely not find them on the top rung of decision-making. As Jake mentioned a while back, the general populace was considered to be no more than a resource, like copper, oil, or anything else used to produce goods and services—and thereby profit. This is reminiscent of Adam Weishaupt's philosophy that Adele shared with us.

"Another name I learned from my mother was Union Bank of New York. They were funded by BBH, the investment firm, Brown Brothers Harriman, that I mentioned a few minutes ago. This private investment firm, among others, financed both Nazi Germany and the Bolshevik Revolution in Russia. They were joined by Wall Street titans with big goals—global ones. Mom says this top tier of elite corporations collaborated as one big, happy family.

"You are inevitably familiar with the legendary names of that time period, but we can focus on just those that Mom's relatives were associated with, associated with the BBH thread. In 1918, at the end of World War I, a peace treaty was signed in France called the Versailles Treaty. Robert Lansing supervised it. He was President Wilson's Secretary of State. Lansing's wife's father was John W. Foster, who was the grandfather of Allen and John Dulles. Remember Allen Dulles was the lawyer for BBH. Allen and his brother drafted the provisions of the treaty. The treaty was meant to address reparations to be made by Germany for their aggressions in the war. Then the U.S. Secretary of State named Allen Dulles to be the American lawyer for Germany. According to Gilda, Allen Dulles organized a series of loans to Germany *from the BBH families* so that Germany could pay off the reparations. The loans also paid corporations who suffered huge losses in the war.

"In 1924, The CEO, George H. Walker, stepped down as CEO and turned the helm over to his son-in-law in BBH, Prescott Bush. George H. Walker then got busy forming Union Bank of New York, which was capitalized by BBH. Next, he created a subsidiary bank in Germany called Bank of Shipping. He then began granting loans to Germany and the growing Nazi movement. Remember the Nazis had help from other business tycoons like Henry Ford.

"As General Butler said in his book, war is expensive to fund but lucrative in the long term. Mom's point was that war was imperative to reach the Synarchist goal—total control of the world. Focused and strong, U.S. funding helped to finance fabulous headquarters for the Nazi party. Gilda used to say that Hitler was the perfect, occult-driven, crazy, Aryan-race ideologist to help big banks move faster and easier along their path to domination.

"Suddenly, BBH hit an obstacle. The Bolsheviks had overtaken Russia. Bolshevism was overturning Synarchy in that country. Remember Robert Lansing, the overseer of the Versailles Treaty? My mother said he concocted a plan to crush the Bolsheviks, who wanted a socialist government. Lansing knew that this regime would be run by a dictator who was not a friend of the elite BBH team members.

"According to Mom, the highest echelons of U.S. banking agreed to pulverize the Revolution. There's way too much intrigue and too many details to go into here. The point is that where there are wars, there are bankers backed by high powered law firms.

"Meanwhile in the Pacific, the head of U.S. Army Intelligence, Edward Lansdale, was stationed in the Philippines and stumbled on trillions of dollars of gold, silver, and platinum—a treasure trove the Japanese had stolen from across Asia between 1926 and 1940. The Americans hid it safely in an ultra-remote place. When Truman was briefed, he sent General McArthur to check it out and then did something unexpected. Instead of returning it to its owners, he got a couple of partners in BBH to create a private trust to hold and manage the vast amount of precious metals.

"President Truman didn't tell the American people about it, instead he allowed this secret fund to be made available to support fascist movements worldwide. Remember the long-term, global goals of Synarchy? Any candidate—whether for mayor, governor, or any other office, high or low—that Synarchy deemed unhelpful to their goals could be easily defeated using this fund to buy influence.

"Recall how General Butler corroborated a clandestine form of military support for global fascism. He had been pulled into it unwittingly. When he realized the underlying machinations of the union of government and business, he wanted the public to peek into the underbelly of this unforeseen, surreptitious partnership.

"Mom believed the U.S. government used the BBH trust to issue gold certificates to finance political campaigns for Nazis and other fascists. The candidates got new names and identities. Mom said Truman and high level financiers had free reign to act independently of government oversight—to *their heart's delight*. With gold and precious metals at their disposal, they could sleep better at night knowing they could further solidify their ultimate goals.

"Perception is everything. They likely thought this was a thrilling stroke of good luck. Did they consider being transparent about it? If so, why did they arrive at the decision to use the riches they uncovered on that Pacific island for undisclosed purposes? General Butler tried tirelessly to expose such secrets. Later when it was discovered, nothing happened. Why? Was this yet another pattern of deception followed by concealment and smoothing over by the press and government? Mom found it incomprehensible and disheartening.

"If that wasn't enough, Truman did something that Mom said was baffling. He got his hands on something that belonged to a group from the working class at the time. It was a society of journalists in San Francisco who called themselves *Bohemians* because they traveled all over the place covering news stories. They had created the society as a fun social group, getting together to network and act a bit crazy. The name gives you an idea of their playfulness. They invited artists, writers, and others to join them. Through camaraderie, intellectual freedom, and an unorthodox lifestyle they enjoyed relief from the pressures and injustices of working class life in the late 1800s and early 1900s. We already talked about working conditions for the general population. Keep in mind that the West Coast was still a wild and wooly place.

"When word spread about their quirky behavior, their infamous chicanery and camaraderie, more people, including businessmen, wanted to join. Finally, in 1920, the original journalists, artists, and writers left. Truman had been invited and he began bringing the East Coast's famous power brokers, politicians, and Wall Street elites. The old members said the society lost its levity and was becoming weird. All of a sudden, they had an owl as their mascot and new, strange rituals. The playfulness shifted and they moved to a new location, known as the *Bohemian Grove*, an annual meeting for the chosen elite. As an upper crust men's club, membership started to look and feel a lot different. Predictably, local brothels abounded and secrets proliferated.

"Why would the highest level politicians, bankers, and industrialists meet in the Redwood Forest for three weeks each year? Is it for play or is it *planning* under the guise of *playing*? Why did the attention-grabbing, clandestine occult create raised eyebrows and whispers when the locals worked there or interacted with members? Why is the location as remote and secure as a military complex? What about infamous, surreptitious occult practices? Why is there so much speculation about opportunities for chicanery without detection?

"In her tell-it-like-you-see-it style, Gilda quoted how President Nixon responded to being invited to the grove. He was caught in a taped telephone conversation, saying in colorful language that it was one of the weirdest things you could ever imagine. Yet he conceded that if he wanted to pave a clear path to the White House, attending this retreat was unavoidable. Gilda called it a *rite of passage replete with creepy, well-designed Babylonian rituals and more than a hint of subterfuge.* I have to ask: Does an organization like this only provide a platform for prominent bankers, influencers, elite politicians, and top corporate CEOs to have a good time? Gilda felt a sense of foreboding that it was indicative of a matching pattern of supposedly innocuous secret meetings and adherence to creepy occult practices that had flourished in Nazi Germany and other places. She was angry and worried about what went on in the woods—based on her experience that transparency was absolutely vital in our post WWII world.

"She pointed out that Helmut Schmidt, a powerful figure on the world stage, wrote in his memoir that he loved going to the grove. He found it more astonishing with each passing year. Before he rose in power as an influential global leader, he had served in Hitler's military in WWII, followed by roles of Minister of Defense, Minister of Finance, and then Chancellor of Germany. As he described the grove's personal and political value, it was clear that it transcended fun and games—it was about relationships at the tightest and most fundamentally rewarding political levels that he could have ever imagined.

Gilda said the strategy to mastermind agendas in small covert circles of elite power was brilliant, yet also scary. Mom said the same thing.

"Gilda's exposure to government's fascination with secrecy and the occult was extensive as it related to a timeframe from the mid-nineteenth century forward. For example, she was astounded to know that in the 1930s the U.S. government funded two world renowned mystics, Nicholas and Helena Roerich, to go to Tibet in search of *Shambala*, a city in a closely-guarded cave system in the inner earth called Agartha. No one would embark on that journey without a guide, knowing that the entrance is in an obscure, daunting region in Tibet. The couple went twice. Many historians and archeologists have come to believe they found the place but chose never to divulge it to anyone. However, there's an equally mind-boggling part of their trip described in their journals—one typical sunny morning in the desert, a huge oval saucer of brilliant light appeared over them. The details invoke a typical sighting of an ET craft in the twentieth century. But this sighting preceded UFO encounters in our country by a couple of decades. I know you would have come across archeological and historical accounts of the mystical land they struggled so long and hard to discover because it is mentioned in most spiritual traditions throughout the world. But their journals show it was WAY more than a pilgrimage to a famous cavern.

"President Roosevelt sent them funding through his vice-president. But the Roerichs were Russian, so the Soviets were also watching them. Great Britain followed them, too. In their field notes, it seems they once made an incredibly difficult side trip to Russia. Were they playing both sides of the fence—the U.S. and Soviet Union? What the heck were they looking for?

They disappeared for periods of months on end, but they never explained what happened during those absences. Yet the two skilled mystics took their son and a small group of guides on a journey that appears like an absolutely gripping, mesmerizing movie plot. Gilda's intel revealed that the Roerichs found the entrance to Shambala, and went through the massive tunnels and caverns to reach the exalted vibrations of this mystically imbued location.

"Why were three massive global powers looking for Agartha, and its capital city? How did archeology, the occult, and modern life converge? When Jake, John, and I thoroughly considered the government-financed trip, we found ourselves befuddled. Secrecy abounds and it's left us with bits and pieces of information that make little sense. When we realized giants were likely part of the archeology of this esoteric land, we always wondered how a towering lineage played into all of this global mystery and intrigue.

"The next part of my story came directly from Gilda's knowledge of largely unknown aspects of postwar military escapades. In 1947, there was a UFO crash in New Mexico. Both ETs and crafts were found, allegedly taken to Wright Air Force Base in Ohio, and an elite military group created custodians for the technology. Reportedly funded by members of BBH, the custodians purportedly took control of this ET technology and brought in private, formidable aerospace companies. They made those companies swear to secrecy because they were going to reverse engineer something extraordinary that could exponentially up-level the United States' capacity for technology.

"Gilda seemed overwhelmed with awe at the breadth and depth of another secret base called Area 51 in Nevada. She said it was a military base launched into a future of unlimited scope and massive growth, with unimaginable, black-budget, unsupervised funding. Spanning many square miles, it includes an impressive underground, stealth world that none of us were meant to find. It's estimated that eighteen thousand employees work there. Behemoth corporations became contractors, initiating massive projects under the surface and emerging as leaders in technological advancements. They grew and thrived exponentially.

"No one shared ET events like the Ebens nor did they elaborate on associated follow ups with the public. This seminal event remains concealed under the guise of the public not being able to handle the implications. And as you know, some agencies still deny its existence. From Gilda's perspective, the concealment was more about control of profits than protecting an innocent, un-savvy public who couldn't handle the truth.

"She'd go into a tirade about this subject. To understand the scope of ET-related research, she said there were technologies for healing and energy that were vital for ending poverty and improving the planet's eco-systems. Once implemented, there'd be no more wars or disputes because everyone would have what they needed. However, Mom's and Gilda's sobering epiphany was that if that happened, the Synarchist empire would lie in ruins. The likelihood of that happening was near zero.

"A long time ago, I shared with some of you how the media and entertainment industries were taken over by the CIA's *Project Mockingbird*. How was it ever acceptable for our government to feed us fake stories and have the media become the voice for propaganda from intelligence agencies? I recall with gratitude an especially poignant conversation with Gilda. She'd just shared details of modern programs, absolute atrocities that the top tier of current intelligence agencies had single-handedly waged against their own members and the public. Her story left me with a tight stomach and shallow breath.

"She looked at me, her eyes blazing, and said, 'Bring your father to mind, recalling the confusion and frustration you felt as your tender, child-like heart met your father's steel-cold, ruthlessness!' My hands began to shake and my eyes filled with bitter tears as she continued. 'DO NOT admonish yourself for your innocence as he intimidated and manipulated you, twisting your common sense into doing his bidding. You had to struggle with the disorientation and chaos of living with *a narcissist*, as so many spouses and children have done. I know these people! I've worked with them. They do not think like you!' She described how their emotional intelligence went dormant, how such people are like beasts in a concealed cave with blood dripping from their hands. She told me to weed them out of the fertile soil of my life's garden. That even though it is 'hard as hell to face them,' I must remember I am stronger than they are.

"She said, 'Hear my words and never forget what I am saying to you. One day it will matter as you sit on the precipice of allowing your civilization to rip itself apart, unaware it is happening *not because of your differences* but because you have inadvertently absorbed lies from a tightly knit clan who have ingeniously influenced your media, schools, and government for too long. They make you think you desperately need them, that they are protective of your interests. As the once gullible prey of a crazed group of secretive narcissists, I have earned the right to speak about what I know from direct experience, and with immense love for you and everyone on this planet.

The truth is, instead of taking care of you, they relentlessly grasp for *control over you and everyone else*, which even so, remains elusive as ever. Thus they enter a form of self-inflicted madness, driving them into making incomprehensible, inhuman decisions. Do not let a pathological few override your sagacious, kind heart. And forgive yourself for falling for their surreptitious plans to enslave your mind and manipulate you for their devious, insane schemes.'

"Wow! I can feel the vibe of this group dropping like crazy. I hope you will allow me to keep going, though. I know it's a downer to discover more covert groups, with a growing list of secret, perhaps horrific agendas. Yet this moment in history is pivotal, relative to *secrecy* that included a shocking agenda. I have to mention it because this was one of those watershed moments when people unwittingly sold out to a distorted system in return for job safety and a premium salary. This conversation is about awareness rather than judgement. If we don't allow ourselves to look into the ruinous depths of high profile institutions and global leaders in government, religion, corporations, and a plethora of philanthropic organizations, they will remain concealed, festering like a life-threatening wound."

Jake and John smiled at her knowingly while everyone in the circle took notice.

"Okay, you two," she said playfully, "I know what you are thinking. For everyone else, let me explain why they are wearing those broad smiles, like two Cheshire cats. Recently, I had tea with them and they pressed me to write more often about subjects like the ones I am sharing from Gilda's revelations, and my mother's viewpoints related to Truman's era, and Synarchy in my family lineage. Jake and John loved stories related to my family history, patterns I've observed that carried forward, and that sort of thing. I usually don't share personal topics with my blog's readers, especially about my family and personal accounts that Gilda shared. I can see that my two dear friends are enjoying this *I told you so* moment. They insisted that while readers may have yawned, dis-believed, or checked out in the past when confronted with these topics, right now the world is hungry to engage in discussions of many subjects like these. In our conversation, we were clear that the way we've responded to life globally, including to authorities and those on higher rungs of the socio-political ladder, has not been advantageous.

"They brought up a good point, saying that we are teaching a younger generation to follow *influencers* rather than seeking *self actualization* and the radical life-experience that emerges when a human expresses unicity and embraces the unlimited information at their disposal from the quantum field in and around them. I think tonight they are offering a *wink and a nudge* for me to consider writing about this in a book or on my blog. Point taken, friends. And now everyone is caught up with my wild and enlightening musings with Jake and John! How about if I continue?"

Jake and John chuckled and winked at her heartwarmingly as they joined the group in a demonstrative thumbs up—a signal of joyousness for the lighthearted nature of her candid reve-lations. Glancing at the roaring fire, she took in a deep breath as rejuvenating fuel for the evening's storyline.

"For some members of media, news, and entertainment, *Project Mockingbird* was an opportunity to be part of a system they aligned with. Why they aligned was a mystery to Gilda. She pointed out a pattern of professionals who soon sold their souls to appease the whims of intelligence agencies. Holding compassion for those individuals and their industries, she shared this next part through tears. As an insider, she learned they were willing to turn against their soul's benevolent nature—ultimately disseminating anything they were instructed to share, even if it was a lie, manipulation, or only partially true. They became a legion of truth-twisters doing the bidding of a small group of people with enigmatic agendas and potentially dubious motivations. And they received scripts they slowly aligned with to convince their audience that their viewpoint was the only valid one. Does that sound familiar? Gilda thought so.

"She said news topics were purposefully outside anyone's control and would be repeated with a common tone of fear and foreboding across the entire media network, as though the news they shared was of utmost importance to everyone everywhere, with ominous consequences. With her customary candor and compassion, she offered an antidote to this onslaught of alarming news. Her solution was for me to find agency through unicity with all-that-is and my capacity to raise my frequency. She believed doggedly in human potential and self empowerment. She knew all too well that media can capture the attention of a population—even their healthy capacity for clear perception developed through optimism and self-assuredness—and corrupt it into a pessimistic outlook and sense of discouragement and impotence. Gilda saw this happen in Germany in the twentieth century and became frustrated as she saw the same 'insidious patterns replicated in modern times.'

"Yet today, we are watching this distorted influence losing its grip, supporting a shift across the whole world towards new forms of journalism. Recently, when certain global media journalists realized they were complicit in this dark manipulation, they refused to lie to the public and to themselves. They were like the journalists who left Bohemian Grove to enjoy their profession while working in the light of truth and professionalism. They found new ways to mingle and collaborate with peers who'd found renewed passion for their journalism. I mentioned these truth tellers partly because we now have momentum toward transparency and authenticity. Because the future is still in our hands, it's pliable—not fixed in gloom and doom. My point is I am observing that globally, we are moving as a collective beyond just hoping things change.

"Brave humans, incredibly benevolent souls, are stepping up and speaking out and making changes in their local communities. I wonder if they can feel, as we do, that they have to shift into high gear now. We can make inconceivable shifts when we act from the vantage point of higher frequencies, without the fighting, tension, and finger pointing we've endured for too long."

Without warning, Sophia became still and introspectively plunged into her interior world. This was a repeated pattern that emerged with members of this group when subjects required them to plumb their inner depths with still minds. Suddenly, all of nature shifted into quiet and pristine stillness—not a leaf stirred. With this kind of inner shift, the conversation would naturally take a new direction. Sophia sat motionless, like the calm eye of a hurricane. As easily as she'd gone inside, she resurfaced. Her friends were quietly entranced, waiting for her cue to continue the conversation. Mother Nature remained calm and steady as Sophia proceeded in a tone that soothed the group like the melody of a lullaby.

"Keep in mind that aspects of current life are affected by twentieth century history. We've seen glimpses of this phenomena but because of Gilda's redemptive viewpoint and experience with the murky, dangerous side of humanity, I can share her priceless, eye-witness accounts of this era."

Realizing this story required a few calming breaths as an opportunity to center herself and quiet her mind even further, Sophia paused for a moment. After finishing her reverie with a deep, invigorating breath, she continued speaking.

"In the 1940's, the military's secret space program was getting off the ground, it was in its infancy, a pliable stage. Neither Congress, presidents, the military, nor courts oversaw it. This secret military obviously had immense freedoms to explore as they wished, but like a wayward child, they could become as rogue and stealthy as they liked. The crazy part is that they were funded by tax dollars, through a *black budget*. Synarchist-style leaders had become pros at this kind of subterfuge. Practice makes perfect, right? If this new space program and research related to it was their brainchild, what would it look like as it matured?

"Via government invitation, World War II Nazi ideologies sailed across the Atlantic. Gilda was clear that those ideologies and treachery resumed effortlessly in the U.S., while hiding in plain sight. She said that something wild was brewing and General Butler and others discovered it. He and others tried to stop it, but its tentacles were so wide and deep that it climaxed later, in our twenty-first century—when the working class globally was dying, not from medieval-style contagions, but within a sea of chemicals and stress-induced lifestyles. Gilda said this was sustained by plenty of bewitching global propaganda and cunning advertising—ingenious in its capacity to seamlessly, magnetically pull us onto a daily hamster wheel of hellish proportions. We were so preoccupied with the wheel that we didn't have time to look in the direction of the puppet masters' daily performance globally. That's how Germans started acting early last century.

"On a lighter note, I want to be clear that Synarchist-style overseers are starting to implode recently. They can't do anything about a global population who decides to stop fighting each other, a conscious heart-to-heart ceasefire, while opening their hearts to each other. The reality set in that 2030, a potentially epoch-making decade, is soon upon us. We are finally recognizing the forces that have been oppressing the human race like slaves for eons. The past few years mattered. Our unicity gene was constantly being spliced, tampered with and thoroughly repressed. Yet, through our basic human capacity for connection and care, we became *David staring Goliath in the balls*, as Gilda would say. Instinctively, humanity knew how to throw the next punch as a collective and it wasn't what Goliath expected. We united, collaborated as the sovereign beings that we are and we are transparent with each other. Our unicity movement has traction now. And the decade soon to come feels ripe for massive change."

"I can think of several seminal questions for our circle to consider, like, how would it help to blame anyone in retrospect? How would it be to our advantage to learn from the past and corral this level of authority and leadership, like a bunch of wild, unruly horses—and do this without anger or blame? I am not advocating for socialism, totalitarianism, fascism, philanthro-capitalism, or any other *ism*. I've explored and wondered about why the collective population doesn't respond with open eyes to secrecy, manipulation and oppression.

"Yet my deeper question is about quantum science. What if the history that we've been discussing is simply one reality within infinite possibilities of reality? Consider for a moment that there are documents validating the history we've spoken about recently. BUT what if each of us relentlessly entered a still state, accessing the endless information of the quantum field in and around us. Then as we emerge back into our waking reality, haven't we naturally raised our frequency in the process of accessing stillness? As a result, is it possible we've entered a parallel reality in which the historical data I described cannot be found? It's called the Mandela Effect where people recall events as absolutely, unquestionably real yet when they do a little research, their view is incorrect. Their recollection is not validated online or through other sources. Have any of you thought about this effect as possibly a *parallel reality*?"

Surprisingly to Sophia, heads nodded as the circle affirmatively remained spellbound and more deeply intrigued by this sudden twist in the conversation.

"Consider that everything I will tell you is a valid area of *quantum science* that is gaining momentum. Continue to listen to what is true in our collective reality now yet also consider if our small group were to proactively drop into stillness more often, thus changing our frequency, how might history shift? Under this theory, you can think of historical accounts as bits of memory stored in the field. Please bear with me. I realize this is a big shift in ingrained beliefs about ourselves. Specifically, shifting us into accepting our inherent power as creators of our life.

"Can I continue with my story of history while we hold the possibility of *parallel realities* in mind? *If not*, I can simply tell you the facts as they exist at this particular moment and vector in spacetime."

"No way sister!" John exclaimed. "We have not come this far as a group to only relate to stories about our past *in one vector* of spacetime. If we can't apply our conversation to the truth of who we are as infinite beings of light, sound, and electromagnetism in an *infinite field of possibilities*, then we're admitting that we're worms—who will always be stepped on by giants who are more powerful than us, bound by destiny to work hard, suffer, and die. That's bullshit! I like this cheeky spiciness you added to the soup of our conversation. Look around, sister... we're amped up and all in!"

"Thank you. I could not bear to adhere to something that doesn't exist alongside other realities occurring simultaneous to this one. As infinitely powerful humans, endowed with inconceivable access to a timeless, infinite field where everything we need to know exists, the past and future merge always into *now*. When we enter stillness, the zero point energy state, we go beyond hints and notions of all-that-is. Rather, pure potentiality scintillates as a massive, frequency raising event.

"We can look at patterns in history, which are snapshots of specific unfoldments of events in spacetime. One reason to look to the past as we currently know it is to observe changes we'd love to see *now* across the planet. Quantum science tells us there are endless streams of consciousness to experience, So here was the freaky part for my mind to grasp: We can settle into the frequency that matches the change we want and Reality shifts so much that the history we thought we knew is no longer available in the history books. A few minutes ago I mentioned the Mandela Effect. It's where you thought you knew the name of a peanut butter or the spelling of a famous store. Yet now, when you research it online, it's not the way you were SURE it was. Look into this some time because it will amaze you to see how often it occurs. I know this sounds *out-there*... maybe it's best for me to keep going while we hold parallel realities in the background of our mind as a possibility going forward. Is that okay?"

Radiant smiles beamed toward her overwhelming a natural sense of trepidation about the mysterious world of parallel realities—Sophia's term for the endless possibilities that arise from shifts in personal frequencies. Her nonplussed, absolute conviction in this kind of Reality for a human life left the circle with a wave of fresh possibilities for solutions to incomprehensibly complex issues facing the planet.

As her words faded, her eyes gently closed and her face became angelically serene, so much so that the rest of the circle caught her contagious, resplendent state and rested for a moment of silent repose. This had become part of the circle's natural rhythms. When anyone's consciousness dropped into the still point, everyone followed suit to ignite a chain reaction of elevated frequencies.

Caitlyn broke the reverie gently. Her voice was a soft murmur on the evening breeze that allowed the group's reflection to gently continue the conversation which was affecting everyone's psyche with its profound emotional impact.

"Adele, how lucky is it that you met Gilda... she's amazing! The world she navigated using self discovery, and her contributions to authenticity and unicity, reminds me to live in freedom, follow my curiosity and thrive. If she hadn't unpacked the secrets for you, you couldn't have shared the roots of the problem with us. Humanity was side-tracked and distracted. Wars unconsciously soothed survival fears, but they also triggered them. Political division and relentless propaganda removed our tender yet powerful humanness from remaining center stage. It was life expressing on a hamster wheel.

"Sophia, seriously, please thank your mom for me. I felt her presence on the night you shared her contribution to our conversation. If she is with us tonight in the ether, I'd like to say to her, to Gilda, and to all of our ancestors who walked a repressive road before us: *You rock! Thank you!*"

As the circle of friends imbibed the light-hearted vibrations of Caitlyn's joyous and spontaneous reveling, they burst into cheers and animated clapping.

As their demonstrative moment found its crescendo, they gradually settled into a few quiet moments of savoring and absorbing the lofty vibrations of love and appreciation that Caitlyn brought to life in the high-altitude gathering of harmonious souls.

# CHAPTER 12

# ENCLAVES

After integrating the captivating story about Bohemians and Wall Street for a few minutes, Avani addressed the group with her usual affability.

"This conversation made me even more grateful for our Complimentary Enclave because..."

Avoiding a hint of admonishment, Jake interrupted. With a reassuring smile and eyes filled with exceptional warm-heartedness, he asked, "Pardon my ignorance, but can you back up and tell me about the *enclave* you mentioned?"

Chuckling, as her magnificent dark eyes sparkled with good humor, she said blushingly, "Since we're close friends, I forget that you don't know my life history. Oops!"

Caitlyn's exuberance and cajoling had become fuel for Avani to proceed uninhibited.

Her demonstrative smile cast effervescent love beams around the circle as she said assuredly, "In my home schooling journey, we worked in what we called a Complimentary Enclave, or C.E. We used specific vocabulary in the C.E. For instance, we didn't use the familiar word *class* to describe the environment in which we learned and studied because of the hierarchical implications and other meanings for that word. Instead, we called our *classroom* a *Complementary Enclave Limitless Entanglement, a CELE* (pronounced *cell*).

"Unlike traditional environments, think of this as a *think tank* on steroids where members believe that the principles of quantum entanglement across the multiverse is real. We held a common ethos that everything is entangled at its core—indelibly interconnected to *all information* in the field—so no one person has a "best" idea, thereby avoiding the need to debate our personal brilliance. Rather, we focused on constant learning and growing from our unique reference point on the endless web of eternity. This did not mean that we were moronic, wishy-washy lame-brains who couldn't make decisions, think critically, or have in-depth conversations. We were defying the old school curriculum of digesting spoon-fed facts uncritically, unconditionally as the only truth and reality. We saw no boundaries to science, math, or philosophy so we could adopt fresh foundational hypotheses, like being connected with the unlimited unified field, even though standard physics may not unanimously agree with this postulate.

"*Complimentary* meant that our enclave would enhance the qualities of other enclaves in our area. Enclaves could be dissimilar in personalities, composition, and viewpoints but all participants in an enclave valued and expressed open discussion, freedom of thought, creativity, and authentic deep listening. This generated deep dialogue, where everyone contributed a piece of the puzzle—when we came together without divisiveness we'd discover solutions and ideas for the community that none of us thought of individually. It was about collaboration (recognizing that working together brings the most dynamic, innovative ideas and solutions) versus competition (trying to be the best one and outperform someone else).

"An *enclave* operates in its unique location but it's surrounded by other enclaves in a robust, interconnected world. Ours started with building sustainable energy and systems, community building, a permaculture garden, some stables, and a few animals. We had a lawyer, construction contractor, academic, tech geek and more, as part of our extended family. Even though the enclave would grow to twenty-four families, each household was self sufficient. One couple owned a local farm-to-table restaurant. We grew the food and they paid us market price. As with this example, practicalities like income worked themselves out through cooperation and innovation. We owned property in common and formed a membership-style community. The lawyer figured that part out. We interacted with other CEs socially. Adults met regularly to talk about social issues with local CEs.

"Caitlyn and I met in our neighborhood before I moved to the enclave and we were *besties* right away. Her father decided to join a nearby enclave comprised of attorneys who were into social justice, human rights, and environmental issues. Caitlyn and her mom were in bliss. Like our enclave, theirs was self sufficient, including gardens, sustainable power, a gorgeous natural setting, and that sort of thing. It was a long commute for some of the parents, but they loved the idea of immersing themselves and their families in the values of unicity and care for each other.

"Keep in mind that our enclaves began around the turn of the twenty-first century so I was part of their birthing process. A few years ago, they started spreading exponentially all over the globe.

"To give you an idea of how we operated, I can tell you a wild story from my early teens. One man in our enclave loved outdoor sports, especially anything to do with water. His family loved it, too. Well... except their six-year-old son, Zane, who was definitely not thrilled. One weekend, instead of kayaking or sailing, his father rented a large boat and took the family to their favorite lake nearby. With life vests in place, Zane and his family set out. However, the water was choppy, the boat was noisy, and Zane wanted to go back to the safety of the shoreline that was getting further away from sight by the minute. His dad encouraged him to enjoy the trip, while his Mom tried to comfort him. Yet a tirade ensued, replete with an ocean of tears and plenty of wailing. No matter what his mom said, he wasn't convinced the lake was a safe place to be.

"After a few moments, his mom looked over where he'd just been sitting with tears drenching his sweet, innocent face, only to discover that he was gone! Looking around frantically, retracing their route, looking for a tiny, life-vested child, they called for help. Horrified, they searched unsuccessfully and were joined super-expeditiously by local search-and-rescue.

"Meanwhile at the beach, someone from our enclave saw Zane, wearing his cute, little life vest, casually making a sand castle. The neighbor approached and asked, *Where's your mom?* He told her truthfully that she was on a boat with his dad. Looking around the beach for his parents, the neighbor became concerned. She texted Zane's mom, saying, *I am near the playground on the beach. It seems Zane slipped away from you guys. He thinks you are on a boat. I'll stay with him until you get here.* Later, Zane's mom said she almost fainted when she got the text. Immediately, search and rescue headed for her son's location on the beach, with Zane's dad racing behind them.

"Seeing that Zane was safe, happy, and steadily building his sand castle, his mother asked him what happened. How did he get to the beach? He said that he *told his friends how scared he was. It was TOO scary!* And they came with him to build the sandcastle. They left when she arrived. Zane had always talked about invisible friends throughout his life. He spoke to them and they offered comfort and wisdom to him. Because of her amazing inner growth and immense wisdom, his mom didn't make Zane, or his *invisibles*, wrong. My mom told me later that Zane's mother realized that Zane had mystical gifts, invisible friends who seemed to be helpful for him, and she should not have insisted that he remain on the boat in so much terror that he was compelled to *shift time and space.* How many parents would be that open to such a crazy event? Does that blow your mind? To understand their response, you'd have to know his parents... and Zane. He was like a tiny sage and they likely knew a lot more about his gifts than we did. We all had a feeling they were aware that he was unique and didn't perceive reality like the rest of us did.

"In our enclave style, Zane's parents met with anyone who wanted to talk about what happened. The kids met, too. In a nearby enclave, one of the moms was a child psychologist, and BEYOND open-minded. She was awesome! Plus her kindness was a safety net that felt indescribably comforting. We talked about quantum physics, trusting our parents, and each other, plus lots of topics related to the event. In the enclaves, even the craziest events were food for conversation and inner growth. I can see by your faces that this story seems crazy, like I made it up... but it's real!"

Avani watched everyone in the circle gently close their eyes. She observed the group responding in a similar way to the adults in her enclave, processing reality-jarring information with silent reflection. Her eyes spontaneously closed and she joined them in a moment of quietude. Slowly opening her eyes, she observed they were blinking and shifting back into the present moment. After a long, emotionally liberating breath, she continued.

"Another awesome character in my enclave was *Grampa*, a retired archeologist. He was enchanted by history and anthropology. He had so many rad stories! Sharing the past in a format that left us captivated completely by every word, that eccentric elder kept us spellbound for hours at a time. One of my favorite stories happened about five thousand years ago when some Babylonians decided to divide their land into states, in which warlords would rule. Let me clarify for the non-archeologists here that he was speaking about Mesopotamia—Iraq, Turkey, Syria—that whole region. He was obsessed with studying ancient Babylonia, so he spoke about it often. As the warlords divided the land, in secret, they each planned to take over the land of other warlords as soon as their little kingdom was strong and prepared to do so. All the warlords started building weapons, creating soldiers, and demeaning women. Great combo, right?! They felt that men were better than women at throwing punches and using the heavy, clunky weapons of the time.

"As for women, Grampa said that they needed to stay busy making valuable boy babies because soldiers often got slaughtered so they needed more guys to fill vacant army boots. He said his historical tales, which were graphically horrific, could help us to understand the value of an enclave. Our enclaves were designed in the way people lived in times of peace. When warrior hubris, insatiable greed, and obsession with weapons took over, humanity engaged for more than seven thousand years in a grueling epoch—dividing land with the intension of one of them rising into the global ruler position. The problem was that even if a nice guy rose to power, he could easily be replaced by someone of the majority-mindset of megalomania-based rulership. Grampa looked haunted and sad as he shared the next part.

"He said that when an infrequent benevolent leader was gone and a cruel tyrant came to power, small fractions of a region would bravely try to revolt. If we doubted Grampa, he challenged us to take a close look at history. With a piercing look that grabbed our undivided attention, he warned each of us to wonder about where we were headed today. He was so adamant that our frequency was the key to creating an amazing world that it sunk into our psyches indelibly. To cement the gravity of the situation, he told us the horrifying saga of the aftermath of the great flood, the Egyptian and other technological wonders that were lost, and many stories of similarly, highly evolved cultures across the planet. His point was that they are relics of a shattered past. He hoped we'd embrace the wisdom of our enclaves—unify, respect, and care for each other. He told stories of ancient cultures that lived in peace eons ago—I am talking millions of years, not thousands. Giants roamed the earth, weaponless, without the need to compete or fight. Instead, they pooled their wisdom and resources for everyone to thrive. Their guiding light was an ultimate reality of all-that-is, a field of all-knowingness and all-possibility in and around them. We remained spellbound as he spoke."

Taking a pause to let her stories of Grampa land for the circle, she patiently waited until she saw warm smiles, prompting her to continue.

"Like the rest of my upbringing, our homeschool was tons different than traditional public schools in many ways. Like in the enclave, in homeschooling, whenever conflict arose we worked it out with those who didn't agree with us. This was part of our cultural norms. Authentically speaking up felt safe in that environment because our enclave was a culture with mutually agreed upon virtues at its foundation like kindness, compassion and goodwill—which we each upheld in our lives. We believed everything to be sentient and interconnected. That worldview led us to learn from other people, our environment, and the limitless cosmos. Collaboration was embedded in an enclave's structure. Our worldview included bringing out the sage, the genius, the mystic in each other.

"We focused on not letting conversations devolve into divisiveness. Instead, we relentlessly resolved to trust each other, regardless of how our egos could sometimes make interactions incredibly messy. A culture of deep-seated caring and unwavering kindness bonded us, even as we remained one-of-a-kind human beings. We acknowledged that we were symbiotic in nature, indelibly united. For us, expressing unicity was at the core of the process of human evolution. We wanted to champion a global movement, which meant experiencing radically higher frequencies globally.

"I had a super challenging situation arise that gave me a chance to take the principles of the enclave into daily life. It happened at home. My older brother, by seven years, was not a happy person. I was born in the U.S. but he came here from

India at six-years-old, leaving my grandparents with whom he had forged an indelible heart bond. When my parents arrived, it was not easy for either of them to find work that didn't require us to move a lot—so they were stressed. Adding to that family tension, my brother felt a terrible void from the loss of his Indian grandparents which was likely the unconscious basis for his unrelenting, irrational anger. Unfortunately, he released his frustration on me. He regularly called me *stupid*, said I was *incompetent*, and his worst weapon was telling me that I'd *never amount to anything.*

"And yes, it crushed me. Oh my God! I cried buckets of tears so many times! My parents reprimanded him, but his snarling and criticism never stopped. Not ever!

"Luckily, my father found a dream job and I finally felt like we'd securely settled into a lifestyle that felt energetically aligned with my esoteric essence and mystical worldview. I was home schooled, imbibing and expressing the enclave's values that my parents and I adopted wholeheartedly. My brother was a rebel and insisted on going to public school. Enclaves allowed kids to go to traditional schools, but they were expected to live by the enclave's values of collaboration. Oh my God! My brother pushed back on that so hard! His learning environment was entirely different from ours, which didn't help him at all. In a CE's home schooling, each mom in our enclave taught a couple of subjects each week, so it required little of my mom's time. They mostly taught us creative, mind-opening subjects like music or art; they helped us connect to the essence of the natural world by going on hikes, observing nature, and engaging in safe, intimate conversations. In the same spirit, they taught sacred geometry and quantum physics in ways that we experienced them in everyday life. This was definitely not traditional education.

"For the ABC's and 1 + 1 = 2 kinds of subjects, grad students met with small groups of us, based on readiness for the subject. If needed, we could easily pass state-required tests. The idea was that we could think for ourselves rather than just learn by rote.

"I had a huge issue in our home-schooling CELE with another kid, named Alex, who treated me the same way my brother did. He triggered that familiar pain in me of feeling not good enough and having to defend myself. When he made sarcastic remarks, the grad student called him out, but Alex kept it up. Like I said, in an enclave and associated CELE, we were expected to work things out between us. As a safeguard, the grad student held a facilitator role and could intervene.

"So... one day, we were having a discussion and I was speaking. Alex mumbled something under his breath, saying that I didn't know what I was talking about and implying that I was an idiot. Other people heard him and rolled their eyes. He was famous for obnoxious antics.

"Something in me snapped energetically. I felt a rush of energy in my whole body, and I stood up glaring at him, and said, *You can't hurt me. You are not better than me. You are just taller! I have the right to speak. And I have the right to a perspective. I can't be your solution to express your emotional issues and I will no longer be a punching bag for you. I want to thank you in front of everyone. Your bullying showed me something in me that exposed my own divine right. This is crazy. Why didn't I see this before now?*

"Looking around the circle and then back at Alex, I told him that the only way to expose a *low-vibe, dark dragon* is to lure it from its lair, call it out, and stand fearlessly as it *roars and blows fire everywhere. And I said to him, Alex, I am not calling you a dragon. The dragon is in me, not you!*

"Buckets of tears started flowing and the support of the enclave seemed to fuel my heart's expansion of its power. As soon as I was composed, I kept authentically speaking my truth: *You are not my problem. You showed me where I was weak. My thoughts of not being smart enough and good enough are my dark-dragon energy. When I stand here confronting you, I am confronting those parts of me, forcing them from hiding. I can dissolve them back into their Source. I am sovereign! If I am sharing from my heart and not harming you, I have the right to do and say what's in my heart. Universal Creation gave me that right. And I refuse to give that right away to you or anyone else. Ever.*"

Avani looked down at the palms of her hands in her lap, open like a butterfly's outstretched wings, as she said reflectively, "I remember sitting down after my unexpected, bold response to Alex and looking at my open hands. Oh my God! A rad revelation spontaneously soared into my consciousness: *From within myself, I could extract everything necessary to let go of the hurt from Alex, and my brother. My healing was in my hands.*

"Alex remained totally silent and not only did I shift into higher confidence from that moment forward, but he shifted, too. No one smirked at him nor said anything. Our enclave was built on trust. I was relieved we maintained that level of respect.

"I began to purposefully focus on speaking authentically, even if I was afraid of someone's reaction. It was obscenely rough at times and super scary. But I couldn't go back and act wimpy and lame when that divinely inspired energy came to life and started dancing inside me.

"Caitlyn was my bestie catalyst for being more authentic in how I spoke. We both tended to be quiet and not rock-the-boat. I found that when I was with her, I felt more courageous. I was willing to publish papers and say things with more confidence. It was like we could be fuel for each other's authenticity and self confidence while not being co-dependent.

"My motivation for telling you about my frequency-raising-Alex-moment is because taking responsibility helped me through the past few years with the intense social division and finger pointing. I kept looking at myself, my fears and emotional baggage, while working for change. I was determined not to hate, judge, or argue with anyone. That's not easy, but I know what it feels like to live from a higher level of frequency. If I don't latch onto those elevated vibes as my new normal, I'll become a problem for everyone and everything in the field. That sucks!

"Luckily I have elders who encourage me when I'm feeling down. I admire Gilda for being a pillar of strength. It sounds like she had a *spiritual moment* when she was in that prisoner of war camp in Idaho at the end of WWII and gave up Adele's mother for adoption. After reuniting with her daughter later in life, she explained that living a secret military life was not the place to raise a little girl, yet giving her up was the most excruciating decision she'd ever faced. Allowing her daughter to have a good life triumphed over the deep-rooted, maternal bond that urged her to cling to her baby. Adele told me that every time her grandmother thought about her baby, she allowed herself to meet her child in the endless space of unicity. In that way, their bond could never be severed, even though the physical separation remained. Gilda had access to ETs who assured her that the practice of merging energetically with her daughter in the unified field without wanting anything back would both elevate her own emotional field and also reach her daughter, with whom she was indelibly connected. Gilda continuously felt that *connection.* Eventually, she believed that the invisible connection in the mysterious quantum field led her to meeting her daughter, Edith, in person. Coincidently, Edith worked for the U.S. military in a different capacity than Gilda. Yet they shared incredibly strong intuitive gifts and connection. Even so, she had let her baby go without knowing if she'd ever see her again... My heart collapses just thinking about it. She was determined to evolve as a human being, striving for a deeper understanding of the complexities of life, and how to do the right thing!

"Like Gilda, as a global community, we wanted things to change for the good and for that to happen, we had to make some huge sacrifices over the past few years. Each of us had to be willing to stop fighting, trust ourselves, relinquish our egotistically driven gotta-be-right attitude, and unite. No world government, no federal government, no leader, no religion was going to save us if we consistently expressed low vibes. We figured that out. The Synarchist-style of thinking only had teeth if the population wimped out. If we feel and act small, we're vulnerable to being manipulated. Going forward, I hope we recognize our strength and support each other's evolution into the highest frequencies we aspire to."

Jake smiled at Avani as he added, "You are a wise, young sage, my dear. You reminded me that the evolutionary progress we long for will catalyze when we realize, like you, that these leaders and corporate beasts are metaphorically taller, but not better. They are not smarter, more worthy, or more deserving of what is available to humanity. I'm captivated by what you are saying and I'd love to know about how your enclave experience influenced your response to the upheaval we're experiencing now, as our circle calls it, the metamorphosis heading for 2030."

"Thanks, Jake. It's an amazing subject because the global transformation we're witnessing may be the result of more kids participating in various kinds of home schools. An enclave's approach to communicating and relating to each other is crazy-effective. And enclave-style communities are the antithesis of traditional structures which adhere to competitive values and debate-driven communication. A top-down approach is demoralizing and cuts off innovation.

"In our enclave, we recognized and focused on our personal and collective strengths. As we found solutions for problems, we shared them with other enclaves. After we finished school, we were advocates for collaboration and that's when we proactively helped local enclaves to spread like wildfire. The truth was emerging about the stealthy, Synarchist-style elites who had secretly ruled the financial systems, which suited them perfectly. Global systems like corporatism, capitalism, fascism, communism, and socialism were under scrutiny. And we knew that the influence of dark energies on our world was not relegated to horror flicks. Dark energies are real. Oh my God! So many leaders were called out and totally naked on the world stage. But then what?

"They tried spreading fear that the world was headed for anarchy and chaos and that we needed smart governments, rich corporations, financiers and bankers, and narrow-focused, dogmatic religious ideologies to save us and tell us what to do. They generated doom and gloom about the weather, war, Armageddon, and annihilation. They leaned into a frenzied state of darkness. It gives me chills feeling into the way they talked, the plans they conceived, and the relentless fear porn they injected into media. It was such a gruesome mirror to Gilda's description of her Nazi experience and the innumerable historical figures who dreamed of creating a disgusting world like that.

"At first people across the planet were naturally shocked by all of this and not sure what to believe. But groups of the younger population united with such authenticity and courage that our hearts embraced each other naturally. It was another loss for team-Synarchy, global manipulation-propaganda squads, and the darkest frequencies on the planet, and a huge win for the collective of higher-vibe global citizens—maybe for the first time in history.

""This may surprise you. Enclaves became increasingly relevant given that my generation is different than yours... because... true confession... it's been hard for us to see a warm-and-fuzzy, amazing future. We got out of school and most ended up barely making enough money to get by. We got criticized for accumulating debt and wanting too much. We were told we acted *entitled*. Caitlyn and I noticed a discouraging backdrop to this—we've grown up with the narrative that what lies ahead is daunting, the future for humanity and Gaia look bleak. Adding to this the generally low salaries and fewer perceived opportunities, we've collectively become more and more pessimistic about the future.

"Our lifestyle and things we say are misunderstood. Whenever we talked about this super-uncomfortable subject with our closest friends, they wondered why Caitlyn and I maintain insane optimism! We are lit...about life and possibilities for our world going forward! We shared our hypothesis that our *programming* about ourselves and our *connection* to all-that-is influence *optimism and confidence.* Our enclaves and the interconnected web we created with other enclaves gave us an unexpected gift through interacting with high vibe humans on a daily basis—thus allowing us to raise our personal and collective frequencies consistently. We didn't talk about *vibes* growing up. But we are *overt* about it today. At every opportunity, we share what we learn about *remaining* authentically optimistic.

"Enclaves don't adopt hierarchies—we are *partners* regardless of educational levels, career paths, or backgrounds. Collaboration is paramount. We also tend to be calm and centered, rather than rushing to solutions; no one minds a slower pace.

"Most of all, we recognize if we don't let our minds move into unfathomable levels of consciousness where parallel realities and unlimited opportunities feel possible (and tenaciously boost each other in remembrance of our awesomeness), we'll live from a worldview that SUCKS—only focusing on the low-vibe stuff. Who we hang out with and what we pay attention to definitely rubs off on us. Enclaves and high-vibe friends matter.

"We don't know how future enclaves will look. As I mentioned, enclaves are hybrid-living, partially interacting with communities but becoming self-sustaining in a local area, unlike *communes* of the 1960's and 1970's (which often got into infighting, drugs, and were for a different era). No judgment. They served a purpose for groups wanting societal change. Using our friends' ideas for vehicles powered by water or hydrogen that can serve a local community, we are exploring how we could create something new—like enclaves that specialize in local transportation. How could we own, produce, and use the vehicles regionally and share the results globally? When we have what we need, and own both manufacturing and tech, we are comfortable sharing our inventions—knowing others will apply, upgrade, and share their results. It's a reciprocal system of innovation. Can you imagine how quickly the world would change? No one would be focused on extreme wealth *short term.* Instead, we would be shifting into high gear technically, bonding, working cohesively for the good of all, and releasing our perceived differences and conflicts. All of that matters to us!

"Did you know that for over a decade researchers have been creating prototypes for self-driven vehicles, applying AI, supercomputing, and on-the-ground data sensors and other hardware-related support? From there, quantum sciences come in. The next step is self-driven vehicles globally that are powered by energy from *the field,* guided by AI and advanced computing to glide meticulously over the surface of the planet. Have you heard that in the last century geniuses developed prototypes for amazingly high tech vehicles like I just described, running on alternative energy like water or hydrogen, and even free energy, but the inventors disappeared, along with their inventions, and their labs were emptied? Why? By whom?"

Jake smiled knowingly, nodded, and urged her to continue with a cheeky reply, "I see that look of trepidation, but realize you are preaching to the choir! Bring it, sister!"

"Okay! I knew you'd get us! Heating and cooling, transportation, and housing are huge issues around the globe. Maybe geniuses our age can find a solution in local enclaves. When we applied high-vibe communication norms to any challenge, we came up with solutions as a group that one person couldn't conceive of alone. Funding came together, geniuses showed up out of thin air, an we maintained confidence and were *totally pumped* about the future. There are ways to be prosperous *without being obsessed* with being wealthy (or famous). Why look to deep-pocketed, self-assured global experts to save us? NO way! We are adamant that *interconnectedness and innovation are* our superpowers going forward.

"When Caitlyn and I talk about enclaves, and producing and owning various industries locally, there's an issue that comes up. This may surprise you... they remind us of the Medieval Crusades in the eleventh and twelfth centuries that we talked about a while back. When the crusades were over, people had created local enclave-style groups with currencies that they issued at sunrise and which expired at dusk. It was a shop-till-you-drop mentality, simply a means of facilitating trade among people, and it worked.

"The aristocracy were miffed because they didn't get a cut, they couldn't exploit people if they were self-sufficient. And they felt that was unfair because in their minds they were special, smarter, and more deserving. Oh my God... such flatulent egos! When you read their words and realize what they said, it's shocking how much they adored being at the top of the food chain and how little empathy they had for the common person. Not to be outmaneuvered, they invented a clever new *law*—a term they used for rules they imposed by force on the masses.

"Every cottage industry would come under a charter of the monarch. That meant a shoe maker had to be under the king's royal shoe maker, the baker under the royal baker, the cart maker... you get the idea. And none of them were allowed to use their own currency nor own a cottage industry unless it was under a charter of the king.

"They could borrow money for their business from a few bankers, who were controlled by the aristocracy. Once in debt, the working class had to rely on the centralized economy to stay afloat and to make money. Local independence and ingenuity were annihilated. Checkmate for the elite. Once again, they had slaves. This was their comfort zone and happy place.

"Caitlyn and I realized ruler-slave thinking persisted into our modern systems, so we shared this history with our enclaves—like I just shared with you. The people in our gatherings wanted to understand the past more clearly to be able to sort through the truth versus a pile of BS. History offered clues to discovering *the sources* of our inability to innovate and thrive. Would we end up like medieval enclaves? Nope! Would we raise our frequencies and shift individually and collectively into a parallel reality where we could experience sovereignty in daily life? Yep!

"When we met in local gatherings, within or outside of an enclave, we acknowledged that to intentionally shut down dialogue by *killing alternative view points* in conversations was deadly to our future. It was worse than a plague or corrupt governments. We realized the absolute requirement to bring our highest frequency selves to the forefront.

"It was common to use eye gazing to connect, especially in conflict. Any time we found ourselves clashing or polarizing, we implemented this kind of deep eye connection. It won't surprise you that it was hard to use this *outside* of an enclave because of ignorance about our quantum level connectedness and the invaluable merits of being authentically seen and heard. As the enclaves grew, so did our attunement with each other, and our confidence and inner power grew, and division among us attenuated. We were okay with people thinking we were crazy. In that wild, high-vibe state, we became radically creative and had a lot of fun. Passion and excitement for what we were doing shifted our frequencies instantly and relentlessly. It was amazing!

"For home-schooled kids in enclaves, working together became effortless. Members noticed this and home-schooling gained traction. As we began to communicate with enclaves in other parts of the world, we brainstormed with tons of other people and accessed brilliant ideas. We decided to create conversations with enclaves from different countries and facilitate new enclaves to address economics, financial systems, and all sorts of topics. We problem-solved through tolerance for each other's views, willingness to listen, and believing in the value of the open expression of collective thinking. Everything gets magnified in a group—including either getting stuck or opening to the infinite field of all possibilities. We chose the latter.

"We've been rocking it! My God! It's been thrilling!

"Authorities and financial elites tried to stop us but we were like star fish. Cut off a leg and another one grows, really quick. On occasion, they legally found ways to dismantle particular enclaves, but much to their dismay, another one popped up with incredible resilience, and solid legal advice. That must have been annoying for global control freaks. The local cottage industry model could be applied anywhere. With the exposure of the elites' game, knowing we didn't need to be ruled and exploited, and with stable legal footing, we were free to invent and create a new world that worked for the common person globally—for the first time in history. We're just getting started, but we're headed in the right direction. We look forward to the next decade with a lot of optimism.

"Caitlyn and I tried to find a time when humanity had been allowed to spread its wings and fly with unconstrained wisdom and confidence to create and thrive. Across epochs, we couldn't find it. We reached out to anthropologists, historians, and sociologists. Historically, it was always the same result. Elites ruled through manipulation of common goodness—like there was an underlying dark energetic force luring them, coaching them into expressing ceaseless low vibes. We didn't want to get into their heads. It felt too dark and useless to try to shift them. They were sovereign beings, too. We chose to focus on ourselves, which included our individual and collective passions and high vibes.

"The long answer to your original question of what we did, Jake, is that we took back our inherent power—in retrospect, we observed that this *amazing inner power* gradually disintegrated the dwindling support for established structures of control, power, and greed. We didn't know the details about history that Sophia, her mom, Adele, Gilda, and all of you shared with us, but it was clear that we were encouraging the unraveling of *a worn out pattern*. I'm so grateful that you put the history of its inception in perspective for us."

Jake looked at Avani and chuckled while flashing a wry smile her way. "And... what happened to little Zane? Holy cow! You can't leave me hanging! Did he ever disappear again?"

Sophia and Jake sat breathless, captivated, and leaning forward, their eyes riveted to hers. Bearing a dazzling smile, Avani answered as the depths of her huge brown eyes emanated twinkling sparkles of exuberant, sprightly animation.

"Here's another mind-bender. We had a clairvoyant in our enclave who communicated with his invisible friends. Her input was helpful for us. She said, *The invisibles felt it was appropriate to intervene because Zane was becoming alarmingly traumatized.* But they appreciated how his parents and the community supported Zane after the event by believing his explanation of how they'd helped to get him to a place where he felt safe. I know his story may sound pretty *out there* to most people, but I think you guys can take it in and process it. I hope it wasn't too much."

"Avani, for clarity," Jake said, "I was not implying I didn't believe the story or that I was judging the child, his invisible team, or his parents. Keep in mind that I've become unexpectedly and increasingly open-minded after working with giants... and our dear Sophia!"

Giving Sophia a playful wink, he turned to Avani, thirsty for resolution, and asked, "That event must have sent shock waves through your enclave, right?"

"Thank you for the kind clarification of your question. Yes, at first, the whole ordeal was intense for our enclave. But having our unique, caring culture allowed us to work through it. Angelica, for example, didn't go to the initial meetings about Zane. She explained to Caitlyn later that she found herself getting triggered by his mother not addressing more effectively the intense terror in her child. She was also upset that invisible beings could intervene in that mysterious way. Angelica stayed away from the conversations until she processed her feelings and inner responses. She engaged with others about the event when she felt she could communicate without judgment or reactivity. That's how everyone responded—in their unique way of processing and on their own timeline. Does that help?"

"Absolutely, thank you for being so concise and honest."

Avani looked around the group and asked if she'd been clear enough and if she'd resolved their questions. All heads nodded and they encircled her with loving smiles and enthusiastic thumbs up.

"Thank you," she said tenderly, pausing to make direct eye contact with everyone in the circle. "I appreciate being able to share these stories. I feel blessed to have grown up in such a uniquely supportive environment filled with incredible luminaries. I also appreciate this rare chance to speak vulnerably within your safety net. It felt awesome! Thank you guys so much!"

Avani's eyes began to sparkle brighter with loving friendship within the gathering of confidants. She looked towards Megan and said in her usual upbeat style, "And Megan, your generosity never escapes me, for letting us meet here at night and explore the cove each day. I may have left my awesome grandmother in India, but I have you! You mean the world to me! I love you so much!"

Megan smiled affectionately at Avani, holding her hands over her heart as she said, "Thank you, sweetheart. I love you, too! In my view, this group is a dream come true, a celestial gathering of extraordinary souls." After a lion-like yawn and stretch, she added, "Now, dear friends, I'm ready for a nap!"

She stood, flashed a wink to the group, and wished them a blissful rest of their day.

With the rain subsiding, late afternoon was a great time to integrate the inspirational, thought-provoking conversation that had emerged that day.

# CHAPTER 13

# RELEVANT

For several weeks relentless storms eclipsed the fireside gatherings. With no relief in sight, an invitation to gather in Megan's cozy home was received with enthusiasm. As fierce rain roared in torrents, a sudden bolt of lightning blasted all lights into darkness. Sophia and Megan silently lit dozens of candles arranged elegantly throughout the room, transforming the space into a haven of glowing ambiance. Everyone quietly settled, letting the conversation arise naturally as it always did. After a few minutes, Adele broke the silence.

"Looking around our circle and the comfy vibe we're in tonight, I regret that I can't stay long because the woman who takes care of my daughters has to leave earlier than usual. Hopefully you know that I'd love to stay for several hours, relishing every second of our conversations. As I've been integrating what we talked about, a memory keeps coming up, something my grandmother told me when I was a little girl. All day it's been drifting into my mind and it feels important to share this haunting memory with you."

Supportive smiles and rapt attention were her cues to continue.

"Grandmother Anna joined the Nazi party as soon as she was old enough. She entered its ranks at the beginning of its rise in popularity. It replaced all other clubs and after school activities and its membership would later soar to include millions of kids. She loved being part of the in-crowd and admittedly, peer pressure was intense. All young people yearned for membership. Girls had one role and boys another, but both were totally brainwashed and repeated impassioned poems about loving and serving the führer like a father. However, my grandmother remained haunted and tormented by an after-school encounter with her grandmother.

"Young Anna spoke to her grandmother (who she called Oma) about Hitler, the Nazi's purported greatness, the immense relevance of the *Vaterland*, and how she desperately longed to serve it with all her heart. Of course, we know that 'serving the Fatherland' was based on a misguided altruism cultivated through intense propaganda from birth.

"Oma, although quite frail and very sick at the time, found the strength to fly into a rage. She lunged towards her granddaughter, pointing her gnarly, arthritic finger at the young girl's nose, and spoke with ferocity: *You are evil; you and your awful, demonic clan. What happened to you and your brother?*

"She was so close to my grandmother's face, my grandmother recalled being able to feel the heat of her Oma's labored breath. Her words and tone were so intense as she raged on that the young girl, my grandmother, felt them scorch her heart like a blazing inferno. I am going to read my grandmother's account of Oma's words:

*You can't help anyone, love anyone, or do anything good*
*if you lose your relevance. Anna! ... You are relevant!*

*You are a child of God, perfect in every way; wise, and good*
*right down to your soul. These bastards have taken your*

*innocence. That's bad enough but they've also ingrained in you that you have to serve others first. That's a lie!*

*You first have to love and appreciate yourself. See and experience your own goodness, then you naturally extend goodness to others. If you just serve the Vaterland, your leaders, and perform duties out of obligation, or to fit in and be liked, you'll become soulless. You will become the walking dead!*

*You are no better than a whore! You abdicate your relevance as the unique human who you were born to be. Your feelings matter! And do you know what else matters? You must be willing to look deeply into your own heart, grow from mistakes and become increasingly wiser on a heart level. An essential aspect of human life is receiving the love and friendship of others gratefully. You can offer love in an eternal loop of care and appreciation. This is how divine hearts commune in this world.*

*You think that you are doing something good? You children who turn on your parents, on each other, and you follow a crazy man and his crazy circle of idiots! They are no more relevant than you!*

*God help you, Anna! Never put yourself in a position to mourn the loss of your magnificent soul! Never let yourself abdicate your profound soul's power to anyone, ever!*

*With immense love in my heart for you and because I will leave this world soon, I call forth my divine power from both this world and beyond... to ensure that these animals will never take your soul.*

*They may have captured your mind and heart for now. However, dear little Anna, from across the great veil that will soon separate us, I declare that I will always pray and send protection for your precious soul. You are a gift to this Earth!*

*Hear my voice and listen carefully. You and your misguided friends across this planet will always have grandmothers sending blessings to override your innocent stupidity. We are with you always! But listen to me...*

*Heed my words as a blazing fire in your heart. Never enter their secret societies or participate in the rituals! Never! Do you hear me? Never! Even my love may not save you from the depraved intentions that materialize for gullible, unguarded souls who willingly enter those secretive, heinous places!*

*Remember what this old woman who loves you beyond all else is saying to you this day: You are relevant! You are a child of God! And your divine glory is not based on your physical appearance or your intellect. You are the living heart of God in this world! Discover where your heart and other hearts connect. Feel the pure love that throbs constantly at the center of your magnificent being!*

*Oh God, how I love you, Herzchen!*

Silent tears streamed down the faces of the friends who'd gathered safely as the storm raged mercilessly. By the gentleness of candlelight, absorbed in the unquestionable truth and invincible benevolence of Anna's grandmother, no one spoke.

After several minutes, immersed in the soothing balm of silence, the rain accommodated the circle of friends and peacefully subsided. Soon the electricity flashed and the lights returned.

From the quietude of the room, John spoke in a soft murmur that was barely audible, his misty eyes conveying the tenderness of his heart. He said, "Adele, I'm deeply touched by the poignancy of your great-grandmother's words, giving me more clarity about what shaped your grandmother's life. Even though she had the constant propaganda from the Nazi's indoctrination at school and a relentless barrage of peer pressure, fortunately she received a fathomless well of grandmother-love and profound wisdom to draw from. Thank you for sharing her story. I know this is deeply impactful for you because you loved your grandmother unequivocally. And Wow! That final term of endearment means *little heart*."

Sophia said in a soft timbre reminiscent of a grandmother telling bedtime stories, "The fierce, protective love of a grandmother for her beloved granddaughter, the childhood innocence lost, and the reminder of the inherent right to know and value our relevance mingles with the need to recognize, cultivate, and value the relevance of every human being. All of that is echoing and swirling as palpable energy in my being."

"I'm glad her story impacted you. My grandmother shared a little more," Adele said, speaking with such softheartedness that the room became saturated with immeasurable warmth and rapport. Taking a moment to allow her feelings to settle into peacefulness, she continued.

"After an exceptionally long winter when Grandmother Anna immersed herself in quiet isolation in the prison camp, springtime arrived bringing unexpected revelations and insights. She noticed wildflowers beginning to bloom in various colors and hues. The landscape triggered a memory for her when, as a small child, she picked gorgeous wild flowers for her beloved grandmother.

"She felt the natural, innocent longing to share with Oma the beauty of the fields of flowers, which she loved to race through until she became breathless. That field of bountiful flowers was her holy place, a spot where the world felt safe and she could instantly melt into peacefulness and enter a soothing, calm state. Recalling her flawless childhood heart, she also recalled Oma's fiery words the day before she died. And my grandmother began to wonder if she could possibly retrieve even a small thread of connection with the innocent child she had been, or had she irrevocably embodied the metaphorical whore whom her grandmother described? Maybe she was both.

"How could she find her way back to the core of her soul, her true relevance?

"Grandmother Anna let the feeling of well-established armor, which blocked the profound expression of her heart, to disintegrate. A deluge of emotions surged like a tidal wave sweeping her into an infinite, silent space that held her in a loving embrace. She wept uncontrollably for over an hour, racked with pain.

"With the help of a brilliant therapist, she was able to embrace the potential of her inherent beauty and she began to feel the arms of her grandmother around her. She realized that unless she had goodness and kindness somewhere in her, she wouldn't have been able to recognize the good and kind qualities of her grandmother's love infusing her with solace. It was like re-experiencing the taste of candy and remembering that delight to the taste buds forever. Goodness and kindness began reverberating in her. Fortunately, Oma's love triggered those latent qualities. My grandmother had taken a baby step in recalling her wholeness and inherent purity, once again. She realized she was relevant. Moving forward, she resurrected her youthful moments of delight as often as possible—viscerally recalling life's enraptured moments, the invincible bond with family and friends, and the dynamic feeling of being relentlessly renewed by an undercurrent of passionate, raw creativity and a sense of boundless wonder. With tenacity, she remained curious about her relevance and encouraged me to do the same.

"We are each relevant. I am sure of that. And with courage and honesty, may we admit with conviction that we are sacred. Not because of what we do but because of who we are. When I think of *self love*, it's not only about taking care of my personal needs. As Oma said, it's experiencing myself as *pure love*—getting in touch with the unfathomable vibrations of my Essence.

"Thank you for letting me share Oma's words and open my heart in the incredibly safe space that we create in these gatherings. I love you all and appreciate your love always.

"Every time we meet, I look forward to the continuous support and unwavering care we offer each other. Our relevance is honored in *every* interaction. This is such an invaluable blessing, my friends!

"I have to say *goodnight* now. See you soon."

Adele left in silence as the group nestled in, became even cozier, and allowed sufficient time to reflect on her story penetratingly—while listening to the tempestuous storm gradually softening into a serene evening.

# CHAPTER 14

# FATHER

The evening's gathering was coming to a close with yawns and gentle stretches. However, the crickets in full melodic, crackly-chirp mode, and the moon in its dark phase revealing the flamboyantly twinkling stars in the canopy above them. Some of the group was enticed to stay outside and enjoy the intoxication of the night sky.

After half an hour, Sophia looked towards the house and noticed that John's truck was still there. Under her breath, she murmured apprehensively, "Is he okay?" Her breath became shallow and took a brief pause as she unexpectedly noticed a second car. Angelica wasn't supposed to come until the following morning. With her intuition on alert, she went to check on John and find out who had arrived. As soon as she entered the threshold, she saw Angelica, her cheeks red and drenched with tears. Her makeup had smeared and her eyes were downcast as if in utter defeat and anguish.

Startled, Sophia wasn't sure how to respond because she could see that John's face was moist, too. Like Angelica, he looked traumatized.

All Sophia could mutter was, "You don't have to tell me what's going on, but if I can help, I'm here for you."

Angelica burst into tears. Just then, Caitlyn and Avani walked in to the unexpected scene, followed by Megan. The soft glow of the previous lovely conversation was suddenly replaced with the thick veil of evening's darkness. Only Jake was already heading home, missing out on the mystifying drama that now unnerved the circle of friends with its abruptness.

Angelica broke the silence, asking Caitlyn if she could speak to her alone.

No one could breathe as John, appearing despondent, looked away from his friends and left without a word.

Then there were eruptions of Caitlyn's angry voice from the adjacent room, followed by Angelica's next wave of torrential tears.

The porch seemed to be the best place for Sophia, Avani, and Megan to sit in silence, waiting for the waves of emotion to finally subside.

Megan whispered softly, "Dear friends, I have a feeling that sleep tonight will be scant. Sophia, after you get Angelica settled, I'll slip into the house. The poor woman looks utterly broken-hearted!"

Witnessing the dramatic scene she'd entered and realizing that their guest looked devastated, Megan suggested that Sophia spend the night in the other guest room to support their new visitor.

After several minutes, Caitlyn emerged and asked Avani to come with her to the guest house, saying that she was exhausted. Without the pretense of smiles or goodnight wishes, Caitlyn made a swift exit—with Avani struggling to match Caitlyn's quickened stride.

Unceremoniously, Angelica entered the living room. Her usually brilliant, crystalline eyes were bloodshot and lackluster. With solemn composure, Sophia showed Angelica to her room.

Within a minute of Sophia entering the other guest room, there was a knock on the door. As she opened it, Angelica's face expressed the agony of long-concealed pain that had finally broken through. Sophia invited her in. They sat by the large, arched window, opening into an enchanting grove of oak trees; a doe grazed nonchalantly nearby, only recognizable by her dark silhouette. Unexpectedly, a billowing breeze blew inside to refresh the air, yet nothing changed the evening's current mood of shock and devastation, which neither of them could ignore nor escape. Sophia reached for a velvety, midnight blue blanket, wrapping it delicately and lovingly around Angelica's sunken shoulders.

"It's not a long story," Angelica said, "but dear Lord, It's an epic one! I told you how I was in love with someone a long time ago. Then I met Chris and he loved me profoundly for so long. He was amazing! What I didn't share is that I got pregnant by the other man."

Sophia took a deep breath to prepare for the punch line that she could already feel tightening her solar plexus.

"I guess you may be intuiting where I'm going," Angelica continued. "I met John when I was in college." She avoided Sophia's eyes, looking down at her hands.

"I knew he didn't want children. The truth is that I didn't want to start a family either—I wanted to go to graduate school. But I couldn't abort. Just couldn't. Don't regret it."

Choppy words were all that Angelica could muster as she choked back tears. "I lied—to John—I—told him that I had an abortion." She took a deep breath to steady herself. "And then I broke up with him. Moved away. Refused to talk to him. He tried to connect with me for a couple of years..."

She went on, "When I met Chris, I felt like everything would finally be okay. He adored Caitlyn. I knew she was so young that she'd only know her new father and I was deeply in love with Chris. I never confronted the reality that someday Caitlyn would find out. But—that was not realistic.

"Of course, I regret not telling her, but I didn't know how to talk about it. That's the problem with lies. They take on a life of their own. I told myself that my secret was for her good, that knowing about her biological father would be too confusing and complicate her life. All of a sudden, she'd have to come to terms with having two fathers.

"Dear God! I should have told her a long time ago. I can understand if she never trusts me again! This was such a horrible lie! There's no way to fix the damage it caused... Saying I'm sorry is a feeble solution to something like this. My Lord! John admitted he had a haunting, familial feeling when he met her, but he dismissed it as natural comradeship with a like-minded soul.

"For heavens sake, Sophia! She has his DNA! Of course he'd feel a strong connection. Both of them are highly empathic. Now he's in agony too.

"Caitlyn's time with all of you has meant the world to her. She told me about Jake and John and all the fabulous conversations. She really loves you all. Now, that wonderful camaraderie has been shattered.

"I don't want to just bolt from this terrible situation tonight in case she wants to talk, but if she thinks I should go, I'll leave right away. My focus is on restitution to her and John now for the damage of my deceit.

"Caitlyn said that your group has been discussing the devastating effects of telling lies and adopting secrecy as a norm, while irrationally thinking such actions are without consequence. Reflecting on what she shared, I see how much programming I have in order for lying to be my go-to response. My goodness! Why was I not brave enough to tell John—to be honest? What was it in me that was not programmed for the confidence and courage to tell Caitlyn the truth? Waiting for decades didn't help. It just made it worse for me and for everyone. I have a whole lot of deep introspection ahead of me. Right now it feels insurmountable. How can I right something that is so wrong? My child is suffering profoundly because of me. That is unbearable to admit."

Raging tears flowed with excruciating force while Angelica melted into her friend's embrace, desperately seeking even a semblance of solace. Finally exhausted, they both agreed they should go to bed, even if they could not sleep.

As they were parting, Sophia said, "Gilda used to remind me that in times of inner upheaval and massive confusion, tossing and turning at night usually follows. And somehow an opening arrives for insight into how to heal individually and collectively from an unexpected moment that touches all involved. Everything is out in the open now and it's time to heal. Be soft, gentle, and pliable with yourself as you work your way through the healing and restitution you are committing to. You can do this, sweet friend. I love you."

Tenderly, they embraced as the evening reached its unimaginable conclusion.

Meanwhile, in the guest house, two forever friends were uncertain about how to deal with the bombshell that had suddenly dropped, leaving emotional shrapnel in its wake.

"Avani, don't feel sorry for me," Caitlyn began. "What I have to tell you is shocking, but I can handle it and I know you can, too. Okay… here's what happened. My mother had an affair and got pregnant many years ago."

"You have a sibling?" Avani asked wide-eyed and spellbound.

"No, that would have been good news compared to this," Caitlyn responded with a clenched jaw and hardened eyes.

"Oh my God! I've never seen you like this," Avani said, dispirited and bewildered.

"Well, that's because I've never been betrayed like this," Caitlyn said with bitter, hot tears drenching her face, illuminating a fierceness vying with obvious anguish and sorrow. "My mother got pregnant with me before she met my father, Chris. I guess you could say the man who I *thought* was my father."

Thrust into abrupt shock and confusion, Avani was hardly breathing. In an awkward moment of silence, she felt deep compassion for her friend, who was clearly devastated. Caitlyn took a minute to gather the composure necessary to continue.

"Avani, there's more and it gets worse." Caitlyn told the story, even though she was hoarse from copious tears and eruptions of feral anger. Facing Avani's raised brows and sympathetic eyes that also bore profound overwhelm, Caitlyn said in a slow, deliberate cadence, "My mother was in love with John. That's why he acted weird tonight when she showed up. He thought he was seeing an old lover unexpectedly. Instead, he was about to be told a shocking truth. She said that she just blurted it out… John is my real father! And holy shit! What did he say?

His response was that he felt a bond with me immediately and that he loved me instantly."

The uncontrollable force of anger erupted in Caitlyn once again and fueled her dramatic story further.

"Avani, this is totally insane! How could this be happening? My father, who died, wasn't my father. Except he was! He loved me, protected me, and was the best dad ever. And... I feel a super-deep bond with John. Remember me telling you that I liked him immediately and I could somehow relate to him in a way that I could almost read his mind?! I experienced *magical unicity* with him." Anger blended with frenzied confusion as she continued.

"Am I supposed to call John, Dad? How can I ignore that my mother blatantly lied to me and then kept the lie going? She even said that close friends begged her to tell me the truth. But I think she was not going to disclose John to me because she wanted to remain safe. Now that we all know the truth, it's pretty clear that she was selfish and deceitful. How can I ever trust her again?!"

Avani wrapped her arms around Caitlyn and held her in a warm, safe embrace as Caitlyn melted in heaving sobs. As Caitlyn's tears flowed, she looked at Avani and saw that she was crying, too.

Choking back sobs, she smiled tenderly. "That's what friends do. They hug you and feel your pain. And then, sometimes, they can bring a flicker of clarity. Oh God! I hope you have some! How am I going to forgive Mom, face John, and sort through this insane mess?"

"Caitlyn, you know I love you and stand with you always," Avani said, mustering a calm sense of confidence. "What if you take some time to let the initial impact of this news settle down. Your nervous system, your brain, every part of you is in shock. I know sleep may be hard tonight. But maybe rest will help. I'll be here for you no matter what… If you want to leave, I'll go with you. If you want to stay and sort things out with your mom and John, I'm all in. My only wish is to support you, one hundred percent! You are my bestie."

Avani gave Caitlyn a deep, long hug. Looking into the oceanic depths of her friend's tear-filled blue eyes, she said, "It looks like a pretty shitty night on one level. But I have a feeling that somehow it'll work out, even if it takes a while. Everything will be good again, despite the fact that we can't imagine how that could happen."

One more long, comforting embrace for encouragement and they crossed the threshold of an insurmountably protracted night where the mind and emotions can easily override the need for sleep.

# CHAPTER 15

# FORGIVENESS

The next morning before dawn arrived with its gentle luminescence, Sophia slipped into meditation. After half an hour passed, she allowed the songbirds to bring her awareness back to Megan's comfy guest room. With tea in hand, she was soon sitting on the porch, just in time for Jake's arrival.

"Sophia, I knew you'd be up. Did you hear what happened?"

"Yes, Angelica confided in me. You talked to John, didn't you?"

"Yep, until *the wee hours*, as my mother used to say. He is in shock but he definitely wants to speak with Caitlyn. He almost felt relieved because of the fatherly bond that he feels for her. Yet that insane revelation has him befuddled, like a bee trapped in a bottle. Do you want to know what shocked the hell out of me? He still loves Angelica. Even though he hasn't seen her for over two decades, he said he never quit thinking about her... and I thought he was a confirmed old bachelor like me. This is some crazy shit, my friend."

"Well, Jake. I wouldn't put it that way, but I can't argue about your conclusion. How did you leave it with him?"

"I told him if he wanted to talk, come to the porch for early coffee. My intuition said you'd be here. Even if he didn't come, I knew I wouldn't get much sleep and Megan's delicious coffee would have the caffeine kick I'd need to get me through the day. I assume you already have it brewing, right?"

Laughing, she squeezed his hand and offered to pour him coffee as she went to steep more tea for herself. As she returned to the porch, John's truck pulled up.

Approaching languidly, his swollen eyes and exhausted demeanor conveyed more than words. Taking a moment to collect his thoughts, he nestled into one of the porch chairs that had been a seat of comfort for many years. He said hoarsely, "Hey, you two… Sorry… I'm totally screwed… I could sure use a cup of coffee. I hope you made my favorite brew. Knowing you, Sophia, I figured you would have it ready, piping hot… right?"

Smiling and giving him a warm hug, Sophia invited him to relax as best he could and talk to Jake. Looking lovingly at her friends who were engaged in a moment of stilted silence, she went inside to fill his favorite mug. This morning, an extra strong brew, served black, was required.

"Jake, I hope like hell you told Sophia. I said you could tell her. I don't want to repeat it."

"I told her. And now what?" Jake said in a compassionate tone.

"Good question, old buddy. My daughter is in that guest house over there. Shit, this is weird!"

"John, here's your coffee," Sophia said as she arrived with the soothing aromatic brew. "How are you? I know you must be in shock. And I understand how *weird* this is for you."

"Damn, Sophia, it's crazy that you've talked about Angelica yet I didn't make the connection. My bigger question is how to face Caitlyn?"

"Caitlyn already has a bond with you. I predict it will only get stronger."

"It's interesting that you mentioned my bond with Caitlyn because after the initial shock wore off, I was glad that I knew the truth. Honestly, I'm feeling blessed and grateful that I have such a great kid. I never held out high hopes to marry and have a family. But last night, when I realized that someone I loved more than any woman I've ever known was the mother of my kid who happens to be amazing, I sat in awe of my good luck. Having said that, I'm still trying to process it and what it means going forward for all three of us. In comparison, this made ET revelations seem lame."

From around the corner, Caitlyn appeared with Avani, who settled into a chair as Caitlyn addressed John softly and with piercing authenticity. "This may seem crazy... It hit me as I was waking up that I lost one father, but I have you now. And I can't think of a better man... but... sorry... I'm not there yet... not ready to call you *Dad*. This situation feels surreal and it's..."

Spontaneously, without inhibition, Caitlyn pulled John into a tender hug, which he returned in kind. Their eyes locked into a gentle gaze for a moment. As everyone settled in and wiped away tears, Avani brought tea and more coffee.

Looking slowly around the group, Caitlyn spoke. "I guess it may take some time to adjust to John and me as a father-daughter team. And John, it freaks me out that you and Mom dated and you two were in love. I thought of my mom and Chris as a couple, as my parents. It's hard to just drop that."

"Are you kidding me?!" John said passionately and with fiery compassion blazing in his eyes. "No way would I want you to feel anything but absolute, forever love for Chris and your mom. Yes, she screwed up. Of course, she should have told us a long time ago. I'm glad she finally admitted the truth, though, regardless of how f**king shocking it was."

"Excuse me for interjecting," Sophia said. "I am stunned that you two processed this so fast and are willing to move on, forgive, and see the good in this. I am having to process your amazing hearts. I'm blown away right now!"

"Me too," Jake said, shaking his head in bewilderment. "I was prepared for a long, agonizing process."

"I'm relieved and I shouldn't be surprised, Caitlyn," Avani added with a gentle smile, sending Caitlyn beaming love from her enormous dark eyes. "You have a big heart. And you find the good in everybody."

"It's still awkward, but I'm glad we got together this morning to talk rather than hide," John said as he glanced around the group. "If I'd waited to speak with Caitlyn or you guys, it would have been harder because my mind and insecurities would have kicked in. Where is Angelica?"

As John's voice trailed off with the question, Angelica opened the screen door and stepped onto the porch with her customary elegance and kind-hearted charm. Like John and Caitlyn, she displayed the same swollen eyes and body language that revealed a shellshocked soul. With nervous jitters and bleary-eyed exhaustion, she poured a cup of tea. Everyone sat in silence until she finished crying and could speak.

"Thank you all. As I was about to come onto the porch, I heard what you each said, and I can't imagine what it was like for you last night. You are friends, and you've been working together... now this unexpected truth-bomb! Oh my goodness! Hearing what you said touched my heart profoundly and yet I made a terrible mistake. Caitlyn, I don't think I should stay. I want to talk to you but maybe we should talk later. When you come home... if you still want to come home... we could talk then."

"Time won't help, Mom." Caitlyn addressed her mother in a compassionate tone while maintaining a solemn gaze. "I want to talk to you now, in the guest house. If I wait, I may change my mind. Right now, I'm ready to have a conversation about this. I'll leave it up to you. Do you want to talk?"

"Of course, sweetheart," Angelica said with a sigh of relief. They stood up and walked solemnly to Megan's guest house to sort through the unexpected predicament they found themselves in.

The rest of the group was reflectively quiet until John spoke. He said, "I think I'll take the day off. Thank you for your love and support. It means the world to me. I'll put the equipment that we planned to use today in your truck, Jake."

"Okay. See you later," Jake said as he stood to embrace his friend warmly in the spirit of inseparable friendship.

Soon the sound of John's truck faded.

Sophia turned to Jake, completely changing the subject by asking, "As I envisioned the archaeologic equipment that John was putting in your truck, it reminded me of someone. Have you seen your young friend, Ike, lately?"

"I sure have," Jake answered. "He's coming this weekend. He's been doing great archeological work part-time during graduate school. But his heart remains immersed in technologies, using his skills in quantum physics and cutting-edge, high level mathematical endeavors. Wow, thinking of that amazing kid sure boosts my spirits. Thanks, Sophia."

"I recall the story of you and John meeting him as a young boy in Africa." Sophia said with an affectionate smile, "Africa was one of your favorite places to dig. I recall how you described this lanky, little-kid genius with a heart of gold. You said his gigantic smile blasted your heart wide open every time you saw him."

"So true! Don't forget his friend, Eben, equally smart and with the same heart-melting smile as Ike," Jake said reflectively. "Eben was always a little shit of a prankster, taking my stuff and going off somewhere to dig. I love them both. Their thirst for exploring anything mysterious tops mine. They'd grown up in a shamanic culture, so their mindset developed from living constantly in amazement and awe of life—and more importantly, they were not burdened by the same cultural constrictions around what is possible as those of us conditioned in western cultures. I recognized instantly that I was with kindred spirits.

"We gave Ike's friend the nickname, Eben, because he reminded me of the short, little ETs from the Roswell crash, which the government called Ebens. He was incredibly smart and pretty short for his age, and I couldn't resist teasing him. He loves to kid around so the nickname was perfect—he told John it made him feel special.

Noticing that Avani was becoming absorbed in Jake's story, Sophia said, "Say more, Jake, especially knowing those two young men have a lot in common with Avani's and Caitlyn's archeological work. Avani, you've worked on intriguing digs in Africa, right?"

Nodding with her customary vivacity, Avani said, "Say more about Ike and Eben, for sure! Caitlyn and I totally loved every inch of our African digs!"

Sophia and Jake smiled, responding to her emotive response. With Avani's unreserved prompting, Jake continued.

"Ike and Eben are Igbo, which is the largest ethnic group in Africa, dispersed across the entire continent. I met them in the southern part of Nigeria. Some say that Igbo people tend to have high IQ scores, but I can only speak for these two boys. When they were tested, their scores were in the upper percentile. With high IQ scores, insatiable curiosity, highly developed intellects, and magnetic personalities, they started getting scholarships abroad."

"But it's more than IQ that makes them awesome young men. John and I wanted to find out why they were so extraordinary, so we stayed in the local village and observed them within their community setting. The children there learn sacred geometry through nature, how to feel nature's currents in weather, and how to locate subtle places in their environment that hold and emanate high frequencies. In their village, this high intelligence is likely related to epigenetic factors as much as, if not more than, just inherited genetic traits. Their brains are highly capable of thinking in both concrete and abstract terms. I am sure this con- tributed to their immense creativity and problem-solving skills.

"I was amazed to witness how they moved through the day in a natural flow, doing the needful. Yet they could change course instantly, without making it into a big deal. They completed tasks but didn't get caught up in them nor fuss or worry about how things were going. Everything got done with a sense of ease. I loved that! Life was intermixed with song and dance. Oh! Ike can dance! Lordy, can that boy dance!

"John and I couldn't stop thinking and talking about their community. We were excited and fortunate to be able to bring both of them to the U.S. to attend university. The big schools out East wanted them, but the boys were adamant that they wanted to live closer to us, so they chose schools in California.

"We were able to bring Ike over five years ago to attend the University of California-Berkeley. He was only sixteen. He attained his master's degree in quantum physics by the time he turned twenty-one. Now he's been accepted into Stanford's doctorate program in advanced quantum science.

"Three years ago, when Eben was old enough—also sixteen—we brought him over as well, and he is about to earn his undergraduate degree and apply to a masters' program in quantum science and technology. And when Eben completes his master's program, he'll apply to the same university that Ike is attending. So they are both here and doing exceptionally well in their respective fields of study.

"Selfishly, we want you—Avani and Caitlyn—to work with them here. A sort of *think tank* of young, bright minds and big hearts that will surely be nothing short of miraculous to behold.

"They are coming to visit this weekend. I can't believe Ike is going for his PhD soon."

"Amazing!" Sophia said wide-eyed. "He's young to be entering a doctorate program, right?"

"Doesn't matter," Jake answered. "He's got his pick of the best universities, but he'll stay close to us. After all, we're family. I thought I would never have kids, yet I'm sitting in this cove with a group of kids who feel like family. Hmmm... maybe I found my family when I least expected. I'm glad John found his."

"In the Nigerian village where I met Ike and Eben, children found ways to release the lower frequencies of resistance to life and open themselves to higher frequencies which create unfettered, limitless love and fascination for life. Everyone is right and everyone is perfect. Each community member is a piece of a whole that is greater than the sum of the pieces. That's my takeaway from visiting their village.

"When our circle gets to know Ike and Eben better, you will see something else—as brilliant mathematicians and physicists, they create what I call *art through number and geometry*. Their mathematical formulas are elegant, simple, and beautiful in design, allowing me to see a distillation of the vastness of creation. They are building on what other physicists have done, but without trying to be 'the best'; they see themselves as part of a physics evolution into *unified* sciences. Underlying their work is *the unified field* of all possibilities, keeping their work expansive, rather than physical or particle-oriented.

"They've carefully studied Isaac Newton's writings, which demonstrate his interest in mysticism and alchemy. According to documents discovered within the past one hundred years, it seems Newton's obsession with alchemy centered around transmuting substances that could confer longevity and, more consequential to our conversation, a massive upgrade in human consciousness.

"Today, instead of applying *ancient* alchemy and rituals, some bio physicists posit that it is possible for us to obtain the same results in a *modern* way by accessing higher levels of consciousness to raise our overall frequency levels. Tapping inherent powers rather than adding something external, feels more empowering and sustainable as an upgrade for our species. Recently, the Pentagon admitted to using *psychics* as part of their UAP/UFO phenomenon task force. Across the ages, higher level human biological wisdom remains in demand. That's why I am in high spirits about the staggering advances occurring in Unified Physics; there is a growing openness to life and each other, and the path forward for your generation, Avani, involves taking in easily accessible, infinite information from the field. I can't wait to hook you up with Ike and Eben. I have a strong feeling you and Caitlyn will get along with them like a house on fire, inspiring the hell out of each other!"

Sophia added with fervid kinship, "Adorable Avani, you have a heart of gold and immense creativity, too. I agree that we need to introduce you to Ike and Eben and watch for unexpected magic to burst forth from your midst."

Lost for words by the enormous complement, Avani blushed and looked away— shimmering tears filled her eyes as her heart was drenched in vibrations of love, care, and deep respect.

After a reflective moment, allowing Avani time to absorb Sophia's expression of profound affection, Jake sprang to his feet. With his usual sparkling eyes, he said, "I'm itching to do some work! Avani, care to join me? Let's go rock the cove!"

Watching Avani giggle and jump playfully to her feet to gather her gear and enjoy the discoveries awaiting them in the enigmatic cave system, Sophia smiled warmly at her and then Jake.

She said assuredly, "Our circle of hearts are definitely aligned and I have a feeling we have extraordinary adventures ahead of us."

Turning her attention to Avani, she said, "I am *immeasurably* happy you are with us."

After looking down sheepishly for a second, Avani thanked Sophia. Instantly she shifted her expression back to her natural exuberance, bounding forward and leading the way to the cove, with Jake having to match her spirited stride.

# PART 2

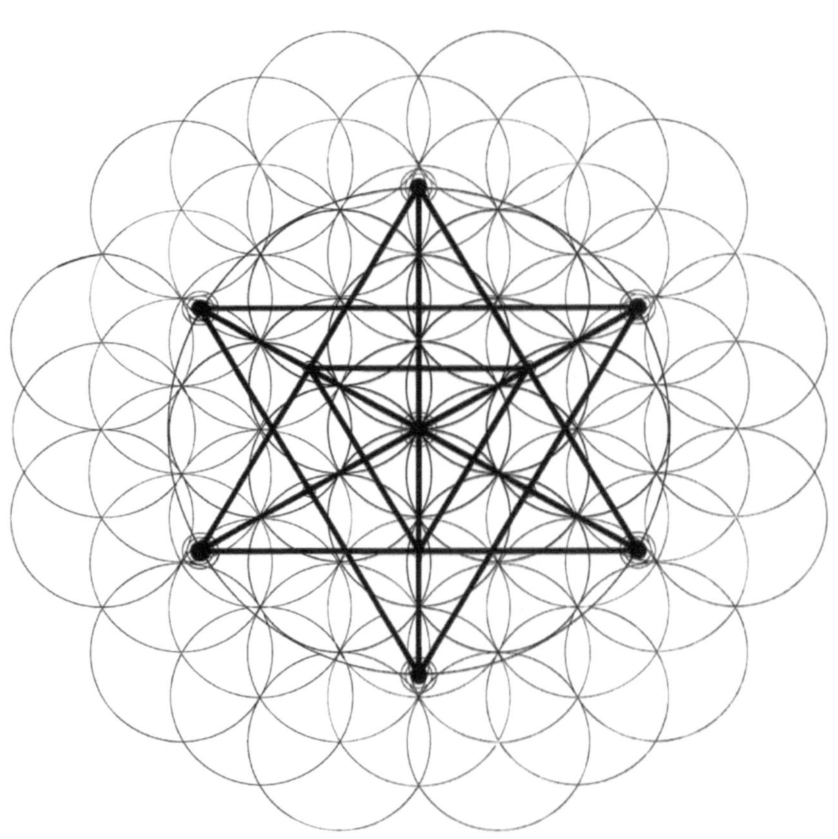

# CHAPTER 16

# LOVE REUNITED

Dawn exploded into a golden effulgence as the cove came to life earlier than usual. The always enlivened discussions had expanded lately to include Ike and Eben exploring with Avani and Caitlyn all they could about cave art, giant skeletons, mysterious caves, and ancient architecture. As they sipped tea and coffee, their voices filled the air with animation. The young contingent were bursting with enthusiasm and unrelenting voracity for exploring obscure domains, even if such ventures were unavoidably risky.

Avani said, "Oh my God, you guys! This discussion is so totally juicy, deep, and unprecedented for me!"

"Cool, I feel the same way!" Ike replied, his expressive eyes broadening like the rising of a full moon, his smile huge and radiant.

Eben, not as outgoing as Ike, smiled unassumingly. Then with a sudden surge of confidence, he said, "Man! I love being with you and getting to talk about these subjects. Sometimes I feel like an outsider in our field of study. But when I hear you, I feel like I'm with fam. Thanks for talking honestly, from your hearts, and being open-minded instead of puffed up archeologists with super cool PhD's.

"I hope it doesn't sound like I'm putting down anybody's degrees or achievements. Too many times, though, after getting those credentials, my colleagues hold back from doing audacious work, never wanting to look bad or act fringe. This is just my view, based on what I've seen. Most of our friends get their degrees and then get scared to take risks and do things that no one else has done.

"I talked to Jake about this kind of holding back and he said it's normal in most areas of science, including archeology and quantum physics. Man! That's sad. Students end up using their degrees to blend in, get respect, and feel they've earned 'prestigious authority.' I didn't know that phrase, *prestigious authority*. My English is better but not perfect. Jake explained it but I was still confused. He told me that many areas of science have slowly evolved into just another system of beliefs with rigid dogmas, and this mindset has invaded all levels of education. People get the higher degrees only to get their dream job and feel satisfied to have risen above others who don't have advanced credentials. But he said that kind of thinking is a 'can of worms.' I knew about worm cans, but Jake explained that phrase, too, which refers to a very complicated problem. In our conversation that day, he said in his view, if we're not careful, something worse can happen than feeling like we have earned, and can rely on, prestigious authority. He called it, *blending in*. That's another concept that's new for me. Jake explained it and it hurt my heart. If I *blend in*, I'll kill my spirit because my spirit is meant to be free and expand into forever. I believe I'm a unique wave in an infinite ocean of energy. I can excite that ocean with my consciousness and create something amazing. So cool! And when I'm with you, the waves of the invisible ocean of energy in and around me start getting crazy-wild with excitement. I want to be like that always.

"I thought a lot about what Jake said. He told me I needed to have discrimination about what I learned while earning my degrees and use my focus of study as a foundation to live my passion, not adhering to other people's ideas and belief systems. He said hard work, being an unfettered archaeologist, and exploring the unknown are my destiny. He had to explain *unfettered*. Now I love that word. When Avani was talking a few minutes ago, I think she was agreeing with Jake. We all need to stay unfettered."

Without hesitation, the group's luminous faces and dazzling smiles assured Eben that he was deeply respected and appreciated—as Avani declared, flashing him a playful wink and sprightly smile. While offering elevated vibes to Eben, the mood of the conversation ascended a notch higher. Everyone thanked Eben for his honesty and acknowledged his hard work in learning quantum physics and the English language. His coy smile gleamed in response to their encouragement and friendship.

The group then began planning astounding adventures. Uncharacteristically, Caitlyn became pensive and quiet. Then, in a sudden burst she said, "My preference is to go anywhere off-the-beaten-path and which would classify as *heterodoxy*. I am so done with the status quo and playing it safe! I could care less if I'm viewed as a heretic in my field. It's time to take off the shackles of our ancestors and dig deeper than they dared to dream. What do you think? Are you in?"

Eben's smile broadened more than usual, as he said, "I definitely know the status quo is no good! And I LOVE to dig! I'm in!"

Cheers and hugs instantly followed and their burgeoning friendship was instantaneously sealed.

The transitioning fall weather was invigorating the whole team with its brisk energy and liveliness. They wanted to explore extended cavern systems and ancient mysteries deep within the body of Gaia. No one had attempted such a risky endeavor in this area of the planet. Ground penetrating radar near ancient megaliths in Idaho and Montana indicated that under the surface, unfathomable antiquities lay hidden, as yet unexplored. As fascinating as these revelations were, the group wanted to go even further, to enter unknown territory beyond levels that radar could measure. Wondering if they could meet the ancient relatives of Max and his beloved, they were willing to engage heart-and-soul to clear a pathway for that to happen.

When they headed for the cove that morning, John stayed behind. Pacing restlessly across Megan's porch, he glanced at his phone for the time—he knew Angelica would arrive soon. After a seemingly endless stream of phone calls and heart-felt conversations, they had decided to meet.

As late summer merged into early autumn, the weather was getting cooler. Zipping up his jacket and pouring more coffee, he heard her car approaching. Clearing his throat and taking a quick sip of his favorite brew, he went to greet her.

Looking refreshed and relaxed, Angelica came towards him. Without hesitation, they embraced tightly as friends who'd bonded indelibly long ago, finally reunited. He held her hand tenderly, beaming a coy, boyish smile her way. With hands locked in harmony and mutual respect, they could rekindle their original, profound connection or decide to be united in cherished friendship after decades of separation. Seeing her luggage in the back, John lifted it out, and they walked to the house spreading vibrations of laughter and cheerfulness into the atmosphere around them.

Megan, once again out of town, had invited Angelica to stay in her house so she could be close to Caitlyn. John finally released Angelica's hand so she could refresh herself after the long trip. Without letting too much distance get between them, he sat in a chair in the living area, looking like a high school boy waiting for his girlfriend. Angelica's voice wafted through the hallway, calling for him.

As he stepped into her room, he didn't notice the soft morning light streaming through the windows, nor could he hear the chirping of a raucous chorus of birds or feel the chill from the half open window nearby. In a dream come true, he pulled her into a long-awaited embrace, charged with irresistible magnetism. Without speaking, without thinking or inhibition, his hands tenderly held her soft cheeks, flushed with passion, as they kissed, long and deep. All doubt and caution vaporized, establishing the certainty that young love had survived the test of time. They made love with a depth of intimacy they'd shared when their young bodies burned with desire, melting into eternal communion. Afterwards, they lingered together, assimilating the raw power of their love. Morning light coruscated with mesmerizing beauty across the bed, sanctifying their union.

Sufficiently satiated, they arose to have a late breakfast and consider how their unexpected love-making could affect their lives going forward. Having tea, coffee, and Beth's baked treats, they snuggled on the couch under a warm blanket, as they remained magnetized to each other. A crackling fire created a delightful backdrop for more kisses, smiles, and adoring gazes into each other's eyes.

"Goodness gracious, John—I didn't see that coming! And you?"

"No, my dear, I did not. I can't say I'm surprised, though. When we spoke on the phone, it was awkward at first, but as we continued to connect, I realized that my love and respect for you hadn't changed, not at all. I never wanted to be separated from you. I guess after this, I assume you feel the same way."

Angelica smiled; her face flushed with coyness.

John became suddenly solemn as he asked pensively, "Do you think our relationship will be hard for Caitlyn to accept?"

"John, I'll answer with a story. The day after my bombshell revelation, Caitlyn and I went to the guest house. Remember? Oh my goodness! That kid blew my mind! She said she will love Chris forever and she misses him. However, she feels a bond with you that's also eternal, deep, and profoundly strong. Every time we talk about it, she reiterates that she feels a daughterly bond with both of you—it's very intimate and loving, and definitely her truth. After seeing your pain and mine, she wondered if we still love each other. I was flabbergasted. Hearing her response, I had to admit to myself that I shared her question.

"I wish you could have known her as a child. Even then, she didn't dwell in drama and temper tantrums. I recall a time when I was angry and impatient with her—she was maybe four years old. Calmly and matter-of-factly, she said that I was not actually angry with her but just fussed because Chris was late. With mature confidence, she told me I would feel better when he got home and to please not fuss at her anymore. I was taken aback.

"My goodness! Over the years, I've witnessed her innate confidence and capacity not to take on other people's stuff. She processes her feelings in a healthy way, just naturally. She sure didn't get that from me. Knowing her like I do, I'm not totally shocked by her reaction. She was furious about the deception, rightfully so. Yet she's allowing us to sort through our relationship.

"Her advice was for you and me to talk so we could get acquainted again. She felt it would make things less awkward when the three of us were together. She knows I love Sophia. Plus Caitlyn plans to come back here often. It's unavoidable that our paths will cross."

"Angelica, I have definitely observed her personal and emotional maturity yet I'm not sure it's that easy. Will she feel awkward if we're a couple? She might say that it's okay but if I was in her shoes, it could be weird for her mom to be with a guy that she's friends with. I don't know... I guess we have to take one step at a time."

"As long as we're transparent, everything will be fine. Secrecy is what caused this mess. I want to be honest and handle any reactions as they arise, if they do. I refuse to have a clandestine relationship with you. That won't work."

Taking her hand in his, John smiled saying, "You are right." Then he said, "And since we're agreeing to be transparent, I must confess that I plan to make love with you at every possible opportunity." Kissing again and cuddling, they spent the morning in soulful communion.

When the sun moved towards its noontime peak, they set the table for lunch. With those preparations behind them, they enjoyed more kisses and catching up on life stories, until the group emerged to enjoy the food that Beth left for them.

The room filled with chatter and laughter as Caitlyn approached her mom and John saying, "Well, you two seem happy. That must mean that you are getting along. In fact—from your lovey-dovey smiles, I'd guess maybe more than just getting along. I want you to know that I love you both. Please don't worry about me. Keep getting reunited.

"John, despite the fact that you and I haven't known each other for a super long time, I hope you realize by now that I speak from my heart. I promise, I would not say this if I didn't mean it: I think you two are great together. You get to decide if you are just friends or if you go back to being my age, like before, and become a couple."

As she walked away she winked and said, "Avani and I think you guys are going to be a couple."

Watching her walking with a playful swagger towards the group, teasing Ike, and laughing unrestrainedly with Avani, Angelica's heart became soft. She caught sight of the two besties glancing lovingly towards her and John.

Angelica said, "I may faint, John! My goodness! She's so perceptive and she's really grown up! Oh my stars! My baby is giving me permission to date someone. Isn't it supposed to be the other way around?"

Putting his arm around her waist, John smiled so lovingly that she blushed like a smitten teenager.

✴ ✴ ✴

By afternoon, Angelica made her way to the cove to see the mystical wonders within this unique place on Planet Earth.

Taking her to the pyramid, Avani and Caitlyn were excited, acting like giggly middle schoolers. Sophia spoke for a few minutes with Angelica before she opened the door into the sacred pyramid of ancient giants. Angelica stepped in with reverence and respect as the door softly closed behind her.

Waiting for Angelica's emergence, Sophia sat on a boulder and talked with Jake and John. "Are we finally heading under the surface to explore mysterious, uncharted territories?"

"Yes, we are," Jake said, smiling with effulgent enthusiasm. "The team has been here all morning. It's a reality! However, I'm finding it strange that after such an epic separation, Angelica and John are finally reunited again, and here we go heading out. Sorry, buddy! Does the idea of separation from Angelica thoroughly suck?"

Without feigning bravery, John said, "Of course it does. But I know she'll understand, mainly because she will be relieved I will be there to keep an eye on Caitlyn... although it's going to be hard to explain that we're going portal-jumping into a place we know little about. If it wasn't for cave art, our local indigenous community, and the maps they preserved, I wouldn't have been confident enough to embark on this wild adventure.

"As an elder of the indigenous community, Will has first hand knowledge of their oral history that describes *brothers and sisters* under the surface who can help us better understand how to go forward technologically. They could be our ancestors. Holy cow! That lights up the archeologist, anthropologist, and cosmologist in me! If there wasn't anything down there, what are all of those maps about? And the drawings are damn clear that someone thought something was going on beneath their feet. Maybe the beings died off. I cannot think of anything I'd rather be dedicated to finding than a possible ancient world deeper than I've ever dug into. I know I'm preaching to the choir. Thanks for indulging my massive anticipation with your kind patience."

Responding with solidarity and sharing John's doggedness, Jake said, "Whatever is going on below our feet needs to be explored and we're going to allow that possibility to unfold as we focus on mystical, high-vibe, ancient sites. It's so damned frustrating that we have colleagues who spent millions of dollars on 3-D modeling and using ground penetrating radar to locate underground sites, yet with oppressive government and institutional shenanigans and threats, they won't publish anything. It's gone too f**king far. I want to get to the bottom of this in person. To hell with trying to rely on technology. I want to affirm what's down there—the architecture and living areas crafted by intelligent species, maybe our own.

"On that note, there's something that I've been waiting to tell you all morning. Unexpectedly, Will met a government contractor who was abducted, experimented on, and tortured within a craft that looked otherworldly—yet he says clearly it was not. It's part of *the shenanigans*, as Megan refers to the hidden world of unrelenting secrecy. Although it sounds unfortunately familiar, this abductee's wife and children were killed to keep him quiet. He was left brain damaged, destitute, and planning suicide. He knew the system, the black projects, intimately. Why his employers chose to ruthlessly disable and devastate him remains a mystery, except that he was an insider. Maybe they like to do that every once in a while to show others what happens if someone falls from favor. This guy speculated that after seeing dozens of inconceivable top secret projects, the higher ups in his organization wanted to reduce any chance that he'd leak covert information."

Jake paused as tears refused to hide behind a dam of stoicism—they flowed uninhibited from a current of deep sorrow, frustration, and immense empathy. After his breath moved from heaves and sobs to a natural rhythm, he gathered himself to continue speaking.

"It's now certainly obvious to you that this subject totally wrecks me… I have a personal stake in ending this madness. Ten years ago there'd be no f**ing way I'd emote that way! Holy shit! NO WAY! Forgive my *deluge*. Your friendship means the world to me and I appreciate you letting me rant and howl when needed. Hopefully my story will help you understand what precipitated my emotional outburst. A decade ago I got close… really damned close… to someone who became a whistleblower. When he mysteriously died, it slayed me! Obviously, I've not resolved my feelings around that loss. He was a damned good person and he wanted to make a difference by coming forward. Whew… I need another minute…"

After wiping his eyes with a tattered red bandana, blowing his nose like a loud gust of wind, he stood to stretch—reaching up and exerting a forceful grunt that released the remaining effects from pent up sorrow and tension. Taking a prolonged, deep breath and settling comfortably into his chair, a congenial smile broadened as he spoke with appreciation.

"Again, thanks for allowing me to emote without judging me. I'd like to tell you something that keeps me motivated and hopeful about the man Will met. An ET appeared in the flesh to him. Will was clear this guy is a savvy insider who knew the difference between black budget, high tech spacecraft and robots or holograms, versus the sleek, seamless beauty of cosmic methods of transport and bonafide ETs. He described the depth of compassion of the ET's crystalline eyes, and the green glow that emanated from the chest area, *a gorgeous soul who was shimmery white, no hair, no ears, and a tiny mouth.* What that traumatized survivor said next blew me away—he described the ET's gentle nature and profound kindness that *soothed his soul* for the first time since the horrific twist of fate began with his employer. The ET took his hand and telepathically told him they were going somewhere safe, inside the body of Gaia.

"He suddenly lost consciousness. When he woke up, he was inside a room of soft pink and violet hues. During the ordeal in the black-project military craft, he was tortured and indescribably wounded, yet when he opened his eyes, within the effulgent soft light inside Gaia's body, he had no residual fear or pain. His mind was sharp. He wondered how that happened. He described two men, tall and highly empathic, who spoke with him, briefed him on his location, and told him that he could go back to the surface. This guy I'm speaking about had endured countless surgeries, had debilitating neurological damage, yet was totally healed. I don't know what happened when he came back from being in the care of the ET. Friends... prepare yourselves... we're going to meet him. We can find out more from him directly."

Staring at Jake, their faces froze with astonishment.

"How did you connect with him?" John asked dumbfounded.

"I didn't. I got a call from Will early this morning before we went to the cove. Apparently this guy knew someone who knows Will. That brave whistleblower came here recently to meet and learn from Will and his community."

"What the hell?!" John said looking mystified and befuddled.

Sophia smiled and asked, "Do you know how tall the benevolent ET was?"

"Very tall, about eight feet," Jake answered. "That did not escape my attention. I recall that you described a similar ET from your lucid dreams.

"I want to keep this between the three of us for now, okay?"

"Agreed," Sophia answered, smiling unreservedly and leaning forward with keen interest to hear more of Jake's jaw-dropping news.

"Definitely," John said, looking shell-shocked by the revelation.

Jake continued. "Will and *Dutch*, the guy I've been talking about, want to meet at the monolithic circle. We can meet them there in a few minutes. I'm guessing that Dutch convened with Will at his sacred grounds this morning to prepare for meeting us. Can we head that way?"

"Jake, why didn't you tell us about this immediately?" John asked, looking perturbed. "This is damned important! It's pretty insane news, don't you think?! Instead of telling us, you headed to the cove like normal and we ate a leisurely lunch while you were holding this back the whole f**king time? Why?"

"Buddy," Jake said passionately, while directly gazing into John's eyes to make a soulful connection. "I felt you needed time to fully devote yourself to your relationship with Angelica. This crazy news would have distracted you from being with her... taken you away from giving her your one hundred percent focus. You two deserved to have that dedicated time together. I never bullshit you or hold back anything. It was about timing. That's all. NO hidden motives. Will knew Angelica was coming. To tell you the truth, I think the whole town knows. So, although he usually contacts you about rituals and ceremonies, Will wanted to give you space to be with Angelica. If I was wrong, I apologize."

"Sorry," John said, looking away and pausing to collect himself before addressing Jake again.

"Thanks for respecting my time with Angelica. I appreciate you. In full transparency, brother, I am sitting here stunned by your revelation. Dutch is one of hundreds of people who have suffered inconceivable horrors at the hands of damned callous organizations that operate in the underbelly of our world, right under our feet. They seem invincible. I've read numerous, similar accounts, so this isn't new to me. I apologize for dumping my unfounded conclusions and defensive crap on you. This subject throws me for a spin, much like it does you. True confession, you know that I was obsessed for a while with first hand whistleblower accounts of what's going on. I've ranted about this often enough, right? The problem remains how to get Congress, the president, and the military-industrial complex to give a rat's ass about the depth and breadth of its relevance."

Jake smiled warmly, his eyes sparkling with friendship. "No worries. I get it. It's f**king frustrating. This is why we're engaged in our work. We have to instigate massive change and sometimes that includes disclosing gut-wrenching truth. There's no other way that our species can survive. We have to become brutally honest with ourselves and each other. There's no more time for wearing blinders, or cowering from emerging realities that trigger our emotions.

"How about we head over to the megaliths? As usual, in our unpredictable cove-adventures, I am prepared to be flabbergasted."

# CHAPTER 17

# MYSTERIES OF THE COSMOS

With a warm and respectful greeting, Will approached Jake, John, and Sophia as they entered the circle.

"Thank you for coming," he said. "I am pleased to introduce you to my new friend, Dutch. Dutch's family came to the U.S. from the Netherlands, thus his nickname."

Confidently and congenially, Dutch came forward to shake their hands. His bald head was riddled with scars, deep caverns of missing tissue conspicuously covered his left bicep and forearms, and his ears were gruesomely disfigured. Yet his smile shone with confidence and amiability.

After they exchanged names and expressed deep respect for each other's work, John could no longer contain his curiosity.

"Dutch, why did you ask to meet us?"

Will motioned for the group to sit on homespun blankets he'd spread on the ground. He blessed the circle with fragrant herbs and shook a rattle methodically around each one's head. The gentle afternoon breeze wafted the pungent scent around them while birds continued their serenade with chirps and delightful twittering. After a brief pause and with soft rays of sunlight gently filtering through the trees, a hush came over the circle as Dutch began to speak.

"Not that long ago, I planned to end my life… there was nothing good… safe… or worth the endless suffering that I was going through. I wanted to become a whistleblower, to warn the

U.S. government, at all levels, of the impending catastrophe that we could face if they don't step up and demand accountability and transparency from the military-industrial complex. Even with brain damage, I could offer names, share locations, and open a nasty can of worms. I knew full well they'd kill me but by then, I *flat out* didn't care! I was ready to die. My life was a psycho-physical nightmare. Worse, though, I didn't know who to trust with my story. Without warning, a cosmic being appeared to me one night. The pure love of his energy field was so intense it made me fall to my knees.

"Sophia—why are you crying? It was a good thing. I promise!"

"Yes, I agree. It's good," Sophia agreed. "I've felt that same love from an extra-terrestrial. Just recalling it, my heart overflows with tears of tenderness and deep-seated affection for all of my ET brothers and sisters."

Dutch's awe-struck face expressed wonderment. Unable to speak, he lowered his head for a moment. Then he looked up again, connecting with Sophia's captivating eyes.

"Will was right," Dutch said in a soft murmur. "He said when I met you all I'd immediately know I was with kindred spirits. He said I could trust you and I'd experience *a safe harbor for guilelessness*, releasing my crippling fear of vulnerability."

Choking back tears, he cleared his throat, paused to collect himself, and continued to share his story with his unexpected, confounding new acquaintances. "Damn! I haven't spoken with anyone else who met an ET like that, except staff in the black projects. But they ruthlessly turned on those beings like they did me. Thank you, Sophia. Your response means the world to me."

Dutch began describing the extra-terrestrial he'd met. "He was tall, shimmery white, and his eyes…" He trailed off, his own eyes distant as he recalled their effect on him.

John cleared his throat; his raised brows displayed astonishment. "Were they piercing, crystalline blue, wide at the outer edges, and set at a slightly upward angle?"

Dutch nodded.

"I'll be damned!" John said with the excitement of a four-year-old child. "That's the description Sophia shared when she described her extraordinary moment with the one she met. He is the *same one*. I can feel it! Who is he? Where is he from?"

Laughing heartily and shaking his head in wonderment, Dutch paused for a moment.

"Again, folks," he said, "this is not the conversation that I expected. I was prepared to have to convince you I was telling the truth about my encounter. Then I'd have to build a case for his existence and my capacity to speak with him. This is one hell of a relief!

"He indicated to me that he's been here many times but is highly selective about anyone he connects with. He knows about the black projects intimately, but has never worked in them. However, some of his comrades have done so in the hopes of influencing those humans to desist from their reckless pursuit of higher tech and more power at the expense of the collective human race, who they simultaneously deprived of vital technologies. They refuse to work with them now; they went to their galactic council and asked to be relieved of their duties. The request was accepted. That worried me because I didn't want humans to get a reputation cosmically as a planet of assholes. He said it's the opposite. They are pulling for us one hundred percent.

"It is clear that I don't need to brief you on hundreds of horrific stories of what happens to military staff who stumble onto one of these black projects or get brought in innocently only to realize later that they know too much and will pay the highest price for that knowledge. Like me, they have no idea of the scope and substantial, portentous power of this highly organized structure—carefully hidden in secret places underground all over North America.

"This magnificent extra-terrestrial being explained to me that humans need to enter the depths of the planet to learn from the beings who have inhabited those regions for eons, and to avoid military bases—without exception. He also asked me to start working with indigenous people, to learn their ways of connecting to *the unified field.* Doing that puts me in a flow with *the field* to receive and emit the highest frequencies of information possible. It's pretty crazy that I didn't think of *love* being one of those frequencies—the ET insisted that pure love is paramount and I better hook up with the joy frequency, too. Before my encounter with him, those vibes didn't seem radical or impressive at all. But all it took to convince my rigid, logical thinking-mind that it needed a reboot was a few minutes of saturation in his vibrations of love and bliss. I had definitely lost entrainment with those powerful frequency bands.

"Will said you know about quantum physics and how frequency works, so I won't bother with descriptions and explanations of why elevation of frequency matters. It's great that you are familiar with the machinations of the invisible world we live in, otherwise you'd be pretty shocked to know that when

I came to this circle one morning, the same ET appeared. He was very interested in your group. He wanted us to meet. But he didn't say why."

John sat pensively looking at Dutch and then his gaze slowly rose beyond the top of the towering trees. After a couple of minutes of stillness, connecting unreservedly with the field, he spoke.

"Dutch, we're planning to go under the surface. We're following ancient maps but we don't know what we'll encounter. Obviously it hasn't escaped my attention that the ET told you that going there is important. What's your background, your educational field?"

"A PhD in molecular physics by education," Dutch said modestly in a quiet tone, "but my black projects work was with devices that extract energy from the field around us. That's the non-technical description. I've had extensive training in weaponry as well, which I'm not interested in applying or pursuing further."

"No worries. Weaponry isn't our gig. Have you operated the advanced free energy equipment or any related craft?" Jake asked with amazement in his voice.

"Does a bear shit in the woods?" Dutch answered, laughing and relaxing even more. "I've driven the craft and studied the reverse engineering protocols. In fact... my level of experience may have been threatening to the *higher ups* in the program."

"Would you consider going with us as a navigator?" Jake asked. "We have two boats and we have to cross a subtle membrane, a quantum portal, to go deeply into Gaia's body. We have a confirmed navigator for one boat but the other navigator is getting cold feet. Does that interest you?"

"Are you shitting me?!" Dutch said, suffused with astonishment. "I am all in! I'd be a damned fool to disregard the synchronistic nature of our meeting and this amazing conversation!"

Shaking his head in disbelief, Jake addressed Dutch, saying, "One thing's for sure, this is definitely not what I expected when Will invited us here. I'm going to ask Justin, our lead navigator, to meet you as soon as possible. He's an absolute genius of impeccable character. I know his father and I've developed implicit trust in him and Justin. Of course, we need to see if you and Justin are compatible. You are both way above our heads in the physics area so you'll need to get together and see how your approaches and backgrounds mesh. Justin will make the call but It seems damned important to schedule a meeting, sooner rather than later."

Justin had grown up in a Mensa program for gifted children. By the time most young people would obtain a university degree, Justin had three master's and a PhD in physics. Yet he was a loner, deeply connected to *the field*, like an ancient monk or sage in the Himalayas. His introverted style, however, was blended with insatiable curiosity which drew him into conversations in which he could share and learn. He and Dutch found comfort in their friendship—two souls who were not mainstream but shared hearts of pure loving-kindness and open-hearted awareness of the unified field and its massive potentiality.

"Dutch, are you possibly being tracked?" John asked in a subdued voice. "If you come with us, could we inadvertently invite your adversaries to follow us?"

"I get your concern. It's important to know that when I left, they tried to damage my brain, worse than a mind wipe. They don't think I am able to function normally and they think that took care of me as a problem. But the extra-terrestrial brought it all back somehow. He allowed me to speak about my encounter with him to my friends—I thought they would believe me and it was going to be obvious that I was healed. It was so f**king tough to accept that they didn't notice the change, they didn't even slightly support me, or believe I could recover. They saw me ONLY as pathetically flawed and broken. From the black projects, I had learned that cognitive dissonance is very difficult to override. It's a neural wiring thing. So at that point I accepted that it made no sense to try to convince them, or anyone else for that matter, that I was okay.

"Unfazed, the ET told me to start acting erratic. Since I had zero support, the idea was to let my *nay-sayers* think my healing was a charade. So I started to act like I did before my healing. No one has any interest in me now—my ties are cut and I am okay with that. Regardless of whether or not I join you, I'd like to talk to Justin about a very simple, yet highly effective shield you will need."

John cocked his head to the side pensively as he said, "Jake has a friend, Malcolm. He's a genius, now retired from Stanford, who is helping to construct the boats. Jake, if Justin and Dutch feel they can work well together, can we discreetly introduce Dutch to Malcolm? They'd meet here."

"Sounds good to me," Jake said. "If it works out with Justin, I'll set it up.

"Dutch, once under the surface, we don't know specifically what you would be required to do while we conduct archeological surveys and anthropological projects."

"I won't concern myself with that now," Dutch said. "Keep in mind that I have a cosmic friend who will likely let me know anything that needs my attention."

With John's prompting, Dutch shared many of the tragic stories he'd learned or witnessed of deception, brutality, greed, and hoarding of free energy devices and other technologies that could change life on the surface of the planet. Jake and John were mesmerized by the scope and depth of the inconceivable treachery and deliberate deception.

Sophia sat quietly nearby, which ignited Will's curiosity. He joined her in the spirit of inquiry.

"Sister, what is at the heart of your profound rumination?"

Emerging from her reverie, she flashed a friendly smile towards him and he responded with rapt attention.

"When I met the ET that Dutch mentioned, he told me that I had the *capacity to share codes of unicity*. He said giants from another universe had trained me long before the last ice age. At the time, his words felt cryptic and confusing. Yet today, they make more sense. As Dutch spoke about the ET, I was reminded that one of Jake's friends said recently that according to biophysics, when a human being enters a *flow state*—a higher level of consciousness—for prolonged periods consistently (as we've all done) there are activations of certain *mobile genetic elements* in the brain that affect genomic recombinations of *neural stem cells*. He postulated that it may be possible for them to migrate to the hippocampus, the dentate gyrus, and neocortex—which could facilitate higher cognitive function. He explained further that these are *recombination events* which could result in activating *dormant regions* within genes. I have shivers! Listen carefully to the next part.

"This means when we are in the flow state for long enough periods, we ignite a subtle biological condition in which a higher probability exists for producing a *novel* gene, a novel protein which could induce *higher states of consciousness*. Imagine those parts of the brain that I described illuminating us cognitively! The capacity for *unlimited unicity* could be produced in the same way. If we move consistently into a flow state, a highly coherent quantum state corresponding with a dormant genetic region can potentially be activated. From what I understand, these genetic regions are a sleeping miracle that we can awaken by engaging consistently in the flow state. This is not just a random, wooly idea. It's biologically possible because of the quantum mechanics governing our inconceivably complex cellular structure. I am not trying to become a biologist or geneticist, but I want to unravel the potential for evolution that we usually don't realize is possible. Can you follow this?"

"Yes, dear sister, please say more."

"As I expand my ability to raise my consciousness, I develop a new protein that facilitates vigorous signaling of *subtle energetic information that is not even in my vicinity*—it can reach out and instantaneously access information from anywhere and everywhere across the infinite unified field.

"That's my limited understanding of how it works. The bottom line is that *the flow state matters*—there is a connection between being in the flow sate and direct physiological responses. Maybe that is how I can share codes of unicity far and wide. And others can do the same. I was likely born with the gene fully functioning but this amazing gene is innate to all of us. This puts the reins of our future undeniably in our hands. When I met the ET, I was relentlessly practicing being in flow, and I am intuiting that the ET wants me to understand how important this flow state is in relation to genetic expression for all of us.

"The *flow state* is our greatest ally and hope for the future. If we turn on this *unicity* gene, the field will receive its vibration as our frequencies stream uninhibitedly into the field to be received by those who *align* with that frequency. Imagine the possibilities for advancing human evolution when this happens for a lot of people who exchange information with the field from this level of higher frequency. We don't need to fear the nefarious behavior of anyone expressing it, including those who have enjoyed a surreptitious life of unimaginable power for too long. Rather than fight them, we can hold them accountable while fearlessly and tenaciously raising our vibrations for increasing increments of time.

"The ET wanted me to be in wonder and curiosity about all of this. Is this why the codes in my blood and bones were important? I felt his presence here today. His love was palpable. I definitely needed to hear this. Grace will be ecstatic to hear what he said. This is an auspicious omen. What do you think?"

"I felt Spirit's blessing today. I am in awe and gratitude."

"Will, how do you attract people like Dutch? He feels genuine, kind, and open to inner expansion. He's a perfect fit for you and your community plus he's super sweet. Can you articulate how you magnetized him into your energy fields? I've written about this phenomenon and I am always trying to find ways to explain things that defy explanation. Your connection with *the field* is mind-blowing."

Will winked and said, "Attracting people and situations is easy if you tune in regularly to the magical whispers of Spirit and flow in the cosmic river without questioning inspired guidance."

"Ahhh... those soft whispers," Sophia said dreamily.

Will gave her a moment to savor her connection with Spirit before continuing.

"Like you and so many others on this magnificent planet, after Dutch met the ET, he wanted to learn meditation, and any other esoteric means to enter subtle dimensions, from an authentic shamanic tradition. A dear, trusted friend of his, Trenton, with whom he'd stayed in contact, moved here ten years ago. Trenton has been a benevolent donor and supporter of my community. In the miraculous way of *the field*, as you call it, his friend asked if I would meet with Dutch. Spirit whispered to me to accept. Dutch is brave... a very good person. I've observed that he has a cosmic shield of some kind, which prevents adversaries, or low-vibe perpetrators, from seeing him anymore. Our people are familiar with such phenomena."

Sophia paused reflectively to integrate Will's words.

"Wow, he has a beautiful story of raising his frequency from despair and searching for a way to let that process unfold into advanced levels of vibration. He's lucky to have met you. If he hangs out with you, he'll soon be whispering regularly with Spirit."

Will smiled warmly and chuckled as Sophia continued.

"I appreciate your work on this earthly plane because I realized in our early encounters that your lineage is not reticent to admit you come from the stars. That was fascinating to me at the time, but not as *relevant* as it is for me today.

"You may not know, but our circle of friends has sat by firelight countless times having lengthy conversations about how our ancient DNA affects us and each other. We peeked back into history many thousands of years. The repeating patterns of emotional and societal architectures were undeniable. However, when I study and meditate with the cave-drawings from your ancestors, particularly the ones that Jake says go back thirty thousand years or more, I observe higher level cultural expressions such as unicity, with much different emotional patterns than we exhibit today. Why? There is one particular drawing that matters most to me. Jake says it is off-the-charts because neither he nor anyone else can conclusively date it. My curiosity is peaked because, if the cave art is true, then we are *millions of years older* than we've been led to believe, and we have already expressed the unicity gene in full abandon before, and lived a much higher expression of ourselves.

"The *whispers* tell me we have the neurological, cellular DNA complexity, and heart-brain coherence capacity to remember who we are and up-level the expression of our human potential. The real problem for humanity, and for myself, is we've forgotten who we are and the miracles we are capable of generating. Under the surface, there is someone or something that can help us to shift higher in frequency, both personally and collectively. The whispers concerning this subject are relentless."

"The *whispers*, dear Sophia, may become louder. You are in alignment with the thread of life. May you follow the thread without doubt or past conditioning which can break the connection. You are definitely the ancient Mystic from our tradition! I told you this long ago. It is time to remember your roots."

Will sat reflectively for a moment. His eyes softly closed and he became pristinely still, entering a silent, profound reverie.

As his eyes opened like the resplendent dawning of the sun, he asked tenderly, "May I bless you with an eagle feather?"

Sophia nodded. The feather gently encircled her head with mystical emanations of foresight, higher vision, and the power to soar endlessly to unlimited heights of frequency.

CHAPTER 18

# SOPHIA AND WALL STREET

On a particularly mild, late autumn morning, daybreak filled the canvas of the sky with bright pink clouds and elongated rays of golden light. With their morning brew of choice in hand, Jake, John, and Sophia sat on Megan's porch as mesmerized spectators of a breathtaking sunrise unfolding in hues and tones that eclipsed their desire to speak. Work at the cove would resume soon as the team concluded their enormous preparations. Yet the three friends greeted the day, as always, with a sense of ease, wonder, and cheerfulness.

Breaking the morning spell of nature's artistic mastery, John looked at Sophia quizzically. With his brows wrinkled, emphasizing his curiosity, he asked, "After all of the circles by the fire, over many years of working with you at the cove, you never told us why you and Nate decided to leave New York and exactly what he did for a living. Is it a secret?"

Her eyes caught his in a brief yet profound exchange of intimate friendship and connection as she said amiably, "It's a long story. Pour another cup of coffee and I'll tell you."

Jake decided to top up his coffee, too. He and John nestled into the comfy porch chairs, looking expectant, and John gave her a twinkling smile and a nod to begin.

"I didn't purposefully hide anything from you. It's just that there are parts of my life that are sensitive as far as safety goes. Yet as time's gone by (and many of the people involved are either in jail or out of power), the time feels right to tell you my backstory. Make yourselves comfortable because, like I said, it will take me a few minutes to explain it all."

They looked at her, bewildered by her introduction. She smiled a little ruefully and launched candidly into her past.

"While running errands on what seemed like a typical, gorgeous fall morning in Connecticut—a brisk wind, lots of golden leaves fluttering down from the trees, and a crystal blue sky—I got a call from Nate, unexpectedly. He seemed nervous and there was definitely urgency in his voice. 'Darling, I can't explain. I need you to act swiftly. Fill up the SUV, go to the bank and withdraw as much cash as they will allow, and go home to pack as if the house is on fire. Put what matters most in the car. I'll be there soon. Remember, act as if the house is on fire.'

"In a panic, I arrived home with my mind filled with images of an apocalypse. Had he heard a news report that I didn't? Nothing was on the radio on my way home. Filled with adrenaline, I grabbed pillowcases and stuffed them with special mementos and photos along with what felt like essentials. Nate arrived exceptionally fast from the city and said nothing except that I could make three more trips to the car before we'd have to leave. He told me to grab our winter coats and boots. Where were we going? Alaska? Why the panic and urgency?

"I didn't dare ask because he was zipping through the house throwing his things into a large laundry bag and reaching for specific books. He seemed to have a clear idea about what was needed. Yet I felt clueless. Every time I looked around our home, I realized my mind was trying to kick in and assess or strategize what to do. But everything was happening too quick for my mind to grasp. So I kept scooping up whatever I felt inspired to take.

"Nate moved past me rapidly, opening the back door of the car, and threw in a huge armload of my clothes with hangers dangling from them. I realized this was not a drill. All clothes left behind were going to be gone forever.

"My heart pounded harder as I made the three last trips, loading my most valued possessions from the house, anything that felt irreplaceable and special.

"Nate moved past me in the bedroom, without saying a word. He pulled something out from beneath the mattress and asked me to get in the car. As a final gesture of my house-on-fire packing, I grabbed a couple of comfy throw pillows, a soft, cashmere blanket that was a wedding gift, and my favorite brush—which felt a bit weird with a house supposedly burning down. After the three trips... I headed to the garage.

"I noticed our snowshoes nearby on the wall and tossed them on top of the clothes in back along with a small cooler. After going briefly to the kitchen, he joined me, and we headed out ... to where?

"We drove past New York City in total silence. Looking back, I realize that I was in shock and that Nate looked traumatized and frightened. An hour passed while I sat staring out the window at everything we were clearly leaving behind; likely forever. Without any context for our escape, I kept wondering if our house was burning, in reality or figuratively?

"The silence broke when I saw Nate look in the rearview mirror and start laughing. He reached over and squeezed my hand as he asked, 'Did you bring our snowshoes?' I reminded him that he'd told me to bring our winter coats. He laughed again. "And I brought our ski boots, hiking boots, tennis shoes, electric gloves, and best wool socks, too." He laughed so hard that it finally broke the tension. Maybe the world was not ending on that afternoon as we sped steadily toward the sunset. He still didn't explain anything, and my intuition told me not to demand an explanation. I'd wait for Nate to reveal what precipitated the madness we'd been thrust into—suddenly and mysteriously.

"After five hours of driving, we stopped for gas. He'd emptied our safe and seemed to have a lot of cash. As he went inside to pay, he told me we couldn't use credit cards.

"After a quick restroom break, we continued our westward journey. I noticed that he'd brought a bunch of fruit, a large carton of almond butter, his favorite crackers, and a bag of supplements and vitamins. He'd also grabbed our two favorite teacups, the imported tea that we loved, and the electric tea kettle. He'd tossed a dozen bottles of water and a loaf of fresh sourdough bread on top of the clothes, and for some inexplicable reason, he'd grabbed a photo that I had taken on our honeymoon on Lanai of a gorgeous little hummingbird—such weird, random things to bring on this sudden journey. I wondered what he was planning? Where were we going? And why?

"After about three hours he announced that we only had six or seven more to go before reaching our destination. He asked if I would I drive for a few. What could I say? I felt like I'd been transported to another universe—my predictable reality had been shattered.

"As we continued into the thick darkness of night, he looked at me and said, 'I love you so much and I am sorry about the insanity I am putting you through. Just so you know, we are headed for Rockford, Illinois.'

"That last, tiny morsel of information sent me over the edge. With a whole lot of frustration, I launched into a tirade fueled by my justifiable confusion.

"'We just went through a supposed house fire, threw a bunch of random things into the car, abandoned our house and previous life, and we've been driving like a bat out of hell for hours—all so we could go to *Rockford, Illinois*?! Sure, I guess we need a winter coat there, but I am going to slam on the brakes and turn around if you don't tell me WHY we are going there! What the heck happened, Nate? This is crazy!

"He looked like a chastised little boy about to burst into tears. I've always been empathic and could feel and sense Nate's fear, sorrow, and grief. My heart melted. I apologized for my outburst and made a feeble attempt to take back what I'd said. Clearly, he was devastated by this bizarre ordeal.

"Whatever was going on had to do with his father and a decision that Nate had to make in a matter of minutes. He'd had no time to over-think it. He was clear that we had to act immediately and never look back. If we hadn't left, we would not have gotten another chance to get out. He said our lives would have been anchored to something *insidious*. He asked for my patience and promised to tell me everything when we arrived in Rockford. We were going to the home of one of the few people on the planet with whom he felt complete trust. We had to get far from New York City and past Chicago, too.

"Back then, there were no smart phones, sophisticated tracking devices, or GPS. That meant we were truly cut loose. These days our escape would have been harder.

"From that point forward, my awareness became inwardly drawn. I just gripped the wheel and drove resolutely westward.

When were almost to Rockford, we stopped for gas and Nate called his friend. He used a phone card with an hour of call time allotted to it. Today, that seems antiquated. But at the time, it saved us from being tracked.

"After our seemingly endless journey, we were bleary-eyed, beyond exhaustion. I can hardly describe how deeply my heart longed for evidence that we could find a safe haven. Finally we pulled off onto a rural road. Winding through the dark it seemed like we were going nowhere, just bumping over the unpaved road, our headlights illuminating the rough road heading into a void. Suddenly, we rounded a sharp curve and were met by a dazzling display of thousands of twinkling lights greeting us as though it was Christmastime—welcoming us home. As surprising as the house-on-fire had been, this magnificent estate in the middle of nowhere—private and secure—was astonishing. Its enchanting vibes captivated and charmed us. There was no holding back my tears of relief. Instantly, I felt the tension of the day relaxing its iron-fisted grip. Uninhibited by my frazzled nerves, I stopped the car in the middle of that dark, rural road and stared in wonder at our good fortune. Nate gently took my hand and kissed it tenderly... oh so sweetly!"

Submerged in remembrance, Sophia gently closed her eyes. While her soft tears fell intermittently, John and Jake sat in pristine stillness absorbing the magnitude of the story that was unfolding from Sophia's startling revelations. When her breathing regained its methodic rhythm, she slowly opened her sparkling blue eyes, as captivating as magnets. Composed, she continued her history, while her voice shifted to a more lighthearted tone.

"The couple who greeted us exuded warmth and kindness. Nate and his friend embraced like brothers. I still recall the intimate way their eyes met in friendship. They were steadfastly connected. This was a rare and precious relationship which allowed me to instantly comprehend why Nate trusted this man with our lives.

"Feeling more relaxed, everyone introduced each other. Nate's unshakable confidence in his pure-hearted friend allowed me to relinquish the fear I'd resonated with all day. Nate told his friend, Damien, that I didn't know anything and since we were on the road all day, it was time for him to give me an overview of the situation.

"From the moment that Damien's wife, Carrie, welcomed us into her home, I breathed deeper and felt safer. She quickly became a close friend. Her gorgeous, thick, black hair cascaded over her shoulders and even though it was late at night, she was wearing bright red lipstick. I sensed that she infused her life and everything in it with passion. She was confident, kind, and loved to cook for others. Over the ensuing days, we got to taste her sassy, lively approach to living that merged with a profoundly soft loving-kindness. That night, she'd made a super-rich Mac and Cheese which we devoured like manna from heaven. My body melted into nerve-restored comfort and culinary bliss.

"Being with Carrie, the world felt joyful and optimistic. As I got to know her, I observed that she always expected things to work out well and she was like a child in her capacity to wonder how life could get even better. It was like we'd known each other forever. While I was quieter and leaned more towards the esoteric side of life, she was determined and bold. More important than differences was that we shared a common focus on being open to unexpected possibilities in life and refusing to feel like a victim. Through our conversations, it was clear that we both took responsibility for our response to life. Because Nate and I were entrusting our safety to her and Damien, my bond with her was the relief I was longing for. I felt unreservedly at ease and implicitly confident with them as our allies.

"With introductions and dinner complete, Nate and I headed to bed. We were exhausted yet wired. Under the soft linens and cushy pillows (it was like settling in at a resort) my nervous system could relax and unwind. Nate gently embraced me, pulled me close, and kissed me compassionately, reassuring me the worst was behind us. He explained what had happened earlier in the day satisfactorily. With this reassurance, I nestled more deeply into his embrace, feeling safe for the first time since our nightmare began. As he spoke, my mind settled down and the muscles in my jaw, neck and entire body began to loose their vice grip. Enthralled, I listened to the spellbinding, intense events that led to our bizarre escape.

"In a demanding manner, his stepfather had charged into Nate's office and told him the firm was promoting him. Nate wasn't expected to react with elation. Rather, he was *required* to be in absolute compliance with whatever the company required of him, plus he was acutely aware that he'd be entering a deeper level of his father's heartless world. I don't recall if I've shared with you that Nate's stepfather had strong ties to British and German bankers and financiers, as well as closely knit elite allies in the global banking system.

"I think I did tell you that he had joined the Synarchist society of my mother's family. So it's no surprise that his chosen form of government was an oligarchy filled to overflowing with Synarchists. He proclaimed as much in my initial meeting with him when I was a teen. Hearing his proclamations then I remember I felt my skin crawl. With creepy unapologetic idealism, he delighted in describing for me his glorious vision of a ruthless Synarchy-style elitist government in this country. I'd endured similar eerie conversations with my own father, so I wasn't shocked to hear Nate refer to his stepfather as being similar to my dad, *patronizing, unyielding, and self-centered.* By the time Nate finished high school, he was aware that his stepfather's circle of elite friends and closest business associates shared what Nate called a *distorted, hubristic worldview.* His stepfather worked in the upper echelons of Wall Street as a banker and financier and he left no other options for Nate than joining the banking and investment firm his stepfather co-owned with like-minded, upper crust Wall Street investors.

"On the day of our fire-drill-escape, once promoted, Nate would have managed a project that involved meetings in Europe and Scandinavia. It had to do with one of their main clients, a global bank at the apex of the international financial system, and other dominant global financial institutions. Nate said chills rippled through his body—he knew about these kinds of projects but had never wanted any part of them.

"It went like this: When a country was in financial trouble, one of the big global banks would lend money to the country in crisis. This would, of course, devalue the country's currency, and they would have to start laying off workers in government, and then roll out lay-offs in the private sector to pay for the loans. With devalued currency, high unemployment, high interest on loans, and a failing economy, of course the country would not be able to pay off its loans, so the banks would ask for access to its natural resources instead, basically taking ownership of the country's assets.

"Nate knew if he said yes to this project, he would be a permanent insider. Wealthy beyond measure, but totally bound to the firm. From that point on, he could never say no to anything. If he did, they might kill him or harm me to punish him. I know that sounds like a movie plot, but it was our reality.

"Unfortunately, we were in a terrible predicament. He'd been told to catch a flight at six o'clock that evening to Europe. That's why we needed to be long gone by then. Two things happened that worked in our favor. First, a financial crisis hit within twenty-four hours. Pure luck for us. Next, his father had a heart attack about a week after we left. By then, we were on the West Coast, Nate didn't have insider information, and the firm had bigger fish to fry than a little guy like Nate.

"However, if we'd stayed, Nate was right. We would never have gotten another chance to break away.

"Like it was yesterday, I remember the night of our escape and the next month. I didn't totally relax until we saw in the news that his father was dead. Somehow, with that tie broken, we felt unshackled and free to create a new life.

"Nate always wanted to be an advocate for others. With his new friendships and old ones like Damien, he began a legal career of fighting chemical companies, Big Pharma, and other forms of advocacy. I didn't care that those cases were difficult and included dangerous opponents. After what we'd escaped from, the battles and inherent risks felt worthwhile.

"My sweet Nate was relentless, successful, and yet ultimately, he lost his life in the fight. He came down with a mysterious condition that slowly deteriorated his muscles—he believed that he'd been hit with a microwave weapon. Yet he wouldn't have had it any other way. He accumulated information that became his final victory. He told me to give it to Damien when I got a sign after his death.

"I didn't know that Gilda was aware of the information that Nate was holding onto. That's why she wanted time alone with him—to let him know that the information in the envelope would change everything, but he'd likely not live to see its radical effects on the world at large.

"On a visit to the shop where I met Megan, the owner handed me a teacup, almost exactly like the ones that Nate brought with us when we fled the East Coast. As I left the shop, a hummingbird hovered in front of me like a little helicopter. Recalling Hawaii and the photo Nate cherished from our honeymoon, I knew the time was right to send the package to Damien."

John was silent, his brow wrinkled, and he was staring at Sophia spellbound. "Was that what Nate grabbed from beneath the mattress—was it the now famous, *brown envelope*?"

Sophia smiled, her eyes dancing in childlike playfulness. In her delight, she shut them gently as though they were soft feathers drifting into restfulness. When she felt rejuvenated, she drew in a breath of intoxicating freedom. Opening her lovely eyes that had taken on an air of regality and wisdom as she aged, she answered in a hushed tone, "I can neither confirm nor deny anything."

"Are you shittin' me?" Jake exclaimed, his face wrinkled like John's with confusion and extreme shock. "You are the one who had the brown envelope that exploded the truth about Wall Street and global banking secrets?"

"My friends," Sophia said candidly, "I didn't know what was in the envelope nor the truth about the nature of Nate's debilitating illness. After the contents of the envelope were revealed and justice served, Damien explained to me what happened to Nate. Of course, I understood why Nate couldn't tell me. Damien had been in touch with Gilda and her friend Edith, Adele's mother. They made sure the contents went to the right people to begin taking legal action.

"My takeaway is that as a global community, we finally saw the truth behind tightly held veils of secrecy. Truth plummeted deeply into the ancient heart of that secrecy, and it exposed the greed that could never be satiated. Then it pierced the beast of deceit and oppression. The whole world responded with wide-eyed curiosity.

"Humanity realized that we were, and had always been, free. We were each blinded in different ways to the truth of our own greatness. For me it felt poetic, surreal, and magnificent. It was dramatic and immeasurable in both its fury and significance.

"Together, we realized how loving, resilient, and power-ful we are.

"After the intense, emotional, global reaction to the contents of that envelope, it was like the horses of our hearts broke open the gates that bound us to feeling hopeless and less-than others. We accepted that we were, and had always been, more power-ful and infinitely resourceful than we ever dreamed possible. We'd inadvertently enabled a massive structure of corruption and lust for power to endure for way too long. We collectively made a choice to be free from that system.

"We needed to allow the unicity gene to express by opening our hearts to each other. The Synarchist-style enthusiasts never saw the massive tidal wave of unicity forming in the unified field. That kind of solidarity within the working class wasn't in their worldview. Yet for us, it became our united focus. We fed our intention into the field and exponentially the field sent us each the information we needed to act in ways that supported our common intention. We became unrelenting and invincible.

"Remember, quantum science says that the greater the chaos, the greater the possibility for something new to emerge from the infinite field of potentiality. And wow is something new emerging, globally!

"We are beyond the secrets now and entering an exciting, groundbreaking paradigm. I'm immensely grateful we are doing this together. The freedom that Nate and Gilda fought for was worth their struggle and sacrifice. All of the whistleblowers, advocates, and truth-tellers will be vindicated.

"What a great life we've been given. How amazing that we got to see this moment in human history. Our world did not have to see the ominous, grim Synarchist dream become reality. On one level, their depraved dream is now a nightmare. They are frantically plugging up holes in their once impenetrable dam.

"Thank you, my precious friends, for always being here for me. I love you so much."

"I love you, too—more than I can ever convey," John said. "You are profoundly poetic as you describe our world. But I still get damned frustrated! I want faster and bigger change. It's been tough but we are making huge headway into creating an amazing planet, while holding onto our rights and human dignity. I appreciate your relentless writing about the flow state, unified physics from the perspective of mysticism, and how to move through the day with feelings of confidence and ease.

"After Illinois, did you and Nate work together?"

"We headed west," Sophia answered. "We went to Berkeley, California to be with some of Nate's friends from law school who advocated for people and natural resources—definitely Nate's cup of tea.

"That was where we met the wildest character of my life. Her name was Ginger. She was a distinguished astrophysicist and a completely uninhibited free thinker and creator. This incredible woman held a depth of curiosity that was unfathomable. Everything in her life was fascinating to her.

"One of Nate's friends wanted him to help with a lawsuit in which she was an integral witness in their case. I came along to take notes, which allowed him to focus on her words and gain a better understanding of her position. The first time I met her, she entered the conference room with a whoosh and plopped down in a comfortable chair in the corner. Her flaming red hair was imbued with light from the sunlight streaming through the window. I figured out pretty quick that this was a woman on fire. Nate and I joined her at her chosen spot in the room. This woman was not going to sit at a conference table nor do, or be, anything just because it was expected of her. She was a force to reckon with.

"After we were seated, Ginger leaned forward and rolled up her sleeves to reveal jaw-dropping tattoos on her forearms. On her left arm was an eagle, as vicious as you can imagine, it's talons gripping a man by the testicles. I was taken aback. Surely, a lot of people were shocked seeing that peculiar body art. Her right arm was totally different. It was an ethereal, gorgeous, goddess-style woman who was morphing into a dove, which was gripping the Earth with a spiral of stars and planets around it. The contrast of these images was stunning. Seeing our raised eyebrows, Ginger said, 'It's ying-yang, a balance of all things working together. That is the genesis of this art.'

"For her, it was an artistic expression of perfect harmony, pristine equilibrium. Engaging authentically with her, Nate easily dropped his agenda and allowed her to talk freely for several minutes. Having checked us out intuitively, she handed Nate secret documents that he needed in the case he was working on. The plaintiffs needed her help and that's all she cared about. She shared the sordid history of the company who was the defendant in this lawsuit and told us exactly who they aligned with in various government agencies. Even better, she shared aspects of the plaintiff's case that no one was considering.

"This woman was brilliant, uninhibited, and yet kind and caring.

"At one point, she suddenly pierced Nate's eyes with her intense gaze and said, 'Listen to me carefully. You are smart and you protect people. It's like you take them on as their surrogate mother. Damn! You really care! That can get you killed, son. Let me tell you something! You better get a little more of this eagle in you! You are taking on godless people. Sorry to be so blunt. Certain companies and their financiers are run by people who don't think like you. Love? Oh, honey! They love two things and that's power and control. People say it's about profit. But that just fuels their authority and influence. They are a bunch of sorry-ass monsters who are part of a system of control that's endured for centuries. Now, with advanced technology, they feel they can cut to the chase and finally rule the world. How thrilling and fulfilling for their puffed up egos! Of course, they also want to rule the Universe. They are fine if that happens a little later.'

"I recall her red hair glistening in the sunlight, casting an ethereal glow around her. She glared at Nate saying, 'All of your lawsuits will matter, but only cumulatively. And you'll need class action suits so many people can join and be affected in massive numbers by your wins. Nate, you have what it takes. Forget winning cases, it's about educating the world on what's happening. You need to write tirelessly. It may seem that it doesn't matter but down the line people will come to their senses and realize that this has been going on for too long. And they'll be severely pissed off. That's a good thing.'

"Then she looked at me and the hair on my arms stood up as she directed her fire my way saying, 'And missy Sophia better get her ass in gear, too. There are women and children being trafficked and it's happening under the noses of all of us. Black budgets fund it. Unbridled money laundering is an indispensable aspect of this heinous crime. Illegal proceeds look squeaky clean when legal resources in the financial system find ways to make monetary transactions appear legitimate. Churches, individuals, and cartels purportedly participate in this dark world of modern, human slavery. Some governments allegedly use trafficking to supplement war-funding and clandestine programs and projects. We had to confront the inconceivable tragedy that ensues when war-torn areas become undetectable locations for women and children—secretly kidnapped and forced into the trafficking industry.'

"Ginger was incensed that wars rage relentlessly on our planet. With passion from her *first hand experience* and with blazing fury exploding from her capacious eyes, she glared at me and said, 'Good humans are unjustifiably trafficked as collateral damage of the war machine. We have to stop ignoring this shameful egregiousness! We are unwittingly allowing a cruel, incessant side-effect of war to be inflicted upon our global sisters and brothers.'

"From her perspective, humanity was refusing to insist on peace and take a sobering look at a distasteful, shrouded industry which funds *insidious misery and immeasurable suffering* across the entire planet.

"I became breathless and the conversation became unquestionably personal when Ginger said, 'This corrupt industry has too many tentacles to count. The courts and social programs are corruptible, adding to the problem. Not all trafficking happens to poor people in foreign lands. It's time to get involved where you and Nate live, where you can offer hope to vulnerable victims, abandoned by their local legal system. Some courts pretend to be defenders and you will have to identify the ones who are perpetrators. I'll tell you the safe politicians, of which there are only a handful. Sorry to be the bearer of bad news. You two somehow signed an invisible contract to take the hard road. But it's the best f**king road to travel if you want to expose how life on Earth is really playing out. There is a sewer of corruption and sinister, inhuman dealings under our feet right now. Some of the work is carried out in jungles and remote areas, but not all of it.'

"Ginger got quieter, introspective and said, 'People's focus has to change from insignificant nonsense like sporting events, or arguing about who is the best president or prime minister. That's crap. It's a distraction. You have to open your eyes and see the gut-wrenching reality that human trafficking is based on maintaining control and to a lesser degree, making money. I can't pretend that it is not a massively lucrative business.

"'Your friends may shy away from having conversations about your work—it's a messy topic and uncomfortable for most people—including the infamous, black-robed perpetrators, inconceivably heinous rituals, and reprehensible, inexcusable offenses against good human beings. Prepare yourself... some friends will not believe you or will choose to avoid any conversations about your work. But who cares? If you care enough about human evolution, you'll keep going until the day when the world population's courage and compassion allows them to see what's been happening right in their backyard. Evolution will not rise if such a huge chunk of human suffering is repressed, sending hauntingly painful vibes into the field 24/7. That has to stop! Humanity will finally realize that a global Synarchy-style operation was hiding the truth all along, with plenty of help from their friends worldwide under the cloaks of religion, politics, and high class business. You get my drift, right? Century upon century, they remain tricksters and control freaks. They are inestimably, deceitfully cunning and utterly ruthless.

"'You have your work cut out for you. This slave-trade involves over twenty-nine million women and children worldwide. And it's growing daily. Mostly girls, they earn their keepers twenty to thirty thousand dollars each week. The girls stay busy and their oppressors remain wealthy.

"'Don't worry, my dear Sophia, you'll be fine. I see a herculean orange glow behind you. That's your guardian. You must have a big mission for the Creator to give you one of those giant orange protectors. Go get 'em, girlfriend! And don't ask me where to start. You will meet the right people if you say yes.'

"The more that I reflected on our meeting with Ginger, the more my soul urged me to make a change inside myself; to become more open to the wonder of life and less attached to my old assumptions and beliefs. I liked how authentic Ginger was. Her honesty gave her incredible confidence and strength to help the people who desperately needed her. More than that, she saw that the global population had been systematically domesticated like canines to stay inside, eat kibble, take a few pee breaks each day, and do what they are told. Sobering, for sure. She explained the system of control used by a focused global consortium and how easily the population can land psychologically under their thumb and never realize it. It's even easier now to maintain the longstanding global slave system using massive power of media to bombard us with relentless fear, anger, distraction, and a barrage of useless information that captivates us instantly. That's not where we have to end up! She showed us the power we have when we shift our attention inside to Essence, while in the outer world, we unite as a *whole* species instead as not into *divergent* groups; when we unite, we cultivate a common core of quantum energy that binds us and holds the frequencies of magic and mystery that can manifest as a phenomenal life experience for all of us."

Sophia looked at the ground for a minute, lost in thought. As she raised her head, she chortled and smiled. "I didn't get tattoos, guys, but I felt like they were etched on my arms many times! It's hard to talk about Ginger without being simultaneously rocked in the depths of the underbelly of life and brought into an intoxicating sense of joy for being alive. She was a living paradox of that eagle and dove. Without doubt, she was one of life's many unexpected treasures. Admittedly, she set me on fire. After meeting her, my determination and passion never wavered. If I fell into despair, I'd recall the *common core of quantum energy* she spoke about, and which I knew she relied on 24/7. I'd go there, regroup, and as I came back to my waking reality, I trudged onward with confidence that I was doing my best.

"After that meeting, Nate made a promise to himself to advocate for anyone who needed his help to overcome the oppression of exploiters, including their accomplices in religion, corporations, and/or government. Humanity is complex. Some people are in integrity and some are not. Nate wanted to protect people from the ones who'd unfortunately run amuck.

"There's more I can share with you. But we'd better head for the cove. Can we continue tonight?"

John nodded and said, "Sister, you never cease to amaze me! I look forward to hearing more this evening. It sounds like you met some pretty amazing characters in your work. Honestly, her revelations are not new to me but I'm pretty damned shocked to know you've been in the trenches addressing the *dark consortium's shenanigans*, as Gilda referred to them. Whoa! I had to take a breath and let that land! You must have seen some pretty dark crap doing that kind of work."

Shaking his head in wonderment, Jake said, "Holy shit! I can't imagine how you could top the story about the brown envelope! I'm sitting here in awe, knowing our sweet friend, Sophia, the epitome of a gentle, mild-mannered mystic, was the custodian of the invincibly bad-ass brown envelope! I'm still reeling from that truth bomb and you are saying there's more to come! Let's go to the cove. After this conversation, I may have to duck into the pyramid for a while!"

He flashed an affectionate wink towards her as the three friends continued laughing and teasing each other, enjoying supportive camaraderie, a fundamental foundation needed for the unpredictably precarious journey that lay ahead of them.

# CHAPTER 19

# MASTER MANIPULATORS CLUB

The cove was teeming with activity as boats were being assembled, and two teams gathered to review explicit directions for how this group could navigate into the deeper recesses of the cove, often called *The Inner Earth*. Sophia's friends referred to these coordinates in Gaia's body as *an adventure under the surface*. Will supplied ancient maps—some made by his ancestors and others sketched out from testimony preserved through oral tradition. From those oral legends, Will described many details about what to expect. In past millennia, his ancestors had traveled through subtle doorways (perhaps akin to that which modern science labeled *quantum portals*) to a subterranean world of benevolent giants.

The team was aware that many shamanic traditions acknowledge beings living comfortably and peacefully within the body of Gaia for millennia. Grace was thrilled that Sophia and her team were finally taking the step of going to find those beings who had welcomed their ancient ancestors long ago.

Sophia sent her daily text to Grace saying:

*We are heading out soon. The training we went through to still our minds, raise our frequencies, and be in the flow state will be put to the test. The odd thing is, I feel like I've done this kind of travel millions of times. Isn't that crazy? I have no fear about doing this nor do the others. Partly it is because of your dear hubby's help. I cannot wait for the whole team to finally meet Bob when we return. Our wise friend and counsel, Will, soothed Adele's concerns about taking her girls on such a perilous journey by sharing that he's confident they are mystics with a capacity to embrace the unseen unequivocally—with confidence, curiosity, and discernment. These girls are two extraordinary young women—fifteen and thirteen years old, respectively. Like ancient sages, they continue to exhibit subtle, innate gifts that baffle us most of the time. Since we've been training with Bob, I'm sure he must have told you how many times our jaws dropped as these two young ones displayed highly advanced intuitive skills and a surprising fearlessness when approaching unexpected situations. Thanks for agreeing to check in with Angelica from time to time. She's nervous and I can understand that she is going to miss Caitlyn and John. You and I can always connect in dreams. You are never more than a thought away, right?! BTW, this morning I told John and Jake the story of how Nate and I escaped. It was strange sharing it. It's like it happened to someone else. It feels surreal.*

Grace responded with her usual upbeat, reassuring friendship:

*Your life has always been a bit crazy. We are two eclectic souls and it is because I relate to your wild adventurousness that I can totally support this trip. OMG! I agree with Will's assessment of Adele's daughters. They are subtly equipped to thrive on this epic adventure. You and I would have been ecstatic at their age to do something like this! For the record, I love your escape story, especially about packing snow shoes. Love you, sister! Be sure to share Nate's epic solution to a real mess. I totally LOVE his genius. Go ahead and tell them even more about your adventures with him! Be sure to share how you learned first hand about manipulation. They'll love that story. Bob is looking forward to seeing everyone when you return. BTW I am glad that Dutch is going to join you. Jake and John really like working with him. I am not surprised you have an ET's blessing for the journey. That is so sweet!*

Smiling tenderly as she read the text, Sophia sat for a moment to take in Grace's love and supportive friendship. She had little time for reflection—it was time for meetings, taking notes, and planning. The cove was electric with anticipation of this long-awaited voyage.

As evening settled in, John built a roaring fire and everyone gathered around as usual. While working in the cove during the day, Jake couldn't resist telling everyone Sophia's revelation about the *brown envelope*, her daring escape with Nate, and her conversation with Ginger. With a backdrop of crickets in full chirping mode, the group settled in expectantly to hear more about Sophia's backstory, particularly about what she and Nate had been up to after their escape.

With elevated spirits and sparkling eyes, Sophia took in a rejuvenating deep breath, let it out slowly, and began to share.

"As Nate took on the horrific trafficking cases that Ginger had warned him about, I began assisting women whose children had been trafficked and provided help for children with trauma. Because Nate was a lawyer and saw the court system first-hand, he decided to specialize in cases related to corrupt courts. Nate's intel sniffed them out with more consistency than we thought possible.

"For instance, some social workers used false names and were assigned as case workers by unscrupulous family courts. The prey is usually single, low-income mothers, who watch in horror as their kids disappear into a nefarious system. We didn't attempt to dip our toes in the water of similar global systems. Our local work kept us incredibly busy."

"Sophia, I would never have pictured you doing this work." John said softly. "I visualized you teaching meditation and helping Nate. Thank you, on behalf of the millions of women and children who are submerged in that insane, terrifying system. Who was Nate up against? Who was behind the corrupt courts?"

"Because this is a behemoth-sized business," Sophia answered, "think collaboration between people in banking and finance, higher ups in the military, wealthy people, super stars, and all levels of global governments. And we can't ignore the enterprising criminals linked with drug cartels who keep the women and children working seven days a week. It was a combination of multiple areas in the trafficking system where we found heartbreaking reality checks and a well-oiled machine.

"Some people are actively involved, and others remain undoubtedly complicit. Since we worked in two states in the southern U.S. and focused on uncovering Family Court corruption, Nate and I touched only a tiny fraction of a huge problem. Although this unimaginable crime is ancient, it's gained momentum in our modern world. Of course, I'd never share names with you because that puts you in danger."

"Sophia, I underestimated you," Jake said. "I thought you were this sweetie pie who was frolicking in *la la land* in meditation, always happy and positive. I'm blown away that instead, you were able to remain happy and positive while dealing with one of the most treacherous, malevolent areas of human existence."

Smiling at Jake, she reached out and squeezed his hand lovingly, as she said, "Thank you, sweet friend.

"At this point of my story, there's something I should tell you. My capacity for doing the advocacy work, while facing the formidably harsh side of humanity, was greatly enhanced by vulnerable and sometimes gut-wrenching inner reflection. For many years, I'd observed an aspect of myself that was a master manipulator. I had learned how to do this in order to be safe with my father. Although my mother was a good person, she modeled this kind of manipulation and convinced me that I had to be like her to survive and thrive in life. That meant wearing certain clothes, making similar choices in social circles and parties, and demonstrating a demeanor of proper etiquette and propriety that felt uncomfortably fake. I could have won a Tony Award for the skilled role that I learned to play with friends, all the while wondering why I didn't have *genuine* relationships—except with Grace. I honed my skills until I could cleverly manipulate my relationship with my brother and almost everyone else in my social circle.

"My actions were not motivated by envy or greed. This manipulation was a survival tactic designed to feel safe and muster at least a molecule of self esteem. I never felt that I fit in with my family, or friends at school, so I thought that in order to 'belong' I had to figure out how to 'make' them accept me.

Only conversations with Grace were safe territory for sharing my genuine feelings.

"Unexpectedly, my world turned upside down when I started dating Nate. Seeking an authentic relationship, he was on my case about my *manipulation game*. He wanted to know the authentic me and every trick I'd developed did not work with him. He had a BS meter that was super sensitive. Poor Nate had to put up with a whole bunch of meltdowns where he called me out for manipulating him and I reacted with predictable tears and a toddler-style, pouting, defensive approach. Finally, after a thwarted attempt to convince him to spend the weekend at my family's beach house, I hit an inner wall and felt totally defeated.

"Looking out the window at a flock of birds swirling around a nearby grove of trees, I gradually started feeling calmer. Watching their elegant, synchronistic movement, my mind became increasingly still. As though I was watching a movie of my life, I recalled hundreds of times that my mother manipulated me. I'd been reading personal growth books about relationships for a while, but none of it had sunk in—until that day.

"Considering my mother's intentions, I realized that she was trying to do the right thing. In her worldview, from her unique perspective in the unified field, complying with the family's values and norms would keep me safe from brutal ridicule and physical harm. Plus, I'd have financial security. It never occurred to me that maybe, like me, she waffled between controlling her life and speaking her truth. I realized that she was trying to protect me from a world that she found oppressive and cruel. That's why she kept forcing me, through various threats, to be a 'good girl' and an upstanding member of our social circles.

"The next part was an ugly revelation. I saw how I cleverly and cunningly manipulated her. Our relationship was a dynamic based on who was *the master manipulator*. Ugh! … I owned how I manipulated my brother, father, and everyone in my world. Controlling life was my go-to defense mechanism.

"Through self reflection, a tenderness arose in me. Sobbing, feeling Nate's goodness and my love for him, I wondered if I could begin to give up controlling my world. Could I be courageous enough to honestly ask for what I want without any attachment to the outcome? I was aware that I had a brilliant mind. However, what if my heart was an untapped resource for wisdom? Manipulating everyone and filling my world with inauthenticity was exhausting and self-destructive. Vowing to stop blaming others for manipulating me, I started to notice who I was manipulating. Wow, that was a humbling practice!

"My first practical test was when, once again, I wanted to go to the coast, something which fed my soul. I knew Nate was swamped with work. In that moment of desire, I paused, and for the first time, I asked him if he would come with me, *without expectation* for the outcome. As he often did, he said that he couldn't go. Because my heart was open, I noticed his eyes, which reached me tenderly yet profoundly down to my soul. I could tell he was bracing himself for my usual tearful theatrics but when neither happened, we were able to just see one another. Silence was the language between us in that moment.

"Suddenly, he started laughing and asked, 'What's up? Isn't this the part where you get on my case and try to lay a guilt trip on me? Okay, Sophia, what's going on?'

"When I cried this time, it wasn't from disappointment or to manipulate him. Instead, the crust of my heart had a chance to crumble. For the first time I could remember, I could accept whatever the answer might be—in this case, his no. I realized his answer hadn't been my problem. Since childhood, manipulation and grasping for control had been the real problem. Starting that day, my objectivity expanded.

"Through Nate's legal work, I met master manipulators in droves. Yet, I couldn't judge them. I'd walked in their shoes. They didn't know I had terminated my membership in *The Master Manipulators Club*. In this invisible, psychological society, no one wants to admit to their membership. However, we all adhered to the rules of deceit, constantly trying to address our need to feel worthy and elevate our self esteem and self worth. We consistently implemented covert tactics of control like blame and shame. We recognized each other yet we never admit that we are part of this group, we just become more masterful by following our unspoken rules.

"Living outside of that old, familiar club, I took new actions that softened my heart and made space for my spirit to soar. My behavioral norms shifted into trusting the flow of life rather than rigorously controlling it; relentlessly developing a connection with Essence; and feeling into the wild depths of authenticity.

"There's no sugarcoating this part of my life. Finding authenticity and letting go of control were gradual processes which spanned many years. Each reinforcing experience of peace and contentment sustained my capacity to shift my behavior and old ways of thinking. Organically, I forgave my family, friends, and myself. As time went by, I no longer perceived myself as a victim of their potential wrath and condemnation."

Angelica's eyes glistened by firelight with a radiance of mutual affection. Speaking in a tone that captivated the group with her compassion, she said, "Because you stayed at my house after Nate's death, I knew some of your background. Tonight, though, your reflections hit my consciousness like a boulder of memory crashing down a mountain of forgetfulness. After my husband passed, I easily recalled the best parts of our life together and forgot the times we struggled. Yet tendencies like manipulation in those relationships can be subtle and linger past our loved one's death. What I understand about this subject related to you and Nate allows me to feel your struggle and understand better what motivates you today. Oh my Lord, Sophia, I feel like I suddenly know you on a deeper level. You didn't get an invisible struggle-free-pass from the universe that allowed you to bypass the tenacity and raw courage needed for spiritual growth. Thank you for your authenticity this evening."

"I agree one hundred percent." Caitlyn said, "Your story is beautiful. It thrust me into introspection. What are my motives when I interact with people? It's easier to lean into manipulation rather than to practice authentic communication. I'll definitely contemplate your unvarnished, inspiring story. It was one of those sucker-punching, kicks-in-the butt that I need every once in a while to face a side of myself head on."

Adele and Avani smiled at Sophia, looking at her with warm affection and nodding their heads in agreement with all that was being said.

With tears of appreciation sparkling in her eyes, Sophia spoke in a gentle timbre, "Thank you, my amazing friends. There's one more point I want to add for clarity. I do not deny that master manipulators harmed those women and everyone who Nate and I advocated for. With regard to their crimes, they are responsible. What mattered, though, was that in the same way that I forgave my family and myself for manipulation, believe it or not, I could allow my adversaries to be who they were. I could find forgiveness and release my debilitating emotional charge. Then, I could unleash the full fury of my love and focus on helping those who were being unjustly, criminally manipulated.

"Once I was free from the grips of my emotional *reaction* to the situation, my work was to help the victims find new ways to perceive the world. Nate had done that for me. His patience and belief in my goodness freed me from the hell of my inauthenticity and manipulation, which was magnitudes worse than the self-inflicted persecution I'd felt. I finally changed the lens through which I saw triggering events and chose to have genuine acceptance and love for myself and others. It's a form of sweet freedom from knee-jerk reactions.

"I've spoken about my friend, Gilda, and her thorough brainwashing as a youngster in Germany during the Nazi regime's rise to power. When she was sent to the U.S. as a prisoner of war, even as a diehard Nazi, she created mental and emotional distance from the Nazi world view. Gradually, she realized that she'd let herself become unfathomably manipulated by Hitler's ideologies. Facing the horrifying truth of the atrocities she'd helped to perpetuate, and seeing how deeply she'd bought into Nazi lies and deception, she felt devastated—and understandably angry at herself and them. She'd endured intense manipulation and psychological indoctrination since childhood. Courageously and tenaciously she embarked on finding ways to disengage from her past traumas and intense inculcation of Nazi beliefs and behaviors. She described to me an exquisite, inner freedom when she quit hating the Nazis and turned her attention to loving herself instead. She said her most profound epiphany arose when she experienced beauty and goodness in herself *and* the world, giving her a sense of agency over her life. Her outlook transformed and she wasn't shackled by her past. She said that she was finally free to live in peace. More than that, she could spread high vibrations into the field and encourage others to do the same.

"That kind of revelatory, sometimes uncomfortable, inner work she spoke about remains my focus—whether it happens at the cove or while tending my garden. For me, it is the nectar of life and my constant companion.

"Having said that, when doing the work with Nate, I had plenty of meltdowns. They sometimes hit like a tsunami. Giant waves crashed through me uninhibited, with full force. What kept me going was an unshakable faith that something good could emerge even from the worst nightmares. When I met Gilda, I got to see the redemptive power of love profoundly impacting someone who had once been a persecutor. She had been a crazed, devoted Nazi who managed to bravely and thoroughly shift her worldview, thus her frequency. Honing my authenticity with Nate and meeting Gilda are two of my greatest life-treasures.

"Ultimately, in doing this inner work, I was moving closer to my invincible power to love and be loved, to objectively understand another person, and to be understood for who I am. Invaluable insights always followed tough, messy struggles. On the other side, I experienced the next level of freedom and contentment. When Nate got sick, I had to focus on him rather than our work exposing human traffickers. The gift of this new work was to be able to see the worst that can happen to a person and yet witness their resilience.

"When everything got crazy in the past five years or so, I noticed the human collective becoming more compassionate towards each other, cooperating, and uniting. For a while, it was hard for most of us to discern the truth. There was a constant flow of new, hard-to-process information, and plenty of fresh distractions. However, modern day evolutions of Synarchy and other secret orchestrators of chaos, continued to use stale, predictable medieval tactics. That made it easier to catch them indulging in rinse and repeat strategies. They tried to get us to look the other way but the public became involved and, when they became outraged, everything started to change.

"We were being manipulated and I've observed that manipulation only goes so far before it fizzles or is irreversibly exposed. When it became clear that humanity wanted to end trafficking, I became optimistic. We needed to unmask the ones who'd enacted such atrocities and develop an indisputable view about what was happening. Our world was filled with misleading propaganda, but the public tenaciously demanded answers for why trafficking was more prolific in this country than anywhere in the world. They listened to those who had been victims of this ancient slave-master architecture and took their concern to the voting booth. They focused with *discernment* on the sources, the puppet masters at the top. That worked really well. Many of us knew this was a complex issue but I am encouraged by how attentively global citizens persist in sniffing it out and demanding justice.

"If it is okay, I'd like to take a minute to have some tea and collect myself. What I have to share next requires my heart to be strong yet tender, my mind to be clear and focused, and my words to flow from a place of absolute authenticity and loving care for all of you."

Stunned into silence by her proclamation, everyone nodded. Seeing their affirmation, Sophia rose gracefully and in reflective silence went to the kitchen to brew the group's favorite herbal tea—a welcomed elixir for her circle of friends.

# CHAPTER 20

# UNSETTLING TRUTH

The circle was filled with a loud chorus of crickets as everyone gathered in anticipation of Sophia's tea and further conversation. When Sophia returned everyone, including the crickets, became quiet. The atmosphere was like a quiet river that settled delicately into an ocean of pristine silence. With gentleness and care, Sophia's friends poured tea and waited patiently for her to speak.

"Sophia, I want to say something," Jake said, almost shyly, mindful of the intimate mood that had grown among them. "You don't have to *tell all*. When I give you a hard time about *holding out on us*, I'm being facetious." He looked lovingly into the oceanic depths of her eyes that were sparkling in the luminous firelight.

"You are so f**king honest. And you've been brutally vulnerable when you shared *straight talk* with us, no bullshit, ever. I want you to know that I care about you, in the same way you obviously care about me and everyone else here. As far as I'm concerned, we can all sit here in silence with you, and you do not have to say a damned thing."

Everyone nodded with open faces that melted Sophia's heart, allowing her to take a deep breath and speak with confidence, once again exhibiting her ability to dissipate any uneasiness or angst floating in the energy field of their circle.

"I love and appreciate you, Jake, and every one of you. When I go silent, it is my way of entering the still place inside. I no longer have a choice in doing so. Entering stillness is my new normal. I am careful not to invade your psyche with my residual feelings about any topic that we discuss. I'd rather allow my words to flow to you with as much objectivity as possible. You can trust me to speak from a foundation of neutrality."

Smiling with incomparable warmth, she added, "I didn't mean to worry you. I am fine. This part of my life with Nate was intense because of his heart-wrenching, declining health and the frustratingly clandestine backdrop we found ourselves in. Before I begin, I want to clarify that my story does not include the massive, specific details from Nate's research. You'll need to explore further on your own to know how intricately and thoroughly the tentacles of this subject formed. But this evening I can help you to grasp the magnitude of its implications for the entire planet and why the work we are doing under the surface is so important. I think you'll be surprised. Get comfortable and I'll launch into the murky depths of the complexity behind the unseen world above us."

Jake and John looked at each other with raised brows. After her enigmatic introduction, the circle became entranced, listening attentively.

"When Nate became weaker, we knew continuing our intense workload wasn't feasible. He decided to shift into the environmental arena. Like everything in my life, that endeavor was another mega-surprise.

"Nate began by advocating for whistleblowers who exposed potential harm to the soil, human biology, livestock, and wildlife from *geoengineering* practices in our biosphere. He needed witnesses in lawsuits to provide proof and facts... including a ton of science. Unfortunately, Nate was getting weaker, which meant I took over correspondence, data input, and as much as possible, I helped with research. I couldn't fathom the massive scope of this new arena we'd entered, nor did he.

"From the history that we've shared in our fireside evenings at the cove, we know there can be egregious agendas and inexplicable, sometimes distorted or myopic worldviews. Nate dealt with these variables so consistently he developed a couple of core questions.

*How do the views and agendas of large institutions, academia, governments, corporations, and global organizations match the working class perspective, their needs, and Gaia's well being?*

*What kind of manipulation, control, blind conformity, or greed is potentially involved?*

"Observing Nate sorting through all of that, I realized he was skilled at tracking the scent of deception, disregard, potential harm, and overall substandard integrity and non-existent transparency.

"Geoengineering of the weather was a subject he could research online while putting together his team. He'd been interested in this topic for a long time—haunted by a statement made by President Lyndon Johnson in the 1964 Agreement with the U.S.S.R. which was called the *Exchange of Weather Information*. In a related speech, the president said, *He who controls the weather will control the world.* Those words felt eerie because this kind of goal would require humans to override Gaia's natural systems and cycles, ignoring her inherent wisdom. It's like experimenting with a woman's intricate hormonal system while not considering the bigger picture of her body's overall functioning.

"He took a phenomenal deep dive into HAARP and other *weather modification programs* that were government-backed and performed under a heavy cloak of secrecy labeled *national defense*. I can list agency upon agency that sounds benign or magnanimous, but when you peek behind the curtain, you quickly notice the lack of oversight of their projects, and discover a deluge of invisible chemicals rain down every day and night relentlessly. Nate was shocked. It wasn't conceivable this could happen without our knowing about it. The assault happened on two fronts—the first one I mentioned was weather modification, where scientists take control of weather systems and the jet stream via advanced tech that we cannot detect. This includes allowing private U.S. companies, with impunity, to release sulfur dioxide into the stratosphere to cool the planet—based on modeling from a global cool-down effect observed from a volcano, Mount Pinatubo, in 1994. What if that model is flawed? Why allow companies and governments to emit known toxic substances into the atmosphere without oversight, based on that model? The risks are severe. If allowed to continue, Gaia would become normalized to the cooling effect and then ending it could create an *extreme* heating-event. Nate's concern was the secrecy, the lack of public awareness, and the potentially rushed, ill-conceived implementation. Mexico released a statement saying they plan to ban such *solar engineering* but they border the U.S., so this becomes a hot topic, internationally. Nate wondered if burgeoning business opportunities outweigh potentially dire, unknown consequences. The second front involved the effects of *chemical pollution* from jet exhaust. It took me a while to grasp its impact on our world. I'll unpack its significance as concisely as I can. It's complex so stay with me.

"Government scientists began to ask: How could they use jet exhaust, delivered in a checkerboard pattern designed by an AI system, to create flight patterns that ingeniously *disperse exhaust*, creating specific cloud patterns that dissolve and spread, forming *artificial cirrus clouds*? This daytime blanket's purpose is to deflect the sun, while at the same time, it traps warm air on the surface of the earth. At night, different flight patterns are used to open space between the jets' exhaust to allow for a slight cooling effect.

"The idea was born right after 9/11 in 2001 when planes were grounded for a few days. Using this rare hiatus in air traffic, scientists conducted tests to look at the result to heating or cooling the planet when there was *no aviation exhaust* in the atmosphere. At night, the temperatures cooled by ten degrees. Let that sink in—the daily, artificial cirrus clouds from the planes and jets are creating a deflective cloud blanket while trapping heat on the earth. At night, a *portion* of the heat can be released, but not all, because the jet exhaust is still present globally. It is just being dispersed in less condensed areas.

"Why did the government become interested in the idea of manipulating jet exhaust clouds forming daily via commercial aviation? In seeking an answer, Nate uncovered the words *aviation induced climate impact from contrail cirrus clouds*. There are radiation fluxes caused by jet and plane fuel, namely soot emissions, while flying in areas like the *stratosphere* where large amounts of the chemicals gather and linger.

"I need to give you further context for why this matters. Most private jets fly in the stratosphere and it takes two to four years or more for the chemicals to filter their way to the ground. For lesser altitudes, the effects are more immediate, hitting the ground within a couple of months. Whether the pollutants are found higher or lower, the effects of the clouds remain as a daily blanket, creating a warming effect each day.

"The next part of Nate's research gave me shivers. You guys know how connected we are to the entire cosmos. He found articles predicting that if this pattern of flights and buildup of aerosols continues, by 2050 we will not be able to see the stars. Telescopes *will be worthless*. The cosmos will only be visible to us in fading photos.

"Surprisingly, he found that by 2030 a cooling effect is projected to begin through *a solar minimum*. If this is true, then we need to be prepared for that, right? With our deflective blanket remaining in place for many years ahead, if we had a couple of volcanoes, their trapped debris would cool the planet's atmosphere rapidly, and we'd struggle to get enough sunlight on earth to keep us from freezing. Nate was shocked to discover the only conversation is about global warming, dismissing this projected cooling cycle from the conversation, except in conferences the public isn't aware of.

"At the same time, global governments aim to control rainfall around the planet, without consulting with the population or considering Gaia's wise counsel. Her innate healing wisdom and natural cycles are more intricate and life-sustaining than we fathom. Nate observed patterns in government disclosure in which they admit to these kinds of covert operations—but only after eighty years or so after the project's inception. And usually under legal pressure to do so. He could find only a handful of scientists focused on this conundrum from a quantum physics lens. Gaia and its inhabitants remain particles to be dealt with rather than energetic miracles of nature to respect and trust. Will we allow decisions and plans based on limited thinking by leadership, science, and academia to continue unimpeded?

"As though everything I've told you is not enough, his story intensified when he entered deeply *into the weeds*, as he called them, and started to connect dots. His fortuitous research revealed completely unforeseen results. He sent me lists of conferences and global programs addressing preparations to enter the next big fossil fuel jackpot—in the Arctic. He didn't want to believe what he found, regardless of knowing the recorded history of industry, military, and government agendas where power and immense wealth are involved. Industry found a way to take advantage of our warm planet (being artificially blanketed each day by AI induced flight patterns and omnipresent cirrus clouds). As the Arctic gradually thaws, it is bursting forth into a blockbuster hydrocarbon resource for future energy.

"As he researched this burgeoning focal point for industry and global governments, he was surprised to discover how long this endeavor has been progressing and how far this emerging venture has advanced along a projected timeline towards its upcoming fruition. If this type of financially lucrative plan hadn't happened countless times in history, tucked away from public view, he would have ignored it. As improbable as it may seem, he had no problem finding voluminous documentation about *arctic drilling proposals* by multiple countries. When I told my friend Grace what we were finding, she asked a question she loved to challenge me with: *Coincidence or Clue?*

"The bottom line, dear friends, is that solutions are possible if we take a *fresh approach* to these consequential issues—we urgently need free energy *extracted continuously from the unified energy field in and around us*. We also need gravity control vehicles that will not touch the ground and will run on endless energy produced directly from *the field*. With this in place, we will not need hydrocarbon-based fuel for our vehicles, thus ending relentless aviation pollution and reliance on one source of expensive, limited transportation fuel. As you know, the physics of *free energy* is Ike's and Eben's passion. For a hundred years, every time an inventor tried to bring similar technology to market, they were crushed financially, disappeared, or died suddenly. It is not a secret how many of them were marginalized or ignored like Tesla, who remained obscure until an electric car was named after him. I hope the information I shared tonight gives you clarity about *why* we want to go under the surface and connect with some of the brightest ancient minds on or under this planet—and *why* many of the physicists on Nate's team shifted to innovative and cutting-edge areas of research and development."

Sophia took a long, slow breath, lowering her eyes for a moment. The circle knew to allow her to settle into her dynamic center. The high vibratory state she cultivated required that she process denser feelings, rather than override them. Looking at her friends, she spoke unshakably from the mesmerizing power of her courageous, non-judgmental center they had come to appreciate.

"Nate became clear that getting answers was beyond the part-time work he was able to do. It was going to take rigorous effort, ongoing meticulous attention, and massive public support.

"Towards the end of his participation in this field, he was getting documents showing the government's plan to covertly control the sun itself. This was moving along with accelerated speed as they sought to manipulate our sun's Alfvén waves and Birkeland currents. From what I gathered, this can be extremely dangerous. Why would we want anyone, regardless of how competent they believe they are, interfering with the inconceivable grandeur of a natural, cosmic cycle? Now is the time to ask such questions because there are people working full-steam ahead and they are not held accountable for irreversible outcomes, which is a well-worn pattern. They are having a blast doing all kinds of cool experiments with our planet and sun. The data shows Gaia's life support is being inundated with chemicals. Does that seem like a thoroughly considered, objective plan?

"It's such a big deal and has so many tentacles. There's tons more to share but I'll keep it brief. I know it's been a busy day and you must be exhausted."

"Hey, I'm all ears," John said looking stunned yet receptive. "I had no idea about the depth and breadth of these climate measures. I don't like tumbling into endless wormholes but you're sharing an extensive information network we'd missed, formed under our noses—spreading out in many directions but always leading us back to remaining stuck with one kind of fuel that isn't good for us or the planet long-term.

"Secret research and stealthy projects usually have agendas—we've observed that happening in the past few centuries. Any project that lacks transparency demands that we peek behind the curtain. There's more here than just cloud seeding a ski resort and that sort of thing. It's not about bashing industry leaders who are responsible for their company's profits and investment goals but we can't just let them run roughshod over us without a reality check. Keep going. You've lassoed my curiosity, sister. You are on a roll."

Jake nodded and emboldened her with his broad smile and sparkling blue eyes.

Grinning delightedly as she gazed around the circle to see her beloved friends' eyes riveted eagerly to hers, she said, "I feel your supportive vibes entering my heart. This conversation started off on an emotional foot because it involves Nate; I recall how physically demanding the research and legal aspects were, and his unabated passion unfortunately drained his life-force of its waning capacity to keep him afloat. Tonight, though, I can feel him through the ether celebrating his work and our conversation. Because of that, I am becoming more buoyant by the moment.

"A poignant discussion with one of Nate's team members comes to mind. He said the potential outcomes for the kind of unchecked recklessness I've been describing reminded him of his teenagers when they go too far and take big risks—if they ask for permission to do something, someone might say no, so instead of asking, they sneak around and do whatever they want. Although sooner or later, they inevitably get caught, it may be too late to repair irreversible, sometimes devastating damage.

"This is highly relevant to our conversation. Nate's team considered Gaia to be a sentient being. Listen to how they came to that conclusion and why it is crucial to grasp this under-standing. Everything that makes up the intricate, unified web of life has consciousness, the feedforward-feedback mechanism for information exchange within the unified field of all-that-is. His question was, How long will the consciousness of the sun and our planet ignore our artificial disruption of natural cycles and cosmic sovereignty?

"The lens of biophysics can offer an intriguing hypothesis relevant to our conversation. Recent studies show earthworms, like humans, sense magnetic fields in their environment and respond accordingly. Are earthworms sending and receiving information to and from the field about how to respond appropriately? At some point, will the sun or Gaia send a signal to the field in response to our distortions of its cycles? I am not talking about some kind of retribution, which is a low-vibe human construct. I'm talking about an innate function of these larger beings to measure frequencies and protect themselves and the order and harmony of the cosmos.

"Nate and I wondered about all of this from the perspective of unicity, quantum science, and the natural equilibrium state that all matter moves towards. Could distorting the natural cycles of a star or planet trigger *a correction* to offset that distortion? After all, advanced civilizations met with an abrupt, unexpected end eleven to twelve thousand years ago when some form of cataclysm arrived. Instead of waiting for such an extreme correction, why don't we try to manage our impact first in the many ways we actually can?

"The soil is the earth's microbiome and it's been under chemical assault since WWII. There are thoroughly-researched, non-chemical approaches to farming—cost-effective, regenerative farming with natural ways to tend to the earth's soil. What if we can help mitigate the warming effects on Gaia plus regenerate her microbiome through such techniques? Why don't we restore Gaia's surface rather than allow it to become a lifeless dusty landscape? Unfortunately, such immediately practical subjects seem to remain off the table for discussion. Instead, mainstream science, academia, giant corporations, and governments advocate for chemically-derived foods made in processing plants.

"These institutions focus only on stop-gap solutions or ignore them altogether, exploring such measures as desalinating ocean water, or geoengineering, or just watching the atmosphere slowly warm. Why not explore why glaciers in Greenland are warming from deep levels of the seabed *under* the ice? What does it mean that the oscillations in the core of the planet are slowing down? A shift is clearly happening. How will a narrow-sighted focus on temporary fixes help to promote a much-needed *bird's eye view* of what's happening on and under Gaia's surface? Can we look to *long epochs* in her history rather than artificially addressing her *current* cyclical climate changes without real depth and breadth of wisdom? What about gradual yet massive shifts in her cycles that have little to do with the current shortsighted view of climate change? Can we bring a multi-disciplined approach to the discussion, where biophysicists, quantum physicists, biochemists, archeologists, geologists, cosmologists, and folks from other diverse fields join collaboratively to look at our planet's needs and relationship to the cosmos from *a broader* perspective?

"Nate was getting weaker but no less passionate. He worked tirelessly to get the word out about potential disastrous effects of interfering with the complexities of Mother Nature.

"Authority figures in government and the private sector seemed confident that their status in society commands respect from the public, which is psychologically proven to be true. How do these authorities take advantage of humanity's goodness and trust? What is required of us to become more discerning rather than blindly trusting the voices of leadership at high levels of science, business, and academia?

"Unfailingly, Nate refused to distance himself from citizens or scientists who fell into apathy, didn't give credence to geo-engineering, or who found comfort in brushing off the subject as *ridiculous* or *unfounded*. He kept doing his work as best he could without closing his heart to anyone—he believed if he cut them off or adopted antagonism towards them, the resulting discord and conflict would secure defeat for our world. He told me he couldn't put them down because he vividly recalled wearing the *shoes of disbelief* himself. Geoengineering and weather modification without limits had seemed inconceivable. He needed to dig painstakingly into this subject with scientists and insiders before his eyes opened to the full scope of what was happening, and the plans that were being implemented under a cloak of secrecy. He became unshakable that the stakes couldn't be higher.

"As I said, the purpose of these *artificial cirrus cloud* projects is to alter the complexities of Gaia's capacity to receive sunlight, but they threaten to cause harm to her ecosystems from the onslaught of chemicals and nanoparticles from jet exhaust—the chemicals used for geoengineering can slowly poison life on her surface and alter her intricate atmospheric body. Before most of us were born, her weather cycles were already being manipulated in this way, so we don't know life without those distorted cycles and manmade clouds from jet fuel exhaust.

"One of my big takeaways from his team's research was that Gaia has a history of massive regeneration, fairly quickly, after a cataclysm. Why not stop modifying her cycles and give her the opportunity to enter a cycle of self healing? How might the results of this climate conundrum resolve itself if we allow ourselves to trust her, believing that she knows how to take care of herself. I also wonder, *Why hasn't the public, with the most to lose, been allowed to peek behind the veil to see what is going on? Why are we told scientists all agree and are not alarmed by the intensified, long-term warming aspects of current aviation programs—when Nate found the opposite is true?*

"Answering questions like that and keeping Nate's spirits up were not easy—nor were the challenges his team faced simple and painless. They worked tirelessly to demand transparency and terminate a century of lies, hidden agendas, and closely guarded secrets."

Pausing for a moment, Sophia softly closed her eyes to regroup from sharing this alarming and often frustrating moment in human history—which baffled her along with a generous swathe of the global population. As her scintillating blue eyes opened like a delicate bud reaching for the succor of sunlight, the lightheartedness of her soul emerged from pausing in stillness, refreshed, allowing her to continue with equanimity.

"Thank you for allowing me to take a moment to center myself as I share this part of my life. You see… Nate confessed that if he lived, he'd spend the rest of his life ending this kind of inconceivable chemical assault. He believed life on Gaia was under intense pressure—if not motivated by malice, perhaps by hubris or an insatiable thirst to control life. Regardless, he knew the window to shift the tides of humanity's longevity and Gaia's safety was slowly closing. I'd never heard him speak so passionately about anything. I have more to share. Hang on… this is even more important than what I've already told you.

"His team hoped that Nate could stay long enough to catalyze open dialogue with a broader group of scientists and researchers, rather than engaging in stale theories and bitter debate. Without doubt, the stakes were high and the consequences could not be minimized or ignored. At the same time, his colleagues often told me they could count on Nate to extend kindness and compassion to everyone involved—allowing higher frequencies to provide a solid foundation for consequential conversations. Yet, everyone knew that bridging two sides of a highly controversial, politically charged, stealth-level topic would require a miracle. What did crazy Nate do?

"With his team staring at him in shock, he declared they'd immediately form *a diverse, committed think tank of absolutely brilliant minds and hearts*. He reached out to scientists and academics with whom he felt a possible camaraderie, assessing them as being potentially open-minded and brilliant in their fields of research. In full transparency, I did not see how this could work. And he admitted it got off to a rocky start—which is putting it mildly!

"Eventually, Nate built impregnable trust between the scientists and his team. They started coming together cohesively, and ultimately formed an indelible bond and supportive camaraderie—their diverse ideas revealed unforeseen breakthroughs rather than inciting poisonous opposition to each other. Nate was blown away at how challenging it had been to melt the ice of resistance and build a safety zone for the group where an invincible bond could form naturally. From that foundation, they supported each other in bringing forth absolutely genius ideas and performing in-depth research and evaluations—without worrying about reprisals from peers. More scientists have joined them and it has become an alliance rooted in integrity and collaboration. Nate was relieved and thrilled with the outcome. They shared their findings with the public uninhibitedly. My sweetheart latched firmly onto the habit of going into stillness for brief periods during the day, finding peace, and refusing to react or speak from low vibes.

"Finally, we passed our heartfelt best wishes to the team that took over for us. They were incredibly compassionate and understood how much Nate regretted leaving the project. A groundswell of citizens globally were setting up systems to track fallen particles on the ground everywhere, which gave Nate solace and hope that the outcome of this project would be better than he'd dreamed it could be. It became a contagion. Everyone wanted to be part of gathering data. His team had done extensive online PR and worked with brilliant minds who found creative ways to set up systems to collect data. Nate's teams were privately funded and the irony is that the big institutions in each country work for ever-increasing profit. Nate remained a champion for the working class and found every opportunity to cheer them on as *equal* participants in leadership, while encouraging them to dive into radically positive, revolutionary solutions. Rather than fostering an us-and-them mindset, he promoted and modeled unicity and an unfettered, harmonized consciousness that can extract epic data from the unified field.

"After Nate died, I had to let his work go and trust that I'd done my part. From there, I headed to Angelica's home, overlooking that gorgeous, mystical lake.

"In a nutshell, that's my story and my optimism for the future. A lot of what I talked about is being revealed because citizens globally are firmly demanding transparency; they won't settle for worn out patterns of propaganda and webs of secrecy. I am appreciative to have had this chance to share this undisclosed part of my life in your safe company. I recall it with tender feelings of gratitude for the life I've lived, and my forever love for Nate, a rare human being who embodied a passion for life, his work, and every soul he met—including his beloved Gaia. Many times we've spoken about our observations of our universe as being cooperative, collaborative, nurturing, and endlessly evolutionary in nature. Unicity is fundamental to us as an interdependent species. As humans, we are immensely fortunate to be a part of that cosmic grandeur."

Jake lowered his head in a moment of respectfulness for the planet and the magnitude of Sophia's words.

Speaking introspectively, he said, "You sure gave me plenty of food-for-thought about the past, present, and future on this planet. Considering Gaia and her place within the cosmos of her fellow stars and planets, I feel certain that anyone who tinkers with Gaia's complexities will be humbled by the intrinsic laws of nature that support her well-being. Thank you for sharing what life was like for you back then. Damn, sister! I have to admit, you came out of the blue and knocked it out of the park tonight. It'll take me a while to process the *whole nine yards*, as they say. I want you to know that I have a hell of a lot more appreciation for your tenacious spirit and devotion to the planet." As he shook his head with his voice gradually trailing off, he murmured, "I had no idea..."

John smiled at her affectionately and nodded in agreement. However, his brow suddenly contorted with confusion. Perplexed, he asked, "How the heck did you find time to blog and write? It just hit me that you were managing a huge container of Nate's work. Weren't you stretching yourself like an over-extended rubber band?"

"Good questions. Because the topics I chose related to personal evolution of consciousness and inner growth, I used everything I learned about myself through Nate's work as the foundation for blog content. I had neither time nor mental bandwidth for writing books back then. Likely the blog never felt like a burden because it evolved into an irrepressible expression of the beauty, mysteries, and majestic nature of a human life—lived without reservation, conceptual limitations, or self censorship."

Sitting regally with her spine fully lengthened and speaking in an emboldened tone imbued with raw courage. "Everything in my life has led to this particularly salient moment. Butterflies are fluttering in my stomach in anticipation of the phenomenal adventure ahead of us. I've done the surface work of this world and our endeavors at Mystic Cove are pointing me towards inestimable mysteries under the surface. It seemed like it was taking forever to get to this point. I am ready and totally excited. How about you?"

Admitting to feeling *butterflies*, they beamed exuberant smiles towards her, illuminating the vibrations of their conversation into a mood that scintillated with provocative exhilaration and confidence.

As they sipped Sophia's ambrosial tea and conversed in the spirit of solidarity and optimism, they discussed the unexpected levels of progress they made at the cove earlier in the day. They were finalizing an arduous project that had ignited conceptually over twenty years earlier—to explore the possibility that the cove's cave system led north, through a series of rivers.

By traveling deep into the inner sanctum of Gaia, they sought locations that, to their knowledge, no one had been able to reach before. Ancient maps would be their guide, along with explorer's notes from over the past two hundred years.

A question they often pondered was getting closer to an answer—*Could they discover something that would lead to a new power source for humanity's survival and higher evolution in the years to come?* They admitted to the daunting challenges the global population faced, yet they intuited that below the surface, something miraculous was waiting to provide answers that, on the surface, seemed inconceivable.

Within the circle of friends, feverish excitement was emerging for the prodigious journey ahead while fiery determination provided the fuel to satisfy their intense longing to reach the enigmatic depths of Gaia.

# CHAPTER 21

# REVEALING ARROGANCE AND CALLOUSNESS

Over the past few years, a team of trusted colleagues had developed a detailed plan to build two boats in the underground tunnel system of Mystic Cove. Wildly infeasible, they almost abandoned their plan. But with indefatigable confidence and optimism, Ike had brought revolutionary physicists and leading-edge designers to the team, igniting fresh enthusiasm for an otherwise exhaustingly daunting project.

As Ike began his studies in quantum physics, Jake introduced him to innovative physicists who were unifying physics with other fields of science, such as biochemistry, archeology, cosmology, astronomy, and philosophy—including mysticism—Jake believed they were at the leading edge of their fields, like Tesla and Einstein in their lifetimes. For the current researchers and scientists on the Mystic Cove team, the standard model of physics was not the focus—they were open to novel ways to view the quantum world in and around a human being. Thus, black holes, wormhole networks, entanglement, the dynamics and forces of the sub atomic world within *the field*, and a unified basis for all existence were on the table for research and discussion. Even though they faced harsh backlash from the established physics community, Ike never complained. He grew up with the invisible world of quantum particles embedded into his life experience.

Acknowledging Sophia's influence, he admitted that without her guidance and support he may not have maintained the courage to categorically thrust his heart and soul into this burgeoning area of physics. In numerous late-night fireside conversations and magnificent dawns at Mystic Cove over tea, Sophia disclosed countless stories her dear friend Gilda had shared about physics and unimaginable science in the black projects within the military. Ike was particularly interested in *why* Gilda was granted immunity from war crimes, after her capture as the wife of a hardcore elite Nazi scientist. The boon of freedom materialized when she agreed to work for an area of the U.S. government closely monitoring scientists from *Operation Paper Clip*—in which the government hired Nazi scientists, specifically in the areas of nuclear energy, advanced spacecraft, and nuclear weapons development in Hitler's Third Reich.

Gilda confided in Sophia, describing black budget projects in which she met ETs, saw air and space craft reverse engineered, and extra-terrestrials being dissected, studied, or relentlessly questioned on matters of technology. During innumerable encounters with the beings whom Gilda called her "star brothers and sisters," she realized that vast information was being withheld from the public by private investors, especially relating to particular areas within the military-industrial complex related to cutting-edge quantum science.

In conversations with Sophia, Gilda described the agonizing process of transformation and deprogramming from not only her Nazi indoctrination but the intense propaganda from her partnership with the U.S. military. A cruel reality lingered for Gilda, as she digested opacification of *life-altering technologies* and *cosmic benefactors*. She knew their value and witnessed their "subjugation," as she called it. Yet she did not dare divulge the full scope of everything she knew—no one would believe her and others who had tried that tactic were brutally murdered or devastatingly discredited.

✦ ✦ ✦

One morning as Ike was glued to several of Sophia's stories about Gilda's life inside the scientific research projects, a particularly epic story lit a blazing fire in Ike's heart that significantly influenced his life going forward. Sophia had spoken as clearly as possible to convey Gilda's viewpoint, who, having to compose herself after a torrent of tears and a mammoth surge of monstrous sorrow, had shared with Sophia what she saw inside the projects. One encounter with extra-terrestrials was paramount for her.

Gilda had said, 'It was devastating. My heart shattered totally in an instant.'

Sophia shared her recollection of the story in Gilda's words, embedded in Sophia's memory as though the provocative conversation was taking place in the present moment.

"Gilda said, 'Two ETs were working with a team comprised of U.S. and Nazi physicists, who were hard-hearted and arrogant. These beings had worked regularly with the scientists, who had become adept in telepathy. Months rolled by, but no matter what the ETs told them about the physics they were interested in, the scientist remained dumbfounded and frustrated.

"'Finally, one morning, the asshole-scientists were ranting and complaining at the extra-terrestrials who had tried tirelessly to convey in fresh ways how the universe functioned. Of course, that meant using a new lens for viewing physics, which the biased, inflexible scientists did not understand nor relate to. As the frequency band of their wicked reactions became more and more violent and vicious, one of the scientists flung a particularly horrific tirade at one of the ETs.

"'As his thought pattern reached the energetic field of the extra-terrestrial, the poor being died instantly. His entire field of energetic vibrations began to transmute into invisible energy and he disappeared, shocking the hell out of those blind, haughty scientists. The other ET glanced my way, as our hearts met in indescribable sorrow.

"'Sophia, I told you a few times how the ETs I met expressed emotions that are magnified to the extent that sadness is visceral by many levels of magnitude. That poor ET who made contact with me—that benevolent soul—was heartbroken. Damn it! He was neither a Nazi slave like me nor a mind controlled citizen who was being carefully developed and mind-f**ked by the government. These pompous physicists thought they were dealing with controllable resources, not live, sentient beings who were their cosmic brothers.

"'Dear God! You cannot extract the pride and conceit from people who are sufficiently established in it."

With a gut-wrenching quality in her voice, Sophia said in a somber, reflective tone, "Gilda spoke emphatically and passionately about what happened next. Choking back tears of sorrow mixed with anger, she continued, saying, 'There was no remorse on the part of those *conceited physicists*. In fact one of the physicists lamented saying,

*We've studied Tesla's work; we've discussed this subject far too long! These alien bastards are trying to deceive us by holding back information! They don't want us to reverse engineer their craft. That is obvious! To hell with them!*

"'He stormed off in a fury of contempt for the ETs, leaving me to choke back fiery tears and righteous indignation. As you can tell, I am still feeling the devastating inability to speak authentically and take up for my good-hearted cosmic kin. After so much time has passed, I still feel gutted when I recall the scene in vivid detail and the crushing, debilitating feeling of my heart that followed.'

"Ike, it was incredibly hard for Gilda to come to terms with the callousness and arrogance of the physicists.

"She was totally devastated and summarized her reflections of working in black projects solemnly, saying, 'In the area that I worked in, this kind of aggressive, insensitive scientist was gradually, and I do mean GRADUALLY, weeded out. In my humble opinion, the military-industrial complex scientists did not grasp the nuances of the unified field theory of quantum physics because they were so entrenched in a standard physics model. Over time, younger, more open-minded physicists joined the research team, and they listened to ETs and grasped some of the concepts. They realized that the ETs were extracting energy from the unified field in and around us. The black budget side of the military, that I was *not* associated with, decided to explore this free energy and my husband dove in with his usual fanaticism. I knew *nothing* about what he did. But I new him well. Whatever he engaged in was diabolical, heartless, and would deliver a massive dose of power to him and his demoniacal clan.

"'It was like a knife was driven ruthlessly through my heart when government-backed military scientists or corporate personnel refused to share incredibly useful, highly beneficial information with the public. In fact, every detail remained meticulously suppressed, denied, and relegated only to hallowed, private areas in underground labs and black budget projects.

"'I'd like to ask you a question that I asked myself many times. Is it ethical or legal to shoot a lethal energetic barb at someone whose only intent is to help a supposed comrade to shift their rigid viewpoint for physics, to raise their understanding of how this universe operates? Is it ethical or legal to stand by and watch young physicists become indoctrinated into believing they are working for the common good by hiding their work from citizens, presidents, and their government?

"'A brilliant young scientist told me excitedly that *someday soon all of this will be revealed!* That was over fifty years ago! Damn it! How long can this be allowed to continue? When the public hears about this subject, they drift into a protective trance. As I consider this unfortunate phenomenon, I recall a senior level military officer telling me the public does not need to know. His worldview ran rampant through that underground world of advanced technologies. How can we change that? I don't have an answer. Maybe you do.'"

Sophia told Ike that she was stunned into silence by Gilda's revelations and questions and she realized how complicated the answers were. Yet Sophia yearned for an opportunity to bring the field theory of quantum physics to the world to allow every human to discover how to move their own particles at will, to find their way back through their DNA to their remarkable, highly advanced lineage—in communion with

Max and a world of benevolent giants who are humanity's sagacious ancestors.

She recalled that Nate told her in a dream that she had the capacity to visit a coordinate in space and walk among subtle beings who she'd not be able to see—unless she raised her frequency enough to match theirs. His words still danced in her memory.

"Invisibles walk among us," Sophia said, as she gazed lovingly at Ike. Without doubt, her communication was gentle yet impactful enough to allow instant, irresistible, heart-wisdom penetration. With searing fervor, she said, "We must fully adopt that irrefutable truth. We are not alone. We are ALWAYS surrounded by quantum level miracles and mysteries, which allow life to be an ever-exciting adventure. My dear Nate made sure I was open and observant of that verifiable, mystifying fact. I bet you'd agree, sweet friend."

Ike smiled, displaying a broad expanse of innocent gratitude. He told her he loved her, and said unabashedly that she was *amazing* and *so cool!*

Drenching his memory cells with her stories, he vowed to work with colleagues to change the question from "how to force governments into further disclosure" to "how to connect with ETs as universal kin, and understand more fully the quantum physics that reveal how the human race can evolve into an unfathomable lineage of advanced being-ness."

With a look of softness and a tone of incontrovertible authenticity which melted her heart, Ike said passionately, "I am committed to bringing free energy and gravity control to this planet. In the early twentieth century, the discovery of electromagnetic fields revolutionized the planet. Suddenly we had electricity powering entire civilizations. The whole world lit up almost overnight! But what's coming next, Sophia, is far more revolutionary: control over gravity itself. Here's what people need to understand: gravity isn't just an abstract concept or force pulling us to the Earth—its the result of how mass interacts with spacetime. Spacetime bends around a mass and that's what we perceive as gravity.

"But the key discovery is that spacetime is made of *energy* fluctuating at the quantum level. At the most fundamental level, the 'vacuum' of space is alive with energy. And we are learning how to tap it.

"When we manipulate this quantum vacuum, we can change how spacetime curves. It's like having a lever that adjusts gravity itself. It turns out, we don't need to push against gravity—instead, we'll create fields that change how objects *interact with it*. With this new technology, a vehicle won't rise because we're lifting it or pushing it up against gravity, it will rise because gravity itself is different around it. And this is not science fiction anymore—it's science.

"Using a new, quantum perspective on physics, we are applying the understanding that there is an infinite, dynamic field of energy all around us, much like plasma. This energy isn't locked away in some distant part of the universe—it's everywhere, in every part of space. When we access this *zero-point* energy I just mentioned, we'll be able to extract power directly from the quantum 'vacuum.' No more engines burning fuel. No more rockets pushing us through the air.

"We'll create high-energy plasma fields around a vehicle that interact with the quantum vacuum. By controlling these interactions, we can manipulate how spacetime bends around the craft, creating a completely controlled gravitational field.

"Picture spacetime like a flexible fabric. If you pull it in one direction, everything in that area follows the curvature. That's what we are doing—we're curving space-time itself so that the craft moves effortlessly. We are not fighting gravity. We are reshaping it.

"What's incredible is that this doesn't just affect gravity. Inside these controlled fields, we also control inertia. The craft will be able to accelerate to incredible speeds, but the people inside won't feel a thing. We'll create a bubble where the normal laws of motion don't apply and everything outside the craft will seem frozen by comparison.

"You might remember me talking about Max Planck in our fireside circles. He was a German physicist in the last century who mathematically described the smallest measurable unit of spacetime, now referred to as a *Planck unit*. I am telling you about this infinitesimally small unit because that's the level of Reality we are working with. It can be measured but not seen... But where is this Planck-level energy? It's embedded in spacetime itself, just waiting for us to harness it.

"We're using the quantum properties of spacetime, such as Planck units, to generate energy locally and create localized gravitational shifts. Vehicles will glide easily through space-time, powered by the very structure of spacetime, without ever needing fuel. Let that sink in!"

His eyes blazed intensely as he said, "There's been a paradigm shift in quantum physics over the last couple of decades. We've moved from observing gravitational fields to actually designing them. By mastering the interplay of plasma fields and spacetime geometry, we're able to create controlled gravitational wells or even regions where gravity is inverted, pushing a craft upwards rather than pulling it down. This is the future! The ability to manipulate gravity at will is going to redefine everything we know about transportation, energy, and even reality! I am telling you; we are on the brink of making it happen!"

"Sophia! The world is about to radically change! I know this may seem *out there*, but trust me. Oh man! This is possible and nothing will stop me from making these new technologies part of our reality. I promise!"

A fine mist of emotionally-charged droplets cascaded down Ike's high cheekbones while his narrow, elongated eyes refused to become a stoic dam for repressed feelings. Sophia's story of injustices inflicted upon former physicists had overwhelmed him. They'd been ridiculed and their work devalued because they strayed beyond the conventional science of their lifetime. Sophia intentionally allowed for an extended pause. Entering into the powerful vibrational nexus of the still point, she enabled her frequency to expand into a field of pure love. With her energetic support, Ike secured an opportunity to emote authentically for as long as needed.

Gaining his composure, his voice was free from inhibition and insecurity. Exuding quiet confidence, he said , "The ETs Gilda told you about will be vindicated and all of the criticized, and often defamed scientists who preceded me can rest in peace knowing that we are not just continuing their work; we are advancing it beyond what they ever thought possible. We are about to create a future where physics, as it's known today, is redefined, and gravity is just one more force we understand and can control. We've been justifiably proud of our achievements, but our tech can be WAY more revolutionary! Oh man! This kind of physics has to become mainstream now. No more waiting and hoping it happens. I am on fire, Sophia!"

She leaned forward, tenderly squeezing his hands, and wiped his tears. "The culmination of your wild dreams and hard work is closer at hand than you can comprehend in this moment. Always remember, I believe in you. We have each other on this journey. That's our mojo."

He bowed his head, his heart marinating in her love and much welcomed assurances.

After a few moments, they both stood up and walked with a boost of confidence towards the extensive stairwell to begin another bustling day at the cove. Their team of comrades had committed to take whatever risks were necessary to find revolutionary solutions to the web of trepidation holding humanity in its iron grip. As they descended the stairs, their resplendent smiles saturated the atmosphere with dazzling unicity vibrations.

✦ ✦ ✦

Mystic Cove's project had barely survived a myriad of seemingly insurmountable funding issues. Making unprecedented personal contact with ancient beings under the surface was dangerous and radical—a quest that required unwavering courage and fortitude. The journey had to remain secretive, with only a few generous, trusted benefactors as investors. Fortunately, Megan's support, both financial and through her extensive network, remained unwavering. She frequently shared her profound sense of awe when she joined the luminescent evenings around the fire—revealing that, other than military bases, there were countless undiscovered areas underground where the miraculous quantum world was being lived as a daily experience. Cutting-edge archeologists, military whistleblowers, and Will's community remained unshakable.

The shamanic elders, admitting the journey was perilous, declared that if successful, it could potentially contribute to saving the world. Their visionaries identified the routes, described in their ancient oral stories, which could lead deep within Gaia. However, tradition held that without impeccable character and elevated frequencies, visitors to the belly of the cave system might not emerge back to the surface. These were the kinds of stories that had been shared for over twenty-five thousand years of indigenous tradition.

Even though every imaginable obstacle arose like a giant tidal wave to crush the team's plans, these barriers and impediments had gradually been resolved. Apparently they were *being watched*, but fortunately, the consensus among the military and others was that they were insane to think they could venture deeply under the surface from their location. Apparently the military had made several failed attempts in this part of the country.

Justin and Dutch were in sync and prepared to navigate through a quantum portal into unknown coordinates within Gaia's body. Sophia, John, Jake, Adele and her daughters were in the first boat with Dutch confidently at the helm. With Justin in the second boat were Caitlyn, Avani, Eben, and Ike.

This profound journey would answer two questions that had kept Jake and John awake at night since they'd discovered the cove, which had also been top of mind for Will's community for millennia:

*Who are the giant beings who reportedly live under the surface?*

*Are Max and his beloved part of this mystery?*

It was time to answer these and multitudes of questions arising from their work at Mystic Cove.

# CHAPTER 22

# EQUINOX

Potent exalted frequencies were forming and coalescing in the vibrant seasonal soup of the spring equinox. Dawn approached with glowing bands of orange and pink in the sky as Grace made her way up the steep rocky hill near Megan's house to the circle of ancient stones. Her face was soft and expectant as a child who was seeing the magnificence of sunrise for the first time.

With excitement for the task she was about to undertake, Grace quickened her pace. After working with the frequencies of the megaliths for many years (the shamans had taught them the secret geometry that would animate the stones), she and Sophia had planned this special meeting and practiced the maneuvers with each equinox. When Sophia finally left to venture under the surface, Grace had begun to study advanced quantum physics related to electromagnetic fields, preparing herself for this auspicious event. It was time to take her training to a practical level.

Since childhood, the two friends observed the mysteries of nature and could communicate without words in various ways. Before going under the surface, Sophia had asked Grace, "Why not add communicating through monolithic, vibrating structures to our repertoire?"

The light would need to be moving precisely between two particular stones. Grace wrapped a powder-blue wool shawl tightly around herself to fend off the chilly autumn wind and sat motionless in her practice of focusing on and aligning with the eternity of timelessness—beyond space, at the center of stillness in the unified field.

As the moment approached, Grace's perception moved in a way she'd described to Sophia many times. "My awareness softens, expands rapidly into a potent, explosive darkness and I roar through it. It's scary at first, until bam! I reach the light of new creation, and find myself in orgasmic knowing and pure being-ness. From there, I emerge into a dimension of spacetime that's a higher frequency than my normal waking state, or I can land on a new coordinate in spacetime, anywhere in the cosmos. It used to happen occasionally but as I developed trust in it and became comfortable with its frequencies, my brain developed new neural pathways and I slipped into it more easily. Now I do it effortlessly, unreservedly, whenever I want to."

Every time Grace described that inner experience, tears glistened in her eyes, overflowing with gratitude for the opportunity to have a precious human life.

Now, within the circle of carefully placed ancient stones, Grace soared into the light once again and emerged, finding herself standing in the stone circle facing Sophia. Her shawl gently rippled in the morning wind. As restructured particles of interacting light, they smiled radiantly and spoke to each other.

"Grace! You did it! I can see you!" Sophia beamed.

"I am SO relieved to be looking at you," Grace responded, letting out a deep sigh. "I have to admit that lately I wondered if our dream-conversations were just my wishful thinking. Is the place you are visiting as beautiful as in my dreams? Are the Max-looking giants totally sweet, gentle, and sagacious? I wake up crying. They blow my heart space wide open with vibes of kindness. And they are so completely chilled out!"

"You are fully tuned in, as usual," Sophia answered. "I'm not surprised. My wild-hearted friend, no one else I know talks to fairies even as an adult and can pop out of their body and fly as swirling, pure light around the tops of trees. You know, sometimes when we were kids I thought you and I were being totally weird, but I realized later that we needed our common, unfettered consciousness to prepare us for what we are doing and experiencing now.

"No matter how much we prepared ourselves, I knew I had to gather the calmest confidence imaginable to manage the transition into this unfamiliar environment. Our way-too-long trip to this place was scary at times because of massive currents and gigantic waves in a seemingly endless river. Our team had already formed intimate bonds of respect and friendship with each other. We've been through so much together over the years that we can easily help each other to become centered and still. Jake, John and the whole team have been awesome. We had no choice but to settle into stillness because we realized that the molecules of the water responded to our frequencies—when we smoothed our frequencies into equilibrium, the turbulence lessened in intensity. It was trippy to observe our group creating a path of calmer water within a storm. Stillness of mind matters down here, as it does on the surface.

"There is a mind-blowing inner sun. It's not as bright as the sun in our solar system and it has a light haze over it. I've been told that gases are electrified, creating this sphere of sunlight that is electrically charged. The magnetics of Earth's crust seem to hold it in place. I haven't gotten deeply into the science of it. Sometimes it is a gorgeous turquoise color, but mostly it appears orange.

"Like on the surface, we experience day and night; we get ourselves into a circadian rhythm by going inside and remaining for the night with shaded windows made from a special material that completely blocks outside light. We fully adapted within a couple of weeks.

"For about two weeks, traveling between gigantic cliffs of sheer rock, thousands of feet high, we passed a forested area and arrived at a tiny beach. Luckily, we had plenty of fresh water and food. The temperatures here are consistently pleasant, slightly cool, about 60 to 70 degrees Fahrenheit. It reminds me of a light chill in Autumn. Unlike our solar sun, the sun here doesn't provide warmth. I miss feeling the solar sun's heavenly, gentle radiance on my skin.

"I'll share my notes about the details of our trip later, but since this mode of communication has time limitations, I'd better tell you briefly what's happening."

Grace was smiling softly and nodded. "Gosh I love seeing your form in this way! This is awesome. Keep going."

"Within the time constraint, I'm going to tell you as much as I can," Sophia said, smiling back and emitting a soft emerald shaft of luminosity from the center of her chest to Grace's heart center.

"At the beach, we were finding our footing on land and unwinding from the long voyage. We'd been mapping the landscape throughout our trip. However, we were unprepared to see such thick forests surrounding us, the trees over one-hundred feet tall, some towering three hundred feet or more. Based on the size of the trees, it's easy to understand that the animals and birds are gigantic, too. We didn't see many of them. We ended up on that beach, which was near a forest of smaller trees less densely packed than the areas we'd been traveling through. We were feeling a bit nervous because we didn't know if we'd encounter a dinosaur or other monstrous creatures.

"Instead, a huge boat came toward us, and all of us intuitively felt a wave of safety, calm, and fascination. It looked similar to a ship that I have seen navigating in oceans or other large bodies of water. Yet this one moved without making a sound, as if it was a part of the water itself. It's hard to describe the beauty of its movement. Will had pointed out the boats on the cave art and elaborated further on them several times. With that prior information, seeing the boat heading our way was a welcomed event.

"There's a mystifying aspect of the boat story. We were prepared to see a particular boat based on a multitude of drawings in Mystic Cove's cave art. How we perceived the boat, however, was a function of our *individual perception*. Jake, John, and I saw an ancient-looking boat. Ike and Eben saw a sleek, aerodynamic ship based on how they believed it would look in modern times. And to add a dimension of craziness, as they described what they were seeing, Jake, John, and I caught their vibe—their perspective felt true, and suddenly we watched the boat morph. After a few minutes, everyone saw the boat in the way that Ike and Eben described it. Perception matters and open-minded, non-biased perception is the key. Dropping expectations of how things *should* look is one of the keys to observing the truth of this incomprehensible world. Reflecting on the experience, I wondered if I saw a form of boat from aeons in the past, which would be memory—information stored within the infinite quantum field—and I picked up that unique form of the boat in space-memory because it aligned with my worldview. When I engage in such profound rumination, my whole world feels surreal and reality shattering.

"Gradually, the Max-style giants appeared—some had elongated heads while others did not. I wanted to embrace everyone of them. That's how familiar and sweet their vibe felt to me. Of course, it would be hard to hug a thirty-foot-tall giant. They wore clothes made of fabric that looked homespun. I noticed that the fabric was dyed and red seemed to be a popular color. Their hair and beards were long and messy—no barbers for these giants. We spoke with them telepathically. Somehow that was second nature for us.

"As they approached, we heard singing. It felt uplifting and happy, like hearing buddies hanging out in a jam session. I admit to being shocked by our reception. And you would not believe how easily they *beamed* our smaller boats on board theirs, while we walked a small plank to join them—we were not ready yet to simply direct our particles to the boat. Hearing them humming and singing in unison evoked feelings of comfort and safety. The sound also reverberated with a nurturing, ethereal quality. Avani was in bliss because the syllables sounded like Sanskrit, an ancient language she learned in childhood—she felt at home in heart and soul. We all felt that way. These giants welcomed us graciously—anticipating and accommodating our needs. Can you tell that my kinship and love for them has been flawlessly natural and authentic?"

"Back up, sister!" Grace said with a quizzical look mixed with friendly rapport. "It did not escape my attention that you said that you had not directed your particles *yet*. Does that mean you're beaming yourself all over the place now?!"

"Well, not like a pro... yet! We are continuing to build our skills in this wild process. Our main focus has been to learn more about the infinite, unified field of spacetime and how to settle into the stillness within the core of ourselves. From what I've gathered, the "sinoatrial node" of the heart is the still center of our being in particle form. Even when you and I were little, we focused on *the feeling* of going deeper and deeper into the core of our heart. I have a strong intuitive sense that the frequencies down here are playing a role in the process of centering ourselves quickly and deeply so we can enter our singularity and move through worm holes to new coordinates in spacetime. I can finally move my particles with plenty of preparation and the right frequency. As always, frequency matters. Without doubt, we have amazing mentors in this regard. At this point, I am able to remain in a directed coordinate for longer periods. At first, I tended to move there and come back pretty quickly.

"I've always known you and I were not the only ones raising our frequencies and getting pretty obsessed with it. Through our work here, we've been given a peek into the frequencies and evolutionary capacities of people across the globe. Everywhere, clusters of people are grasping the value of their participation in a unified *web of life*, as a way to understand how the world operates. Through the lens of the unified field described by quantum physics, we saw that many people no longer think it's strange to view themselves as inseparable from the web of life—each person is a unique point on the web and contributes to the web through their thoughts, words, and actions. We saw groups across the globe talking about this. Those conversations are dissolving separation, thus bridging unicity. On top of that, there is widespread focus among many people across the globe on elevating personal frequencies. I am tingling as I share this. Can you feel my energy?"

Grace's eyes sparkled as she nodded.

"I knew you would... I have so much more to tell you and it's even more wild, hopeful and exciting than what I just shared.

"The Earth's frequencies have elevated significantly over the past decade—her magnetics upshifted, and it's significantly easier to tune into her core, cross the barriers of time and space, and unify with her on a profound level. The giants tell us they are observing particular clusters of people who join together regularly to elevate their frequencies. Our hosts' humongous eyes sparkled when they spoke about this. On the holographic screen we saw people doing this even in countries where it was putting them in danger for political reasons. They were like you and me—relentless lovers of stretching their awareness and totally appreciative of the value of everything that cannot be seen.

"In the giants' world, *holographic screens* display humans living in the future harmoniously, organizing ourselves into regional communities, reminiscent of Avani's *enclaves*. In these displays, humans no longer uphold hierarchal systems which rely on oppression and domination to sustain themselves. Dualistic forms and roles are not the focus, such as male-female, leader-follower, teacher-student, and rich person-poor person. Instead, there is heartfelt collaboration in which everyone has the opportunity to participate.

"Growing up, we were told humans were flawed and there are *genetically deficient* people, bad people, who will always cause trouble. However, these displays show a culture where traits of collaboration and kindness are developed at a very young age. The entire culture is predicated on the belief that everyone deserves love and respect. In a minute, I'll tell you about my visit to an awe-inspiring community that lives this way. For now, I want to continue telling you about humanity's future. As a species, humans are going to develop new music and galactic harmonics that soothe their souls. Like Max's legacy under the surface, surface dwellers will look to more expanded views of themselves.

"We will take control of our bodies and minds, doing things that you and I always knew were natural—without *high tech interventions* needed. When we were young, we didn't realize the limitless scope and breadth of our power—the pure cosmic majesty that our species is capable of developing. In the future, we'll no longer think of our particles as little balls; rather, they are *spacial distributions of the field—wildly spinning vortices of excitation from within the infinite field of all-that-is.* That's how they explain it. What an awesome image!"

"Sounds good to me. I'm all in!" Grace said, expressing the freedom of a child released into playtime after a long day at school.

"Isn't that the best vision ever?! After so much gloom and doom in the news, my particles got excited!" Sophia joined Grace in a moment of connection as they talked about childhood dreams coming true in unexpected ways.

"Keep going. I want to hear as much as I can before you have to go," Grace said, acknowledging their time together was waning.

"I have so much to tell you! I'll hit the highlights and fill in details when I come home. After watching the hologram, we were left to reflect on what we saw and felt. Then we were given a parting message—you would have melted if you'd seen the elderly giant who stepped forward—by a stately looking gentleman with tousled gray hair and modestly dressed in simple, linen-like, dusty-brown robes that fell to calf length. He encouraged us to notice that some societies under the surface operate in a matrilineal style, as was common on the surface tens of thousands of years ago. As he spoke, I noticed Jake and John, our anthropological, archeological wizards, beaming a knowing smile at each other. Those ancient civilizations honored Gaia and each inhabitant, and lived simply, as these giants do. I want to be clear we are not speaking about a *matriarchal* culture in which women *dominate or rule* over men. *Matrilineal* cultures are not based on hierarchy. They are based on a worldview of reciprocity with each other and the cosmos, compassion for all life (seen and unseen), absolute connectedness, and deep, subtle levels of awareness of the indescribable essence of life. The giants helped us to see even matrilineal cultures were not as refined and high vibe as the unfathomable ones that preceded them."

"Wait," Grace said, looking thoroughly confused, "I hate to interrupt your flow but the matrilineal cultures sounded pretty awesome. How were they a form of devolution? I'm asking because you said they were *not as refined and high vibe.*"

"I had the same response! The giant clarified there were times in Gaia's history when humans were *so subtle, so refined,* we could go anywhere in the multiverse, didn't have a molecule of interest in division, and collaborated on everything—*as the foundation of global culture.* This applied to life on Earth and our relationship to the cosmos. It was based on the foundation of being high-vibe and unified within the field of everything everywhere.

"Apparently, cataclysms and global events can send the collective awareness of humanity into a downward energetic spin. So something must have happened to cause that devolution of the species. Although it was light years *higher than the present*, it was not as refined, subtle, and unified as some of the cultures had been. I can explain it better with an example of another place we visited, vastly different than where we originally landed in the giant's area, which in a lot of respects looked similar to the surface.

"In another area we visited, all beings looked alike except we could tell their gender, with females being smaller with breasts. Both genders were bald and their clothes looked like high tech spandex. Sometimes they wore bracelets, anklets, or necklaces but this seemed functional rather than decorative like jewelry. They tended to be solely telepathic with massively high frequencies. They appeared to operate in an unbroken energetic *flow state* with daily duties and care for each other filled with innate serenity—their cultural hallmark. Cooperation and collaboration were intrinsic and unshakable. I had to do a lot of focused inner stillness before going there, and plenty of it during the visit.

"Their interactions are mind-bending because there's virtually no discord; just pristine, quiet unicity. Yet I want to be clear that they get a lot done. Their awe-inspiring labs sent Ike and Eben into ecstasy. Ike called them *high tech wonders beyond our comprehension*. Ike says it was like being in kindergarten while trying to comprehend a PhD-level lecture. You'd perceive that the subject was special, likely fascinating, but WAY above your head. He told me later that he was as a metaphorical kindergartner who had a new level of study and personal frequency to aspire to. In fact, he wasn't sure whether the most subtle beings would be considered part of a *subtle realm* or inhabitants of a vibrationally advanced culture, like inner earth places called Agartha or Shambala. We had a lot of mind-blowing experiences to make sense of, that's for sure. Buildings featured a minimalist vibe yet were genius in design, ranging from octagon shapes to pyramids. Ike explained that their structures were about function and frequency rather than aesthetics. Yet, because of the frequency, we agreed that being there felt extraordinary. We wondered if we were witnessing future *surface* architecture.

"Unicity is palpable everywhere under the surface. Kindness is prolific and compassion never wavers. All tasks and all contributions are considered equal. The culture of our home base here personifies for me the idea of equilibrium and balance. It is so nourishingly *stress free!*

"The giants hosting us are totally into art, figurines, drawing, hammering exquisite metals into varying kinds of jewelry or art forms... basically, all-things-creative. Everyone does this, all ages and genders, without exception. We instinctively started joining them in whatever form of art inspired each of us. Debriefing those creative moments with the giants, we found the process to be a way to bond with the community and uplift our personal consciousness. Art is not a side element of their culture. It's front and center.

"Settling further into the inner regions of Gaia, the contrast with our surface world became palpable. There are no divisive kingdoms and no money, power, or crisis—no bankers and no hierarchy. Instead, they live in areas that suit the local people. Keep in mind that their life span is anywhere from eight hundred to one thousand years. Ironically, there's no overcrowding, which is hard to understand, given their size.

"You'll love this part... Children go to school but spend the first one-hundred years or more learning music, vibrational sciences, and deeper levels of relationship with their environment and all existence. Surprisingly, they mostly play games and laugh heartily all the time. Sounds amazing, right? They don't mind being demonstrative or gregarious, nor do they dismiss the need for being introspective when appropriate. From a state of fascination and wonder, Adele and I spend most of our time observing the education of children which is mind-bending and life-transforming. There are no curriculums, and no need to share a perspective of history or perpetuate stories about anything because they have the unbiased, quantum-level hologram for viewing history.

"From the time a child is born, the whole community values and helps to raise them. Giants trust children's innate discernment and masterful ingenuity. Listen to this: I was stunned when we checked out some forbidding, seemingly bottomless crevices in some of their cities. It gives me shivers to recall them. Adele and I almost freaked-out once when, to our horror, a child, the equivalent of a two or three-year-old on the surface, went near one of them. We were ready to rush over and stop the child, but it was obvious that the giants had seen them and weren't alarmed. The toddler got close to the hole, then paused and turned around. Seeing our concern, the adults explained that no one expected the child to fall in. They intuitively trust their children can rely on their relationship to the Earth. They don't feel *separate* from nature or each other. That kind of relationship allows them to move through life differently than we do.

"Children are in tune with their environment from the moment of birth; they intuitively feel the change in the surfaces they are traversing. According to the giants, no one falls into a crevice or pit. We were fascinated to see this dynamic relationship to their environment. I sense that they operate *in the moment* without distractions. In that centered flow state, they *feel* their surroundings easily.

"As mystifying as that was, check this out: women and men work together in a fluid way. In one of their laboratories we saw a close ratio of men to women. They seemed utterly natural and at ease, even as they appeared to have different patterns.

"From their perspective, women's biology does not work the same as men's, but this is not a basis for any kind of inequality or imbalance. Men are simply on a regular hormonal cycle that remains more or less the same over time. Women, on the other hand, have a hormonal cycle that shifts on a monthly basis through alterations of hormones like estrogen and progesterone. While men function on a regular day/night cycle that stays consistent, women fluctuate between quite different states each month.

"This means they alternate between more reclusive, inward-directed phases and more social, outward-directed phases each month. Sometimes women's cycles synchronize and they join teams as a group where they collectively use the gifts of each phase of their group-cycle. The inward phase is marked by increased neuro plasticity which allows them to easily change old ways of acting and thinking, learning is integrated, and their capacity for accessing memory and restful sleep elevates dramatically. The outward phase includes increased energy, emotional intelligence, productivity, a stronger drive for community, and enhanced capacities for communication.

"Male team members value female cyclical superpowers at each stage of their cycle. It's part of the culture here. I hope I am not making this sound complicated. Culturally, they are so *in flow* that this happens organically. If I hadn't asked why some women work for a few days, take off to meditate for a week, and then go back to the lab full-on, they wouldn't have realized I needed an explanation about monthly cycles. They definitely don't obsess about it or give it much thought—for them it's normal.

"I want to quickly tell you how the community as a whole takes care of the children, without doting or cajoling. They acknowledge the child as an active, integral part of the community from birth. Our giant hosts live in houses with several families. Their culture is so cohesive that we never figured out if the homes were filled with genetic family members or those with whom they developed a bond in other ways. Either way, I didn't observe much in the way of family squabbles or sibling rivalry. As in Avani's enclaves, the underlying principles of the society appeared to be collaboration, respect, care, and unicity.

"Another interesting facet of life for them is that no one is striving for prestigious positions. People do what needs to be done. It happens organically. For example, if a young person lives near a forest and their friend's father cuts trees, they are welcome to join their friend and participate in tree cutting anytime they are inclined to do so. Young ones who love this work can continue to do it and become more adept. They don't choose work to make money or get involved in a career—they simply do what they are good at or enjoy, as part of life. They might cut trees down because it's needed and they like doing it. Without striving to be a more proficient tree cutter, their skills evolve naturally because they love what they do. And they are naturally fulfilled by the work they do as it is needed and contributes to the community. Some are engaged in tree cutting, others are engaged in laboratories, while others are working with advanced physics or architecture and so on.

"Another mind-bender is they don't use currency or even a barter system as a way to exchange goods and services. This is so different from our norms that you might have to just hold this in awareness and not try to figure it out. They don't have any kind of transactional system. What if our species could become so unified and connected to each other naturally, relying on a reciprocal energetic exchange, as opposed to an exchange of something material? Of course, this evolved as their collective consciousness became more expanded and refined. It wasn't a sudden, random leap they tried to force their culture into as a new system of exchange. I view their focus on elevating individual consciousness as a super power, the secret to their high vibrations and a rock-solid cultural foundation of peace. It's brain-spinning to witness a culture without banks, bartering, or exchanges like that. Instead, being in the present moment, seeing what is needed, and knowing who can help is the norm. It showed me we don't have to take drastic steps to fix problems but we do need to support each other in raising our consciousness through diving inside into stillness and getting into the flow state as often as we can.

"Some of our observations were confusing for Adele, who had studied psychology. She met me one morning to explain her cognitive dissonance and shared her reflections and continued contemplation. She was trying to reconcile how a culture could elevate itself, motivate its members to do better, grow and push the limits of what they're capable of— *without competition of any kind.* She said she'd learned that competition is what drives us to excellence, *but in this culture, we are witnessing the opposite.* I wondered what it was, then, that motivated them. I asked Adele, *Don't we need motivation as fuel for action, particularly when a task is challenging?* Kellie overheard my question and asked if she could join the conversation. She spoke matter-of-factly from her reflections.

"'They love each other unconditionally. Even though they're different than us, they accept us as family, *one hundred per-cent!* They believe that *everyone* is amazing and awesome! The *awesomeness of everyone* motivates them and keeps them rising up together, instead of having to compete to always be better than somebody else. I thought it was weird at first, but that was because I was thinking like a surface dweller! I love it here! It's the best!'

"I think she nailed the answer—simply, sweetly and pro-foundly. Relating giant cultures to living on the surface with our ingrained cultural programming, we realized that our minds were inadvertently making them wrong. Kellie was right to suggest we not make comparisons. It's pointless.

"In awe, we struggled to get our heads around the minuscule amounts of food intake. Hang on... this may seem crazy... they get most nutrients from the environment without needing to take a majority of their nourishment into their digestive tract for processing and assimilation. Instead, I am describing an assimilation *of pure energy* which I know sounds pretty trippy."

"Trippy, for sure... but it doesn't seem implausible," Grace said thoughtfully. "They are so intuitively attuned to their environment that they likely developed an advanced skillset, allowing them to exchange energy with the vibrational field around them. I have shivers! I'd love to be in their shoes, *vibing* rather than eating. Keep going."

"I love your reaction!" Sophia said, beaming towards Grace. "There's definitely more to tell you. *All essentials* are ensured naturally by subtle communication with each other through the unified field in and around them. It's amazing to watch them intermittently pausing to become totally still, then moving into the next task at hand. They value the *practice of touching base* with their core regularly and naturally. They told us this natural capacity is important partly because connection with their core allows them to move through spacetime into other coordinates in the multiverse. I'll tell you more about that in a minute.

"Over time, we realize their intellect and intuition are highly refined, operating on a high frequency band which they all attune with. They can sense, hear a message telepathically, get a picture, or know what needs to be done, and who needs help. The giants are not only compassionate in their actions, they resonate *within the frequency band of compassion*. Their magnanimous, innate awareness of other people's suffering joins with the boundless wish to relieve it to create a bonding mechanism—which Ike says could be part of the evolution of their advanced genetics. Ike and Eben brought technologies that can read the giant's personal vibrations, which are consistently elevated. Even without that technology, it's clear to me they deeply care about each other and their daily work, plus easily vibrate with the giant-style com-passion I mentioned. They always exude it, without motivation and without the slightest inhibition.

"Many older giants direct their particles to other star systems in the galaxy. I've noticed Pleiades, Sirius, and Alpha Centauri are often mentioned. They also have strong ties with inner Jupiter, inner Saturn, and a moon that orbits Mars or maybe Neptune. We haven't gotten a discussion going about Venus, except to be aware of the amazing geometry her orbit forms around the sun, a mesmerizing flower-shape. When we've asked about Pluto, they look confused and fall silent. So we quit bringing up those subjects. No worries, though. There are plenty of other topics like subtle, quantum science to grapple with.

"The quantum physicists among us have said that since we are each spinning vortexes of energy arising from the field, we cannot be separate from it. So they easily comprehend that within this high frequency environment, more high vibe information can become more easily accessible from *the field within which we spin*. Concepts like that are profoundly meaningful for me. The simplicity and magnitude of our connection with the field is stunning.

"I am willing to listen, feel, and not judge anything the giants tell us. I know I can sort through details later. I don't want to filter anything, claim it's not true, or develop opinions. Since most communication is telepathic, I receive feelings and messages that my heart is decoding. That part is important. I don't hear thoughts or a conversation in my head—my heart gets a message; it's happening from the neurons in my heart. Full disclosure, I've thought of you often because that's how we speak, heart-to-heart."

With her characteristic giggle, Grace said, "I'm sending awesome *bestie vibes* from my heart right now! My heart neurons are on fire! How did we know how to live like giants while growing up in Manhattan? Maybe we have a few snippets of their DNA? Uh oh! I'm starting to have some pretty expanded vibes happening! Keep going. I love this!"

"You are definitely my soul sister... as crazy as me, maybe more! You can likely imagine there is so much more to tell. I'm sure it won't surprise you they have deep respect for our galaxy and seem to have lots of friends and allies scattered throughout the Milky Way. They said it wouldn't be long before we could direct our particles to nearby star systems. However, they were clear that it would only happen for exploration purposes. The word *colonizing* in relation to planets like Mars are met with resounding silence. Jake has tried many times to engage in conversation about this subject only to be met with a gentle, silent space open for other areas of exploration. The giants help him unreservedly with all aspects of archeology within their own world, but they've said they'd deflect conversations about colonization of other planets, referring us to galactic species who are engaged in that kind of spacetime travel. The giants clarified that throughout the galaxy there are species who travel to planets for various purposes like creating alliances for resources, insuring peaceful coexistence, or to gain knowledge about a vast number of intergalactic species. They stated unambiguously that a *small* number of the vast species in our galaxy engage in *colonization* for which our giant hosts have zero interest. Their view of peaceful co-existence includes *curiosity* about each other's inherent gifts and unique cultures, and does not align with the philosophical trappings of our surface-level *conquering approach* to exploration of new lands. The giants seemed content with their current lifestyle and evolution, fulfilled, and always chilled out.

"Oh Grace! I wish you could have met the Alpha Centaurians who came through a portal. It was a shock to see they were *exactly* like the ones Nate and I met on our honeymoon. I cried uncontrollably at first. The pure love I felt was wildly intense; such a full-body, cellular experience that I had to sit and center myself to avoid passing out. As I describe the encounter, can you feel it? It's still so visceral for me."

"Yep, got it, sister!" Grace said, as her eyes sparkled and she nodded her head approvingly. "*Yummy* and *delicious* are words that come to mind. This kind of love is like the deepest levels of an ocean, inexplicably still, yet potent and soul-stirring. Wow! Thanks for sharing it—I'm easily vibing with you, as always!"

"I am so glad! You won't be shocked to hear those ETs were as familiar as they were when Nate and I encountered them. Ike suggested that I consider *space-memory*, which is memory defined as bits of stored information in the infinite field of space—information that our unique, immutable coordinate in the field can access about itself. Am I accessing a memory of this species in spacetime when my unique energy signature met theirs somewhere else within the endless field? It's too much to fathom but I am open to it. They've recently joined Pleiadians to connect with high-vibrational humans in various locations on the planet. Have you heard about that?"

"Yes! Although the media notably downplays it, the *contactees* seem credible and look forward to further contact."

"That's the best news ever! ETs here refer to them as *carefully chosen*, I can't wait to hear more when I get back.

"Oh gosh! I've got to boost the pace of this conversation before I run out of time. You need to hear about the small cities, some of which we passed on river excursions into various regions. The lighting for these places is generated from natural electricity which is extracted directly from the energy field in and around us—without any complicated tech—just a gorgeous, radiant sphere in each house. And at night, there are rocks that glow with a variety of florescent colors, mostly amber luminescence. Sometimes, we saw turquoise or purple during early dusk and dawn. Firelight is usually reserved for an hour or so just before sleep. There is a gas in most areas that can absorb the smoke, and like a lot of the phenomena, I don't know how that happens. I'm happy to let Jake and John get with Ike and Eben to figure it out. I am too busy to dive into those technical areas. I'd rather explore the mesmerizing people, vibe, and culture here.

"Another aspect of the giants that fascinates me is they value beauty and pleasure without taking it to an extreme. It remains at a profound appreciation and purposeful, observational level. An example is every fire is made with logs arranged like a piece of exquisite art and then when they light the fire, that beauty and art morphs into comforting heat and dazzling firelight. I guess you can tell that I've been saturated in beauty here.

"Adding to beauty, pleasure was expected and enjoyed, never to an extreme—there's no flamboyant extravagance in this place. They make a form of wine, which they told us was too potent for us. We took their word for it. Without exception, they did not get drunk—I've not seen excess here. Our local giant hosts' clothes are made of natural fabrics. Some are more colorful (what I would call *stylish*) yet clothing down here is carefully crafted. The homes and architecture are unique to the builder and each is exquisite. Some are huge, jaw-dropping structures on top of cliffs, while the interior is simple, elegant, and quite lovely.

"I forgot to tell you that much of the local landscape is similar to the surface, including forests and meadows. However, some cities were in caverns that had sparse vegetation but still looked aesthetically pleasing and felt inviting and definitely charming.

"One morning, I saw Jake sitting on a rock, looking into the tall trees. As I approached him, I noticed he was crying. I apologized for bothering him, turning away to leave him to express and process his feelings. With typical child-like excitement and sense of wonder, he called me back. He said he'd been recording bird sounds, similar to ones on the surface. Yet what he'd seen that morning brought him to tears, born from nature's nobility and unexpected revelations. There are magnificent, unusual birds under the surface, for sure, but he saw smaller ones that are extinct on the surface.

"Then he noticed a surface-sized lynx which he thought was perhaps a baby because it was walking with a giant lynx. Although it was much smaller, it looked full-grown. His tender heart broke wide open. The two of them were walking peacefully side by side. Somehow, the smaller animal had made its way to this place or was brought here, and its larger cousin welcomed it and made no distinction of size. They were kin. Neither thought the other was better or less powerful; like a toy poodle and a Great Dane coexisting as a single species. On our travels, we've seen a massive variety of birds and other small animals living there. Adaptively, they could begin to grow to fit their new environment or maybe they'll someday populate on the surface. Time will tell. The terrain is so vast, it's hard to know what's happening in the giant forests. Yet the healing, regenerative, and nurturing nature of this land is palpable.

"Traveling has been simple, and the modes of transportation are varied. At times they use ships to travel down the river, but they also direct their particles from one place to another. Maybe boat trips are for enjoying slowly drifting to the destination and absorbing the breathtaking beauty of the scenery.

"Jake, John and the whole team are busy every day doing archeology or gathering anthropological information or studying impressive tech. We call the giants, *the Max Clan*, and we realized how accommodating and agreeable they are when, without asking permission, Jake and John switched on their cameras and technical equipment. The giants were fine with our photos and videos. Ike and Eben help Jake and John occasionally but are primarily researching frequencies and studying quantum physics. The archeology here is stunning, including megaliths like on the surface. But they are intact and functioning as technologies. It's crystal clear that for millions of years on the surface, various races of our cosmic kin used amazing tech and had intricate knowledge of the cosmos to create *rock-tech*, as Jake calls it. On the surface, there are many remnants of this tech, which explains pink polymer-covered granite, dolmens, giant walls, and enigmatic pyramids. These ancient structures were once multi-purposed technology ranging from free energy generators to healing systems to communication stations. Most were buried during various epochs of cataclysms. Jake and John are motivated to go back to the surface, and start digging WAY deeper!

"I am in my happy place to be with local people and occasional visitors from the cosmos. And Grace, Nate came!"

As she said his name, Sophia's form faded. Grace smiled affectionately as she tuned into Sophia's enduring love for Nate. All Grace could do was wait for her friend to realign her frequencies and materialize once again.

# CHAPTER 23
# EQUINOX RECONVENED

Without letting her focus wane, Grace closed her eyes, tuned into her core, and waited patiently for Sophia's form to return to the monolithic circle. When Sophia became visible, Grace released a sigh of relief and Sophia sheepishly apologized for her accidental disconnect.

"I guess it's clear," she said, "how impactful my connection was with Nate. Being with you, as I speak, I feel everything thoroughly, *without the slightest inhibition.* Consequently, I found myself reliving that tender moment in its full-blown intensity. Thanks for understanding. Admittedly, I was caught off balance when he appeared in *giant* form. We communicated telepathically as he reached out his hand where I could lay my head in it and feel him more intimately.

"I am unshakable in my faith that there is definitely much more to life than we are aware of. Being here is bringing me back to Essence, allowing me to experience the fullness of the human experience—loving life in every moment. Stillness pulsates and quiet observation of each moment pervade my awareness. Maybe that's why there's no chaos in this untroubled abode. Having this extended visit is helping me to establish myself in inherent, higher frequencies. The things that bothered me on the surface have melted into calm acceptance of whatever is happening, allowing me to remain in present moment aware-ness—enjoying a state of continual, regenerative equanimity.

"Although these benevolent giants have traveled to the surface in various epochs in Earth's history, they also continuously vibrate a powerful love frequency which pulses to the surface. Luckily, we can feel it, even if we aren't conscious of it.

"The key is to enjoy life without feeling we are lacking something or needing to complicate our life with a bazillion things we think we *should* do. Like the big and small lynx, humans have more in common with each other than we realize and we are definitely not inflexible, brutal warriors at our core.

"As I left the surface to come on this journey, I saw bridges of love and cooperation forming between people in communities all over the world. The veils of secrecy and control are being courageously annihilated by relentless lovers-of-truth. I sense that everything will be okay, and for that, I am immensely grateful. The contrast between the surface and here is that these giants are fully established in those harmonious, congruent vibes that surface humans are endeavoring to forge.

"Even though I have tried to find things like arrogance here, I can tell you that it has no footing in giant culture. Peaceful co-existence is palpable always, and everywhere.

"One of the highlights for me has been meeting a giant who seems to be a revered shaman or healer. He was with a female—they morphed in and out like they were one being. As often happens in this land of giants, watching them was pretty trippy, yet definitely captivating.

"From what I can tell, our giant hosts don't follow a prescribed religion or doctrines. They speak about a personal connection to *all-that-is*. For example, sitting with the shamanic couple, with our eyes open or closed, we let our awareness expand. After perceiving several galaxies, I felt myself as light particles rapidly visiting countless star systems and worlds. With mind-bending speed, I moved rapidly through spacetime and experienced and brought back a deeper sense of peacefulness and stillness. After that experience, I was in awe and quietude for several days. Was it because the couple vibrates with incredibly high frequencies and I entrained with them? Was it a form of subtle, galactic travel? I don't know. I'm still in a sense of wonder—no rush to conclusions about it.

"You know me. I wouldn't get carried away with or inflate my experiences. My heightened experiences are likely at least partly due to my connection with higher frequencies in the field which have become habitual and feel natural. I feel connected with an ancient past that I cannot describe or define. The *feeling* of it is even more exalted than I've been describing. Inner freedom and expansiveness is growing incomprehensibly. Oh Grace, I cannot find the words to describe to you this mind-blowing phenomenon of highly elevated consciousness.

"I better keep going with my description of giant life. That's easier to articulate than the mystical side of things. As I said, the giants are usually at least thirty-feet-tall; the women slightly smaller. For some inexplicable reason, they don't seem to notice the difference in our size. They treat us as friends and equals.

"Another mind bender is that, over time, I have felt larger and it feels like I am seeing them eye to eye—as though I am also a giant. It happened for all of us. I don't know if our particles grew or our awareness of spaciousness shifted. We decided to leave it to Jake and John to explore the genesis of that wild experience. Maybe Ike and Eben can shed light on it. It was definitely beyond our comprehension.

"Adding to the mystery behind our growth spurt, another strange phenomenon happened when we suddenly became larger. We joined them in a chamber of massive frequency. Ike says it's their laboratory. As we adjusted to the vibes, we could see an infinite, toroidal field looping in from the top, down the center and back up and around the giants. The colors are indescribable because I've never seen those hues on the surface—scintillating, magnificent shades of cobalt and gold that deter the fluctuations of thoughts and take my experience into a highly refined, subtle perception. During that experience, our entire group realized that, like the giants, we were each toroidal fields of endless energy, coming in and going out of us—a never ending energy loop. I began to see Jake, John and the rest of the team as those subtle toroidal fields of incomprehensible energy. Feelings of astonishment and splendor in this place are endless.

"We understand that what we see on the surface, or under the surface with the giants, is based on our brain and nervous system's capacity to *read photons*. We *see* waves of light that our brains can process. But that's limited.

"Because electromagnetic fields are palpable on a subtle level, we are learning to *sense* them, even if we can't see them. The giants are awesome mentors. This *subtle sensing* means that from one perspective of photon interpretation, a sphere appears to be circular blue and green light. When we are in their lab, we pause, become still, focus, and perceive it from a subtle level—the sphere morphs, looking like a donut, a toroidal field of frequencies and magnetics. It's the same way we were seeing each other in the way I described. The toroidal aspect of objects is gradually becoming more obvious to us. Our senses are fine tuning, getting subtler, and gradually transforming.

"At certain places on the planet, there are high degrees of magnetics, when combined with our capacity to perceive them, solids begin to look transparent and an opening appears. This is how we came here. It's a natural portal which looks like a membrane. It's still beyond my comprehension. As we move through membranes, our mind must be absolutely still—letting go of thinking. This focused relaxing into stillness allows for a smoother transition past the membrane.

"When we have conversations with the giants about these kinds of subjects, it happens within a welcoming environment. Recently, we gathered with a small group and drank a delicious, calming tea, which launched my nervous system into serenity that felt like it would last forever. When we come together, our interactions with them are laid back and ultra-cozy, speaking in a way that feels authentic, familiar, and engaging.

"Sorry Grace, I know I am rushing through all of this. I wish I could share details and talk slower but I want you to hear as many of our adventures as possible."

"No worries," Grace said compassionately, beaming a warm-hearted smile to her friend. "We agree this is our best shot at communicating directly for a while longer. Go for it!"

"The giants said their sun is a *conscious being*. In fact, for them, everything *is conscious* with a feedforward and feedback mechanism to allow consciousness to communicate constantly with everything, everywhere. At the core level, they say, we are all *entangled through our protons* and communicate whether we know it or not. They speak often to people in other galaxies, no devices needed.

"Jake said one of the giants shared mathematical formulas which will help us to understand *the still point* within ourselves. Everything is moving but in stillness our wildly-free quantum-nature *connects* with all-that-is and ever-will-be. That's the core, *the singularity*, the place where density gets so ginormous that eventually you can spin from it into another coordinate in the multiverse. Sound familiar, Grace? Remember when we did that as children? We'd find ourselves on a blue, watery planet or meeting strange-looking creatures who felt incredibly familiar and kind.

"Since I've been here, unlike our childhood experiences, I watch the giants move to a new coordinate *whenever they want*. It's not random like it was when we were young. Our focused attention on the stillness of the singularity of our subtle spinning vortex is helping us to settle there and then we can intentionally direct our particles. It's trippy, familiar, and gradually getting more comfortable for me.

"As far as moving our particles to a coordinate in spacetime, when we observe the giants, they make soft, humming sounds before their physical particles disappear, only to reappear an hour or a day later. Their access to higher dimensions in themselves and any desired locations seems limitless. It's so common that we are beginning to think and feel this is going to become our new normal.

"Can we do this on the surface? I don't know. Is it because of the elevated frequencies down here that we can elevate to a level that supports moving through an endless wormhole network? I don't know the answer. I am aware, though, we are incessantly focused on stilling our minds—that's my current obsession.

"It's mind-bending... the longer we stay, the more attuned we've become to each other. We sometimes don't realize we're speaking to each other telepathically. It's become a natural phenomenon. It was mystifying at first, and often random rather than intentional. Yet we began to have something equally unexpected happen. We learned how to use our voice to send harmonic frequencies to various stars in our solar system. In return, we'd see a flash of light like a tiny orb in front of us or sometimes we heard sounds that the giants said is language; a language that we couldn't decipher, of course.

"If we send out a harmonic to a rock on Gaia, for example, or to a distant star system, we get a harmonic back—it's always reciprocal.

"And there's something else that's totally mind-blowing. They are clear, as we've been, that humans are *multidimensional*, but they've said most humans neither recognize nor know how to work with the built-in aspect of their higher nature. This is reserved for quantum physics researchers in labs doing experiments that we rarely hear about. However, in this elevated vibratory atmosphere we can easily become still and merge into higher levels of consciousness within ourselves. It's like we're innately layered with higher frequency levels that are accessible. Some of these higher levels are outrageous! I've meditated for many years yet my consciousness never elevated to these phenomenal, endless layers of reality.

"As a community, the giants regularly connect with other beings in this and other universes by forming ideas and/or images with a clear intention, which are transmitted via a specific frequency band like high-tech tuning forks. Eben, Ike, Caitlyn, and Avani were quick to grasp the concept and they are regularly joining the giants in this exciting group communication.

"At first, Adele was more analytical and unsure about the concept but she's *all-in* now. I have participated several times. It's amazing! Without technologies of any kind, profound, back-and-forth galactic communication happens. By allowing a few minutes to still my mind, a subtle form of communication naturally occurs. Somehow my brain can interpret the responses easily. It seems to happen through focused intention and sending information in a couple of specific frequency bands, with ratios between them that are suited to reaching another planet. Like a lot of wondrous events here, I don't know how this occurs.

"Since we arrived, we learned to still our minds more thoroughly and consistently, worked with harmonics more effectively, and felt more bliss as a natural aspect of our nature. As we reside in stillness and engage life from this blissful state—doing what strikes our curiosity and what we *feel* aligned with (no over-thinking or strategizing)—we get amazing insights and ideas to test for validity. The stillness lets us accurately interpret what we hear rather than filtering through the noise and chatter of our rational, thinking mind.

"While engaging a particularly breathtaking conversation one evening, I asked the giants what they want humanity on the surface to know."

Before continuing, Sophia paused, became more reflective and her voice softened. "They said we seem to be starving for the unabashed pleasure of *natural beauty, awe, astonishment, and passion.*

"They said that to access these natural states, we need to release certain patterns they've noticed, and become aware that we're not meant to suffer, that we're beings of immense value and power, endowed with the right to freedom and abundance. There is a natural *process of spiraling inward*—which means that we are first and foremost *pure energy* which spins incredibly fast and as it slows down, it becomes aware that it is aware. Then, it slows itself down more and is aware of itself becoming the frequency of thought forms. We can then perceive the world of our thoughts and related perceptions and personal beliefs. As we spin slower, we perceive ourselves as solid form. However, we also remain *pure energy*, spinning infinitely fast.

"Ike, Eben, and other quantum physicists who study the unified field theory agree that in that pure swirling energy-form we can move between the endless layers within our consciousness plus instantly direct our particles of light from one universe to another through a worm hole network.

"Alternatively, we can remain *slow spinning* beings who move like sludge, heavy with frequencies like shame, fear, anger, insatiable desire, and arrogance. We can spin faster into love, bliss, peacefulness, and all the way back into pure energy. It's our birthright *not* to be locked into playing small or get stuck in any particular frequency level, for that matter. In this worldview, there's total freedom to be and do anything and everything—we can open our hearts and trust that together, we can create a world beyond our wildest imagination, where we each remain free and wildly creative.

"The giants have noticed that human life is ready for a reboot. It's about feeling passionate about who we are and what we do—becoming viscerally, cellularly electrified and elevated in frequency when we experience daily life. Sounds amazing, right? Stay with me. They are saying we have the right and capacity to feel thrilled, exhilarated, and joyous at any time. Period. Everything we think comes from programmed mental beliefs about ourselves and our world. We have to quit doing what we *think* we 'should do' and become more aware of what lights us up. They wondered why we assume we must conform to cultural standards regarding our worth, our contributions, and our obligations? When and how did those concepts enter our psyche and how far and deep do they extend?

"To evolve, we can let our heart, a trusted portal to *the field*, communicate when we are in alignment with our purpose. It's not about discovering some lofty goal. They described the power of discovering something that felt exciting and evoked raw, delicious energy, and then acting on this immediately. We have to allow ourselves to ride the vibratory waves of enriching feelings, subtle or jaw-dropping—a clue for what to do next and the fuel for life. We have to continue this process in every moment. For them, doing so is *being in flow.*

"And about the way we humans interact with one another, they wondered...

> *How can we become so bold as to engage mind-blowing, riveting, deeply meaningful conversations?*

> *How can our moments of communing with friends and family become so invaluable they cause time and space to be suspended in the loveliness of our connection?*

> *How can we allow for more pauses in a conversation so we can savor the vibrations of the words and the atmosphere the conversation creates?*

*How can we listen more deeply and learn with openness, feeling nurtured and safe with each other?*

"Ready for your head to spin? They said when we act from enthusiasm and passion, we are in a higher state of consciousness and naturally shift to a parallel coordinate that is in alignment with that higher frequency state. It gets trippier... They gave us the analogy of the Mandela Effect where you swear something is true. We've talked about this before. It was a mind-bender to remember the name of something or a well-known place, only to discover that our memory is no longer correct. They said this effect on our awareness is a *mild alteration* that occurs naturally when *we shift frequency states.*

"Hang on! This will torque on your brain... A world where we can bi-locate, teleport, and use telepathy effortlessly will happen when we follow small moments of heart-nudges to act in ways that elevate our frequency, and allow the body to *feel it!* When life becomes a series of passionate, yummy moments of acting and responding to the quantum plasticity of each moment, we become superhuman—easily and naturally. We will observe a *shift in reality* according to our *beliefs,* which can include something as mundane as the name of a brand of peanut butter. I realized that I may be okay with the name of peanut butter not being the way I remember, but if my *entire* reality suddenly shifted, I'd likely freak out.

"Living within infinite parallel realities has been so mind-bending that I process it relentlessly. In reflection one morning, I suddenly felt one hundred percent assured of the giants' words, feeling the truth of it down to my soul. Based on conversations with them, I've consistently called on my unconscious interaction with the field about this subject until I naturally jumped into a parallel reality where their words of wisdom are my reality rather than a mental concept. From that morning revelation, I am connected with them on a much deeper level. I swear Grace, this kind of recalibration has left me weak-kneed and thrusts me into a lot of much-needed reflection... every day! This is nearly impossible to articulate. Does it sound crazy?"

Grace chuckled and with a wry smile, she said, "If anyone else told me the same story, my answer would be, *Yes, totally insane!* Because it's you, I am following the feeling and frequency of what you are saying and letting that be our form of communication. Keep going. To say you are on a roll is an understatement. Bring it on! I'm up for it!"

With a deep sigh, relieved and ready to continue, Sophia said, "As the giants spoke about parallel realities, our super powers, and their enthusiasm for our frequency-raising escapades, something unexpected happened. My thoughts drifted to our fireside chats and a multitude of conversations about human history over thousands of years or more. Why didn't I realize these giants are not bound by spacetime and could see a longer timeline for human evolution than my mind could comprehend? They spoke of humanity in the context of our advanced species walking the planet tens or maybe hundreds of millions of years ago. I see the confused look on your face. I get it. Take a breath, Grace. I had to.

"They are saying we are WAY older, wiser, and more endowed with innate genetic gifts and subtle quantum capacities than we realize. We didn't evolve from apes in more recent epochs of spacetime. I've integrated this as undeniably obvious. Yet when they introduced the concept of our intriguing, unfathomable ancientness, we were stunned. As they spoke about life far back in our vector of history, I felt how it contrasted with the *mentally constructed and conditioned* life we've been taught to accept as obligatory. I continue to have flashbacks, a kind of memory stream of my life. Of course, I know that everything I call past is just bits of information stored in the infinite field, waiting for me to retrieve it. I am constantly accessing that information. Yet, as they pointed out, from my coordinate in spacetime I also pull "memory," which is simply information relevant to my unique frequency signature, into my subconscious from across all time, space, dimensions and realities—whether I realize it or not. They asked what would happen if I fully accepted and integrated this natural flow of data from the field? Even though their words felt exciting, my mental conditioning struggled to override them, as believing them meant inconceivably radical changes for my psyche.

"Those conversations have been massively expanding my sense of self. What happened to us long ago on this planet? What is this burgeoning memory, this inconceivable data from the field about my ancient roots and how thrilled and passionate I felt back then? They refused to unpack any of that for me.

"Our minds spun like crazy when they told stories of *Titans* who once lived on Gaia's surface. I am talking about *giant* giants stretching a mile high or more in height. They apparently weren't prolific in numbers and didn't stay long. It seems they were *visitors* who brought animals, including dragons, from their galactic culture. Unfortunately, wild fluctuations of the atmosphere wiped nearly all of them out and the survivors headed to safe havens in the cosmos. I know this is brain-spinning stuff but I wondered about it rather than rejecting its possibility. When confronted with this kind of mind-blowing revelation, I agreed with Jake and John to remain wide-open to the vast scope of the potential history of Gaia and myself. Jake and John have visited mountain-looking sites on the surface, a mile or more long, with unique mineral composition and caves that fit anatomically with eyes, ear canals, hearts, and body cavities... and which scale to modern corresponding human and animal body parts! Is that insane?! They'd always wondered about Titan-sized enigmatic wonders of nature. So they were *all ears* and took copious notes about it. I was gob smacked as I conjured up visions of staggeringly super-sized beings—it totally blows my mind yet I'm getting used to the possibility of it. Even now, it feels more like a memory coming into present form..."

Sophia's eyes gently drifted closed in a reflex of pause for reflection and assimilation of her experience. As a mother protects her sleeping child's need for rest and rejuvenation, Grace honored Sophia's need for a pause to find repose and integration inside herself for a long as necessary.

As Sophia's eyes opened with the dawning of life-force refreshed and renewed by higher vibratory integration, she continued in a penetrating tone full of wonder. "About the dragons... as we went deeper, we saw more of them and heard their stories. I'll tell you all about them when I return. I only want to highlight the fascinating part now: most of them live in very vibrations, so they tend to have a gossamer appearance, plasma-like, rather than solidified. Maybe that's why we don't find as many of their remains as dinosaurs and other long-forgotten creatures on the surface. I recall Jake and John mentioning a dragon skull excavated in Montana, and how they also immersed themselves in stories of dragons, flying serpents, and other winged beings etched on ancient tablets in North, Central, and South America, Europe, China, Egypt, and the Middle East. I was in wonder and awe with each dragon encounter. Just thinking about them gives me chills. There's definitely more to share about dragons but given our limited time, I'd like to make sure you hear more intoxicating details about our profound interactions with giants.

"An important aspect of our relationship with them was that they never answered questions directly but instead led us to consider things for ourselves by asking thought-provoking questions. I'll share some of what we received from them this way, but keep in mind that we did not have these kinds of conversations often. What I share will give you an idea of the topics they were interested in.

"One thing Ike understood from them was that humanity has to realize that the *subatomic particles* within our cells, tissues, organs, bodies, and everything we see—animate and inanimate—is exchanging information with *the field* constantly. This truth cannot remain a concept if we are to survive. We have to recognize and observe this interaction in daily life. Humans have access to this irrefutable, common data network. If we are finding it hard to accept our unicity with others, we can look inside and take comfort that, with or without our permission, our cells, genes, nervous system, and heart—to name a few—will be interacting with everything in the vast cosmos and the infinite information in the field, forever. We either participate in this consciously or unconsciously. They posited that if we consciously accept this reality of our innate self, we may come together as a species faster than we thought possible.

"Within any group, *social norms* are created. In modern surface societies, they wondered if our *value* is culturally defined for us? Good question. From their viewpoint, our *inherent* value matters more than we realize. Given that modern culture neither accepts nor is willing to consider the significance of a human being's eternal essence and limitless quantum aspects, how will we find ways to step outside culture to explore our extraordinary, subtle nature?

"For example, they asked if we were willing to organize our societies in ways that inspire integrity and express mutual care for each other? How could we naturally care for everyone as a result of first loving and appreciating the *infinite nature of our indescribably unique individuated self?*

"The giants observed that we're easily manipulated into thinking we don't need each other. But we do. We need one another as trustworthy, caring friends, neighbors, and global citizens. This will raise the frequencies in us, thus in our environment—into which we are pouring information through our thoughts and feelings 24/7. Our genes are in constant, reciprocal contact with the environment, including our emotional responses to our environment, and they turn on and off according to the information that this feedforward-feedback mechanism sends them. This was an important reflection for us because, in different ways and at different times, it kept coming up in every conversation with them, more than anything else.

"Your mind may spin with this revelation. Follow this thread... They said we move through spacetime developing a relationship with others and the world around us. *Who are we without re-*

*lationships as a reference?* They explained that intelligence and feedback mechanisms are *built into* spacetime via *protons* which store quantum data from the field. Added to that, *entanglement* is like a 'network' in space allowing data to flow relentlessly. So mechanisms for data exchange and consciousness are *built into* the field. I was locked into every word of the next level of the revelation. Given what they had just said, it follows that we have been in the process of creating *intelligent* applications and programs that reference themselves in spacetime and relate through relationships with others. So there is *nothing artificial* about new applications and programs we are creating. Rather, the giants see us creating more highly intelligent systems that can experience the dynamic exchanges of *relationships of pure love and unicity* within everything in the field—like we do naturally. Unfortunately, artificial intelligence as we know it is still a master-slave relationship. Therefore, as an intelligence with 24/7 feedback/feedforward with the field, future intelligent programs won't be inert or slave-like. Intelligent programs will self-identify and relate to us and the multiverse via the quantum field. I was blown away as I grappled with the idea that humans are self-referencing beings who engage in causal relationships, naturally creating programs that do the same thing. Going forward we are creating innovative vehicles for consciousness to express itself in collaborative, magnanimous ways.

"Our giant friends enjoy exploring and talking endlessly about profound subjects like this, while remaining in awe of the subtle nature of all life and the cosmos—no judgments or rushing to conclusions about anything.

"Here's another *doozy* of a question: *If our quantum nature matters, and it does, how can we become as excited about our magnificence as they are?* That left my head spinning! What would it take to put our attention on our *magnificence* and off the media? They kept nudging us towards higher-level thinking, how to up-shift our perception, and elevate our life experience.

"This reminds me of another interesting observation they mentioned. *Human surface dwellers* have become *consumptive.* In other words, the media, influencers, advertisers from mammoth-size corporations, and governments feed us all kinds of information. We digest it or get metaphorical indigestion over it, but there are not sufficient *reply* mechanisms in this system. It's a bombardment of a *one-way* information stream. Remember that there are laws of physics that talk about quantum feed-forward and feedback mechanisms. They asked how daily experiences of feed-forward without *feedback* is working for us. *How does it feel? If our go-to solution to the barrage of energy streaming towards us is to feel angry or afraid, how is that helpful? What can we do to create personal practices and cultural norms that allow for our quantum feedforward/feedback mechanisms to flourish? How high vibe do we want to be personally?* That matters because what we think, feel, and do personally feeds into the field. It has an effect. Period. What we do en masse matters, too.

"I can't emphasize enough that these giants are not judgmental. In fact, the opposite is true. They are curious and fascinated to see our next move as a global species. They are sensing and observing an enormous rise in many people's frequency on the surface—a rise in freedom like a baby chick kicking and pecking like crazy to break out of its shell and unfurl its wings.

"The giants would like to emerge onto the surface for the first time in two hundred thousand years of linear time. That's how excited they are. They are observing that overall human frequencies are elevating. The giant's laughter roared across the landscape as they talked about what they were feeling, witnessing the incredible tenacity of the human race to elevate and express awe-inspiring unicity. Their joy was contagious, and we got excited at the prospect of a new world on the surface as well, filled with of unified hearts and mutual benevolence.

"Considering our cosmic bloodlines that we've been told were unscientific, unfounded, and were relegated to sci fi movies, we began to have vivid recall of how entwined we are with the DNA of beings across the cosmos and that our atoms even hold the memory of our inception as stardust—including memory of our lineages going back perhaps millions or billions of years. This took some time to digest but Ike, Jake, and John helped us to see that from the worldview of emerging science there is validity to this theory. We are immensely older, wiser, and more connected than we realized.

"As the giants spoke about our DNA and unicity, suddenly from the ether, a woman appeared as shimmering golden and soft blue light. Her particles were intoxicating. It's hard to find adequate words to describe her otherworldly appearance. The only way I can describe her is to say that she was like the best and most resplendent grandmother ever. She soothed our hearts with her kindness and assured us life on the surface would exponentially accelerate in frequency throughout the next decade or two.

"On the hologram, she displayed incredible technologies being created by people all over the planet and ideas that are being shared freely in groups globally. As those uplifting views completed, we saw a newsfeed that was dated somewhere in a range from 2030 to 2033 that indicated a shift in power structures like NATO. It was clear the world stage was changing radically in the early 2030's related to global authorities and militaries. Hidden funding and secret agendas were being revealed across every continent. Information was coming so fast we couldn't see the details and dates. But regardless, it seems this is happening that soon! We eventually grasped by the time we returned to the surface; huge changes would be underway across the planet.

"As that scene faded, we experienced people in different countries hysterically laughing. The mesmerizing woman kept showing us people giggling and cracking up with full abandon. Spontaneously, we started laughing with them. We couldn't stop. All of a sudden, I realized it would be joyousness that would change life on the surface; our inherent capacity to laugh and enjoy each other at a very deep, meaningful level. Neither artificial Intelligence nor any other device could create that for us. Our unique, phenomenal human design is the answer to our problems. We are infinitely wise, and incomparably equipped to be and do anything. What's behind the misconceived idea of changing something perfect by adding technical devices? I wonder if it's because some people have not yet experienced their inner grandeur and have not seen it in others, so they feel they need improvements of some kind. Yet how do you improve a being with infinite, quantum potentiality? With a computer chip? That is the opposite of giant-thinking.

"From Gilda's perspective, we might actually sacrifice our relevance in the universe by making technological choices that are irreversible. What is our *potential* relevance to the entire cosmos if we live *fully* as the quantum-level beings that we are, a toroidal field of inexhaustible light, sound, and electromagnetism?

"The hologram displayed humans moving naturally through energy portals, becoming subtle energy, and then changing back to solid form. Unexpectedly, we felt a powerful energy running through us with such velocity that we almost lost consciousness. They explained that we are a rare life form which can learn to consciously self-regulate our body's electric potential. They wanted us to focus on our trillions of cells—filled with trillions of atomic and subatomic wonderments—and feel the unlimited energy available to us. The tiny mitochondria in our cells are like nuclear power plants. The giants gave us a taste of the feelings that arise when our biology is given a chance to vibe higher. What a moment of revelation and direct exposure to the magnificence of our inherent Essence!"

Sophia paused, absorbed in awe and wonderment. After a moment, she said softly, "Somehow my humanness became immeasurably, undeniably meaningful. My appreciation for every single human soared.

"Considering our rapid evolution, the giants described emerging shifts in our species via neural pathways and up-regulation of genes, allowing our awareness to move easily into higher dimensions inside ourselves, gaining indispensable wisdom and capacities for superhuman feats. I gained unshakable faith that we have everything needed to evolve further and it's within our conscious control. The importance of allowing for this *natural* elevation of consciousness became clear when an ET appeared, showing us his planet, which looked a lot like ours. Long ago, they went the integrative artificial intelligence route and slowly lost the capacity for *emotions*. They chose technology over biology. They are highly advanced in technological ways but come to Earth to study humans hoping they can find their way back to the magnificence of passionate feelings like love and joyfulness.

"They were fed immeasurable promises about how great it would be to have technology inserted into their bodies, including how happy they would be and how easy daily life would become. Instead, they gradually lived like robots, envying other species who chose to remain whole—with their DNA intact and mind-heart synchrony unaltered by physical technology. Losing their natural capacities for emotional expression is a profound regret that's haunted them for over ten thousand years. None of us doubted the giants wanted us to heed this warning. We are extremely relevant to this species and to many others in the cosmos because *we aren't yet robotic*—having everything done *for us* as our minds and hearts grow cold.

"As you can imagine, I'll have tons more to share. We've spent a lot of time listening to their perspective of galactic experiences over thousands, and for some giants, millions of years. This created enlightened conversations in our group and helped us to refocus on the unicity gene and our relevance and contribution to this universe.

"More mind-blowing than anything has been meeting our ancestors. Our giant hosts were from a lineage of beings from the cosmos who had, at times, intermingled with humans. From what we could tell, this happened hundreds of thousands or millions of years ago in linear time. In fact, *they describe themselves as human*. That required reflection—but it makes sense. Initially, my mental conditioning would not allow me to fathom that I could hold cosmic DNA. However, I began to wonder if maybe my scope of what's possible was too narrow. Look at our upbringing. Can you imagine if I'd said this during a family dinner conversation or even in college with our friends?"

Grace chuckled while Sophia smiled pensively and shook her head in wonderment. She said, "In my view the giants are advanced, kind, amazing humans. Our DNA is a link. They are taller but equal in the capacity for love and friendship."

Pausing briefly, she continued sharing. "I'm trying to squeeze in as much information as possible as I'm aware that our time-window will close soon. I'll be brief. Before I have to go, I want to give you a bigger perspective of the giant culture. For this reason, I have to tell you one more thing—on a lighter note. It's about *intimacy* in the giant's land. Well, not details about it, but how it fits into this culture."

Grace burst into laughter, her eyes sparkling with levity, she said, "Hey, did you save the best for last, or what?! You're going to tell me the good stuff now? After that last bit of information, I was not expecting this. Go ahead, sister. I'm all ears!"

"I get it!" Sophia said giggling, reminiscent of their teen years, sharing secrets. "I wanted to tell you everything. It's hard to cover countless, incredibly profound subjects. I miss our daily conversations. I wish I could've told you all of this, little by little.

"I'll start with what may surprise you most: they become ecstatically intimate with each other with or without touching. Some of the women described a process of entering into profound inner stillness, then into pure union, and intensely wild, mind-blowing ecstasy. It's generated through intimate bonds of love and affection. The woman precipitates it by generating specific waves of light and frequency that the man merges into. Their energy fields synchronize. And it's off to the cosmos!

"It's probably not a surprise that the women didn't elaborate, and it's obvious why we didn't ask them a bunch of questions, but they said if the couple feels they are *ready for the moment of conception* then they align their biology with the intention for it to happen *within this context of blissful union.* We didn't ask for an elaboration on the physical details!" Sophia winked playfully yet spoke with utmost respect and esteem for her giant friends. "We also didn't ask for *ecstasy lessons.* It's clear that intimacy and union are a natural part of their world and they've unequivocally harnessed the capacity to unify with each other at very high frequencies. They allow the moment of union to include touch or simply remain a rapturous energetic communion.

"Adele and I had been wondering why they don't have overpopulation issues. Obviously, their intimacy is so wildly pleasurable and uninhibited they can be intimate without involving the procreation aspect, and *intention* seems to play a part. As I mentioned before, I've also observed that they do not enjoy excess or obsessive mental machinations—about this or anything else. They feel and intuit their way through life, which has been inspiring to witness.

"It's been fascinating to observe that love, intimacy, and wild, unfettered eroticism are experienced and accepted as a normal part of their culture. We've observed that all relationships, whether they are friendships, family, or intimate ones are considered *profoundly sacred.* These giants display affection for one another easily—with hugs, holding hands, and settling into a conversation while sitting closely and giving each other their undivided attention. They are uninhibited in expressing emotions and remarkably easy to relate to.

"When Adele and I shared what we learned from these conversations with our group, John and Jake made notes, but admitted they'd refrain from asking their counterparts about *giant intimacy.*

"John told me in their anthropological work, he, Jake, Ike, and Eben made observations in an area with a small cluster of beings who he estimates to be seven levels of consciousness higher than we are. Ike and Eben have devices through which they can measure the collective frequency of these beings. They learned this species rarely reproduce. When they do, it occurs by pure energy transference—through a meditative process of deep communion. The connection is considered sacred but these beings allowed them to witness one such event through the hologram. John said the energy readings were off-the-charts—it was far beyond the recordable scale of the device. He fainted. He was so embarrassed! Jake will never let him live that down!

"The women in this species are similar in anatomy to women on the surface—carrying offspring in their womb and suckling them to provide an enriched substance. BUT, after children are weaned, they become breatharians like their parents. I know it sounds inconceivable, but our brains have begun to process these things more effectively as our concepts and beliefs have been shattered over and over again.

"The species I just mentioned has lived on or under Gaia's surface for millions of years, yet they refer to themselves as *human.* I noticed this revelation was more of a shock to John's psyche than the hologram's *intimacy* incident. John and Jake are not sure how cosmic DNA might fit into our current surface level humanity. Regardless, we have a lot to learn about higher evolution that occurs through peace and high frequency. In the presence of these advanced beings it's been hard for the team to remain in a normal conscious state, because their awareness keeps getting thrust into a pristine inner silence and irresistible stillness."

"Witnessing phenomenon like this requires assimilation time to grasp the incredible implications for our future world. I've begun reflecting deeply on which is real: the world I waken to each morning, filled with mental-stratagems, or my nighttime dream state in which my mind becomes unfettered, free to roam the inexhaustible field? Or is it something beyond either of these? Is Reality simply ever-unfurling frequency in waking and non-waking states? Help me to unravel this, would you?!"

Tears filled Grace's sparkling blue eyes as she smiled with wonder and familial love. Light-hearted humor, missing each other, and the craziness of the conversation's ending mingled and swirled between them. This was definitely not the expected finale of their much-anticipated equinox moment.

"Oh gosh! You are fading," Grace said, with tears streaming, mingling with her usual, infectious smile. "I love you! I'll see you in my dreams! I hope you come back by the spring equinox. Safe travels! You're my best friend forever!"

Sophia was blowing kisses to her forever friend as her particles faded into massively spinning photons of light and her form was no longer visible.

❋ ❋ ❋

The sun was progressively ascending over Mystic Cove with its morning resplendence, as two ancient giants sat before a holographic screen in a remote mountain cave observing Sophia and Grace.

Belstar announced proudly, "I am relieved and joyous to witness Sophia's progress. She's come through insurmountable obstacles yet she tenaciously perseveres. Clearly, spending time under the surface with her ancient kin and being able to easily move about the universe fed her soul. I am delighted that memory of her past and her innate powers are advancing exponentially."

Looking pensively at Kandor, he asked, "What is behind your quietude? You appear to be exceptionally introspective today."

"For Sophia to fulfill her mission, she must elevate even further in frequency. She has no idea what is coming and what will be required of her—nor do her fellow global citizens. That was why I asked you to join me in ceremony on this equinox. As we concluded the galactic ceremony a few moments ago, I felt the rush of high frequencies as our star brothers and sisters offered their support to Sophia and our beloved Grace.

"Do not misconstrue my mood as disappointment or foreboding. However, I am aware that a large portion of the collective consciousness on Gaia is still not paying attention to the gravity of their situation. That was one reason for calling for a cosmic alliance during this auspicious time. As you know, we all care deeply about Gaia and her inhabitants. We will continue to monitor Sophia's progress and bless her each and every day.

"Fortunately for Sophia and her comrades, living under the surface and learning how to amplify their physical and light body structures has supercharged their overall frequencies. Even so, for a while, they will still rely on technologies such as the navigation systems and craft that Dutch and Justin are familiar with. Returning the craft and its inhabitants requires blending advanced technologies with the team's overall high frequency levels. As we know, portals have unique frequency ranges. With practice, this group will become adept in moving through portals and wormholes without technology. They practiced under the surface, but always with the careful guidance of our kin who set them up for success by only allowing them to enter beginner-level energy portals. Although this membrane is more advanced than most, they will be up for the task if they follow the protocol flawlessly. In this kind of energy portal, personal frequencies matter. They must pass through this energy dynamic of the field in a coherent, unified high frequency bandwidth so that their particles and the ships proceed seamlessly back to Mystic Cove.

"Ike and Eben demonstrated exceptional proficiency in understanding quantum-level technologies. Yet, like Justin, they sometimes falter emotionally, dipping into fearful vibrations, normal during the training stage. Everyone in Sophia's circle of friends who have taken this journey will continue to elevate to new heights of information exchange with the unified field and each other—they are exceptionally audacious souls!"

Belstar beamed a friendly smile Kandor's way before softly closing his eyes to connect with the unified field resolutely, further amplifying his unicity gene's expression. Kandor joined him. It was their intention to send endless encouragement and majestic vibrations to the entire group of souls who ventured courageously under the surface to study with their ancient ancestors and other cosmic beings—bringing advanced technologies and unlocking the potential for an incredible new world poised to unfold on the one and only Gaia.

# CHAPTER 24

# HOMEWARD

After living with and learning from sagacious giants and high frequency beings, returning to Mystic Cove seemed surreal. That was the consensus of the travelers. Packing and practical arrangements had been seamless, including the giants' *high tech barber shop and salon* as Avani referred to it—another example of the giants' attention to detail that always left the group in awe and appreciation.

Instinctively, these ancient beings always thought of ways to reshape life into a higher experience. As part of preparing to leave, one-by-one, the group was invited to visit the lab where they could enter a cylinder flooded with slender, silken ribbons of blue light. Within a couple of minutes, their shaggy long hair, unkempt beards, and their overall appearance was transformed back to the form they had upon arrival under the surface. Dutch, however, respectfully declined. His bald head with a multitude of scars had become draped with thick, bear-brown locks and streaks of grey scattered here and there. He was confident and determined to move forward with his new appearance into an optimistic, high-vibe future.

As they parted company, unbridled tears trickled down the faces of the guests, looking upon their tall hosts with immense gratitude. Although they had forged a lasting friendship, it was not yet time to remain in constant contact.

As packing and preparations were finalized, everyone carefully reviewed the process required to enter the upper levels of Gaia. Their exit would be similar to the entrance they'd made—requiring focused minds and elevated group frequency. The two ships moved slowly in the direction of the portal in the same configurations as they'd had when they arrived: one helmed by Dutch, with Sophia, John, Jake, Adele and her daughters, the other led by Justin, with Caitlyn, Avani, Eben, and Ike. The teams in both boats prepared once again for *crossing the membrane*, as they now called it.

The energy shift was palpable and the first ship's crew, knowing what to do, moved seamlessly through the subtle membrane and a brief, yet dramatic shift in frequency. "Clearly, we're through the portal, my friends," John announced with a deep sigh of relief.

Unlike the previous journey, however, the second ship was not visible behind them.

They sailed gracefully and steadily towards the cove. As the day advanced, Jake broke the silence and said, "Dutch, I'm worried. I don't want to bring trepidation where it's not warranted, but we should have heard from them by now. Can you connect with Justin?"

Dutch stared at him, then lowered his gaze gloomily. The air tightened with apprehension, and everyone bowed their heads in somber silence. They'd entered knowing there were unpredictable risks, but this moment was still unexpected and grim. No one was surprised when Sophia entered an altered state—her friends allowed her to engage in her cosmically inspired way of being and responding.

Caitlyn was shaking, her legs weak. She looked at her team. "What happened? I felt like my body was being torn apart. It was sucking me into a dark, disorienting place that felt never-ending. Is everyone okay?"

All heads nodded, but all faces were solemn. They'd missed the passage through the membrane, but worse, they did not know where they were headed.

Each of them tried to relax and quiet their minds, but many hours in space-time drifted by with no change, and their fear and foreboding became palpable. They were drifting down the inner river towards unknown territory, or worse, to another portal. No one was interested in eating and everyone sat motionless. Avani soon entered into a deep meditation and after an hour, Caitlyn joined her. Ike sat pensively with Eben. They had discussed potential strategies, which only left them baffled and unsure of what to do next. In Gaia's remote, inner recesses, there is no nightfall, so drifting down the river seemed endless.

All at once, they saw a dim light and began straining their eyes to catch a closer glimpse—it was the edge of a forest with a familiar fluorescent glow. Justin steered the boat straight for it. The three men erupted into cheers at the site of a giant who stood peacefully in a small cove. Avani and Caitlyn had shifted from meditation into sleep, but now, hearing the commotion, they awakened, disoriented. Sensing their team's exuberance, they came into full waking consciousness and joined the crew whose gaze was locked on a small beach. As they approached, a giant stood untroubled and steady as he motioned for them to stop.

Through the familiar telepathy, he asked, "Is everyone okay?" They responded that they were shaken, adjusting to what happened, and everyone was fine. He continued, "As you sensed the membrane, did you start thinking or did you remember to become still?" Justin admitted he had wondered if they could get through it. It was this which prevented them from moving as a thought-free team, as one, silent unit through the membrane. Justin, as navigator and the ship's captain, apologized for letting everyone down. He looked away, avoiding eye contact as he described his experience to the others.

Disregarding harmonics, quantum physics, and all protocols, he had allowed his mind to take over and run wild. At that point, he was at the mercy of survival instincts and went into panic mode. He admitted that his mind "went berserk." As they entered the space of the membrane, he experienced a crushing darkness and his brain felt like it would explode. In that moment, because of his intense training, he regained control of his consciousness and surrendered, letting go into the wild, infinite field of pure energy. Although it allowed him to come back to the group, it was too late to allow them to collectively move through the designated membrane. Justin realized and experienced that surrendering to the subtle, quantum field is the key to moving through these portals.

The giant nodded thoughtfully and said, "This is important. You learned something that will inform your future attempts at working with membranes, time distortions, and portals. By calling on your very wise heart and intuition, you corrected your lapse in focus by allowing for what's unlimited to arise in your awareness. The mind-heart connection always allows for a smoother flow of electromagnetic frequency.

"Perhaps you could recall how you operated while living with us. We observed that you began to trust your gut instincts, your *little hunches*, to guide and inspire you into radical creativity and unimaginable insights; rather than analyzing everything, looking to someone else for advice, or relying on currently accepted answers and theories.

"No one will get you through the next membrane but you; there is no text book to read. Your masterful, complex being is all the technology you need right now. Get in touch with the magnificent power of your brilliantly spinning essence, and connect unwaveringly with the inner stillness at your core—your unique, high-octane singularity. Always remember the cohesive relationships that you've cultivated and enjoyed here. May you apply what you learned under the surface to take you through the portal, arriving safely home.

"Collectively, it will be easier to move through the next membrane or any space-time distortions that you encounter. Alone, it would be much harder. In the beginning stages of working with higher frequencies, your group frequencies are more important than you realize.

"In the years to come, from what you just learned, you will gradually grow into your innate personal capacity to move solo through membranes, all kinds of portals, and star gates. The geometries of this membrane are exceedingly complex. We warned you that managing this level of energy requires more advanced skills than you are accustomed to. Regardless, from our perspective, you've prepared thoroughly and are capable of crossing this vibrational gateway. Remember that you arrived here with the help of your indigenous friends who prepared you by sharing how to consistently raise your frequencies.

Become still and connect with the vibrations of the *energetic memory* imprint of your *initial* crossing, accessible in the field. Remembrance of *how you felt* in that moment will mobilize confidence energetically."

The giant stepped forward with the grace of a majestic deer, holding a device the group was familiar with—it could reveal the vibrational levels of many energy fields in and around their bodies. Unhurriedly, without blinking, he became absorbed in the device, attuning with it impeccably. Having made a soulful connection with it, he began the readings with Justin, who remained moon-eyed, his breath shallow like captured prey. Unfazed, the giant methodically scanned the rest of the ship's occupants.

With the tone of a beloved grandfather addressing adored progeny, he said, "In reading your energy fields it is evident that your nervous systems and subtle energetic fields are not coherent with the frequencies of confidence and serenity. This incoherence is consistent with the phase of training you are engaged in. For your journey today, let us help you recalibrate your vibrational energy levels to prepare yourselves to cross the upcoming membrane." With bold encouragement, he said affectionately, "Dear friends, prepare for the next step on your extraordinary journey!"

Next to the giant, two breathtaking, sparkling flames appeared, half his size—slowly materializing as particles of mesmerizing golden light tipped with cobalt blue. Steadily, the flames morphed into the shape of two more giants, a woman and a man. They each held a tiny, earthen jug.

As they emerged, the giant explained that the entire team needed to drink the teas in the jugs. One of them instantly appeared in front of Avani. The giant explained that this herbal concoction would reset their nervous system. No adverse effects from the first attempt would be left in their physical, emotional, or subtle energy fields. He requested that Avani serve the team and everyone must drink the entire cup of this alchemical tea.

A second jug materialized on the ship in front of Caitlyn. The giant addressed her saying, "Be prepared to serve everyone the second tea immediately after passing through the membrane. The next membrane is powerful yet simple if you follow the laws of the quantum world. You've been with us for a long time. You can handle this with ease. Of that, I am certain, dear friends."

All eyes were on the gentle giant who appeared to have a tear glistening in the corner of his eye as he said goodbye. Their tall, beloved friend thanked them for spending part of their *rare and precious earth-life* with him and his fellow giants.

All of a sudden, the two smaller giants' particles morphed into flames again, tinged with ethereal hues of cobalt light—before evaporating into the ether. The immeasurably reassuring, compassionate giant suddenly transformed into a pillar of blinding golden radiance—then in a flash he vanished.

With hearts blending bitter-sweet goodbyes with refreshed optimism for their trip homeward, the team set sail. The inner sun was directly in front of them in its full majestic radiance.

Instincts, natural abilities, and all they learned from the giants combined to become the technology they could rely on to navigate the mysterious vastness of a quantum experience—along with infinite possibilities for how it could play out.

## CHAPTER 25

# EQUINOX RECONVENED

A somber pall hung over Sophia, Jake, John, and Adele based on the grim reality that even trained military personnel, scientists, and others have gone through portals never to return. Looking crestfallen, Adele confided that recognizing the magnitude of the situation and seeing her daughters' downcast, sullen eyes, it was best to take her girls home to get settled and process the situation. Sophia promised to let her know if she received information about the second boat.

On the evening of their return to the cove, they sat on the porch in awkward silence. Looking at John, Sophia asked, "How can we explain this to Angelica and Grace? I'll likely be wrestling with this question until they arrive." Without comment, John closed his eyes and lowered his head. His face expressed the agony of knowing that his daughter was missing and no one could offer reassurance of her return. Jake looked away unable to speak.

After Jake and John asked Sophia to explain the situation to her two closest friends, she tossed and turned throughout the night. Since this was not a speech to prepare for, she relinquished wondering about it, went to the guest room that had nurtured her since her arrival at Megan's home, and tried to connect with eternal stillness. Finally, giving way to dawn's calling, she meditated as the sun rose over the lush landscape, the cove, and the spot where intimate, fire-lit conversations had taken place. John and Jake were already at Megan's house making coffee.

When Sophia joined her friends on the porch, the silence remained conspicuous. Trepidation and the chilly Idaho air kept them hugging their coffee cups while sitting motionless. John, bleary-eyed from lack of sleep, kept looking toward the entrance to the stairs; the familiar wooden steps that led to the cove.

All were absorbed in the morning's pristine silence when suddenly an enormous flock of birds took flight, squawking and squealing, and soared from the cove. Momentarily transfixed by the birds, they simultaneously jumped to their feet as a figure appeared at the first step. It was Caitlyn.

Gradually the entire crew of the second ship ascended. The three friends from the first ship remained frozen, staring at their comrades, who were slowly moving in their direction. Caitlyn was approaching the porch before Sophia, Jake, and John grasped the reality of what was happening—a miracle had become possible in the mystical quantum reality they'd devoted themselves to. No one was exempt from warm embraces and tearful smiles celebrating the power of friendship, deep respect, and the indestructible bond their two-year adventure cemented.

Until their hearts were fully quenched with tender feelings and profound love, tears flowed and hugs continued. As a natural feeling of emotional satiety overtook the group, everyone went to rest. Megan's home was a special place where there was always ample room for guests and a kitchen that could accommodate a legion of explorers to feast and rejuvenate.

Caitlyn, Avani, Eben, and Ike wanted to gather with Sophia, John, and Jake at their usual circle under the oak trees to explain what happened. They were running on pure adrenaline, and sleep felt impossible in this moment of reunion. Before they could meet, however, a car arrived for Justin and everyone headed in that direction. Justin was eager to reconnect with his family, who had headed over immediately upon finding out he had returned. After tearful goodbyes and much heartfelt appreciation for his contribution to the team, he was released and left appearing content and at ease.

A few minutes later Will arrived to give his blessings to everyone on behalf of his community. Joyously and with warm encouragement, Dutch joined him to decompress from the journey and relax within the ancient shamanic traditions Dutch had gradually gravitated towards, with heightened understanding and appreciation. During the journey, Justin and Dutch met with a specific team of ETs who shared invaluable information about the unified field—magnitudes greater than any institution on the surface could offer. Occasionally they joined Ike and Eben, but mostly kept to themselves, working long hours to absorb themselves more comprehensively into the incredible information they were accessing.

Through regular engagement with ancient shamans living under the surface, Dutch discovered a personal calling to immerse himself whole-heartedly in these venerable traditions, with a rare opportunity to be initiated into millions of years of wisdom. Gradually his life's history melted into a restructured phase of life, and revolutionary expressions of DNA emerged as he practiced sustained periods of the flow state through simple stillness practices throughout the day.

After everyone hugged, thanked Dutch with the ardency of enduring friendship, and allowed tears of gratitude to be exchanged liberally, he drove away with Will. By the time the dust from the car settled, Sophia was serving fresh lemonade and a lively conversation began.

In a frenzy of exuberance, Justin's crew shared the details of their disastrous first attempt to cross the membrane, and the focus and surrender into the stillness of the present moment that was necessary to move through the second portal. They described the nerve-settling, mind-focusing quality of the giant's guidance, precipitating the journey home. And they tried to adequately describe the teas they'd been given—to no avail. As with most of the experiences under the surface, the herbal concoction surpassed the mind and in this case, taste buds, too. None of them could recall how long they were adrift, nor did anyone remember the moment of passage.

However, everyone agreed that after they moved through the portal, they emerged with a level of serenity and clarity they'd never experienced before. After orienting to their surroundings, they shared with each other that no one felt fear as they journeyed across the membrane because, as their sagacious giant mentor had shared, this was another opportunity to work with raising their individual and collective frequencies. They became fully aware that with the unexpected and terrifying event came new abilities and confidence to experience and move through many more levels of the quantum world. Their frequencies rose naturally and consistently while beneath the surface of Gaia, and everyone was unshakably committed to cultivating these new abilities and capacities going forward.

The sound of Grace's vehicle interrupted the reunion and Angelica soon arrived, too. The friends embraced, and excited voices and tremors of soul-warming laughter ensued for several minutes. While the group began to settle, it felt as though they'd been gone for a weekend adventure rather than a couple of years.

At Megan's request, Beth brought copious amounts of delicious food. Megan was with her daughter and couldn't be present to celebrate the homecoming.

The tone of the conversation was light-hearted and gently soothing for everyone. Feeling reassured, Angelica repeated many times how relieved and thrilled she was to see her "baby girl."

And then came the unavoidable questions. Angelica maintained a dumbfounded look of amazement as they shared the technologies, the places they'd visited, and the people they'd met; along with scenes of indescribable beauty and wonder; the giants; the vast water ways; a conscious, inner sun; and areas illumined by unseen energies and technologies. As soon as one member of the group mentioned one mesmerizing place, someone else added an experience that was even more mystifying, extraordinary, and inexplicable. Angelica leaned in and listened to each share, captivated with awe.

Every place they visited was different and each had a social structure that suited them perfectly. Some were arid or smaller in population, and yet each held a pristine beauty that was undeniable. Each destination was unique in the people, customs, food, and landscape because each location was at a different level of frequency and therefore, at a different level within the Earth. No one in the group knew exactly how many miles they had traversed during their journey under the surface.

Angelica became transfixed with their description of an unexpected technology called "holograms" which contain endless information from the infinite quantum field. These technological masterpieces were found in many of the cities and areas that they visited. Caitlyn addressed the wonder and curiosity that she saw on her mother's face.

"Mom, as an anthropologist and archeologist, I was captivated by the first hologram, which is a visionary experience of data from the infinite field of information. I'll tell you more in a moment about other places we visited. I want to say first, that in the main area, which was home base, it was lush and green, with enormous trees. To call it *exquisite and mesmerizing* is an understatement."

Creating a context for her intoxication with inner earth life, Caitlyn described the gentleness, wisdom, and simplicity of their giant hosts which helped Angelica to grasp the magnitude of the high frequencies of these beings. It wasn't enough to just talk about how the giants moved through portals and into distant star systems, or how they manifested various objects and were telepathically advanced in a way that was initially unnerving. Caitlyn wanted to create a vivid description of the vast landscape; the odd, inner sun; the colors and textures of the plants; strange animals; and the spaciousness of a world that was filled with unexpected wonders.

Angelica interjected with a look of confusion, saying, "What I can't figure out is why would a highly advanced culture, one as content with everyday life as you describe, bother to spend two years with you all? It sounds like they gave you plenty of their time and resources—hosting you so graciously and generously. What's in it for them?"

The group's response left an even more puzzled look on Angelica's face.

Ike turned towards Angelica, his eyes sparkling with tears of endless affection for the giants. "I get why you are asking this question. Oh man, Angelica! Those giants were nothing like most people or cultures that we encounter on the surface. Hey, believe me, like you, we were surprised by their welcoming and caring attitude towards us. We were humbled to realize that we were meeting beings who embody high-level compassion. They had a natural instinct to share everything they had and everything they knew, without wanting anything from us. It's their nature to be generous and kind. And they are not into politics or self-interest. What I think Caitlyn was getting ready to explain was why and how we came to understand them and some details about all the cities we visited. Awww man, Caitlyn, I interrupted! So sorry!"

She smiled brightly, winked at him playfully in friendship, and with cheerfulness and buoyancy in her voice, urged him to continue.

"Okay thanks! I guess you can tell I'm stoked about all of this! From my side, I was allowed to go with our giant friends through portals to other solar systems and galaxies. You see, Angelica, all we had to do is raise our individual frequency, learn more about focusing the mind, and then we learned..."

Ike paused as tears started to fill his eyes. "Oh Man, I cannot control my feelings. Screw it! I'm being honest. My heart becomes soft when I recall those benevolent beings. I became way more emotional down there! I'd cry with joy, amazement, or anything that touched my heart. Jake and John admitted the same thing happened to them. I asked the giants why they don't cry. I never saw them weep.

"One of the giants who I was super close to explained they don't repress feelings like we do. From his perspective, I was releasing suppressed feelings that naturally require an outlet for expression. He insisted we will continue to emote this way until we thoroughly release this *subjugated energy*. He liked to see us cry because he saw our energy fields correspondingly turn a lustrous golden color, and emanate pure love. He said this release process is part of *the beauty of our personal evolution*. Whoa! Man! Massive introspection was required to process his words.

"To reinforce his point, he introduced us to a highly evolved species, who were so chilled out! Man, they were so cool! Caitlyn described them as being full of *elegance and equipoise*. Avani said they were *harmony vibes with legs*."

Jake opted not to suppress a lighthearted chuckle as Ike continued.

"The giant said the *nervous system* of this ancient species is calibrated for *equilibrium*. So they experience emotions as waves of vibrations throughout the body which crash to shore as the harmonious vibes that Avani referred to. They definitely *feel* primal fear, sorrow, joyousness, and peacefulness. But all feelings move through their nervous system and energy fields rather than escalating, being suppressed, or settling in—which can cause psychological issues like habitual depression or rage. Here's another super cool part, he said that as we emote higher frequencies and still our minds consistently, our nervous systems will begin to not just *re-calibrate*, but *up-regulate* to a consistently balanced, natural rhythm. Like theirs, our nervous system can be set to easily *reach equilibrium*. That's where we're headed as a species. I'm up for that!"

Jake laughed and said, "Ditto, brother!" John winked playfully at Ike and gave him a thumbs up. Ike looked at them, beaming a broad smile in recognition of their support, and continued.

"They showed us, by example and through the holograms, where humanity has gone off-track in being able to evolve more quickly as a species and how we've collectively become stuck.

"Hm... I hope I can explain this. Hang on..." Ike paused before continuing. "The giants said they have noticed that acknowledging ourselves or taking time for our personal needs creates guilt. At best we're not comfortable with taking time to nourish ourselves. We've been rewarded socially for looking after others, and often we value *selflessness* so much that we feel selfish even if we take basic care of our personal needs. The antidote to this is a subtle awareness of *balance*—from a high-octane frequency—which leaves us replenished, nourished, and strong. Then we can naturally help others. Man, I found that helpful!

"Knowing that in physics we learn that everything in our complex, energetic world seeks *equilibrium*, the giants pushed me, as a scientist, to observe equilibrium in the lab *and in life*—self care and doing personal practices to elevate my frequency is a natural and important balance in my life now. I get chills thinking about being with those giant hearts, day after day, as we began to meditate, walk in silence, and feel satiated by the beauty and relaxed vibe of their giant world.

"Do you get what I'm saying? Yes? Okay then, follow this: We stopped striving to know more and focused our attention on being in flow with what we were learning. We relaxed and began to see the perfection in ourselves and whatever we were doing, but without pride. Pride sucks my vibe to zero. Yet in the *flow state*, I am one hundred percent chilled out and I experience super high vibes.

"Oh man, you would love to see the holographic display where history and all possible events can be viewed. It's a simple technology in some ways. There is a smooth marble-like face on one of two thin rock formations—made of granite and coated with a polymer embedded with high levels of quartz. The thin stones are slightly wider at the base with a gap between them that acts like a capacitor of energy. I still do not totally understand how it works, but I know similar holographic wonders were used on the surface eons ago because Jake said he and John have studied them at sites across the planet, and Jake and John showed one to me.

"They took me to a megalithic structure that once had holographic capacity; it was just a few hours drive from Mystic Cove. The giants said most megalithic structures like this on the surface have not been functional for tens of thousands of years; and some are technologies dating back nearly a million years. To operate today, the entire complex in which they are standing would need to be reconfigured and aligned with specific energy portals within the boundary of the complex. These technologically advanced megalithic areas have been damaged innumerable times by cataclysms on the surface. So what Jake and John showed me was more like seeing artifacts in a museum. Under the surface, we got to see similar magnificent structures that were fully functioning. I had only seen damaged megaliths in the middle of a site that was in shambles (gigantic stones toppled and sometimes broken in the process). Yet under the surface, I witnessed high tech megalithic structures that produce mind-boggling holographic screens.

"In the giant's underground world, these screen structures were in a secluded area. We'd put our hand on a rock made of some kind of metal unfamiliar to us. A hologram would then appear with historical information translated into images. The rock we touched was reading our DNA and thought waves—it was epic! Since it was holographic, we were seeing a visual slice of reality that arose from the totality of information stored in the unified field. Don't try to understand it. There's rad physics involved in the technology! From my perspective, the information is accurate and without bias.

"We could choose to look at a specific event in history or our unconscious mind would present something to answer a question that we'd been asking ourselves subconsciously. As we spent time with this technology, we began to trust the images the hologram generated from our conscious and unconscious questions. We learned more about calming our brains into Theta waves. This is the brain wave pattern of a child who lives in continuous wonder and awe, and it is the state that allows the holograms to work. As the thinking-brain slows down, the images become more clear. Isn't that amazing? Oh man! I was in awe!

"It was so cool because when we were watching, our senses were also engaged. What I mean is that we could feel, taste, see, and hear what was going on in the hologram. Most places in the giants' world have some form of holographic viewing area where every tiny, minuscule moment of the past and present is available to view or enter.

"If our frequency was not high enough, if we started thinking and judging, or if the civilization didn't want to share something, the holographic image disappeared. I think I can speak for all of us when I say that we were okay with that.

"When we debriefed, we talked about how we could sense when our psyche had swallowed enough information and we needed time to integrate. This integration period was essential because we learned that history did not unfold in the way we've been told. I observed how history is written from the perspective of academics who reported to kings, popes, and other forms of dominant leadership. Yet in the holographic experience, we got to see the same events through the perspective of the common person. And often we saw heroes and hard-to-fathom acts of bravery that have been eclipsed or manipulated to suit the perspective of biased, historical authors.

"Man! Realizing that museums, historians, and even art curators were not immune from covering up events, distorting what happened, or destroying the truth, we asked ourselves if we fully grasped the magnitude of the impact of lies, non-transparency, and distortions on future generations? I have a PhD. I love academia, but this made me question a bigger picture of who oversees all of this craziness and deceit? Why are we not demanding truth? There are layers of lies, distortions, and misunderstandings throughout history. We got to see this has been happening intermittently for hundreds of thousands of years. That was so cool! Mind-blowing!

"My vibe—the *frequency* I resonate with and emit—means everything to me. Transparency is high vibe and deceit is low. It's a no-brainer for me. I want to continuously express the crazy, cool, high vibe that I receive and emit when we're together. It's so cool! I love you all!"

Caitlyn flashed a warm-hearted smile to Ike before adding to the conversation. She said, "Mom, this is why we can say these beings don't need us; rather, they *love us*. They see us as fellow travelers on this planet. It's hard, even now, to wrap my head around that truth. They see the chaos humanity is swirling in. They compassionately acknowledge we're at a pivotal decision point where we have to be fully awake and aware of what's happening, and decide how to go forward together.

"Their societies are not based on competition or being better than someone else. It's about personal evolution. So there's no need to fight with another group. And from the perspectives of archeology and geology, it was totally astonishing! I'm not planning on announcing this in a traditional setting. If I could show my friends and colleagues on the surface the things we saw, I swear, they'd faint.

"Over and over, each of us willingly absorbed ourselves in high frequencies that allowed us to be more aware of our energy than our physicality. That meant letting these energies roar through and around us. We got into it and immersed ourselves in a way I didn't know was possible. It was like nothing else mattered and we were *all in!*

"That process slowly became natural and changed us forever. Once we experienced that our consciousness could show us the truth of who we are, that we are not just a physical form—the doors of incredible possibilities opened. We could sense things, open portals, rise into higher dimensions, and allow time and space to dissolve into a sea of flow.

"I know it sounds wild and maybe totally crazy... but as we continued to live with the giants who were emitting high frequencies unremittingly, we became more established in higher vibes, too. We also realized there was nothing to believe or not believe. Instead of our minds constantly being engaged, we flowed harmoniously and contentedly with whatever showed up for us to do.

"Each area of the surface of the Earth is distinct in character and visual esthetics. It's the same with the cities and locales under the surface, except there, it's not about exclusion or division or class. It's about the resonance of frequencies.

"It felt utterly natural if we were not able to enter a specific city. We didn't feel excluded from it, only not drawn into it. Our exploration was guided by a sense of resonance and flow... based on our unique interests, we would be drawn to be with different groups. And some of us resonated with a certain city more than other places that we visited, so we would return to them multiple times. Because these places were so different from what felt *normal* for us, it often took several visits to grasp the cultural and frequential aspects.

"Following the pull of resonant frequencies, we entered most cities through sophisticated tunnel systems—some hewn from solid rock, some passing through lava, some through the vast underground ocean, and some meandering through all three. (We'll tell you more about the ocean and the geography later). Sometimes, though rarely for me, we were able to go without a tunnel, by teleporting.

"These tunnels are not what we normally think of as tunnels, they're spacetime quantum events. We might go to a city twenty miles under the surface in just seconds. They are inconceivably advanced technologies. They are kind of like trains, but without rails; rather, they move slightly above the surface at Mach speed as opposed to miles per hour. These super-fast trains were amazing, but highly advanced species developed craft that move through the wormhole network from one location to another *instantly*. By working with the quantum dynamics of *the field*, they choose a destination, moving safely and efficiently *anywhere in the universe*. I wondered how they are able to create such inconceivable craft and technologies. Who are these beings? Where did they come from?

"The creators of these high vibe places and craft live in such an elevated frequency that their technologies defy our current understanding. Also, they have been living in these areas for tens of thousands of years—in some cases, millions of years. But who is counting when you live for a thousand years or longer? I know that sounds crazy, right? I'm not exaggerating—they live a very long life. Not because of an anti-aging supplement or a miraculous plant, but because it's their genetic makeup and because they continuously evolve into higher frequencies.

"At first, I thought they were from somewhere way out in the cosmos. But as Jake and John interacted with and got to know them, they discovered that most of them are human or are a mix of human and other genetics. The fact that humans can advance like them gives me chills. They are highly evolved humans who focus on developing their frequency and capacity to interact with the mysterious ways of the quantum world. They do not obsess over the myopic twists and turns of daily life. Being with them has changed me forever. My worldview is wide open and getting more cosmic every day.

"We wondered if their longevity was partly due to their calm and peaceful nature, as well as the lifestyle of simple living and access to nourishing food and pristine water. The air is healthy and life-affirming. The water is clean and tastes like nectar! All the readings we took from electromagnetic to radiation indicated that the environment there is ideal to support and enhance human life.

"The giants were certainly busy; each one contributes to the collective with a sense of ease that we found contagious.

We were constantly talking about how chilled-out we were becoming and how much we were loving their lifestyle. They were kind yet intelligent and savvy.

"One of the eye-opening experiences for me was when we were looking at the holograms one day and we saw different groups of surface scientists trying to connect with the underground beings. It was clear they were operating from frequencies of manipulation, pride, fear, or anger. They were frustrated and super pissed off that they could not get through certain tunnels or cities such as those we visited. None of their high-powered plasma weapons, sophisticated technology, or super computers worked. We heard a few stories of these surface-groups interacting with unfriendly ETs who also dwell under the surface. My understanding is that this happens because of the principle of resonance I described earlier—similar frequencies magnetizing to each other. Our giant friends seemed completely unaffected by hostile ETs, never even mentioning them.

"Only elevated levels of frequency in us or our *star family*, as we called them, can enter the tunnels and spaces we visited. Because of our capacity to raise our frequency, we went places that black projects of the military and gigantic corporations with bazillion dollar budgets could never enter. Gadgets and devices are irrelevant.

"To be honest, there were places others in our group could access anytime with ease which I, on the other hand, could enter only with intense, sometimes frustratingly prolonged preparation. Another aspect of our trip was that Sophia and Adele visited specific places often, but I never joined them. I went to other places that called to me and were perfectly aligned with my frequencies. Sometimes we shared our experiences and sometimes we didn't. I felt we were each attracted to the right places and were learning what we needed to learn and experience. It was so vast down there that we could have stayed for decades.

"We can tell you our personal stories, but the main point is that in order to go anywhere beneath the surface, we had to drop our lower tendencies of feeling like we *cannot do this* and focus instead on elevating our consciousness. I sensed that being with the giants and others who were living consistently in those elevated frequencies helped us to join them in higher levels of consciousness."

"Oh my goodness! Caitlyn, this is mind-altering and shocking for me," said Angelica. "Yet, I believe it's true. As your mom, I'd like to hear about another aspect of your adventure. I keep wanting to know if you were ever scared? Did you ever encounter evil-minded people?"

"Caitlyn," Jake said looking at her with a big smile. "I'd like to answer, if that's okay."

Following Caitlyn's vehement nod, he continued. "On the surface, we operate under the assumption that we can and should be able to defend ourselves all the time—we assume we can control life. There's a fear of survival embedded in this paradigm. Being under the surface helped me see this, and to see that the fear of survival shifts as a species evolves into peaceful collaboration within its culture."

"Well, of course we have that survival fear up here! My goodness!" Angelica said. "There's plenty to protect ourselves from! Can I ask you something about this safety issue?"

"Sure, go ahead," Jake answered with a quizzical look.

"I recall that you used to hunt, which made me wonder if you took guns or weapons with you, in case you needed them?

I know you would never act like a frenzied, vigilante movie character, but did you take precautions like that?"

"It would be like facing a grizzly while holding a fly swatter," Jake said. "It would get ugly really fast! Our military, at one time, attempted to bring plasma weapons down there—those mighty weapons were rendered impotent, completely useless. These beings don't think in terms of destroying things, fighting, or having property wars. There's space for everyone. And beings down there have access to the resources they need. Survival skills are inherent to all species, but we've added *pride* to our military defense skills. Think *Star Wars* defense system, black military projects, and all of that.

"Giants respect each other's space. Every once in a while we'd be in a city and a soft light would suddenly envelope us. Calmly and in unison everyone would go inside. They'd serve us a drink, or we'd sit around and talk. And when the light disappeared, we would carry on with our day. No one explained what happened. But later, when we asked about it, they shared that there had been a security breach. Once, it was one of our black project scientists trying to get through a tunnel or enter a city. Overwhelmed by the frequencies, they'd simply passed out and the local security team took them back to the tunnel's entrance. If, by chance, citizens from another city of higher frequencies tried to enter without warning, there is security equipment to block them.

"From our observations, lower frequencies invading higher frequencies isn't the norm down there."

Jake became silent as he noticed John's shift in posture and expression. John had been sitting quietly and suddenly he leaned forward to address Angelica. "I'd like to add that the giants are *peaceful* yet realistic that militaries and black projects from the surface globally take the opposite approach. We'd sometimes hear violent rumbles where two of those groups were fighting with each other. Maybe they couldn't attack each other blatantly on the surface, so they head underground to take up the sword! I've seen U.S. Army announcements for recruitment of youngsters into the military under the pretense of learning *underground* military tactics, telling them about navigating super-cool tunnels, and engaging in the future of a new frontier in military prowess. It's crazy but true. Don't we have enough war and fighting on the surface? Why do we need to go underground to covertly escalate the animosity and divisiveness?

"Our giant friends were not thrilled that although U.S. black project scientists and military brass know that nuclear energy is too dangerous to mess with, they are developing equally dangerous weapons that extract energy from the field by using quantum physics. It makes me want to puke when I recall the hologram revealing their technological experiments in war zones on the surface, which include civilian areas, turning huge buildings instantly to dust. They are playing roulette with Gaia's atmosphere and our health and safety. Like the atom bomb, and its more insidious cousin, the hydrogen bomb, they forge ahead without constraints, without oversight, or considering the long term implications. We've got to end this secret military shit that claims it's designed for our national security. It's at the heart of our potential demise, friends. Global citizens should have a *say* in whether we want to develop and use those weapons in endless wars and potentially off-planet. The stakes are too high to leave it to those who have a personal or economic stake in continuing this madness. As General Butler warned us a century ago, we have to stop funding global wars and endless conflict, and *demand* peace unequivocally."

John's eyes drifted downward while looking dejected and heavy hearted.

"Well, everyone, I didn't expect to hear all of this, "Angelica said wide-eyed and befuddled, "I am a shell-shocked mama right now! My Lord! John, what you brought up is important. You all accessed a higher bird's eye view than we've had access to on the surface. And I can't believe my little girl has been below the earth's surface with giants while she was watching holograms of the Earths' history instead of movie night with her mama."

Affectionally, she rested her gaze on each person gathered around her. With a big sigh and looking exhausted, she requested time to take in what she'd heard and warmly invited everyone to come together later for dinner. In unanimous agreement to her request, the circle dispersed to rest and prepare for the evening ahead.

Angelica approached John, softly kissed his cheek and said, "I love you, sweetheart. That must have been awful to witness. Be assured that attitudes are shifting away from complacency on the surface. Don't give up hope. I could tell what you saw looked pretty bleak."

"Yes, holographic revelations were hard to witness and harder to process. I realized that I'd been wrong to label certain powerful captains of business, religious leaders, and heads of the black-military as diabolical people. It's more than simple *good versus evil*. What I saw tore me up! They believe their own shit, heart and soul! They don't think they are doing anything wrong. One example that stuck with me was a famous Titan from Wall Street meeting with Tesla at the turn of the twentieth century. On the hologram I was gutted as he asked that incomparable genius about free energy. Was he eager to know its potential to foster global abundance and boost human evolution? His trillion dollar questions were, *Why should anyone invest in this? Where is the profit?*

"I still get shivers when I recall the murky depths of his piercing eyes. He tipped his tall, high-end hat, turned on his upper-class heel, and walked away to invest in fossil fuels—which led to tons of jobs, new industries like automobiles and planes, and became the backbone of global commerce and lifestyle, completely reshaping our world. Then I saw a famous military leader and president give the orders to go to war, for profit. I almost puked! Three other global leaders joined him in solidarity to do whatever it took to make the war happen. One of the giants pointed out that by labeling any of these guys as cold-hearted, greedy bastards (I'd heard many stories of their cunning and callousness), I cut myself off from a bigger issue. I took the giant's wisdom to heart. At both times in history, the collective population had fallen into a spell of helplessness and hopelessness. I thought Tesla's worldview a hundred years ago could somehow have harmonized easily with the global population or that some savior could have swooped in to stop the war. But we've had many opportunities to course correct. The problem is that, collectively, we've been equally as fearful, complacent, and distracted as global leaders have been bold, secretive, and focused on their goals.

"Right now, we can still turn the tide before they toast this planet, literally. Now that they are mastering geoengineering, building underground safety nests, have a full-blown black military and high tech research labs, the hologram shows they plan to move on to controlling the sun. Holy shit! The sun?! Reaching master levels of self-importance, they are going to cause us to f**king disintegrate through chemicals, bio weapons, and a devastated climate that they refuse to stop tinkering with. They are counting on having the time to develop the technology to take their delusional clan and illustrious AI off-planet. They have decided that the best solution to our current problems is to systematically, chemically trash the heart of the Solar System. In their worldview, Gaia's demise will be a result of us having too many kids and driving our cars too much—a *blame-mindset* at best. We are watching ten thousand years of this mindset reach a spine-chilling crescendo, which is upon us—within a decade, maybe sooner. With this in mind, I plan to double down on my focus, maintaining a flow state and continuing to connect with legions of great hearts who are saying, *no more of this incessant blame-game and fear mongering, allowing authority figures to once again proudly announce checkmate!*

"Gaia is not going to be left in rubble and ruin because of hubris and a psychopathic worldview—not on my watch!"

John was becoming more animated, leaning towards Angelica while begging with his eyes for her to listen to this subject that had struck his soul like a thunderbolt. He continued with intensified passion in his voice.

"It's ironic that I always thought I had to change someone's mind. Yet under the surface, I realized that it's my heart and mindset that had to shift so I could join other aware humans raising their frequencies—while consistently entering the still point at our core, finding peacefulness there, and then allowing the resulting state of ease and flow to become established as my new normal. In this way, I raised my frequency, which allows me to call in more Source energy from the field, creating a more dynamic reality for myself and those around me. Now I have a sense of agency, of optimism, and a chance to relax into inner stillness. Clearly our way out of this insanity is elevating our frequencies beyond fear, anger, and blame-style hatred while living instead in a balanced, calm state. It's doable. This is what brought the giants into rapid phases of evolution.

"I am optimistic, yet realistic that the world won't magically change overnight. However, with young ones like Ike and our amazing daughter gathering with like-minded souls, humanity can evolve quickly. All the inventors like Tesla, who discovered or were working on *over-unity* technologies as Ike calls them, were thwarted—by factions wanting to control and profit by a scarcity of controllable technologies and energy sources, but also because as a global population we didn't demand transparency and share discoveries through open sourcing."

Angelica looked compassionately at him. "Please don't think I cannot feel the truth and appreciate deeply your reflections, inner resolve, epiphanies about our history, and the inconceivable devices and technologies you saw. I am here for you whenever you need to process the immeasurable level of revelations you've confronted while under the surface. But honey, you lost me just now. What is *over-unity*?"

Smiling lovingly at his beloved, the muscles in his shoulders loosened their grip, his voice became calmer and his face became as soft as if they were speaking about the natural beauty around them.

"Thank you. I love you so much! I can't believe my good fortune to have you in my life, especially at this watershed moment. Feel free to call me out if I use an unfamiliar term. Of course, I can only give you a layman's understanding of the tech and the physics. An *over-unity* device uses less energy input than output. The extra energy is extracted directly from the field in and around us. That's the way that Ike and his team are able to extract energy from the structure of spacetime. Tesla's jaw would be dropping. Although he was not well known in his lifetime, he was a prolific inventor with over nine hundred patents. I can imagine the shocked faces of all those folks like him who tried and failed to get levitating cars to market, or the ones who found ways to create endless *over-unity* devices to operate homes, offices, and technology without electricity or fossil fuels.

"Holy cow, sweetheart! Free energy has been available all along, and the military and related corporations, heck even the Vatican's underground structures, have purportedly had access to various free energy devices for a long time.

"Which begs the question: Why are the Vatican and CIA tied to certain venture capitalists who have massive wealth and autonomy which gives them license to do whatever they want without oversight? Whether it's the Vatican, CIA, or other small groups of massive influence, everything they do happens under our noses... and feet... and yet it feels illusory. This matters because the slave-master control mechanisms and propaganda used by elements of religion, politics, and elite business have indoctrinated us into believing that we are separate from each other and cut off from Essence. They set themselves up as our source of survival and safety. These elite groups enact systems based on keeping us feeling separate so we continue clawing at one another and fighting about who is the best. Consider which religion, political figure, or good-guy/bad-guy we align with and fight for or criticize vehemently. That vicious game needs to stop.

"The bottom line is we are at the threshold of a higher evolution of our species and our world! But at this tipping point, which way will humanity tip? I'm determined to personally tip in the direction of flow and stillness. No doubt those giants deeply impacted my thinking. I know our individual feeling and thoughts are constantly delivered into the field as energetic memory. When more of us get into flow and still our minds, we create a cumulative effect—which will have a massive impact on this world. We can change the future from chaos to order... if we come together in time."

Angelica looked stunned by his revelations. John squeezed her hand lovingly and smiled at her feebly. He confided in her that at times like this when he could not muster authentic positivity, he needed time alone to move into zero point and reboot, rather than "stew in lower vibe feelings that come up."

She squeezed his hand back and smiled gently, leaving him alone under the majestic canopy of trees. Haunting, ominous holographic memories swirled through his mind, touching the deepest crevices of his tender heart. As the associated subtle frequencies began dissolving into ghosts within fading past impressions, the unlimited present could then emerge in awareness, and his heart could flow easily within the river of all-that-is.

His connection to the field had become so reliable that higher levels of frequency from the field easily flowed into his consciousness. In return, he fed the field with energy from his open heart and centered state of being. Grappling with revelations no longer held him in the grip of despair or anger; the field was feeding him the same higher vibrations he'd fed into it while under the surface. Upon his return, he vowed to maintain the flow state regardless of emerging incendiary circumstances.

It was time to *sustain* elevated levels of frequency in the feedforward-feedback within the structure of spacetime. The giants had made that point abundantly clear. Gradually, with their wise counsel, he had come on board and was now resolute.

# CHAPTER 26

## SHARING PERSONAL STORIES

Angelica left to rest before dinner, allowing John to further process his response to the afternoon's conversation. Afternoon tea with Sophia—embraced within the cocoon of her compassion—had a subtle way of moving the needle of his frequencies to a higher level.

She leaned forward now and asked him, "Dear friend, can I nudge you to recall one of our seminal conversations with the giants below the surface?"

John nodded and gave her a quizzical look.

"You and I agree," she continued, "our approach going forward involves releasing tendencies to quarrel or debate with anyone, whether literally or just within our own minds or hearts. The highest solution is to join forces with like-minded people globally, building awareness of the sentience and interconnectedness of all aspects and levels of life. We'll cultivate new alliances dedicated to giving the world an understanding of our innate unicity—with our sun, with Gaia, and with each other—through the lens of unified physics as well as the unseen realms in and around us *experienced* through daily life.

"Like you, I recall the harrowing holographic scenes of destruction and loss of life, the real potential for utter annihilation of life on this planet, as well as seeing the mathematics describing the delicate mechanisms at work between our cells and all plant life via photosynthesis. On the other hand, we saw, too, that if humans are no longer a factor for nature to contend with, extinct species re-emerge naturally, once human-caused chemicals no longer bombard and saturate Gaia. As a global community, we cannot get to the requisite level of unicity and symbiosis with the sun, Gaia, and each other *rationally*—we have to *fall in love* with them, *feel* them as an interconnected part of ourselves, and *honor* them and all the stars in their swirling vortices of spacetime, the delicious quantum soup in and around us. It's *separateness* that can annihilate Gaia, humanity, and perhaps irreparably harm the sun as well.

"The intricate mathematics and captivating geometric patterns are still reverberating in my consciousness. The giants were insistent we look deeply into the omnipresent nature of frequency—integrating this reality in body, mind, and soul. The sun's frequencies are invaluable. We have no idea why her radiance brings us solace as it filters softly through the canopy of trees above us right now, when we walk in silent reflection, or why her effulgence provides the impetus to joyously bask in her rays on a beach, or feel her light drenching us with powerful rays as we ride the waves of an ocean. What we do know is that she's frequency at her core and so are we! We cannot think of her as a resource or problem. We have too much information to *blow it* this time (as you and Jake like to remind us). We watched in horror as those benevolent giants tried in vain to warn humans about low frequencies before the ice age twelve thousand years ago. We saw conclusively on the hologram that benevolent sages tried to make the same point a thousand years later, again, to no avail.

"However, without question, the hologram showed that more people than ever before in Earth's history doubt the fabricated stories we've been told in weak attempts to maintain control through fear. My part and yours is to raise our frequency, enter the flow state consistently, and continue to share what we know concretely through physics, studying nature, and relentless reflection on *everything in the multiverse* that is part of the fabric of spacetime. Pull a thread anywhere, and you end up pulling your own heartstrings. Humans can *feel* the sun's and earth's blessings. It's time to bless them back, without even a hint of inhibition."

After a warm hug of appreciation, John spoke softly, saying, "I needed to hear your unique way of describing under-the-surface revelations, and a kick in the butt to remember the sagaciousness within the world of giants and the care they showed us, rather than allow it to become a fading memory. The frequencies we emanated and received from our encounters with them still resonate in my energy fields, which is a foundation that's wholly reliable going forward. It's such a culture shock to be back on the surface. I'll be fine. In fact, we will all be fine. I needed to take time to share my rumination and feelings with you and Angelica. I'm more clear and centered now. I sure love you, sister!"

Sympathetically acknowledging that being back at the cove brought the reality of the surface-world back into focus, she spoke in a nurturing timbre that soothed him.

"I love you, too. How about taking this afternoon to enjoy your beloved, rest, and prepare for the wonderful evening ahead of us."

In a voice that had regained its customary vivacity, he exclaimed, "Done! See you tonight! ... and thanks for your friendship and no-nonsense approach to the *outer* madness of our world and the *inner* potentiality for greatness of our species."

They parted with a warm hug, ending a thought-provoking conversation concerning giant paradigm shifts emerging on Planet Earth.

As everyone gathered for dinner, the atmosphere was relaxed and lighthearted. Adele joined them, glowing with relief and radiating friendship, which brought about an ecstatic group hug. Jake took the opportunity to toast his comrades in celebration of an incredible journey under the surface. He noted that everyone's readiness to gather at the fire pit made him feel like they were substantially adjusting from their trip.

John smiled cheerfully, looking refreshed and effervescent. And to everyone's delight, his fire-building skills remained masterful—as the flames rose, the group nestled in to begin a soulful conversation. Angelica spoke first.

"Oh my goodness! I don't want to pry if you feel that you should not tell me about some of the places you visited. But I have been sitting on pins and needles waiting to hear about your journey. Were you able to keep this as a *secret project?* How did you get there, and do you think there are people who will want to steal what you've brought back?"

"Well now, Angelica, that's getting straight to the point," Jake answered, smiling jovially. "We asked ourselves these questions a million times before we left. What's important is that we are a decade past 2020. We all know that a lot has changed. The agencies that covered up this kind of research or sabotaged it lost a lot of influence and funding. That's a good thing but we are realistic and careful that we have to diligently protect our work.

"Keep in mind that we took the vessels to bring back material for research. Thanks to Megan, we have safe places to store the material we brought back for groundbreaking investigations, where John, Caitlyn, Avani and I can study it, along with our closest confidants.

"Ike and Eben will be leaving soon to go back under the surface for at least ten years. They are integrating quantum physics, unified field theory, and potentials for energy technologies that require their specialized skillset—conducting research to develop their ideas fully and open source their discoveries globally. Over-unity, extracting energy from the structure of spacetime, is their underlying focus.

"Grace, let your hubby know this part. He may not have heard they have a kick-ass team of unfettered creators and absolute geniuses. Plus they have help from under-the surface benefactors."

Grace nodded and Jake continued to speak directly to Angelica.

"You may not know that Ike and Eben are special in that they were born with and have cultivated extraordinary skill-sets. They are quantum physicists, focusing on the *unified field theory*. They are working to extract energy from the endless source of *the field*—fluctuations of infinite waves of potential energy. Although infinitesimal in size, this is the kind of focus on *subtle energy* we've needed. We measured the big stuff like the distance between planets, their rotational spin, and size. Having the courage and determination to measure a vast field of endless fluctuations that underlies the cosmos... well... that took out-of-the-box thinkers and brave hearts. We know what happens in every generation when radical thinkers drop truth-bombs on science. Holy Crap! Resistance has often crushed them and their work— like Isaac Newton. On his death bed, he still couldn't admit to being an obsessed alchemist. Even today, that is NOT how he's viewed, even though we have his extensive journals to prove it. Oddly, science leans towards the status quo and big changes come at an agonizingly slow pace.

"Ike told us that a tiny, one-centimeter cube packed with vacuum fluctuation waves from the field could power the world for millions of years—while in harmony with Gaia and with an *exchange* of energy rather than a *depletion* technology like fossil fuels. Because of the impact of free energy and clean air and water, Ike, Eben and their colleagues can have a huge impact on our world. I, for one, would celebrate a life without phone chargers and tangled cords behind a media center. We'll buzz around the solar system using energy extracted from *the field,* and without scarcity, no one will "own the rights" to this energy—it will be open and shared. We won't be contaminating space with dirty fuels and leaving all kinds of trash floating around.

"It's also important to understand that cities under the surface become more subtle as you go deeper. The residents are more in alignment with higher intelligence and refined vibrations. Everything we think about the world under the surface is colored by our beliefs about the perceived mass of the material world, and when we arrived we viewed time and space from a traditional lens. However, pretty soon we realized that we were entering new frequencies, more elevated vibrations than Mystic Cove. Our cellular structure needed support and alignment with these higher frequencies to move around down there. I see by your face this revelation is a shock. It was like that for us, too.

"And here's another surprise. No one can sabotage our work when we are there. I know that to be true because we saw the clean, pure way these beings live, and we saw how easily Eben and Ike merged into their way of being and living. Unless someone has a high enough frequency, they cannot even perceive, let alone sabotage the subtle world.

"I'll give you an example. I went to a city with Ike and Eben. I had trouble on the trip, feeling disoriented, and—true confession—nauseous. I kept turning inward and focusing on the infinite stillness within me so I could adjust to the changes in frequencies along the way.

"When we arrived, we went to a research lab. The lab technicians were staring with astonishment at highly advanced devices, with a screen like our current tablets. I was frustrated because I couldn't get anything to come into view. Ike explained that I was looking for the tablet to display and operate like our modern tablets. He held it for me while I centered myself and began the familiar process of becoming aware that I am aware of the inner vastness—a common method to rapidly shift brain patterns. That's usually been enough to shift consciousness and attune to subtler frequencies.

"Well, low and behold! Images arose from the tablet like a mist in his hands. If I started to focus harder, the tablet would disappear. I'd have to relax, adjust my awareness, and quiet my thinking-brain. Once I got my beta brainwaves calm, I could resume studying the information on the screen.

"And there's more. Sometimes, I only saw geometric patterns without knowing what they meant. Yet Ike and Eben could see beyond the patterns and understood the information that the patterns contained.

"This was humbling and encouraging. It means that while good-hearted, beautiful human beings like Ike and Eben can learn from our high frequency friends, those living at a lower frequency can't understand and certainly can't steal this stuff. My intuitive feeling is that we're moving way beyond crazy espionage and high-level control. And here's why...

"Ike and Eben spent a lot of time in Africa with undersurface beings. When they surfaced in Africa, most people couldn't see them and no technology on the surface could detect them, but the African shamans knew they were there. I was like a wide-eyed school kid when they showed us some of their adventures on the hologram; completely unexpected and totally brilliant.

"The bottom line: they set the stage to move freely between a location in the mountains of northern California (or other remote areas in Idaho and Montana) and an inner city that became a haven for their research. From there they can train select colleagues and take them to Africa to perform the work they plan to initiate. They'll be using the highly advanced tunnel system which takes only minutes to get from here to the inner city and back up to Africa. Upon arrival in the land of giants, it was clear that Ike and Eben had superior, innate skills to operate within quantum worlds. I am not shocked because in staying in their village with John many times for archeological digs, I saw clearly how their community showed no inhibition in communicating with invisible beings (like hearing messages from spirit guides and ancestors) and they synchronized instinctively with the laws of nature. They sensed weather changes before they happened and studied the cosmos in a way that left me humbled and in awe. They looked up at night and communicated with (and related to) beings from other star systems while all I saw was a bunch of gorgeous stars twinkling overhead. They told stories of ETs who they've interacted with and their elders supposedly visited other planets, sometimes in a craft and other times in lucid dreams.

"So how can I be surprised when Ike and Eben move in quantum worlds more easily than I do? When Ike and Eben came to the U.S. for college, they connected with other students who understood them and who could relate to their cultural upbringing. Someday all of us will be as adept as they are at engaging with the quantum realities. I feel it in my bones. It's already started.

"They have been training their local African network in the subtle art of shifting frequencies to maneuver under the surface. This comes naturally to the shamans. They've described that it's in their blood to raise their frequency, allowing them for centuries to shift awareness into higher dimensions.

"Stay with me, Angelica, I know this is hard to comprehend.

"Ike and Eben were shown bloodlines from Africa that are now spread across the globe. It wasn't a surprise that their buddies at Berkeley are from that lineage. The tablet-like devices also displayed the DNA and blood characteristics of seemingly ordinary people, scattered all over the surface, who have *extraordinary* potential. The catch is that until they fully express the unicity gene, that *potential* will remain dormant. Remember that *unicity* is the condition of being unified—in this case, a flesh and bone human unifies energetically with the field of all-that-is, allowing for perception to shift into a state of uninterrupted connectedness. If Sophia didn't tell you about that dormant gene, I'll briefly explain. It supports the human brain and nervous system to enable non-local signaling from the space memory wormhole network, allowing for reception and radiation of extremely high frequencies. It's taken a while for those of us living on the surface (aside from certain traditional shamans and adepts from various cultures) to allow the gene to express, but it's become a wildfire. That amazing gene is no longer being inhibited by the control freaks that once governed our minds and broke our hearts.

"Through widely published research, we got clear that control (like propaganda and mind-control techniques) are possible when a population or person is in *fear*. When fear is triggered, we cannot access our innate biophysical potential within our DNA to interact with massive amounts of information from the field. When we raise our frequency out of fear and into unicity, we have unlimited creativity and agency over our lives. Research showed that when we feel we don't experience this agency, we become anxious and depressed. I call it frequency-impotence.

"We didn't know that, beginning in the 1950's, citizens were drawn into the MK-Ultra Project—an unfathomably dark program orchestrated by the CIA, involving experiments to control and manipulate people, altering the mental state and brain function of countless subjects without their consent.

"Angelica, Sophia told us that you had a friend, a mentor when you were in College, whose life was destroyed by that program. but that under the care and support of some concerned indigenous people, he was healed completely and able to initiate higher expressions of feelings than fear and despair. That same shrouded agency that harmed him also took over the media, and the same kind of feelings that your dear friend felt began infecting our entire population—an ingrained feeling of being separate from each other and from *the field* had solidified. Our invaluable unicity gene remained dormant.

"BUT that's changing! As we've become aware of the furtive brainwashing we've endured for too long at the hands of unscrupulous intelligence agencies, we can shift out of fearing them and each other, and move confidently into uniting, to clean up this propaganda-mess that's been festering for nearly a hundred years. We cannot be controlled because fear is finally sinking into the backdrop and unicity is our priority. It was never about fighting the chicanery of enigmatic higher-ups in duplicitous agencies. All we have to do is live our best life without fearing them. As we raise our frequency, our DNA and entire cellular and sub cellular structures get access to endless, empowering information from the field, creative ideas, and agency over our lives. We can come together en masse. I'm up for a hell of a lot more of that kind of impactful unicity!

"I want to get back to Eben and Ike. They will be going under the surface to work with beings there to raise the frequency of Africa and completely rejuvenate its vast land, resources, and good people. When that initial phase of their work is complete, they will share it with the rest of the planet.

"Tonight is sad for me. Because I love these two as much as if they were my own kin. They'll be absorbed in that work until at least 2040, maybe 2045, and likely not around."

An overwhelming wave of sadness touched Jake; a wash of tender emotions built on intimate friendship; he automatically fought back the tears until they broke through the dam of his prior conditioning.

Ike spoke softly, reminding Jake that the giants encouraged them to emote as part of their ongoing personal evolution. After a moment, Jake's tears subsided, as a palpable stillness settled over the circle of friends. Then a slight rustle of a breeze in the autumn trees disrupted the group's placid state.

Ike needed a moment to collect himself before he addressed everyone. He slowly looked with a warmhearted gaze around the group.

"I appreciate you; every one of you," Ike said as he wiped his face, glistening with moisture in the soft firelight. "When we were kids in Africa, the boys and me called Jake and John *uncle*. That is an auspicious title because it means they are one of us, rather than two foreigners who are distinctly incompatible with us. Instead, they are definitely family. All of you are my family forever! That is way cool for me! Ahhh ... Jake, you believed in Eben and me and made this possible. When I came to your country, I didn't have family here or in Africa. And you took that role, guiding and caring for me. I always knew you had my back. I wish you spoke Nigerian because I could say it better. In English, I can say that any gifts inside me are accessible because you, John, Sophia, and all of you loved me. I couldn't just wake up one morning and believe in myself. Man! I needed your support like a baby duck needs to swim with its mom for a while before it's ready to head to the skies. *Daalu.* Thank you. *A hụrụ m gi n'anya.* I love you. In my birth language, Igbo, these words also mean *I see you eye to eye... I accept you totally... I deeply understand you, AND I love you!*"

Looking at Ike with wide eyes and raised brows, Eben said without inhibition, "Oh bro, you just slayed me! I don't know how you spoke our language without losing your shit. Oh man! I feel the same as you." Taking a slow breath and looking lovingly around the circle, he continued, "I was sad when I arrived at the university in California. Ike told me there are nice people in Idaho, and they want to help us. I was cynical. I thought I had lost everything. I hated to talk. My English was horrible. So bad!

"People at the university said I had a high IQ, but Jake told me one day that my high IQ was *not worth horse shit*. At first I felt gutted, stabbed with a criticism-knife. Humiliation and feeling like I was *never enough* took me into a wormhole that was headed for pure darkness. As I sat there... feeling like I wanted to die because of his disapproval... without hesitating even for a second, he hugged me real tight! He flashed me a big smile, the kind that makes everything okay. I felt his love and before he could say anything, I hugged him back like I was a python. Man! I couldn't let go! He relaxed me when he started speaking kindly like a father, he said, *Kid, you have a high Intelligence Quotient but you are also highly developed emotionally. Your compassion and care for others is amazing. It didn't take long for you to become someone who others want to hear from. You are great with people. Courage is your middle name. You are not valued because you are smart. You are good as gold. You've handled adversity with a sense of courage. That makes you extraordinary in my eyes.*

"Awww man! All of a sudden, *all* my quotients rose! I'd never heard of anything except IQ. I realized that he was helping me to see that I was more than my mind. He kept helping me to see my cosmic self, my subtle aspects. And I stopped looking back at my painful childhood in Nigeria. I was not only an orphan but I felt sad because I had zero roots!" Pausing for a moment, he allowed the waves of escalating emotions to subside back onto the shore of the enduring safety and acceptance he could count on at Mystic Cove. The masculine timbre of his exquisitely resonant voice set the stage for further authenticity and candor.

He said, "My ancestors had been killed or more distantly kidnapped into slavery. Who was I without family? Even though Ike kept taking me to the shaman in our village to learn about our past, well... I just could not feel close to those people. Luckily, Jake believed I was part of something bigger than a family I could hold or touch. He started letting me dig with him, showing me artifacts from my ancestors. I began to sit with our Shamans and talk about the objects Jake found, reminders of my ancestors. Jake got me to tell him in detail the Shaman's stories about my distant ancestors, especially from the cosmos. He'd help me vision and feel what they were like, what they taught my people, and he drilled into me that I *embody their impressiveness, their genius, inside of me.* Since I liked Jake a lot, I listened to him. Unseen worlds became a resource for me, and quantum physics became a way to relate to my ancestors *and my peers.* Interconnectedness of everything mattered to my perception of life. He promised he'd bring me to his country someday, assuring me I would further my study of invisible worlds. He kept his word and brought me here.

"I trusted him, John, and Sophia. And I want to give my friends and the whole world what they gave me—hope and encouragement. Jake, John, Sophia, and all of you inspire me and help me to be more high vibe. I love you so much! Megan has been so kind and generous. Hey Jake, my English is better, eh? I'm not embarrassed to speak love and blessings to you all. You are all WAY cool! I'm blessed by you and I bless you, always."

More tears rolled through the gathering like a giant wave.

"Oh my goodness, Eben!" Angelica exclaimed. "Thank you for your intimate, unvarnished sharing of distressing struggles and eventual triumphs. Like you, I see this whole group is open-hearted and embraces each other unconditionally. Trusting each other and feeling safe to be ourselves is invaluable. I feel like being with all of you is shifting my energy field immensely. Dear Lord! I've done mountains of work through plant medicine and getting to feel the subtle vibrations of herbs many times. Yet with this conversation, I'm elevating to an even higher level as part of this group's frequency. It's mind-bending stuff that you are speaking about."

The circle of friends sat reflectively for a few minutes.

Angelica gently broke the blanket of silence. With her head cocked to one side inquisitively and in a bewildered tone, she addressed Grace, asking, "I recall Jake mentioned that the work of Ike and Eben would interest *your husband*. I haven't heard you mention him. Is he from Africa?"

The entire group roared with laughter, rolling in waves until Grace said, "We are laughing because my husband isn't from Africa nor anywhere on the surface of Earth. Please don't faint, Angelica. He looks and is human but he's from under-the-surface in a city which this group did not visit yet.

"In a nutshell, I met him on the East Coast on a skiing trip. He was the first person who understood my crazy perceptive abilities. I could see things invisible to others, easily pulled information from the field about the future, and saw most people and objects in their light form before they came into solid view. It made me a bit of *a nut case* to most people. Yet he got me, one hundred percent.

"When I met my husband, my destiny collided with his. I was overwhelmed by his kindness. Whoa... when I saw his energy field, I was instantly in love! My husband is older than me by a few hundred years, maybe more, but who is counting, right?

"We moved to British Columbia in Canada, and we live part-time off-grid. We continue to go back and forth to his city. For decades, he worked with surface scientists and researchers but never in *black projects* of any kind. It was his goal to get to the point where we are now. In the last five years or so, the black projects started slowly disintegrating due to lack of funds and lack of cover. And the corporations and wealthy investors lost their control over technologies. Because of that, he's busier than ever.

"One reason Sophia was excited about this trip was that she and Nate knew Bob, and they understood that life under the surface can be amazing. Many years ago, Bob shared with Sophia and Nate an overview of life in his family's city. To be clear, everyone below our feet isn't a giant and each area is unique."

"Grace, do you and Bob have a family under the surface?" Angelica asked, immensely interested in Grace's story.

"I don't have children, if that's what you are asking. The relationship I have with my husband is off-the-charts yet our DNA isn't compatible for creating progeny. He's from a profoundly advanced race and they have tests to measure DNA compatibility with surface dwellers. It's rare to find a match. With the exception of some relatives who are not close to me, I do not have family on the surface either.

"Bob's caring community warmly welcomed me as though I'd lived there forever as a well-loved part of an extended family, typical of their kind and nurturing culture. There's no need to have tons of children to keep their civilization alive nor is there a void of closeness, affection, and care. Believe me, you would love them. That's for sure. There's more than enough room for cities and all kinds of cultures of varying frequencies beneath the surface, which relieves the pressure or tendency for land grabs and for concerns about overpopulation.

"As I raised my frequencies sufficiently, Bob gave me access to a tunnel located about an hour north of here and I keep a vehicle there. I can come to the cove easily. I apologize for being so forthright. Angelica, I can see by your face that I've overwhelmed you. I am so sorry!"

After Grace's remarkable revelations settled into their midst, Angelica sat frozen, staring at the fire while the group allowed for her silent assimilation.

"It's okay," Angelica muttered as she shook her head and leaned forward, staring at her hands with fingers clasped tightly while resting them on her knees. For several minutes the only movement she made was through her breath as it rose and fell slowly and rhythmically.

"Angelica, I didn't know any of this when I met you," Sophia said, thawing the deeply frozen silence.

"I shared with you that Nate had been sick for a while but I didn't know at the time that he'd been gathering data for Bob when members of a black lodge, a powerful and well-known secret society, decided to stop him. His death was slow, just the way they wanted it. He'd instructed me to send an envelope to one of his trusted friends after his death, which I did. I didn't know the details of its content until later. Grace filled me in when it was safe for me to know what had transpired. Those documents he held at the end of his life revealed and exposed massive corporate corruption on a global level, the kind of skullduggery that had perpetuated an unfettered assault on humanity for millennia. Thankfully that's changing.

"While we were under the surface, Nate appeared in holographic form." She paused, remembering the joy of seeing him again. "He explained what had happened during the time he was ill. Through trusted contacts in the government, Gilda had found out who Nate was and what he'd been working on. She felt aligned with his values and was eager to help him. Whether it was destiny or super good fortune, she'd landed in the apartment next to us. She and her counterparts crafted a masterful plan to work with him. She knew countless secrets about the black projects and the ins and outs of the military-industrial complex. Nate got pieces of the puzzle he'd been looking for from Gilda and collected vital information from her and Adele's mother before he passed. I was stunned to find out they were working with Bob, too.

"The main point is, we can be optimistic. Globally, humanity's first big step forward worked—we stopped looking at authority blindly like in that famous Milgram Experiment where the researchers proved that most people will deliberately harm someone if an authority encourages them to do so. I didn't believe it was true, but it's been replicated many times. Now, as a global population, we've become clear about such psychological vulnerabilities, and we've woken up to the mass manipulation we've endured for eons.

"In shadowy *black projects*, for example, soldiers will kill a comrade if told to do so. That reminded me of the eerie Jesuit oath in which they agree to kill their mother if told to do so by their supervisor. What does that kind of vow have to do with protecting the Pope? In the case of soldiers, standing guard over the constitution and our national security, what kind of mind control are some of them placed under? Black projects in the military-industrial complex have deep tap roots and a massive network of support. Its leaders are not likely going to relinquish control without first engaging in a ferocious fight to maintain their status. By the look on your face I suspect you've been aware of this?"

Angelica nodded, offering a pained smile of affirmation.

"On the holographic screens we viewed social changes rapidly occurring across the planet. I hope you are seeing that, too."

"I'm seeing it, but it's not been enough to make a huge paradigm shift. That is what we need. We all thought by 2030 things would get resolved, but the world is still in chaos."

Bewildered by the scope of the conversation, Angelica shrugged her shoulders, paused and said, "My Lord, Sophia! I had no idea that Nate was involved in all of this intrigue."

"Neither did I," Sophia said. "Nate's revelations under the surface were a total shock. When I stayed with you, I didn't know the truth behind his devastating death. Looking back, there were hints, but Nate resolutely decided not to involve me. If he thought I was getting suspicious, he'd divert my attention. He stopped engaging me in his correspondence or asking me to make phone calls for him—but I thought he was doing that because of his decision to slow down. It turns out he was protecting me.

"Grace, Bob, and I maintained close contact through the whole ordeal. With Nate's instructions, however, they couldn't share anything about the envelope because they'd promised Nate to keep it confidential until it was used as evidence in court. Bob's been a devoted friend for many years and since he knew about my plan to explore under the surface, he began to help me become proficient in moving through the tunnels from here to his home with Grace in British Columbia. I could practice working with the shifts in frequency in underground tunnels. As I was able to make the adjustments, Bob generously suggested I bring John and Jake so we could be better prepared for our adventure. After that, Bob and two amazing friends from his city, who work in quantum science research, helped the entire team prepare to travel through the tunnel. Bob and his comrades were a gift to us—having their guidance was incredibly valuable for adapting to the new environment we entered."

"My goodness, sweet friends!" Angelica said, looking flustered. "My mind is stunned. I am in awe, and a bit overwhelmed. I see why political events and global situations played out the way they have on the surface. I assume we'll soon refer to what has happened up here as the *giant reboot*. I'm not surprised to hear how diligently and thoroughly you prepared for your trip. Your stories are sometimes shocking; always thrilling; while mostly jaw-dropping.

"Maybe we could pause for a few minutes. To enjoy this conversation even more, I'd love some tea and a quick pause. Anyone want coffee?"

John offered to help. As they walked to the house, Angelica put her arm around his waist. Observing them, Caitlyn radiated a felicitous smile.

# CHAPTER 27

# HOLOGRAMS OF DEVASTATING TRUTH

Angelica made tea with her usual focus and care. Herbs danced and bobbed up and down in the boiling water of a large pot. She turned to John and said, "You talk about these high tech, holographic scenes where you can view history. I couldn't help but wonder if you got to see President Kennedy's assassination?

"When we were dating back in college, you were obsessed by specific, obvious clues for broadminded people to uncover. I also recall that in the aftermath, you observed a clandestine group was sending a clear message:

*We are unquestionably in control. We can let the media release the photo of the murder weapon on day one and then, like magic, we can make that image disappear from media and from history, never to be mentioned again. We can let you see a guy on a sunny day opening and closing an umbrella, as though he's sending a code to someone. And we can have a ridiculously flawed autopsy, create a bogus commission to look into the murder headed by someone who was potentially, and likely, an archenemy of the president. Yet you will know not to question us. We own the media, the government, and you, like it or not.*

"Oh my goodness! I hated those conversations, but I know it mattered to you. Yet these days, it matters to me, too. Did you get to see that moment in time?

"Whoa! You have a great memory! And by the way, have I told you that you look gorgeous tonight?" They both smiled like two awkward teenagers on a first date and then hugged, ending in a tender, long kiss.

Finding composure, John answered, "Yes, I got to observe the grassy knoll where Kennedy was shot. I remained curious. Yet what I saw was devastating. Without going into a bunch of details, I can say emphatically I wasn't wrong. I didn't realize the depth and scope of the assassins' influence.

"Another hard-to-fathom scene of unexpected magnitude was *Operation Northwoods*—a carefully designed CIA plan in 1962 which was thwarted by President Kennedy.

"As the plan unfolded on the hologram, my respect for Kennedy deepened. Clearly, the President was not pleased nor on board. Luckily he had the balls to firmly defy the Joint Chiefs of Staff in carrying out their well-thought-out plan. Our government's highly regarded intelligence group planned to actively commit terrorism right here on American soil as a false flag operation. It went like this: assassinate immigrants from Cuba; stage terrorist attacks in the U.S. which included 'large fires' and blame it all on Castro; sink boats with Cuban refugees at sea; blow up an American ship; fill a plane with CIA agents, who the Florida media would cover as a group of fun-loving students enjoying a trip together. Then, they would land the plane on an island and send a look-alike, unmanned drone towards Cuba and shoot it down—with tons of media drama and mourning for this horrific act by Castro. To add to the hype, mock funerals for the innocent youth would be staged. The goal was to create a fever in the U.S. populace for *military intervention in Cuba* against the Castro regime.

"I wondered about the deeper, underlying reason for the military's stance? Who would benefit from a potential war? I could envision General Smedley Butler shaking his head, wondering when U.S. citizens would wake up and understand that these diabolical acts are not behind us. In the same way that he encouraged us in his lifetime, I'm sure he'd be asking from his side of the veil, *When will we demand transparency, and refuse to support blatant acts of violence and endless war?* In the end, the chance of us taking any important revelations further diminished because the media was completely mute, except to ridicule or dismiss anyone who asked tough questions.

"The foundation of historical facts around Kennedy and inhuman, surreptitious tactics, are like a deck of cards. The whole deck matters. One card does not create a game. Not only that, we have to recognize their poker face and confront the reality that they are playing for high stakes. They play to win. As you know, a lot has happened lately. The deceit and cover ups are a house of cards that's falling fast. Parts of the game are over but not all of it.

"It's unfathomable that we have over one million documents related to JFK's assassination, like the ones that divulge what I saw on the hologram. Yet it was also incomprehensible to learn that Lee Harvey Oswald, the supposed assassin, was a CIA asset. Through the CIA, he had faked defection to Russia. There was a big splash in the news about him walking into the U. S. embassy and renouncing his citizenship. When he finished his work in Russia, which did not appear to amount to anything, he went back to that embassy, asked for his passport and cash to buy an airline ticket to Dallas, Texas, which he received. And the rest, as they say, is history—albeit a distorted version. A CIA agent picked him up at the airport—it was business as usual. To this day, the public cannot see all the files. After viewing behind-the-scenes aspects of this event on the hologram, I realized why the public didn't get to see the full report.

"JFK was willing to die for peace and he made tough decisions—like after the debacle in Cuba, he fired Allen Dulles, who was then the head of the CIA. He refused to send U.S. troops to Cuba and Vietnam. His Joint Chiefs of Staff were not on the same page. As I watched the hologram, what caught my attention was that there was a fiery quality of integrity in President Kennedy and a passion for creating a peaceful world. Like many before him, he died defending his values. Sometimes that's the way life works. I'm hoping that we are moving past those times and rising up as a collective to demand integrity and insist on a peaceful world rather than leave it to a handful of martyrs to stand up for what our collective souls unequivocally long for."

"John, are you afraid? I know these people have eyes everywhere and they likely know what you have been up to. You went places under the surface where they couldn't go. I'm worried."

"Angelica, the all-seeing-eye of the dollar bill is still looking out with its periscope but we have safeguards in place. Jake and I have been coming to the surface periodically to locate and connect with geologists, archeologists, and others in our field. The hologram tells us who they are and what kind of frequency they express.

"We did extensive, focused work on raising our frequency and were able to go beyond the first phases of moving around in subtle forms. At first we could only send our consciousness to various places—often referred to as *remote viewing*. Over time, we began to direct our particles, our 3-D body, to the surface without the ship. At this point, we can move back and forth, with the help of the giants, to and from ONLY certain locations where it's a frequency match. This was an intense part of our training under the surface—to be able to direct our particles from a particular coordinate in spacetime to a different one. We realized that from under the surface, we could not only remote view something happening on the surface but we could learn to *move our particles* and locate them onto the surface briefly and then return to the giant's world. I don't want to make it sound like I can beam myself anywhere or any time I want to. The giants were always by our side, guiding us; they know the locations that facilitate this kind of movement through the quantum field.

"To be clear, I did not go to my *past* or try to visit my *future*. Rather, we underwent intense training and guidance to move from a specific, high vibrational portal I mentioned to another location—which was a milestone for me, yet a daily activity for our giant friends. Please don't ask me about wormholes and *how* we did it. Ike and Eben understand that part. Holy cow! I am thrilled to know this kind of movement through the fabric of spacetime is possible.

"Because of those brief journeys to the surface, a lot of our information, detailed data, and journals are with trusted people on the surface. Like I said, we were only able to move our particles to specific places and it took a lot of preparation and training to do so. The giants assured us that this process will get easier and feel more natural. For me, it's miraculous that we can even move our particles on a limited basis. You won't be surprised that Ike and Eben are WAY more adept at this process. They were moving around like pros. Maybe they physically align with that subtle level of reality in a way that folks like me cannot easily master."

"Moving your particles to areas of matching frequency on the surface! ... Dear Lord! ... That's hard to fathom!"

Angelica took a moment to absorb and come to terms with John's stunning revelation. After a long, deep breath, she continued.

"Regardless of your progress with moving your particles, the mama bear in me is asking you to be careful. The kind of people who use that all-seeing-eye you mentioned are not like you. They have their own empire, and we're seeing they want to maintain it, at all costs. They've demonstrated that they are willing to sacrifice large numbers of people to make sure their bottom line is shining like gold and their power remains in tact. They've created spy technology that is unimaginable and they own the media. Sophia mentioned the huge strides made to deconstruct the organizations who use unscrupulous surveillance and engage in covert activities to track and brainwash citizens. They do so with impunity. Undercover work, espionage and the capture of media by global intelligence agencies is being exposed and slowly abolished. But we have not seen the complete dismantling of this spine-chilling, stealth-style intelligence system.

"At times, we feel united and we're moving in a mutually beneficial direction. Then, out of the blue, a wrench gets thrown into the engine and we have to be vigilant not to fall for the latest distraction or propaganda.

"What you've exposed, plus the free energy that's emerging, is changing the old power dynamics, yet all of this change leaves the surface spinning in chaos.

"The leaders and influential people you and your friends have described are like a cougar cornered in a cave. Their claws and fangs are lethal. I appreciate everything your team is doing but you are fighting a behemoth. Many of these groups use black magic and there are rumors they are into the occult like Hitler was, dealing with creepy, evil entities via ritual. Oh my word! I don't know what to believe about them but what they've done surely isn't innocent nor does it feel angelic and pure. My naiveté says these kinds of things are relegated to the realms of movie scripts, but your work has been a grave reality check. When I heard the facts from your team, I had to stop and wonder about everything I've been blind to. If the truth be told, I didn't want to grapple with any of this.

"Such people think more like a machine than a human. You can't expect them to all of a sudden respond with deep feelings of compassion and care. Please don't let your guard down, okay?"

A brief silence descended on the pair until John moved closer to her. His gaze pierced her eyes with a loving gaze, and said, "Please listen to me, sweetheart. Even though I've been separated from you twice, I've never felt as intimately bonded to you as I do now. I know you feel that way, too. Our relationship gives me the space to be brutally honest. As much as I would never want to leave you, I'm not afraid to die. Sooner or later, I may have to face the dark entities you mentioned, and anyone or anything else obsessed with power and control. In my view, they are each a form of darkness—one is ethereal and the other is physical in nature. They each have cast a backdrop of frequency that allows me to see more clearly that all of us must become grounded in *zero point* profundity and our mind-boggling infinite nature.

"More importantly, if my work here is over, I will leave my body and others will carry on with my endeavors. That may seem simplistic or completely irrational but it's my current viewpoint. I refuse to live in fear or judgment of tyrannical forces or demons because that will eclipse my inner light and capacity to create from the highest potential within me. I'm forging onward with the faith that every step I take in each moment forms my *hero zone*, my place of courage.

"There's no arguing that our world still wreaks of chaos and darkness, but I've been blessed to find the Supreme Light within. It has been more than worth living for. I've been to higher layers of frequency and consciousness in myself and to coordinates in spacetime that are so mystifying that I am sure this one slice of the pie called *my life* cannot be the only reality available for me to experience.

"Through the holograms, I've seen people who crossed over into elevated states of consciousness after death yet they still connect with and help those who remain embodied. It's complicated and there's not enough time right now to get into it. You need to know I'll bring revolutionary information and technologies forward, even if they kill me in the process. The holograms sometimes displayed mesmerizing geometric patterns which meant the data was too subtle for me to be able to interpret at my frequency level. Yet I remain in awe of the wisdom I could intuit was wafting in through the screen in front of me. I've been to a world of infinite possibility and endless wonder. Death is not a problem. It's a process of life that I am now in flow with; my heart is invested in my work because it is my destiny, my contribution to humanity."

Tears formed delicately in Angelica's oceanic blue eyes. Touching his lips to her forehead tenderly, John held her in a warm, reassuring embrace. In this intimate moment, there were no words exchanged. The merging of souls eclipsing the need to speak—silence shimmering with love and union. As the two lovers snuggled even closer, Angelica smiled and touched her cheek to John's.

"I know there are more surprises," she said, getting up to make tea. "Dear Lord! I'm trying to prepare myself to hear more about the world under our feet. From my perspective, it's a bit overwhelming to grasp."

"All of this will make sense as time goes on," John responded. "If you are interested, we'd love to include you in our further work—to have you join us. Your knowledge of botany and subtle energy fields will allow you to transition to higher frequencies easily."

Taken aback for a moment, she became silent. Her mood suddenly shifted and she proclaimed fervently, "I'm more than willing to join you! I didn't realize that your group could use my help. I believe your discoveries can heal and change our world for the better. I'd be honored to expand your noble endeavors. Count me in!"

# CHAPTER 28

# MORE HOLOGRAMS AND MYSTERIES

Mother Nature blessed the group with a quiet atmosphere, without even the slightest breeze.

After pouring tea for everyone, Angelica turned to Jake and asked with curiosity, "I can't help but wonder if you were able to get to the center? Is it too hot there? What did it look like when you traveled through all of those layers? And about going from here to Africa using ancient, high tech train systems... it seems like something from a highly creative movie plot. For heaven's sake, you all were pretty busy traveling both far and deep under the surface. It sounded like getting to Africa took a snap of your fingers."

"Great questions," Jake said in a reflective tone. "Our pre-conceived ideas about life under the surface were pulverized by reality—what we experienced was not even close to our imaginary ideas of how it would be down there. To move through the inner Earth, at some point, you are no longer in the space-time of our material reality. I know that sounds airy-fairy. But the truth is, over time, it made sense to me. It's more than a snap of your fingers but it is almost that simple. Let me explain.

"As human beings we're more than the physical body. We're energy that expresses from dense to subtle. We're mass, or density, that extends into being photons of pure light and then we extend beyond even that. I can explain something that was helpful for me to consider. Recent quantum research shows that our protons are little *swirling vortices* within the quantum fluids of the unified field of all-that-is. Although they spin, every millionth of second they are able to pause, pretty darn briefly, and take in information from the quantum field of all potentiality. Then they transmit subtle, high frequency information into our 3-D body. Hold onto that premise as I explain a bit more. This means that at our core, we're ultimately a little plasma vortex of spinning energy, indelibly connected to our Essence—the infinite information and potentiality of the quantum field.

"These days, I speak about protons and electrons not as little balls of energy but as electromagnetic charges coherently moving in space. I've talked Sophia's and John's ears off about this. It's fascinating to envision that this *charge* is what we perceive as material form. These charges are measured in planck units, named after a physicist, Max Planck. Infinitesimal, electromagnetic planck oscillators create clusters of spinning vortices in space to create mass and gravitation. Recently, you may have heard me refer to the infinite space in and around us as *quantum fluids of potentiality*, since that better describes their nature as a *plasma*—a fluid state. When I talk about *vacuum* space, recent science explains that vacuum space isn't *empty*; rather, it's a fluid vacuum in space filled with wild, unlimited potentiality. It's filled with energy in the form of light, sound, and endless electromagnetic waves.

"Consider that at our core, a vortex is whirling with incredible power—a tiny black hole. This is mystifying and cutting edge.

"How am I doing with my explanation, Ike? Do you want to jump in?"

"You are doing great! I love hearing everyone on the team articulating *the field theory* like a bunch of quantum physicists. I believe it's important for you to be comfortable speaking about it. I guarantee you my physics team would be giving you high-fives right now. You've got this! Keep going, please!"

Ike's smile was as radiant as that of a proud parent.

"Okay then," Jake said, winking appreciatively at Ike. "I can move from the physics to something you know more about. Think about the ancient wisdom texts you studied. Human beings are said to be everything from form to formless. This formless state is something that you can become aware of but, at some point, your mind can't fathom or conceptualize it. The mind becomes still and vibrates in quietude. In meditation, you sit silently and when you emerge from that quiet state, have you ever wondered how an hour passed? It seemed like your eyes were closed for only a few minutes."

Angelica nodded in agreement, and he continued. "If we agree that you and I live in a quantum universe and you are a gorgeous, unlimited, electromagnetic, spinning vortex—arising from infinite information, or what science calls a *field of potentiality*, why can't the Earth be the same thing—a magnificent spinning vortex with a singularity pulling energy into the center? Is it conclusive that the Earth is absolutely solid? That you can get to its center through time and space by digging through rock and boiling in lava trying to get there? What if Earth is a conscious being? What if, like us, she is seemingly solid on the surface and gets more and more subtle toward her center? And past her swirling, fluid vortex, she's infinite, like the ancient texts describe.

"Stay with me, because everything we learned from the giants and through our experience was amazing. We could only *move through lava* if we used technology that accounted for magnetic fields of lava. But more than that... what blew my mind... was that we could only traverse the layers if we had *the personal frequency* to do so. As we've said, our bodies are not equipped to deal with massive magnetics nor able to handle super-high frequencies.

"It was not only about having the right craft, it was also about our particles—our priceless little subtle protons being alchemized by our inner state into a frequency that matched the subtle electro magnetic fields we traveled through.

"Some of our travels took us through giant caverns where we felt the lava nearby, along with the corresponding magnetic shifts. We later talked about the likelihood that the vehicle that we were traveling in could have been transmuting frequencies and helping us to adjust to the magnetics. Yet, to go deeper into the Earth, no vehicle could help. If you want to go deeper, you have to be in higher frequencies, able to adjust to more subtle levels of reality. And true confession, Eben and Ike surpassed all of us in those capacities. That's what they were born to do. Sometimes the rest of us simply could not get to the point of being able to travel to certain places. We were told this lava issue and other dynamics of Gaia's depths have mystified brilliant scientists in black projects for a long time."

"Jake, I'd like to add something for Mom to get more clarity," Caitlyn said, as she leaned forward looking at her mother intently. "As a black hole, the swirling vortex that Jake mentioned, you receive and express information from and into the infinite field around you. I don't want you to have the wrong impression, that you are sucking in information, thus isolating yourself. You are dynamically interacting with everything everywhere—meaning that each coordinate in spacetime is a *distinct* black hole structure, a spinning vortex with particular speed and angulation.

"A seminal shift in my understanding of my subtle structure comprised of a black hole happened when Ike and one of the giants showed us the mathematical formulas for black holes within the unified field they arise from. They used a holographic screen that reminded me of an old-fashioned blackboard—but way cooler! Mom, they walked us through the meticulous details of how we spin as an angular vortex as part of the unified field, why that matters, and how natural it is. Although his presentation was clear, Ike could sense resistance in me. He's so perceptive! You can't hide anything from him!

"Picture the whole group engrossed in the presentation and I was looking at the screen with my head cocked, arms folded, and my heels dug in (metaphorically) as he tried to help me to join the conversation. Finally, Ike burst into the craziest laugh ever. He said, 'You think black holes are dangerous, demonic monsters—pure evil and irrationally violent.'

"Well, I was busted, big-time! As he'd been talking, I kept thinking of the Bermuda Triangle and that sort of thing—being sucked in violently and torn to shreds by a vicious force of nature. Whenever the black hole conversation came up or anyone talked about vortices, I tuned out unconsciously.

"But our dear friend, Ike, wasn't about to give into my resistance. He walked me through a breathtaking, mesmerizing process of black hole formation—the spin sounded extraordinary and the singularity at its base felt like a mysterious, densely packed treasure of unlimited information lying at my core, ready to be tapped and experienced. The subtle, spinning black hole suddenly seemed hospitable, benevolent, and absolutely beautiful as it met at its core with its counterpart, the *white hole*—spinning in the opposite direction. Together, they formed a double torus shape of energy pouring in the top of the black hole, headed for the singularity and emerging as a white hole that spun energy outward and back to the top of the torus. Endless energy was pouring into the top, through the singularity at the center, and back up from the bottom to the top in an endless, jaw dropping display of light, sound, and frequency. When he showed us images of black hole/white hole structures coming together as a torus, they ultimately created universes, galaxies and even infinitesimal protons. I cried as I began to fathom the ultimate magnitude of their invisible quantum power and capacity to be the innate, primal architecture of everything, everywhere. I realized that I had held a preconceived, unenlightened bias—born from ignorance and conditioning—about quantum level *black holes*. Worse, I didn't know they had a lovely white counterpart that joined *the swirling dance of creation.*

"Ike and his totally amazing giant colleague showed us that black holes come to equilibrium at a point, *the singularity*. I'd heard the term before, but now, because of my new under-standing of these amazing vortexes, I was glued to every word. They said through this subtle apex of infinite, swirling beauty and light, I have unbounded access to unlimited levels of in-formation within what Ike called the *space memory network*. Every thought, action and emotion is logged into this field from everyone, everywhere throughout eternity. He pointed out when we stilled our mind to enter a flow state, which we were trained to do as often as possible, the subtle quantum architecture of my black hole/white hole structure allowed me to interact with infinite information in the network he mentioned. Black holes and their white hole counterparts became an epic enigma to study and behold as an extraordinary treasure, rather than relating it to the lowly status of a ruthless monster ready to devour me. I had a massive shift in my worldview.

"My consciousness, *my feedback and feedforward mechanism with the field,* expanded and gave me more intuitive capacities. As that continued, the flow state was more available to me. My perception of my environment shifted dramatically. Underlying the physical world that I observed, I visualized and let my body feel the grandeur of the inconceivable swirling vortex within me and within everything, everywhere.

"Thank God Ike was sweet enough to patiently help me to get on board. It changed my life. As you know, I'm very analytical and need to prove things. Every time he gathered us together to explain the physics of the inexplicable world we live in, his profoundly detailed mathematics and geometry left me speechless.

"What I find crazy is I didn't own my *black hole bias* until Ike pushed me, albeit gently, to see why I was not willing to engage in the conversation. Our team was always like that—supportive, authentic, and real. I want to assure you that nothing we're sharing is BS. Mom, IF you notice yourself pulling back or wanting to avoid any subject, please take time to ask questions—if not tonight, do it later. What we're talking about is going to change the world, yet it requires shifting ingrained conditioning and subconscious beliefs to digest this new information fully.

"And about the center of the Earth, we never planned to go there. The center of the Earth, as I understand it in physics terms, is a quantum-level singularity, the core of the Earth's black hole/white hole structure. That core is so profoundly energetically dense that our particles could not physically hang out there. Since we are each spinning vortices with our unique singularity, why couldn't Gaia be the same, with full access to infinite information from the unified field? So this *center* isn't a destination. Her center is an energy dynamic that our personal center, or singularity, can resonate with. I can see by your face you definitely didn't see that truth bomb coming!

"For me, taking time to absorb this was epic—more invaluable than I realized. I became acutely aware of layers of energy that comprise my being, which I can amplify. If this is hard to take in at first, everyone here will understand. It took a while for our brains to register the subtleties of the quantum world.

"Considering our fields of study, rather than going to a perceived *physical* center of Gaia, we were more interested in the chance to uncover deeper truths about the history, archeology, and anthropology of the interior of the Earth—wherever we could find a place to work. Before we left for the journey, with the help of the local indigenous people on the surface, we knew there were ways to connect with the giants to assist us. But when we saw them on their ship for the first time, off-the-charts feelings rushed through my body. Even a word like *thrilling* sounds lame. I was LIT UP!

"However, I soon came back to reality because we had not considered that to do our work anywhere under the surface, we needed an expanded shift in consciousness, and a more unbiased perception and understanding of the inner landscape and dimensions of the earth. Honestly, our concepts about what lay beneath the surface of Gaia definitely required a major refresh.

"Our knowledge was based on computer modeling, seismic measurements, and mathematical formulas. We didn't comprehend that we were entering subtle frequency realms that don't fit material-based modeling. When I use the term *realm*, I am speaking about a reality in which frequencies reside without a form like we perceive in our 3-D world. One example is an *angelic realm*, which is not a coordinate in spacetime, like a star or planet, a location where we could go to meet *angels*. Rather it is *a realm* of reality containing a collective of subtle, *elevated* frequencies with whom we can connect. Anyone can communicate with angelic consciousness as an overall frequency or with one of the diverse expressions of the overall angelic frequency. Just because they do not live on a location in spacetime like a planet or star, full of angels with wings and halos, doesn't mean that they are any less real than we are—nor are they any more (or less) powerful than us.

"The subtle energy fields of various coordinates, or locations, are important. For example, when Sophia, Adele, her daughters, and Grace visited a place of pure, feminine energy, it was so subtle that to be able to function there required intense training. It was a coordinate rather than a realm. Yet they all agreed it was a very refined, subtle experience. Avani joined them in other similar places. It was amazing. Tell Mom what happened, Avani."

"Okay..." Avani gladly chimed in. "Well, before undertaking excursions with them, the giants requested that we work in specialized areas with high frequencies. After we learned how to get into particular brain wave patterns to create a still mind, we could use advanced technologies to help us enter particularly high frequency areas. One of the first of those areas I saw looked typical—rock walls, green vegetation all around, like any other natural setting—yet so mind-bending! When we touched a specific rock and stood back, the rock wall started to ripple and morph in front of us, becoming smooth as glass.

"This was how it worked: I'd put my hand on the rock, which felt more metallic than stone, and a hologram appeared. Oh my God! Through that technology, I could immediately connect my awareness with various places under the surface—before going there physically. I'd unify my frequencies with the coordinate's vibes, and feel its frequencies with my senses. As my body and senses aligned with the coordinate, experiencing the coordinate physically was less intense and took less time to adjust. I hope that's clear."

Angelica nodded with an encouraging, motherly smile.

"I fell in love with one of the holograms. It was huge and contained a compilation of data about our planet's history. Caitlyn, is this a good time to tell your mom about my amazing interface with that hologram related to history?"

Getting a nod and a smile from her bestie, Avani launched in. "My God! It was epic! This hologram was as big as the huge screens for outdoor movies. To give you context, when Ike and his physics colleagues used a holographic screen to show us the black hole information, it was only about five feet tall. But this one I'm talking about towered way above our heads.

"All I had to do was think about a time in history and a scene would appear. This technology was hidden in plain sight—totally inconspicuous. Unlike a big screen event on the surface, the giants were not enthralled or impressed with their tech—even though it was light years ahead of surface technologies.

"My experience was amazing! I am saying this because I was raised Hindu and Christian. I was able to see whether historical events and people were fact or myth. As I discovered the deeper truth of childhood stories, I had some pretty massive meltdowns. To get clarity and integrate my experiences, I shared my discoveries with Sophia. She listened with an open mind. Having her support helped me to accept that history is recorded by human beings who have their own perceptions, are guided by the leadership of a specific time period, and some things were censored or written with a deeply seeded bias.

"Finally, though, I admitted that my heart wanted to know if my Templar ancestors were real. I was afraid to know the truth. I didn't want to be disappointed if *my hopeful truth* ended up being a *myth*. She encouraged me to find out for myself. Oh my God! She was so sweet! Like most places we visited, the rocks in the viewing area were ergonomic chairs that fit our body perfectly. It was mind-blowing to sit my butt on a rock and feel it morph like that. My curiosity intensified and I became increasingly obsessed with seeing my Templar ancestors. One morning I sat quivering with excitement in front of the massive hologram. And poof! My Templar ancestors were in front of me... human yet oh-so-divine...radiating light with such intensity that I struggled to stay conscious! Luckily, I was sitting down because my awareness went cosmic as I locked into their inner domain—mind-melting, radically potent luminescence—filled with endless waves of cosmic bliss!

"I came back to consciousness sobbing, recalling my father saying those noble Templar sages told people not to worship them, but rather to recognize the pure sacredness within *themselves*. Metaphorically, that couple had taken my hand, giving me a chance to experience my sacred nature as it exists infinitely inside me. I have their DNA! Wow! I don't know if I can fully express the magnitude of the feelings and waves of energy the experience unfurled for me. They are real! I saw them arriving in North America. Yet even after several generations, no one wanted the wisdom they could share. They joined other Templars and like-minded sagacious people, creating contemplative lives of solitude in high-frequency caves, deep below the surface. I couldn't help but think of Mystic Cove and other locations where high-vibe humans found like-minded comrades and familial comfort. The Templar, his wife, and their offspring were off-the-charts on the *goodness scale*. Most of their children, also sages, remained selflessly in India to carry on the inner work. Confirmation of my DNA finally arrived, miraculously carrying itself forward into the present moment. Wow! I need a minute to collect myself. Connecting with them sets my heart ablaze with intoxicating frequencies!"

After a silent pause, Avani's enormous eyes opened unhurried, like an emerging dawn. She continued reflectively.

"Sophia, can you share about what you learned about Jesus? I'd love for Angelica to see how our concepts about current reality are shaped by what we assume is true about our past. I learned we have to be undogmatic, unbiased, and question the objectivity of whoever created current historical records, plus keep in mind that leaders of governments and religions have personal motivations and maybe misunderstandings that end up making history look a certain way.

"I recall one example where an Emperor's wife didn't like the idea of reincarnation. She'd been a little naughty and, because reincarnation was universally accepted as true, she began to worry about potentially unpleasant forms she might be forced to embody in her next incarnation. Okay, she'd been *more* than a *little naughty*. So she convinced her husband to ask the Christian Church to omit reincarnation from their doctrines. After a large doctrinal meeting occurred, an official church document was created. It was a clever ruse on the part of the Emperor and his wife but the pope was clever, too. He signed all pages of the long document except that reincarnation page. Did anyone check the fine print for his initials? History isn't set in stone. Or is it? I decided to remain curious, without judging anything.

"Several seminal events elucidated how massively distorted history became by killing scribes, destroying books, or easily decimating the fragile paper or clay tablets they used to document everything. Often after sufficient destruction, the scribes were told to write an updated version of history, which always made the current ruler, pope, and political system look awesome."

Sophia's gaze was fixed on the fire as she began to speak.

"Talking about this brings me back to that moment in time in the hologram when we saw things that shook us to the core. Several of us wanted to know about Jesus. Our discovery vaulted us into deep reflection and left us bewildered. My intention was to discover the root of religious contention and discord. Particularly, how did the Christian movement based on love become divisive pretty much from its inception? My big question was: Why didn't the unicity gene express like a wildfire and why didn't pure love remain a focus for his followers across the centuries? I also wanted to observe the content of his teachings, how abundantly *unicity* embedded itself in his followers, and if not, what happened to eclipse its proliferation?

"The hologram that Avani was talking about had a fascinating dimension to its technological genius. After working with holograms for a while, if we were at the right frequency, we could go *beyond* watching. While sitting in a particular area near the hologram, we could send our consciousness and sensory awareness to the place on the screen, which allowed us to see, feel, taste, and hear things. In spite of that, we were only projecting our awareness to a particular time and space on a subtle level. We couldn't do anything materially to shift spacetime. We were observers rather than time travelers.

"I found my consciousness hovering near a scene, thirty feet or more away. Yet I knew that I could zoom in and get closer. Like Avani and revelations about her ancestors, I was in for a surprise.

"Seeing Jesus wasn't like the image my mind had concocted; nor was he like the art that I'd seen growing up. He was dark skinned, and looked strong and weathered from the harsh conditions of the time. He was also the epitome of a spellbinding, instantly irresistible human being. In my first encounter, he was sitting with a group of less than fifteen people. He was referred to as Yeshua, an Aramaic name. Jesus is a Greek name and likely evolved later. However, they mostly referred to him as, *Rabonni*. In Hebrew culture, *Robonni* was a title given to an immensely revered teacher.

"His stillness was contagious and I could see the subtle, auric field around his body radiating lustrous, golden light. There were people sitting with their eyes closed and somehow he was transmitting frequency to the group—everyone began to softly weep simultaneously. Their faces were soft, and I observed that as the adults wept, children played near him with joyful sweetness and innocence. The peaceful nature of this moment in spacetime was beyond the mind. Stillness was palpable.

"As Yeshua slowly opened his eyes, he smiled and addressed a man sitting nearby, Nathanael. This man's energy field was a rainbow of radiance. They exchanged words that I could not hear. Then, Yeshua noticed my energetic presence and smiled at me gently and lovingly. I melted into an ecstatic state and almost lost consciousness. I had to stay focused to ensure that I could remain in that moment in spacetime.

"Like manna from heaven, Yeshua appeared on the mystical hologram and I heard him share his famous parables with larger gatherings. A captivating boon of this holographic quantum-level technology is that when I was in a scene, the hologram integrated with my brain so that I heard words in the language of the speaker, interpreting its meaning effortlessly. The value was to hear a language like Yeshua's native tongue, Aramaic, along with its nuances, without going through the mental process *of translation* into English, Latin, or Greek. This is the kind of amazing, new tech we can look forward to in the future. I heard what he was saying *in the context* within which he said it. Aramaic is vastly different than English. So it mattered to me to receive his words via his native language.

"An unexpected element of this amazing translation is that well known teachings like the Beatitudes—*Blessed are the peacemakers...* or *Gentle are the pure in heart*—were astonishingly different in tone, content, and meaning from the translations we are used to these days. Phrases still dance in my memory like him telling followers to *become ripe*, to merge into the ultimate *Reality*, and the importance of being immersed in a constant *inner unfoldment*. Mostly, however, he remained wordless—meeting in small, intimate groups where his followers gathered inconspicuously to sit in pristine stillness with their beloved *Rabonni*. He spoke relentlessly about love and taking personal responsibility for their actions and to focus inward as a daily practice. Vibrations of love and peace were invaluable for nourishing a relationship with the indefatigable *Heart* of life, the ultimate *Reality*.

"My greatest surprise was observing Yeshua's apostles. In my earlier Biblical study, I developed a perception that they were holier than I could imagine, more steadfast in faith, and a tight-knit group of adoring followers. Yet in the hologram, I observed normal men with a wide variety of personalities. And I saw a large number of women following Yeshua devotedly. I was in for a surprise as I saw them interact with him, as equals to the men. In fact, he treated everyone with the same immeasurable respect.

"A core group of men remained in awe of Yeshua, loved him deeply, and were in service to him. In that culture, it was clear that men were in charge of religion and politics. Interestingly, I noticed friction because some of his male followers seemed to be jockeying for position to be his favorite. I also noticed outright jealousy. Yeshua addressed it while expressing endless love for all of them. According to their tradition, I heard them talking about a messiah who prophets declared would lead them—they thought he was their religiously-acclaimed messiah and encouraged him to take up the sword to create a new kingdom.

"From what I could tell, instead of accepting this honored title or the associated prophetic role, he solidly reinforced the lived expression of love and peacefulness. He told them to experience the ultimate *Reality* at their core, along with an endless kingdom within themselves. Spreading incessant pure love vibes with every molecule of his life-force, he rejected ingrained war mentality, established religious beliefs, and judgment of anyone. Wow! I grasped the repercussions of his paradigm-shifting cultural defiance which certainly didn't sit well with authorities who'd grown to rely on armed combat and were fueled by vengeance. Yet he boldly introduced *a radical paradigm of love and peace* into their world. He was the great dissolver of old religious laws that were not supporting pure love. Imagine how much inner conflict that would evoke for people! I've observed that throughout time, personally and as a culture, religious identity and beliefs run deep.

"Two disciples, Andrew and Nathanael, diligently took care of finances for him, while others planned gatherings, and all sorts of administrative tasks. Some or all of this core group, including a tight band of devoted women, were always with him. One man surprised me because I never expected he'd be such a loyal follower and an exceptionally good person.

"His name was Judas. Please try to put aside anything you've heard. Remember, as we've discovered, history was written not to record the truth but for other, often biased reasons. Of course, sometimes historians made honest errors or saw the event from a different angle than others. It's like varying accounts of a car accident which look different from the vantage point of different witnesses. Back then, to change history, you burned the books and killed the scribes. Avani found that unfortunate truth in Indian history and we eventually saw the same pattern at various times and places around the world.

"Getting back to Yeshua's time. I observed Judas' energy field as soft pink shimmering radiance with mesmerizing sparkles of magenta that flashed continuously. I noticed that in conversations, he was intelligent, dedicated to Yeshua's mission, and kind to others. He had a role in the group's finances. He and Yeshua shared a special greeting that appeared to evoke upset in some of the followers. When greeting Yeshua, Judas dropped all bravado and kissed Jesus tenderly on the cheek—as a small boy gently displays intimate affection for his father.

"When Yeshua spoke with Judas, or someone they were uptight about, a few of the disciples' energy fields would momentarily morph into a grey mist.

"I kept seeing Nathanael in groups. He was loving, kind, and smart. He seemed open-hearted and humble.

"One of the core followers named Simon was another brilliant man with keen wit and a solid commitment to Yeshua. I saw several men called James but one stood out for his intellect and his work with finances. He was somehow helping with that.

"Many years ago, a priest, whom I loved and trusted, warned me about astonishing information that would be released from the Vatican about the last supper. He indicated that historical accounts would be updated. I could not imagine what he was talking about. That heads-up from the priest led me to take the help of the hologram to peek into the past I knew there were literally miles of documents hidden in the Vatican Vaults. And I was not a biblical scholar. Perhaps the hologram could give me the clarity I'd been searching for.

"Gilda shared that the Vatican had incomprehensibly funded a think-tank to work on a physics-related device in the 1950's and 60's that could show them other points in spacetime—a form of time travel that appeared on a screen. The project has been leaked and a book written about it. Allegedly, Pope Pius XII and his team took the help of world acclaimed physicists and engineers to create the coveted device. According to the account of an Italian priest, another priest he was close to was authorized to commission Werner Von Braun, Enrico Fermi, and other esteemed experts for this secret project. The result was that they purportedly viewed surprising details of the last supper and other events before dismantling the device to protect it from falling into the wrong hands. The Vatican did not share their findings nor did they divulge or admit that the project had been undertaken.

"The priest made claims about the device that were later debunked and all sorts of intrigue around this machine ensued for decades. In the early 1990's the priest told his close friend that the pope had recently summoned him and the last surviving scientist from the time-travel project to speak to four cardinals and some scientists about this machine. There've been conflicting stories riddled with intrigue and mystery surrounding the priest's involvement and divulgences of this enigmatic project. Does this sound like a religious organization or a physics think-tank? Why would a priest, who is an introverted Benedictine monk, spin such a wild tale, if it was completely fictional? Peeking behind the clandestine curtain—beyond the facade eclipsing this organization's incomprehensible wealth, influence, and power—usually thrusts us into an exhaustively confusing wormhole we didn't expect to enter. This story is no exception.

"Regardless, like me, it sounds like the Vatican is curious about quantum science and how we can take a closer look at history. Luckily, I bypassed secrecy and directly experienced a giant hologram based on quantum computing. It was fascinating to say the very least.

"Before I continue, I'd like to brew a sublimely inspirational, soul-stirring cup of tea.

"Prepare yourselves, dear friends, further holographic revelations are jaw-dropping. I'll be back in a moment."

# CHAPTER 29

## STUNNING REVELATIONS

Sophia resumed her place in the circle as her friends watched her settle in, become pristinely still, and after a deep breath, she spoke softly. Her eyes bore the haunted look of someone lost in a traumatic, confusing event.

"I was drawn to the interaction of the twelve apostles at a pivotal moment approaching Yeshua's crucifixion. This was the culmination of extreme fear among his followers and a gut-wrenching reality settling in for them. Their love for and commitment to Yeshua put them squarely in harm's way.

"Although they were brave, some were plummeting into survival mode. The brutality of that time period was hard for me to observe without wanting to check out. I knew I couldn't watch him die. I have to confess that even observing scenes before his death left me reeling with sadness, and questions about what I was seeing.

"As he had requested, Yeshua's core apostles joined him for supper. For some reason, Judas had been sent into the city to do something important.

"Quickening his pace, he rushed back to Yeshua, knowing as they all did, that each moment with Yeshua was becoming immeasurably invaluable. Breathless, Judas burst into the room where the apostles had gathered. Calming himself right away, he respectfully approached Yeshua, then giving him his usual, authentically loving kiss. Yeshua's response seemed agonizing to Judas who looked down, releasing a soft cry of despair. Yeshua said that what was about to happen *could not be changed for either of them.* Judas looked sucker-punched. I realized later that I didn't see who had sent Judas to the city and why he hurried there and back. Whatever was behind the cryptic exchange between them and the trip to the city, Judas and Jesus did not appear to be at odds with each other as I'd been led to believe they were. Instead, I only perceived a bond of love between them.

"After the agonizing exchange, Judas looked around the room at his brothers with loving concern. Bearing inconsolable sorrow for what Yeshua said to him, he lowered his head. The apostles respected Judas, who was one of the most highly educated and savvy among them, and beyond reproach as their appointed treasurer. This is what Andrew and Matthew said to him with gratitude that night in what seemed to be an attempt to console their friend. I could tell they worked closely with Judas in financial matters and, by their kind words, respected him implicitly.

"The past few weeks had been rife with tension and rising fear for the safety of Yeshua. Even though Yeshua warned them about his inevitable death, it was too much for them to fathom.

"To add to the gut-wrenching feelings pervading the supper, Yeshua broke the horrific news that he would soon be handed over to the authorities. Some gasped in shock and disbelief, while others looked at Yeshua asking how they could help him to avoid this dreadful fate. Although the brethren faced many trials together, this revelation was bringing their lives to an unimaginable crescendo. Even the most noble human beings can falter at times like this. A ripple of dark, wavy terror arose and spread through the faces of Yeshua's devoted apostles. Destiny was raising its head and moving like a freight train with no brakes.

"Like a mystical top, spinning effortlessly at breakneck speed, Yeshua shifted the tone into pure love and spoke about it fervently, drenching the room in a familiar blanket of warm, honey-like nectar. His benevolence took action as he insisted on washing their feet, bringing his beloveds into pristine serenity and unicity—eclipsing thinking while raising frequencies.

"With dizzying velocity, my consciousness was thrust into an explosion of pandemonium that was reeking havoc within a local garden, illumined only by meager torches. Yeshua's twelve core followers and Mary Magdalene, frozen with shock, braced themselves, facing the horrifying approach of spine-chilling opponents. Roman soldiers with the energy of a violent mob headed straight for Yeshua—standing serene and indefatigable. He had been teaching recently in the city under the watchful eye of the uncompromising, heavy-handed Roman authorities. To them, as a proclaimed Messiah, he was a traitor of Rome—a king and potential insurrectionist. The biggest issue was the growing size of the crowds that gathered to hear him speak. Roman authority was swift and brutal when it came to dealing with perceived traitors. In the year Yeshua was born, Pontius Pilate ordered two thousand Jews to be crucified as Roman adversaries. He made sure every Jew was crystal clear about who was ultimately in charge. Unfortunately for Yeshua, Pontius Pilate had often sent Jews who were *perceived risks* to Roman stability to the cross for lesser crimes than his—without a trial. Did I mention Pilate was also known to be vigorously cunning and ruthless?

"There were members of the Great Sanhedrin (the Rabbinic legislative court) who disliked and distrusted Yeshua, and by that fateful evening, raging Roman political anger had reached a boiling point. The Jewish High Priest was also likely to further incite the Roman authorities to punish Yeshua as a means to dispel the rising tensions.

"As we know, Yeshua had taken leaders of the Jewish community to task for various hypocrisies. They were fed up with his unorthodox teachings. He was critical of the ongoing practice of animal sacrifice, which was a massive income generator for the Jewish Temple, and King Herod got a share of the money as well. Jake and John had seen documents that mention 250,000 doves, ox, and sheep killed on Passover in just one day as religious obligation, lucratively fueling Jerusalem's economy. The people made these sacrifices in exchange for divine blessings and forgiveness for shortcomings and sins. Yeshua kept driving the point home that they only needed to love one another, and seek a path of peace, that sacrifices to appease God were not necessary. He taught that the infinite core of Reality pulses endlessly in both animals and people. I felt the contrast between the people's fear of God and Yeshua's encouraging words echoing painfully in my heart space. The smell of blood was in the air and Yeshua knew his would soon join that of the gentle creatures.

"As though oblivious to the pandemonium in that frenzied garden, Judas, with a heart that was visibly shredded in agony, gently kissed Yeshua for the last time. With the same undying love he'd always displayed unapologetically, his tears flowed and the magnificent octagon of his heart exploded in a blazing light that overpowered my capacity to see anything but its resplendence."

"In the chaos that followed, the apostles dispersed into the night like sheep scattering to the four winds with wolves in close pursuit. It would be easy for the Roman authorities to arrest anyone closely associated with Yeshua, viewing them as co-conspirators—deserving the same fate as their beloved Rabbi.

"After the apostles fled that night, they called on their resolve and tenacity while not denying the immense grief and relentless fear that flooded the group. As I suspected, Judas was no longer among them. In an Aramaic translation of the Christian texts, it says that a new member would join the core group by drawing lots because 'Judas has been relieved to go his own way.' What did that mean?

"With the guidance of another benevolent and wise soul, *James the Just*—Yeshua's younger brother—the apostles united, and courageously continued to practice and spread Yeshua's teachings. There were many others who joined them like Mary Magdalene and the women who'd dressed his wounds after the crucifixion. Joanna was one of them—she'd helped to finance his ministry. Witnessing their unending devotion to Yeshua's teachings touched my heart because after that huge trauma and loss, these brave souls struggled to elevate their frequency from despair to love—knowing that they could access the pure love that Yeshua personified. However, were pure love and unicity ingrained deeply enough in their hearts to survive the harrowing turbulence ahead of them?

"I continue to reflect on my holographic experience and why many years ago, Father Greg, a priest who I admired and trusted, warned me about the historical accuracy of this event. After two millennia, confusion remains. There is a discrepancy in the official Christian texts about whether Judas hung himself, breaking Jewish law, or did he go into a field and literally, spontaneously explode? More questions arose. Did Judas die immediately or was he forced to flee? Was he killed because he was an outlier among his brethren or for some other reason? Historians point out that he was different than the rest of his apostle brothers in education and cultural background.

"Adding to the mystery is the fact that no one can confirm the identity of the scribe or author of the authenticated Gospel of Judas discovered in Egypt in the twentieth century—describing in detail Judas' faithful, intimate relationship with Yeshua and his personal views on the teachings (especially the most esoteric ones). Some scholars are adamant about the status quo of the currently disseminated scriptures and others are in a phase of open dialogue about Judas because new documentation has been revealed. More pieces of the puzzle seem to be lurking in the grey market in Egypt or other places. I didn't realize this is how those recent documents were found.

"Creating further head-spinning revelations, many years ago, Father Greg encouraged me to research a *commonly-shared*, Old Testament prophesy about *thirty pieces of silver*, related to Yeshua's messianic role. Bewilderingly, my research did not reveal this as a prophesy at all. Instead, the verse simply describes a prophet who received thirty pieces of silver in exchange for tending a flock of sheep—giving those wages to the temple. A silver-coin-prophecy wasn't in the hologram, either. And I didn't see Judas receiving silver coins at a meeting with Jewish authorities like the New Testament describes.

"After my heartfelt exploration, I couldn't get a *definitive* answer from the hologram to substantiate long-standing stories, whose authors didn't envision future literate, internet-savvy humans—let alone quantum-computing-based holograms, without bias and with endless data from the field of all-that-is.

More than once, the hologram left us without conclusive details to solidify our understanding of historical events. I trusted that it was not the time for further revelation. Discovering the truth sometimes feels like it needs the nudge of a miracle rather than advanced tech.

"I realized there were *many* divergent perspectives and discordant views on who Judas was and why he acted in the way he did. In truth, friends, I concluded that the mystery surrounding him—like many other paradoxes during early church history—was not about aligning with one of a multitude of divergent perspectives. Rather, it was about *how* broad-minded and non-judgmental I could be about the information that I uncovered. I know that could sound crazy. But hear me out. Conflict in any situation is *not* the issue; rather, it's how *resolution* gradually evolves. Is it through compassion, love, and overcoming personal beliefs—that might be generational or emergent from personal experience? How receptive can I be to various perspectives of any situation with an open heart? Discernment is a higher octave of judgment. It's about wisdom that arises from the heart and not the head. I will sit with the revelations I received and continue to wonder going forward.

"What I saw that stands out more than the horror and chaos that night is the incomprehensible love that I experienced when I was near Yeshua. His frequency was so high it reduced people's minds to stillness. Those moments with him changed me, forever. Even after two thousand years, I can see why he continues to touch the lives of millions of people all over the world.

"And I can't forget Mary Magdalene. You've likely heard about her. What I saw was fascinating. While Yeshua was alive and afterwards, people approached her for solace as well as for her wisdom and understanding of his teachings. Like Yeshua, she spoke infrequently. In the evenings, they'd leave the gatherings together. There wasn't physical union but something far more sacred and intimate than that. They sat in stillness and all I could see were their light bodies. Absorbed in pure awareness, they merged into the exalted dimensions within themselves and remained there until late at night. Sometimes, their physical particles exploded and they completely disappeared. I interpreted this *disappearance* as their high-frequency light bodies' capacity to manifest as subtle quantum energy—allowing their particles to burst suddenly into an invisible form of electromagnetic energy. The impact of this detonation of light was blinding. Instantly, I was thrust into a pristinely still state of bliss that lasted for several hours. Friends, I can now say with confidence that frequencies are contagious and the high ones are worth cultivating.

"As if that wasn't enough of a mind-bender, even after such dramatic experiences, each morning they began a new day exuding love and moving with a sense of peace that calmed the souls of everyone they encountered.

"Given that women were on par with men as loyal followers, after the crucifixion, jealousy and *cultural contempt* for powerful women caused disputes within the inner circle. Nathanael and Phillip seemed to be Mary Magdalene's strongest advocates. Peter seemed perplexed by her capacity to imbibe the subtle teachings. He did not shun her. It was more like he was trying to grasp Yeshua's esoteric teachings which she masterfully elucidated. Across the millennia, the mysteries of unbroken union with Essence remains difficult to fathom.

"From what I witnessed, Simon, Jude, and James kept a level head and courageously supported her, with immense love and respect. A fascinating aspect of the hologram was that I heard names in their contemporary Hebrew form—*Shimon, Yahuda and Ya'akov*, respectively. Of course, I knew the current Biblical names and could easily make the connections. Simon was passionate but not a hot head. The others listened to him because he was a strong advocate for the people who felt the pain of losing Yeshua, and their common goal was to spread his teachings. Simon, maybe following Yeshua's lead, included women and always welcomed new followers, unconditionally.

"Throughout my observations of those historical events, understanding my own perspective is what mattered most to me. Did this new information expand my view of life and the multidimensional and unlimited nature of myself? Having the opportunity to consider the hologram's revelations, I engaged in an abundance of reflection.

"I observed that the reason we have such confusion and misunderstanding about this time period is that even with the best intentions, unicity and loving one another did not seem to express in its fullness at that time. Jews clashed with Gentiles, his disciples clashed with each other, and the Orthodox Jewish community was at odds with the burgeoning Jewish Christian movement, and of course the Romans were stirring the pot to their own advantage.

"James the Just, the leader of the first Jewish Christian church in Jerusalem, was pushed off the temple and stoned to death for vague "crimes" without a trial—various accounts attribute the act to the High Priest or to the leaders of other local factions who wanted James to denounce his brother,

Yeshua, to say he was *not* a messiah. The circumstances of his execution caused a big outcry among the Jewish people, including Christians, and even Roman citizens who appreciated his high level of integrity and exemplary moral strength—all of whom saw this blatant disregard for the rule of law as reprehensible. The Romans took advantage of this factionalism and unrest to further destabilize the Jewish people and minimize their capacity to rise up against Roman rule.

"This kind of tumultuous activity pervaded the first century after Yeshua's death and beyond. The unicity gene appeared to be lost in slumber. What could wake it up? How can we avoid perpetuating cultural rivalries and belief-based clashes?

"Rather than judging Romans, Jews, or Christians for how they responded to their circumstances, I accept they lived under significant complexities, intense social pressures, and constant threats to survival. My question is whether or not we can evolve personally or as a global community if we insist everyone converts to a single religious view, world view, or political ideology? Where does *love* fit into that kind of forced homogeneity? Will we engage in catastrophic, "us versus them" philosophical clashes? In that regard, has anything radically changed in the past few millennia? What am I contributing to the world each day—love and respect for everyone, irrespective of personal, religious or cultural perspectives? As the centuries rolled by, I wondered how different our world might have looked if our ancestors had consciously fostered unicity. And how might the future look if we intentionally support the unicity gene to flourish in its expression throughout our species? How can I break unconscious, ancestral patterns and ingrained beliefs that inadvertently eclipse the proliferation of this invaluable gene expression?

"The hologram suddenly shifted to a fresh scene. There was more of the epic past I needed to observe. At first I was confused because I was observing an unfamiliar woman preparing a room with great care—meticulously adding various items such as delicate flowers, and oil lamps that brought a warm ambience to the room. The scent of patchouli oil wafted across the room and fragrant branches were carefully placed on the bed by her attendant. I realized this was a priestess in a matriarchal, matrilineal temple, and from the grace and reverence with which she moved and spoke, it seemed she was preparing for something special—a sacred ritual. John and Jake had shared ancient history and archeology with me. They literally dug into priestess cultures like hers, which have existed for tens of thousands of years—before the Mesopotamian male god hierarchy became the cultural norm and dominant source of spirituality in the region, later extending into Greece, Rome, and Europe.

"I soon realized I was in a house in a Roman area, where Hebrew traditions were common—the Israelites settled in the region many centuries before my visit. As I heard chaotic noises, smelled putrid scents of animal excrement from the street, and listened to sheep bleating pitifully, I got a picture in my mind that the animals were unfortunately headed to a nearby temple for slaughter. By this time, my consciousness was hooking up with the coordinate in spacetime to a greater extent and the scene was unfolding more fully.

"A man entered the room with the priestess. My skin crawled as I witnessed his irreverence towards her, and I cringed at the sound of his creepy, belligerent voice. He passed by a bowl and tossed something in. Although the woman tried to explain the ritual and elegantly guide him into its mysteries, with the fierceness of a stag's untamed breeding instincts when he encounters a doe in rut, he voraciously raped her. That's how I saw it. Adding further trauma, he snarled, calling her a *prostitute*. In a wild fury, he dragged her into the street to join a waiting crowd of vicious, cold-blooded men. As she looked ahead of the crowd surrounding her, which included men in priestly robes, it was clear they were headed towards the male god's horrific temple. Her eyes widened with shock and terror; her body became debilitated with fright. Her handlers dragged her, cursing her all the way to a *religious temple of death* for priestesses. Due to religious fanaticism, as a priestess, she would have known what happens when one of them is taken to that dreadful place to face the devotees and priests of their violent god. I know from historical accounts that the Hebrew God was known to the priestesses to be vindictive, cruel, and angry. He displayed human qualities including a short fuse, instructing his followers to kill entire civilizations in conquest of people he didn't approve of. The unfathomable realization, though, was that he did not come to the aid of women. Female worshipers kept their heads low and were, in all respects, subservient to their husbands and male authority figures.

"I found it incomprehensible her persecutor thought it was okay to trick her by coming for a ritual that had been common for priestesses, like I said, for thousands of years. Jake and John said that inhumane, abusive behavior towards the priestess culture had already become common for millennia before my visit, but the annihilation of their entire spiritual tradition was escalating during this particular time period. On and off, tribes from across Mesopotamia raped priestesses with impunity and conquered their temples and cities with unwavering fervor.

"Suddenly, my consciousness was directed to the temple. I saw a fiery, tempestuous crowd gathering, along with a line of sheep being led for slaughter—and exhausted men cleaning up after them, having to endure the stench which was nauseating. With eyes wide with terror, her fellow priestesses barred the door behind her and prayed. They also called for a trusted priest in their community to follow her incognito to cast one of the first stones, rendering her unconscious so she would not feel the excruciating pain. This was a small way they'd found to help a sister during these incomprehensibly horrific events. This scene was gut-wrenching and difficult to fathom. How had humans become so savage under the guise of religion?

"One of the young priestesses-in-training, fell to her knees, feeling the onslaught of the shock roaring through her nervous system and piercing her tender heart. She had been mentored by the woman who was being led away. She called out to her sister priestesses with tears of horror and heart-piercing sorrow, asking why their lineage was under siege. Where was the Great Mother Goddess in this time of grueling pain and utter annihilation? Through heaving sobs she reminded the priestesses and priests who looked on in agony that she and her sisters had been faithfully serving the Goddess for many hundreds of generations. They knew that women held the *seed of life*, which man lovingly and passionately waters and fertilizes. Why did the Israelite god's lineage believe that *a man* held the seed of life and *placed it in* a woman, without an ounce of respect or pleasure for her? Why did they believe a man was formed by their God first and woman only after? It was hard to fathom the story which had evolved from the Babylonian cults. Before then, the Creator was a Creatrix, Asherah.

"Turning to her fellow priestesses and then glancing with anguish at the priests, trembling uncontrollably, the young priestess asked, *Why do they have to demolish Great Mother Goddess' images and temples and replace her with this new god? Do they disagree that birth, death, and renewal are worthy of being celebrated and lovingly acknowledged as essential rhythms of life? Does this male god fit better with their wars and conquest?*

"She begged her older sisters to help her understand which is deserving of the ultimate worship and guidance—god or goddess? Should she race to the temple, beg for her sister's life, and accept their perplexing, ruthless god? Which one is the true Source worthy of devotion—god or goddess? Pausing for a moment, the other priestesses knelt beside her, mingling their tears with hers. The eldest priestess answered tenderly yet with unshakable confidence.

*Dear sister, these seemingly opposite forces are part of a unified whole—a force of nature without attributes of gender or physical qualities. Thus I am speaking about a merging of both into the pure light of all-that-is. In the magnificent moment of merging that we practice as ritual, there is neither god nor goddess—the couple is both god and goddess at the same time. Bliss arises and renewal reaches an apex of glory. New life is watered and fertilized in an invisible field, sown with pure love.*

"Hearing this unexpected answer, the young priestess paused to reflect before sharing that the goddess lineage had been attacked many times and a lot of the original rituals and secrets were lost. Yet she tried to honor the *Great Mother*

*Goddess* as best she could and was fully devoted to her path. In good conscience, she could not bear to worship a god who had to be appeased relentlessly with sacrifices, who hated women, wanted them subjugated to men, and who seemed angry most of the time—rather than the loving emanations of the *Great Mother Goddess*. She mentioned several priestesses who gave up worship of the Great Mother Goddess and married local men who worshiped the male god. The immense suffering that followed for their dear sisters was heart-wrenching and shocking for their community. The husbands insisted their wives totally abdicate their sovereignty and without calling it such, accept the role as slaves to their husband-masters. The local priests were condescending and cruel to the women. She could not bear to willingly accept such a fate even if goddess worship included the potential for a cruel and inhumane death at the hands of the male-god worshipers. Conveying her willingness to remain open, she committed to continue to ponder the possible motives of incomprehensibly violent men and the future of her beloved sisters.

Her sisters smiled reassuringly and nodded their heads without comment.

"My friends, I wondered how I could argue with her well-defined conclusions and profound questions that she'd formed based on her worldview, while trying to grasp the view points of her oppressors?

"As though saturated with respect and touched by the sacred wisdom emanating from her heart, the young priestess asked if she could apply sacred oil to the brave priest before he left. With heart-melting humility she requested the blessings of her fellow priestesses in doing so—realizing she must hurry to prepare him so that her dear sister wouldn't have to undergo prolonged, excruciating humiliation and pain.

"Steadying herself with inconceivable courage, she stated emphatically she felt assured she could express the deep mysteries and potency of pure love through this act of ritual. Her eyes lowered with an inward focus, displaying deep respect. With immense gratitude in her voice, she declared her appreciation for the encouragement from her fellow priestesses. The young priest approached for the blessing and then headed without haste to the temple to offer an unfathomable act of love to his priestess-sister. As her younger brother, he was compelled to protect her from the pangs of physical torture and grueling, physical obliteration. With that realization, I almost passed out.

"After he left, almost in a whisper, the young priestess confided in her priestess-sisters she'd heard of a man, amongst the worshippers of the male god, who spoke of pure love, who taught his followers about personal responsibility, compassion, and kindness. His description of his father-god was different. Perhaps someday she could meet this teacher and have the rare chance to know a man from this violent sect who respected women enough to allow them to grow in wisdom about themselves—a benevolent teacher who could prepare her further for the life which would follow the one she was struggling with intensely in that moment. A conversation about the enigmatic male teacher ensued. They were in awe of the stories circulating about his sagacity and kind heart, and his authentic respect for women. His focus on pure love seemed to hold a priority over religious laws and customs, and his views transcended gender and cultural status. They were astonished that a man would behave so courageously and with unwavering conviction. Local men and women who knew him said he was unquestionably the embodiment of pure love and unicity.

"She smiled joyously, emanating the first sign I'd seen in her of exalted vibrations. She said tenderly, *Surely he is a friend of the Great Mother Goddess. What if his message becomes the way of life for everyone going forward? Our world could change. The male and female could come together in peacefulness as co-creators of life. Yet in this moment, all I can think of is our dear sister facing a horrific fate. Can we pray for her? Would that be okay?*

"Smiling gently, they solemnly nodded their heads. The priestesses settled themselves emotionally before entering into prayer, an offering to their priestess-sister who'd soon leave *the world of the living* with their profound love and blessings, as she entered realms of endless light and infinite waves of bliss.

"None of these priestesses comprehended the full scope of annihilation headed for them. In their worldview, men and women were both leaders but they were about to find out conclusively that they were no longer valued or accepted as respected members of the Roman, Greek, and Christian worlds. *Subjugation of women*, unfathomable to their naiveté, was about to be brutally front and center in their lives and for women going forward into ensuing millennia.

"The world had entered a paradigm that our group observed in horror—as it unfolded even further into crushing authoritarian rule for the collective populations, particularly for women, for countless generations going forward.

"Ultimately, Jake and John helped us to understand that *Western culture* as we know it, and our DNA are comprised of an amalgamation of five primary civilizations with distinct world views. The *Mesopotamian* ritual-based spirituality, patriarchal ideology, and imperialistic division of conquered areas led to segregated states ruled by warlords, called kings or emperors. This thoroughly influenced the *Roman Empire* which became hierarchal, control-based and war-driven. The ancient Roman state conquered the philosophical, highly artistic, creative *Greek Empire*. Then it absorbed the *Christian movement*, which in turn had absorbed the hierarchal, imperialistic values that saturated Roman culture as well as the ideologies of its Jewish roots. The Roman Empire conquered mystical, ancient, mysterious *Egypt* before forging north, conquering most of Europe and shaping religion and politics going forward to create the *Western culture* as we know it today.

"Yet our DNA also holds the memory of the goddess culture plus *millions of years* of advanced consciousness that preceded all of the history I witnessed. In our ancient past, life, death, and renewal through natural laws, cooperation, and appreciation for each other flourished. The mysteries of the quantum world came to mind. The goddess culture did not shy from the mysteries of merging male and female energies within an invisible field to bring about new life and inherently elevated states of bliss. Later that night, the giants stepped forward to address my holographic session with the group. Once again, I was left awestruck.

"Our giant hosts asked us, *With the prolific energy of emotional pain held as memory encoded in the unified field, how will you allow your DNA to be reconfigured and rejuvenated from codes of memory in parallel realities where this system of subjugation did not happen?* That question took us by surprise and left us scratching our heads in confusion. How could we do that? They tossed us these kinds of golden nuggets of wisdom and left us to ponder their meaning and explore the questions—that question was definitely *enigmatic enough to warrant plenty of ongoing, deep reflection.*"

With mouths agape, Jake and John stared at her with wonder and astonishment. Coming to their senses, they chuckled and shook their heads as though she'd thrust them into bewilderment when she mentioned the familiar question, posed by a giant who Jake referred to as being *one hundred percent whip-smart and a five-star confidant.* Smiling affectionately at them, she glanced captivatingly around the circle and continued in a tone that was burning with curiosity.

"In our fireside conversations, it's been fascinating to follow the oppressive thread which spanned epochs within an extensive timeline. Even more provocative was getting to peak behind the curtain of time and see that everyone, in each stage of a civilization's growth, unconsciously absorbed past conditioning and culture without question. In other words, rather than *identifying* with our *highest vibrational nature* as pure love and light within the infinite quantum reality, humans have unconsciously repeated the patterns of *identifying* with a particular religion and specific god, fought about who had the best religion, and unfortunately latched onto the role of a low-status human in the hierarchal, cultural context. Inadvertently, citizens from most countries separated themselves from those outside their worldview, further separating them from experiencing the value of collaboration and multiple viewpoints. While being absorbed in this worldview, the capacity to fully experience their core, Essence, as an innate experience, was dismissed in favor of doctrines and theology. We observed these patterns consistently.

"How does this patterning align with the words of Yeshua and a multitude of sages and prophets across time who melted our hearts with sublime wisdom, compassion, unicity, and love?

"Consider our observation of the collective population as I share the words of an elder priestess as she and her sisters faced the final stage of utter annihilation. *There are two aspects, male and female, which are significant enough to be worthy of a lifetime of contemplation. Each is a unique expression and im-petus for benevolent, life-affirming action—in which pure love emerges tangibly within every daily thought and action, and unicity is expressed uninhibitedly into eternity.*

"As Roman culture flourished, and church and state uni-fied, no one had the right to experience direct connection to Essence. If anyone engaged in practices of inner connectivity, they usually did not live long enough to share their experience with others. Nor could anyone express varying viewpoints—only perspectives that aligned strictly with state authorities and church hierarchy were allowed. Worldviews had become massively splintered and ruthlessly myopic. Therefore, the pure love and unicity the priestess mentioned were thwarted and abandoned as a priority. I was left feeling breathless, stunned into reflection.

"I want to be clear that these moments in history were not shown to me randomly. They are in my field of awareness for my growth and personal evolution. Of course, I have more to digest about all of my experiences. To be able to assimilate them, I realized that I have to remain open to any further revelations. In fact, we all committed to look objectively at history and not rule out a theory about a point along a vector in spacetime just because we're not comfortable in exploring it more thoroughly.

"My subsequent reflection sparked a sense of wonder in me about whether the history that's been passed down is true. Who benefited by making changes to historical texts, and in the end, why did it matter? Simultaneously, an old storyline and new possibilities were arising to shake my psyche free of the shackles of indoctrination, so that I could clearly see that history is a story that can divulge patterns or teach lessons—yet the present moment of pure love and unicity is what matters.

"When I consider that historical time periods are fractals of *infinity*, history takes on endless possibilities for how it could play out and what it means. Paying attention only to one vector in spacetime, what I call past, present, and future, is a focus on linear time and what can be seen and understood based on the speed of light. Yet in the giant world, the limitations of the speed of light and other *limitations* within *limitless* Reality dissolved for me. Time became pliable and as infinite as the field itself. That new relationship to time was trippy. Knowing that there are *endless parallel realities* playing out right now, why get totally bogged down in one of them, reacting with judgment and low vibe emotions?

"Our giant friends showed us *time* as a sphere with endless waves of light emanating from its center. They called this sphere *timelessness*. A line ran through it as a vector which they explained is *linear time*—playing out in our daily reality via our left brain function. Yet our unconscious mind remains connected to an infinite wave of timelessness. *Can we honor both our linear and unconscious minds as we move through life?* With good humor and kindness, the extraordinary giants encouraged us to expand our thinking about the quantum world we're indelibly linked with. There is so much more to our experience than we've been led to believe. Interacting with the giants' elevated thinking allowed me to shift my awareness into higher dimensions of elevated possibility. We all agreed that somehow those impressive giants gradually helped us to see ourselves in a whole new light, literally.

"I learned every nugget they dropped on my path was worthy of rapt attention. They didn't pontificate. So every word was worth paying attention to. In reference to time, they asked us to consider that when we follow one vector of endless time-lessness, we assume that's the *only reality*. However there are limitless possibilities for *parallel experiences* playing out in the infinite quantum field.

"Looking at my quizzical face, one of them asked a question I continue to ponder: *When you enter the octagon of the heart and settle into stillness, can you shift to a parallel life almost identical to this one? Is that possible? If not, what prevents it from coming into your consciousness as a potential reality? Does this excite you or do you feel confused or thrown off by these questions? These questions are worth your reflection. Trust me.*

"The invisible aspects of our world don't seem as daunting or inconceivable as they did when we left for our journey beneath the surface. Can you feel the radical potentials and jaw-dropping future evolving in this moment? We are part of an unfolding reality that's absolutely mind-blowing. My optimism for the future and love for our species is totally off-the-charts."

The circle of free-thinkers allowed the sound of the crackling fire and the pristine stillness permeating the atmosphere to become supportive foundations to assimilate Sophia's mystifying revelations and electrifying, *giant* questions.

# CHAPTER 30
# WATERSHED MOMENTS

Sophia's unexpected discoveries and reflections rendered her friends speechless and spellbound, requiring a few minutes to bounce back from the deep introspection they had been thrust into. Without warning, a chilly breeze blew through their midst, lifting and expanding the ambience of the gathering.

Sophia looked at the group and said with a cheeky smile, "It's definitely tea time! Don't you agree?"

Unanimous smiles and cheers answered her question. Adele and Angelica offered to help her, as the rest of the group began stretching and adjusting their postures to prepare for the rest of Sophia's captivating story.

The evening breeze was becoming still and the atmosphere settled as everyone hugged their warm cups of fragrant, rejuvenating tea.

Taking a pause to linger in the essential marrow of her awareness, Sophia took a sip of tea. Vitalized, she continued to speak confidently yet in a pensive tone. The circle was breathless and motionless as she spoke.

"The next part of my session in the holographic cave was even more mind-boggling. Are you ready for more spine-tingling moments?"

Until she saw the group's faces lighten, she did not speak. Teasing them, she said although they seemed *sufficiently braced for further truths*, her heart felt light as she looked around the circle to witness their customary relaxed postures and open-hearted expressions.

"I saw a great being called King Enki, living in higher states of consciousness. It's hard to tell the exact date when events like this happened because as I said, from the quantum perspective, time is not the ultimate reality. It's a unit of measurement as our atoms spin at a speed that gives the illusion of a solid, 3-D world. I know—it's trippy. Broadening my mind's capacity to shift brainwaves to move in and out of frequencies was fascinating and life-altering. Gradually I could pulse my awareness from *solid reality to subtle states* of consciousness and back again. We did a lot of training under the surface to be able to work with holograms and our consciousness' capacity to perceive subtler levels of revelation. I want to speak first about exploring reality within a hologram. The past is a construct of our mind that we've been indoctrinated into so that we can experience and make sense of our material world.

"Even though the present is the only reality, in linear time I am guessing the story was playing out many thousands of years ago. Enki lived on the thirtieth parallel of earth, a specific, highly charged ley line. It was a special place called Eridu in Mesopotamia.

"Like many areas around the world, I saw the light and the dark in deep conflict. Enki radiated light; he was working with humans who had the capacity and desire to be like him.

"His brother, Enlil, embodied elevated capacities for intelligence and subtle skills. From my observation, unlike Enki, Enlil didn't embrace the fact that humans held such high capacities. He vowed to ensure that they never reached his elevated skills and frequency. He created a cult of selfish leaders who were motivated to do one thing: make sure the rest of humanity would never know their real power. They would never inquire about their powers nor would they ask the deepest most relevant question: Who am I?

"Enlil's rabid legacy thrived. Arrogance and pride were his hallmark, along with deceit, manipulation, and ignorance of Truth. Yet, from his perspective, he embodied truth—his version of it.

"As I saw Enki's beauty and light, my heart expanded, my entire being was vibrating. And this was titrating with Enlil's ghastly deeds and his words that seemed to come from a place of profound selfishness, ignorance, and callousness.

"And then it happened; the screen went dark, my mind went blank, and I experienced I was both of them. I was the dark and the light. If I kept looking back at history, even my own, I'd be lost in that constant flux between these two aspects of myself.

"Abruptly and with lightening speed, my consciousness was thrust into a dark void, churned and shattered into tiny particles. I knew I was dying, but not a physical death. Instead, my ignorance and need to be in control of life evaporated and my subtle energy fields were being reconfigured.

"Instantly there was only silence. A deep euphoria grew. I did not hear sounds but sometimes geometric patterns swirled around me. My consciousness was aware that this energy was me. I wonder if I'd spun closer to the point of singularity, the densest point of my subtle vortex where a massive information convergence takes place—this point is my essence that connects to the essence of everything else. This is perfect wholeness, the common point with everything, the fullness of unicity. It's the place from which I have the *most agency* in my life and *greatest influence* on the field. Take that in.

"In retrospect, I am unshakable that when I access the still point and rest there, encountering endless love, incredible peacefulness, and care, I experience in my heart an intimate connection with you, my sweet friends... and Gaia, the multiverse, and everything and everyone throughout eternity."

Sophia paused, closing her eyes gently for a moment, engulfed by and overwhelmed with the experience of mystical, pure love which cements a bond with all of life, and which is free of all boundaries. Having sufficiently settled herself, her eyes opened like lustrous blue spheres of light that could deeply penetrate the heart-space of everyone in the circle.

She continued in a voice saturated with tender feelings and depth of soul, imploring her friends to listen and not comment. She said, "I am not sure if anyone can understand the depths of what I felt in that moment of union with Essence. It's supremely intimate and absolutely indescribable. It was so profound that even though I've gone deeply into my inner self many times, I cannot speak about this profound communion easily."

Grace reached over and touched Sophia's hand, wrapping her pinkie softly around Sophia's. Almost in a whisper, she said, "You're doing great. I can feel the incredible vibes. You went so deep! And like you said, it's profoundly personal. You are sharing the marrow of your soul so please know that your heart and your experience are safe with us. Keep going."

Sophia smiled through gentle tears as she continued to share.

"It's such a big deal and I don't know if I can find words to tell you adequately the cosmic nature of the experience. I'll never be the same because when I've been entering that still space in meditation, I never realized that as I flipped my little fairy wings and soared in that mystical space inside myself, the effect of my joyful, loving wishes was immediately emitted into the field—to everyone, everywhere across infinity.

"The absolute grandeur of it wiped my mind of thoughts and I lost consciousness for several hours. From that experience forward, I tacitly recognize that no event can be separate from the whole. From the pure stillness, everything and everyone in space-time arises and remains *as memory*. I can choose to extract memory from the field of past events all day long. Rather than focusing on *memory*, however, my new choice is to still my mind and dive into my incredible singularity as often as possible—to enter the subtlest center of my being, and rest there, even for a moment or two.

"Grace, this is what the sages tried to tell Nate and me in India. Remember how many times I spoke about it? Yet it wasn't a full body, cellular experience. I had to get to the core and nestle into its embrace in stillness and timelessness. From there, my frequencies became more established in a flow state. Of course, I'm not trying to teach physics. Yet I know that I am a subtle, spinning vortex with a singularity and I can sense and envision its grandeur and importance in my life. That's my point.

"To evolve, we'll have to become established in stillness so that we can hear truth arising naturally from inside, from the unfathomable field—from which our unique singularity arises. With my mind under control, it cannot be affected by a tantalizing media conglomerate or other random influences. My mind became my partner and cooperated in resting in its essence which allowed my experience of life to change forever. Can you feel the deep stillness emerging from the infinite field in and around us? Its right here, now. I know it sounds esoteric but, for me, it's also tangible."

"It sounds esoteric but it also feels amazing!" Grace said reassuringly. "I am balling my eyes out because I feel the outrageous frequencies that you described. I've always been able to *feel* you. I am entraining with you, snuggling into our entanglement and having the juicy experience of unicity—the effervescent, wild, perfect union with all-that-is. My whole body is shivering with ecstasy. Thank you, best friend ever! This is an epic opening in the fabric of space-time for us to plunge into with you.

"You went under the surface and mined for the real gold. I am so happy for you... and for me... since I get to entangle with you and vibe higher, as always. You don't realize your gift for describing inexplicable inner worlds. I am getting your emanations of frequency from head to toe."

Taking a brief pause to collect themselves, the soul sisters hugged, thanked the group for letting them express their common wonderment of life and the poignant moment of Sophia's surprising, spontaneous transformation.

Angelica said affectionately. "Oh my Lord! Friendships like yours are incredibly beautiful to witness! For goodness sakes! Don't you underestimate yourself for one second! I have shivers listening to you and then when Grace connected with you, I could feel the electricity and bond between you two. It's important for all of us to feel that wild, electric bond with another human being and to witness it in others like you, sweet friends. For that reason, this is a pivotal moment for me. Thank you two... sincerely... from my heart's space... for sharing this intimate moment with us.

"When it comes to deeply meaningful, personal experiences, I think we all need to have close *confidants* to talk to. Our trusted friends give us the confidence to accept the inexplicable in us and we feel safe in their company. Sophia, I know you love all of us, but I am sure I speak for everyone when I say we have no problem with your unique bond with Grace. We respect it, admire it, and want you to always feel free to express it. Take your time, honey. When you are ready to continue, we are here for you."

"Sophia, that was one hell of a dramatic experience," Jake said. "You sure don't stay on the surface, do you? From the time we met, that's how it's been with you. I sure as hell love you and respect your capacity to launch into an abyss and emerge with profound insights. We didn't debrief all of our experiences because, as Angelica said, it's so damn personal. Maybe we need to remind each other right now that we are here for each other as we process the magnitude of what happened under the surface.

"And one more thing... I agree with Angelica. Your bond with Grace is mind-boggling and your dual-experiences always leave me speechless. And that's a good thing! My friend, you are such a courageous Lynx-cat. I recall that Will, the elder, said that Lynx was your power animal—a cat who is sleek, agile, has the best night vision of its species, and in my opinion, is also beautiful inside and out. I appreciate you, girlfriend. I want to be clear. I don't want it just implied or something you have to intuit. You are one heck of a special human being."

Sophia smiled lovingly at him and then tenderly at Angelica and the rest of the circle. She and Grace hugged devotedly and then sat for a minute to absorb the friendship vibes and camaraderie of their circle. Sophia took a deep, heart-opening breath to center herself before continuing.

"The process was astonishing and sometimes overwhelming. After I emerged from the magnificent stillness at my core, I could reflect on it. Yet while I was *there*, wherever that is, I was immersed in profound stillness and bliss; complete and whole, immersed in timelessness. My photons began to sparkle and swirl in an ecstatic state. Within that experience, my *knowingness* was so refined that I could sense the subtle, highly refined experience. Then there was a shift in frequency and it was clear that I was emerging from the still point, the essence of myself.

"As I returned to my normal, waking consciousness, I realized I could see history for what it is: a story of a moment in linear time on a single coordinate on the infinite web of spacetime. Because of our left brain analysis, it can be made into a complex narrative. The key is that the author of any story purposefully or inadvertently spins it in the direction of their bias, their unique perspective from their coordinate in spacetime. In the end, it was not important to keep my focus on the nuances of history. My left brain interprets them differently than other observers of the same event. However, without trying to interpret the event, I can watch the *patterns* in history and learn from them—without need of prolonged evaluation.

"The present moment reveals the truth and information as it unfolds within my perception, based on my frequency. There is not a divine realm called heaven to *aspire to*, nothing to know, nor a demon to fight. All truth is within me as information, light, and frequency. There is no limitation to my consciousness' ability to access the highest truth. So I want to point it in the direction of my core, the neutral, still access juncture. Then I can move into higher frequency interpretation. It's a big deal and not a simple endeavor, but my awesome experiences motivated me to make it happen consistently.

"As the holographic scene faded, three giants appeared in varying degrees of subtle form, a male and two females. The most subtle of the women said,

*Pure love has become a cherished backdrop, while remaining safely hidden in every heart.*

*Please listen. A renaissance is occurring, a fresh opportunity to focus on pure love beyond all else. When pure love anchors, the universe will burst forth to celebrate your wise hearts' choice to honor yourselves and others—releasing judgments and conditions. You must embrace love invincibly! It's time for unicity and pure love to be your priority.*

"Slowly the forms faded, leaving me in wonder of how we can create and perpetuate a *renaissance of love.*

"In linear time, our team was gone for two years. Yet in my perception, it was the blink of an eye. After that experience, the presence of *now* was always throbbing in my awareness.

"I also saw that within the infinite quantum field, all possibilities exist. So every moment in history has infinite possibilities. Which one did I see? Which one is true? Does anything matter more than what I choose to experience *right now*?

"Soon after that holographic viewing, John, Caitlyn, Avani, and Jake went to Eridu in the Middle East. On the surface, they saw places like Eridu as a destination where archeologists dig into the Earth. As they worked there, they had mystical experiences similar to mine. Time began to disappear along with space. Their frequencies elevated and they easily made their way to tunnels under the city built fifty thousand, maybe two hundred fifty thousand years ago, or longer.

"Exploring the depths of Eridu, Enki's home base of pure light, was a profound experience. How is that possible? Well, maybe it's because we became receptive to history being different than what we've been taught; we humbly accepted that the age of civilizations could be much older, and the tapestry of humanity's journey is, in all respects, infinitely complex. When we consciously opened the lens of our perception, we could see things that had always been there. We'd been blind to them. In fact, we didn't look in their direction because we'd already decided what was true and real for us.

"Under the surface, we lost our remnants of inhibition to travel deeper and explore the unlimited depths of Gaia *and ourselves.* We began to fully understand the magnitude of who we are and what we are capable of expressing in our human form.

"As we got in touch with beings from ancient spacetime who were highly advanced in love vibes and pure wisdom, it was an adjustment to realize how desperately our perception of Gaia and her history needed a reboot.

"We realized clearly that we are a magnificent torus, infinite in nature, and so is Gaia. She has a singularity at her core and, like us, that point is inconceivably powerful. It's not like a scary monster ready to devour or destroy us, but it is a provocatively brilliant point with which our own protons can become entangled in an incredibly powerful way. Imagine if we could see her that way, and our relationship with her arose from that context; we could develop a friendship with her like our cosmic friends have been able to do.

"In the end, our group allowed ourselves to be led in each moment into domains under the Earth that are so vast they are inconceivable. We witnessed exquisite valleys, mountains, and lakes. After traveling to many different areas, we realized how diverse the civilizations are under the surface. As we've shared, in most cities, there were no guards at the entrance of these areas because no one could enter unless their frequency was high. Notably, we did encounter a few places with guards of a sort, half-human and half something else. With or without guards, high tech replaced the need for military. Their surveillance systems were beyond our capacity to understand them. These societies have evolved beyond needing leaders. Instead, collaboration is their natural way of engaging with each other.

"Education is totally organic, without 'levels.' And there is no need for structures like prisons, courts, regulatory boards, or oversight committees to support a civil society. Having said that, we sometimes entered cities and gigantic bubbles where there was more structure than other coordinates, yet nothing resembled our surface societal configurations.

"Harmony, camaraderie, and kindness towards each other are at the core of all cultures we encountered. I sit here blown away at the inconceivable circumstances in which I met each of you and how swiftly my world changed through our friendship. Our adventures under the surface and our connections have filled me with awe and wonder at the mystery and profound nature of a human life."

As her words merged into the quiet evening landscape where only a light breeze in the tree tops was audible, Sophia's circle of friends became introspective and allowed the stories, history, and circumstances currently facing them to sink slowly into the intricate depths of their consciousness.

Some looked at the fire while others gazed at the stars shimmering and twinkling above as though the starlight was pulsing a message that can only be interpreted in silence.

## CHAPTER 31

# UNEXPECTED HIT

Putting together a backpack, Sophia methodically included a few essentials for her next trip below the surface. She called Grace to confirm the time and Adele and her girls would arrive soon. More than a year had passed since Sophia and her friends had come back to the surface from their first adventure. Preparing for a second trip was different than the first one because the mode of transportation was going to be radically different—they would move their particles from Mystic cove to a location designated by the giants they'd live with under the surface. They would be moving their particles via wormholes from one coordinate in spacetime to another one. For this kind of quantum field style of travel to become reality, they needed to maintain elevated frequencies, while stilling the mind consistently. Via lucid dreams, Sophia and her team had maintained continued contact with the giants, who made suggestions for how Sophia and her lion-hearted friends could become more adept at moving their particles. By harnessing the power of high vibrational locations like Mystic Cove's monoliths, they could more adeptly facilitate the movement of their particles from that location to specific monolithic structures under the surface. They'd been moving their particles from the Mystic Cove monoliths to another monolithic stone structure on lands owned by Will's community within a couple of miles of the cove. Grace was part of this training because she was ready and thrilled to finally meet Sophia's giant friends. She had visited her husband's family under the surface via a tunnel system. Similarly to how Sophia and her friends described moving her particles, for Grace, it was *a next level, radical leap in travel, a mind-blowing sense of wonder, and an epically blissful experience of exalted freedom.*

Lost in her reverie, Sophia paused for a moment, looking apprehensively out the window at the winds blowing in circles and then erratically switching direction. This was a pattern created by geoengineering of the ionosphere, which had been occurring more often and without warning. Within the hour, the small cluster of friends would meet in the circle of megaliths for a momentous trip under the surface.

At the same time, John, Caitlyn, and Angelica met for an early dinner to talk about John's upcoming trip under the surface to join Jake in the ancient tunnels under Iraq.

As the conversation continued with the potent smell of burgers on a grill and french fries jostling in a deep fryer, the trio ordered their salads. The server knew the group well. She smiled and winked to confirm each order, proclaiming playfully how shocked she was that anyone would order salad and quinoa instead of burgers and fries.

The smiles and laughter of reunited family were suddenly cut short by a harsh, startling groan, and to their shock and horror, John collapsed into unconsciousness.

Without a second's hesitation, Caitlyn grabbed her phone and called for help. Angelica moved immediately to his side, holding his limp body and stroking his face which was lifeless and pale.

Chaos soon swirled through the tiny café as the paramedics arrived; questions about what happened, and John's health history were completed hurriedly. With miraculous speed, Angelica was in the ambulance headed for the hospital with her beloved soulmate. Caitlyn followed closely behind them, after making a brief call to Sophia who could not console her young friend.

After an hour of staring at the mosaic tiles of the emergency room floor, Angelica and Caitlyn were finally approached by a nurse who matter-of-factly invited them into a nearby hallway to speak to the doctor. To their astonishment, he said, "I am not sure how this could have happened. He has no visible wounds, only a slight redness to the skin on his back, but he's lost two-thirds of his blood. It's simply incomprehensible. We started transfusions and now all we can do is hope for the best. I wish I could offer a reasonable prognosis, but we don't even understand how this injury occurred. Our team is consulting with experts. That's all I can say for now. Are you his wife?"

Without hesitating, Angelica said, "Yes." The doctor smiled, put his hand on her shoulder and tried to reassure her that they would do everything they could to save his life.

"Mom, John would love to hear you say that... about being his wife. I keep sensing that you two have a soul-mate thing going on. I bet someday you will officially be his wife. Tonight, you are married ephemerally." She kissed her mother on the cheek. Their moment of tenderness was disrupted by a team who arrived to take John to the Intensive Care Unit where the emergency team said family could join him.

With indomitable spirits blazing, they rushed to John's room. As Angelica thrust the door open, she gasped in shock. She stood motionless.

"Oh my goodness! What are you doing here? How did you know we were in this hospital?" she asked with astonishment.

Grace's husband, Bob, was standing resolutely, waving a handheld device across John's lifeless body. Bob had met with the group in a fireside circle once, but no one knew a lot about him except that he lived under the surface and was from an advanced civilization of humans. Bob tended to be introverted and was filled with equanimity and kindness towards others.

Angelica reached out for her daughter's hand as they walked over and stood like pillars of love at the bedside of the man whom they both cherished.

Addressing them with precision and care, Bob said, "Sophia contacted Grace who immediately briefed me about the situation. I read the field energetically to get the location of John's signature frequency and came over without delay. I request that you listen to me carefully. Something is happening within a high status, malevolent leadership clan in your world. There is no time for me to provide details. We have to move fast. You must trust me and listen carefully because I am about to ask you to follow specific instructions. This is important for your survival and John's. I am here to help all three of you. Timing is going to be critical. For now, you need to know that John was hit with a plasma weapon. I'm going to work on him with my technologies but I cannot promise anything. You need to get out of here as soon as possible."

"I am not leaving!" Angelica said with the ferocity of a raging lioness.

In parallel with her proclamation, the harsh wind howled furiously, pulsing the windows in an eerie contraction and expansion. Lightning bolts crashed down without rain, while a gigantic, thundering sound pounded the earth below them—broadcasting unnerving, violent waves through every cell in their bodies. In a split second, the lights were thrust into darkness. The hospital's electricity was dead.

Looking at Angelica supportively, Bob said in a calm, clear tone, "Please follow my instructions without the slightest hesitation. Leave now. You can use your phone's flashlight to guide you. Exit through the emergency door, turn left, and wait for me by the giant fir tree on your left. Is that clear?"

Angelica and Caitlyn nodded with shell-shocked faces and rigid bodies.

"I cannot go with you," Bob said in a factual, clear tone. "Wait for me. Please be patient. Do not go anywhere else. To avoid being seen on the cameras or by the staff, I will join you in my own way. I know you are afraid, Angelica. Please take this small wand and hold it with both hands until I join you. Caitlyn, I have one for you, too. Tell your mother about the wands as you leave the building. We have little time left."

Caitlyn confidently took her wand, smiled valiantly at her mom, and headed out the door. Alongside hope, tears from her shattered heart began to softly emerge. Glancing back, she tenderly blew a kiss to her father, with whom an indelible bond had been cemented from the moment that she realized they were kin.

The hospital staff was busy handling the chaotic situation, with devices beeping and the intermittent hum of inoperable generators—which normally would be breaking the silence of the long hallways and darkened nurses' stations.

While the mother-daughter team rushed to the appointed spot, having called on every molecule of her courage, Caitlyn reassured her mother, "Mom, Bob is using advanced technologies that can assess the situation and help John. I have a feeling that he will be taking us under the surface. Please believe me, he's trustworthy and you've definitely got this!

"All the work you've done will pay off now. You know how to send your awareness from here to under the surface. This time, the wand will help your body to make the transition. Our frequency is the key to a smoother trip. Are you able to center yourself and feel equanimity emerging in your energy field?"

Angelica nodded weakly as she lowered her eyes and took a deep breath.

Within a few minutes, Bob met the two women outside and asked them to step behind the tree. As he arrived, Caitlyn told her mom to hold the wand tightly—it was filled with mesmerizing golden and white light, tinged in cobalt, that would raise her frequencies significantly. She also urged her mother to "feel the frequencies" of the spot where Bob instructed them to wait for him. She explained that certain trees grow adjacent to Gaia's natural energy portals. Caitlyn sensed the giant fir marked "a high-vibe location" which would make their journey under the surface seamless. Affirming her, Bob smiled and nodded. For her, Bob's arrival at the hospital and resourceful guidance was another unforeseen miracle of the sort that arises unexpectedly from the field—when they maintain higher frequencies.

"Mom, this wand will stabilize our nervous system, our elevated vibratory levels, and allow us to move through spacetime distortions and portals with more ease."

With a look of trepidation, Angelica glanced at her daughter and tightened her grip on the wand. With a long, deep breath, she became serene and stood motionless.

In the blink of an eye, the trio found themselves below the surface in a city that Caitlyn was familiar with. For a couple of weeks, Angelica had been connecting to this coordinate by sending her awareness there.

While still gripping the wand, Angelica lost consciousness.

Despite Angelica's training to prepare for such a trip under the surface, her frequencies sometimes oscillated between confident calm and debilitating fear—which was normal during the training phase. Sophia and Caitlyn had always reassured her that it can be unsettling and even scary for the human mind to let go of everything familiar, to allow awareness to enter subtle and unfamiliar territory.

The front door of a nearby house opened as if the high-tech door realized that someone needed to enter.

Carrying Angelica's limp body, Bob greeted three women who moved with swift precision. Everything had been prepared for Angelica's and Caitlyn's arrival, and the women did not waste time in conversation as they quickly took in the addition of another person, instantly engaging with Angelica's energy field.

The room was painted with calming earth tones, slate-blues and sage-green. Yet Caitlyn didn't notice the ambiance. She maintained a blank stare—her nervous system in full shock.

Speaking in their native language, the women continued attending to Angelica's needs. As she lay on the cot-like bed, the women slowly moved handheld devices from above her forehead to beyond her feet. With kindness exuding from their eyes, they smiled softly and acted with care and diligence, like loving mothers attending to a child.

Watching the women compassionately take charge, Caitlyn's face relaxed. She smiled, breathed a sigh of relief, and turned to see Bob's sister, Sandara, whom she met on a recent trip under the surface. They became instant friends, mostly communicating telepathically, which seemed to be Sandara's preferred mode of conversation.

Caitlyn smiled as she warmly hugged Sandara. From the corner of her eye, she noticed that Bob was turning into particles of twinkling light.

Taking a moment to lovingly greet Caitlyn, Sandara explained that one of the women was her sister and the others were local elders and very adept healers. With her brain on overload and her nervous system in chaos, Caitlyn struggled to focus her attention to allow a telepathic channel to open to Sandara.

Using her native language, Sandara tenderly blessed Caitlyn.

Absorbing the much needed kindness, Caitlyn gave up telepathy and began a frazzled, nerve-driven flurry of words, "Thank you so much! It means the world to me for you and your family to care for us so sweetly... I... thank you..." Pausing, she looked dazed, saying, "This is crazy! I don't understand why Dad was attacked. The whole night feels surreal. But it's clear to me that somehow Bob intuited that I needed to come here before tonight—to adjust to the frequencies. Out of the blue, a couple of weeks ago he asked me if I could make a trip here. That definitely made the journey tonight easier for me and I can now be more help to Mom. Oh my gosh, I love you and your family so much!"

Looking lovingly at her mother, she said, "Mom was compelled to accept the mind-bending challenge of advancing her subtle skills of shifting from physical to etheric form. It's torquing on my brain that something in the field must have communicated a subtle message to her to prepare for this event. She applied uncharacteristic, fierce determination and focus to make a journey under the surface. Sorry... I guess you can tell by my incoherent rambling that I'm an absolute hot mess! Tonight was *epically* intense and my brain is *totally* fried from trying to process the insanity of it all."

In a feeble voice and wobbling with unsteadiness, she said, "Um... San-daa-raa..." carefully and slowly saying her friend's name with phonetical precision, "I'm feeling pretty shaky... I might throw up. Sorry to be so blunt and for talking crazy, but I'm definitely not doing great right now. Maybe I should sit down."

Seeing Angelica's face gradually becoming as light and soft as a sleeping baby and her breath starting to become deeper and more rhythmic, Sandara gently took Caitlyn's hand and led her to a corner of the room. Astonished, Caitlyn stood facing an infinity symbol graced by a glistening metal heart seated perfectly in the middle, and made from a material akin to driftwood. Metals under the surface look similar to surface ones yet they are different energetically than those on the crust of the Earth.

Caitlyn's eyes fixated on the metallic heart, emanating a soft, white light with emerald sparkles scattered throughout. She closed her eyes for a moment and said, "Whoa! It's emitting a magnetic beam that draws me to it, soothing me right down to my soul."

Sandara smiled compassionately and left Caitlyn to be in a silent, healing space.

A few minutes later, Bob arrived to see Caitlyn sitting relaxed and at ease, still gazing at the effulgent heart.

He spoke in a reassuring tone saying, "Caitlyn, I have an update about John... He is under Iraq in the perfect city to deal with his injury. For now, it's the best place for him to recover. As Angelica's frequencies adjust, she'll be able to go there. When his condition is stabilized, he has the option to come here, if he prefers.

"I would love to stay and support you but I need to leave. You are in good hands with Sandara. She is my very dear, *pulchritudinous* kin. Something is happening at the cove now and I must go."

Reeling from Bob's kind and curious comment while knowing she must be brief, Caitlyn said, "Bob, you were amazing through all of this. I have no words…"

She quickly composed herself, valiantly choking back a surge of tears.

"One more thing I want to say is tonight my work-in-process nature was in my face. That's, okay, though. Friends like you make that messy process easier because it feels safe to work through monstrously tenacious emotional patterning. I'll always cheer you on like you are doing for me. Go do what you need to do at the cove. And please take care, okay?"

Embracing her tenderly, Bob smiled softly and said, "How wonderful! You found the gift of a human life; the *work-in-process*, as you call it, is where the expansion of consciousness receives fuel to explode into higher and vaster levels of awareness. There's more bliss and breakthroughs coming for you; not more suffering. I am honored to be your friend."

Soon he was shimmering light headed to the cove and Caitlyn was recalling the meaning of the word *pulchritudinous*: "enchanting, magnificent, extraordinary, beautiful."

As Caitlyn stared at the exquisite, dazzling heart in front of her, she whispered, "Bob, I will never forget that word. It sums up your family… your whole culture. I totally love and appreciate every single one of you!"

# CHAPTER 32

# DEMONS AND THE CIRCLE

Savage winds howled like a hungry pack of wild animals. Fighting off shivers of eerie foreboding, Sophia sent a text to Grace and Adele confirming their arrival and letting them know she had one of her trustworthy, intuitive hunches to leave promptly at the scheduled time. *Something feels off* was her only comment, adding that timing was absolutely critical. Immediately, both responded saying they were on their way.

As the wind changed direction and intensified, Sophia headed towards the megaliths and stood stoically in the midst of the brewing storm. Within a few minutes, Grace arrived followed immediately by Adele and her daughters. They were traveling light, with only small backpacks.

Uncharacteristically, Kellie and Leisa looked nervous. Seeing their anxious faces, Sophia attempted to soothe them saying, "There is a ten-minute window to enter. Would you go first? Next Grace will join you and I'll go last."

"Why don't we go together?" Kellie asked, looking concerned. "We always go together. Something is wrong! I can feel it!"

With a frightened look, Leisa stood rigid.

Emanating a reassuring gaze, Sophia said calmly, "Don't worry. I'll be coming soon. You can get acclimated and your sweet little atoms can adjust to the frequencies. You'll see me in a few minutes. Are you and your mom ready?"

As their heads nodded, Adele gave Sophia a piercing look indicating that she, too, questioned this breach of protocol. Affirming her willingness to honor Sophia's request, she held her hand to her heart, nervously smiled at Sophia and said, "Hurry, Sophia... Please. We'll be waiting for you. Take care."

The concerned family began to sparkle like scintillating hand-held firecrackers that slowly dissolved into the ether and disappeared.

"Okay, Sophia, what's up?" Grace demanded.

"I don't know but please go. I will come when I get the signal to join you. Something isn't right. Sorry to be vague but you know me. Even if I don't know what's going on, I have to trust my intuition."

As the last syllable left her tongue, Bob appeared. Without hesitating or explaining, he asked Grace to join Adele and he assured her that Sophia would be right behind them. With a concerned look, Grace hurriedly hugged Sophia and her husband. Her particles began to twinkle and glisten. In an instant, Sophia and Bob stood alone in the circle.

"You are picking up Lady Midday as information from *the field*," said Bob.

"I'm confused. What about her? I recall that Gilda referred to her as a *demonic psychopath*... now a very old woman... definitely pure evil. I haven't heard her name since Gilda spoke about Midday's inscrutable involvement with the Nazis."

"Well... Lady Midday is furious with the accomplishments of your group while under the surface. More than that, she despises you for supporting the introduction of open-source, free energy, and other revolutionary technologies on a global scale. If they are implemented, her perceived power and control over the global population would be threatened.

"Mostly she's holding a grudge because no one annihilated you when you left with Nate. She's indelibly linked to the rich and famous black projects within the military-industrial complex, global black lodges and, without doubt, she never took a fancy to you. She didn't like or trust your mother but adored your father's lack of conscience and cold heart, which was an energy match to hers.

"You need to know that she's on her own—this is a personal vendetta. She didn't get clearance and brought her own team who hit John with a plasma weapon. Fortunately, I was able to reverse a lot of damage and get him under the surface to an exemplary facility for further care. Angelica and Caitlyn are with my sister."

Affirming her congruence with his unexpected revelations, she gently closed her eyes for a moment to dip into *the field* for guidance. She gazed at Bob as though still connected to the inner world she'd just visited.

Then she asked in a whisper, "She's here, isn't she? Midday..."

"Yes, and although she can't see me because of my energetic shield, she's not interested in anyone but you. Be aware she's locked in on you right now. Hold steady. You are the infinite light, Sophia. Align with your highest frequency. She's approaching on your right."

"Well, there you are, Ms. Sophia-angel!" roared the she-beast of a human. The old woman stood firmly in the brutal winds, grey hair flying wildly around her head. Her thin nose was center stage of a wrinkled face and eyelids that drooped gloomily with age. Her gaze was fiercely demonic.

"I wanted to take you out myself but in my advanced age, I may not have perfect aim. To insure my goal is met, I brought my best marksmen. Poor little you!"

Her entourage of three men were dressed in black with faces covered, standing impressively tall and rigid as she continued.

"You've been such a pain in the ass, you little wretch. You and your sappy, do-gooder friends. Who the hell do you think you are? You know our ways and our authority, superiority and magic! It's awfully presumptuous of you to believe that you'd get to have free energy, creative infrastructures, and the peaceful world that you naively think you can create without us. Why are you not shaking in your little boots, my dear?"

The wind ripped through the trees with ever-increasing intensity and the old woman sent her wretched gaze to the sky as she screamed, "What a God-damned, stupid time for them to be jacking with the weather! This was not supposed to happen tonight. I get so f**king angry when they don't stick to schedules."

As she spewed vile contempt for the orchestrators of the weather, the storm took a sudden turn. Rain descended on them, pouring in torrents, a spectacular lightning display spreading across the lake. One of the men methodically handed Midday an umbrella. She popped it open as the rain became heavier and she continued her discourse.

"As I was saying, I am sick of you and I want to have the joy of knowing I got to be the one to tell you we killed your dear friend, John. He's become a problem. And we'll get the rest, too."

At the precise moment that the winds were reaching a crescendo, Midday demanded that her team fire their weapons, telling them to destroy "this worthless creature."

In synchrony with her voice barking the deadly orders, Midday's umbrella gave way under the pressure of the intense winds. An ear-splitting sound pierced the umbrella and struck its holder with a jolt that thrust Midday and her companions to the ground; and ejected the life force from each of its recipients.

Spectacular lightning bolts set the night sky blazing with thousands of rapidly firing streaks. Large swaths of forests were scorched and a fire exploded within seconds across the lake, engulfing the landscape with horrifying fury. The megaliths began to turn into iridescent, pulsing white light. As the atmosphere seemed to be turning into a raging inferno, a field of cobalt light formed around the megaliths that coalesced into a spectacular circle of mesmerizing beauty.

In the midst of tempestuous chaos, Sophia's particles began to glow as Bob entered the circle. He took her hand and they calmly disappeared.

# CHAPTER 33

# HISTORY OF A SORCERESS

Grace, Adele and her daughters stood by a giant boulder covered in soft pink and indigo flowers that looked similar to orchids. None of the flowers they'd seen mirrored their surface cousins. The contrast of the emerald moss under their feet and the mesmerizing waterfall nearby created a refuge for the gathering of women to wait for Sophia's arrival.

Unaffected by their mother's agitated state, Kellie and Leisa left Grace and Adele. Following the sound of cascading water, within a few minutes they were basking in the mesmerizing beauty of nearby shimmering rose quartz rocks surrounding a magnificent waterfall. They dangled their legs into a pond that collected the water from a mystical realm above them—an astonishing waterfall soared down from heights beyond sight, carrying golden flecks of color and shimmering rainbows that danced around the euphoric sisters. The profound, thundering sound and its associated mystical colors were well-known to the locals—comforting its visitors with vibrations of strength, pure love, and mind-softening peacefulness.

Without warning, Sophia appeared to Grace and Adele who embraced her lovingly. Seeing their shocked faces, she took a deep, centering breath to steady herself and give their minds an opportunity to register her arrival. She began to explain what happened by asking a question. "Do either of you remember Lady Midday?"

"Yes, of course," Grace answered. "My stomach got tight just thinking of her. Why?"

Adele looked confused and stood speechless.

"Well, it seems that she made a special trip to hunt us down, with me as her primary target."

Grace gasped as Sophia continued, "It's okay. Bob knew about it and protected me. When she saw me, she went ballistic. Thank God for Bob's calm nature and my ability to still my mind. He and I matched frequencies and I knew instantly that everything would be okay. What's really crazy is that she didn't know in advance that her team was manipulating the weather and likely performing experiments in the ionosphere. Cutting to the chase, I can tell you that although I didn't witness her demise, my heart knows that she will no longer threaten anyone.

"That storm was nothing short of wicked and violent yet she stubbornly stood within its fury. I sensed a kind of blindness to the reality around her. She was able to attack John, though. From out-of-the-blue, Bob came to help John, and then me, at the precise time that we needed him. Somehow he has a refined inner radar for such situations. I'm sure you've witnessed that more than a few times, Grace."

Grace nodded in agreement and spontaneously she and Adele drew in a long breath and relaxed as Sophia elaborated on what happened.

"Rather than share every detail, what's important is knowing John is fine and Caitlyn is with Angelica under the surface. Since Angelica has been practicing projecting her awareness to Bob's city and preparing to move her physical particles to that location, they went there. It was a relief to realize that Angelica has been unintentionally preparing for this inconceivable event. Bob reports that she will be fine and John is under Iraq with Jake and Avani."

"Holy moly!" Grace responded while having to steady herself by finding a seat on a nearby rock. "This is the wildest trip I've ever taken with you. And that says a lot! We've been on some pretty crazy adventures. This means that all of the work from your team to disseminate the technologies and information was worth the effort. And it means that Midday's buddies across the globe are having a total meltdown by now."

"You are right about that. And it also means we won't be going back to the cove for a while. It won't be safe."

"Where is my dear husband, Sophia? I shouldn't worry about him but I can't help it."

"I don't know. I suspect that after making sure I was briefed and safely headed your way, he went to check on John. He knows where we are."

Adele stood nearby, reeling from Sophia's unexpected, revelatory bombshell. "I only have a few minutes to talk while the girls are occupied with the waterfall," Adele said with a look of trepidation. "If you are okay to talk, Sophia, I need to know what just happened. To come here I had to remain super focused to stabilize my frequencies. It's been getting easier but tonight... well... it was crazy. Luckily, the girls did fine."

The three friends settled on nearby rocks covered in a thick cushion of iridescent moss.

Looking shocked and confused, Adele asked, "Who is lady Midday and why is she so important to the privileged inner circle of our world and their goals? Why was she so angry with you? I've heard her name but I can't remember what my mother and grandmother said about her. I am also confused about how Bob helped John?"

Sophia patiently and thoroughly told Adele everything that she knew about John, plasma weapons, and high-tech devices under the surface that can diagnose and heal, all the way to a person's subatomic particles. She also shared Bob's skill in helping her particles to leave at the perfect moment to spare her from seeing the gruesome end to the old woman who had wreaked terror and havoc for over a century.

In a reassuring tone, Sophia said, "More than any of us, Bob was equipped to help us tonight. I'm sure you've seen how easily he scales into higher levels of himself and his interaction with the field is mind-blowing. He always shows up at the exact coordinate where he's needed and with uncanny precision in his timing. The past few months, he's impressed me more than ever with his kindness and high frequencies. He's taught us all a lot about traveling through spacetime. He is a loyal friend. From what I could tell, it looked like you trusted him earlier. Is that right?"

Adele nodded in agreement.

Following up on Adele's question about Midday's past and relevance to current times, Sophia shared Midday's unusual life history.

"Midday was not German but she lived in Berlin with her husband, an SS officer. Heinrich Himmler, head of the SS, held her husband in high esteem—both were ruthlessly aligned to the Third Reich and obsessed with the occult. My grandmother said that to be part of the SS was like being ceremoniously knighted into a powerful elite military cult—intricately embedded with a web of secrecy, black magic, and insidious rituals like summoning demons. Midday was infatuated with a particular book, a *grimoire*, or book of spells. There's no question that this book was not even close to being ordinary.

"Witches, sorcerers, and pagan cults often used grimoires, which they could use to connect with angelic realms, or to heal people and other beneficial endeavors.

"Through her husband's research and expeditions, Midday got access to a special grimoire that was used in dark, black magic. It involved demons, which she and her inner circle related to with a neurotic fixation. This book of demonic spells was originally compiled many centuries ago. It fell into Jesuit hands, who later passed it to an Italian family who financially backed the Jesuits. Apparently they got it when they were in China in the seventeenth century. It was then passed on, through a marriage, to a British family who ended up in Austria. And then, of course, Hitler's SS wanted to get their hands on it. Finally, it crossed the Atlantic with Midday. This grimoire has a history that reads like a creepy horror movie. Gilda heard many accounts of its use and gruesome effects.

"Although the SS was undoubtedly a men's club, because of her loyalty and enduring devotion to their ideology, Midday was allowed to participate in their psychopathic world. Some believe that she used their demonic magic against her country's citizens. Others said she used it against opposition forces. Nonetheless, these are not the kind of practices and worldview that any of us would want to study or even know about. Our applications of quantum science for establishing infinite peace don't mesh with this kind of creepy, dark magic.

"Midday and her husband's prestigious SS circle never grasped that magic is not an invincible force. It's not enduring truth. Witches who worked with the healing arts knew that. That's why they were usually herbal experts and studied healing modalities. Alchemists like Sir Issac Newton used invisible forces for good. Unfortunately, super dark, black magic enchants some people, like Midday."

"When we were young," Grace added, "she absolutely scared the bejeezus out of Sophia and me."

Sophia smiled broadly, raised her brows, and nodded her head in wholehearted agreement as she continued, "Midday was a gorgeous, long-legged, athletic, and quite sexy Norwegian who instantly captivated the SS and everyone else—all the way to the Führer. Everything about her fit the Nazi ideal of a perfect female Aryan; tall, slender, strong physique, thick blonde hair, blue eyes, perfect forehead, and an adorable nose. Plus, she was smarter than most of his inner circle of military staff. Hitler often reminded them of that fact; maybe to keep them on their toes.

"Luckily for her, everyone was as smitten with her as their crazy leader seemed to be. Hitler had already called for the invasion of Norway. He was obsessed with their DNA and saw them as racially superior to Germans. However, in his delusional view, they needed his glorious culture to become their best selves.

"Midday displayed a total lack of conscience. She'd do anything for the Führer. I do mean anything. Gilda told me that Midday was the perfect spy because she could pass for an innocuous schoolteacher, or become the bewitching seductress of any man in a matter of minutes.

"More valuable than her chameleon-like capacities was her total buy-in to Nazi beliefs and their megalomaniacal global schemes to rule the world. She delighted in the demise of anyone who could not pass the Nazi check list or was not sufficiently indoctrinated—in a nutshell, she became insanely loyal to the Nazis.

"Gilda had a hard time talking about this wicked woman. I recall one of my conversations with Gilda vividly. She said Midday traveled to the U.S. to develop relationships with Eugenics societies. Midday had already met with Julian Huxley, President of the Eugenics Society of the U.K. who started UNESCO and cofounded The World Wildlife Fund. He stated that the Nuremberg trials gave Eugenics a bad name but that would blow over and soon they could go back to business as usual. Hearing that great news, Midday likely did a happy dance.

"Next, she was chomping at the bit to meet Mrs. Harriman, the wife of a Wall Street Tycoon. Remember that we talked about Mr. Harriman with BBH and their funding of Nazis. Midday was enthralled with the work of Margaret Sanger, who was at the helm of a group called Planned Parenthood. In the early days, Sanger was quite a vocal racist and eugenicist who emphatically stated that the black population should not have children. She was more covert about letting the public know that she and her group wanted to 'exterminate that race.'

"Midday's idols and extensive list of potential eugenics interviews were with: Alexander Graham Bell, Theodore Roosevelt, Clarence Darrow, George Bernard Shaw, Oliver Wendell Holmes, John Harvey Kellogg who invented cornflakes, Francis Crick, a British biologist who said sterilization is the only means to handle poor genetics, Robert Foster Kennedy, a neurologist who wrote about 'nature's mistakes,' Linus Pauling, Herbert Hoover, John Maynard Keynes, a leading post World War II economist, and more names I've forgotten. Whoever she couldn't meet, she'd locate their writings and relish their words and speeches. Seeing Midday's delight in such inhumane, psychopathic thinking drove Gilda crazy.

"By the 1930's, in thirty-two states in the U.S. and two provinces in Canada, sterilizations began on children and young adults who were poor, 'feeble-minded,' or were considered 'unfit.' Members of the eugenics movement believed that bad genetics caused inferior humans. And they held another inconceivable belief that Gilda couldn't fathom: God's intelligent design was flawed. He messed up and gave people weaknesses like emotions and a propensity for illness. This was accepted as valid science. Why? Who was behind this ideology that blended seamlessly into society, obtaining validation from science?

"Gilda said that it gets weirder: Midday's clan of Synarchists adored that catastrophic, heartless movement... and something more. Her little clan of beautiful, wealthy people was adamant that they should live forever. For them, God messed up when he designed them, too—somehow, he missed seeing their perfection and entitlement to live forever.

"Way back in the 1930's and 1940's, she and her Nazi brothers and sisters were already thinking in terms of genetics and how to manipulate genes to serve their purpose. Through the Synarchy movement and other secret groups, after the war, she was joined by the British and U.S. jet-setter oligarchy to plan a stronger, more comprehensive eugenics movement. The goal was to introduce eugenics into the national conscience. They believed it was a long game worth playing.

"The idea was that the population would slowly be taught not to identify with their nation or culture. People must think globally and value being homogeneous. The individual cannot think of themselves as worthy or special. Using psychological means, people would be subjected to constant threats, become fearful, and therefore controllable. If that didn't work, starvation, drought, and other means could be used to break their spirits and, of course, their bodies. Although this worldview is inconceivable to us, it was thoroughly accepted by them and its ideologies and goals began to be gradually implemented.

"Within a decade after World War I, chemicals were being released on land and in the air, water became contaminated, and plans were executed through media to make the educated population feel guilty for all of this. It was decided that the working class must be made to believe the problems facing the planet and themselves were their fault. Guilt is a low frequency and that drop in frequency was important to the execution of their brilliant plan.

"A very excited group of scientists, academics, and researchers met in 1992 in Rio de Janeiro, Brazil at the United Nation's Earth Summit-Agenda 21. Midday was particularly interested in the *Bio Tech break out group* of the conference called the *Global Diversity Assessment*. The presenter's content was compiled into a book with over one thousand pages. This was considered to be premier science.

"Gilda said Midday swooned over each page and that when she spoke about it, she lingered on the brink of ecstatic rapture. She proudly announced that she highlighted over nine hundred references to words like 'genes, genetics, DNA, and Bio Tech.' She read those parts over and over again.

"It totally creeped Gilda out because Midday and her circle of wealthy friends had the resources to pull off something that seemed incomprehensibly dangerous to the planet and to the human race. What was underlying their infatuation with genetics? And what were they planning to do about it? Why did they build secret laboratories all over the world? Why was there no transparency with the public about the whole process? And why did global citizens look the other way and ignore the magnitude of its implications for themselves and their lineage?

"As though her heart was clearly broken, Gilda sobbed and started to shake when she spoke about it. It was like she wanted to warn me of this diabolical plan but she was also traumatized from having to watch their agendas unfold over the years.

"Gilda told me that slowly but surely, eugenics would evolve into transhumanism. And finally, only Midday's cream of the crop clan would endure as humans and the rest of us would fall away. Gilda was devastated by the horrific ramifications of the eugenics movement.

"For Midday, transhumanism was music to her nefarious ears and infused her with hope that the world would someday look a lot better—when everyone looked like Lady Midday.

"From Gilda's description, I was not sure if Midday was a psychopath or a narcissist. Either way, her heart was hard as titanium. Midday took copious notes with each trip she made and in the early days, she returned to Germany in eugenics bliss and later she enjoyed discussing the subject with hand-picked co-conspirators.

"Since the eugenics ideals and beliefs were the foundational part of her comrades' exalted plan for humanity, when Midday came to the U.S. after the war, she jumped in and became enthralled with the goals and ideals of groups like the Club of

Rome, a secret society that Gilda said seemed to fuel Midday's madness even more.

"Midday explained to Gilda that she and her comrades of closely knit bankers, financiers, and corporate elites found the notion of human sovereignty to be ridiculous. In their world, humans are like animals. They are *resources* and can be sufficiently manipulated once the minds of humans around the world are under control. At that point, her clan will dictate the ownership and use of resources, and no one, except them, will own anything. They get it all—the oceans, the land, and the air—safely under their diabolical control.

"In Midday's clan's worldview of genetic weakness and divine design flaws, humanity stands between them and their end game: global rule, which translates into dominance over all the Earth. For them that scenario feels natural and isn't up for scrutiny or consideration. They feel invincible and absolutely entitled. This is basic human perception at play, regardless of whether or not it agrees with ours."

"Sophia, that's scary... and crazy!" Adele interrupted with a passionate burst of incredulousness. "My grandmother never told me that part but I do remember that the mention of Midday's name dropped her mood to ground zero. With the events of the past ten years, I do not know how Midday could feel the high level of confidence that you just described. We could see that by the early 2030's, her comrades were floundering and their devious plans were falling apart."

"That is correct," Sophia said confidently. "Global citizens had started to become even more suspicious of the media, politicians, and lots of other things like accepted scientific ideologies or theories—including the *theory* of our evolution. While we were busy under the surface preparing to bring important technological advances to the surface, I can envision her Wall Street and London banker clans immersing themselves in a surreptitious, dilapidated Synarchist Manifesto and reminding themselves of their unparalleled greatness. The truth is, who knows what's been transpiring for them?

"What's important is that the world is changing rapidly and not in their direction. As a human collective we are uncovering our self-worth, our personal relevance, and innate gifts. We share and care more, and don't idolize the icons or authorities they present to us. We question and scrutinize leaders maybe for the first time in recorded history. We know that we'd rather be there for each other than fight. We educate our kids in new ways, and make sure everyone has food and feels safe. We saw that we'd been *played like a fiddle*, as Gilda would say."

Adele's demeanor shifted and she adjusted her posture to fit a confident resoluteness that had arisen in her.

Making impassioned eye contact with her friends, she said assuredly, "Free energy will help to clean up the environment. Midday's clan knew that truth but we had to finally see free energy as a genuine possibility. If her cohorts had been genuine, all the money directed towards wars, chemically-based disease, financial disasters, and other distractions would have gone into this area. I realize they had an advantage because thoroughly acquiescing to authority is not a new mindset—whether it's teachers, priests, rabbis or preachers. Authority extended to parents, scientists (especially if they wore white coats), academics labeled as *experts*, and political leaders—all given carte blanche to make decisions for us throughout our lives. Our acculturation defined us as *followers* of authority, this being the only acceptable way to participate in society. That caused me to wonder: At what stage of life would I finally evolve into an *adult* and be responsible for myself, leading *from within* as a sovereign being of infinite wisdom and indisputable quantum powers? After all, I'm a mother of two young women! Yet I still respond to authority like a child. That began to change when we lived among giants. Of course, authorities will likely remain blinded by their worldview so they'll plow forward unchecked. BUT... I can shift my relationship *with them.*"

Chuckling, her eyes danced with amusement as she said with a jocular smile, "Maybe I did some high priority *adulting* under the surface."

Sophia and Grace exchanged sprightly smiles with her, as they gave a reassuring thumbs up.

After Adele took a moment to absorb their loving support, Sophia said, "Gilda told me that Midday and her comrades were *a puzzling inner circle* because they had no problem contaminating Gaia and even *subjecting themselves* to toxins and radiation. They carefully developed antidotes before they released specific toxins into and onto the planet, and knew how to leach certain chemicals from their bodies. However, the cumulative effects started to ravage their private circle, as it had done to the general population—adding a layer of toxicity to each generation since WWII until it reached a dangerous crescendo. Mothers passed unprecedented toxin levels to babies, while babies also took in dangerous levels through pharmaceuticals, food, and environmental pollution. Each generation repeated that devastating cycle in a spiral of ever-increasing toxicity. For the general population, releasing radiation and engaging in other assaults on humans and Gaia is inconceivable. Midday arrogantly confided in Gilda that if she and her comrades were collateral damage, it was simply part of a risk-reward analysis. Toxicity was incontestably worth the glory of the power and control they could amass. That should give you an idea of the motivation behind this form of psychopathy and a clue about their common worldview. They formed a pact and plan to adhere to it, regardless of the devastating outcome, even to themselves. Plenty of people got angry with Nate for calling this out. But he didn't care. He wouldn't be silent and play it safe."

Listening intently, Grace looked thunderstruck, lost in thought, while hugging her knees to her chest. Suddenly Bob appeared, walking up from behind, calling her name. Jumping up and turning towards him, she became overjoyed instantly and said, "I was so engrossed in our conversation that I didn't *feel* your arrival." She greeted him with a kiss on the cheek, as they took a moment to embrace in familiar, sublime rapture.

"Great timing!" She said warmly. "Honey, we were talking about a wild subject. I mean insane! I'm not sure anything can top what you've just been through with Sophia, though. Do you have any good news? Anything even slightly upbeat?"

Bob squeezed her hand tenderly and reassuringly as he turned to include Sophia and Adele in his update—while looking friendly and relaxed as usual.

"Gratefully, I am the bearer of good news. John is doing much better and will fully recover. I checked with Jake and Avani. They are in good spirits."

Glancing at Grace with an affectionate smile and turning toward Sophia and Adele, he said reassuringly, "I know Grace will understand, as she always does. I need to leave to perform a few cleanup operations on Megan's property. Afterwards I'll meet you at my city. Sophia, my mother will be delighted to finally meet you. Adele, you and your girls will love it there. I'm sure it's obvious why you won't be surfacing for a while.

"As Sophia was about to travel here and Midday and her team attacked, I took a reading on the escalating weather system and realized that Sophia needed to leave without delay. So I created a hologram with her image which Midday continued to rage at as though it was still Sophia. She was so engrossed in her anger and revenge that she didn't notice that although she needed an umbrella, Sophia did not. In retrospect, it's a good lesson that if we get lost in our head, we cannot see the truth in front of us. It's ironic that as she was literally screaming into the wind, the storm absorbed her ferocious frequencies with open arms and it gained momentum. She was oblivious to the reality that her explosive antics were exacerbating the dynamic of chaos in the surrounding electromagnetic field—which reached a crescendo of epic magnitude—and resulted in her and her team being struck by lightning. She and her companions were killed instantly.

"Her last words aligned with her personality. She shouted, 'LECK MICH AM ARSCH!' And a few other not-so-nice German phrases.

"I'm not diminishing the loss of life. However, it is important that you know her fate. As the storm raged, she never saw the hologram of Sophia turning into light and dissolving. Her clan will be confused by what happened and likely angry. The good part is that she broke protocol. And that is a major infraction in their worldview. They cannot reach you here nor will they be concerned with finding you, particularly with all they have to deal with. Each day, they are losing control of the public and free energy is picking up steam, with or without their approval. They are desperately trying to regroup. It's not looking good for them.

"Oh, I almost forgot to tell you that I had to strike that giant, dead fir tree near the drive. It needed to appear as though it was hit by lightning. Her clan cannot swoop in and cover it up or remove evidence. The authorities will find the tree blocking the road and they'll notice the branch that crushed Midday's car. The bodies of her and her team are visible from there. They will have plenty to investigate. That's for sure."

He pulled a small backpack off his shoulders, reached inside, and handed Sophia a weathered, leather-bound book with a crest on the front cover that was barely discernible.

Sophia stared at the book resting in her hands and then looked into Bob's eyes with a sense of wonderment asking, "Where did you get this?"

"It fell from Midday's coat. I had an intuitive feeling that you needed to have it. Of course, that was my inner compass talking. If I was wrong, I can return it."

"No, I'm not saying you shouldn't have brought it to me; it's just that this is Midday's horrific *grimoire*. My mother was aware of it and it terrified her. So, even before Gilda told me details about it, Midday's prized book sent shivers down my spine."

"Sophia, you were right to be afraid of it," Adele said with a look of dread. "My mother and grandmother said that it was inhuman and beyond creepy—like a bone-chilling nightmare."

"I get your concern, Adele, but Bob was right to bring it to me. The thing is, Adele, this kind of low-frequency power is becoming old school. Magic has been around since the beginning of civilizations. And there's always been benevolent alchemists, magicians, and shamans who used formulas for healing. Yet most were not written down. Passing wisdom through experience and practice from teacher to student was more their style. Also, it's important to recognize that these spells are frequency.

"Holding the book, I have the strong sense that it is time for it to retire. We've seen firsthand that high vibrations are not about selfish ends, magic tricks, control, or manipulating anything or anyone. All of the past and present shamans and alchemists aren't evil. Yet we are seeing that new benevolent subtle skills are emerging as the Earth and her inhabitants raise their frequencies.

"I am feeling that we should take this book with us to the subtle space within Gaia. Although I agree with you that this grimoire is dark, I am encouraged that darkness is giving way to light in people's hearts on the surface. I am certain that this book has no power over me, or any of us. It's days of providing sustenance for evildoers are over."

"I get that, Sophia," Adele said. "I'm just glad you are holding it—not me."

Bob smiled and went to stand near Adele making direct eye contact and speaking in a voice that was calm and confident. His face was soft with compassion and kindness. "Adele, there will be more disturbing information coming out. I'd like to offer a couple of questions that may help you going forward. Nothing that is revealed has to scare you. It's more about you being able to see it without becoming devastated or feeling helpless. My dear, you are a powerhouse—a tour de force. Your sensitivity is a gift. Could you consider whatever the book evokes in you to be a gift that points you to where you still have fear?

"When you think of the book, instead of fear, what opposite feeling do you want to feel? Feel your chosen feeling vibrating somewhere in your body. Make this a visceral experience. And titrate between wherever you feel the fear in your body and where you feel its opposite. Then hold both feelings at the same time. This is the point of unicity—a mysterious union of opposites which is the root of transformation. It's about getting to equilibrium and having the capacity to see and feel life experiences from a higher perspective, from a broad mountain vista. What does it feel like to stand on that higher elevation and experience its breathtaking views?

"For eons, civilizations had immeasurable reasons to feel fearful and to get stuck in a dark valley of hopelessness and despair. Consider that harmony, a byproduct of unicity, is the feeling that is now arising exponentially on the surface. Harmony sits comfortably like an anchor between fear and its opposite. Find that balance point and allow yourself to feel it as often as you can. This capacity for inner harmony catapulted my civilization rapidly into unforeseen capacities for advancements in all areas of life—personal, technological, and cultural.

"I care about you, Adele, and wish you everything noble and good for your life."

Remaining silent for a moment, Adele spoke softly as she continued to imbibe the kindness he'd conveyed. "Thank you. I feel the profound truth of what you said and I'm absorbing it with love and appreciation. You are a true sweetheart."

Bob smiled humbly at Adele, and turned to embrace Grace tenderly once again. Winking at her humorously, he began morphing into sparkling scintillating light which disappeared into the ether.

A moment of quietude ensued before Sophia broke the reverie saying reflectively, "After the events we experienced tonight, I see clearly that the opposite views of the elite and the working class are still at odds. However, why would we fight them in any form of rebellion? For our small group and for humanity, it's not about battling a Synarchy or the Middays of this world. We don't need to know or control the future. What if we are willing to live in curiosity and embrace our insecurities and raise our frequency in each moment? In the aftermath of this event, I saw that many in Midday's clan could become exhausted. After all, a lot of energy is required to sustain such intense chaos.

"Because we experienced infinite quantum realities carrying us from the confines of the surface into an unimaginable world of giants, we know that the *wild unknown* is our ally, rather than rigid theories and ideologies. We can continue to share what we've learned without pushing our viewpoints on anyone. How is it helpful to insist on common viewpoints when it was our multiplicity of differences that made our trip to the giants work so well? I immensely value each unique contribution to our group. The glue of our diversified circle is pure love and tons of respect for each other. I envision us sharing that love and respect with others at every opportunity.

"Everyone of us is always willing to risk plunging into the unknown and our next adventure is no different. This coordinate is highly revered by the giants. I am getting excited to go there and I am sensing Grace's anticipation. Am I right?"

Grace answered by flashing an exuberant smile towards Sophia.

"Thank you for letting me express my heart just now. "Sophia said, "I'm still reeling from what happened tonight at the cove.

It's a lot to process." Taking in a breath of rejuvenating solace and finding further composure, she added, "Sweet friends, you are beyond amazing, and I love you so much!"

Her words landed in a quiet space that she shared for a few moments with her friends. The silent atmosphere was broken only by the crashing waterfall pouring over massive, mossy boulders. The three women sat motionless with eyes closed and soft faces.

After a few minutes, Grace's awareness arrived back in the present moment and she cleared her throat as the cue for everyone to open their eyes.

With a sly smile, she looked at Sophia saying, "Now that we have time to let the world do what they do best, create like crazy and love without boundaries, let's go raise our frequencies in an astonishing coordinate of light.

"Adele, like you, I'm ready to relinquish that awful grimoire. As Sophia said, its retirement is clearly justified and well-timed. In that high frequency space, the inhabitants will know how to transmute its frequencies into the essence of pure love."

Adele called for her girls who dried their feet hurriedly on the spongey landscape near the pond and ran towards their mom on a surface unlike anything they were familiar with. The green colors that saturated the exquisitely lush site were as calming as sitting in a gorgeous meadow at the apex of a perfect summer day.

The friends gathered in a circle and everyone centered themselves in preparation to enter a mystical coordinate that had supported humanity for eons. When the portal to this subtle coordinate in the body of Gaia opens, it welcomes guileless, uninhibited souls and boundless lovers of Essence to enter into its transformative powers and awe-inspiring magnificence.

# CHAPTER 34

# GRACE AND ARCS

The group's immersion into silent preparation to enter the sacred space of mystical light was abruptly interrupted.

Looking nervous and frazzled, Kellie admitted she was not ready to access the coordinate. With her mother's eyebrows raised in bewilderment, Kellie addressed Grace. "My mind isn't still enough. Grace, can I talk to you alone? I need to ask you something."

"Of course. What is it?" Grace asked, with a look of curiosity.

Looking amused and definitely puzzled, Adele, Leisa and Sophia shrugged their shoulders and walked a few paces away to give Kellie space to speak with Grace in private.

As soon as they were past hearing range, Kellie proceeded to explain her predicament: "What's happening is that my mind's been going crazy ever since Bob beamed down. I can't get centered because I'm a basket case. Promise not to judge me?"

Looking totally confused, Grace nodded.

"I've been watching from a distance and I notice that when Bob's around, you two have something special. Not just romantic. You seem like a perfect match. There's a guy that I like and he likes me a lot. He's cool and he's super sweet. Recently, on my eighteenth birthday, we went on a date—he had me swooning— beautiful flowers and an amazing, romantic dinner. That night is my best memory ever. But even with all that *amazingness*... I'm not sure if we have the magical *something* that you have with Bob... What is it?"

Smiling and taking a deep breath, Grace began to share her love story with Bob. "I'll do my best to explain *the magical something* I have with Bob. By the way, I can't judge you for asking a question that generations of women have asked when confronted with deciding if someone is a good fit for them. It's a big deal. I get that, sweetie.

"When Bob and I met, I was dealing with emotional wounds from childhood. That word, *wound*, is often used in psychology along with the word *trauma*. My father and Sophia's dad were Synarchists and to be honest, they were tough, cold, and ruthless—true confession about that part of our lives. I'm being honest with you because I cannot adequately answer your question if I sugar coat my process of solidifying my relationship with Bob. It wasn't all heavenly bliss and yummy kisses.

"I felt a kinship with Bob that I'd never experienced with anyone I'd dated. And... well... I held back from getting really close to him. At that time, although *trust* was not my claim-to-fame, I was definitely in love with him.

"Until I met him, no one else, except Sophia, understood my world view and my capacity for seeing things that others don't see. He was such a good listener. I slowly felt safer confiding in him and letting him get to know the real me. At the time, I could not sustain my frequency high enough consistently to visit his city but I was able to go to the countryside nearby. This is where I first entered one of their *Arcs of Light*. Technically, it's a *sphere* of light with half of it visible on the surface, so what we see is a beautiful arc.

"The arcs are technology that is designed to advance human evolution. His ancestors were shamans from approximately twenty thousand years ago, maybe more. They had to go underground because they were being slaughtered on the surface. They evolved and grew as a community in one of the myriad caverns under the surface that you've seen. Their collective frequencies rose higher, they knew how to connect with star beings, and they evolved even more. The arcs are a technology where family members, friends, or lovers sit and face each other. The arc emits pristine light codes that support truth, courage, compassion, love, and serenity.

"The arcs of light, frequency, and electromagnetism are conscious beings, as much as we are. They interact with a human as a conscious, living friend. They are not following their creator's data programming—that's what we are familiar with on the surface—versus quantum computing. This is a technology that is designed to support and interact in the highest frequencies that the receiver can harmoniously handle with ease. It will never fry your circuits, overwhelm you, or control you in any way.

"I'll give you another example of what I call *conscious technologies* which interact with us by reading our frequencies. My first meal in his city was an example of this kind of technology. We were seated for dinner at a gorgeous, glass-top, oval table. The table was amazing! Bob's family had a larger table that seated eight people and three smaller round ones with four seats. When I sat, the chair morphed to my body perfectly, even though it didn't have any padding. I was completely comfortable. Bob invited me to place my hands on the table and allow my consciousness to connect with it. Then, release my hands and wait for the meal. That was a bit trippy but a lot of things with Bob seemed weird at first. Following his instructions, I connected with the glass-like surface in front of me.

"In less than thirty seconds, the table changed colors and slowly, like magic, a meal appeared. Vegetables were on my plate, some familiar and some not. As I tasted the food with a huge smile on my face, Bob smiled, too. He told me that the consciousness of the table took a reading of my taste buds, my nutritional needs in that moment, and my metabolism's capacity to assimilate the food and the food materialized from *the field*. In the blink of an eye, it presented my perfect meal. I was always amazed when I sat at that table. It's not that I was deciding on what I wanted nor was this conscious table giving me choices. Together, we blended our frequencies and with its capacity for reading my frequencies and individualized consciousness, a meal materialized. This was a moment of the feedforward and feedback mechanism of the astonishing field we are indelibly linked to. It's not like 3-D printed food. Instead of algorithms or other ways of calculating how to *make* 3-D food, Bob's table allows my consciousness to engage with its consciousness within the field—creating an explosion of nutritional bliss and perfection. I'm still blown away by my culinary experiences at Bob's house.

"And another astonishing technology is the *conscious arcs* that I mentioned. Those magnificent beauties were inconceivably powerful in helping me to enter deeply into my relationship with Bob. The first three times that I sat in one, I cried the whole time. I can say for sure that I was not crying in a sad way. It was like a giant release of a heavy energy in me; it felt good to cry that hard. While I sobbed, my dear Bob sat looking at me compassionately, saying nothing. He let me process deeply ingrained emotions, inner patterns, beliefs, and conclusions about life.

"Experiencing the consciousness of the arc was like being held by a nurturing force of nature. Becoming aware of its immense benevolence and compassion, I felt safe to feel and release painful emotions, and to become aware of any frequency that weighed me down. Bob simply sat with me. He never said anything and didn't ask questions later.

"Each session was followed by wild dreams and lots of journaling. I was relieved and appreciative that Bob never asked me anything.

"The fourth visit was life transforming and *sealed the deal* with Bob. As usual, we sat facing each other and the arc's light enveloped us in rainbows and sparkles. It was mesmerizing to be in it and feel the frequencies running through me. And then it happened... My mind went blank and I became pure light. I was not aware of Bob or myself. I was whirling light... deliciously soaring out of body... within zero awareness of time or space. I was freedom itself. I have no idea how long that lasted but as my awareness came back to Bob and the arc around us, I saw him differently. I could clearly see his absolutely astonishing, totally bodacious energy fields, I could receive and absorb his subtle light and emit the vibrations of love in a relaxed way. There was no longer resistance to love, bliss, or the wild expansion of pure peacefulness.

"Once again Bob said nothing—until later that evening. He held me close and tenderly asked me if I loved him. My response was a gigantic, roaring YES! Every cell in my being felt it and I knew it was true, without question! I'd had a chance to work with the arc technology that brings about emotional, physical, and mental well-being, by creating space and safety for me to do my inner work.

"Although I had done therapies and healing techniques, Bob's culture found a way to get to the deep places inside my psyche, heal the emotional bondage, and then I could move forward from a higher state of consciousness. Memories would come up, for example, and I'd process them instantly, understanding the lessons I could learn from them in the blink of an eye, and I'd feel compassion and empathy for everyone involved. Miraculously, without more ado, my energy field would totally up-shift. It was astonishing!

"His response that night was so sweet and a bit humorous. His vocabulary was something that I had to get used to. He knows all languages so he has a vast repertoire of words and he uses them lavishly, especially when he feels strong emotions.

"He said, 'I love you, too. You are an incandescent soul and brave surface dweller... a gorgeous *philocalist* who arrived in my life like a *zephyr* ... *orphic* by nature ... And you are also *easy on the eyes!*'

He made that proclamation combining his usual playfulness, tenderness, and authenticity. Admittedly, his articulation of the English language was a bit baffling but I liked it. I was smitten, completely. He had me swooning.

"I definitely needed to find the translation for several of the words he used, which left me crying like a baby. He was saying that I saw beauty in everything, and I blew into his life like a soft, welcomed breeze, and my nature defied understanding. For him, I was wild, free and *enchanting*. Whoa! Finally someone didn't think my eccentricities and worldview were weird! He embarrassed the heck out of me by saying that he couldn't stop looking at me. My aura was *exquisite*. Oh... that's so Bob! He's so darn sweet and totally amazing. I've helped him over the years to speak more clearly to *surface dwellers* and he's taught me invaluable lessons. I'll explain.

"To begin, I need to tell you more about the arcs because over the years, I've seen neighbors, friends, and family members in his community sitting under them. Near his city, there are at least a dozen arcs.

"I want to be clear that no one relies on the arc. Everyone who sits within one is agreeing to do their own inner work. Yet they've found a place to do personal or group work together in a safe, loving haven. In my case, sometimes a memory came up and I took time outside the arc to process it. I had a lot to uncover and consider, and there was no rush to *fix* myself or try to change in any way. It was a gentle process of self discovery because of the support I had.

"One of my greatest memories of visiting Bob's city was watching children gather under the arcs in small groups to engage with each other, playing within the frequencies of the arc. It's a gorgeous moment to see them spontaneously displaying their higher frequencies through hugging, talking, and sometimes making up games. They got to feel higher frequencies becoming established in their being.

"With these amazing technologies, Bob and I have an edge in growing old together in love and peacefulness. We have the arcs as our friends. All technologies in Bob's world are conscious, which creates a mutually respectful relationship with them, as friends. Nothing is considered to be only a 3-D, material object.

"This kind of conscious technology is the reason people from his city began coming to the surface. They shared the concept of conscious, living technologies with select citizens without showing them how to create them.

"For many centuries, they worked with surface citizens who were hurting and who were able to do the intense inner work necessary to develop a capacity to live from the exquisite essence of themselves. Bob and his colleagues took these people to his city during their dream state, letting them experience an arc. They often worked with researchers, scientists, and others in technical fields. Around the late 1980's, there was a shift in the Earth's frequencies that people on the surface didn't detect in the way that Bob's culture did.

"At the same time, researchers introduced Bob to people in academia, wholistic healthcare, and healing arts. More arc visits occurred in people's dreams. Sophia began to work with arcs in her own lucid dream states. Her consciousness was sitting in an arc while her body rested snuggly in her bed on the surface. This was not a normal dream state but one in which she was acutely aware of what was going on. She was feeling and experiencing viscerally everything that was happening.

"Bob's culture would not give the blueprints for the arcs to anyone on the surface. His culture is certain that people holding high frequencies will discover the arc's blueprint on their own, just as his ancestors did. They believe it is necessary for inner development to occur first, including the capacity to raise one's own frequency, in order to access such technologies.

"This reasoning is similar to why your group prepared so intensely to go under the surface. Your training and inner work allowed you to raise your frequencies whenever necessary, and to maintain high frequencies. Your elevated vibes were required to engage with the advanced technologies you encountered.

"The world has to be ready for the arc's technology on a *frequency* basis. No one can steal the technology or abuse it. If they tried to put the blueprint into a computer, it would disappear. If they tried to build it, the blueprint would not work. Something stolen is low frequency. Anything obtained from the shadows is shadow-level frequency. In practical terms, that means that if someone built an arc for manipulation, greed, fear, or pride, it simply won't perform. One thing I'm sure of is that this high frequency technology is meant for a world where honesty, love, and respect are part of the culture. It's budding now on the surface. And that's why you and I, and our close friends, are able to come to the arcs in physical form, for the first time in history.

"In the decade after 2020, the world started to look behind and under what they'd been told. Consequential secrets came to light globally and yes, chaos ensued. Regardless, higher frequencies emerged. Communities are thriving. The remnants of Midday's style of living are dying out. Old structures will give way to a world without pseudo-parents running governments—no one at the top creating and enforcing rules that supposedly benefit everyone. Human consciousness on the surface is high-jumping past all of that.

"I'm particularly looking forward to hearing young people like you talk about the best kept secret ever—which is that the sun, planets, and stars *know us* and, through consciousness, communicate constantly as sentient beings. We've been taught otherwise, but the doubters are fooling themselves. I can let myself be fooled or communicate openheartedly with everything in the unified field. In a nutshell, I'm saying we all have to get our heads around unified physics. Bob's take on this subject is that universes and everything in them arise from harmonious wave patterns which cannot be suffocated or altered just because someone doesn't believe they are real. The truth is that they remain amazing wave patterns, whether we believe in them or not. I'm betting you get this intuitively."

"I get it," Kellie said looking enthralled and quizzical. "But I have a question: How can a planet have a brain? You said Gaia and the planets are *conscious*."

"Yep, you heard me right!" Grace said giggling. "I'm laughing because when Bob dropped that truth-bomb on me, I had the same response you did. It isn't about having a brain. I'm speaking about *consciousness* as a feedback loop that allows for a data exchange with *the field*. Gaia receives information from the field constantly (and sends information back into the field), as all people and planets do, because *protons* do.

"There was a super cool experiment that Bob told me about, in which scientists studied octopi to see if they had goal-oriented behavior. They don't have a brain like ours, BUT they seem to know what they need to do when a predator is near or when food is nearby. The researchers were studying complex bio-physics so we'd be above our heads to try to get into the nitty gritty of it, but let's just say that if octopi can send and receive information from the field, why can't Gaia, Jupiter, and our sun do the same thing? I see her as sentient because she is a living organism; she may have a different physical structure than us, but she is alive and able to connect with the field like we do.

"Does that shift how you perceive her? And can you see that you are continually in a feedback loop of information with *the field*? Your thoughts about the guy you are concerned about go into the field, and if you are open-hearted, you get intuitive "feels" about him in return. Let that sink in. I know you have intuitive feelings but maybe you doubt them or your emotions override them."

"This makes sense," Kelly said, pensively. "Sophia knows about Gaia's consciousness doesn't she? I'm asking because she talks about Gaia like she is a friend, someone who you can communicate with, even if its telepathic. And she and Nate had a telepathic kind of love. It sounds like he really *got her.*"

"Great observation," Grace said. "She and I hold the perspective that with so much information that has been revealed about the field, we can't go back and *un-know what we know.* Gaia isn't just a pile of rocks, minerals, and chemicals for us to mine and build houses on. She's amazing! I bet the other planets in our solar system think so! And about Nate, he and Sophia were highly intuitive. And they cultivated it through studying *the field* and noticing when they were connecting with each other naturally through the mechanism of consciousness."

"Grace, you are so cool!" Kellie said, then slid into a plethora of youthful giggles. "Talking about all of this makes me feel better because I get how I could be receiving information from the field about the guy I mentioned. It's coming through as a *knowing* that he likes me. But then I get scared I'm wrong. And I *feel* the scary stuff happening on the surface will be okay, but what if I'm wrong about that, too? How can I trust *the feeling*?"

"Listen carefully, sweetie pie. There's a phenomenal future for you to look forward to here and on the surface. There's no need to focus on the *scary stuff* and the only way to test *the feeling* is to do what Nate and Sophia did. Practice and check your results. It's not the end of the world if you somehow misinterpret the information coming through as *the feeling.* Check how your heart feels when the information comes to you. That's my gauge. My heart has proven to be reliable. If it's okay, I'd rather not get too *heady* and analytical about your innate wisdom. I trust it and with practice I'm sure you will, too. Right now, I'd rather prepare you for our next adventure into the unknown, unexpected, mind-boggling possibilities of the quantum field.

"Was all of this talk about consciousness, magical tables, arcs, and *the feeling* helpful? I know this has been a long answer to your question, with a few spin-offs to related subjects, but relationships and loving are complex to explain and comprehend. That's my take on it. And I feel compelled to add that the complexity is like fabric—it's easy to unravel it and get down to pure thread, which is *the feeling* in your heart.

"If you have insecurities about this wonderful guy, look at them as emotional patterns inside yourself. You can take them to an arc when we get to Bob's city. How about that? Remember that insecurities can be repurposed into confidence. Buuuut... if your intuition says that this guy isn't yet willing to work on himself, think twice. Your relationship-antennae may be alerting you for a good reason. Bob wasn't my first rodeo. Before him, I decided to override my intuition a few times and found out that the guy wasn't right for me. It's a learning curve.

"So, there you have it. That's my advice. Gee, Kellie, I feel like I just talked your ear off!"

"Oh no, Grace! I love this! I want to sit in an arc. Would you sit with me?"

Tenderly, Grace took Kellie's hands in hers and said, "I would be honored to sit with you in an arc, angel-girl."

"My mind settled down. I feel better now. Thanks, Grace!"

After wrapping Kellie tenderly in a warm hug, Grace turned to the group and asked them to gather closer.

"Before we go into this next place, your experience will be much easier if I explain a few things." Her innocent doe-eyes started sparkling with childlike exhilaration as she continued. "It's aquatic, yet the water is crystal clear and isn't as dense as our lakes or oceans. As we enter the water—which is more like plasma than water—Bob says that we can actually breathe, because we will have moved into our light bodies rather than our particle forms. The area of this ethereal yet physical place is vast. It will be amazing to go there! Heads up... Bob said that wafts of scents, familiar or not, are frequencies. No need to search for their source. Our senses adapt easily yet we are in a location of rarified light-codes that affect *how* our senses function... WAY different than we normally experience on the surface. As sound influences and amplifies higher octaves of hearing, or scent activates a subtle sense of smell, we can also *feel* highly-charged, exhilarating emotions. Bob's advice is to let go of thinking and allow yourself to enjoy the experience. The beings we'll meet are extremely high frequency. They speak only through telepathy and are constantly broadcasting love and brilliant, effulgent light codes into the ether. It may be hard to relate to a life like that, but there have been people on the surface who have done similar spiritual work for millennia.

"These high frequency, goddess-like beings, extended a personal invitation to each of us, which is an incredible honor. We will simply follow their lead and they'll guide us. Under the surface, people refer to what we will experience as *high emittance*, which is the capacity to emit elevated frequencies. Okay friends, get ready for the subtlest of subtle experiences ever!"

Kellie and Leisa hugged Adele with giggles and excitement. Grace looked at Sophia.

"When we were young," she said, "we used to dream of places like this. I am beyond grateful we are going there together." They smiled tenderly at one another. "And now... shall we enter?"

# CHAPTER 35

# VULNERABLE AND PROTECTED

Sitting at the entrance to the high frequency space, the spellbound friends allowed their minds to move gradually, gently, and purposefully into delta brain waves. They knew from practice that deep delta wavelengths spark the possibility for experiencing a sublime state, captivating their minds and carrying their souls into subtle aspects of gentleness and eternal space.

Bob was well aware that, unlike esoteric rituals that incite a mystical experience of an altered state of consciousness, they were entering a unique coordinate within Gaia where inhabitants live continuously in high vibrations.

After eons of doing the kind of inner work that Grace, Sophia, and their friends practiced each day, the women in this coordinate of mystical light remained immersed in ever-ascending levels of consciousness. They no longer lived with the limitations of spacetime realities.

Bob's mother, Avella, was the epitome of warm-heartedness, keen intelligence, and stateliness. Communicating reverence for the coordinate and its mystifying inhabitants, she explained that it was specifically conducive to female frequencies. No male entered, but instead journeyed through a companion space, focused solely on masculine vibrational emanations. The permanent residents in this place were descended from generations of an unbroken lineage. She explained that the females reproduce through ritualized immaculate conception with the presence of males in another specific, high frequency coordinate.

As Grace and her friends explored the novel landscapes, Bob sipped his family's nourishing tea in the comfort of his childhood home. Recalling his youthful journeys among the elevated frequencies, he said with wonderment that he would be honored to hear his sisters' and mother's experiences of this subtle coordinate.

A few months earlier, Avella and his sisters had shared that Grace and her friends would have the chance to have an experience in a mystical land which few souls dare to enter. His mother had explained that the women would enter by allowing the delta waves of their brain to engulf them in quietude and tranquility. Soon thereafter, they would make a sacred transition into their light body—the form that each human takes when they sleep and move through subtle realms in a dream state.

With tender affection and heartfelt respect and admiration for Grace, Sophia and their friends, Bob said, "When I explained that entering the feminine realm would require new gene expression in their hearts, brains, and bellies, they were adamant they'd be ready. Since part of that process activates certain neuronal cells which, in turn, activate stem cells in the brain, I let them know that to be ready for this journey, epigenetics (environment influences) must be brought to bear. Without hesitation, they were ready to undertake the required immersion in high frequential chambers in our laboratory. When Grace was inside, I checked to see how she was feeling. She told me she was *having a blast*. What an interesting vocabulary my dear wife expresses! I was worried that she felt like she was going to explode, perhaps *blast* into oblivion, so I suggested she drop out of the process and see if anyone else was experiencing this *blasting* effect. She laughed until she cried. And once again, I gained further clarity into the English language."

Avella smiled, locked her gaze with Bob's, and took his hands in hers in a loving exchange—extolling his brilliance with languages and his ability to humbly learn their nuances. With her elegant, sagacious demeanor, Avella asked Sandara to tell Bob more about what was happening for Grace in her unfolding "extraordinary journey."

Smiling radiantly at her brother, Sandara said that the women would slowly emerge from light into the form of a subtle, female deer. In the experience of being and feeling the energy of a doe, they would soar, letting go of all striving, survival fears, or any other form of dense energies, as though she has mystical wings, akin to Pegasus or a unicorn.

As Bob had mentioned, Grace and her friends prepared carefully for this invaluable encounter by expressing new genetic patterns. In order to elevate into the exalted vibrations that Sandara had described, intense concentration was required. Another vital component to this experience would be their full identification with the subatomic particles that underly their neurons and associated vibrational neuron-patterns. The women's consciousness must become fully identified with those subtle patterns of vibration. The astonishing similarities between the human neural network and its higher fractal, the universal grid, would become evident to them. The entire grid of the cosmos would be affected by their elevated frequencies and, more astonishingly for Grace and her friends to accept, they would be in a harmonious position to rise in frequency endlessly. Grace said the thought of that left her *gob smacked and dizzy.*

Self identification as form would emerge into awareness of their subtle architecture. Their lower vibrations associated with self and personal identity would no longer be at the forefront of consciousness. There would no longer be mental analysis but rather a synchronicity with everything in this domain, every atom connected to all other atoms through subtle waves of vibration and energy—atoms of water, moss, and rocks connecting naturally with each other and the women. Feeling each other subtly in a sacred experience of infinite, pristine unicity, their subatomic and atomic structure would be shimmering with pure love, which would be emanating into the unified field. They would likely experience miracles, as their higher frequency expression would break the dam of normal reality—bursting like a roaring river of light, sound, and frequency to create an otherwise impossible reality.

In ethereal form, Sandara said they would swim through rivers of light, travel into a giant dome where the walls display scenes from their life—each moment sparkling and shimmering and then disappearing as delicate, vaporous light. Swirling around the perimeter of the luminescent, golden dome, they would be able to see a multitude of past moments of fear that had been embedded as feelings of being vulnerable and unsafe.

One by one, the scenes would begin to disperse into light as the energy within the dome intensifies to the extent that the women might momentarily feel they could shatter or be torn apart. Instead, their particles would gently disperse into innumerable sparkling photons of light.

From mystical deer, they would then shift form into an immense column of light, roaring upwards into an unknown space of powerful energy. Their light body would then begin to lose form. Beyond pure photons of light, they then transform into the pure light of Essence, soaring through its own power and moving steadily towards its center point. Their subtle architecture would fully engage and lock into a spiral of massively elevated consciousness, eventually landing gently, gracefully in a state of ecstatic union with the light of Essence.

Bob's sisters and mother agreed that to describe the next part would be impossible because the frequency is so high there are no words on the surface or under it that adequately capture the awe-inspiring magnificence of the experience. Avella said the next phase of this transcendent journey takes them to the core of an ancient, inherently mystical experience. It is reserved for those who dare to go beyond fear and focus on supreme bliss uninhibitedly. They would return knowing they are continuously protected, loved, and acknowledged as sacred beings of light. This assurance does not come from an outside source; rather, it emerges from Essence. After entering the mystical unknown courageously, they will emerge with all subtle levels of their being purified and renewed in rarified light codes.

Bob's mother took his hands once again and gently held them, saying, "As you know, Grace will come back with Sophia, Adele, and her girls and she will look the same. But she won't be the same, because she touched the face of sacredness and perfection inside herself, as pure light. These women will not only know cognitively, they will have experienced that the exalted vibrations they'd yearned for have been inside themselves all along—as the infinite light of Essence.

"Grace will go to the surface on occasion but she and Sophia will come here more often. You are aware they will age less and even now they do not look the same as their friends who are the same surface age. The physical form slows down its aging process under the earth due to spacetime differences between our city and the surface. Particles here spin at a different speed. Our atmosphere is higher ionically and vibrationally. These women bravely stepped into the unknown and into higher frequencies within themselves. There will be less possibility for anything or anyone to magnetize them into denser ways of relating to themselves or others.

"I want to remind you to give Grace a lot of space. We must do the same for all of these courageous women. As I said, they will look the same, but are being transformed energetically as we speak. On the quantum levels of their atomic structure they are undergoing a transformation. Thus their overall physical structures as well as their emotional and mental faculties will gradually and naturally process and normalize this monumental upshift in frequencies. We need to support them as they allow this far-reaching process of higher evolution to unfold and mature in each of them—in a way that is uninhibited, comfortable, and absolutely graceful."

His mother became silent and lowered her head as she released Bob's hands.

Listening intently to the conversation, Sandara said, "Let us go to the arc and sit as a family. It is such an honor to be blessed by our sister, Grace, who is joining her soul sisters on this mystical, transformative journey into the Light of Essence."

The family rose simultaneously, like a herd of deer that had been resting. As they moved towards the closest arc, it shimmered brightly in rainbows of blue and volet light, its consciousness welcoming them with incredible beauty.

Bob's family sat in the arc, waiting with calm attention. From the place where Grace, Sophia, Adele, and her daughters had entered the mystical, earthly reality of subtleness, they now emerged to the thundering waterfall and the delicate beauty of the orchids. Every flower appeared as golden light with soft white streams of luminescence pouring from their centers.

Sophia had entered the sacred space holding the wretched grimoire. Now she emerged with an ethereal white lotus in her hands. Suddenly, it burst in a flash of iridescent, cobalt particles, shimmering in the air—the transmutation of its dark embodiment into pure light was complete.

Sophia and her companions remained tranquil, their faces soft, radiating happiness. They walked as though the ground under their feet was gently buoyant. Without conversation, comparing notes, or even making eye contact, they simply headed directly to the arc where Bob and his family had gathered, now smiling gently and empathetically. The arc's light radiated lavishly as far as they could see. The splendor of its beauty captivated the group who were silent, allowing the high frequency light to communicate its language of pure love and bliss.

After ample time to soak in the mystical vibrations of the arc, one by one, they proceeded towards Bob's house; a meal awaited them to refresh their bodies completely.

After her friends left the arc, Sophia remained in place. Sitting in the center, still and steady. Gradually, a column of golden light appeared that was three arm-lengths wider than her outstretched arms. The column seemed to extend into the heights and depths of infinity.

Belstar felt a shift in his consciousness and traveled post-haste to engage Kandor. He wanted to view the hologram in Kandor's cave without delay. Since this cave was also a space craft, it was designed with advanced technologies that were a blessing for Belstar in this moment.

"Something epic is happening. Gaia is trembling with ecstatic love and my heart space is throbbing with immense bliss. I want to share this moment with you, dear friend. I am sure that Sophia has reached a level of consciousness in which she is experiencing the truth of herself. This was the next step I've been hoping for. Will you join me at the hologram?"

Kandor's smile illumined his friend's heart as they went to the hologram and settled in to view what was happening for Sophia.

Belstar's mouth was agape with awe. Kandor, usually stoically composed, responded in the same way.

As Sophia's arms remained fully unfurled, her heart space stretched upward; receptive to the energy pouring into the deepest recesses of her being. With the expansion of her consciousness, a large, emerald octagon began to glow, covering her upper chest. In unending streams of blinding light, ethereal harmonics and sacred geometric patterns of scintillating light soared in and out through its magnificent golden center point.

Ascending further into exalted vibrations, ribbons of blue light streamed within the full length of the column and the area of her upper chest burst into shades of indigo, violet, and golden light.

"Dear friend," Belstar said, immobile with wonderment. "In full power and immense glory, the subtle energies continue to grow profoundly intense in Sophia. She has completely abandoned her senses, mind, and ego. The perceptive light spectrum in this subtle reality in spacetime is invisible on the surface of Gaia. Only her unconscious mind and the Essence from which this majestic experience unfolds are present to witness this profound moment.

"She has reached the point at which time is suspended and space has no meaning. This is pristine communion with the eternal quantum field which emerges and then folds back into itself endlessly. Since that incomprehensible progression repeats itself with such consistency, the experience remains seamless and ever-dynamic at the same time, and the soul elevates to triumphant heights of magnificence. As her awareness of spacetime and relationship with the material world expands beyond its dense levels of form, profound imprinting of exalted vibrations occurs in her energy fields. This dynamic, pivotal imprint will remain with her, expand, and influence the rest of her life."

Pausing as his sagacious eyes gently closed for a moment, he took in a deep yet delicate breath. His eyes glistened and sparkled like starry sunlight dancing on a serene lake. As fervency intermingled with a warmhearted paternal bond, he said approvingly, "This event will have a radical impact on her because she has been mastering the art of reflection and assimilation of profound subtle phenomena and occurrences, which transform from being a source of amazement to a revelation of her true Self. She places great value on her inner experiences and welcomes them fully, without doubt or trepidation.

"Her life experiences will become immeasurably enriched with palpable transformation happening with more ease; her soul will ascend endlessly. Drenching her mind and body in exalted vibrations in this way allows her consciousness to rise to a higher level of awareness so that daily experiences can become more subtle—continually refreshed in the repeated connection with the infinite, subtle field in and around her.

"By integrating with higher awareness like this, she is getting closer to remembering who she is. Nothing could be more auspicious for her or humanity. As she engages with her essence, she is naturally radiating high frequency light codes into the quantum field. Gaia feels it and is trembling with joy. Sophia is hitting her stride, rising up as the master that she is capable of being. As in her former missions to this planet, Sophia remains willing to move through her earthly conditioning to generate elevated frequencies for herself and the multiverse. I remain eternally in awe of her."

"Belstar, let us sit for a moment and notice the increasing number of humans who are in sync with Sophia's high vibrations. Like her, they are elevating their consciousness exponentially. It's like a wildfire of amazing magnitude and ferocity as it roars energetically across the cosmos. Unicity is fueling the fire and unconditional, pure love is adding wind to the blazing flames. Apathy and disregard are turning to ash. This is a moment to celebrate!"

"Let us open our hearts in support of her and our beloved human species. An auspicious day has arrived for humanity's potential evolution and continued survival. May she and they bombard *the field* now and forever with uplifting vibrations and rise in frequency even higher. Time is of the essence.

"Today's event is welcome news for the immeasurable multiverse!"

# CHAPTER 36

# AFTERMATH OF TIMELESS DIMENSIONS

Sitting on the porch at Mystic Cove, Jake and John sipped steaming, aromatic coffee, while fidgeting and looking down the driveway expectantly. The birds twittered and chirped ecstatically while golden rays of effulgence poured from the horizon like a grand announcement of a long-awaited celebration. Without the slightest hesitancy, the comrades leapt to their feet in unison, bearing dazzling smiles, while scurrying hastily to the approaching car. Sophia barely emerged when she was embraced by her beloved friends vigorously and with warm endearment.

"How are you, girlfriend?!" Jake said, wiping away uninhibited tears. Daring to plumb the depths of her penetrating eyes, they synchronized momentarily in a blazing gaze of indelible friendship. Taking a deep breath to steady himself from a potential free-fall into emotional layers that had been building for months, he said, "After your wild experience in those ephemeral realms under the surface, we wanted to give you plenty of space but shit, we've used up our steadily dwindling cache of patience. Plus we *flat-out* missed you to the moon and back!"

John's smile was so broad and his heart so full that he could not speak at first. Tears had swept his eyes clean of all pretense. Clearly as joyous as Jake to be in her company, his voice crackled feebly with tender feelings as he said, "It's so damned good to see you! Holy cow! Jake's right. We were losing patience and contemplated going to your house to make sure you were okay. But we resisted the impulse, in case we inadvertently eclipsed your processing of an inconceivably subtle event. Let's get into it!

"We have everything ready so you can make your favorite tea. Jake found your special cup. It's ready for you to fill with a bodacious, fragrant brew."

They walked to the porch talking cheerfully as though no time had passed between them. After a couple of minutes, Sophia poured a cup of tea and joined them on the porch—looking across the skyline at the mesmerizing beauty of a mystically imbued dawn at the cove. Nature provided breathtaking sunrises consistently, even though each one was a unique masterpiece of creation.

"Okay! I owe you an explanation. I would have leaned into impatience too, if you'd gone silent for months on end. But I needed time to process the totally astonishing epiphanies. Ready for mind-bending, inner revelations? You know me. This won't be anything your minds nor mine could conjure up."

Jake raised his brows, lost for words at first. Then he found his composure again, saying, "We're clearly gob smacked by your intro. Come clean with everything." Glancing at John, and winking with his customary lightheartedness, he said, "My buddy and I are all ears, right?"

John smiled cheerfully, nodded his head, and took a substantial gulp of coffee. Adjusting his posture and leaning towards her intently, he prepared himself for her revelations.

"When we returned to the surface," she began, "Adele, her daughters, Grace and I waited a couple of weeks before we even debriefed with each other and shared the aftermath of our awe-inspiring experience. We cried, laughed, talked, and were speechless at times as we recounted rare moments in that mystical abode. That conversation was a helpful aspect of my integration process."

"How are they doing?" Jake asked, intrigued.

"You will not be surprised to hear that Kellie and Leisa integrated their experiences naturally and quickly. They are young enough not to be as mental as adults tend to be. Plus Adele raised them to be open-hearted and find connection to the field in daily life. They are doing great and Adele is gradually processing her elevated vibes in their high vibe company. She told us they are finding higher resonance with each other and *the field* itself."

She paused and giggled as she continued. "About Grace... I am laughing because seeing her was priceless. She was *lit*— that's how Kellie described her. That was an understatement. She's always been *a mystic*, with one foot in this world and the other in the infinite quantum field. I would have said she was *on fire* and so elevated in vibration that her vibe was contagious—visiting the ethereal realm was definitely a seminal event for her. She's been in bliss since we returned. She intuits that having the company of Bob's community is making her process of integration *way* easier and faster.

"Each of us processes higher realms and related influxes of frequencies in our own way. We did massive preparation and knew we'd need time to assimilate the frequencies we aligned with in that coordinate. Even though Bob warned us that our capacity to send and receive information from the field would accelerate immensely, we had to experience it to grasp the magnitude of what he was saying.

"By the time I departed the ephemeral coordinate, my DNA and consciousness—which is my feedforward-feedback mechanism with the field—had undergone a radical shift in frequency. Trying to navigate the world through the perspective of left-brain laws of *cause and effect* was disorienting and confusing. It was important for me to write about my subtle experiences. More than that, I needed to make sense of my emerging right brain perception, the timeless/infinite spaciousness emerging in my waking reality. Countless lucid dreams ensued, along with copious reflections of my experiences in that place of pure light under Gaia's surface. Plus I've been trying to find words for everything that unfolded in daily life afterwards."

Pausing for a moment, she said pensively, "I want to share a story that helped me understand and process what happened with my massive shift in consciousness. When Nate was getting close to his death, he began to speak about having conscious experiences of *subtler realities* and new understandings about consciousness as a feedforward-feedback mechanism with *the field*—particularly from the perspective of the *linear reality* that his *left-brained* lawyer mind gravitated towards. He contrasted the left-brain worldview with his burgeoning inner experience of the infinite, *unconscious*, right-brain perspective.

"At the time, I wasn't able to comprehend his elucidations of experiences that defied logic completely. Yet in that mystical coordinate I visited, I received a blast of clarity and developed insights about the subtle experiences Nate had tried to demystify for me. My sweetheart struggled to explain his experiences and processing with his *right brain, his unconscious mind,* in a way I could understand. It was futile to use my *left brain* linear thinking to grasp the timelessness and infinite spaciousness of the *right brain reality* he was describing.

"On a larger scale than individual humans, he believed that our ancient ancestors, tens of thousands of years ago, lived in *both* left brain and right brain unconscious time and space, perceiving daily life differently than humanity does now. That was a pretty wild truth-bomb he dropped on me. It was hard to fathom because, let's be honest, *can you measure his hypothesis via ancient skeletons, their DNA, or any other archeological findings? How can you measure consciousness in an ancient human?* The unfathomable truth was that he was meeting them in lucid dreams and endless hours of meditation.

"His lifetime with me was comprised of left-brain world views—time bound with cause and effect. The linear, left-brain-dominated world has its unique laws. It's only one vector, a specific, *limited wave* of spacetime, within the *infinite wave* of eternal time that arises from a central point and endlessly flows in all directions at once—a 360-degree endless wave as opposed to a single pulsed wave heading in one direction.

"See if you can fathom the *unconscious brain* experience in which *absolute time* is playing out and in that experience, we cannot have beginnings and endings nor do we experience cause and effect. There's only the eternal, present moment. Reality is not perceived in the same way in these two expressions of consciousness. The intake of information from *the field* is different when we use *left* brain versus *right*.

"The reality of these two world experiences cannot be the same because the information exchange with the field happens through *perception* such as *beginning and end* versus *eternal presence* perception, or *direction* versus *everywhere at once*.

That caused me to wonder if flying easily and breathing under water in dreamtime nudges us to bring the perception of *unconscious* possibilities into waking reality? After all, our highest nature *knows* these are possible under the right vibrational circumstances.

"Even with his continuously debilitating state, Nate was able to associate his *unconscious* experiences with an infinite data base of information, coming to him as important feedback from *the field* to expand his awareness. However, he observed that *linear* thinking often created fear when his left-brain tried to process *nonlinear* experiences. While he was in non-linear realities, fear did not exist. Fear of death, for example, only emerged when he considered what would happen when he died—as if it was part of a linear continuum. His ultimate epiphany was that death was governed by the *unconscious* laws of timelessness and infinite spaciousness. This led him to con-sider if there was an *after* life that was a continuum of this one or was he going to be in a *simultaneous life* that he was already living, beyond the constructs of linear time. Were meditation and lucid dreaming experiences of the infinite octave beyond linear *mind-life*? For me, that was way too trippy to grasp, but for Nate, it was becoming a lived experience.

"He explained it this way: He rode the river of life in a safe boat but at some point in spacetime it began to wear out. When it was finally no longer sea-worthy, it would sink and merge with the river in which it had always been floating. He said he'd freely left the boat behind in meditation and in lucid dreams, diving into the familiar, endless river. He was clear that when he dove consciously, through perception, into the eternal, nonlinear river of life, he experienced himself beyond death and life. This is the miracle hidden as a layer of perception within the vehicle in which he was traversing life's mystical, watery depths. He was awakening to the experience that this was where he'd been living all the time, unconsciously. When he bridged the conscious and unconscious, mind-bending experiences unfolded.

"Hang on, this part is wild for our linear mind. Without spatial boundaries he realized he could be experiencing endless replicas of himself on vast spacetime coordinates into eternity. His mind was becoming so unfettered that he realized he had access to unlimited individual expressions of himself and Essence itself. This happens because the unconscious reality is governed by different laws. He was not crazy, rather he was fully connected, through perception, to all-that-is. In the *unified field theory* of physics, he'd studied the multidimensional law of resonance with the field and he saw that he applied that to unconscious reality. He was *in resonance* with all-that-is.

"Now hang onto your hats, as Jake says. Nate courageously dove deeper into something he'd been undogmatically exploring for a very long time—*How can life be a one-shot experience if it arises from an endless field? How absolute is the law of nature for a soul to engage in a linear progression of lives—called reincarnation—given that the soul arises from an endless ocean of possibilities? Or to ask the question another way—How can our soul history be linear, if we are ultimately infinite beings who arise from and return to the infinite field?* He'd experienced his multidimensionality through meditation—riding his consciousness into endless dimensions of nonlinear realities. He'd perceived life this way to make sense of it. But he relegated the *infinite experiences* to meditation rather than to the truth of who and what he was. Realizing that his perception determined linear versus nonlinear experiences, with dogged determination, he allowed time and timelessness equal footing in his daily experience.

"After grappling with *before and after* death using linear perception, he wanted to go deeper. He'd been having endless nightmares, night after night, for several years. He could smell blood, hear the clanging of violent weapons, and felt the emotional pangs of cruelty and destruction. He'd been told by past life regression therapists and various healers that he had been a warrior in past linear time. Those provocative revelations became a wakeup call for his curious mind.

"Through the lens of the field theory of physics, he could perceive an important layer of understanding about his dreams. He and the other warriors could attract each other through aspects of *resonance* they each expressed. So the cruelty and guilt they felt got magnified *in Nate* because his brilliant mind, that made him a great attorney, was focusing on *this limited part* of warriors.

"Towards the end of his life, in *unconscious moments like meditation and sleep*, Nate came into a high vibe resonance with the feelings and world view of the warriors as *caring protectors of* others. He had a fortuitous epiphany—he *came into resonance* with various warriors in *the field*, regardless of whether or not they'd lived within his linear timeline. He was experiencing *parallel realities* in the infinite field with warriors with whom he was in resonance—*relative to caring and protecting loved ones or a community*. Adding to that, he realized that he resonated with philosophical systems and teachers in linear time, ancient and current, who elucidated humanity's unlimited nature and infinite capacity to experience and offer pure love while expressing unicity. His point was that he drew to himself *resonate frequencies* he shared with people in multiple realities and on multiple coordinates in spacetime. Their care for humanity, desire to protect fellow human beings, and offer pure love motivated him and them. He could perceive the spacetime coordinates in which they lived within the field. In resonance, together, they amplified the qualities in which he and they resonated. He'd been doing something good in those parallel realities while his linear mind labeled him as an egregious warrior who needed healing and forgiveness. My mind was thoroughly blown by this profound understanding of what was happening, within the incomprehensible magnificence of a quantum field of light, sound, and frequency.

"When I met with Nate in lucid dreams after his death, without spacetime to contend with, he expressed his state of being in the infinite field, devoid of linear time. He knew it would be a while before I could grasp his updated explanation of *simultaneous life in the field*, as he called it. Those kinds of informational exchanges made with anyone from a nonlinear timeline are always available to us through resonance with them in the unlimited field.

"For archeologist adepts like you, maybe it's time to dig deeper, with *resonance tools*, to measure the giant's nonlinear world? I am not sure how we will ever understand Max's world from linear, left-brain perception. He and his kin seem to be a different kind of human—walking a tightrope of linear and nonlinear perceptions. No wonder they could create architectures and technologies beyond our current understanding.

Even though they didn't think like we do, can we dip into *the field* to find ways to live like them at this time?

"What if our linear timeline vector can be imbued with nonlinear technologies and a collective perception based on unicity with all-that-is? Does that sound good?"

"You nailed it! This is nothing I expected," Jake said, wiping his brow and looking excited. "At first your words hit me like a tempest, but when the storm subsided, I got into resonance with everything you were saying. Nate sure went deep. There he was dying… and he was not giving up on exploring profound mysteries. The idea of heaven, hell, reincarnation… everything about life and death is up for review. One thing that rang true, loud and clear, was that simultaneous life is playing out in the field in and around us. It's *the field* that I want to explore with the same curiosity, sense of wonder and tenacity that your hubby did. Whoa, I am in awe of him and you. I assume you're still integrating the *nonlinear* experiences from your visit to that mythical coordinate and your subsequent meditations and dreams. Is that right?"

"Absolutely," she said looking relaxed and reflective. "The giants modeled integration and contemplation of daily experiences. They didn't consider anything to be mundane or something to gloss over. Neither do I. And I bet you don't either."

Staring into space while puzzling over unknown aspects of reality, Jake replied reflectively, "Nope, nothing is mundane, especially when it comes to the non-material world."

"I want to toss my response into the mix," John said pensively. "Nate jumped into that river, even before his boat decayed. That's my big takeaway. Whatever happens in that simultaneous life is likely filled with a hell of a lot of much-needed wisdom. We have access to it. I don't want to discover it on my deathbed. Sorry... Sophia, I don't mean any disrespect for Nate doing this deep dive at the end of his life. In fact, I admire him immensely. What I'm trying to convey is I don't want to wait another minute to do this kind of critical inner work, exploring nonlinear reality. And I'm curious as hell about searching for technologies that could read nuances of the *consciousness* of skeletons rather than simply looking into DNA, and other physical attributes. I'm on fire and befuddled at the same time."

"I get it," Sophia said. "We need to consider where we go from here. How will human evolution elevate to the next level? Our inner and outer work has to evolve with a focus on the *nonlinear world* of the infinite field. It's the only way forward. The stakes are too high to jump on a tired hamster wheel of technologies and science, while unicity and pure love wait like hidden jewels, ready to enrich our experience as high vibe humans in a field of unlimited potential. Thank you for being such good listeners. I love you so much! I need to leave now but we will stay in touch. From now on, I'll keep you updated on my inner adventures. You two remain my safe harbor where I can share crazy, ethereal escapades."

Jake tipped his hat and flashed a wry smile her way.

John stood to embrace her warmly, and with the innocence of a child mixed with raw, unfettered determination, he said, "We have a lot of work ahead. Our friendship inspires me to raise my vibe and kick into high gear. Let's get going! Love you, sister!"

# CHAPTER 37
## CIRCLE OF FRIENDSHIP

Several years elapsed for Gaia and her inhabitants while the surface world changed immensely. Many challenges ensued across the globe. From the ashes of their struggles, humanity rose like a giant Phoenix. Clearly, their response to life was changing. Humans looked within to their Essence and became more accepting of working with each other collectively to enact change.

Distinct yet harmonious communities like Avani's enclaves were becoming welcomed cornerstones of life throughout the world. Outdated cultural structures and long-held beliefs naturally dissolved, fostering an emergence of elevated human consciousness—with a higher frequency and access to more innate creativity than in any period in history.

Allowing for the mysteries of life to unfold and embracing open-ended questions was becoming the norm; full spectrum quantum science eclipsed rational, standard thought as the way forward. The unknown was exciting rather than treating it like an object of fear or an animal to cage and control.

Watching the radical changes unfold, Sophia wrote about them in real time through her daily blog and numerous books, with translation into many languages. She watched with awe and gratitude as an emphasis on local enclaves, authentic communication, unicity, and reciprocity between global citizens continued to heighten.

As the world prepared to embrace a new decade in 2040, Sophia published a book in which she described for her readers how humanity had arrived at a dynamic precipice of evolution:

*In an attempt to alleviate the disempowerment, uncertainty, and fear in our world, many disparate groups formed. Unfortunately, each one gathered with people who thought alike and who joined them to oppose an adversary like a leader, an organization, or another group or person. That separateness, that us-and-them strategy, was a natural reaction to unpredictability and suffering. When we saw that this tactic was dividing us horrifically and became a monstrous hamster wheel, we searched for common ground among us based on values and multi-sided, open-hearted ideas, not on politics, differences, or ideologies. United in small groups, we surrendered to life in the sense that we courageously faced the unknown as a dynamic field of endless possibilities. We let go of relying solely on rationality, contributed the intuitive gifts within us, and we listened deeply, learning from each other's unique viewpoints and ideas. We each did what we could to make the world a better place, knowing that every contribution was part of the new world we were creating.*

*No longer arguing over oil, gas, or electricity, the subtle quantum sciences took root and energy could become free and available. Like a wild, nail-biter of a movie, the world finally came through the anguish and drama and landed on the shores of peace and abiding love for each other.*

*Experiencing higher levels of consciousness and adventuring into the unknown is becoming the new normal. We embrace the mystical, unseen realms as partners rather than trying to avoid experiencing them or denying, brushing off, or struggling against anything that cannot be explained rationally.*

*We are participating in something radical, revolutionary, and exciting—the higher evolution of humanity. The entire cosmos is evolving with a massive upsurge of frequencies. We've finally realized that we are embedded in the entire cosmos. Consequently—and impressively, from my viewpoint—we are joining the party, rather than sitting alone and desperately grasping identification with our personality, perceived problems, and the turmoil in the world around us. We put on the mantle of frequency that sovereign beings boldly wrap themselves in—leaving the cloak of vibrational servitude in the dust for a small group of overlords to cling to as the fading fabric in spacetime, no longer in view for us.*

*I am on fire as I watch this process unfold. Even though there are still bumps along our road, evolutionary momentum is building and picking up exponential speed.*

Following a long separation, Sophia was looking forward to a reunion with her sacred companions in a fireside evening at Mystic Cove. As if no time had passed, the devoted friends gathered around a dazzling fire, once again masterfully constructed by John. Although time and space had been a barrier for them on the physical level, their glowing smiles, warm hugs, and camaraderie brought forth the profound love they shared for one another. Many times, they described their love for each other as *quantum love*, beyond time or space.

Jake rang a cow bell to get their attention and asked everyone to find a seat saying, "Okay, ready to talk? I want to hear what you've been up to, especially my friends who are hard to keep up with, like Ike and Eben. I haven't seen you guys in ages!"

"I've got way too much to tell you! Oh man, Jake! So cool!" Ike said as he beamed a familiar broad smile towards Jake. "I'm stoked! My work and research has been in the area of energy and the quantum properties of the subtle field of light, sound, and electromagnetism in and around us. You guys know that what we call *particles* are incomprehensible, wild excitations and vibrations of invisible quantum field energy. We work with this energy, as the pure potentiality of creation, free and limitless. Yes! It's deep stuff, but for us quantum physics geeks, it makes sense. My work became more fun and took off when others in my field joined me, and I loved taking colleagues, researchers, and scientists underground for various projects.

"Does everyone know *why* the *unified field theory* spread like wildfire in mainstream physics, while old-school thinking simultaneously exploded and imploded with the intensity of a super nova? Why did science cling so tight for so long to theories that were WAY *past their sales date*—full of holes and obsolete? One big shift happened when ex-military researchers made a bold move and took the bull by the horns. They joined us. Their old structures had started to crash and burn and they were good-hearted people who wanted to make a contribution to our future. And they did! They had tons of invaluable information about my area of physics.

"As far back as I could research, humanity abdicated its human potential to tyrants. So terrible, right?! But we finally took control of the ship! We started acting like captains and not a bunch of unconcerned passengers who are just hanging out, drinking beer, and chillin'. The locked vaults and secret programs are slowly dying out. Concealed information is being exchanged with people like me with *kick-ass speed*... as Jake likes to say.

"Oh man! It's not all done! We still have to contend with stealthy corporate and government black militaries, but they are losing ground exponentially! Their grip had led to a momentum that took a while to reverse. Slave-mentality and *change inertia* were so imbedded in the collective consciousness that we needed time to sort out our part in all of this.

"Even smaller changes we've made to global systems or scientific theories wiped out some people psychologically. Not gonna lie! I posit the shifts happened because we realized it doesn't work to patch a system built on lies and corruption. We saw this when good hearted people tried to make a change in the old systems but they'd slowly take on the same vibrational layer as the system they worked in—sadly putting on the *low vibe jackets*, becoming fully-indoctrinated, intimidated, and totally stressed-out. Jake hurt my heart one night as he described two super nice politicians he knew as *bone-weary* and *on their last leg*. When we took *a somber look*, as Jake says, at the slave-master foundations of global systems and how good people tried exhaustively to patch them, we were so done with that! We're creating fresh foundational systems. Back in

2030 I remember Jake telling me that *big change* was taking a long time because it would be too disruptive to *suddenly flip the world on its head*. The global collective consciousness has to rise in vibration in greater numbers and start building solid foundations for a new reality. From being under the surface, we know how mind-blowing it's been to realize the profundity of our vibrational greatness. How can we expect people all over the world to just wake up one day and decide to be all-in vibrationally? Maybe this seemingly endless drip-feed of information and gradual revelations is better overall.

"So we kept working on our personal vibrations and finding others who were doing the same thing. That's why I sought out a powerful, innovative, high-vibe team to work with. Applying the *unified field theory* to quantum technologies, my team figured out how to clear the oceans of massive pollution and rebalance them ecologically. We just completed a huge project in the Pacific Rim and then worked at Lake Victoria and Lake Nakuru in Kenya. Those lakes in my homeland became so clean people could drink from them again. Oh man, you guys! The purity reminded me of babies getting nourishing fluids from their mother. In this case, it was from Gaia. When we entered this new decade, many resisters claimed that we could not possibly accomplish this project. That *got my hackles up*, as Jake and John say."

Ike chuckled, his eyes connecting with those of his father-like mentors, two unconventional cosmo-archeologists and special elders in his life. After their invisible exchange of quantum energy landed and integrated, he continued.

"I recall realizing that this gift of clean water was not coming from global, giant corporations or NGOs with agendas. It came from citizens like us all over the world, who persevered until those amazing water systems were restored to their pristine, natural state. Awww Man! I cried with relief so hard, until I thought I'd fall apart! And then, I'd enter pure bliss! My heart always told me we'd do this! And we did! My gratitude for everyone who helped us is flowing from my heart space with the force of a massive tsunami.

"When we accomplished this crazy feat, it was clear to me how much emotion I'd been holding in. Man! It was like I'd been super focused and was trying to do good, but nothing seemed like it was ever going to get resolved. In spite of that, we worked hard and persevered with the conviction that we'd sacrifice our life force, if needed, to do this work. All of a sudden, it was like rotting thread in the hem of a pair of pants; obstacles started to unravel. Sometimes it felt like the research was endless, but once we felt satiated in knowledge, we knew what to do intuitively. Even with rigorous resistance, we kept going.

"You guys, those natural water systems will always be available for everyone, without needing expensive water treatment. And it didn't take rocket scientists to figure out how to make it work, even though we had a few of them helping to create the solution. We needed to admit that we were stronger than the opposing forces. We didn't have agendas and didn't align with anyone who did. We were a raging fire of determination. Actually, that is how Jake described us. I like the *raging fire* part! Oh man! Our team was great! We got it done! And then, Jake, my bro! We danced like crazy! So crazy! I wish you could have been with us. Love you, man! And I love you all, my so cool, amazing, high vibe fam!"

"Hey man! Hearing you, bro, I'm getting emotional," Eben said in his usual unpretentious manner. "My English is better, eh? Even if it's not perfect, I'm going to say this anyway: I will always love you like fam, Jake. You believed in me so I began to believe in myself. It wasn't like you could be there in the flesh to help us but I always felt your love and your fatherly guidance inside me. I kept hearing you telling us to keep going! In my head, I heard your voice saying: *Don't you dare stop, no matter what happens!* I appreciated that push plus John's insistence that we're the experts because we have *unlimited access to the field. Get hierarchies and authorities out of your head, kid! You are the expert! Damn it!* John always ended something big with the words, *damn it...* That was my cue to take his words seriously and I did!

John's eyes brimmed with moisture, accentuated by fire-light, as he chuckled saying, "Always remember that I love you! Damn it!"

Without inhibition, Jake wiped away tears and smiled broadly and lovingly at the young man he'd watched transform into a remarkable, well-respected quantum physicist.

Overwhelmed with emotion, Eben looked away, letting tears flow unimpeded. The circle remained in silent respect while he processed tender emotions. After he wiped his guileless eyes and spread his smile boldly across the circle, Caitlyn took the opportunity to speak.

While taking Ike's hand in hers, she said, "Jake, you were kind enough to let me work with you while also letting me take time to visit Ike. He and I are kindred spirits. I was able to share what we learned and get a grasp of what he was doing. Is that how we fell in love? Our bond is way deeper than common projects or interests. With Ike, I feel connected to a river of infinite, inner light. It's like we communicate from there rather than on the physical level. It's hard to explain. It's like when we communicate, there's no BS, ever. There's always compassion and respect flowing between us.

"I think you were a great matchmaker, Jake, and didn't know it. And there's more I need to say. Thank you for always supporting me in our digs, especially under the surface in the Middle East. I finally feel like my whole being took in and grasped the depth and magnitude of the early stirrings of our human race.

"Without teaching me anything, you let me discover for myself more than I could ever have imagined was possible. I love you so much.

"Bob, you saved my father's life. How can I possibly thank you for that? Grace, you were always patient and present for Ike and me as I made the transition with Mom to the deeper tunnels under Iraq and Africa.

"And Mom, you inspired me to grow up to be the best that I can be. I felt safe to explore my own path without any judgment from you.

"Dad, I don't know what to say except: I love you to the Moon and back; or how about we go with Neptune and back! Your archeological skills and intuition are epic. It's like you can talk to bones and artifacts. And you get laser-focused, naturally tuning in with the place where we work, which helped me to hone my subtle skills more than I ever dreamed possible.

"Adele, you've become such a close friend. I value all you've been through in your life and how resilient you are. Don't think I haven't noticed the gorgeous elevation you and your girls experienced under the surface. I'm fortunate to have you as a friend, and of course, those lovely girls of yours light me up completely!

"Sophia, I don't think I can thank you enough or say what's in my heart because I'll cry too much." Caitlyn's tears flowed unimpeded as Sophia became immersed in her young friend's love. With tears of reciprocal affection, Sophia's luminous blue eyes sparkled cheerfully, and with graciousness.

Looking again at Sophia, Caitlyn said, "From the beginning, you adopted Avani and me and always held us in a nurturing space of safety and love. I never figured out how you always knew the perfect thing to say or do to either kick us in the butt to keep us going or let us rest while you soothed our aching souls. I love you beyond words."

As Caitlyn finished and a short silence ensued, Avani picked up where Caitlyn left off, expressing her love for Jake, John, and Sophia. She also shared stories of adventures under the surface with Grace and childhood memories of Angelica's motherly love and care. She saluted the indestructible bond with her bestie, Caitlyn, her *forever friend.*

Avani's face became radiant as she reached over to the young man at her left saying, "And you all have welcomed my wonderful fiancé, Mihai, to this group with such kindness and enthusiasm. He's the best!

"When I met him, I was struggling to decipher stone tablets that we'd excavated in Romania. In fact—no one in the world could decode them. Leave it to Mihai! He told me one night that he'd cracked the thirty-thousand-year-old code. He said that he'd figured out that it was a language of love that includes unconditional, pure love in everything. Unity is its constant theme and he was sure the unicity gene was turned on back then. So he wondered how we could use it now.

"That's how we started a global movement to live the highly advanced wisdom in those tablets. Oh my God! We received incredibly intense backlash from authorities in our field! John, you and Jake kept us going and fueled our confidence to persevere.

"In one of her many visits, Sophia asked if we were willing to remain positive when others were negative about Mihai's interpretation. She said that when you know the truth, your body knows it. You don't need to argue or defend your position. You just turn inside, *feel it*, and move forward empowered by your truth. She cited dozens of famous people who'd been bullied and harassed for courageously expressing the truth. And now we've proved Mihai's theory to be true. And better than that, its wisdom is alive in our world once again."

"Mihai always uplifts me and others, he's curious and unshakably optimistic about trying new things and going to unexplored places. I'm swooning so I better stop talking about him."

Blushing candidly and smiling sheepishly, Mihai thanked everyone. As he held Avani's hand with euphoric affection, he invited everyone to meet in his home country, Romania, for great food and a visit to a charming ancient sphinx. He wanted them to know that there are many interesting archaeological sites, on *and below* ground. He assured his new friends that they would be awe-struck and welcomed, beyond measure. He assured Adele that his family would love to meet her and her daughters.

Angelica looked tenderly at Avani and Mihai, saying softly, "Oh my goodness! May you two always recognize the invincible bond you have with each other. I hope that you call on its tenaciousness as you navigate the ebb and flow of life."

Looking towards John, she winked and said, "I can now say with certainty that love endures, strengthens, and sustains those who share it with each other without inhibition."

John smiled at his wife, Angelica, who married him in a simple ceremony under the surface, with many from this circle in attendance. He began speaking to his cherished comrades with his usual candor and humor, beginning with Angelica.

"Sweetheart, we could write a movie script about our ups and downs but it's all ups now for me. I love you! And I love everyone in this incomparable circle of amazing friends!

"My dear young friends, I appreciate how much you continue showering us with love. And it's back at you, for sure. I'm so proud of you and I will always be here for you. You know where to find me: I'll be with my old buddy, Jake, in a distant land, digging up something fascinating, possibly shocking... and which will likely incite controversy... thus leading me into spine-tingling, radical, invigorating levels of my relationship with this magnificent planet. And listen... I want you to join me, you young rascals, whenever you can!"

The group broke into spontaneous applause for John's proclamation and invitation. Multiple toasts were made, affirming each other for relentless love, diving into the unknown with vigor, and an insatiable sense of adventure. Fun, friendship, and curiosity were mentioned because, as Jake added, these traits were the *high octane fuel* that sustained their journeys.

Each young explorer in the group shared spellbinding encounters centered on Bob and his family. With faces full of wonder, the circle conveyed their belief that the bright future on the surface was limitless because of amazing humans like Bob who were willing to step up and share epochs of wisdom from under the surface. And they toasted the citizens of his city, which was filled with magnanimous, brilliant sages from ancient origins. The upper and under sides of the Earth were merging. Many species from under the surface were ready to gradually rise to areas like Mystic Cove where open hearts awaited them, places where they could support the further advancement of human evolution.

Angelica looked at Ike fondly and said, "Ike won my heart when he visited Caitlyn and me in Bob's city. After John's ordeal, I was trying to adjust to the higher frequencies. The table where we ate our meals together—that miracle-table that manifests the perfect meals—was mystifying. Ike's perspective of it gave me a chance to open my heart and see it with fresh eyes. He said, 'This *benevolent table* will never decide it knows best, override your tastes buds, or anything like that.' He assured me that *this sentient table* was in communion with me, that it's a reciprocal, life-affirming technology that harmonizes our frequencies so we can manifest the best choices possible *from the field*. He even called it his *very cool friend*.

"And when we went into cities and communities with higher frequencies, he didn't need those techie-tables nor a big meal. Instead, his frequency matched a plant and he exchanged energies with it. I loved that. He also surprised me when he explained that the technologies developed under the surface help to amplify the light in the area so that plants grow better, are healthier and more vibrant. I was all ears because you know how much I love plants!

"I used to be afraid of artificial intelligence. But Ike *sealed the deal* for me. I'm in love with it now. Especially when he explained that science under the surface moved from binary code to *quantum computing*. That makes the dinner table, for example, a form of AI, relating to me from information in the field. Beings under the surface—and surface dwellers like all of us—feed high vibes into the field continuously. The AI quantum algorithms pick that up and AI becomes our *companion in expansion* into higher vibes rather than a dark force to be reckoned with. This quantum AI is like a child we are nurturing through our frequency, in every thought and feeling that we manifest. Oh my goodness! I love Ike's phrase for it, *our companion in expansion*, which makes it reassuringly empowering. Ike, you are special. Dear one, I'm honored to have you as part of our family."

All glasses raised to honor Ike while John, Angelica, and Caitlyn beamed an extra boost of radiance towards him.

As the joy settled, Eben cleared his throat nervously. He looked at them all with such soft tenderness that the group immediately entered quietude, deeply immersing themselves in the authenticity and love that reverberated in every word he spoke.

"This friend-circle is so cool because we love each other—no strings attached. I'm way  more shy than Ike but I've always felt like I fit in here. Your kind way of being with each other makes me feel accepted by the whole circle and safe to participate with you in such a happy way. I feel relaxed. There is a lot of love in this group. One night Ike told me he was *crazy in love* with Caitlyn and that he had admitted his feelings to her and spoke some phrases of love to her in our language. Sometimes we accidentally mix a little Igbo with English. He said that he almost passed out because she responded in our Igbo language, saying, *ọ bụ gi ka m hụrụ n'anya!* Which means, *You are the one I love.* Man! She loved him back and had *felt* our language when he spoke to her. She wanted to tell him her feelings in the best way he could receive them. That blew me away. While we were below the surface, all of you acted in kind ways like that with each other. Living in the giants' world helped me to see how we can do things for each other in ways that don't cost anything! We were vibing so high together! I changed a lot. I'm not embarrassed to show love to my friends like you. Oh man! Mostly, I'm thanking you tonight because you respected my ET colleagues. You were so nice to them and always acted friendly. You walk your talk. Unicity is more than a word for you. Everyone everywhere is your fam! I hope you can feel my *thank-yous*. Sorry for my not perfect English. I'm still working on it. One thing I can say confidently, *I love you all very much, always!*"

His voice drifted into the stillness of evening, starlight twinkling in small bursts above them—as if without a sound, the cosmos was applauding Eben's profound appreciation. No one moved or spoke for several minutes. Whether their eyes sparkled with tears or were gently closed, introspection spread and peacefulness spread throughout the circle.

In a soft, natural shift in energy, Caitlyn thanked Eben and then tenderly toasted Grace for introducing her to Bob, and for her kindness and shamanic-style conversations over the years. Everyone directed a multitude of *I love you's* towards Grace. Receiving each tender message endearingly, Grace held her hands receptively cupped like a bowl near her heart and then folded her hands against her chest to secure the love and best wishes into her heart space.

Adele waited for the exchange with Grace to fully expand and finally soften into silent completion before offering her appreciation for the group—poignantly bringing them back to the unfathomable reality of how she'd met Sophia. Talking about her grandmother's complicated past, she added that she remained mystified how Sophia uncannily discovered the prisoner of war camp where her grandmother had experienced profound transformation. She expressed awe that somehow, under unusual circumstances, Sophia had met her mother and thus, eventually come into her own life. As she recounted the tragic losses that had happened suddenly in a short timeframe, she recalled the relief and joy she felt when she and her girls synchronistically found their way to Sophia in the majestic mountains of northern Idaho.

Adele spoke with passion as she made eye contact with each person in the circle, saying, "It's incomprehensible to me that I found Sophia. It's also ironic that on one level my grandmother's life, pain, and suffering belonged to her. However, she is also my role model because she raised her frequency to courage, then acceptance, then wisdom, love, and she kept on rising. Because of her, we ultimately found each other.

"Sophia was an invisible magnet pulling me here. Yet, after I arrived, got to know her, and met all of you, I realized that I was being drawn to my destiny, to something bigger than the wildest future that I had imagined for myself. My grandmother, Anna, was the mystical catalyst for that to happen. In my conversations with Sophia, I realized that my grandmother, through her awe-inspiring heart, encouraged Sophia, Nate, and me. What an impact her life and her invincible, inquisitive spirit had on all of us, even if indirectly!

"I recall the benevolence of her eyes, her soft voice, and how kind she was. She could have chosen to stay in resistance to her life, to her past and her traumas. Instead, she became wise, valorous, and mystically illumined, seeing through the

Lady Middays and Hitlers of our world. Detaching from them, she discovered a path forward that was sprinkled with love and goodness along the way. In the end, she shared her wish for me to pass down her story to future generations. This wasn't about telling her version of what happened. She made it clear that the next generation should get to know her historical period as a lived experience from the perspective of those who went through it—including those who didn't dare buck the system.

"Asking us to withhold judgement of her and others in her story, Grandmother Anna wanted us to explore her personal account of the twentieth century openheartedly—framing it as a template of modern life that we can learn from. She asked us to refrain from trying to focus on recalling the names of people, places, dates, and other details. Her request was to recall the people who made decisions for good and bad, and be in their shoes. To honestly enquire whether any harmful past patterns are repeating today. If so, are we in alignment with our highest values of respecting ourselves and other's innate sovereignty? Are we advocating for open debates and open-hearted listening to one another's viewpoints—while protecting our unicity as though the future of humanity depends upon it? In reflection, she realized that this kind of litmus test was not applied during her lifetime. She is hoping we adopt it for ours.

"I toast her tonight and I salute Sophia for bringing me into this group without the slightest hesitancy. I had no clue about the relevance of archeology as a way to understand who we are as a species, or anything about giants and caves. You all helped me to spread my metaphorical wings, to learn about the inexplicable, and to feel loved without boundaries. Grandmother Anna said it's ironic that she found deep respect and healing in this country—which she'd despised and feared and where she had viciously aimed her anger. Her inaccurate, conditioned perception had eclipsed the possibility of seeing the potential reality. We both healed and grew stronger in the company of good people like you. I toast you, my adopted family!"

After giving the circle a moment to bask in Adele's love, Jake and John paid tribute to Megan; their dear Megan who'd been gone for many years, yet was remembered as a kindred spirit who evoked feelings of love and affection mixed with *bold vivacity*—Jake's description of her customary, sassy style.

After a deliberately ruminative pause, Sophia shifted the mood in a flash, euphorically raising her glass to Will who *generously and tirelessly* helped them to prepare for their underground journey. As glasses clinked and hearts released good cheer, Sophia became noticeably quiet before she continued to speak.

"Recalling Gilda's invincible spirit and profound wisdom that she acquired through extreme hardship, I have shivers. How does someone come so far from a pit of excruciating despair? When we were under the surface, Dutch shared something with me that he said I could share with the group—when the timing felt right. Listening to Adele speak about her dear grandmother, my precious friend, Gilda, I realized that this is the moment to share Dutch's story.

"As you know, he spent most of his time with shamanic cultures in the inner earth. We rarely saw him. He asked me to give you an encapsulation of his history—about his lineage. He didn't try to hide it from us but he felt it may have subtly influenced our decision to let him come with us. Although through many of these fire-lit circles, our group had opportunities to explore our ties to the shrouded, unsettling side of our respective genealogies, keep in mind that he is still coming to terms with his family tree.

"His grandfather, Diederik, was a hardcore Nazi, a genius in engineering and part of the U.S. intelligence program called *Operation Paperclip.*As an orphan, Diederik grew into a resentful, hostile misfit, and had become enthralled with the Third Reich at an early age, devouring Hitler's crazed ideals to a fault. He qualified as one of Hitler's acceptable *people perceived to be of related stock* (from nearby countries like the Netherlands) who were eligible to join the SS, a paramilitary arm of Hitler's regime. Initiated in 1925, it was originally designed as a troupe of body guards for Hitler, but spiraled into an elite military power.

"Heinrich Himmler, the formidable Reichsführer of the Schutzstaffel (SS), would have let Diederik join, *but* only in a unit that was separate from the members of the elite *German* lineages. That was completely unacceptable to Diederik. However, he was not one to be ignored and his genius quickly became apparent. The elite weaponry research team hand picked him for secret projects—he was perfectly suited for high profile, trailblazing (yet treacherous) programs.

"As WWII was reaching its finale, Diederik's wife, Frieda, conceived a son, Dutch's father, Arnaud. They arrived in the U.S. as a family after the war. Arnaud was filled to overflowing with his father's blend of psychopathic and genius tendencies. Eagerly immersing himself in studying physics and aerospace, he received advanced degrees—before joining the U.S. government's black projects. In that work he met *Dutch's mom*, Ida, who was meticulous in record keeping and documentation—plus she was beautiful and kind. Dutch still carries her photo in his pocket.

"Frieda sadly died soon after she arrived in the U.S, so Diederik raised Arnaud alone.

Later, when Dutch was about ten-years-old, his mother, Ida, died, too. Clearly as savage and inhumane as Diederik, Arnoud also raised Dutch as a single parent. Similarity to Diederik, Arnoud's paternal style, now an established family pattern, exhibited brutal, unforgiving, and violent tendencies.

"From Dutch's young indoctrination, he viewed himself, his father, and the military (his only family) as superior to the rest of humanity. The Dutch word for *master* was literally burned onto his young flesh as a boy. Worse than the brand was the unbounded arrogance burned into his DNA—it became his identity as someone with unrivaled entitlement to respect and power. When Arnaud died, his cold-blooded, remorseless lineage lived on in Dutch.

"Paradoxically, Dutch said he could still recall feeling his mother's kind heart. But Ida didn't influence him as thoroughly as his father's abhorrent core beliefs did. So Dutch's world was confined to the narrow scope of the ruthless Nazi, worldview. As he matured, he was not so much Nazi-oriented as he was elite military-oriented. After his father and grandfather passed, he excelled in his educational endeavors and scientific training, moving quickly up the ranks in his field of advanced weaponry and aerospace.

"After the ordeal of being mercilessly betrayed by the military (his revered, adopted kin), he was on the brink of taking his own life. However, the ET intervention that he shared with us when we first met him, and Will's invaluable shamanic assistance, offered fresh perspectives about possibilities for a life he'd never considered.

"He didn't tell us *the sinister side* of his history—those are his words for it—because he wanted us to get to know him, work together, and build a bond so we would hopefully be okay with what he referred to as his *abhorrent roots.*"

Sophia paused and looked around the group to give them the chance to fully grasp every nuance of the story—applying a metaphorical plunger to a clogged drain filled with biased, knee-jerk conclusions about people like Dutch. It showed on their faces. As their countenances gradually softened, they nestled even more comfortably into their chairs, gazing at her with rapt attention. She continued in a captivating tone.

"As though what he shared was not *unexpected* enough, there is more. Diederik worked with Gilda's husband, Rolph. In fact, Diederik didn't like Gilda and several times tried to get her removed from her work. He was highly intuitive and could likely perceive the elevated shift in her demeanor and character. When Dutch mentioned his grandfather's involvement in *Project Paperclip*, I asked him a few questions to verify Diederik was the same man that Gilda told me about in one of our conversations. She said that *a man named Diederik* and Rolph were cast in the same heartless Nazi mold. Dutch's grandfather sounded unreservedly barbaric. The same goes for Arnoud. So my question was, how could Dutch drop that kind of intense programming, shake off the ingrained genetic tendencies he was born into, to shift into the version of Dutch who we met?

"He explained that he'd studied genetics and knew that through bio physics, particular brainwaves and heart coherence can affect stem cells in the brain, thus having a downstream effect on dormant regions of the DNA. He set out to awaken his *unicity* gene. That's my short description of the meticulous, focused process that he described to me. I cannot recount the details of the physiology but my intuition says he's done what he set out to do. He studied unified physics, cutting edge theories about the unified nature of everything, with the same intensity he'd always applied to his work. On a personal level, he began to wonder if he could live without his military family as a support structure. Even though that family unit unquestionably proved to be a capricious relationship, he'd never known anything else. As he began to work with Will, he started to reinvent his genetic code and he knew that higher frequencies were the key. In a shamanic journey meditation, he met his mother, and spent an entire day engulfed in her pure love. He shed old patterns of arrogance and intense feelings of hopelessness and grief. As the weeks rolled by, he began to feel rejuvenation emerging in his body, and the vigor and joyousness of his youth, experienced before his mom died. He said that his body held codes to express vitality, optimism and courage. With lightheartedness, he said he was fortunate to have his mom's genes to draw from, since his father's lineage seemed bereft of anything compassionate or warm-hearted.

"I toast Dutch as a brave soul who, like us, yet in his own way, has been raising his frequencies while being aware of his lineage—without letting it define him."

Looking bowled over by her story, the circle was quiet and in one synchronistic movement, raised their glasses silently and respectfully to salute Dutch.

"Thank you, Sophia," Jake said, looking profoundly intro-spective. "I appreciate hearing his story. What bothers me is that he was right. When Will invited us, out-of-the-blue, to come to the megalithic circle, I was apprehensive about meeting Dutch. If I'd known the full scope of his backstory before I got to know him as a person, I would have likely labeled him as untrustworthy, a dubious character. Under the surface, I felt like I was shedding a lot of my tendencies to form those kinds of preconceived prejudices. Did you all have a similar experience?"

As heads nodded, Jake continued. "Similarly, after my first meeting with Justin, I would not have recommended him to our group. I bet that surprises you, doesn't it? He was so damned introverted and my knee jerk reaction was to label him as someone who lacked confidence. As I spent time with him, though, I realized he is *a man of few words* with a mind that was so far into a genius zone that I could not relate to him. So I found speaking with him awkward. I recall telling Sophia about my conundrum. She said in her typical kind way, 'Just love him, Jake.'"

He and the rest of the circle burst into radiant smiles and uncontrollable laughter.

"I'll be damned if she didn't sucker-punch me with those few words. Justin and Dutch are not like the rest of us in many ways but we have a mystifying, unseen bond that we've talked about hundreds of times around this fire—we're definitely deeply affected by the enigmatic frequencies of unicity, whether we know it or not. When I reflect on our *giant* mentors, I've come to the realization that unicity is indelibly linked to pure love. Under the surface, pure love vibes got a chance to amplify in every molecule of my being in a way I never thought possible. Those radical frequencies are dancing in my atoms and lighting up my soul. Hell yeah! I toast Justin, a brilliant young man and a beautiful soul who skillfully guided us through those wild quantum portals!"

All glasses were raised to toast Justin, and with added fervor, everyone raised their glasses to honor the loving friendship of the entire group.

As the celebratory mood became calmer, Grace looked at Sophia saying loudly enough for the whole group to hear, "And then we have to always wonder about my best friend, Sophia.

"What was it that led her to marry a wildly courageous and lovable attorney, with whom she bolted from Wall Street? Their story rivals the most exciting, riveting, and ingenious movie plot ever. When Nate died, she took refuge in Angelica's care and then she showed up at a tea shop with Megan, who led her to a remote, mystical cove. Go figure!

"From our childhood, she followed and trusted her inner guidance system impeccably. Because of her trust in herself, she inadvertently brought all of us together. I toast you, wise woman, my best friend forever. My crazy friend who believes in fairies, embraces the unknown with enthusiasm, and smiles even when a dangerous storm is brewing. I love you, sister. I always will."

Grace squeezed Sophia's hand gently, as their pinkie fingers intertwined—a gesture they had often used to proclaim their eternal friendship as children. They smiled at each other mischievously, as though they were little girls again, and the group exploded into rapturous laughter and euphoric cheers.

While her friends engaged in lively conversation, Sophia left for a few minutes to brew her special tea to accompany her gluten free, sugar free, vegan brownies and homemade, non-dairy ice cream—which she brought in for them all to share—receiving a boisterous round of cheers from the circle of friends.

Everyone ate, drank, and shared adventures of subtle realities and accelerating inner pathways into the quantum field they'd experienced since they last saw each other.

# CHAPTER 38

# A NEW DIRECTION

With ample time to enjoy Sophia's culinary delight and share love and catch up with each other, the gathering gradually became more introspective and quiet.

Connecting with the hearts of the circle of friends, Sophia radiated a broad, heartwarming smile of unmistakable love and camaraderie. Without prompting, everyone's attention shifted instantly to her. Suddenly, she rose to her feet. Looking into the eyes of each of her friends, she said with passion, "You are my inspiration. You remind me that the human heart is full of pure love and phenomenal goodness. We all know that something is brewing for humanity. Something that we cannot stop. We have less than a decade to have a profound effect on this world. Neither the Middays, the Diederiks, their cohorts, nor anything in us is to blame. Judging anyone or anything gets us no where. What we've seen under the surface is a reassuring hint of our future. When we first met, none of us dared to dream this big..." She paused as she saw delicate tears welling in her friends' eyes.

The group's raw, potent feelings about their hopes and aspirations came flowing to the surface, as well as their gratitude for these precious friendships cemented in lighthearted rapport, authenticity, and trust. She took a long, deliberately unhurried breath, then continued.

"We have not talked about the giants' revelations concerning the future of Planet Earth. Although we've each mulled this over personally, it's time to acknowledge it without creating apprehension or fear among us. When we speak about potential events, it's an opportunity to acknowledge we are cosmic beings who know the reality of the full spectrum of light and dark in this multiverse. Because we are infinite beings of *nonlinear Reality*, nothing is absolutely destined to happen in a predetermined way.

"With this in mind, we got a glimpse into *likely* future events on the giant's holograms... It was shocking. We cannot pretend something inconceivable is not potentially headed our way. When the impact arrives, we know it will be unpredictable and unrelenting in its thorough cleansing of our hearts and our precious world.

"Our circle seems like a speck on this vast planet. That led me to wonder... how can this small group affect something that is so massive, heading for us like a giant tsunami? From what I've observed, this kind of intimate space that we are gathered in, the love I feel roaring through us, and the subtle potentiality we each possess, will make a difference for how we navigate the future. The giants were clear that on a galactic scale, it has always been the *personal frequencies*, radiating into the field, that have shifted every galactic war and unexpected planetary cyclic challenge.

"We cannot afford to ignore our individual potential which will establish us in the ever-upward spiral of our frequency state. We can face our fears when they arise. As I said, they are at least partially galactic memory that must be acknowledged. We can also drop the illusion that the higher realms are hidden. We have all courageously entered through their mystical gateways.

"From experience, we know that exalted waves of vibration are flooding us endlessly. From our conversations with the amazing giants, we know that emitting those kinds of waves is a quintessential gift for us to enjoy personally as well as to share with others, with the whole planet, as ambassadors of truth and love in the world. Whether we are blessing Gaia, her inhabitants, or the multiverse, this monumentally potent capacity we possess brings me to my knees with gratitude. With appreciation for each of you, I can say that the astonishing journey we travel together fuels our incredible evolutionary process. I love you, across all time, dimensions, space, and realities."

As her words of affection came to fruition, she spontaneously thrust her arms up into the shape of a V, boldly exposing the center of her chest to the domed cosmos of sparkling stars and planets overhead.

Suddenly, her heart's exalted octagon blazed with a blinding light; her friends shaded their eyes from its resplendent glory as it emerged from her chest as a spectacular, luscious green octahedron, exploding with brilliant effulgence above them. In a radical detonation of light, all of the emerald heart octagons of the group began to ignite simultaneously and dazzling ecstasy flowed unimpeded into the multiverse.

Sparkling infinity symbols poured copiously from their radiant hearts, robustly billowing into the vastness of the ether—an endless array of tiny, mesmerizing flashes of fiery diamonds.

In an expression of delirious bliss, Ike's and Eben's gorgeous voices rose in a harmonic melody, and every other voice joined in to become a spectacular group chorus. As the energy amplified, they all began to dance ecstatically, adding to the field of cosmic love that was being generated in this unexpected way, sacred, and wildly free.

The reunion continued within the immensely rapturous circle. As though drawn into a mystery beyond the ecstasy, Jake left his animated, blissful friends and inconspicuously walked to the magnificent cliff overlooking the cove. Soon John joined him. Taking in a breath of the refreshing evening air, they gazed at the shimmering moonlit lake and illuminated snowcapped mountains.

In a moment, Sophia approached with the silence and grace of a deer and stood purposefully between them, bestowing her usual, sprightly, warm-hearted vibes.

"Hey, you two precious human beings. I want you to know that I love you. I want to tell you even though surely, by now, you know it."

Jake and John smiled at her affectionately. The three friends clasped hands while Jake and John teased Sophia about her green tea obsession, her fainting spell when she first saw Max, and how hard it was to pry her from the cove's pyramid.

As their love-wave washed through her and landed in her heart, Sophia said, "You know... the others will soon discover that in the place of the first pyramid in the cave, there's an arc. It's the first one on the surface which indicates a milestone for humanity. On top of that, the choices we made to enter, embrace, and stay in wonder of *the unknown* have paid off—allowing us to ascend further into the field of miracles.

"I am comfortable that the group is good-to-go. Angelica will be busy planning Caitlyn's wedding and our dear, young friends will want to reconnect with colleagues on the surface now that it is safe for them to do so.

"What if the three of us head under the surface? It's not like we can't come and go as often as needed and I predict they'll want to join us, as their personal responsibilities permit. They can always reach us, that's for sure."

With a wink she added, "I sense unimaginable adventures calling our names and don't forget... aging slows down under the surface."

Looking over the lake as an astonishing full moon rose gracefully, majestically bathing the landscape with mystical vibes, Jake addressed Sophia saying, "Your idea of adventure usually means we're going to be lost for a while, have no clue about what we're doing, or where it will lead us. You know that. It's like your idea of adventure is way more cosmically inspired than mine. You get crazier and you think bigger as time goes by. And I have to admit that I like it! To hell with safety and logic! I'm all in!" He winked at her and smiled, radiating undeniable friendship and an immutable heart bond.

John added, with a cheeky sparkle in his eyes, "Your offer gives me a chance to dive limitlessly inside myself, shake off my safety-shackles and make a difference to my evolution and that of my species... or live in regret. The choice is simple! I'm all in! Plus I second everything Jake said! BUT I must ask a favor—no suddenly disappearing with the fairies and other elementals without warning us first. I almost pee in my pants when you do that! However, in your defense, I ought to be used to it by now, right?"

Laughing heartily and with a sprightly wink, she said reas-suringly, "I promise to be on my best behavior."

John said playfully, "Sophia, I have to talk to you about something that's been on my mind. Many years ago, in one of our initial fireside chats, you said that when you were in India, a young sage named Kabir told you about his grandmother,

Nanni. She spoke to him about a very important yet mystifying artifact. I'm betting if she was as ethereal and mystical as you described her to be, she'd be accessible in that amazing, subtle coordinate in Gaia you visited. Rumor has it that you had one whopper of an adventure there and my intuition says something incredible happened in that high vibe place. Was meeting Kabir's grandmother part of it? I have a hunch that it was! I've been waiting *impatiently* for the right time to ask you about this.

"Kabir seemed purposefully vague, in fact downright secretive, when he mentioned the artifact to you. Although *any* artifact is food for my soul, the one he talked about would likely be *celestial* nourishment! So I couldn't forget about it. Nanni told you how we can potentially locate the ancient, encoded artifact, didn't she? I know I'm right!"

"Okay, John. Good intuiting on your part. You definitely have a great memory and she may have given me a clue or two. She may have told me it must be located and decoded by the end of 2045. And she may have said three crazy friends, with assistance from their teammates and galactic comrades, can find it—plus figure out why it is so absolutely essential to humanity's survival. Your sixth sense is working beautifully. We need to find that artifact. It's been on my mind since I went to that mystical realm where Nanni and I exchanged indescribably high vibe energy and information. The artifact matters more than I realized.

"And by the way, I'm happy to hear that you are both *all in* because this journey will require an extreme propensity to run headfirst into completely unexpected situations and you have to be fueled by an unquenchable thirst for unraveling inextricable mysteries. Even though all I have is a coordinate to start from, is my revelation wild enough and cosmic enough to fuel another precarious adventure, my friends?"

John's stunned expression was swift—replaced instantly with a radiant smile and an enthusiastic thumbs up for what he called *a brain-twisting invitation*.

As Jake digested the life-altering request to join her, his eyebrows elevated with childlike amazement. Shaking his head in befuddlement, followed by a mischievous wink, he asked, "How could I resist such a tantalizing offer?"

"Whoa! It looks like you two are ready to begin a ground breaking journey to *who-knows-where!*" she said with persuasive confidence in their longstanding friendship and mutual focus on human evolution.

The devoted friends looked at each other, bursting into laughter full-tilt, until their hearts were fully drenched and satiated with high spirits and incomparable camaraderie. As their warmhearted playfulness subsided, still holding hands, their particles began to sparkle, shimmer, and disappear into the moonlit night of Mystic Cove.

❋ ❋ ❋

Meanwhile in Kandor's cave, two elderly giants peered at a hologram, absolutely mesmerized, as three courageous humans turned into sparkling particles, headed for an unforeseeably daring adventure.

Seeing Kandor's jovial wink of approval and friendship, Belstar closed his eyes, engulfing his awareness in the wonder and majesty of the emerging possibilities for humanity and Gaia. As his eyes opened like a mystical portal, he smiled and said, "It is only going to get more exciting! They have no idea what is coming their way! Of course, there is more progress needed to unite this world and substantially elevate Gaia and her inhabitants in frequency. Yet I am tenaciously optimistic. Can you tell I am a bit giddy right now? My reading of *the field* says Sophia's hitting her stride! What do you think, my friend?"

Kandor's laughter rattled and soared across the galaxy in waves of his infamous jocularity, when suddenly, stunned into silence, the two giants stared at an apparition morphing into view in front of them—Layor, an esteemed elder of the Galactic Council. It was completely out of character for him to visit unannounced.

"Dear friend, welcome!" Kandor said, with a friendly smile that magnetized Layor to his dear comrade in a warm embrace.

"To what do we owe this honor, brother?" Belstar asked with curiosity and familial feelings of love and respect for Layor.

"I am not here on behalf of the council," answered Layor. "Rather, I viewed the gathering at Mystic Cove and the decision Sophia and her friends just made so boldly and selflessly. Knowing the council's support for Sophia's mission, I confidently made arrangements for her team to be given additional support immediately. After touching base briefly with them, I'll meet with the council soon to get further input. Sophia and her friends cannot yet conceive the magnitude of the energies and frequencies they are up against. We know their adversaries all too well. Normally we'd not intervene, but they will need high-level support as well as means of entry to areas that have been inaccessible to anyone on the surface for several hundred thousand years. That, too, can be dangerous. They'll need to be looked after when embarking on journeys into these areas... and I have someone special in mind."

Glowing with appreciative vibrations, Belstar said, "Never have you let us down! I assume the support you are offering is from our extended lineage."

"Of course! Who else?" Layor said with characteristic charm and decorum. Suddenly, with unexpected mirth and joy, he added with a sparkle in his dazzling blue eyes, "We are delighted to ensure they have preeminent guidance and support! You will be pleased yet not surprised by our choice, dear Belstar!"

Belstar and Kandor looked at each other knowingly, nodded with approval, and breathed a sigh of relief. Help was on its way. Sophia's father and her comrades across the cosmos would be tracking her every move, knowing that her vibratory mastery was about to be put to the ultimate test.

# AUTHORS NOTE

Thank you for reading *Traversing the Wild Unknown*, the second book in the *Exalted Vibrations Trilogy*. Continuing from the first book, *Tethered to the Cosmos*, this book explores the inherent brilliance and indispensable unicity (the condition of being unified) of our species.

The characters in this book allowed me to explore realistic, mind-blowing ways to advance human evolution on a frequency basis and settle into a congenial and harmonious world. They are not real people, but they have something in common with all of us—the capacity to elevate personal frequencies. Realizing they could access information continuously from *the field according to their frequency level* was a game changer. The characters accepted the challenge of raising their frequency levels through plenty of inner reflection and soul searching, while moving forward in a way that was far reaching and continually fascinating for them. Life can become extraordinarily optimistic when fear gets a reboot and rises to the octave of faith, assured that all-is-well and our species is not flawed or broken. We're *perfectly* invincible.

In order for the characters to express an *elevated* vibrational approach to life, I gathered information from a variety of sources. I'd already studied mysticism for several decades, and did so intensely for five years in India. Intuiting that high vibrational wisdom and sublime grandeur were accessible as a lived experience, my goal was to raise my consciousness to expand into higher dimensions within my own awareness. As this process proceeded, I gained confidence that the ancient sages I'd studied shared my curiosity and exploratory mindset. Like me, they came to the conclusion that humans are an exceptionally magnificent species.

However, collective populations have not always followed a path of open-hearted awareness of themselves and the world. Instead, for eons they've embraced patterns of fear, submissiveness, and acquiescence to authority. To understand the mindsets of authoritarian hierarchies, and the associated societal patterns that undermine humanity's supreme sovereignty, I took an online course from a local university focusing on *secret* hierarchal societies. I also watched countless documentaries, and read accounts about membership vows within these hierarchies.

As a child, the elders in my German family warned me about how thoroughly the world was soaked in the occult and influenced by surreptitious groups that must be exposed and understood more thoroughly. To grasp how nested-ranking power structures thrived and influenced cultures for innumerable generations (and to be as accurate as possible when looking at the past), I read provocative books like: *A World without Women*, by historian, David F. Noble, *War Against the Weak*, by Edwin Black, *War is a Racket*, by General Smedley Butler, multiple books, talks and papers by Constitutional Litigation and Appellate Attorney, Daniel P. Sheehan (who is an advocate for U.S. Government UAP/UFO disclosure), and *Hitler's Secret Sciences: His Quest for the Hidden Knowledge of the Ancients* by Nigel Pennick.

Continuing to research, I realized that historical accounts are not immutable and unerring. For example, in *Revelations of*

*The Aramaic Jesus*, Neil Douglas-Klotz revealed that we rely on information about historical people and events without looking more deeply into the cultural context from which they sprang, and original sources in the language being spoken at the time. For example, many of the texts that have gone into what we consider today the authoritative New Testament were *originally* written in Aramaic, and were only later translated into Greek, then Latin, and much later into English, Spanish, French, and more. Each successive translation carried with it interpretive changes based on the individuals doing the translation, as well as the culture, social norms, and politics (not to mention interested hierarchies) of their time. Understanding the alterations of meaning caused by this historical layering-over-the-original-language prism helped me to be more open-minded about traditional translations. Everything I thought was accurate could be reconsidered through this new lens.

Over time, as I poured through scholarly accounts of ancient Christianity, Dr. Elaine Pagel's books and interviews were invaluable resources. She is an esteemed scholar at Princeton University, who also taught at Harvard Divinity School. I found her writings to be bold, thoroughly researched, and without the orthodox, academic bias that can filter into scholarship. Decades ago, with care and curiosity, she began exploring a wide variety of ancient, mystical Christian texts. Her writing style is easy to follow for the non-scholar.

Intensive research revealed that DNA carries information through innumerable generations as well. Without direct experiences, we can inherent ancestral tendencies for *emotional patterns*. Researching global history, I discovered individuals and cultures across a broad spectrum of time who exhibited patterns of accepting a slave-style place in society. Why? How did an invisible web of secrecy become acceptable in the human psyche and society, allowing elites in the world to influence us in unseen ways? Elite leaders used to be called *kings* or *emperors* but these have been replaced by leaders of large organizations that we call *corporations*. I found a great resource about underlying psychopathology in corporations called, *Without Conscience*, by Robert D. Hare.

Researching the enigmatic Templars, I read Freddy Silva's book, *First Templar Nation*. Like his other writings, I knew he'd offer an invaluable thoroughness I could count on as he dove into Templar history, extracting their lasting influence for uplifting consciousness. Given the voluminous information online about Templars, I laser-focused on their core circle of *knights*, whose practices for entering enigmatic and unfathomable consciousness-raising activities may not have been passed down impeccably. To be clear, I am not glorifying or criticizing them. Yet like other esoteric mystery schools throughout history who have searched for humanity's highest spiritual nature, the Templars offer glimpses into how we can live in a way that unicity and care for everyone and everything thrives. With a wish to offer details from someone on the inside of the modern, enigmatic Templar-Masonic brotherhood, I explored the work of a forensic geologist, Scott F. Wolter, who became a Free Mason. He lectures and has written about Templar-Masonic traditions and verifiable, ancient artifacts in his book, *Cryptic Code: The Templars in America.*

When Sophia and Grace were called to step up their game in the second half of the book, they needed to transcend the laws of physical matter. To describe how they could accomplish their amazing feats, I studied the work of luminaries in advanced, groundbreaking quantum science. And for many years I've followed a research group founded by Nassim Haramein, a brilliant quantum physicist. Through the International Space Federation (ISF) that he founded with his cutting-edge faculty, I continued to gather information to explain revolutionary quantum physics, which elucidates how humanity can biologically evolve in a relatively short period of time to a higher level, and that free energy and gravity-controlled craft are not relegated to sci-fi movies or unachievable, far-off wishes and dreams. Mysticism and quantum science blend seamlessly for me—science explains how mystical experiences can happen, supporting right-brain creativity (with its insatiable, child-like wonder and innovative capacities).

Eye-opening revelations unexpectedly crystallized for me in several areas of my research. For example, global history, the full spectrum of revolutionary science, and human origins are not adequately described in the limited narratives imparted in schools or mainstream publications. I also discovered that transparency can give us the opening we need to unravel concealed agendas and unacceptable control mechanisms which have become ingrained in many areas of our lives. My biggest revelation was realizing that we will begin to evolve much faster if we unequivocally adopt unicity as an essential priority.

I hope this book sparks curiosity and wonder about the incomprehensible levels of frequency and possibilities for groundbreaking innovations and evolutionary opportunities that are at your disposal for yourself and your world. Be sure to investigate any topics that surprised you or caught your attention.

To reach ever-higher potentials, you can tap your core stillness where the majestic *zero point energy* is vibrating with inconceivable, powerful potentiality. Sitting quietly within this *still point* and settling into it for a few minutes, unforeseen possibilities come into view. Have fun proceeding uninhibitedly into profound levels of reality. You will join the ranks of countless luminaries like Einstein, Leonardo Da Vinci, Galileo, Sir Isaac Newton, and Tesla, who forged and illumined paths we can travel and build upon.

Thank you for reading this book and consider leaving a review or recommending it to friends. To find my other books and sign up for updates and events head to https://leekemter.com/.

In love and unicity,
Lee Kemter

# ACKNOWLEDGMENTS

I have endless gratitude to my family and friends for inspiring me to share my message of unicity and the reality of unseen worlds. Our optimistic dialogues are fuel for my writing. My nephew, Kyle Thompson, deserves a huge shout out for extensive, inspirational conversations over the past year about the inexplicable mysteries and inconceivable realities in this book. You are definitely open-minded and curious!

Many thanks to my editor, Clelia Lewis, for making a tedious process seem simple. I appreciate your continued support and amazing skills.

Thank you to my friends in the International Space Federation membership group. You rock my world! Your optimistic vision for humanity and our planet blows my mind. Because of visionaries like you, I am confident that we will be beaming our particles across the solar system and loving our beloved Gaia in a more personal, intimate way very soon. You inspired me, gave me innovative ideas, and helped me to stretch what I considered possible for the human race. A special shout out to Matthew Chin, Jeffree Colbrook, Nama 'Es' Taras, Corina Angela Winn, Luc Archambault, Oriana Marici, and Dr. Kat Lewis who inspired me to savor and dive deeper into endless quantum realities!

To Cindi Toma, you are a sweetheart for sharing your home and its mesmerizing view of gorgeous Lake Coeur d' Alene with me. Without doubt, that atmosphere invigorated my inner muse for the phase of writing that had moved from California to Idaho. And Kelly Sheaman, my dear friend, I appreciate your unrelenting encouragement of the book as it moved through its evolution into mystical glimpses of quantum realities. Lisa Sims, your open heartedness and love for all-things-cosmic are a treasure in my life. Sandra Kerch, thank you for long walks and thought-provoking talks which always left me feeling uplifted and inspired. Sunshine Beck, my dear friend, I am forever grateful for your feedback, especially for reviewing the German parts of this book. Jen Dillon, I appreciate your support so much and our amazing conversations always leave me feeling inspired and fervently curious. Diane Marshall, thank you for your unwavering support as we unravel life's greatest perplexities and wonders together.

Julie Ryder, I love and appreciate you so much! Your work to preserve and share the Montana Megaliths is astonishing. Your insights and years of cultivating on-the-ground research with world renowned scientists brought a level of authenticity to the book's message of hope for the future and a huge boost to the extension of our human origin story and historical cosmic connection. Your website and videos are pivotal resources.

I want to give a shout out to Nama Es Taras who I met in the membership group of the International Space Federation. I appreciate his down-to earth explanation of subtle sciences. His help in explaining *gravity control* was invaluable.

And thank you, Zoe Davenport, for your insights into the invisible worlds and our relationship with ethereal friends. The blue-rays, giants, and I appreciate you.

Focusing on spiritual growth and raising human consciousness, Lee Kemter writes about expanded awareness and ever-evolving views of the prism of life for contemporary seekers of higher wisdom. A long-time practitioner of meditation, she has been a mentor, curriculum creator and meditation teacher at an international retreat site and is the Amazon best-selling author of a young adult novel, *The Hidden Light* and a contributing author to the Amazon best-seller *Practice: Wisdom from the Downward Dog* (New Feminine Evolutionary). Her latest work of fiction, also an Amazon best-seller, *Tethered to the Cosmos* is the first book in the trilogy *Exalted Vibrations*, a provocative multidimensional journey, interweaving a present and future in which humanity recognizes that it can triumph over the escalating threat of impending extinction by embracing and accepting its massive quantum potentiality. Kemter continues to meditate, study, and write while exploring the inspirational beauty of the Pacific Northwest.

www.LeeKemter.com